BEAU TRILOGY
(BEAU GESTE, BEAU SABREUR, BEAU IDEAL)

P.C. WREN

2015 by McAllister Editions (MCALLISTEREDITIONS@GMAIL.COM). This book is a classic, and a product of its time. It does not reflect the same views on race, gender, sexuality, ethnicity, and interpersonal relations as it would if it was written today.

CONTENTS

BEAU TRILOGY 1
(BEAU GESTE, BEAU SABREUR, BEAU IDEAL) 1
P.C. WREN 1

BOOK ONE 1
BEAU GESTE 1
PART I 1
MAJOR HENRI DE BEAUJOLAIS' STORY 1

CHAPTER I. OF THE STRANGE EVENTS AT ZINDERNEUF 1

CHAPTER II. GEORGE LAWRENCE TAKES THE STORY TO LADY BRANDON AT BRANDON ABBAS 37

PART II 45
THE MYSTERY OF THE "BLUE WATER" 45

CHAPTER I. BEAU GESTE AND HIS BAND 45

CHAPTER II. THE DISAPPEARANCE OF THE "BLUE WATER" 55

CHAPTER III. THE GAY ROMANTICS 90

CHAPTER IV. THE DESERT 150

CHAPTER V. THE FORT AT ZINDERNEUF 155

CHAPTER VI. A "VIKING'S FUNERAL" 207

CHAPTER VII. ISHMAELITES 232

BOOK TWO 249
BEAU SABREUR 249
NOTE 249
PART I 250
FAILURE 250
THE MAKING OF A BEAU SABREUR 251

- CHAPTER I. "OUT OF THE DEPTHS I RISE" . 251
- CHAPTER II. UNCLE 253
- CHAPTER III. THE BLUE HUSSAR 256
- CHAPTER IV. A PERFECT DAY 265
- CHAPTER V. BECQUE--AND RAOUL D'AURAY DE REDON 269
- CHAPTER VI. AFRICA 277
- CHAPTER VII. ZAGUIG 284
- CHAPTER VIII. FEMME SOUVENT VARIE ... 298
- CHAPTER IX. THE TOUAREG--AND "DEAR IVAN" 306
- CHAPTER X. MY ABANDONED CHILDREN. 312
- CHAPTER XI. THE CROSS OF DUTY 318
- CHAPTER XII. THE EMIR AND THE VIZIER.. 322
- CHAPTER XIII. "CHOOSE" 330
- CHAPTER XIV. A SECOND STRING 334
- CHAPTER XV. "MEN HAVE THEIR EXITS ..."341
- CHAPTER XVI. FOR MY LADY 350

NOTE 356

PART II 356

SUCCESS 356

- THE MAKING OF A MONARCH 357
- CHAPTER I. LOST 357
- CHAPTER II. EL HAMEL 358
- CHAPTER III. EL HABIBKA 371
- CHAPTER IV. THE CONFEDERATION 379
- CHAPTER V. A VOICE FROM THE PAST 382
- CHAPTER VI. MORE VOICES PROM THE PAST 386
- CHAPTER VII. L'HOMME PROPOSE 397
- CHAPTER VIII. LA FEMME DISPOSE 405

CHAPTER IX. AUTOCRATS AT THE BREAKFAST-TABLE 412

CHAPTER X. THE SITT LEILA NAKHLA, SULEIMAN THE STRONG, AND CERTAIN OTHERS 415

CHAPTER XI. ET VALE 425

BOOK THREE **427**

BEAU IDEAL **427**

PROLOGUE 427

CHAPTER I 449

CHAPTER II 453

CHAPTER III 462

CHAPTER IV 468

CHAPTER V 479

CHAPTER VI 502

CHAPTER VII 509

CHAPTER VIII 518

CHAPTER IX 528

CHAPTER X 532

CHAPTER XI 540

CHAPTER XII 544

CHAPTER XIII 550

CHAPTER XIV 556

CHAPTER XV 566

CHAPTER XVI 576

CHAPTER XVII 590

CHAPTER XVIII 599

CHAPTER XIX 606

EPILOGUE 610

BOOK ONE
BEAU GESTE

PART I

MAJOR HENRI DE BEAUJOLAIS' STORY

CHAPTER I. OF THE STRANGE EVENTS AT ZINDERNEUF

TOLD BY MAJOR HENRI DE BEAUJOLAIS OF THE SPAHIS TO GEORGE LAWRENCE, ESQ., C.M.G., OF THE NIGERIAN CIVIL SERVICE

"Tout ce que je raconte, je l'ai vu, et si j'ai pu me tromper en le voyant, bien certainement je ne vous trompe pas en vous le disant."

"The place was silent and *aware*."

Mr. George Lawrence, C.M.G., First Class District Officer of His Majesty's Civil Service, sat at the door of his tent and viewed the African desert scene with the eye of extreme disfavour. There was beauty neither in the landscape nor in the eye of the beholder.

The landscape consisted of sand, stone, *kerengia* burr-grass, *tafasa* underbrush, yellow, long-stalked with long thin bean-pods; the whole varied by clumps of the coarse and hideous *tumpafia* plant.

The eye was jaundiced, thanks to the heat and foul dust of Bornu, to malaria, dysentery, inferior food, poisonous water, and rapid continuous marching in appalling heat.

Weak and ill in body, Lawrence was worried and anxious in mind, the one reacting on the other.

In the first place, there was the old standing trouble about the Shuwa Patrol; in the second, the truculent Chiboks were waxing insolent again, and their young men were regarding not the words of their elders concerning Sir Garnet Wolseley, and what happened, long, long ago, after the battle of Chibok Hill. Thirdly, the price of grain had risen to six shillings a *saa,* and famine threatened; fourthly, the Shehu and Shuwa sheiks were quarrelling again; and, fifthly, there was a very bad smallpox ju-ju abroad in the land (a secret society whose "secret" was to offer His Majesty's liege subjects the choice between being infected with smallpox, or paying heavy blackmail to the society). Lastly, there was acrimonious correspondence with the All-Wise Ones (of the Secretariat in "Aiki Square" at Zungeru), who, as usual, knew better than the man on the spot, and bade him do either the impossible or the disastrous.

And across all the *Harmattan* was blowing hard, that terrible wind that carries the Saharan dust a hundred miles to sea, not so much as a sand-storm, but as a mist or fog of dust as fine as flour, filling the eyes, the lungs, the pores of the skin, the nose and throat; getting into the locks of rifles, the works of watches and cameras, defiling water, food and everything else; rendering life a burden and a curse.

The fact, moreover, that thirty days' weary travel over burning desert, across oceans of loose wind-blown sand and prairies of burnt grass, through breast-high swamps, and across unbridged boatless rivers, lay between him and Kano, added nothing to his satisfaction. For, in spite of all, satisfaction there was, inasmuch as Kano was rail-head, and the beginning of the first stage of the journey Home. That but another month lay between him and "leave out of Africa," kept George Lawrence on his feet.

From that wonderful and romantic Red City, Kano, sister of Timbuktu, the train would take him, after a three days' dusty journey, to the rubbish-heap called Lagos, on the Bight of Benin of the wicked West African Coast. There he would embark on the good ship *Appam,* greet her commander, Captain Harrison, and sink into a deck-chair with that glorious sigh of relief, known in its perfection only to those weary ones who turn their backs upon the Outposts and set their faces towards Home.

Meanwhile, for George Lawrence--disappointment, worry, frustration, anxiety, heat, sand-flies, mosquitoes, dust, fatigue, fever, dysentery, malarial ulcers, and that great depression which comes of monotony indescribable, weariness unutterable, and loneliness' unspeakable.

And the greatest of these is loneliness.

§ 2

But, in due course, George Lawrence reached Kano and the Nassarawa Gate in the East Wall, which leads to the European segregation, there to wait for a couple of days for the bi-weekly train to Lagos. These days he whiled away in strolling about the wonderful Haussa city, visiting the market-place, exploring its seven square miles of streets of mud houses, with their ant-proof *dôm*-palm beams; watching the ebb and flow of varied black and brown humanity at the thirteen great gates in its mighty earthen ramparts; politely returning the cheery and respectful "*Sanu! Sanu!*" greetings of the Haussas who passed this specimen of the great Bature race, the wonderful white men.

Idly he compared the value of the caravans of salt or of ground-nuts with that of the old slave-caravans which the white man thinks he has recently suppressed; and casually passed the time of day with Touareg camel-drivers, who invited him to hire or buy their piebald, brindled, or white camels, and, occasionally, a rare and valuable beast of the tawny reddish buff variety, so prized for speed and endurance.... .

On the platform of Kano Station (imagine a platform and station at Kano, ancient, mysterious, gigantic, emporium of Central Africa, with its great eleven-mile wall, and its hundred thousand native inhabitants and its twenty white men; Kano, eight hundred miles from the sea, near the border of Northern Nigeria which marches with the French *Territoire Militaire* of Silent Sahara; Kano, whence start the caravan routes to Lake Tchad on the north-east, and Timbuktu on the north-west)--on this incredible platform, George Lawrence was stirred from his weary apathy by a pleasant surprise in the form of his old friend, Major Henri de Beaujolais of the Spahis, now some kind of special staff-officer in the French Soudan.

With de Beaujolais, Lawrence had been at Ainger's House at Eton; and the two occasionally met, as thus, on the Northern Nigerian Railway; on the ships of Messrs. Elder, Dempster; at Lord's; at Longchamps; at Auteuil; and, once or twice, at the house of their mutual admired friend, Lady Brandon, at Brandon Abbas in Devonshire.

For de Beaujolais, Lawrence had a great respect and liking, as a French soldier of the finest type, keen as mustard, hard as nails, a thorough sportsman, and a gentleman according to the exacting English standard. Frequently he paid him the remarkable English compliment, "One would hardly take you for a Frenchman, Jolly, you might almost be English," a bouquet which de Beaujolais received with less concern by reason of the fact that his mother had been a Devonshire Cary.

Although the Spahi officer was heavily bearded, arrayed in what Lawrence considered hopelessly ill-fitting khaki, and partially extinguished by a villainous high-domed white helmet (and looked as truly French as his friend looked truly English), he, however, did not throw himself with a howl of joy upon the bosom of his *cher Georges,* fling his arms about his neck, kiss him upon both cheeks, nor address him as his little cabbage. Rather as his old bean, in fact.

A strong hand-grip, "Well, George!" and, "Hallo! Jolly, old son," sufficed; but de Beaujolais' charming smile and Lawrence's beaming grin showed their mutual delight.

And when the two men were stretched opposite to each other on the long couches of their roomy compartment, and had exchanged plans for spending their leave--yachting, golf, and the Moors, on the one hand; and Paris boulevards, race-courses, and Monte Carlo, on the other--Lawrence found that he need talk no more, for his friend was bursting and bubbling over with a story, an unfathomable intriguing mystery, which he must tell or die.

As the train steamed on from Kano Station and its marvellous medley of Arabs, Haussas, Yorubas, Kroos, Egbas, Beri-Beris, Fulanis, and assorted Nigerians from *sarkin, sheikh, shehu,* and *matlaki,* to peasant, camel-man, agriculturist, herdsman, shopkeeper, clerk, soldier, tin-mine worker, and nomad, with their women and *piccins,* the Frenchman began his tale.

Through Zaria, Minna Junction, and Zungeru, across the Jebba Bridge over the Niger, through Ilorin, Oshogbo, and mighty Ibadan to vast Abeokuta, with brief intervals during which Lawrence frankly snored, de Beaujolais told his tale. But at Abeokuta, George Lawrence received the surprise of his life and the tale suddenly became of the most vital interest to him, and from there to Lagos he was all ears.

And as the *Appam* steamed through the sparkling Atlantic, the Frenchman still told his tale--threshed at its mystery, dissected and discussed it, speculated upon it, and returned to it at the end of every digression. Nor ever could George Lawrence have enough--since it indirectly concerned the woman whom he had always loved.

When the two parted in London, Lawrence took it up and continued it himself, until he, in his turn, brought it back to his friend and told him its beginning and end.

§ 3

And the story, which Major Henri de Beaujolais found so intriguing, he told to George Lawrence as follows:--

"I tell you, my dear George, that it is the most extraordinary and inexplicable thing that ever happened. I shall think of nothing else until I have solved the mystery, and you must help me. You, with your trained official mind, detached and calm; your *phlegme Britannique*.

Yes--you shall be my Sherlock Holmes, and I will be your wonder-stricken little Watson. Figure me then as the little Watson; address me as 'My dear Watson.'

Having heard my tale--and I warn you, you will hear little else for the next two or three weeks--you must unhesitatingly make a pronouncement. Something prompt and precise, my dear friend, *hein?*"

"Quite," replied Lawrence. "But suppose you give me the facts first?"

"It was like this, my dear Holmes.... As you are aware, I am literally buried alive in my present job at Tokotu. But yes, with a burial-alive such as you of the Nigerian Civil Service have no faintest possible conception, in the uttermost Back of Beyond. (You, with your Maiduguri Polo Club! Pouf!) Yes, interred living, in the southernmost outpost of the *Territoire Militaire* of the Sahara, a spot compared with which the very loneliest and vilest Algerian border-hole would seem like Sidi-bel-Abbès itself, Sidi-bel-Abbès like Algiers, Algiers like Paris in Africa, and Paris like God's Own Paradise in Heaven.

Seconded from my beloved regiment, far from a boulevard, a café, a club, far, indeed, from everything that makes life supportable to an intelligent man, am I entombed ..."

"I've had some," interrupted Lawrence unsympathetically. "Get on with the Dark Mystery."

"I see the sun rise and set; I see the sky above, and the desert below; I see my handful of *cafard*-stricken men in my mud fort, black Senegalese, and white mule-mounted infantry whom I train, poor devils; and what else do I see? What else from year's end to year's end? ..."

"I shall weep in a minute," murmured Lawrence. "What about the Dark Mystery?"

"What do I see?" continued the Major, ignoring the unworthy remark. "A vulture. A jackal. A lizard. If I am lucky and God is good, a slave-caravan from Lake Tchad. A band of veiled Touaregs led by a Targui bandit-chief, thirsting for the blood of the hated white *Roumi*--and I bless them even as I open fire or lead the attack of my mule-cavalry-playing-at-Spahis ..."

"The Dark Mystery must have been a perfect godsend, my dear Jolly," smiled Lawrence, as he extracted his cheroot-case and extended it to his eloquent friend, lying facing him on the opposite couch-seat of the uncomfortable carriage of the Nigerian Railway. "What *was* it?"

"A godsend, indeed," replied the Frenchman. "Sent of God, surely to save my reason and my life. But I doubt if the price were not a little high, even for that! The deaths of so many brave men.... And one of those deaths a dastardly cold-blooded murder! The vile assassination of a gallant *sous-officier*... . And by one of his own men. In the very hour of glorious victory... . *One of his own men*--I am certain of it. But why? *Why?* I ask myself night and day. And now I ask you, my friend... . The motive, I ask? ... But you shall hear all--and instantly solve the problem, my dear Holmes, eh! ...

Have you heard of our little post of Zinderneuf (far, far north of Zinder which is in the Aïr country), north of your Nigeria? No? Well you hear of it now, and it is where this incomprehensible tragedy took place.

Behold me then, one devilish hot morning, yawning in my pyjamas over a *gamelle* of coffee, in my quarters, while from the *caserne* of my *légionnaires* come the cries of '*Au jus,*' '*Au jus,*' as one carries round the jug of coffee from bed to bed, and arouses the sleepers to another day in Hell. And then as I wearily light a wretched cigarette of our beastly*caporal,* there comes running my orderly, babbling I know not what of a dying Arab *goum*--they are always dying of fatigue these fellows, if they have hurried a few miles--on a dying camel, who cries at the gate that he is from Zinderneuf, and that there is siege and massacre, battle, murder, and sudden death. All slain and expecting to be killed. All dead and the buglers blowing the Regimental Call, the rally, the charge; making the devil of a row, and so forth... .

'*And is it the dying camel that cries all this?*' I ask, even as I leap into my belts and boots, and rush to the door and shout, '*Aux armes! Aux armes!*' to my splendid fellows and wish to God they were my Spahis. '*But no, Monsieur le Majeur*' declares the orderly, '*it is the dying goum, dying of fatigue on the dying camel.*'

'*Then bid him not die, on pain of death, till I have questioned him,*'I reply as I load my revolver. '*And tell the Sergeant-Major that an advance-party of the Foreign Legion on camels marches en tenue de campagne d'Afrique in nine minutes from when I shouted "Aux armes." The rest of them on mules.*' You know the sort of thing, my friend. You have turned out your guard of Haussas of the West African Frontier Force nearly as quickly and smartly at times, no doubt."

"Oh, nearly, nearly, perhaps. *Toujours la politesse,*" murmured Lawrence.

"As we rode out of the gate of my fort, I gathered from the still-dying *goum*, on the still-dying camel, that a couple of days before, a large force of Touaregs had been sighted from the look-out platform of Zinderneuf fort. Promptly the wise *sous-officier,* in charge and command since the lamented death of Captain Renouf, had turned the *goum* loose on his fast *mehari* camel, with strict orders not to be caught by the Touaregs if they invested the fort, but to clear out and trek with all speed for help--as it appeared to be a case of too heavy odds. If the Touaregs were only playful, and passed the fort by, after a little sporting pot-shotting, he was to follow them, I suppose, see them safe off the premises for a day or two, and discover what they were out for.

Well, away went the *goum*, stood afar off on a sand-hill, saw the Touaregs skirmish up to the oasis, park their camels among the palms, and seriously set about investing the place. He thought it was time for him to go when they had surrounded the fort, were lining the sand-hills, making nice little trenches in the sand, climbing the palm trees, and pouring in a very heavy fire. He estimated them at ten thousand rifles, so I feared that there must be at least five hundred of the cruel fiends. Anyhow, round wheeled Monsieur Goum and rode hell-for-leather, night and day, for help... .

Like *How we brought the good news from Aix to Ghent,* and *Paul Revere's Ride* and all. I christened the *goum,* Paul Revere, straight away, when I heard his tale, and promised him all sorts of good things, including a good hiding if I found he had not exceeded the speed limit all the way from Aix to Ghent. Certainly his 'Roland' looked as if its radiator had boiled all right. And, *Nom d'un nom d'nom de bon Dieu de sort!* but I made a forced march of it, my friend--and when we of the Nineteenth African Division do *that,* even on mules and camels, you can hardly see us go."

"Oh, come now! I am sure your progress is perceptible," said Lawrence politely. "Specially on camels, and all that.... You're too modest," he added.

"I mean you can hardly see us go for dust and small stones, by reason of our swiftness.... Any more than you can see a bullet, witty one," rebuked de Beaujolais.

"Oh, quite, quite," murmured the Englishman.

"Anyhow, I was away with the advance-party on swift *mehari* camels, a mule-squadron was following, and a company of Senegalese would do fifty kilometres a day on foot till they reached Zinderneuf. Yes, and, in what I flatter myself is the unbreakable record time between Tokotu and Zinderneuf, we arrived--and, riding far on in advance of my men, I listened for the sound of firing or of bugle-calls.

I heard no sound whatever, and suddenly topping a ridge I came in sight of the fort-- there below me on the desert plain, near the tiny oasis.

There was no fighting, no sign of Touaregs, no trace of battle or siege. No blackened ruins strewn with mutilated corpses here. The Tri-couleur flew merrily from the flag-staff, and the fort looked absolutely normal--a square grey block of high, thick mud walls, flat castellated roof, flanking towers, and lofty look-out platform. All was well! The honour of the Flag of France had been well defended. I waved my *képi* above my head and shouted aloud in my glee.

Perhaps I began composing my Report then and there, doing modest justice to the readiness, promptitude, and dispatch of my little force, which had maintained the glorious traditions of the Nineteenth African Division; giving due praise to the *sous-officier* commanding Zinderneuf, and not forgetting Paul Revere and his Roland.... Meanwhile, they should know that relief was at hand, and that, be the Touaregs near or be they far, the danger was over and the flag safe. I, Henri de Beaujolais of the Spahis, had brought relief. I fired my revolver half a dozen times in the air. And then I was aware of a small but remarkable fact. The high look-out platform at the top of its long ladder was empty.

Strange! Very strange! Incredibly strange, at the very moment when great marauding bands of Touaregs were known to be about--and one of them had only just been beaten off, and might attack again at any moment. I must offer the *sous-officier* my congratulations upon the excellence of his look-out, as soon as I had embraced and commended him! New as he might be to independent command, this should never have happened. One would have thought he could as soon have forgotten his boots as his sentry on the look-out platform.

A pretty state of affairs, *bon Dieu,* in time of actual war! Here was I approaching the fort in broad light of day, firing my revolver--and not the slightest notice taken! I might have been the entire Touareg nation or the whole German army....

No, there must be something wrong, in spite of the peaceful look of things and the safety of the Flag--and I pulled out my field-glasses to see if they would reveal anything missed by the naked eye.

As I halted and waited for my camel to steady himself, that I might bring the glasses to bear, I wondered if it were possible that this was an ambush.

Could the Arabs have captured the place, put the defenders to the sword, put on their uniforms, cleaned up the mess, closed the gates, left the Flag flying, and now be waiting for a relieving force to ride, in trustful innocence and close formation, up to the muzzles of their rifles? Possible--but quite unlike brother Touareg! You know what *his* way is, when he has rushed a post or broken a square. A dirty fighter, if ever there was one! And as I focussed my glasses on the walls, I rejected the idea.

Moreover, yes, there were the good European faces of the men at the embrasures, bronzed and bearded, but unmistakably not Arab... .

And yet, that again was strange. At every embrasure of the breast-high parapet round the flat roof stood a soldier, staring out across the desert, and most of them staring along their levelled rifles too; some of them straight at me. Why? There was no enemy about. Why were they not sleeping the sleep of tired victors, below on their cots in the *caserne,*while double sentries watched from the high look-out platform? Why no man up there, and yet a man at every embrasure that I could see from where I sat on my camel, a thousand metres distant?

And why did no man move; no man turn to call out to a sergeant that a French officer approached; no man walk to the door leading down from the roof, to inform the Commandant of the fort!

Anyhow, the little force had been extraordinarily lucky, or the shooting of the Arabs extraordinarily bad, that they should still be numerous enough to man the walls in that fashion--'all present and correct,' as you say in your army--and able to stand to arms thus, after two or three days of it, more or less.

As I lowered my glasses and urged my camel forward, I came to the conclusion that I was expected, and that the officer in charge was indulging in a little natural and excusable *fantaisie,* showing off--what you call 'putting on the dog,' eh?

He was going to let me find everything as the Arabs found it when they made their foolish attack--every man at his post and everything *klim-bim*. Yes, that must be it... . Ah, it was! Even as I watched, a couple of shots were fired from the wall. They had seen me... . The fellow, in his joy, was almost shooting *at* me, in fact!

And yet--nobody on the look-out platform! How I would prick that good fellow's little bubble of swank! And I smiled to myself as I rode under the trees of the oasis to approach the gates of the fort.

It was the last time I smiled for quite a little while.

Among the palm trees were little pools of dried and blackened blood where men had fallen, or wounded men had been laid, showing that, however intact the garrison of the fort might be, their assailants had paid toll to the good Lebel rifles of my friends.

And then I rode out from the shade of the oasis and up to the gate.

Here half a dozen or so kept watch, looking out over the wall above, as they leant in the embrasures of the parapet. The nearest was a huge fellow, with a great bushy grey moustache, from beneath which protruded a short wooden pipe. His *képi* was cocked rakishly over one eye, as he stared hard at me with the other, half closed and leering, while he kept his rifle pointed straight at my head.

I was glad to feel certain that he at least was no Arab, but a tough old legionary, a typical *vieille moustache,* and rough soldier of fortune. But I thought his joke a poor one and over-personal, as I looked up into the muzzle of his unwavering rifle... .

'Congratulations, my children,' I cried. 'France and I are proud to salute you,' and raised my *képi* in homage to their courage and their victory.

Not one of them saluted. Not one of them answered. Not one of them stirred. Neither a finger nor an eyelid moved. I was annoyed. If this was 'making *fantaisie*,' as they call it in the Legion, it was making it at the wrong moment and in the wrong manner.

'*Have you of the Foreign Legion no manners?*' I shouted. '*Go, one of you, at once, and call your officer.*' Not a finger nor an eyelid moved.

I then addressed myself particularly to old Grey-Moustache. '*You*,' I said, pointing up straight at his face, '*go at once and tell your Commandant that Major de Beaujolais of the Spahis has arrived from Tokotu with a relieving force--and take that pipe out of your face and step smartly, do you hear?*'

And then, my friend, I grew a little uncomfortable, though the impossible truth did not dawn upon me. Why did the fellow remain like a graven image, silent, motionless, remote--like an Egyptian god on a temple wall, looking with stony and unseeing eye into my puny human face?

Why were they all like stone statues! Why was the fort so utterly and horribly silent? Why did nothing *move*, there in the fierce sunlight of the dawn? Why this tomb-like, charnel-house, inhuman silence and immobility?

Where were the usual sounds and stir of an occupied post? Why had no sentry seen me from afar and cried the news aloud? Why had there been no clang and clatter at the gate? Why had the gate not been opened? Why no voice, no footstep in all the place? Why did these men ignore me as though I were a beetle on the sand? Where was their officer? ...

Was this a nightmare in which I seemed for ever doomed to ride voiceless and invisible, round endless walls, trying to attract the attention of those who could never be aware of me?

When, as in a dream, I rode right round the place, and beheld more and more of those motionless silent forms, with their fixed, unwinking eyes, I clearly saw that one of them, whose *képi* had fallen from his head, had a hole in the centre of his forehead and was dead--although at his post, with chest and elbows leaning on the parapet, and looking as though about to fire his rifle!

I am rather near-sighted, as you know, but then the truth dawned upon me--they were *all* dead!

'*Why were they not sleeping the sleep of tired victors?*' I had asked myself a few minutes before. They *were*... .

Yes, all of them. *Mort sur le champ d'honneur!* ...

My friend, I rode back to where Grey-Moustache kept his last watch, and, baring my head, I made my apologies to him, and the tears came into my eyes. Yes, and I, Henri de Beaujolais of the Spahis, admit it without shame.

I said, '*Forgive me, my friend.*' What would you, an Englishman, have said?"

"What about a spot of tea?" quoth Mr. George Lawrence, reaching beneath the seat for his tiffin-basket.

§ 4

After a dusty meal, impatiently swallowed by Major de Beaujolais, that gentleman resumed his story, with serious earnestness and some gesticulation, while, on the opposite side of the carriage, George Lawrence lay upon his back, his clasped hands beneath his head, idly watching the smoke that curled up from his cheroot. But he was paying closer attention to the Frenchman's tale.

"But, of course, it soon occurred to me," continued that gentleman, "that someone must be alive... . Shots had been fired to welcome me... . Those corpses had not of *themselves* taken up those incredibly life-like attitudes. Whoever had propped them up and arranged them and their rifles in position, must be alive.

For, naturally, not all had been struck by Arab bullets and remained standing in the embrasures. Nine times out of ten, as you know, a man staggers back and falls, when shot standing.

Besides, what about the wounded? There is always a far bigger percentage of wounded than of killed in any engagement. Yes, there must be survivors, possibly all more or less wounded, below in the *caserne.*

But surely *one* of them might have kept a look-out. Probably the Commandant and all the non-commissioned officers were killed.

Even then, though, one would have expected the senior man--even if the survivors were all *soldats deuxième classe*--to have taken that much ordinary military precaution! ...

Well, I would soon solve the problem, for my troop was approaching, my trumpeter with them. I was glad to note that my Sergeant-Major had evidently had a similar idea to mine, for, on coming in sight of the fort, he had opened out and skirmished up in extended order--in spite of the bravely-flying Flag.

When my men arrived, I had the 'rouse,' the 'alarm,' the Regimental Call, sounded by the trumpeter--fully expecting, after each blast, that the gates would open, or at least that someone would come running up from below on to the roof.

Not a sound nor a movement! ... Again and again; call after call... . Not a sound nor a movement!

'Perhaps the last one or two are badly wounded,' thought I. 'There may not be a man able to crawl from his bed. The fellow who propped those corpses up may have been shot in the act, and be lying up there, or on his cot,' and I bade the trumpeter cease. Sending for the *Chef,* as we call the Sergeant-Major, I ordered him to knot camel-cords, sashes, girths, reins, anything, make a rope, and set an active fellow to climb from the back of a camel, into an embrasure, and give me a hoist up.

That Sergeant-Major is one of the bravest and coolest men I have ever known, and his collection of *ferblanterie* includes the Croix and the Medaille given on the field, for valour.

'It is a trap, *mon Commandant,*' said he. 'Do not walk into it. Let me go.' Brave words--but he looked queer, and I knew that though he feared nothing living, he was afraid.

'The dead keep good watch, *Chef,*' said I, and I think he shivered.

'They would warn us, *mon Commandant,*' said he. 'Let me go.'

'We will neither of us go,' said I. 'We will have the courage to remain in our proper place, with our men. It may be a trap, though I doubt it. We will send a man in, and if it is a trap, we shall know--and without losing an officer unnecessarily. If it is not a trap, the gates will be opened in two minutes.'

'The Dead are watching and listening,' said the *Chef,* glancing up, and he crossed himself, averting his eyes.

'Send me that drunken *mauvais sujet,* Rastignac,' said I, and the Sergeant-Major rode away.

'May I go, *mon Commandant?*' said the trumpeter, saluting.

'Silence,' said I. My nerves were getting a little on edge, under that silent, mocking scrutiny of the watching Dead. When the Sergeant-Major returned with a rope, and the rascal Rastignac--whose proper place was in the *Joyeux,* the terrible Penal Battalions of convicted criminals--I ordered him to climb from his camel on to the roof.

'Not I, *mon Officier,*' replied he promptly. 'Let me go to Hell dead, not living. I don't mind joining corpses *as* a corpse. You can shoot me.'

'That can I, of a surety,' I agreed, and drew my revolver. 'Ride your camel under that projecting water-spout,' said I. 'Stand on its back, and spring to the spout. Climb into the embrasure, and then go down and open the gates.'

'Not I, *mon Officier,*' said Rastignac again. I raised my revolver, and the Sergeant-Major snatched the man's rifle.

'Have you *le cafard?*' I asked, referring to the desert-madness that, bred of monotony, boredom, misery, and hardship, attacks European soldiers in these outposts--especially absinthe-drinkers--and makes them do strange things, varying from mutiny, murder, and suicide to dancing about naked, or thinking they are lizards or emperors or clock-pendulums.

'I have a dislike for intruding upon a dead Company that stands to arms and keeps watch,' replied the fellow.

'For the last time--*go*,' said I, aiming between his eyes.

'Go yourself, *Monsieur le Majeur,*' replied Rastignac, and I pulled the trigger.... Was I right, my friend?"

"Dunno," replied Lawrence, yawning.

"There was a click, and Rastignac smiled. I had emptied my revolver when approaching the fort, as I have told you.

'You can live--to be court-martialled and join the *Batt d'Af,*' said I. 'You will be well placed among the *Joyeux*.'

'Better among those than the Watchers above, *mon Officier,*' said my beauty, and I bade the Sergeant-Major take his bayonet and put him under arrest.

'You may show this coward the way,' said I to the trumpeter, and, in a minute, that one had sprung at the spout, clutched it, and was scrambling on to the wall. He was *un brave*.

'We will proceed as though the place were held by an enemy--until the gates are opened,' said I to the Sergeant-Major, and we rode back to the troop and handed Rastignac over to the Corporal, who clearly welcomed him in the rôle of prisoner.

'*Vous--pour la boite,*' smiled the Corporal, licking his lips. And then we watched and waited. I could see that the men were immensely puzzled and intrigued. Not an eye wandered. I would have given something to have known what each man thought concerning this unique experience. A perfectly silent fort, the walls fully manned, the Flag flying--and the gates shut. No vestige of a sign from that motionless garrison staring out into the desert, aiming their rifles at nothing--and at *us*....

We watched and waited. Two minutes passed; five; six; *seven*. What could it mean? *Was* it a trap after all?

'*That* one won't return!' said Rastignac loudly, and gave an eerie jarring laugh. The Corporal smote him on the mouth, and I heard him growl, 'What about a little *crapaudine*[1] and a mouthful of sand, my friend? ... You speak again!' ...

At the end of ten minutes, a very *mauvais quart d'heure,* I beckoned the Sergeant-Major. I could stand the strain no longer.

'I am going in,' said I. 'I cannot send another man, although I ought to do so. Take command... . If you do not see me within ten minutes, and nothing happens, assault the place. Burn down the gates and let a party climb the walls, while another charges in. Keep a half-troop, under the Corporal, in reserve.'

'Let me go, *mon Commandant,*' begged the *Chef,* 'if you will not send another soldier. Or call for a volunteer to go. Suppose you ...'

'Silence, *Chef,*' I replied, 'I am going,' and I rode back to the fort. Was I right, George?"

"Dunno," replied George Lawrence.

"I remember thinking, as I rode back, what a pernicious fool I should look if, under the eyes of all--the living and the dead--I failed to accomplish that, by no means easy, scramble, and had ignominiously to admit my inability to climb up where the trumpeter had gone. It is sad when one's vile body falls below the standard set by the aspiring soul, when the strength of the muscles is inadequate to the courage of the heart... .

However, all went well, and, after an undignified dangling from the spout, and wild groping with the raised foot, I got a leg over the ledge, scrambled up and crawled into an embrasure.

And there I stood astounded and dumbfounded, *tout bouleversé,* unable to believe my eyes.

There, as in life, stood the garrison, their backs to me, their faces to the foe whom they had driven off, their feet in dried pools of their own blood--watching, watching.... . And soon I forgot what might be awaiting me below, I forgot my vanished trumpeter, I forgot my troop waiting without--*for there was something else.*

Lying on his back, his sightless eyes out-staring the sun--lay the Commandant, and through his heart, *a bayonet,* one of our long, thin French sword-bayonets with its single-curved hilt! No--he had not been shot, he was absolutely untouched elsewhere, and there he lay with a French bayonet through his heart. What do you say to that, my friend?"

"Suicide," replied Lawrence.

"And so did I, until I realised that he had a loaded revolver in one hand, one chamber fired, and a crushed letter in the other! *Does* a man drive a bayonet through his heart, and then take a revolver in one hand and a sheet of paper in the other? I think not.

Have you ever seen a man drive a bayonet through his heart, my friend? Believe me, he does not fumble for letters, nor draw a revolver and fire it, after he has done *that*. No. He gasps, stares, staggers. He grips the handle and the *forte* of the blade with both hands, totters, stretches convulsively, and collapses, crashing to the ground... . In any case, does a man commit suicide with a bayonet when he has a loaded revolver? ... Suicide? *Pouf.*

Was it any wonder that my jaw dropped and I forgot all else, as I stared and stared... . *Voyez donc!* A French fort in the Sahara, besieged by Arabs. Every man killed at his post. The Arabs beaten off. The fort inviolate, untrodden by Arab foot. The gates closed. Within--

---

[1] Torture. The hands and feet tied together in a bunch in the middle of the back

-the dead, and one of them slain by a French bayonet while he held a loaded revolver in his hand! ...

But *was* the fort inviolate and untrodden by Arab foot? If so, what had become of my trumpeter? Might not the Arabs be hiding below, waiting their opportunity to catch the relieving force unawares? Might not there be an Arab eye at every rifle-slit? Might not the *caserne,* rooms, offices, sheds, be packed with them?

Absurdly improbable--and why should they have slain the Commandant with a French bayonet? Would they not have hacked him to pieces with sword and spear, and have mutilated and decapitated every corpse in the place? Was it like the wild Touareg to lay so clever a trap with the propped-up bodies, that a relieving force might fall into their hands as well? Never. *Peaudezébie!* Had the Arabs entered here, the place would have been a looted, blackened ruin, defiled, disgusting, strewn with pieces of what had been men. No, this was not Arab work.

These Watchers, I felt certain, had been compelled by this dead man, who lay before me, to continue as defenders of the fort after their deaths... . He was evidently a *man*. A bold, resourceful, undaunted hero, sardonic, of a macabre humour, as the Legion always is.

As each man fell, throughout that long and awful day, he had propped him up, wounded or dead, set the rifle in its place, fired it, and bluffed the Arabs that every wall and every embrasure and loophole of every wall was fully manned. He must, at the last, have run from point to point, firing a rifle from behind its dead defender. Every now and then he must have blown the alarm that the bugler would never blow again, in the hope that it would guide and hasten the relieving force and impress the Arabs with fear that the avengers must be near.

No wonder the Arabs never charged that fort, from each of whose walls a rifle cracked continuously, and from whose every embrasure watched a fearless man whom they could not kill--or whose place seemed to be taken, at once, by another, if they did kill him... .

All this passed through my mind in a few seconds--and as I realised what he had done and how he had died in the hour of victory, *murdered,* my throat swelled though my blood boiled--and I ventured to give myself the proud privilege of kneeling beside him and pinning my own Croix upon his breast--though I could scarcely see to do so. I thought of how France should ring with the news of his heroism, resource, and last glorious fight, and how every Frenchman should clamour for the blood of his murderer.

Only a poor *sous-officier* of the Legion. But a hero for France to honour.... . And I would avenge him!

Such were my thoughts, my friend, as I realised the truth--what are yours?"

"Time for a spot of dinner," said George Lawrence, starting up.

§ 5

Next morning, as the two lay awake on their dusty bedding, begrimed, tousled, pyjama-clad, awaiting the next stop, bath, and breakfast, de Beaujolais lit a cigarette, turned on his side, and fixed his friend with the earnest troubled gaze of his bright brown eye.

"Well, George, *who killed him*--and why?"

"Oh, Ancient Mariner!" yawned Lawrence.

"What?"

"I feel like the Wedding Guest."

"You look like one, my George," smiled the Frenchman.

"Get on with it, Jolly."

"How was the Commandant of that fort killed?"

"Someone 'threatened his life with a railway-share.'"

"Be serious, little George. I want your help. I *must* get to the bottom of this. Where did I leave off?"

"God knows. I was asleep."

"Ah! I was on the roof, pinning my Croix on the breast of the bravest man I have ever met. Your General Gordon in miniature! This obscure and humble soul had kept his country's Flag flying, as that great man did at Khartoum, and, like him, he had been relieved too late. But yes, and there it flapped above my head and recalled me to myself.

I rose, drew my revolver, loaded it, and walked to the door. As I was about to descend into that silence I had a little idea. I looked at each of the Watchers in turn. No. Each man had his bayonet, of course. I had not really supposed that one of them had stabbed his officer and then gone back to his post and died on his feet! He would have fallen--or possibly have hung limply through the embrasure. I raised my weapon and descended the stairs--expecting I know not what, in that sinister stillness--that had swallowed up my trumpeter. And what do you think I found there, my friend?"

"Dunno," said George Lawrence.

"*Nothing*. No one and nothing. Not even the man who had fired the two shots of welcome! ... As I had felt sure, really, all along, no Arab had entered the fort. That leapt to the eye at once. The place was as tight shut as this fist of mine--and as empty of Arab traces. The *caserne* was as orderly and tidy as when the men left it and stood to arms--the *paquetages* on the shelves, the table-apparatus in the hanging cupboards, the *gamelles* and cleaning-bags at the heads of the beds, the bedding folded and straight. There had evidently been room-inspection just before the sentry on the look-out platform had cried, '*Aux armes! Aux armes! Les Arabes!*' and all had rushed to their posts.

No, not a thing was missing or awry. The whole place might just have been made ready by an outgoing garrison, to be taken over by the incoming garrison. No Arab had scaled those walls nor wriggled through the keyhole of the gate. The stores were untouched--the rice, the biscuits, bread, coffee, wine, nothing was missing ..."

"Except a rifle," grunted Lawrence.

"My friend, you've said it! Where was the rifle belonging to the bayonet that was driven through the heart of the murdered officer up above? That was precisely the question that my crazed mind was asking itself as I realised that the fort had never been entered.

Had a corpse bayoneted that *sous-officier,* returned to its post, and flung the rifle to the horizon? Scarcely.

Had an Arab--expert in throwing knife or bayonet as in throwing the *matrak*--possessed himself of a French bayonet, after some desert-massacre of one of our tiny expeditionary columns? And had he got near enough to the fort to throw it? And had it by chance, or skill of the thrower, penetrated the heart of the Commandant of the garrison?"

"Possibly," said Lawrence.

"So I thought for a moment," replied de Beaujolais, "though why a man armed with a breech-loading rifle, should leave the cover of his sand-hill, trench, or palm tree, and go about throwing bayonets, I don't know. And then I remembered that the bayonet went through the breast of the *sous-officier* in a slightly *upward* direction from front to back. Could a bayonet be thrown thus into the middle of a wide roof?"

"Sold again," murmured Lawrence.

"No, I had to abandon that idea. As untenable as the returning-corpse theory. And I was driven, against common sense, to conclude that the officer had been bayoneted by one of his own men, the sole survivor, who had then detached the rifle from the bayonet and fled from the fort. But why?

Why? If such was the explanation of the officer's death--why on earth had not the murderer shot him *and calmly awaited the arrival of the relieving force?*

Naturally all would have supposed that the brave Commandant had been shot, like all the rest, by the Arabs.

Instead of fleeing to certain death from thirst and starvation, or torture at the hands of the Arabs, why had not the murderer awaited, in comfort, the honours, *réclame,* reward, and promotion that would most assuredly have been his? Obviously, the man who--lusting for blood and vengeance on account of some real or fancied wrong--could murder his superior at such a moment, would be the very one to see the beauty of getting a rich and glorious reward as a sequel to his revenge. Without a doubt he would have shot him through the head, propped him up with the rest, and accepted the congratulations of the relieving force for having conceived and executed the whole scheme of outwitting and defeating the Arabs. Wouldn't he, George?"

"*I* would," replied George, scratching his head.

"Yes, you would. And I almost sent that theory to join the other two wild ones--the corpse who returned to its post, and the Arab who threw sword-bayonets from afar. Almost--until I remembered that revolver in the dead man's hand, and the empty cartridge-case in one of its chambers. And then I asked myself, 'Does a man who is conducting the defence of a block-house, against tremendous odds, waste time in taking pot-shots *with a revolver* at concealed enemies, two or three hundred yards distant? Does he do that, with hundreds of rounds of rifle ammunition and a score of rifles to his hand?' Of course not.

That revolver shot was fired at someone *in* the fort. It was fired point-blank at the man who murdered him--and the murderer must have been one of his own men, and that man must have fled from the fort. But again, why? Why? *Why?*

Why not have shot his officer, as I said before? He would never have had even the *need* to deny having done it, for no one would have dreamt of accusing him.

And then I had an idea. I suddenly said to myself, 'Suppose some scoundrel bayoneted the Commandant even before the alarm was given or the attack began--and then organised the defence and died at his post with the others?'

Led a mutiny of the garrison, perhaps; took command; and was shot and propped up in his embrasure by someone else. Yes, but who propped the last man up? He did not do it himself, that was certain--for every single corpse on that roof had been *arranged* before *rigor mortis* set in. The only man who was not 'to the life' was one who lay on his back. It was curious, that recumbent corpse with closed eyes and folded hands, but I did not see that it offered any clue. Whoever had been doing the ghastly work of corpse-drilling had overlooked it--or, indeed, had been going to set the dead man up when the final tragedy, whatever it was, occurred.

It may have been that the brave *sous-officier* was going to arrange this very corpse when he was attacked. Or, as I say, the officer may have been dead the whole time, or part of it, and the last survivor may have had this last work cut short by a bullet, before he had put the man in position.

But if so, where *was* he? ... Was it the man who had fired the two shots in answer to mine--and if so, what had become of him? *Why had he fired if he wished to hide or escape?*

My head spun. I felt I was going mad.

And then I said to myself, '*Courage, mon brave!* Go calmly up to that terrible roof again, and just quietly and clearly make certain of two points. First: Is there any one of those standing corpses who has not quite obviously been arranged, propped up, fixed in position? If so--*that* is the man who killed his officer and was afterwards shot by the Arabs. Secondly: Has any one of those dead men been shot point-blank with a revolver? (That I should be able to tell at a glance.) If so, *that* is the man who killed his officer--(who lived long enough to thrust his assailant into an embrasure)... .'"

"After himself being bayoneted through the heart!" enquired Lawrence.

"Exactly what I said to myself--and groaned aloud as I said it," replied de Beaujolais.

"Anyhow," he continued, "I would go up and see if any man had been shot by a revolver, and if any man lay *naturally* against the slope of an embrasure... . I turned to ascend the stair, and then, George, and not till then, I got the *real* shock of that awful day of shocks. For, *where was my trumpeter?*

I had made a quick but complete tour of the place and now realised in a flash that I had seen no living thing and heard no sound.

'*Trompette! Trompette!*' I shouted. I rushed to the door leading to the courtyard, the little interior, high-walled parade ground.

'*Trompette!*' I shouted and yelled, again and again, till my voice cracked.

Not a sound. Not a movement.

And then, in something like panic, putting all else from my mind, I rushed to the gates, lifted down the great bars, pulled the heavy bolts, turned the great key, and dragged them open--just as the mule-squadron arrived and my good Sergeant-Major was giving them the signal to join the assault!

It was not that I had suddenly remembered that the time I had allowed him must be up, but that I needed to see a human being again, to hear a human voice, after a quarter of an hour in that House of Death, that sinister-abode of tragic mysteries. I felt an urgent and unconquerable yearning for some ..."

"Breakfast," said George Lawrence, as the train slowed down.

§ 6

Bathed, full-fed, and at peace with a noisy world, in so far as choking dust, grilling heat, and the weariness of three days' close confinement in a stuffy carriage allowed, the two *compagnons de voyage* lay and smoked the cheroot of digestion in a brief silence. Brief, because it was not in the power of the impulsive and eloquent *beau sabreur*, of the Spahis, to keep silence for long upon the subject uppermost in his active and ardent mind.

"*Georges, mon vieux,*" he broke silence, "do you believe in spirits, ghosts, devils?"

"I firmly believe in whiskey, the ghost of a salary, and a devil of a thin time. Seen 'em myself," was the reply.

"Because the only solution that my Sergeant-Major could offer was just that... .

'*Spirits! Ghosts! Devils!*' he whispered, when he realised that the *sous-officier* had been murdered apparently by a corpse, and that the trumpeter had absolutely vanished into thin air, leaving not a trace of himself, and effecting the evaporation of his rifle as well as of his trumpet and everything else.

This was not very helpful, strongly as I was tempted to endorse it.

'Sergeant-Major Dufour,' said I, 'I am going to propound theories and you are going to find the weak points in them. The absurdities and idiocies in them.

Post vedettes far out, all round the place, and let the men fall out and water their beasts in the oasis. Sergeant Lebaudy will be in command. Tell him that fires may be lighted and *soupe* made, but that in an hour's time all are to be on grave-digging fatigue. He is to report immediately when mule-scouts from Lieutenant St. Andre's advance Senegalese arrive from Tokotu, or if anything happens meanwhile. If a vedette gives the alarm, all are to enter the fort immediately--otherwise no one is to set foot inside. Put a sentry at the gate.... You and I will look into this *affaire* while Achmet makes us some coffee'--and I gave the good fellow a cake of chocolate and a measure of cognac from my flask. We were both glad of that cognac.

While he was gone on this business I remained on the roof. I preferred the sunlight while I was alone. I freely admit it. I do not object to Arabs, but I dislike 'spirits, ghosts, and devils'--that commit murders and abductions. Perhaps I was not quite myself. But what would you? I had been enjoying fever; I had ridden all night; I was perilously near *cafard* myself; and the presence of those dead Watchers to whom I had spoken, the finding of that incredibly murdered man, the not finding of that more incredibly vanished trumpeter--had shaken me a little.

As I awaited the return of the Sergeant-Major I gazed at the corpse of the *sous-officier*, I stared and stared at the face of the dead man--not too pleasant a sight, George--contorted with rage, and pain, and hate--dead for some hours and it was getting hot on that roof--and there were flies ... flies... .

I stared, I say, as though I would drag the truth from him, compel the secret of this mystery from his dead lips, hypnotise those dead eyes to turn to mine and--but no, it was *he* that hypnotised and compelled, until I was fain to look away.

As I did so, I noticed the man who was lying near. Yes, undoubtedly someone had carefully and reverently laid him out. His eyes had been closed, his head propped up on a pouch, and his hands folded upon his chest. Why had he received such different treatment from that meted out to the others?

And then that bareheaded man. It was he--a very handsome fellow too--who had given me my first shock and brought it home to my wondering mind that the men who watched me were all dead.

You see, all but he had their faces in the deep shade of the big peaks of their *képis*-- whilst he, bareheaded and shot through the centre of the forehead, was dead obviously-- even to shortsighted me, looking up from below against the strong sunlight; even to me, deceived at first by his lifelike attitude.

And, as I glanced at their two *képis* lying there, I noticed something peculiar.

One had been wrenched and torn from within. The lining, newly ripped, was protruding, and the inner leather band was turned down and outward. It was as though something had recently been torn violently out of the cap--something concealed in the lining perhaps? ...

No, it was not the freak of a ricochetting bullet. The standing man had been hit just above the nose and under the cap, the recumbent man was hit in the chest.

'Now what is this?' thought I. 'A man shot through the brain does not remove his cap and tear the lining out. He gives a galvanic start, possibly spins round, and quietly he falls backwards. His limbs stretch once and quiver, and he is still for ever. His tight-fitting cap may, or may not, fall off as he goes down--but there is no tearing out of the lining, no turning down of the leather band.'

Bullets play funny tricks, I know, but not upon things they do not touch. This bullet had been fired, I should say, from a palm tree, and almost on a level with the roof; anyhow, it had entered the head below the cap. There was no hole in *that* whatsoever. To which of these two men did the cap belong?...

Had all been normal in that terrible place, all lying dead as they had fallen, I might never have noticed this torn cap. As it was--where everything was extraordinary, and the mind of the beholder filled with suspicion and a thousand questions, it was most interesting and remarkable. It became portentous. It was one more phenomenon in that focus of phenomena!

And from that cap and its recently torn and still protruding lining--oh yes, most obviously torn quite recently, with its edging of unsoiled threads, frayed but clean--from that cap, I looked quite instinctively at the paper crushed in the left hand of the dead officer. I know not why I connected these two things in my mind. They connected themselves perhaps--and I was about to take the paper from the rigid fist, when I thought, 'No! Everything shall be done in order and with correctness. I will touch nothing, do nothing, until the Sergeant-Major returns and I have a witness.'

If I was to be *procureur, juge d'instruction,* judge and jury, coroner, and perhaps, avenger--everything should be done in due form--and my report upon the impossible affair be of some value, too.

But without touching the paper, I could see, and I saw with surprise--though the *bon Dieu* knows I had not much capacity for surprise left in my stunned mind--that the writing was in English!

Why should *that* be added to my conundrums? ... A paper with English writing on it, in the hand of a dead French officer in a block-house in the heart of the *Territoire Militaire* of the Sahara!"

"Perhaps the bloke was English," suggested Lawrence. "I have heard that there are some in the Legion."

"No," was the immediate reply. "That he most certainly was not. A typical Frenchman of the Midi--a stoutish, florid, blue-jowled fellow of full habit. Perhaps a Provençal--thousands like him in Marseilles, Arles, Nîmes, Avignon, Carcassonne, Tarascon. Might have been the good Tartarin himself. Conceivably a Belgian; *possibly* a Spaniard or Italian, but most certainly not an Englishman... . Still less was the standing man, an olive-cheeked Italian or Sicilian."

"And the recumbent bareheaded chap?" said Lawrence.

"Ah--quite another affair, that! He might very well have been English. In fact, had I been asked to guess at his nationality, I should have said, 'A Northerner certainly, English most probably.' He would have been well in the picture in the Officers' Mess of one of your regiments. Just the type turned out by your Public Schools and Universities by the thousand.

What you are thinking is exactly what occurred to me. English writing on the paper; an English-looking legionary; his cap lying near the man who held the paper crushed in his hand; the lining just torn out of the cap! ... Ha! Here was a little glimmer of light, a possible clue. I was just reconstructing the scene when I heard the Sergeant-Major ascending the stair...

Had this Englishman killed the *sous-officier* while the latter tore some document from the lining of the man's cap? Obviously not. The poor fellow's bayonet was in its sheath at his side, and if he *had* done it--how had he got himself put into position?"

"Might have been shot afterwards," said Lawrence.

"No. He was *arranged,* I tell you," was the reply, "and he most assuredly had not arranged himself. Besides, he was bareheaded. Does a man go about bareheaded in the afternoon sun of the Sahara? But to my mind the question doesn't arise--in view of the fact of that inexplicable bayonet.

One bayonet more than there were soldiers and rifles!

No--I ceased reconstructing the scene with *that* one as the slayer, and I had no reason to select anyone else for the rôle.... Then I heard the bull voice of Sergeant Lebaudy, down in the oasis, roar '*Formez les faisceaux*' and '*Sac à terre,*' and came back to facts as the Sergeant-Major approached and saluted.

'All in order, *mon Commandant*,' reported he, and fell to eyeing the corpses.

'Even to half-smoked cigarettes in their mouths!' he whispered. '*The fallen who were not allowed to fall--the dead forbidden to die.*' Then--'But where in the name of God is Jean the Trumpeter?'

'Tell me that, *Chef,* and I will fill your *képi* with twenty-franc pieces--and give you the Grand Cross of the Legion of Honour,' said I.

The Sergeant-Major blasphemed, crossed himself, and then said, 'Let us get out of here while we can.'

'Are you a Sergeant-Major or a young lady?' I enquired--and as one does, in such circumstances, rated him soundly for feeling exactly as I did myself; and the more I said, the more angry and unreasonable I grew. You know how one's head and one's nerves get, in that accursed desert, George."

"I know, old son," agreed Lawrence. "I have found myself half-ready to murder a *piccin,* for dropping a plate."

"Yes--the best of us get really insane at times, in that hellish heat and unnatural life.... But I got a hold upon myself and felt ashamed--for the good fellow took it well.

'Did Your Excellency make a thorough search?' he asked, rebukingly polite.

'But, my dear *Chef,* what need to make a thorough search for a living man, a hale and hearty, healthy soldier, in a small place into which he had been sent to open a gate? *Mon Dieu!* he has legs! He has a tongue in his head! If he were here, wouldn't he *be* here?' I asked.

'Murdered perhaps,' was the reply.

'By whom? Beetles? Lizards?' I sneered.

He shrugged his shoulders, and pointed to the *sous-officier* with a dramatic gesture.

That one had not been murdered by beetles or lizards!

'Yes,' said I. 'Now we'll reconstruct this crime, first reading what is on this paper,' and I opened the stiffened fingers and took it. There was a dirty crumpled torn envelope there, too. Now *Georges, mon vieux,* prepare yourself. You are going to show a little emotion, my frozen Englishman!"

Lawrence smiled faintly.

"It was a most extraordinary document," continued de Beaujolais. "I'll show it to you when we get on board the ship. It was something like this: On the envelope was, '*To the Chief of Police of Scotland Yard and all whom it may concern.*' And on the paper, '*Confession. Important. Urgent. Please publish.*

For fear that any innocent person may be suspected, I hereby fully and freely confess that it was I, and I alone, who stole the great sapphire known as 'Blue Water.' "...

"What!" shouted George Lawrence, jumping up. "What? *What* are you saying, de Beaujolais?"

"Aha! my little George," smiled the Frenchman, gloating. "And where is the *phlegme Britannique* now, may I ask? That made you sit up, quite literally, didn't it? We do not yawn now, my little George, do we?"

George Lawrence stared at his friend, incredulous, open-mouthed.

"*But that is Lady Brandon's jewel!* ... What on earth ..." stammered Lawrence, sitting down heavily. "Are you romancing, de Beaujolais? Being funny?"

"I am telling you what was written on this paper--which I will show you when I can get at my dispatch-case, my friend," was the reply.

"Good God, man! *Lady Brandon!* ... Do you mean to say that the 'Blue Water' has been pinched--and that the thief took refuge in the Foreign Legion, or drifted there somehow?" asked Lawrence, lying back on his roll of bedding.

"I don't mean to say anything--except to tell my little tale, the dull little tale that has bored you so, my George," replied de Beaujolais, with a malicious grin.

George Lawrence swung his feet to the ground and stood up again. Never had his friend seen this reserved, taciturn, and unemotional man so affected.

"I don't get you. I don't take it in," he said. "Lady Brandon's stone! *Our* Lady Brandon? The 'Blue Water' that we used to be allowed to look at sometimes? Stolen! ... And you have found it?" ...

"I have found nothing, my friend, but a crumpled and bloodstained piece of paper in a dead man's hand," was the reply.

"With Lady Brandon's name on it! It's absurd, man... . In the middle of the Sahara! And *you* found it... . With her name on it! ... Well, I'm absolutely damned!" ejaculated Lawrence.

"Yes, my friend. And perhaps you begin to realise how 'absolutely damned' I was, when I read that paper--sticky with blood. But probably I was not as surprised as you are now. Even that could not have surprised me very much then, I think," said de Beaujolais.

Lawrence sat down.

"Go on, old chap," he begged. "I sincerely apologise for my recent manners. Please tell me everything, and then let us thrash it out... . Lady Brandon! ... The 'Blue Water' stolen!" ...

"No need for apologies, my dear George," smiled his friend. "If you seemed a little unimpressed and bored at times, it only gave me the greater zest for the *dénouement*, when you should hear your ... our ... friend's name come into this extraordinary story."

"You're a wily and patient old devil, Jolly," said the astounded Lawrence. "I salute you, Sir. A logical old cuss, too! Fancy keeping *that* back until now, and telling the yarn neatly, in proper sequence and due order, until the right point in the story was reached, and then ..."

"Aha! the *phlegme Britannique,* eh, George!" chuckled de Beaujolais. "Wonderful how the volatile and impetuous Frenchman could do it, wasn't it? And there is something else to come, my friend. All in 'logical proper sequence and due order' there comes another little surprise."

"Then, for God's sake get on with it, old chap! ... More about Lady Brandon, is it?" replied Lawrence, now all animation and interest.

"Indirectly, *mon cher Georges.* For that paper was signed--*by whom?*"asked the Frenchman, leaning forward, tapping his friend's knee, staring impressively with narrowed eyes into those of that bewildered gentleman.

And into the ensuing silence he slowly and deliberately dropped the words, "*By Michael Geste!*"

Lawrence raised himself on his elbow and stared at his friend incredulous.

"By *Michael Geste!* Her nephew! You don't mean to tell me that *Michael Geste* stole her sapphire and slunk off to the Legion? 'Beau' Geste! *Get* out ..." he said, and fell back.

"I don't mean to tell you anything, my friend, except that the paper was signed 'Michael Geste.'"

"Was the bareheaded man he? Look here, *are* you pulling my leg?"

"I do not know who the man was, George. And I am not pulling your leg. I saw two or three boys and two so beautiful girls, once, at Brandon Abbas, years ago. This man might have been one of them. The age would be about right. And then, again, this man may have had nothing on earth to do with the paper. Nor any other man on that roof, except the *sous-officier*--and he most certainly was not Michael Geste. He was a man of forty or forty-five years, and as I have said, no Englishman."

"Michael would be about twenty or so," said Lawrence. "He was the oldest of the nephews.... But, my dear Jolly, the Gestes don't *steal!* They are her nephews.... I am going to put some ice on my head."

"I have wanted a lot of ice to the head, the last few weeks, George. What, too, of the murdered *sous-officier* and the utterly "vanished trumpeter?"

"Oh, damn your trumpeter and *sous-officier,*" was the explosive reply. "Michael Geste! ... Lady Brandon.... Forgive me, old chap, and finish the story ..." and George Lawrence lay back on his couch and stared at the roof of the carriage.

Lady Brandon! The only woman in the world.

§ 7

And as the train rumbled on through the sweltering coast-lands toward Lagos, Major de Beaujolais, highly pleased with the success of his neat and clever little *coup,* continued his story.

"Well, my George, figure me there, with this new astoundment, this extraordinary accompaniment to the sinister and bewildering mystery of an inexplicable murder and an inexplicable disappearance.... .

And then, 'What is in the paper, might one respectfully enquire, *mon Commandant,*' asked the Sergeant-Major.

'The confession of a thief--that he stole a famous jewel,' I replied.

'Which was the thief?' said he.

'Oh, ask me some questions, my good imbecile!' said I. 'Ask me where the trumpeter is, and whose is this bayonet, and who disposed these dead men as defenders, and who fired two shots, and whether I am mad or dreaming,' I answered--and then pulled myself together. 'Now come with me,' I bade him. 'We will make one more search below, and then *déjeuner,* and a quiet, sensible, reasonable discussion of the facts, before we bury these brave fellows, detail an *escouade* of our men as garrison, and return to Tokotu. I shall leave you in command here until we get orders and reliefs.'

The Sergeant-Major looked distinctly dubious at this. '*Here*--for weeks!' he said softly.

We made our tour below, and, as before, nothing unusual met the eye, and there was no sign of the trumpeter, alive or dead. We had seen him climb on to that parapet and apparently no living eye had beheld him again.

I was past wonder. I accepted things.

Very well, this was a place where Commandants are murdered by non-existent people; soldiers vanish like a whiff of smoke; and English letters concerning one's friends are found in the hands of dead Frenchmen. Very good. Be it so. We would 'carry on' as you say, and do our duty.

'Think hard--and be prepared to pick holes in the theories I shall propound an hour hence,' said I to the Sergeant-Major, as we passed out of the gate, and I proceeded to the oasis where my excellent Achmet had prepared my soup and coffee... .

You do not want to hear my theories, George, and there was no need for the Sergeant-Major to point out the impossibilities and absurdities in them. They leapt to the eye immediately.

It all came back to the bald facts that there must be a soldier of the garrison missing, that he must have taken his rifle and left his bayonet in the *sous-officier,* instead of shooting him and awaiting praise and reward; that my trumpeter had vanished; that the dead *sous-officier* had been in possession of a confession, real or bogus, to the effect that Michael Geste had stolen his aunt's famous sapphire.

There it was--and nothing but lunacy could result from theory-making about the *sous-officier's* murder, the trumpeter's disappearance, or Michael Geste's confession and how it got there.

No--you do not want to hear those perfectly futile theories--those explanations that explained nothing. But it may interest you to hear that I was faced that evening, on top of the rest of my little pleasures, with a military mutiny."

"Good Lord!" ejaculated Lawrence, turning to the speaker.

"Yes. At four o'clock I ordered the Sergeant-Major to fall the men in, and I would tell off the new garrison for Zinderneuf.

In a most unusual manner the Sergeant-Major hung fire, so to speak, instead of stepping smartly off about his duty.

'Well?' said I sharply.

'There is going to be trouble, *mon Commandant,*' he faltered.

'*Mon Dieu,* there is!' I snapped, 'and *I* am going to make it, if I have any nonsense. What do you mean?'

'Sergeant Lebaudy says that Corporal Brille says that the men say ...'

'Name of the Name of the Name of Ten Thousand Thundering Tin Devils,' I shouted... . 'You say that he says that they say that she says,' I mocked. '*Va t'en, grand babbilard!*' I roared at him. 'I'll be on parade outside those gates in ten seconds, and if you and your gibbering chatterboxes are not awaiting me there at attention ...' and my poor Sergeant-Major fled.

I was the more angry at his news, for I had subconsciously expected something of the sort.

What else, with these ignorant, superstitious clods, who were the bravest of the brave against human foes? None like them. Every man a hero in battle... . But what of that House of Death with its Watchers? That place into which their comrade had boldly climbed--and never come forth again.

Rastignac had begun it. And they had seen him face instant death rather than enter it--Rastignac, the fearless reckless devil, whose bravery alone had prevented his escapades from bringing him to a court-martial and the Zephyrs. He, of all men, was afraid of the place. There is nothing so infectious as *that* sort of panic... .

Well! One more fact to accept.

If the men would not enter the fort of Zinderneuf, they would not enter the fort of Zinderneuf--and that was that.

But if the will of these scoundrels was coming into conflict with the will of Henri de Beaujolais, there were exciting times ahead. Since they sought sorrow they should certainly find it--and as I put on my belt and boots again, I felt a certain elation.

'Action is always action, *mon Henri*,' said I to myself, 'and it will be a change from these thrice-accursed theories and attempts to explain the inexplicable and reconcile the irreconcilable.'

Bah! I would teach my little dogs to show their teeth, and I rode, on a mule, over to the fort. There I bade Dufour and Lebaudy select an *escouade* of the worst men, all *mauvais sujets* of that Company. They should garrison either Zinderneuf fort, or else the grave that had been dug for those brave 'fallen who had not been allowed to fall.' ...

As I rode up, the Sergeant-Major Dufour called the men to attention, and they stood like graven images, the selected *escouade* on the right, while I made an eloquent speech, the funeral oration of that brave band to whom we were about to give a military funeral with all the last honours that France could render to the worthy defenders of her honour and her Flag.

Tears stood in my eyes and my voice broke as I concluded by quoting:--

'Soldats de la Légion,
De la Légion Étrangère,
N'ayant pas de nation,
La France est votre mère.'

Then, when the selected new garrison got the order, '*Par files de quatre. En avant. Marche*,' that they might march into the fort and begin their new duties by bringing the dead out for burial--they did something quite otherwise.

Taking the time from the right, with smartness and precision they stooped as one man, laid their rifles on the ground, rose as one man and stood at attention!

The right-hand man, a grizzled veteran of Madagascar, Tonquin, and Dahomey, took a pace forward, saluted, and with wooden face, said, 'We prefer to die with Rastignac.'

This was flat disobedience and rank mutiny. I had hardly expected quite this.

'But Rastignac is not going to die. He is going to live--long years, I hope--in the *Joyeux*. You, however, who are but cowardly sheep, led astray by him, shall have the better fate. You shall die now, or enter Zinderneuf fort and do your duty.... Sergeant-Major, have those rifles collected. Let the remainder of the Company right form, and on the order '*Attention pour les feux de salve*,' the front rank will kneel, and on the order, "*Feu*," every man will do his duty.'

But I knew better, George. That was precisely what they *wouldn't* do; and I felt that this was my last parade. That accursed fort was still exerting its horrible influence. These fools feared that it would kill them if they entered it, and I feared it would kill them if they did not. For let me but handle them wrongly now, and they would shoot me and the non-commissioned officers and march off into the desert to certain death, as they weakened from thirst and starvation. They would be harried and hunted and herded along by the Arabs, and daily reduced in numbers until a sudden rush swept over them and nothing remained for the survivors but horrible tortures.

Mutinous dogs they might be, and fools they were--but no less would the responsibility for their sufferings and deaths be mine if I mishandled the situation. I thought of other desert-mutinies in the Legion.

It was an awkward dilemma, George. If I ordered the Company to fire upon the squad, they would refuse and would thereby become mutineers themselves. They would then feel that they might as well be hung for a sheep as a lamb, and, having shot me, take their chance of escape and freedom.

If, on the other hand, I condoned this refusal of the *escouade*--what of military discipline? Duty to my country came before my duty to these fellows, and I must not allow any pity for their probable fate to come between me and my duty as a French officer.

I decided that if they *would* die, then die they must--but I at least could do my best to save them. Without deviating from the path of duty, I would hold out a hand to them.

If the *escouade* would not enter the fort they must expiate their military crime. If the company would not carry out my orders and fire on the mutineers, they must expiate *their* crime.

If I were to be shot, I should at least be saved the unpleasantness of reporting that my men had mutinied, and I should die in the knowledge that I had done my duty.

Yes--I would make it clear that disobedience to my orders would be death. Swift and sudden for some, lingering and horrible for many, sure and certain for all. Then I would 'carry on' as you say. Was I right, George?"

"I think you were quite right, Jolly," agreed Lawrence.

"As I was deciding thus, all in the space of a few seconds, with every eye upon me and a terrible tension drawing every face," continued de Beaujolais, "the Sergeant-Major approached and saluted. I eyed him coldly. With his back to the men, he whispered:

'They won't do it, *mon Commandant*. For God's sake do not give the order. They are rotten with *cafard* and over-fatigue. That Rastignac is their hero and leader. They will shoot you and desert *en masse*.... A night's rest will work wonders.... Besides, Lieutenant St. André and the Senegalese will be here by midnight. It is full moon to-night.'

'And shall we sit and wait for the Senegalese, Dufour?' I whispered back. 'Would you like to ask these fellows to spare us till they come?'

And looking from him to the men I said loudly:

'You are too merciful, Sergeant-Major. We don't do things thus in the Spahis. But these are not Spahis. However, in consideration of the most excellent march the men have made, I will do as you beg and give these *cafard*-stricken fools till moon-rise. It gives me no pleasure to inflict punishment, and I hope no man will insist on being punished. We are all tired, and since you intercede for your men I grant a four-hour holiday. At moon-rise, our motto is "*Work or die.*" Till then, all may rest. After then, the dead will be buried and the fort garrisoned. I hope there will be no *more* dead to be buried to-night.'

And I rode back to the oasis, hearing as I did so the voice of the Sergeant-Major, exhorting the men and concluding with the order, '*Rompez.*'

He joined me a few minutes later.

'They'll never do it, *mon Commandant*,' said he. 'They'll fear the place worse than ever by moonlight. In the morning we could call for volunteers to accompany us. And then the Senegalese ...'

'That will do, Dufour,' said I. 'They will render instant obedience at moon-rise, or take the consequences. I have strained my military conscience already to satisfy my private conscience. If, after four hours' rest and reflection, they still decide to mutiny--on their heads be it! No responsibility rests on me. If they mutiny, they do it in cold blood. If they obey orders before the Senegalese arrive, no great harm has been done, and discipline has been maintained. That is the very utmost length to which I can go in my desire to save them.'

'To save *them, mon Commandant!* It is *you* I am trying to save,' stammered the good fellow.

Patting him on the shoulder as he turned to go, I bade him send me a couple of the most influential men of the *escouade* and two or three of the best of the remainder--leaders of different cliques, if there were any.

I would point out to them the inevitable and awful results to the men themselves, of disobedience and mutiny. I would speak of the heroism, discipline, and dutifulness of the dead. I would point out to them that in the event of mutiny, they themselves would either be loyal and die at the hands of the mutineers, or become deserters and die at the hands of the Arabs. I would then send them back among their fellows--and abide the issue... .

It was while I awaited their arrival that I wished our army more resembled yours in one particular--the relationship between officers and men. Our fellows get too much noncommissioned officer and too little officer. We are too remote from them. We do not play games with them, get to know them, interest ourselves in them as fellow human beings, in the way that your officers do. Too often it is a case with us of hated non-coms. and stranger-officers. Particularly is this so in the Legion. The non-coms. are all-powerful and tyrannical; the officers are utterly uninterested in the men as individuals, and do not even know their names.

And I was not one of their own officers of the Legion. I was a Spahi officer, superintending the organising of mule-cavalry out of infantry; or rather, making ordinary infantry into mounted infantry, that the Legion might hope to compete with the Touaregs in mobility. We wanted mounted riflemen down there just as you did in the Boer War, or else the Arabs served us as the Boers did you at first.

I certainly had not been unduly harsh or oppressive during the time I had been with this particular lot; but, on the other hand, I certainly had no *personal* influence with them. I did not know them, nor they me, and all our lives seemed likely to be forfeit in consequence... .

However, I talked to the men whom Dufour brought, and did my best under the heavy handicap of not so much as knowing their names. Finally, I dismissed them with the words:

'For your lives, influence your friends wisely and well, and get it into their heads that at moon-rise we will have obedience with honour and safety, or disobedience with dishonour, misery, and death. For at moon-rise, the chosen *escouade* will enter the fort and bring out the dead, or the company will fire upon them.... *Au 'voir, mes enfants.*'

Of course, I knew the danger of making any reference to what would happen if the company refused to fire on the *escouade*--but it was foolish to pretend to ignore the possibility of such a thing. But I made no allusion to the Senegalese, and the coercion or punishment of white men by black.

It *might* be that the company would obey orders, if the *escouade* remained mutinous, and it *might* be that all would reflect upon the coming of the Senegalese.

Anyhow, I was on a knife-edge, and all depended upon the effect on these rascals of a four-hour rest and the words of the men to whom I had talked. There was just a chance that St. André and his Senegalese might arrive in time to influence the course of affairs--but I most certainly could not bring myself to postpone the issue until his arrival, and then take shelter behind the blacks. With the full moon well up in the sky--by its beautiful soft light--we should see what we should see ...

And then, just as the men turned to go, I had an idea. Suppose some of them would volunteer to go over the fort with me; see for themselves that there was nothing to be afraid of; and then report to their fellows that all was well.

Their statement and the inevitable airs of superiority which they would give themselves, might well counteract Rastignac's influence and their superstitious fears. If some of these men, selected for character and influence, went back in the spirit of, 'Well, cowards, *we* have been in there and it is much the same as any other such cursed hole--except that somebody had a great idea for diddling the Arabs,' the others would probably take the line, 'Well, where you can go, we can. Who are *you* to swagger?'

Yes--I would try it. Not as though I were really persuading or beseeching, and anxious to prove that the *escouade* had nothing to fear if sent to garrison the place. No--merely as offering them, superior soldiers, an opportunity of seeing the fort before its remarkable dispositions were disturbed.

'Wait a moment,' said I, as they saluted and turned to go. 'Is there a man of courage among you--a man, *par exemple* such as the trumpeter, brave enough to enter an empty fort with me?'

They looked sheepish for a moment. Someone murmured, 'And where *is* Jean the Trumpeter?' and then I heard a curious whispered remark:

'*Gee! I sure would like to see a ghost, Buddy,*' and the whispered reply:

'*Sure thing, Hank, and I'd like to see ole Brown some more.*'

Two men stepped forward as one, and saluted.

They were in extraordinary contrast in body, and some similarity in face, for one was a giant and the other not more than five feet in height, while both had clean-shaven leathery countenances, somewhat of the bold Red Indian type.

You know what I mean--lean hatchet faces, biggish noses, mouths like a straight gash, and big chins. By their grey eyes they were Northerners, and by their speech Americans.

'You would like to see the fort and how it was manned to the last by heroes--victorious in death?' I asked.

'*Oui, mon Commandant,*' they replied together.

'Isn't there a *Frenchman* among you?' I asked the rest.

Another man, a big sturdy Gascon he looked, saluted and joined the Americans. Then what they now call 'the herd instinct' and 'mob-psychology' came into play, and the others did the same.

Good! I had got the lot. I would take them round the fort as though doing honour to the dead and showing them as an example--and then I suddenly remembered ..."

"The murdered *sous-officier*," said George Lawrence.

"Exactly, George! These fellows must not see him lying there with a French bayonet through him! I must go in first, alone, and give myself the pleasant task of removing the bayonet. I would cover his face, and it would be assumed that he had been shot and had fallen where he lay. Yes, that was it... .

'Good! You shall come with me then,' said I, 'and have the privilege of treading holy ground and seeing a sight of which to talk to your grandchildren when you are old men. You can also tell your comrades of what you have seen, and give them a fresh pride in their glorious Regiment,' and I bade the Sergeant-Major march them over to the fort.

Mounting my mule, which had not been unsaddled, I rode quickly across to the gate. The sentry had been withdrawn.

Dismounting, I hurried up to the roof, to perform the distasteful duty I could not very well have delegated to the Sergeant-Major. I emerged from the darkness of the staircase on to the roof.

And there I stood and stared and stared and rubbed my eyes--and then for a moment felt just a little faint and just a little in sympathy with those poor superstitious fools of the*escouade*... . For, my dear George, *the body of the sous-officier was no longer there!* Nor was that of the bareheaded recumbent man!"

"Good God!" ejaculated Lawrence, raising himself on his elbow and turning to de Beaujolais.

"Yes, that is what I said," continued the other. "What else was there to say? *Were* there djinns, afrites, evil spirits in this cursed desert, even as the inhabitants declared? Was the whole thing a nightmare? Had I dreamt that the body of a French *sous-officier* had lain here, with a French bayonet through it? Or was I dreaming now?

And then I think my temperature went up two or three degrees from the mere hundred and two that one disregards; for I remember entertaining the wild idea that perhaps a living man was shamming dead among these corpses. Moreover, I remember going round from corpse to corpse and questioning them. One or two that seemed extra lifelike I took by the arm, and as I shouted at them, I shook them and pulled at them until they fell to the ground, their rifles clattering down with them.

Suddenly I heard the feet of men upon the stair, and pulled myself together. The Sergeant-Major and the half-dozen or so of legionaries came out on to the roof.

I managed to make my little speech as they stared round in amazement, the most amazed of all being the Sergeant-Major, who gazed at the smeared pool of blood where the body of the *sous-officier* had lain.

The two Americans seemed particularly interested, and appeared to be looking for comrades among the dead.

When would one of the men salute and ask respectfully the first of the hundred questions that must be puzzling them: '*Where is their officer?*'

And what should I reply? They could see for themselves that the Arabs had not entered and carried him off. Perhaps their minds were too full of the question: '*Where is Jean the Trumpeter?*' for the other question to formulate itself.

I had made no reference to the disappearance of the trumpeter; but I knew that they had seen him enter the fort and had waited, as I did, for an astounding quarter of an hour, to see him come out again. They had watched me go in alone, at the end of that time, and had seen me emerge alone. What could I say?

It seemed to me to be best to say nothing on that subject, so I said it.

After a few minutes that seemed like a few hours, I bade Dufour take the men round the outbuildings, and then march them back to the oasis.

As he disappeared, last, down the stair, I called him back and we were alone together. Simultaneously we said the same words: '*Did you move it?*'--and each of us knew that the other knew nothing about it!

I laughed loudly, if not merrily, and the Sergeant-Major produced the oath of a lifetime; in length and originality, remarkable even for the Legion.

'Quite so, *Chef*,' said I... . 'Life grows a little complicated.'

'I'll give a complicated death to this *farceur,* when I find ...' growled he as I motioned him to be off. 'Blood of the devil, I will!'

He clattered down the stairs, and, soon after, I heard his voice below, as he led the group of men across the courtyard.

'Not much here to terrify the great Rastignac, *hein?*' he jeered.

'But there is certainly something here to terrify *me,* my friend,' I observed to myself, and made my way back to my mule and the oasis... . In fact, I fled... .

Well, George, *mon vieux,* what do you think happened! Did the *escouade* obey and enter the fort like lambs, or did they refuse and successfully defy me, secure in the knowledge that the others would not fire on them?"

"You are alive to tell the tale, Jolly," was the reply. "That's the main thing."

"On account of the importance of a part of it to you, my George, eh?" smiled the Frenchman.

"Oh, not at all, old chap," Lawrence hastened to say, with a somewhat guilty smile. "Simply on account of the fact that you are spared to France and to your friends."

"I thank you, my little George. Almost might you be a Frenchman," said de Beaujolais, with an ironical bow. "But tell me, what do you think happened? Did they obey and enter, or did they refuse?"

"Give it up, Jolly. I can only feel sure that one of the two happened," replied Lawrence.

"And that is where you are wrong, my friend, for neither happened," continued de Beaujolais. "They neither obeyed and entered, nor disobeyed and stayed out!"

"Good Lord!" ejaculated Lawrence. "What then?"

And this time it was the Frenchman who suggested a little refreshment.

§ 8

"Well, this is the last 'event' on that remarkable programme, *mon cher Georges,*" resumed de Beaujolais a little later. "A very appropriate and suitable one too... . '*A delightful open-air entertainment concluded with fireworks,*' as the reporters of *fêtes champêtres* say."

"Fireworks? Rifle-fire works do you mean?" asked Lawrence.

"No, my George, nothing to speak of. Just fireworks. Works of fire... . I will tell you... .

I let the moon get well up, and then sent my servant, Achmet, for the Sergeant-Major, and bade that good fellow to parade the men as before, with the fort a hundred paces in their rear, the garrison *escouade* on the right of the line.

This party would either march into the fort or not. If *not*--then the remainder would be ordered to right-form and shoot them where they stood, for disobedience in the field, practically in the presence of the enemy.

The remainder would either obey or not. If *not*--then I would at once give the order to 'pile arms.' If they did this, as they might, from force of habit, they would immediately be marched off to the oasis and would be 'arrested' by the non-commissioned officers and marched back to Tokotu, under escort of the Senegalese, to await court martial. If they did not pile arms, the non-commissioned officers were to come at once to me, and we would prepare to sell our lives dearly--for the men would mutiny and desert. Possibly a few of the men would join us, and there was a ghost of a chance that we might fight our way into the fort and hold it, but it was infinitely more probable that we should be riddled where we stood.

'*Bien, mon Commandant,*' said Dufour, as he saluted, and then, hesitatingly, 'Might I presume to make a request and a suggestion. May I stand by you, and Rastignac stand by me--with the muzzle of my revolver against his liver--it being clear that, at the slightest threat to you, Rastignac's digestion is impaired? If he knows that just this will happen, he also may give good advice to his friends... .'

'Nothing of the sort, Dufour,' I replied. 'Everything will proceed normally and properly, until the men themselves behave abnormally and improperly. We shall lead and command soldiers of France until we have to fight and kill, or be killed by, mutineers against the officers of France in the execution of their duty. Proceed.'

Would you have said the same, George? It seemed to me that this idea of the Sergeant-Major's was not much better than that of waiting for the Senegalese. Would you have done the same in my place?"

"I can only *hope* I should have had the courage to act as bravely and as wisely as you did, Jolly," was the reply.

"Oh, I am no hero, my friend," smiled de Beaujolais, "but it seemed the right thing to do. I had not in any way provoked a mutiny--indeed, I had stretched a point to avert it--and it was my business to go straight ahead, do my duty, and abide the result.

But it was with an anxious heart that I mounted the mule again and cantered over to the fort.

I had thought of going on a camel, for, it is a strange psychological fact, that if your hearers have to look up to you physically, they also have to look up to you metaphysically as it were. If a leader speaks with more authority from a mule than from the ground, and with more weight and power from a horse than from a mule, would he not speak with still more from a camel?

Perhaps--but I felt that I could *do* more, somehow, in case of trouble, if I could dash at assailants with sword and revolver. I am a cavalry man and the *arme blanche* is my weapon. Cold steel and cut and thrust, for me, if I had to go down fighting. You can't charge and use your sword on a camel, so I compromised on the mule--but how I longed for my Arab charger and a few of my Spahis behind me! It would be a fight then, instead of a murder...

It was a weird and not unimpressive scene. That sinister fort, silver and black; the frozen waves of the ocean of sand, an illimitable silver sea; the oasis a big, dark island upon it; the men, statues, inscrutable and still.

What would they do? Would my next words be my last? Would a double line of rifles rise and level themselves at my breast, or would that *escouade,* upon whom everything depended, move off like a machine and enter the fort?

As I faced the men, I was acutely interested, and yet felt like a spectator, impersonal and unafraid. I was about to witness a thrilling drama, depicting the fate of one Henri de Beaujolais, quite probably his death. I hoped he would play a worthy part on this moonlit stage. I hoped that, even more than I hoped to see him survive the play. I was calm. I was detached...."

George Lawrence sighed and struck a match.

"I cast one more look at the glorious moon and took a deep breath. If this was my last order on parade, it should be worthily given, in a voice deep, clear, and firm. Above all firm. And as my mouth opened, and my lower jaw moved in the act of speech--I believe it dropped, George, and my mouth remained open.

For, from that enigmatical, brooding, fatal fort--there shot up a tongue of flame!

'*Mon Dieu! Regardez!*' cried the Sergeant-Major, and pointed. I believe every head turned, and in the perfect silence I heard him whisper, '*Spirits, ghosts, devils!*'

That brought me to myself sharply. 'Yes, imbecile!' I said. 'They carry matches and indulge in arson! Quite noted incendiaries! Where is Rastignac?'

I asked that because it was perfectly obvious that someone was in the fort and had set fire to something highly inflammable. I had been in the place an hour or two before. There was certainly no sign of fire then, and this was a sudden rush of flame.

As I watched, another column of smoke and fire burst forth in a different place.

'He is tied up back there, *mon Commandant,*' replied Dufour.

'The forbidden *crapaudine?*' I asked.

'I *told* Corporal Brille to tie him to a tree,' was the reply.

Anyhow it could not be Rastignac's work, for he would not have entered the place, even had he been left at liberty and had an opportunity to do so.

'Send and see if he is still there--and make sure that everyone else is accounted for,' I ordered.

It was useless to detail a *pompier* squad to put the fire out. We don't have hose and hydrants in the desert, as you know. When a place burns, it burns. And, *mon Dieu, how* it burns in the dry heat of that rainless desert! The place would be gone, even if the men would enter it, by the time we had got our teaspoonfuls of water from the oasis. And, to tell you the truth, I did not care how soon, or how completely it *did* go!

This fire would be the funeral pyre of those brave men. It would keep my fools from their suicidal mutiny. It would purge the place of mystery. Incidentally it would save my life and military reputation, and the new fort that would arise in its place would not be the haunted, hated prison that this place would henceforth have been for those who had to garrison it.

I gave the order to face about, and then to stand at ease. The men should watch it burn, since nothing could be done to save it. Perhaps even they would realise that human agency is required for setting a building on fire--and, moreover, whoever was in there had got to come out or be cremated. They should see him come... . But who? Who? The words *Who?* and *Why?* filled my mind... .

All stood absolutely silent, spellbound.

Suddenly the spell was broken and back we came to earth, at an old familiar sound.

A rifle cracked, again and again. From the sound the firing was towards us.

The Arabs were upon us!

Far to the right and to the left, more shots were fired.

The fort blazing and the Arabs upon us!

Bullets whistled overhead and I saw one or two flashes from a distant sand-hill.

No one was hit, the fort being between us and the enemy. In less time than it takes to tell I had the men turned about and making for the oasis--*au pas gymnastique*--'at the double,' as you call it. There we should have cover and water, and if we could only hold the devils until they were nicely between us and St. Andre's Senegalese, we would avenge the garrison of that blazing fort.

They are grand soldiers, those Légionnaires, George. No better troops in our army. They are to other infantry what my Spahis are to other cavalry. It warmed one's heart to see them double, steady as on parade, back to the darkness of the oasis, every man select his cover and go to ground, his rifle loaded and levelled as he did so.

Our camel vedettes rode in soon after. Two of them had had a desperate fight, and two of them had seen rifle-flashes and fired at them, before returning to the oasis, thinking the Arabs had rushed the fort and burnt it.

In a few minutes from the first burst of fire, the whole place was still, silent, and apparently deserted. Nothing for an enemy to see but a burning fort, and a black brooding oasis, where nothing moved.

How I hoped they would swarm yelling round the fort, thinking to get us like bolted rabbits as we rushed out of it! It is not like the Arabs to make a night attack, but doubtless they had been hovering near, and the fire had brought them down on us.

Had they seen us outside the fort? If so, they would attack the oasis in the morning. If they had not seen us, anything might happen, and the oasis prove a *guet-apens,* with the burning or burnt-out fort as the bait of the trap.

What were they doing now? The firing had ceased entirely. Probably making their dispositions to rush us suddenly at dawn, from behind the nearest sand-hills. Their game would be to lull us into a sense of security throughout a peaceful night and come down upon us at daybreak, like a whirlwind, as we slept.

And what if our waiting rifles caught them at fifty yards, and the survivors turned to flee--on to the muzzles of those of the Senegalese? ...

It was another impressive scene in that weird drama, George. A big fire, by moonlight, in the heart of the Sahara, a fire watched by silent, motionless men, breathlessly awaiting the arrival of other players on the stage.

After gazing into the moonlit distance until my eyes ached, expecting to see a great band of the blue-veiled mysterious Silent Ones suddenly swarm over a range of sand-hills, I bethought me of getting into communication with St. André.

I had ordered him to follow by a forced march, leaving a suitable garrison at Tokotu, when I dashed off with the 'always ready' emergency-detachment on camels, preceding by an hour or so the 'support' emergency-detachment on mules, with water, rations, and ammunition.

These two detachments are more than twice as fast as the best infantry, but I reckoned that St. André would soon be drawing near.

It was quite possible that he might run into the Arabs, while the latter were watching the oasis--if they had seen us enter it, or their skirmishers established the fact of our presence.

So far, we had not fired a shot from the oasis, and it was possible that our presence was unsuspected.

This might, or might not, be the same band that had attacked the place. If they were the same, they might be hanging about in the hope of ambushing a relieving force. If St. André arrived while the fort was burning, they would have no chance of catching him unawares. If he came after the flames had died down, he might march straight into a trap. There would certainly be a Targui scout or two out in the direction of Tokotu, while the main body did business at Zinderneuf.

Anyhow, I must communicate with St. André if possible. It would be a good man that would undertake the job successfully--for both skill and courage would be required. There was the track to find and follow, and there were the Arabs to face.

To lose the former was to die of thirst and starvation; to find the latter was to die of tortures indescribable.

On the whole it might be better to send two. Twice the chance of my message reaching St. André. Possibly more than twice the chance, really, as two men are braver than one, because they hearten each other.

I went round the oasis until I found the Sergeant-Major, who was going from man to man, prohibiting any firing without orders, any smoking or the making of any noise. This was quite sound and I commended him, and then asked for a couple of men of the right stamp for my job.

I was not surprised when he suggested two of the men who had been into the fort with me, and passed the word for the two Americans. He recommended them as men who could use the stars, good scouts, brave, resourceful, and very determined.

They would, at any rate, stand a chance of getting through the Arabs and giving St. André the information that would turn him from their victim into their scourge, if we had any luck.

When the big slow giant and the little quick man appeared and silently saluted, I asked them if they would like to undertake this duty. They were more than ready, and as I explained my plans for trapping the Arabs between two fires, I found them of quick intelligence. Both were able to repeat to me, with perfect lucidity, what I wanted them to say to St. André, that he might be able to attack the attackers at dawn, just when they were attacking me.

The two left the oasis on camels, from the side opposite to the fort, and after they had disappeared over a sand-hill, you may imagine with what anxiety I listened for firing. But all was silent, and the silence of the grave prevailed until morning.

After two or three hours of this unbroken, soundless stillness, the fire having died down in the fort, I felt perfectly certain there would be no attack until dawn.

All who were not on the duty of outposts-by-night slept, and I strolled silently round and round the oasis, waiting for the first hint of sunrise and thinking over the incredible events of that marvellous day--certainly unique in my fairly wide experience of hectic days.

I went over it all again from the moment when I first sighted the accursed fort with its flag flying over its unsealed walls and their dead defenders, to the moment when my eyes refused to believe that the place was on fire and blazing merrily.

At length, leaning against the trunk of a palm tree and longing for a cigarette and some hot coffee to help me keep awake, I faced the east and watched for the paling of the stars. As I did so, my mind grew clearer as my body grew weaker, and I decided to decide that all this was the work of a madman, concealed in the fort, and now burnt to death.

He had, for some reason, murdered the *sous-officier* with a bayonet (certainly he must be mad or he would have shot him); and he had, for some reason, silently killed the trumpeter and hidden his body--all in the few minutes that elapsed before I followed the trumpeter in. (Had the murderer used *another* bayonet for this silent job?) He had for some reason removed the *sous-officier's*, and the other man's, body and concealed those too, and, finally, he had set fire to the fort and perished in the flames.

But where was he while I searched the place, and why had he not killed me also when I entered the fort alone?

The lunacy theory must account for these hopelessly lunatic proceedings--but it hardly accounts for the murdered *sous-officier* having in his hand a confession signed, 'Michael Geste,' to the effect that he had stolen a jewel, does it, my old one?"

"It does *not,* my son, and that, to me, is the most interesting and remarkable fact in your most interesting and remarkable story," replied Lawrence.

"Well, I decided, as I say, to leave it at that--just the mad doings of a madman, garnished by the weird coincidence of the paper," continued de Beaujolais, "and soon afterwards the sky grew grey in the east.

Before a rosy streak could herald the dawn we silently stood to arms, and when the sun peeped over the horizon he beheld St. Andre's Senegalese skirmishing beautifully towards us!

There wasn't so much as the smell of an Arab for miles... . No, St. André had not seen a living thing--not even the two scouts I had sent out to meet him. Nor did anyone else ever see those two brave fellows. I have often wondered what their fate was--Arabs or thirst... .

I soon learnt that one of St. Andre's mule-scouts had ridden back to him, early in the night, to say that he had heard rifle-shots in the direction of Zinderneuf. St. André had increased his pace, alternating the quick march and the *pas gymnastique* until he knew he must be near his goal. All being then perfectly silent he decided to beware of an ambush, to halt for the rest of the night, and to feel his way forward, in attack formation, at dawn.

He had done well, and my one regret was that the Arabs who had caused the destruction of Zinderneuf were not between me and him as he closed upon the oasis.

While the weary troops rested, I told St. André all that had happened, and asked for a theory--reserving mine about the madman. He is a man with a brain, this St. André, ambitious and a real soldier. Although he has private means, he serves France where duty is hardest, and life least attractive. A little dark pocket-Hercules of energy and force.

'What about this, Major?' said he, when I had finished my account, and, having fed, we were sitting, leaning our weary backs against a fallen palm trunk, with coffee and cigarettes at hand.

'Suppose your trumpeter killed the *sous-officier* himself and deserted there and then?'

'*Mon Dieu!*' said I; 'that never occurred to me. But why should he, and why use his bayonet and leave it in the body?'

'Well--as to why he *should*,' replied St. André, 'it might have been revenge. This may have been the first time he had ever been alone with the *sous-officier,* whom he may have sworn to kill at the first opportunity... . Some fancied or real injustice, when he was under this man at Sidi-bel-Abbès or elsewhere. The sight of his enemy, the sole survivor, alone, rejoicing in his hour of victory and triumph, may have further maddened a brain already mad with *cafard,* brooding, lust of vengeance, I know not what of desperation.'

'Possible,' I said, and thought over this idea. 'But no, impossible, my friend. Why had not the *sous-officier* rushed to the wall, or up to the look-out platform when I approached! I fired my revolver six times to attract attention and let them know that relief had come, and two answering rifle-shots were fired! Why was he not waving his *képi* and shouting for joy? Why did he not rush down to the gates and throw them open?'

'Wounded and lying down,' suggested St. André.

'He was not wounded, my friend,' said I. 'He was killed. That bayonet, and nothing else, had done his business.'

'Asleep,' suggested the Lieutenant, 'absolutely worn out. Sleeping like the dead--and thus his enemy, the trumpeter, found him, and drove the bayonet through his heart as he slept. He was going to blow the sleeper's brains out, when he remembered that the shot would be heard and would have to be explained. Therefore he used the bayonet, drove it through the man, and then, and not till then, he realised that the bayonet would betray him. It would leap to the eye, instantly, that *murder* had been committed--and not by one of the garrison. So he fled.'

'And the revolver, with *one* chamber fired?' I asked.

'Oh--fired during the battle, at some daring Arab who rode round the fort, reconnoitring, and came suddenly into view.'

'And the paper in the left hand?'

'I do not know.'

'And who fired the two welcoming shots?'

'I do not know.'

'And how did the trumpeter vanish across the desert--as conspicuous as a negro's head on a pillow--before the eyes of my Company?'

'I do not know.'

'Nor do I,' I said.

And then St. André sat up suddenly.

'*Mon Commandant,*' said he, 'the trumpeter did not escape, of course. He murdered the *sous-officier* and then hid himself. It was he who removed the two bodies when he again found himself alone in the fort. He may have had some idea of removing the bayonet and turning the stab into a bullet-wound. He then meant to return to the Company with some tale of cock and bull. But remembering that you had already seen the body, and might have noticed the bayonet, he determined to set fire to the fort, burn all evidence, and rejoin in the confusion caused by the fire.

He could swear that he had been knocked on the head from behind, and only recovered consciousness in time to escape from the flames kindled by whoever it was who clubbed him. This is all feasible--and if improbable it is no more improbable than the actual facts of the case, is it?'

'Quite so, *mon Lieutenant*,' I agreed. 'And why did he not rejoin in the confusion, with his tale of cock and bull?'

'Well--here's a theory. Suppose the *sous-officier* did shoot at him with the revolver and wounded him so severely that by the time he had completed his little job of arson he was too weak to walk. He fainted from loss of blood and perished miserably in the flames that he himself had kindled. Truly a splendid example of poetic justice.'

'Magnificent,' I agreed. 'The Greek Irony, in effect. Hoist by his own petard. Victim of the mocking Fates, and so forth. The only flaw in the beautiful theory is that *we should have heard the shot*--just as we should have heard a rifle-shot had the trumpeter used his rifle for the murder. In that brooding heavy silence a revolver fired on that open roof would have sounded like a seventy-five.'

'True,' agreed St. André, a little crestfallen. 'The man was mad then. He did everything that was done, and then committed suicide or was burnt alive.'

'Ah, my friend,' said I, 'you have come to the madman theory, eh? So had I. It is the only one. But now I will tell you something. The trumpeter did *not* do all this. He did *not*murder the *sous-officier*, for that unfortunate had been dead *for hours,* and the trumpeter had not been in the place ten *minutes!*'

'And that's that,' said St. André. 'Let's try again.' And he tried again--very ingeniously too. But he could put forward no theory that he himself did not at once ridicule.

We were both, of course, weary to death and more in need of twenty-four hours' sleep than twenty-four conundrums--but I do not know that I have done much better since.

And as I rode back to Tokotu, with my record go of fever, my head opened with a tearing wrench and closed with a shattering bang, at every stride of my camel, to the tune of, '*Who killed the Commandant, and why, why, why?*' till I found I was saying it aloud.

I am saying it still, George." ...

§ 9

Passengers by the *Appam*, from Lagos to Birkenhead, were interested in two friends who sat side by side in Madeira chairs, or walked the promenade deck in close and constant company.

The one, a tall, bronzed, lean Englishman, taciturn, forbidding, and grim, who never used two words where one would suffice; his cold grey eye looking through, or over, those who surrounded him; his iron-grey hair and moustache, his iron-firm chin and mouth, suggesting the iron that had entered into his soul and made him the hard, cold, bitter person that he was, lonely, aloof, and self-sufficing. (Perhaps Lady Brandon of Brandon Abbas, alone of women, knew the real man and what he might have been; and perhaps half a dozen men liked him as greatly as all men respected him.)

The other, a shorter, stouter, more genial person, socially inclined, a fine type of French soldier, suave, courtly, and polished, ruddy of face and brown of eye and hair, and vastly improved by the removal, before Madeira, of a three years' desert beard. He was obviously much attached to the Englishman... .

It appeared these two had something on their minds, for day by day, and night by night, save for brief intervals for eating, sleeping, and playing bridge, they interminably discussed, or rather the Frenchman interminably discussed, and the Englishman intently listened, interjecting monosyllabic replies.

When the Englishman contributed to the one-sided dialogue, a listener would have noted that he spoke most often of a bareheaded man and of a paper, speculating as to the identity of the former and the authorship of the latter.

The Frenchman, on the other hand, talked more of a murder, a disappearance, and a fire... .

"How long is it since you heard from Lady Brandon, Jolly?" enquired George Lawrence, one glorious and invigorating morning, as the *Appam* ploughed her steady way across a blue and smiling Bay of Biscay.

"Oh, years and years," was the reply. "I was at Brandon Abbas for a week of my leave before last. That would be six or seven years ago. I haven't written a line since the letter of thanks after the visit... . Do you correspond with her at all regularly?"

"Er--no. I shouldn't call it regular correspondence exactly," answered George Lawrence. "Are you going to Brandon Abbas this leave?" he continued, with a simulated yawn.

"Well--I feel I ought to go, *mon vieux,* and take that incredible document, but it doesn't fit in with my plans at all. I could post it to her, of course, but it would mean a devil of a long letter of explanation, and I loathe letter-writing 'fatigues' more than anything."

"I'll take it if you like," said Lawrence. "I shall be near Brandon Abbas next week. And knowing Michael Geste, I confess I am curious."

Major de Beaujolais was conscious of the fact that "curious" was not exactly the word he would have used. His self-repressed, taciturn, and unemotional friend had been stirred to the depths of his soul, and had given an exhibition of interest and emotion such as he had never displayed before in all de Beaujolais' experience of him.

What touched Lady Brandon evidently touched him--to an extent that rendered "curious" a curious word to use. He smiled to himself as he gravely replied:

"But excellent, *mon vieux!* That would be splendid. It will save me from writing a letter a mile long, and Lady Brandon cannot feel that I have treated the *affaire* casually, and as if of no importance. I explain the whole matter to you, her old friend, give you the document, and ask you to lay it before her. You could say that while supposing the document to be merely a *canard,* interesting only by reason of how and where it was found, I nevertheless think that she ought to have it, just in case there is anything I can do in the matter."

"Just that," agreed Lawrence. "Of course 'Beau' Geste never stole the sapphire, or anything else; but I suppose, as you say, a document like that ought to go to her and Geste, as their names are mentioned."

"Certainly, *mon ami.* And if the stone *has* been stolen, the paper might be an invaluable clue to its recovery. Handwriting, for example, a splendid clue. She could please herself as to whether she put it in the hands of your Criminal Investigation Department at Scotland Yard and asked them to get in touch with our police... . Assure her of my anxiety to do absolutely anything I can in the matter--if either the jewel or Michael Geste should be missing."

"Righto, Jolly," was the reply. "I'll drop in there one day. Probably the first person I shall see will be 'Beau' Geste himself, and probably I shall see the 'Blue Water' the same evening."

"No doubt, George," agreed de Beaujolais, and added, "Do you know Michael Geste's handwriting?"

"No. Never saw it to my knowledge," was the reply. "Why do you ask? You don't suppose that Beau Geste wrote that, do you?"

"I have given up supposing, my friend," said de Beaujolais. "But I shall open my next letter from you with some alacrity. Either this 'Blue Water' is stolen or it is not. In either case that paper, in a dead man's hand, at Zinderneuf, is uniquely interesting. But if it *has* been stolen, it will be of practical as well as unique interest; whereas if it has not been stolen, the unique interest will be merely theoretical."

"Not very practical from the point of view of recovery, I am afraid. It looks as though the thief and the jewel and the story all ended together in the burning of Zinderneuf fort," mused Lawrence.

"*Mon Dieu!* I never thought of it before. The biggest and finest sapphire in the world, valued at three-quarters of a million francs, may be lying at this moment among the rubble and rubbish of the burnt-out ruins of Zinderneuf fort!" said de Beaujolais.

"By Jove! So it may!" agreed Lawrence. "Suppose it has been stolen.... If I wired to you, could anything be done about making a search there, do you think?"

For a moment George Lawrence had visions of devoting his leave to jewel-hunting, and returning to Brandon Abbas with three-quarters of a million francs' worth of crystallised alumina in his pocket.

"That will require prompt and careful consideration, directly we learn that the stone has gone, George," said de Beaujolais, and added: "This grows more and more interesting... . A treasure hunt at Zinderneuf! Fancy the Arabs if the information got about! Fancy the builders of the new fort, and the garrison! Zinderneuf would become the most popular outpost in Africa, instead of the least--until the sapphire was found. If it *is* there, I suppose the surest way to lose it for ever would be to hint at the fact ... No, we should have to keep it very quiet and do all the searching ourselves, if possible.... Good heavens above us! More complications!" He smiled whimsically.

George Lawrence pursued his vision and the two fell silent for a space.

"Supposing that stone had actually been in the pocket of a man on that roof, when it collapsed into the furnace below," said de Beaujolais as he sat up and felt for his cigarette case, "would the jewel be destroyed when the body of the man was cremated? Does fire affect precious stones?"

"Don't know," replied Lawrence. "We could find that out from any jeweller, I suppose. I rather think not. Aren't they, in fact, formed in the earth by a heat greater than any furnace can produce?"

"Of course," agreed de Beaujolais. "You could make as many diamonds as you wanted if you could get sufficient heat and pressure. They are only crystallised carbon. Fire certainly wouldn't hurt a diamond, and I don't suppose it would hurt any other precious stone."

"No," he mused on. "If the Blue Water has been stolen, it is probably safe and sound at this moment in Zinderneuf, adorning the charred remains of a skeleton"... and George Lawrence day-dreamed awhile, of himself, Lady Brandon, and the sacrifice of his leave to the making of a great restoration. Of his leave? Nay, if necessary, of his career, his whole life.

("Describe me a man's day-dreams and I will describe you the man," said the Philosopher. He might have described George Lawrence as a romantic and quixotic fool-errant, which he was not, or perhaps merely as a man in love, which he was. Possibly the

Philosopher might have added that the descriptions are synonymous, and that therefore George Lawrence was both.)

He was awakened from his reverie by the voice of de Beaujolais.

"Queer, that it never got into the papers, George," mused that gentleman.

"Yes. It is," agreed Lawrence. "I should certainly have seen it if it had. I read my *Telegraph* and *Observer* religiously.... No, I certainly should never have missed it.... Probably the damned thing was never stolen at all."

"Looks like it," said his friend. "Every English paper would have had an account of the theft of a famous jewel like that.... Though it is just possible that Lady Brandon hushed it up for some reason.... What about an *aperitif,* my old one!"

And, his old one agreeing, they once more dropped the subject of Beau Geste, the "Blue Water," Zinderneuf, and its secret.

On parting in London, Major de Beaujolais handed a document to George Lawrence, who promised to deliver it, and also to keep his friend informed as to any developments of the story.

The Major felt that he had the middle of it, and he particularly desired to discover its beginning, and to follow it to the end.

CHAPTER II. GEORGE LAWRENCE TAKES THE STORY TO LADY BRANDON AT BRANDON ABBAS

As his hireling car sped along the country road that led to the park gates of Brandon Abbas, George Lawrence's heart beat like that of a boy going to his first love-tryst.

Had she married him, a quarter of a century ago, when she was plain (but very beautiful) Patricia Rivers, he probably would still have loved her, though he would not have been in love with her.

As it was he had never been anything but in love with her from the time when he had taken her refusal like the man he was, and had sought an outlet and an anodyne in work and Central Africa.

As the car entered the gates and swept up the long, winding avenue of Norman oaks, he actually trembled, and his bronzed face was drawn and changed in tint. He drew off a glove and put it on again, fingered his tie, and tugged at his moustache.

The car swept round a shrubbery-enclosed square at the back of the house, and stopped at a big porch and a hospitably open door. Standing at this, Lawrence looked into a well-remembered panelled hall and ran his eye over its gleaming floor and walls, almost nodding to the two suits of armour that stood one on each side of a big, doorless doorway. This led into another hall, from, and round, which ran a wide staircase and galleries right up to the top of the house, for, from the floor of that hall one could look up to a glass roof three stories above. He pictured it and past scenes enacted in it, and a woman with slow and stately grace, ascending and descending.

Nothing seemed to have changed in those two and a half decades since she had come here, a bride, and he had visited her after seven years of exile. He had come, half in the hope that the sight of her in her own home, the wife of another man, would cure him of the foolish love that kept him a lonely bachelor, half in the hope that it would do the opposite, and be but a renewal of love.

He had been perversely glad to find that he loved the woman, if possible, more than he had loved the girl; that a callow boy's calf-love for a maiden had changed to a young man's devotion to a glorious woman; that she was to be a second Dante's Beatrice.

Again and again, at intervals of years, he had visited the shrine, not so much renewing the ever-burning fire at her altar, as watching it flame up brightly in her presence. Nor did the fact that she regarded him so much as friend that he could never be more, nor less, in any way affect this undeviating unprofitable sentiment.

At thirty, at thirty-five, at forty, at forty-five, he found that his love, if not unchanged, was not diminished, and that she remained, what she had been since their first meeting, the central fact of his life--not so much an obsession, an *idée fixe,* as his reason for existence, his sovereign, and the audience of the play in the theatre of his life.

And, each time he saw her, she was, to his prejudiced eye, more desirable, more beautiful, more wonderful... .

Yes--there was the fifteenth-century chest in which reposed croquet mallets, tennis rackets, and the other paraphernalia of those games. She had once sat on that old chest, beside him, while they waited for the dog-cart to take him to the station and back to Africa, and her hand had rested so kindly in his, as he had tried to find something to say-- something other than what he might not say... .

Opposite to it was the muniment-box, into which many an abbot and holy friar had put many a lead-sealed parchment. It would be full of garden rugs and cushions. On that, she had sat beside him, after his dance with her, one New Year's Eve... .

Same pictures of horse and hound, and bird and beast; same antlers and foxes' masks and brushes; same trophies he had sent from Nigeria, specially good heads of lion, buffalo, gwambaza, and gazelle.

From these his eye travelled to the great fire-place, on each side of which stood a mounted Lake Tchad elephant's foot, doing menial service, while above its stone mantel, a fine trophy of African weapons gleamed. One of his greatest satisfactions had always been to acquire something worthy to be sent to Brandon Abbas--to give her pleasure and to keep him in mind.

And now, perhaps, was his real chance of giving her pleasure and keeping himself, for a space, very much in her mind. He pulled the quaint old handle of a chain, and a distant bell clanged.

A footman approached, a stranger.

He would enquire as to whether her ladyship were at home. But as he turned to go, the butler appeared in the doorway from the inner hall.

"Hallo, Burdon! How are you?" said Lawrence.

"Why, Mr. George, sir!" replied the old man, who had known Lawrence for thirty years, coming forward and looking unwontedly human.

"This is a real pleasure, sir."

It was--a real five-pound note too, when the visitor, a perfect gent, departed. Quite a source of income Mr. Lawrence had been, ever since Henry Burdon had been under-footman in the service of her ladyship's father.

"Her Ladyship is at the Bower, sir, if you'd like to come straight out," he continued, knowing that the visitor was a very old friend indeed, and always welcome. "I will announce you."

Burdon led the way.

"How is Lady Brandon?" enquired Lawrence, impelled to unwonted loquacity by his nervousness.

"She enjoys very good health, sir--considering," replied the butler.

"Considering what?" asked Lawrence.

"Everythink, sir," was the non-committal reply.

The visitor smiled to himself. A good servant, this.

"And how is his Reverence?" he continued.

"Queer, sir, very. And gets queerer, poor gentleman," was the answer.

Lawrence expressed regret at this bad news concerning the chaplain, as the Reverend Maurice Ffolliot was always called in that house.

"Is Mr. Michael here?" he asked.

"No, sir, he ain't. Nor none of the other young gentlemen," was the reply. Was there anything unusual in the old man's tone? ...

Emerging from the shrubbery, crossing a rose-garden, some lawn-tennis courts, and a daisy-pied stretch of cedar-studded sward, the pair entered a wood, followed a path beneath enormous elms and beeches, and came out on to a square of velvet turf.

On two sides, the left and rear, rose the great old trees of a thickly forested hill; on the right, the grey old house; and from the front of this open space the hillside fell away to the famous view.

By wicker table and hammock-stand, a lady reclined in a *chaise longue*. She was reading a book and her back was towards Lawrence, whose heart missed a beat and hastened to make up for the omission by a redoubled speed.

The butler coughed at the right distance and upon the right note, and, as Lady Brandon turned, announced the visitor, hovered, placed a wicker chair, and faded from the scene.

"*George!*" said Lady Brandon, in her soft deep contralto, with a pleased brightening of her wide grey eyes and flash of beautiful teeth. But she did not flush nor pale, and there was no quickening of her breathing. It was upon the man that these symptoms were produced by the meeting, although it was a meeting anticipated by him, unexpected by her.

"*Patricia!*" he said, and extended both hands. She took them frankly and Lawrence kissed them both, with a curiously gentle and reverent manner, an exhibition of a George Lawrence unknown to other people.

"Well, my dear!" he said, and looked long at the unlined, if mature, determined, clever face before him--that of a woman of forty years, of strong character and of aristocratic breeding.

"Yes," he continued.

"Yes 'what,' George?" asked Lady Brandon.

"Yes. You are positively as young and as beautiful as ever," he replied--but with no air of gallantry and compliment, and rather as a sober statement of ascertained fact.

"And you as foolish, George.... Sit down--and tell me why you have disobeyed me and come here before your wedding.... Or--or--are you married, George!" was the smiling reply.

"No, Patricia, I am not married," said Lawrence, relinquishing her hands slowly. "And I have disobeyed you, and come here again without bringing a wife, because I hoped you might be in need of my help.... I mean, I feared you might be in trouble and in need of help, and hoped that I might be able to give it."

Lady Brandon fixed a penetrating gaze on Lawrence's face--neither startled nor alarmed, he felt, but keen and, possibly, to be described as wary, or at least watchful.

"Trouble? In need of help, George? How!" she asked, and whatever of wariness or watchfulness had peeped from her eyes retired, and her face became a beautiful mask, showing no more than reposeful and faintly-amused interest.

"Well--it is a longish story," said Lawrence. "But I need not inflict it on you if you'll tell me if Beau Geste is all right and--er--the 'Blue Water'--er--safe and sound and--er--all that, you know."

"*What?*" ejaculated his hearer sharply.

There was no possible doubt now, as to the significance of the look on Lady Brandon's face. It certainly could be called one of alarm, and her direct gaze was distinctly watchful and wary. Had not she also paled very slightly? Undoubtedly she frowned faintly as she asked:

"What *are* you talking about, George?"

"Beau Geste, and the 'Blue Water,' Patricia," replied Lawrence. "If I appear to be talking through my hat, I am not really, and will produce reason for my wild-but-not-wicked words," he laughed. "There is method in my madness, dear."

"There's madness in your method," replied Lady Brandon a trifle tartly, and added: "Have you seen Michael, then? Or what? Tell me!"

"No. I have not seen him--but ..."

"Then *what* are you talking about? What do you know!" she interrupted, speaking hurriedly, a very sure sign that she was greatly perturbed.

"I don't *know* anything, Patricia, and I'm asking *you,* because I have, most extraordinarily, come into possession of a document that purports to be a confession by Beau that he stole the 'Blue Water,'" began Lawrence.

"Then it *was* ..." whispered Lady Brandon.

"Was what, Patricia?" asked Lawrence.

"Go on, dear," she replied hastily. "How and where did you get this confession? Tell me quickly."

"As I said, it's a long story," replied Lawrence. "It was found by de Beaujolais at a place called Zinderneuf in the French Soudan, in the hand of a dead man ..."

"Not *Michael!*" interrupted Lady Brandon.

"No--a Frenchman. An *adjudant* in charge of a fort that had been attacked by Arabs ..."

"*Our* Henri de Beaujolais?" interrupted Lady Brandon, again. "Who was at school with you? ... Rose Cary's son?"

"Yes. He found it in this dead officer's hand ..." replied Lawrence.

"Er--*has* the sapphire been stolen, Patricia, and--er--excuse the silly question--is this Beau's writing?" and he thrust his hand into the inner pocket of his jacket.

"But of course it isn't," he continued as he produced an envelope and extracted a stained and dirty piece of paper.

Lady Brandon took the latter and looked at it, her face hard, enigmatical, a puzzled frown marring the smoothness of her forehead, her firm shapely mouth more tightly compressed than usual.

She read the document and then looked out into the distance, down the coombe, and across the green and smiling plain, as though communing with herself and deciding how to answer.

"Tell me the whole story from beginning to end, George," she said at length, "if it takes you the week-end. But tell me this quickly. *Do* you know anything more than you have told me, about either Michael or the 'Blue Water'?"

"I know nothing whatever, my dear," was the reply, and the speaker thought he saw a look of relief, or a lessening of the look of alarm on his hearer's face, "but what I have told you. You know as much as I do now--except the details, of course."

George Lawrence noted that Lady Brandon had neither admitted nor denied that the sapphire had been stolen, had neither admitted nor denied that the handwriting was that of her nephew.

Obviously and undoubtedly there was something wrong, something queer, and in connection with Beau Geste too.

For one thing, he was missing and she did not know where he was.

But since all questions as to him, his handwriting, and the safety of the jewel had remained unanswered, he could only refrain from repeating them, and do nothing more but tell his story, and, at the end of it, say: "If the 'Blue Water' is not in this house, Patricia, I am going straight to Zinderneuf to find it for you."

She would then, naturally, give him all the information she could, and every assistance in her power--if the sapphire had been stolen.

If it had not, she would, of course, say so.

But he wished she would be a little less guarded, a little more communicative. It would be so very easy to say: "My dear George, the 'Blue Water' is in the safe in the Priests' Hole as usual, and Michael is in excellent health and spirits," or, on the other hand, to admit at once: "The 'Blue Water' has vanished and so has Michael."

However, what Patricia Brandon did was right. For whatever course of action she pursued, she had some excellent reason, and he had no earthly cause to feel a little hurt at her reticence in the matter.

For example, if the impossible had come to pass, and Beau Geste had stolen the sapphire and bolted, would it not be perfectly natural for her to feel most reluctant to have it known that her nephew was a thief--a despicable creature that robbed his benefactress?

Of course. She would even shield him, very probably--to such an extent as was compatible with the recovery of the jewel.

Or if she were so angry, contemptuous, disgusted, as to feel no inclination to shield him, she would at any rate regard the affair as a disgraceful family scandal, about which the less said the better. Quite so.

But to *him,* who had unswervingly loved her from his boyhood, and whom she frequently called her best friend, the man to whom she would always turn for help, since the pleasure of helping her was the greatest pleasure he could have? Why be reticent, guarded, and uncommunicative to him?

But--her pleasure was her pleasure, and his was to serve it in any way she deigned to indicate... .

"Well, we'll have the details, dear, and tea as well," said Lady Brandon more lightly and easily than she had spoken since he had mentioned the sapphire.

"We'll have it in my boudoir, and I'll be at home to nobody whomsoever. You shall just talk until it is time to dress for dinner, and tell me every least detail as you go along. Everything you think, too; everything that Henri de Beaujolais thought;--and everything you think he thought, as well."

As they strolled back to the house, Lady Brandon slipped her hand through Lawrence's arm, and it was quickly imprisoned.

He glowed with the delightful feeling that this brave and strong woman (whose devoted love for another man was, now, at any rate, almost maternal in its protecting care), was glad to turn to him as others turned to her.

How he yearned to hear her say, when his tale was told:

"Help me, George. I have no one but you, and you are a tower of strength. I am in great trouble."

"You aren't looking too well, George, my dear," she said, as they entered the wood.

"Lot of fever lately," he replied, and added: "I feel as fit as six people *now*," and pressed the hand that he had seized.

"Give it up and come home, George," said Lady Brandon, and he turned quickly toward her, his eyes opening widely. "And let me find you a wife," she continued.

Lawrence sighed and ignored the suggestion.

"How is Ffolliot?" he asked instead.

"Perfectly well, thank you. Why shouldn't he be?" was the reply--in the tone of which a careful listener, such as George Lawrence, might have detected a note of defensiveness, almost of annoyance, of repudiation of an unwarrantable implication.

If Lawrence did detect it, he ignored this also.

"Where is the good Sir Hector Brandon?" he asked, with casual politeness.

"Oh, in Thibet, or Paris, or East Africa, or Monte Carlo, or the South Sea Islands, or Homburg. Actually Kashmir, I believe, thank you, George," replied Lady Brandon, and added: "Have you brought a suit-case or must you wire?"

"I--er--am staying at the Brandon Arms, and have one there," admitted Lawrence.

"And how long have you been at the Brandon Arms, George?" she enquired.

"Five minutes," he answered.

"You must be tired of it then, dear," commented Lady Brandon, and added: "I'll send Robert down for your things."

§ 2

That evening, George Lawrence told Lady Brandon all that Major de Beaujolais had told him, adding his own ideas, suggestions, and theories. But whereas the soldier had been concerned with the inexplicable events of the day, Lawrence was concerned with the inexplicable paper and the means by which it had reached the hand of a dead man, on the roof of a desert outpost in the Sahara.

Throughout his telling of the tale, Lady Brandon maintained an unbroken silence, but her eyes scarcely left his face.

At the end she asked a few questions, but offered no opinion, propounded no theory.

"We'll talk about it after dinner, George," she said.

And after a poignantly delightful dinner *à deux*--it being explained that the Reverend Maurice Ffolliot was dining in his room to-night, owing to a headache--George Lawrence found that the talking was again to be done by him. All that Lady Brandon contributed to the conversation was questions. Again she offered no opinion, propounded no theory.

Nor, as Lawrence reluctantly admitted to himself, when he lay awake in bed that night, did she once admit, nor even imply, that the "Blue Water" had been stolen. His scrupulous care to avoid questioning her on the subject of the whereabouts of the sapphire and of her nephew, Michael Geste, made this easy for her, and she had availed herself of it to the full. The slightly painful realisation, that she now knew all that he did whereas he knew nothing from her, could not be denied.

Again and again it entered his mind and roused the question, "*Why* cannot she confide in me, and at least say whether the sapphire has been stolen or not?"

Again and again he silenced it with the loyal reply, "For some excellent reason... . Whatever she does is right."

After breakfast next day, Lady Brandon took him for a long drive. That the subject which now obsessed him (as it had, in a different way and for a different reason, obsessed de Beaujolais) was also occupying her mind, was demonstrated by the fact that, from time to time, and à propos of nothing in particular, she would suddenly ask him some fresh question bearing on the secret of the tragedy of Zinderneuf.

How he restrained himself from saying, "Where is Michael? *Has* anything happened? *Is* the 'Blue Water' stolen?" he did not know. A hundred times, one or the other of these questions had leapt from his brain to the tip of his tongue, since the moment when, at their first interview, he had seen that she wished to make no communication or statement whatever.

As the carriage turned in at the park gates on their return, he laid his hand on hers and said:

"My dear--I think everything has now been said, except one thing--your instructions to me. All I want now is to be told exactly what you want me to do."

"I will tell you that, George, when you go... . And *thank* you, my dear," replied Lady Brandon.

So he possessed his soul in patience until the hour struck.

§ 3

"Come and rest on this chest a moment, Patricia," he said, on taking his departure next day, when she had telephoned to the garage, "to give me my orders. You are going to make me happier than I have been since you told me that you liked me too much to love me."

Lady Brandon seated herself beside Lawrence and all but loved him for his chivalrous devotion, his unselfishness, his gentle strength, and utter trustworthiness.

"We have sat here before, George," she said, smiling, and, as he took her hand:

"Listen, my dear. This is what I want you to do for me. Just *nothing at all*. The 'Blue Water' is not at Zinderneuf, nor anywhere else in Africa. Where Michael is I do not know. What that paper means, I cannot tell. And thank you so much for wanting to help me, and for asking no questions. And now, good-bye, my dear, dear friend... ."

"Good-bye, my dearest dear," said George Lawrence, most sorely puzzled, and went out to the door a sadder but not a wiser man.

§ 4

As the car drove away, Lady Brandon stood in deep thought, pinching her lip.

"To think of that now!" she said... . "'Be sure your sins.' ... The world *is* a very small place ..." and went in search of the Reverend Maurice Ffolliot.

§ 5

In regard to this same gentleman, George Lawrence entertained feelings which were undeniably mixed.

As a just and honest man, he recognised that the Reverend Maurice Ffolliot was a gentle-souled, sweet-natured, lovable creature, a finished scholar, a polished and cultured gentleman who had never intentionally harmed a living creature.

As the jealous, lifelong admirer and devotee of Lady Brandon, the rejected but undiminished lover, he knew that he hated not so much Ffolliot himself, as the fact of his existence.

Irrationally, George Lawrence felt that Lady Brandon would long outlive that notorious evil-liver, her husband. But for Ffolliot, he believed, his unswerving faithful devotion would then get its reward. Not wholly selfishly, he considered that a truer helpmeet, a sturdier prop, a stouter shield and buckler for this lady of many responsibilities, would be the world-worn and experienced George Lawrence, rather than this poor frail recluse of a chaplain.

Concerning the man's history, all he knew was, that he had been the curate, well-born but penniless, to whom Lady Brandon's father had presented the living which was in his gift. With the beautiful Patricia Rivers, Ffolliot had fallen disastrously and hopelessly in love.

Toward the young man, Patricia Rivers had entertained a sentiment of affection, compounded more of pity than of love.

Under parental pressure, assisted by training and comparative poverty, ambition had triumphed over affection, and the girl, after some refusals, had married wealthy Sir Hector Brandon.

Later, and too late, she had realised the abysmal gulf that must lie between life with a selfish, heartless, gross roué, and that with such a man as the companion of her youth, with whom she had worked and played and whose cleverness, learning, sweet nature, and noble unselfishness she now realised.

Lawrence was aware that Lady Brandon fully believed that the almost fatal nervous breakdown which utterly changed Ffolliot in body and mind, was the direct result of her worldly and loveless marriage with a mean and vicious man. In this belief she had swooped down upon the poor lodgings where Ffolliot lay at death's door, wrecked in body and unhinged of mind, and brought him back with her to Brandon Abbas as soon as he could be moved. From there he had never gone--not for a single day, nor a single hour.

When he recovered, he was installed as chaplain, and as "the Chaplain" he had been known ever since.

Almost reluctantly, George Lawrence admitted that most of what was good, simple, kind, and happy in that house emanated from this gentle presence... .

Pacing the little platform of the wayside station, it occurred to George Lawrence to wonder if he might have more to tell the puzzled de Beaujolais had his visit to Brandon Abbas included the privilege, if not the pleasure, of a conversation with the Reverend Maurice Ffolliot.

PART II

THE MYSTERY OF THE "BLUE WATER"

CHAPTER I. BEAU GESTE AND HIS BAND

"I think, perhaps, that if Very Small Geste were allowed to live, he might retrieve his character and find a hero's grave," said the Lieutenant.

"And what would he do if he found a hero's grave?" enquired the Captain.

"Pinch the flowers off it and sell them, I suppose. As for retrieving his character, it is better not retrieved. Better left where it is--if it is not near inhabited houses, or water used for drinking purposes ..."

"Oh, *please* let him live," interrupted Faithful Hound. "He is very useful at times, if only to try things on."

I was very grateful to Faithful Hound for daring to intercede for me, but felt that she was rating my general usefulness somewhat low.

"Well, we'll try bread and water on him, then," said the Captain after a pause, during which I suffered many things. "We'll also try a flogging," he added, on seeing my face brighten, "and the name of Feeble Geste... . Remove it."

And I was removed by the Lieutenant, Ghastly Gustus, and Queen Claudia, that the law might take its course. It took it, while Faithful Hound wept apart and Queen Claudia watched with deep interest.

I used to dislike the slice of bread and the water, always provided for these occasions, even more than the "six of the best," which was the flogging administered, more in sorrow than in anger, by the Captain himself.

The opprobrious name only lasted for the day upon which it was awarded, but was perhaps the worst feature of a punishment. The others passed and were gone, but the name kept one in the state of unblessedness, disgraced and outcast. Nor was one allowed in any way to retaliate upon the user of the injurious epithet, awarded in punishment after formal trial, however inferior and despicable he might be. One had to answer to it promptly, if not cheerfully, or far worse would befall.

This was part of the Law as laid down by the Captain, and beneath his Law we lived, and strove to live worthily, for we desired his praise and rewards more than we feared his blame and punishments.

The Captain was my brother, Michael Geste, later and generally known as "Beau" Geste, by reason of his remarkable physical beauty, mental brilliance, and general distinction. He was a very unusual person, of irresistible charm, and his charm was enhanced, to me at any rate, by the fact that he was as enigmatic, incalculable, and incomprehensible as he was forceful. He was incurably romantic, and to this trait added the unexpected quality of a bull-dog tenacity. If Michael suddenly and quixotically did some ridiculously romantic thing, he did it thoroughly and completely, and he stuck to it until it was done.

Aunt Patricia, whose great favourite he was, said that he combined the inconsequent romanticism and reckless courage of a youthful d'Artagnan with the staunch tenacity and stubborn determination of a wise old Scotchman!

Little wonder that he exercised an extraordinary fascination over those who lived with him.

The Lieutenant, my brother Digby, was his twin, a quarter of an hour his junior, and his devoted and worshipping shadow. Digby had all Michael's qualities, but to a less marked degree, and he was "easier," both upon himself and other people, than Michael was. He loved fun and laughter, jokes and jollity, and, above all, he loved doing what Michael did.

I was a year younger than these twins, and very much their obedient servant. At preparatory school we were known as Geste, Small Geste, and Very Small Geste, and I was, indeed, Very Small in all things, compared with my brilliant brothers, to please whom was my chief aim in life.

Probably I transferred to them the affection, obedience, and love-hunger that would have been given to my parents in the ordinary course of events; but we were orphans, remembered not our mother nor our father, and lived our youthful lives between school and Brandon Abbas, as soon as we emerged from the Chaplain's tutelage.

Our maternal aunt, Lady Brandon, did more than her duty by us, but certainly concealed any love she may have felt for any of us but Michael.

Childless herself, I think all the maternal love she had to spare was given to him and Claudia, an extraordinarily beautiful girl whose origin was, so far as we were concerned, mysterious, but who was vaguely referred to as a cousin. She and a niece of Aunt Patricia, named Isobel Rivers, also spent a good deal of their childhood at Brandon Abbas, Isobel being, I think, imported as a playmate and companion for Claudia when we were at school. She proved an excellent playmate and companion for us also, and, at an early date, earned and adorned the honorary degree and honourable title of Faithful Hound.

A frequent visitor, Augustus Brandon, nephew of Sir Hector Brandon, often came during our holidays, in spite of the discouragement of the permanent name of Ghastly Gustus and our united and undisguised disapproval.

One could not love Augustus; he was far too like Uncle Hector for one thing, and, for another, he was too certain he was the heir and too disposed to presume upon it. However, Michael dealt with him faithfully, neither sparing the rod nor spoiling the child... .

§ 2

I do not remember the precise crime that had led to my trial and sentence, but I recollect the incident clearly enough, for two reasons.

One was that, on this very day of my fall from grace, I achieved the permanent and inalienable title and status of Stout Fella, when, inverting the usual order of precedence, Pride came after the Fall. The other reason was that, on that evening, we had the exciting privilege of seeing and handling the "Blue Water," as it is called, the great sapphire which Uncle Hector had given to Aunt Patricia as a wedding gift. I believe his great-grandfather, "Wicked Brandon," had "acquired" it when soldiering against Dupleix in India.

It is about the loveliest and most fascinating thing I have ever seen, and it always affected me strangely. I could look at it for hours, and it always gave me a curious longing to put it in my mouth, or crush it to my breast, to hold it to my nose like a flower, or to rub it against my ear.

To look at it was, at one and the same time, most satisfying and most tantalising, for one always longed to do more than merely look--and, moreover, more than merely touch, as well. So wonderful and beautiful an object seemed to demand the exercise of all five senses, instead of one or two, for the full appreciation of all the joy it could offer.

When I first heard the charitable remark, "Sir Hector Brandon bought Patricia Rivers with the 'Blue Water' and now owns the pair," I felt that both statements were true.

For what other reason could a woman like Aunt Patricia have married Uncle Hector, and did not he still own the "Blue Water"--and so retain his sole claim to distinction?

Certainly his wife did not own it, for she could not wear it, nor do anything else with it. She could merely look at it occasionally, like anybody else. That was something anyhow, if it affected her as it did me... .

My degree of S.F. (Stout Fella) I earned in this wise. One of Michael's favourite and most thrilling pastimes was "Naval Engagements." When this delightful pursuit was in being, two stately ships, with sails set and rudders fixed, were simultaneously shoved forth from the concrete edge of the lily-pond, by the Captain and the Lieutenant respectively.

They were crowded with lead soldiers, bore each a battery of three brass cannon, and were, at the outset, about a yard apart. But to each loaded brass cannon was attached a fuse, and, at the Captain's word, the fuses were lighted as the ships were launched from their harbours.

The Captain presided over the destinies of the ship that flew the White Ensign and Union Jack, and the Lieutenant over those of the one that carried the Tri-couleur of France.

There was a glorious uncertainty of result. Each ship might receive a broadside from the other, one alone might suffer, or both might blaze ineffectually into the blue, by reason of a deviation of their courses. After the broadsides had been exchanged, we all sat and gloated upon the attractive scene, as the ships glided on, wreathed in battle-smoke, perhaps with riddled sails and splintered hulls (on one memorable and delightful occasion with the French ship dismasted and the Tri-couleur trailing in the water).

I was then privileged to wade, like Gulliver at Lilliput, into the deep, and bring the ships to harbour where their guns were reloaded by Michael and Digby, and the voyage repeated... .

On this great day, the first combat was ideal. The ships converged, the guns of both fired almost simultaneously, splinters flew, soldiers fell or were sent flying overboard, the ships rocked to the explosions and concussion of the shot, and then drifted together and remained locked in a death-grapple to the shouts of "Boarders ready" and "Prepare to receive boarders," from the Captain and Lieutenant.

"Fetch 'em in, Feeble Geste," said Michael, imagination sated, and tucking up my trousers, I waded in, reversed the ships, and sent them to port.

The next round was more one-sided, for only one of the French ship's guns fired, and that, the feeblest. Neither the big gun amidships, that carried either a buckshot or half a dozen number-sixes, nor the stern-chaser swivel-gun was properly fused.

I waded in again, turned the French ship, and, with a mighty bang, her big gun went off, and I took the charge in my leg. Luckily for me it was a single buckshot. I nearly sat down.

"I'm shot," I yelped.

"Hanging would be more appropriate," said the Captain. "Come here."

Blood oozed from a neat blue hole, and Faithful Hound uttered a dog-like howl of woe and horror.

Claudia asked to be informed exactly how it felt.

"Just like being shot," I replied, and added: "I am going to be sick."

"Do it in the pond then," requested the Captain, producing his pocket-knife and a box of matches.

"Going to cauterise the wound and prevent its turning sceptic?" enquired the Lieutenant, as the Captain struck a match, and held the point of the small blade in the flame.

"No," replied the Captain. "Naval surgery without aesthetics... . Cut out the cannon-ball."

"Now," continued he, turning to me as I sat wondering whether I should shortly have a wooden leg, "will you be gagged or chew on a bullet? I don't want to be disturbed by your beastly yells."

"I shall not yell, Captain," I replied with dignity, and a faint hope that I spoke the truth.

"Sit on his head, Dig," said Michael to the Lieutenant; but waving Digby away, I turned on my side, shut my eyes, and offered up my limb.

"Hold his hoof then," ordered the Captain... .

It was painful beyond words; but I contrived to hold my peace, by biting the clenched knuckle of my forefinger, and to refrain from kicking by realising that it was impossible, with Digby sitting on my leg and Claudia standing on my foot.

After what seemed a much longer time than it was, I heard Michael say, apparently from a long way off: "Here it comes," and then, a cheer from the Band and a dispersal of my torturers, announced the recovery of the buckshot.

"Shove it back in the gun, Dig," said the Captain; "and you, Isobel, sneak up to the cupboard outside our bathroom and bring me the scratch-muck."

The Faithful Hound, mopping her tear-bedewed face, sped away and soon returned with the scratch-muck (the bottle of antiseptic lotion, packet of boric lint, and roll of bandage, which figured as the *sequelæ* to all our minor casualties).

I believe Michael made a really excellent job of digging out the bullet and dressing the wound. Of course, the ball had not penetrated very deeply, or a penknife would hardly have been the appropriate surgical tool; but, as things were, a doctor could not have been very much quicker, nor the healing of the wound more clean and rapid.

And when the bandage was fastened, the Captain, in the presence of the whole Band and some temporary members, visitors, raised me to the seventh heaven of joy and pride by solemnly conferring upon me in perpetuity, the rank and title of Stout Fella, in that I had shed no tear and uttered no sound during a major operation of "naval surgery without aesthetics."

Further, he awarded me the signal and high honour of a full-dress "*Viking's funeral.*"

Now a Viking's funeral cannot be solemnised every day in the week, for it involves, among other things, the destruction of a long-ship.

The dead Viking is laid upon a funeral pyre in the centre of his ship, his spear and shield are laid beside him, his horse and hound are slaughtered and their bodies placed in attendance, the pyre is lighted, and the ship sent out to sea with all sail set.

On this occasion, the offending French ship was dedicated to these ocean obsequies.

A specially selected lead soldier was solemnly endowed with the name and attributes of *The Viking Eorl, John Geste,* laid upon a matchbox filled with explosives, a pyre of matches built round him on the deck of the ship (the ship drenched with paraffin), his horse laid at the head of his pyre, and a small (china) dog at his feet.

All being ready, we bared our heads, Michael, with raised hand, solemnly uttered the beautiful words, "*Ashes to ashes and dust to dust, if God won't have you the devil must,*" and, applying a match to the pyre, shoved the long-ship (late French battleship) well out into the middle of the lily-pond.

Here it burned gloriously, the leaping flames consuming the mast and sail so that the charred wreckage went by the board, and we stood silent, envisaging the horrors of a burning ship at sea.

As the vessel burned down to the water's edge, and then disappeared with hissings and smoking, Michael broke the ensuing silence with words that I was to remember many years later in a very different place. (Apparently Digby remembered them too.)

"*That's* what I call a funeral!" said Michael. "Compare that with being stuck ten feet down in the mud and clay of a beastly cemetery for worms to eat and maggots to wriggle about in you... . Cripes! I'd give something to have one like that when my turn comes... . Good idea! I'll write it down in my will, and none of you dirty little dogs will get anything from me, unless you see it properly done."

"Righto, Beau," said Digby. "I'll give you one, old chap, whenever you like."

"So will I you, Dig, if you die first," replied Michael to his twin, and they solemnly shook hands upon it... .

My gratification for these honours was the greater in that nothing had been further from my thoughts than such promotion and reward. Frequently had I striven in the past to win one of the Band's recognised Orders of Merit--Faithful Hound, Good Egg, Stout Fella, or even Order of Michael (For Valour)--but had never hitherto won any decoration or recognition beyond some such cryptic remark from the Captain as, "We shall have to make John Chaplain to the Band, if he does many more of these Good Deeds... ."

That evening when we were variously employed in the schoolroom, old Burdon, the butler, came and told us that we could go into the drawing-room.

Claudia and Isobel were there, the former talking in a very self-possessed and grown-up way to a jolly-looking foreign person, to whom we were presented. He turned out to be a French cavalry officer, and we were thrilled to discover that he was on leave from Morocco where he had been fighting.

"Bags I we get him up to the schoolroom to-morrow," whispered Michael, as we gathered round a glass dome, like a clock-cover, inverted over a white velvet cushion on which lay the "Blue Water" sapphire.

We looked at it in silence, and, to me, it seemed to grow bigger and bigger until I felt as though I could plunge head first into it.

Young as I was, I distinctly had the feeling that it would not be a good thing to stare too long at that wonderful concentration of living colour. It seemed alive and, though inexpressibly beautiful, a little sinister.

"May we handle it, Aunt Patricia?" asked Claudia, and, as usual, she got her way.

Aunt Patricia lifted off the glass cover and handed the jewel to the Frenchman, who quickly gave it to Claudia.

"That has caused we know not what of strife and sorrow and bloodshed," he said. "What a tale it could tell!"

"Can you tell tales of strife and bloodshed, please?" asked Michael, and as Claudia said, "Why, of course! He leads charges of Arab cavalry like *Under Two Flags*," as though she had known him for years, we all begged him to tell us about his fighting, and he ranked second only to the "Blue Water" as a centre of attraction.

On the following afternoon, the Captain deputed Claudia to get the Frenchman to tell us some tales.

"Decoy yon handsome stranger to our lair," quoth he. "I would wring his secrets from him."

Nothing loth, Claudia exercised her fascinations upon him after lunch, and brought him to our camp in the Bower, a clearing in the woods near the house.

Here he sat on a log and absolutely thrilled us to the marrow of our bones by tales, most graphically and realistically told, of the Spahis, the French Foreign Legion, the Chasseurs d'Afrique, Zouaves, Turcos, and other romantically named regiments.

He told us of desert warfare, of Arab cruelties and chivalries, of hand-to-hand combats wherein swordsman met swordsman on horseback as in days of old, of brave deeds, of veiled Touaregs, veiled women, secret Moorish cities, oases, mirages, sand-storms, and the wonders of Africa.

Then he showed us fencing-tricks and feats of swordsmanship, until, when he left us, after shaking our hands and kissing Claudia, we were his, body and soul... .

"I'm going to join the French Foreign Legion when I leave Eton," announced Michael suddenly. "Get a commission and then join his regiment."

"So am I," said Digby, of course.

"And I," I agreed.

Augustus Brandon looked thoughtful.

"Could I be a *vivandière* and come too!" asked Isobel.

"You shall all visit me in your officers' uniforms," promised Claudia. "French officers always wear them in France. Very nice too." ...

Next day we went back to our preparatory school at Slough.

§ 3

The next time I saw the "Blue Water" was during the holidays before our last half at Eton.

The occasion was the visit of General Sir Basil Malcolmson, an authority on gems, who was, at the time, Keeper of the Jewel House at the Tower of London, and had, I think, something to do with the British Museum. He had written a "popular" history of the well-known jewels of the world, under the title of *Famous Gems,* and was now writing a second volume dealing with less-known stones of smaller value.

He had written to ask if he might include an account of the "Blue Water" sapphire and its history.

I gathered from what Claudia had heard her say, that Aunt Patricia was not extraordinarily delighted about it, and that she had replied that she would be very pleased to show Sir Basil the stone; but that very little was known of its history beyond the fact that it had been "acquired" (kindly word) by the seventh Sir Hector Brandon in India in the eighteenth century, when he was a soldier of fortune in the service of one of the Nawabs or Rajahs of the Deccan, probably Nunjeraj, Sultan of Mysore.

The General was a very interesting talker, and at dinner that night he told us about such stones as the Timour Ruby, the Hope Diamond, and the Stuart Sapphire (which is in the King's crown), until the conversation at times became a monologue, which I, personally, greatly enjoyed.

I remember his telling us that it was he who discovered that the Nadirshah Uncut Emerald was not, as had been supposed, a lump of glass set in cheap and crude Oriental gold-work. It had been brought to this country after the Mutiny as an ordinary example of mediaeval Indian jewel-setting, and was shown as such at the Exhibition at the Crystal Palace. Sir Basil Malcolmson had examined it and found that the "scratches" on it were actually the names of the Moghul Emperors who had owned it and had worn it in their turbans. This had established, once and for all, the fact that it is one of the world's greatest historic gems, was formerly in the Peacock Throne at Delhi, and literally priceless in value. I think he added that it was now in the Regalia at the Tower of London.

I wondered whether the "Blue Water" and the "Nadirshah Emerald" had ever met in India, and whether the blue stone had seen as much of human misery and villainy as the great green one. Quite possibly, the sapphire had faced the emerald, the one in the turban of Shivaji, the Maratha soldier of fortune, and the other in that of Akhbar, the Moghul Emperor.

And I remember wondering whether the stones, the one in the possession of a country gentleman, the other in that of the King of England, had reached the ends of their respective histories of theft, bloodshed, and human suffering.

Certainly it seemed impossible that the "Blue Water" should again "see life" (and death)--until one remembered that such stones are indestructible and immortal, and may be, thousands of years hence, the cause of any crime that greed and covetousness can father... .

Anyhow, I should be glad to see the big sapphire again, and hear anything that Sir Basil might have to say about it.

I remember that Augustus distinguished himself that evening.

"I wonder how much you'd give Aunt for the 'Blue Water,'" he remarked to Sir Basil.

"I am not a dealer," replied that gentleman.

And when Claudia asked Aunt Patricia if she were going to show Sir Basil the Priests' Hole and the hiding-place of the safe in which the sapphire reposed, the interesting youth observed:

"Better not, Aunt. He might come back and pinch it one dark night--the sapphire I mean, not the Hole."

Ignoring him, Aunt Patricia said that she would take Sir Basil and the other guest, a man named Lawrence, a Nigerian official who was an old friend, and show them the Priests' Hole.

The conversation then turned upon the marvellous history of the Hope Diamond, and the incredible but true tale of the misfortune which invariably befell its possessor; upon Priests' Holes and the varying tide of religious persecution which led to the fact that the same hiding-place had sheltered Roman Catholic priests and Protestant pastors in turn; and upon the day when Elizabethan troopers, searching for Father Campion, did damage to our floors, pictures, panelling, and doors (traces of which are still discernible), without discovering the wonderfully-contrived Priests' Hole at all.

It was near the end of this very interesting dinner that our beloved and reverend old friend, the Chaplain, made it more memorable than it otherwise would have been.

He had sat throughout dinner behaving beautifully, talking beautifully, and looking beautiful (with his ivory face and silver hair, which made him look twenty years older than he was), and then, just as Burdon put the decanters in front of him, he suddenly did what he had never done before--"broke out" in Aunt Patricia's presence. We had often known him to be queer, and it was an open secret in the house that he was to be humoured when queer (but if open, it was still a secret nevertheless), though he was always perfectly normal in Aunt Patricia's presence.

And now it happened!

"Burdon," said he, in the quiet voice in which one speaks "aside" to a servant, "could you get me a very beautiful white rabbit with *large* pink eyes, and, if possible, a nice pink ribbon round its neck? A mauve would do... . But on no account pale blue ribbon, Burdon."

It was a bad break and we all did our best to cover it up by talking fast--but Burdon and Michael were splendid.

"Certainly, your Reverence," said Burdon without turning a hair, and marched straight to the screen by the service-door, as one expecting to find a white rabbit on the table behind it.

"That's a novel idea, sir," said Michael. "I suppose it's a modern equivalent of the roast peacock brought to table in its feathers, looking as though it were alive? Great idea ..."

"Yes," Digby took him up. "Boar's head, with glass eyes and all that. Never heard of a rabbit served in its jacket though, I think. Good idea, anyhow."

The Chaplain smiled vacantly, and Augustus Brandon giggled and remarked:

"I knew a man who jugged his last hair, though."

I hastened to join in, and Isobel began to question the Chaplain as to the progress of his book on Old Glass, a book which he had been writing for years, the subject being his pet hobby.

I wondered whether my aunt, at the head of the table, had noticed anything. Glancing at her, I saw that she looked ten years older than she had done before it happened.

As I held the door open, when the ladies retired after dinner, she whispered to me in passing, "Tell Michael to look after the Chaplain this evening. He has been suffering from insomnia and is not himself."

But later, in the drawing-room, when the "Blue Water" was smiling, beguiling, and alluring from its white velvet cushion beneath the glass dome, and we stood round the table on which it lay, the Chaplain certainly was himself, and, if possible, even more learned and interesting on the subject of gems than the great Sir Basil.

I was very thankful indeed, for my heart ached for Aunt Patricia as she watched him; watched him just as a mother would watch an only child of doubtful sanity, balanced between her hope and her fear, her passionate denial of its idiocy, her passionate joy in signs of its normality.

§ 4

Poor Aunt Patricia! She had contracted an alliance with Sir Hector Brandon as one might contract a disease. The one alleviation of this particular affliction being its intermittence; for this monument of selfishness was generally anywhere but at home, he being a mighty hunter before the Lord (or the Devil) and usually in pursuit of prey, biped or quadruped, in distant places. It is a good thing to have a fixed purpose, an aim, and an ambition in life, and Sir Hector boasted one. It was to be able to say that he had killed one of every species of beast and bird and fish in the world, and had courted a woman of every nationality in the world! A great soul fired with a noble ambition.

As children, we did not, of course, realise what Aunt Patricia suffered at the hands of this violent and bad man when he was at home, nor what his tenants and labourers suffered when he was absent.

As we grew older, however, it was impossible to avoid knowing that he was universally hated, and that he bled the estate shamefully and shamelessly, that he might enjoy himself abroad.

Children might die of diphtheria through faulty drains or lack of drains; old people might die of chills and rheumatism through leaking roofs and damply rotting cottages; every farmer might have a cankering grievance; the estate-agent might have the position and task of a flint-skinning slave-owner; but Sir Hector's yacht and Sir Hector's lady-friends would lack for nothing, nor his path through life be paved with anything less than gold.

And Lady Brandon might remain at home to face the music--whether angry growls of wrath, or feeble cries of pain.

But we boys and girls were exceedingly fortunate, a happy band who followed our leader Michael, care-free and joyous... .

§ 5

I think that the feat of Michael's that impressed us most, was his sustaining the rôle of a Man in Armour successfully for what seemed an appallingly long time. (It was nearly long enough to cause my death, anyhow!)

We were in the outer hall one wet afternoon, and the brilliant idea of dressing up in one of the suits of armour occurred to the Captain of the Band.

Nothing loth, we, his henchmen, quickly became Squires of, more or less, High Degree, and with much ingenuity and more string, more or less correctly cased the knight in his armour.

He was just striking an attitude and bidding a caitiff to die, when the sound of a motor-horn anachronistically intruded and the Band dispersed as do rabbits at the report of a gun.

Michael stepped up on to the pedestal and stood at ease. (Ease!) Digby fled up the stairs, the girls dashed into the drawing-room, Augustus and another visitor rushed down a corridor to the service-staircase, and I, like Ginevra, dived into a great old chest on the other side of the hall.

There I lay as though screwed down in a coffin and pride forbade me ignominiously to crawl forth. I realised that I was suffering horribly--and the next thing that I knew was that I was lying on my bed and Michael was smiting my face with a wet sponge while Digby dealt kindly blows upon my chest and stomach.

When sufficiently recovered and sufficiently rebuked for being such an ass, I was informed that Aunt Patricia had driven up with a "black man"--mystery of mysteries!--and had confabulated with him right in front of the Man in Armour, afterwards speeding the "black man" on his way again in her car.

We were much intrigued, and indulged in much speculation--the more, in that Michael would not say a word beyond that such a person *had* come and had gone again, and that he himself had contrived to remain so absolutely still in that heavy armour that not a creak, rustle, clank, or other sound had betrayed the fact that there actually was a Man in the Armour!

In the universal and deserved admiration for this feat, my own poor performance in preferring death to discovery and dishonour passed unpraised.

I must do Michael the justice, however, to state that directly Aunt Patricia had left the hall, he had hurried to raise the lid of the chest in which I was entombed, and had himself carried me upstairs as soon as his armour was removed and restored to its place.

Digby, who, from long and painful practice, was an expert bugler, took down his old coach-horn from its place on the wall and blew what he said was an "honorific fanfare of heralds' trumpets," in recognition of the *tenacity* displayed both by Michael and myself.

I must confess, however, that in spite of Michael's reticence concerning the visit of the "black man," we others discussed the strange event in all its bearings.

We, however, arrived at no conclusion, and were driven to content ourselves with a foolish theory that the strange visitor was in some way connected with a queer boy, now a very distinguished and enlightened ruler in India. He was the oldest son and heir of the Maharajah, his father, and had been at the College for the sons of Ruling Princes in India, I think the Rajkumar College at Ajmir, before coming to Eton.

He was a splendid athlete and sportsman, and devoted to Michael to the point of worship.

Aunt Patricia welcomed him to Brandon Abbas at Michael's request, and when he saw the "Blue Water" *he actually and literally and completely fainted.*

I suppose the sight of the sapphire was the occasion rather than the cause, but the fact remains. It was queer and uncanny beyond words, the more so because he never uttered a sound, and neither then nor subsequently ever said one syllable on the subject of the great jewel!

And so we lived our happy lives at Brandon Abbas, when not at our prep. school, at Eton, or later, at Oxford.

CHAPTER II. THE DISAPPEARANCE OF THE "BLUE WATER"

And then, one autumn evening, the face of life changed as utterly and suddenly as unexpectedly. The act of one person altered the lives of all of us, and brought suffering, exile, and death in its train.

I am neither a student nor a philosopher, but I would like some convinced exponent of the doctrine of Free Will to explain how we are anything but the helpless victims of the consequences of the acts of other people. How I envy the grasp and logic of those great minds that can easily reconcile "*unto the third and fourth generation,*" for example, with this comfortable doctrine!

On this fine autumn evening, so ordinary, so secure and comfortable, so fateful and momentous, we sat in the great drawing-room of Brandon Abbas, after dinner, all together for what proved to be the last time. There were present Aunt Patricia, the Chaplain, Claudia, Isobel, Michael, Digby, Augustus Brandon, and myself.

Aunt Patricia asked Claudia to sing, and that young lady excused herself on the score of being out of sorts and not feeling like it. She certainly looked pale and somewhat below her usual sparkling standard of health and spirits. I had thought for some days that she had seemed preoccupied and worried, and I had wondered if her bridge-debts and dressmakers' bills were the cause of it.

With her wonted desire to be helpful and obliging, Isobel went to the piano, and for some time we sat listening to her sweet and sympathetic voice, while my aunt knitted, the Chaplain twiddled his thumbs, Claudia wrestled with some unpleasant problem in frowning abstraction, Augustus shuffled and tapped his cigarette-case with a cigarette he dared not light, Digby turned over the leaves of a magazine, and Michael watched Claudia.

Presently Isobel rose and closed the piano.

"What about a game of pills?" said Augustus, and before anyone replied, Claudia said:

"Oh, Aunt, *do* let's have the 'Blue Water' down for a little while. I haven't seen it for ages."

"Rather!" agreed Michael. "Let's do a gloat, Aunt," and the Chaplain supported him and said he'd be delighted to get it, if Lady Brandon would give permission.

Only he and Aunt Patricia knew the *secret* of the Priests' Hole (excepting Sir Hector, of course), and I believe it would have taken an extraordinarily ingenious burglar to have discovered it, even given unlimited opportunity, before tackling the safe in which the "Blue Water," with other valuables, reposed. (I know that Michael, Digby, and I had spent countless hours, with the knowledge and consent of our aunt, in trying to find, without the slightest success, the trick of this hiding-place of more than one hunted divine. It became an obsession with Michael.) ...

Aunt Patricia agreed at once, and the Chaplain disappeared. He had a key which gave access to the hiding-place of the keys of the safe which the Priests' Hole guarded.

"What *is* the 'Blue Water' worth, Aunt Patricia?" asked Claudia.

"To whom, dear?" was the reply.

"Well--what would a Hatton Garden person give for it?"

"About a half what he thought his principal would be willing to offer, perhaps."

"And what would that be, about, do you suppose?"

"I don't know, Claudia. If some American millionaire were very anxious to buy it, I suppose he'd try to find out the lowest sum that would be considered," was the reply.

"What *would* you ask, supposing you *were* going to sell it?" persisted Claudia.

"I certainly am not going to sell it," said Aunt Patricia, in a voice that should have closed the conversation. She had that day received a letter from her husband announcing his early return from India, and it had not cheered her at all.

"I did hear someone say once that Uncle Hector was offered thirty thousand pounds for it," said Augustus.

"Did you?" replied Aunt Patricia, and at that moment the Chaplain returned, carrying the sapphire on its white velvet cushion, under its glass dome. He placed it on a table under the big hanging chandelier, with its countless cut-glass pendants and circle of electric bulbs.

There it lay, its incredible, ineffable, glowing blue fascinating us as we gazed upon it.

"It *is* a wonderful thing," said Isobel, and I wondered how often those very words had been said of it.

"Oh, let me kiss it," cried Claudia, and with one hand the Chaplain raised the glass dome, and with the other handed the sapphire to Aunt Patricia, who examined it as though she had not handled it a thousand times. She looked through it at the light. She then passed it to Claudia, who fondled it awhile.

We all took it in turn, Augustus throwing it up and catching it as he murmured, "Thirty thousand pounds for a bit of glass!"

When Michael got it, I thought he was never going to pass it on. He weighed and rubbed and examined it, more in the manner of a dealer than an admirer of the beautiful.

Finally, the Chaplain put it back on its cushion and replaced the glass cover.

We sat and stood around for a few minutes, while the Chaplain said something about Indian Rajahs and their marvellous hereditary and historical jewels.

I was standing close to the table, bending over and peering into the depths of the sapphire again; Augustus was reiterating, "Who says a game of pills, pills, pills?" when, suddenly, as occasionally happened, the electric light failed, and we were plunged in complete darkness.

"What's Fergusson up to now?" said Digby, alluding to the head chauffeur, who was responsible for the engine.

"It'll come on again in a minute," said Aunt Patricia, and added, "Burdon will bring candles if it doesn't.... Don't wander about, anybody, and knock things over."

Somebody brushed lightly against me as I stood by the table.

"Ghosts and goblins!" said Isobel in a sepulchral voice. "Who's got a match? A skeleton hand is about to clutch my throat. I can see ..."

"Everybody," I remarked, as the light came on again, and we blinked at each other in the dazzling glare, so suddenly succeeding the velvet darkness.

"Saved!" said Isobel, with an exaggerated sigh of relief, and then, as I looked at her, she stared wide-eyed and open-mouthed, and then pointed speechless....

The "Blue Water" had vanished. The white velvet cushion was bare, and the glass cover covered nothing but the cushion.

§ 2

We must have looked a foolish band as we stood and stared, for a second or two, at that extraordinarily empty-looking abode of the great sapphire. I never saw anything look so empty in my life. Aunt Patricia broke the silence and the spell.

"*Your* joke, Augustus?" she enquired, in that rarely-used tone of hers that would have made an elephant feel small.

"Eh? *Me?* No, Aunt! Really! I swear! *I* never touched it," declared the youth, colouring warmly.

"Well--there's someone with a sense of humour all his own," she observed, and I was glad that I was not the misguided humorist. Also I was glad that she had regarded the joke as more probably Augustan than otherwise.

"You were standing by the table, John," she continued, turning to me. "Are you the jester?"

"No, Aunt," I replied with feeble wit, "only the Geste."

As Digby and Michael both flatly denied any part in this poor practical joke, Aunt Patricia turned to the girls.

"Surely not?" she said, raising her fine eyebrows.

"No, Aunt, I was too busy with ghosts and goblins and the skeleton hand, to use my own hand for sticking and peeling--I mean picking and stealing," said Isobel.

"*I* haven't got it," said Claudia.

Lady Brandon and the Reverend Maurice Ffolliot eyed the six of us with cold severity.

"Let us say nothing of the good taste displayed, either in the act or in the denial," said the former, "but agree that the brilliant joke has been carried far enough, shall we?"

"Put the brilliant joke back, John," said Augustus. "You were the only one near it when the light went out."

"I have said that I didn't touch the sapphire," I replied.

"Suppose *you* put it back, Ghastly," said Digby, and his voice had an edge on it.

"And suppose *you* do!" blustered Augustus angrily.

Digby, who was standing behind him, suddenly raised his right knee with sufficient force to propel the speaker in the direction of the table--an exhibition of ill manners and violence that passed unrebuked by Aunt Patricia.

"I haven't *got* the beastly thing, I tell you," shouted the smitten one, turning ferociously upon Digby. "It's one of you three rotters."

It was an absurd situation, rapidly degenerating into an unpleasant one, and my aunt's lips were growing thinner, and her eyebrows beginning to contract toward her high-bridged nose.

"Look here, sillies!" said Isobel, as we brothers glared at Augustus and he glared at us, "I am going to turn all the lights out again for two minutes. Whoever played the trick, and told the fib, is to put the 'Blue Water' back. Then no one will know who did it. See?" and she walked away to the door, by which were the electric-light switches.

"Now!" she said. "Everybody keep still except the villain, and when I switch the lights on again, there will be the 'Blue Water' laughing at us."

"Oh, rot," said Augustus, and out went the lights before Aunt Patricia or the Chaplain made any comment.

Now it occurred to me that it would be very interesting to know who had played this silly practical joke and told a silly lie after it. I therefore promptly stepped towards the table, felt the edge of it with my right hand and then, with a couple of tentative dabs, laid my left hand on top of the glass dome. Whoever came to return the sapphire must touch me, and him I would promptly seize. I might not have felt so interested in the matter had it not been twice pointed out that it was I who stood against the table when the light failed.

Isobel's device for securing the prompt return of the sapphire was an excellent one, but I saw no reason why I should linger under the suspicion of having been an ass and a liar, for the benefit of Augustus.

So there I stood and waited.

While doing so, it occurred to me to wonder what would happen if the joker did not have the good sense to take advantage of the opportunity provided by Isobel... .

Perfect silence reigned in the big room.

"I can't do it, my boots creak," said Digby suddenly.

"I can't find the cover," said Michael.

"Another minute, villain," said Isobel. "Hurry up."

And then I was conscious that someone was breathing very near me. I felt a faint touch on my elbow. A hand came down lightly against my wrist--and I grabbed.

My left hand was round a coat-sleeve, beneath which was the stiff cuff of a dress shirt, and my right grasped a wrist. I was very glad that it was a man's arm. Had it been a girl's I should have let go. Ghastly Gustus, of course... . It was just the silly sort of thing he would do, and it was just like him to take advantage of the darkness, when he found the joke had fallen remarkably flat. I did not envy him the look that would appear on Aunt Patricia's face when the light went up and he was discovered in my grip.

I would have let him go, I think, had he not endeavoured to put the blame on me, and insisted on my nearness to the table when the light failed.

I was a little surprised that he did not struggle, and I was prepared for a sudden violent twist and a swift evasion in the dark.

He kept perfectly still.

"I am going to count ten, and then up goes the light. Are you ready, villain?" came the voice of Isobel from the door.

"Yes, I've put it back," said Digby.

"So have I," said Michael, close to me.

"And I," echoed Claudia.

Then Isobel switched on the light, and I found that my hands were clenched on the right arm of--my brother Michael!

I was more surprised than I can say.

It was only a small matter, of course; a pointless practical joke and a pointless lie, but it was so utterly unlike Michael. It was unlike him to do it, and more unlike him flatly to deny having done it. And my surprise increased when Michael, looking at me queerly, actually remarked:

"So it was *me*, John, was it? Oh, *Feeble* Geste!"

I felt absurdly hurt, and turning to Augustus said, "I apologise, Gussie. I admit I thought it was you."

"Oh, don't add insult to injury," he replied. "Put the beastly thing back, and stop being a funny ass. Enough of you is too much."

Put the beastly thing back! I turned and looked at the cushion. It was empty still. I looked at Michael and Michael looked at me.

"Oh, shove it back, Beau," I said. "It's all been most extraordinarily clever and amusing, I'm sure. But I'm inclined to agree with Gussie."

Michael gave me one of his long, thoughtful, penetrating looks. "H'm," said he.

Isobel came over from the door.

"I *do* think you might have played up, sillies," said she. "Put it back, Beau, and let's have a dance. May we, Aunt?"

"Certainly," said Aunt Patricia, "as soon as ever the great humorist in our midst has received our felicitations," and I really pitied the said humorist, when he should make his avowal, annoyed with him as I felt.

The Chaplain looked from face to face of the six of us and said nothing. Aunt Patricia did the same.

We all stood silent.

"Now stop this fooling," said she. "Unless the 'Blue Water' is produced at once, I shall be very seriously annoyed."

"Come on, somebody," said Digby.

Another minute's silence.

It began to grow unbearable.

"I am waiting," said Lady Brandon at last, and her foot began to tap.

From that moment the matter became anything but a joke, swiftly growing unpleasant and increasingly so.

§ 3

I shall not forget the succeeding hours in a hurry, and their horrible atmosphere of suspicion--seven people suspecting one of the other seven, and the eighth person pretending to do so.

My capable and incisive aunt quickly brought things to a clear issue, upon getting no reply to her "I am waiting," and her deliberate look from face to face of the angry and uncomfortable group around her.

"Maurice," said she to the Chaplain, laying her hand upon his sleeve, her face softening and sweetening incredibly, "come and sit by me until I have asked each of these young people a question. Then I want you to go to bed, for it's getting late," and she led him to a big and deep chesterfield that stood on a low dais in a big window recess.

Seating herself with the air and presence of a queen on a throne, she said, quietly and very coldly:

"This is getting serious, and unless it ends at once, the consequences will be serious too. For the last time I ask the boy, or girl, who moved the 'Blue Water,' to give it to me, and we will end the silly business now and here, and make no further reference to it. If not ... Come, this is absurd and ridiculous... ."

"Oh, come off it, John," said Augustus, "for God's sake."

Nobody else spoke.

"Very well," said my aunt, "since the fool won't leave his folly... . Come here, Claudia... . Have you touched the 'Blue Water' since the Chaplain restored it to its place?" She laid her hand on Claudia's arm, drew her close, and looked into her eyes.

"No, Aunt... ."

"No, Aunt," said Claudia again.

"Of course not," said Aunt Patricia. "Go to bed, dear. Good night."

And Claudia departed, not without an indignant glance at me.

"Come here, Isobel," continued my aunt. "Have you touched the 'Blue Water' since the Chaplain put it back in its place?"

"No, Aunt, I have not," replied Isobel.

"I am sure you have not. Go to bed. Good night," said Lady Brandon.

Isobel turned to go and then stopped.

"But I might have done, Aunt, if the idea had occurred to me," she said. "It is just a joke, of course."

"Bed," rejoined her aunt, and Isobel departed with a kind glance at me.

Aunt Patricia turned to Augustus.

"Come here," she said coldly, and with a hard stare into his somewhat shifty eyes. "Please answer absolutely truthfully--for your own sake. If you have got the 'Blue Water,' and give it to me now, I shall not say another word about the matter. Have you?"

"I swear to God, Aunt ..." broke out Augustus.

"You need not swear to God, nor to me, Augustus," was the cold reply. "Yes or No. Have you got it?"

"*No,* Aunt! I take my solemn oath I ..." the unhappy youth replied vehemently, when the cold voice interrupted:

"Have you touched the sapphire since the Chaplain put it under its cover?"

"No, Aunt. *Really,* I haven't! I assure you I ..." began Augustus, to be again interrupted by the cold question:

"Do you know where the 'Blue Water' is now?"

"No, Aunt," promptly replied he, "upon my soul I don't. If I did, I'd jolly well ..."

"John," said my aunt, without further notice of Augustus, "do you know where the stone is?"

"No, Aunt," I replied, and added, "nor have I touched it since the Chaplain did."

She favoured me with a long, long look, which I was able to meet quite calmly, and I hope not at all rudely. As I looked away, my eyes met Michael's. He was watching me queerly.

Then came Digby's turn. He said quite simply and plainly that he knew nothing about the jewel's disappearance and had not touched it since it was passed to him by Claudia, and handed on by him to Isobel.

There remained Michael. He was the culprit, or else one of us had told a most deliberate, calculated, and circumstantial lie, inexcusable and disgraceful.

I felt angrier with Michael than I had ever done in my life, yet I was angry rather *for* him than with him. It was so utterly unlike him to do such a stupid thing, and to allow all this unpleasant and undignified inquisition to go on, when a word from him would have ended it.

Why must my idol act as though he had feet of clay--or, at any rate, smear clay upon his feet? The joke was unworthy, but the lie was really painfully so.

I have no objection to the good thumping lie that is "a very present help in time of trouble," told at the right time and in the right cause (such as to save the other fellow's bacon). But I have the strongest distaste for a silly lie that merely gives annoyance to other people, and puts blame upon an innocent person.

From the moment I had caught him in the act of trying to return the jewel secretly, I had felt sick with indignation, and literally and physically sick when, his effort frustrated by me, he had pretended innocence and held on for another opportunity of returning the thing unseen.

Had I not myself caught him in the very act, he was, of all of us, the last person whom I should have suspected. He and Isobel, that is to say. I should have strongly suspected Augustus, and, his innocence established, I should have supposed that Digby had fallen a victim to his incurable love of joking--though I should have been greatly surprised.

Had Digby then been proved innocent, I am afraid I should have suspected Claudia of wishing to turn the limelight on herself by an innocently naughty escapade--before I should ever have entertained the idea of Michael doing it and denying it.

Now that all had firmly and categorically declared their absolute innocence and ignorance in the matter, I had no option (especially in view of my catching him at the spot) but to conclude that Michael had been what I had never known him to be before--a fool, a cad, and a liar.

I could have struck him for hurting himself so.

"Michael," said Aunt Patricia very gravely, very coldly, and very sadly, "I'm sorry. More so than I can tell you, Michael. Please put the 'Blue Water' back, and I will say no more. But I doubt whether I shall feel like calling you 'Beau' for some time."

"I *can't* put it back, Aunt, for I haven't got it," said Michael quietly, and my heart bounded.

"Do you know where it is, Michael?" asked my aunt.

"I do not, Aunt," was the immediate reply.

"Have you touched the sapphire since the Chaplain did, Michael?" was the next question.

"I have not, Aunt," was the quiet answer.

"Do you know anything about its disappearance, Michael?" asked the hard level voice.

"I only know that *I* have had nothing whatever to do with its disappearance, Aunt," answered my brother, and I was aghast.

"Do you declare that all you have just said is the absolute truth, Michael?" was the final question.

"I declare it to be the whole truth, and nothing but the truth," was the final answer.

§ 4

What was I to think? Certainly I could not think that Michael was lying. Equally certainly I could not forget that I had caught his hand on the glass cover.

On the whole, if I had to doubt either Michael or the evidence of my senses, I preferred to do the latter. When we got out of that terrible room, I would go to him when he was alone, and say, "Beau, old chap, just tell *me* you didn't touch the thing--and if you say you didn't, there's an absolute end of it." And so there would be as far as I was concerned... .

On hearing his last words, my aunt sat and stared at Michael. The silence grew horrible. At length she began to speak in a low frozen voice.

"This is inexpressibly vulgar and disgusting," she began. "One of half a dozen boys and girls, who have practically grown up here, is a despicable liar and, apparently, a common thief--or an uncommon one. I am still unable to think the latter... . Listen... . I shall leave the cover where it is and I shall lock the doors of this room at midnight and keep the keys, except the key of that one. Bring it to me, Digby... . Thank you.

"This key I shall put in the old brass box on the ledge above the fire-place in the outer hall. The servants will have gone to bed and will know nothing of its whereabouts. I ask the liar, who is present, to take the opportunity of returning the sapphire during the night, relocking the door, and replacing the key in the brass box. If this is *not* done by the time I come down to-morrow, I shall have to conclude that the liar *is* also a thief, and act accordingly. For form's sake I shall tell Claudia and Isobel."

"Come, Maurice," she added, rising and taking the Chaplain's arm. "I do hope you won't let this worry you, and give you a sleepless night."

The poor Chaplain looked too unhappy, bewildered, and bemused to speak.

Having locked two of the doors, Lady Brandon, followed by the Chaplain, swept from the room without a "Good night" to any of us.

I think we each heaved a sigh of relief as the door shut. I certainly did.

And now, what?

Digby turned upon Augustus.

"Oh, you unutterable cheese-mite," he said, apparently more in sorrow than in anger. "I think de-bagging is indicated... . And a leather belt," he added, "unless anyone's pumps are nice and swishy."

I said nothing. It was not the hand of Augustus that I had caught feeling for the cover.

He glared from one to the other of us like a trapped rat, and almost shrieked as Digby seized him.

"You lying swine," he shouted. "Who was by the table when the light failed and came on again? Who was grabbing who, when Isobel turned it on?"

I looked at Michael, and Michael looked at me.

"Yes," screamed Augustus seeing the look, and wriggling free.

"By Jove!" said Digby, "if he pinched it, he's *got* it... . Come to my arms, Gus!" and in a moment he was sitting upon the prostrate form of the hysterically indignant youth, and feeling the pockets of his dinner-jacket from the outside.

"Not in his breast-pockets ... side ... waistcoat ... trousers ... no--the beggar hasn't got it unless he has swallowed it," announced Digby. Then ..." Might have shoved it behind a cushion or dropped it somewhere... . Come on, out with it, Gus, and let's get to bed."

"You filthy, lying, beastly cad," blubbered Augustus in reply, showing the courage of the cornered rat.

I don't think he had ever defied or insulted either of my brothers before in his life.

I expected to see him promptly suffer grief and pain at their hands, but Michael did the unexpected, as usual.

"Why, I believe the little man's innocent after all," he said quite kindly.

"You *know* I am, you damned hypocrite," shouted Augustus. "Weren't you and John fumbling at the cover when she turned the light on--you cowardly blackguards."

Digby's hand closed on the scruff of the boy's neck.

"If I have accused you wrongly, Gussie, I'll humbly apologise and make it up to you," said he. "But if we find you *did* do it--oh, my little Gussie ... !"

"And if you find it was Michael, or John, or yourself!" sneered the dishevelled and shaking Augustus.

Michael looked hard at me and I looked hard at him.

"Look here," said Digby, "presumably the thing is in the room. Aunt wouldn't pinch her own jewel. The Chaplain has no use for it nor for thirty thousand pounds. No one supposes Isobel did it--nor Claudia. That leaves us four, and we haven't been out of the room. Come on, find it. Find it, Gussie, and I'll swear that *I* put it there," and Digby began throwing cushions from sofas and chairs, moving footstools, turning up rugs, and generally hunting about, the while he encouraged himself, and presumably Augustus, with cries of "Good dog! ... Fetch 'em, boy! ... Seize 'em, Gussie! ... Sick 'em, pup! ... Worry 'im, Gus!" and joyful barks.

Michael and I searched methodically and minutely, until it was perfectly clear that the "Blue Water" was not in the room, unless far more skilfully concealed than would have been possible in the dark and in the few minutes at the disposal of anyone who wished to hide it.

"Well, that's that," said Digby at last. "We'd better push off before Aunt comes down to lock the door. I don't want to see her again to-night. Damned if I don't feel guilty as soon as she looks at me."

"Perhaps you are!" snarled Augustus.

"You never know, do you?" grinned Digby.

"Better tidy up a bit before we go," suggested Michael. "Servants'll smell a rat if it's like this to-morrow."

"Smell a herd of elephants, I should think," answered Digby, and we three straightened the disordered room, while Augustus sullenly watched us, with an angry, bitter sneer, and an occasional snarl of "Beastly humbugs," or, "Lying hypocrites."

"Come to the smoking-room, you two?" said Digby to Michael and me, when we had finished.

"Yes--go and fix it up, cads," urged Augustus.

"Go to bed, Ghastly," replied Digby, "and don't forget the key will be in the brass box on the ledge over the fireplace in the outer hall. Bung off."

"For two damns I'd sit in the hall all night, and see who comes for it," was the reply, and the speaker glanced at me.

"Don't let *me* find you there, or I shall slap you," said Digby.

"No, I shouldn't be popular if I went there now and refused to budge, should I?" was the angry retort.

"Lord! It's a long worm that has no turning," cryptically remarked Digby, as Augustus took what was meant to be a dignified departure. "And a long lane that has no public-house," he added.

"Either that lad's innocent or he's a really accomplished young actor," I observed, looking after the retreating Augustus as we crossed the hall, where we said "Good night" to a yawning footman, and made our way down a corridor to the smoking-room.

§ 5

"Well, my sons, what about it!" said Michael, poking up the fire, as we threw ourselves into deep leather arm-chairs and produced pipes.

"Pretty go if the damned thing isn't there in the morning," said Digby.

"I wonder if she'd send to Scotland Yard?" he added, blowing a long cloud of smoke towards the ceiling.

"Filthy business," said Michael. "Fancy a fat mystery-merchant prowling about here and questioning everybody!"

"What a lark!" chuckled Digby. "Jolly glad the servants are out of it all right, poor beggars."

"Beastly vulgar business, as Aunt said," observed Michael.

"And a bit rough on her too--apart from any question of thirty thousand pounds," said I.

"Shake her faith a bit in human nature, what?" said Digby. "But, damn it--the beastly thing will be there all right in the morning."

"I hope to God it will," said I from the bottom of my heart, and found that Michael and I were staring at each other again.

"Reconstruct the dreadful crime," suggested Digby. "Wash out Aunt and the Chaplain."

"And the girls," said Michael. "If anyone even glanced at the possibility of Claudia stealing, I'd wring his beastly neck until he could see all down his beastly back."

"I'd wring the neck of anyone who even glanced at the possibility of Isobel stealing--until he hadn't a head to see with," added Digby.

"Wouldn't it be too silly to be worth noticing at all!" I asked. I was thinking more particularly of Isobel.

"Let's go and *beat* young Gussie," said Digby.

"Gussie doesn't know a thing about it," said Michael. "Nothing but genuine injured innocence would have given him the pluck to call us 'Filthy liars,' and 'Damned hypocrites.' You know, if he'd been guilty, he'd have been conciliatory, voluble, and tearful--oh, altogether different. A much more humble parishioner."

"Believe you're right, Beau," agreed Digby. "Nothing like a sense of injustice to put you up on the bough.... 'Sides, young Gus hasn't the guts to pinch anything really valuable.... And if he'd taken it for a lark and hadn't been able to put it back, he'd have hidden it behind a cushion till he could. I quite expected to find it in some such place. That's why I gave him the chance.... If he *has* got it, he'll shove it back to-night," he added.

"He hasn't," said Michael--and again Michael and I found ourselves looking at each other.

"Well--that leaves us three then," said I.

"It does," said Michael.

"You can count me out, old son," grinned Digby. "Search me."

"Which reminds one, by the way, that we didn't search ourselves, or each other, when we searched Gussie," said I. "It would have been fairer ..."

"Most undignified and unnecessary," put in Michael.

"So Gussie seemed to find," chuckled Digby.

"Then that leaves you and me, John," said Michael.

"Yes, it leaves me and you, Beau," I agreed, and again we stared at each other.

"I did not take the 'Blue Water,' Beau," I said.

"*Nor did I,* John," said Michael.

"Then there's a misdeal somewhere," remarked Digby, "and Gussie *must* have done it. Anyhow--it'll be put back in the night. Must be."

"What do you say to our sitting here until we hear somebody come down to the hall? That door always makes a frightful row," I suggested.

"Certainly not," said Michael sharply.

"Why not?" I asked, eyeing him.

"Why, you ass, it might not be ... I mean we might ... Anyhow, we've no right to interfere with Aunt's arrangements. She has given the person a chance ..."

Michael was by no means fluent. He turned to Digby.

"Don't you think so, Dig?" he asked.

"Any ass can sit up who wants to," was the prompt reply. "I have had enough of to-day, myself. Who's coming up?" He rose and yawned.

"I say," he chuckled, "what a lark to pinch the key and hide it."

"Don't be a fool," said Michael. "Let's go to bed," and we went with our usual curt "Good nights." ...

But it was easier, for me at least, to go to bed than to go to sleep, although my brain seemed somewhat numbed and dulled. I lay and tossed and turned, refusing to believe that Michael had done this disgusting thing, and unable, somehow, to believe that Augustus had. It did not occur to me to doubt Digby--and, as I have said, I should never have dreamt of doubting Michael, had I not caught him.

Leaving out Aunt Patricia, the Chaplain, Digby, and Augustus, there remained Isobel, Claudia, Michael, and I. Eliminating Isobel, there remained Claudia, Michael, and I. It could not be Claudia. How *could* it be Michael?

Had *I* done it myself?

Such was my mental condition by this time that I actually entertained the idea. I had read a book not so long before, in which, after a most tremendous mystery and bother, it turned out that the innocent hero had committed the crime while in a somnambulistic condition.

That could not apply in my case, of course... . There was no question or possibility of sleep-walking or trance about it--but might I not, absolutely unconsciously or subconsciously, have put the thing in my pocket without knowing it? People undoubtedly did do absurd things in fits of absent-mindedness, to their subsequent incredulous astonishment. I had never done such things myself--but might I not have begun doing them now? It was certainly as possible as it was utterly improbable. I actually got up and searched my clothes.

Of course I found nothing, and hour after hour of cogitation and reiterated argument brought me nearer and nearer to the conclusion that either Augustus or Michael was the culprit.

Having repeatedly arrived at this inevitable point, I delivered myself of the unhelpful verdict, "*Augustus or Michael--guilty. And I believe Augustus isn't, and Michael couldn't be!*"

Anyhow, daylight would find the wretched stone back in its place, and the whole business would be merely a very unsatisfactory and annoying puzzle, until it faded from the memories of the eight people who knew of it.

I turned over and made another resolute effort to go to sleep--a foolish thing to do, as it is one of the best ways of ensuring wakefulness.

My mind went off on a new tack. Suppose the "Blue Water" were not put back during the night? What exactly would happen?

One thing would be clear at any rate--that a determined effort was being made to steal the jewel, by somebody who intended to convert it into money.

Certainly Lady Brandon, that *maîtresse femme,* was not the person to accept that "lying down," and she would surely take precisely the same steps for its recovery that she would have taken had it been stolen by burglars or a servant. She would communicate with the police, and see that no one left the house until the matter was in official hands.

It would be inexpressibly unpleasant and degrading. I imagined the questioning, the searching, the loathsome sense of being under suspicion--even Isobel and Claudia. At four o'clock in the morning the whole affair looked unutterably beastly.

And then I pulled myself together. *Of course* it would be all right. The idiot who had played the fool trick, and been too feeble to own up, would have replaced the jewel. Probably it was there now. The said idiot would have been only too anxious to get rid of it as soon as Aunt Patricia had put the key in the brass box... . Why not go and make sure?

Of course--and then one could put the silly business out of one's mind and get some sleep.

I got out of bed, pulled on my dressing-gown, and put my feet into bedroom slippers. Lighting one of the emergency candles which stood on the mantelpiece, I made my way down the corridor to the upper of the two galleries that ran round the four sides of the central hall, and descended the stairs that led to the gallery below, and thence to the hall. Crossing this, I entered the outer hall, avoided the protruding hand and sword-hilt of a figure in armour, and made my silent way to the big stone fire-place.

On the broad shelf or mantelpiece, some six feet from the ground, was the ancient brass box, dating from the days of pack-horse travel, in which my aunt had placed the key.

Only she hadn't--or someone had removed it--for the box was quite empty!

Was this a trap, a trick of Lady Brandon's to catch the guilty one? Justly or unjustly, I thought she was quite capable of it.

If so, presumably I was caught again in this indiscriminating trap that another should have adorned. I was reminded of the occasion many years before, when she suddenly entered the schoolroom and said, "The naughty child that has been in the still-room has got jam on its chin," and my innocent and foolish hand promptly went up to my face to see if, by some wild mischance, it were jammy.

Well--the best thing to do now was to fade swiftly and silently away ere the trap closed; and I turned, wondering whether Aunt Patricia were watching.

That was an absurd idea, of course.

Then I wondered if the box contained some scent of indelible odour, which would betray the guilty hand that had come in contact with it.

Equally absurd.

As I crossed the hall, I also thought of finger-prints.

Had she polished the lid and front of the box with the intention of having it examined by experts for the identification of the owner of the fingers that touched it during the night? Less absurd, perhaps, but utterly improbable. Such an idea might have occurred to her had it been certain that the "Blue Water" was really stolen by a thief who had meant to get away with it.

And supposing that were really the case, and the jewel were not replaced during the night?

There were my finger-prints, anyhow, if she had really thought of this plan! And there they were if it occurred to her later, in the event of the sapphire not being restored. I re-entered the central hall--not more than half a minute later than I had left it--and saw someone coming toward me. He, or she, carried no light, and, of course, could identify me, the candle being just in front of my face.

"Well, Gussie," said I. "Cold morning."

"Well, John. Looking for the key?" said the voice of my brother Michael.

"Yes, Beau," I answered. "It's not there."

"No, John," said Michael quietly. "It's here," and he held it out towards me.

"*Beau!*" I said miserably.

"*John!*" he mocked me.

A wave of sick disgust passed over me. What *had* come over my splendid brother?

"Good night," I said, turning away.

"Or morning," replied Michael, and, with a short laugh, he went into the outer hall.

I heard him strike a match and there followed the rattle of the key and the clang of a falling lid. He had evidently thrown the key carelessly into the box, and dropped the lid without any attempt at avoiding noise.

I went back to bed and, the affair being over and the mystery solved, fell into a broken sleep.

§ 6

I was awakened at the usual time by David, the under-footman, with my hot water.

"Half-past seven, sir," said he; "a fine morning when the mist clears."

"Thank you, David," I replied, and sat up.

What was wrong? Of course--that idiotic affair of last night, and Michael's heavy fall from his pedestal. Well, there are spots on the sun, and no man is always himself. Why dwell on one fault rather than on a hundred virtues? But it *was* unlike Michael to tell such silly pointless lies to cover a silly pointless trick.

I dressed and went downstairs, taking a mashie and a ball from the glory-hole, a small room or large cupboard off the corridor that leads to the smoking-room. I would do a few approach-shots from the tennis-courts to the paddock and back, before the breakfast-gong went at half-past eight.

Crossing the rose-garden I ran into Claudia. This surprised me, for she was more noted for being the last arrival at breakfast than for early rising. It struck me that she looked seedy and worried, and she was certainly deep in some unpleasant slough of thought when she saw me.

As she did so, her face cleared and brightened, rather too suddenly and artificially, I thought.

"Hullo, early worm," said she.

"Hullo, early bird," I replied. "What's up?"

"What do you mean?" asked Claudia.

"I thought you looked a bit off colour and bothered," replied I, with masculine tactlessness.

"Rubbish," said Claudia, and passed on.

I dropped my ball at the back of the tennis-courts, and strove in vain to smite it. I scooped generous areas of turf from the lawn, topped my ball, sliced it into a holly bush, threw my club after it, and slouched off, my hands deep in my pockets and anger (with Michael) deep in my soul.

Returning to the house I saw Burdon crossing the hall, the gong-stick in his hand. The brass box leered at me cynically as I passed.

Having washed my hands in the lavatory by the glory-hole, I went into the dining-room.

The fire was blazing merrily, a silver kettle was simmering on its spirit-stand on the table, a delicious smell came from the sideboard, where three or four covered silver dishes sat on their metal platform, beneath which burnt spirit-lamps. The huge-room--with its long windows, looking on two sides to the loveliest view in Devon; its great warm-tinted Turkey carpet hiding most of the ancient oak floor; its beautifully appointed table, flooded with sunshine; its panelled walls and arched ceiling--was a picture of solid, settled comfort, established and secure.

Digby was wandering about the room, a plate of porridge in one hand, and a busy spoon in the other. Augustus was at the sideboard removing cover after cover, and adding sausages to eggs and rashers of bacon.

"Good effort, Gus," said Digby, eyeing the piled mass as he passed him with his empty porridge plate. "Shove some kedgeree on top."

"Had it," said Augustus. "This is going on top of the kedgeree."

"Stout citizen," approved Digby, getting himself a clean plate.

Isobel was sitting in her place, and I went to see what I could get for her.

As I stood by her chair she put her left hand up to mine and gave it a squeeze.

"I'll wait for Aunt Patricia, John," she said.

Michael came in.

"Aunt come down?" he asked, and added a belated "'Morning, everybody."

"No," replied Digby. "Watch me gobble and go. I'm not meeting Aunt till the day's been aired a bit."

"Claudia down yet?" enquired Michael, ignoring him.

"I saw her in the garden," I said.

"I'll tell her breakfast's ready," he observed, rising and going out.

"Take her a kidney on a fork," shouted Digby, as the door closed.

We sat down, and conversation was in abeyance for a few minutes in favour of the business of breakfast.

"I suppose the Crown Jewels are all present and correct by now?" said Digby suddenly, voicing what was uppermost in all our thoughts. "Door's still locked. I tried it."

"Of course it's all right," I said.

"Seen it?" asked Augustus.

"Or was it too dark?" he added, with a sneer.

"No--I haven't seen it," I replied. "But of course, it's there all right."

"You should know, of course," said Augustus.

"Shut it, Ghastly," said Digby, "or I'll have your breakfast back."

"You're a coarse lout, Digby," remarked Augustus calmly.

"'Streuth!" murmured Digby to the world in general. "Isn't the gentleman's courage coming on?"

It struck me that it was. I had never known Augustus so daring, assured, and insolent before. I felt more and more convinced that, as Michael had said, nothing but genuine injured innocence and a sense of injustice could have wrought this change.

The door opened, and Claudia, followed by Michael, entered. She looked very white and Michael very wooden and *boutonné*. I saw Isobel give her a sharp glance as she sat down and said:

"'Morning ... Aunt not been down yet?"

"No, no. Gobble and go. If asked about sapphires, say you don't know," chanted Digby, beating time with a spoon on his cup.

Michael foraged at the sideboard for Claudia, and then went to the coffee-table. I watched his face as he took the coffee-pot and milk-jug from their tray and held them poised one in each hand, over the cup. His face was perfectly inscrutable and his hands absolutely steady--but I knew there was something very wrong.

He looked up and saw me watching him.

"'Morning, bun-face," quoth he. "Sleep well?"

"Except for one unpleasant dream, Beau," I replied.

"H'm," said Michael, and I tried to analyse the sound, but found it as non-committal as his face.

He returned to his place beside Claudia, and as he seated himself, Aunt Patricia entered the room.

We rose, and I drew back her chair, and then we stood petrified in a complete silence.

One look at her face was sufficient, as she stopped halfway from the door. I knew before she spoke almost the words she was going to say.

"I have come to request that none of you--*none* of you--leave the house to-day," she said. "Unless, that is, one of you cares to say, even now at the eleventh hour, 'A fool and a liar I am, but a criminal I am not!'"

No one spoke or moved. I looked at Michael and he at me.

"No?" continued Lady Brandon. "Very well. But please understand that if I go out of this room without the 'Blue Water,' I will have no mercy. The thief shall pay a thief's penalty--*whoever* it may be."

She paused and fixed her coldly angry gaze on me, on Augustus, on Michael, on Digby, on Isobel, on Claudia.

No one spoke or moved, and for a full minute Lady Brandon waited.

"Ah!" said she at last, and then, "One other thing please note very carefully. The servants know *nothing* of this, and they are to know nothing. We will keep it to ourselves--as long as possible, of course--that one of you six is a treacherous, ungrateful, lying thief."

And then Michael spoke:

"Say one of us four, please, Aunt Patricia."

"Thank you, Michael," she replied cuttingly. "You four are among the six. And I will apply to you when I need the help of your wisdom in choosing my words."

"I think you might say 'one of you three brothers,'" Augustus had the audacity to remark.

"Hold your miserable tongue," was Lady Brandon's discouraging reply.

"As I was saying," she continued, "the servants are to know nothing--and neither is anybody else. Until, of course, the police-court reporters have the story, and the newspapers are adorned with the portrait of one of your faces."

Once again her scornful glance swept us in turn, this time beginning with Michael and going on to Augustus.

"Very well, then," she went on. "No one leaves the house, and no one breathes a word of this to anyone but the eight people who already know of it ..."

"Except to a detective or the police, of course," she added, with an ominous note and a disdainful edge to her voice. "The Chaplain is ill," she concluded, "and I don't wonder at it."

She turned and walked to the door. Before opening it, she faced us once again.

"Have you anything to say--Michael?" she asked.

"Leave the girls out of it--and Augustus," he replied.

"Have you anything to say, Digby?"

"No, Aunt. Awful sorry, and all that," replied Digby, and I seemed to see his lips forming the words, "No, no. Gobble and go... ."

"John?" and she looked even more disdainful, I thought.

"No, Aunt--except that I agree with Michael, *very* strongly," I answered.

"Augustus?"

"It's a damned shame ..." blustered Augustus.

"Very helpful," Lady Brandon cut him short with cruel contempt.

"Claudia?"

"No, Aunt."

"Isobel?"

"No, Aunt," answered Isobel. "But please, please wait another day and ..."

"... And give the thief time to dispose of it, were you going to say?" interrupted Aunt Patricia.

She opened the door.

"Then that is all, is it?" she asked. "No one has anything to say? ... *Very well!*" and she went out, closing the door quietly behind her.

§ 7

"I hate skilly and loathe picking oakum, don't you, Ghastly?" remarked Digby conversationally, as we stared at each other in utter consternation.

"You foul, filthy, utter cads," spluttered Augustus, looking from Digby to me and then to Michael.

"Cuts no ice, Gus. Shut it," said Michael, in a perfectly friendly voice, and added, "Run along and play if you can't be serious... . Come with me, John," and turning to the girls, said, "Do me a favour, Queen Claudia and Faithful Hound."

"Of course," said Isobel.

"What is it?" asked Claudia.

"Put this wretched business out of both your minds, by means of my absolute assurance and solemn promise that it will be settled and cleared up to-day."

"How?" asked Claudia.

"Oh, *Michael*, dear!" said Isobel, and glanced at me.

"Never mind how, for the minute, Claudia," replied Michael. "Just believe and rest assured. Before you go to bed to-night, everything will be as clear as crystal."

"Or as blue as sapphire," said Digby, and added, "By Jove! I've got an idea! A theory! ... My dog Joss got alarmed at the sudden darkness, jumped on a chair to avoid the crush, wagged his tail to show faith and hope, knocked over the cover, reversed his engine, and smelt round to see what he'd done, found nothing and yawned in boredom--and inhaled the 'Blue Water.'"

"Perhaps he was thirsty and *drank* the 'Blue Water'?" amended Isobel.

"Both very sound theories. Sounder still if Joss had been in the room," said Michael. "Come, John."

I followed my brother out into the hall. He led the way to his room.

"Take a pew, Johnny. I would hold converse with thee on certain dark matters," he said as we entered.

Having locked the door, he put his tobacco-jar on the low table beside the low arm-chair in which I was sitting.

"You leave the carbon cake too long in your pipes," he said. "That's what cracks them. Unequal expansion of the carbon and the wood, I suppose. You ought to scrape it out once a month or so."

He seated himself opposite to me and sprawled in the low chair, with his knees higher than his head.

"Oh, I like a well-caked pipe," I replied. "Nuttier and cooler."

"Ah, well! So long as you can afford to crack your pipes," he said lazily, and sat silent for a minute or two.

I was quite under his spell again, and had to keep whipping my feelings up into a state of resentment and disgust to maintain them in the condition that common justice demanded. If he were going to restore the sapphire that evening as he had hinted, why on earth couldn't he have done it just now? For the matter of that, why on earth couldn't he have returned it last night when he went to the drawing-room? Why had he ever denied taking the thing at all?

"Well, son, what about it?" he said suddenly.

"Yes, what about it, Beau?" I replied.

He looked at me quizzically.

"What's the game, should you think, Johnny?" he asked.

"That's what I want to know," I answered. "It seems a damned silly one, anyhow."

"Quite," agreed Michael. "Quite very. *Very* quite. *And* a little rough on the girls and our good Augustus."

"Exactly," said I. "And on Aunt Patricia."

An uncomfortable silence followed.

"Well?" said Michael, at length.

"Oh, put it back, Beau," I implored. "God alone knows what you're playing at! Do *you*?"

Michael sat up and stared at me.

"Oh? You say '*Put it back*,' do you, John?" he said slowly and thoughtfully.

"I do," I replied. "Or look here, Beau. Aunt thinks a lot of you, and devilish little of me. It would be doing her a real kindness not to let her know it was you after all. Give it here, and I'll ..." I coloured and felt a fool.

"*Eric, or Little by Little. A Story of School Life*... . *The Boy with the Marble Brow*," murmured Michael, smiling. But his voice was very kind... .

"This grows interesting, Johnny," he went on. "If I go and fetch the 'Blue Water' now, will you take it to Aunt Patricia and say, '*Alone I did it. I cannot tell a lie. It is a far, far better thing I do ... ?*"

"Those very words, Beau," I grinned. "On condition you tell me what the game was, and why you did such a damned silly thing."

Thank God the wretched business was going to end--and yet, and yet ... I felt quite sure that Michael would not let me take the blame--much as I would have preferred that to the wretched feeling of our Michael being the object of Aunt Patricia's scorn and contempt. The more she liked him and approved him now, the more would she dislike and despise him then. She might forbid him the house.

Michael rose.

"You really will?" he asked. "If I go and get it now, you'll take it straight to Aunt Patricia and say you pinched it for a lark?"

"Only too glad of the chance, Beau," I answered. "To get the beastly business over and done with and forgotten--and the girls and Gussie and Digby out of the silly mess."

"H'm," said Michael, sitting down. "You would, eh!"

"And might I ask you a question or two, John?" he went on.

"What were you doing with your hand on the glass cover when I put my hand on it last night?"

"Waiting to catch the ass that was returning the 'Blue Water,'" I replied.

"H'm! Why did you want to catch him?"

"Because I had twice been accused of the fool trick--just because I was standing close to the table when the light failed."

"So you were, too... . And what were you doing downstairs last night when I found you in the hall?"

"Looking for the key, Beau, as I told you," I answered.

"And what did you want the key for?"

"To see whether the sapphire had been put back--and to get some peace of mind and sleep, if it had."

"Did you go into the drawing-room?"

"No," I answered.

"Why not?"

"What need! I took it for granted that you had returned it," replied I.

"H'm!" said Michael. "Suppose a vote were taken among the eight of us, as to who is likeliest to be the thief, who do you suppose would top the poll?"

"Augustus," I stated promptly.

"Do you think he is the culprit?" asked my brother.

"No, I do *not*," I replied significantly.

"Nor I," answered the enigmatic Michael. "In fact, I know he's not."

He sat silent, smoking reflectively for a few minutes.

"Go through the list," he said suddenly. "Would Aunt pinch her own jewel?"

"Hardly," said I.

"Would the Chaplain?"

"Still less," said I.

"Would Claudia?" he asked next--almost anxiously, I fancied (absurdly, no doubt).

"Don't be a fool," I replied.

"Would Isobel?"

"Don't be a cad," I said.

"Would Digby?"

"Utterly preposterous and absurd," I answered.

"Would Augustus?"

"I feel certain that he *didn't* anyhow," I answered.

"Would you?"

"I didn't, as it happens," I assured him.

"Would I?"

"I should have thought you almost the last person in the world, Beau," I assured him.

"Looks as though I did it, then, doesn't it?" he asked. "Because if Augustus and Digby and you didn't do it--who the devil did, if I didn't? Yes--it looks as though I am the thief."

"It does--to me only though. Nobody else knows that I found you downstairs," I said. "Why *didn't* you put it back then, Beau?" I asked.

"*Wish I had,*" he said.

There came a bang at the door.

"Who's there?" cried Michael.

"Me," bawled the ungrammatical Digby.

Michael unlocked the door.

"What's up?" he asked.

"Isobel wants to speak to us three. She's been looking for you two. A thought has struck her. Blow severe but not fatal. All about the Painful Event... ."

"Where is she?" asked Michael.

"I said I'd lead you by the ear to the smoking-room at an early date--unless either of you had done a bunk with the loot," replied Digby.

"Well--I haven't fled yet, but I shall want a Bradshaw after lunch," said Michael, adding, "Let's go and hear Isobel's great thought. Generally worth hearing."

We went downstairs and made our way to the smoking-room. The brass box caught my eye, and an idea also struck me with some violence, as I noticed that the lid and front seemed brighter than the rest of it.

"Don't expose me yet, John," said Michael as we crossed the hall.

"John been catching you out?" asked Digby.

"Caught me last night, didn't you, John?" replied Michael.

"Red-handed," said I.

"It's blue-handed that Aunt wants to cop someone," said Digby, opening the door of the smoking-room. "Sapphire-blue."

Isobel was sitting by the fire looking tearful and depressed. It was at me that she looked as we entered.

"Caught them both in the act of bolting, Isobel," said Digby. "They've each got a half of the 'Blue Water'--about a pint apiece. But they are willing to hear your words if you are quick."

"Oh, I *am* so miserable," moaned Isobel. "I have been such a wicked, *wicked* beast. But I can't bear it any longer."

"Leave it with us, dear," said Digby, "and forget it. We'll smuggle it back, and share Aunt's few well-chosen words among us, won't we, Beau?"

"What's the trouble, child?" asked Michael.

"I've let Augustus take the blame all this time," she sobbed.

"Didn't notice him taking any," observed Digby. "Must be a secret blame-taker, I suppose."

"Augustus is perfectly innocent and I could have proved it, the moment Aunt began to question us last night. A word from me would have saved him from all suspicion--and I never said it," she went on.

"Why, dear?" I asked her.

"Oh, I don't know... . Yes, I do. It would have looked like exculpating myself too," she replied. "Besides, I didn't know *who* had done it. And it was more or less of a silly practical joke last night... . And, of course, I thought the person who had taken it would say so, or at least put it back. But now--it's awful. And I can't keep quiet any longer, I thought I'd tell you three before I told Aunt."

"Well--what is it, Faithful Hound?" asked Michael.

"Why, when the light went out--you know I said, '*Ghosts and goblins and skeleton hands,*' or something! Well, I half frightened myself and half pretended, and I clutched somebody's arm. When the light went up I found it was Augustus I was hugging--and let go so quickly that nobody noticed, I suppose."

"That settles it," said Digby. "It wasn't poor Gussie." "Couldn't have been," he added, "unless those two were one and did it together."

"Don't be an ass, Dig," I said, for poor Isobel was really upset about it.

"Oh, never!" said Digby. "Absolutely never!"

"Well--I like our Augustus all the better for not having adduced this bit of evidence himself," said I.

"Bless the dear boy," said Digby, "and I searched all his little pockets. I must find him and forgive him."

"Have you told Claudia this?" asked Michael.

"Yes," replied Isobel. "But she seems to think that I may have been mistaken."

"Which is absurd, of course," she added.

"Well--friend Gussie ought to be much obliged to you, both for hanging on to him in the dark, and for remembering it, Isobel," said Michael.

"Yes," chimed in Digby, "now he can bark and wag his tail and gambol around the feet of Aunt Patricia, while we walk in outer darkness."

"Tell her at once and get it off your conscientious chest, Isobel," said I.

She looked at me long and miserably, almost apologetically I thought, and went out of the room.

"Say, citizens," said Digby as the door closed, "what I want to know is this. Who pinched this here gem we're being bothered about? Officious and offensive fella, I consider--but Gussie now being out of it, it must be one of us three.... . Excuse my mentioning it then, but me being out of it, it must be one of you *two*. Now unless you really want the damned thing, I say, '*Put it back.*'"

Michael and I once again looked at each other, Michael's face being perfectly expressionless.

"I think of bolting with it, as I told Isobel just now," said Michael.

"John going with his half too?" asked Digby.

"No," replied Michael for me. "I'm taking it all."

"Well, old horse," said Digby, looking at his watch, "could you go soon after lunch? I want to run up to town to see a man about a dog, and Aunt seems to have other views for us--until the matter is cleared up."

"Do my best to oblige," said Michael, as I quietly slipped from the room to carry out the idea which had occurred to me as I crossed the hall.

I went to the brass box. Finger-prints were very faintly discernible on its highly-polished lid and front. Going to the wash-basin in the room opening off the neighbouring corridor, I damped my handkerchief, and rubbed soap, hard, on the wet surface. The hall was still empty when I returned, and I promptly began scouring the lid and front of the box.

It was easier, however, to remove the finger-marks than to remove the signs of their removal. I did not wish it to be obvious that someone had been doing--what I was doing.

Under a heavy curtain, in a recess in the panelling, hung overcoats, caps, mufflers, and such outdoor garments. A silk scarf of Digby's struck me as being just the thing I wanted.

I had restored to the box the brilliance which had been its before I soaped it, and was giving it a final wipe with the silk, when the door from the corridor swung open, Michael entered, and I was caught in the act.

And then I saw that in his hand was a piece of wash-leather and a silver-duster, presumably purloined from the butler's pantry!

"Ah!" he said. "Removing all traces of the crime?"

"All--I hope, Beau," I replied.

"Sound plan too," he observed. "Just going to do it myself," and he passed on.

Having finished my task, I placed the fingers of my right hand on top of the box, my thumb on the front, and left as fair and clear a set of finger-prints as I could contrive.

How could it possibly matter to me if a detective identified them as mine? I hadn't taken the "Blue Water," and nobody could prove that I had.

And why was Michael so anxious that his finger-marks should not be found there as a piece of evidence to be coupled with the fact that I had been seen holding his wrist, above the glass cover, when the lights were turned on?

I went up to my room despairing, and trying to recall what I had read, somewhere, about the method of examining finger-prints. I believe they blow a fine powder on to them and then apply carbon-paper or tissue-paper, and take a photograph of the result.

Anyhow, if Aunt had been wily enough to polish the box, just where we would touch it, so that she could get the fingerprints of the person who opened it, she'd get mine all right and those of nobody else, when the detectives came.

§ 8

Aunt Patricia did not appear at lunch, nor did Claudia. The Chaplain was still ill in bed.

As Burdon and a footman always waited at that meal, there was no general conversation on the one subject of interest to us all.

It was a painful meal, to me at any rate, though Digby seemed perfectly happy, and Michael unconcerned. The only reference to the theft was during a brief absence of the servants.

"Did you tell Aunt what you proposed to tell her? What did she say?" asked Michael of Isobel.

"Yes.... She said, somewhat cryptically, '*Virtue is its own reward,*' and nothing else," replied Isobel.

"Gussie," said Digby, "Isobel has--one cannot say 'bearded' of a lady--let us say faced--Aunt Patricia in her wrath, in order to tell her that you must be absolutely innocent of sin, and quite above or beneath suspicion."

"What do you mean?" snarled Augustus.

"She very kindly went to the lioness's den," continued Digby, "to say that she seized you and hung on to you last night while the lights were out--and that, therefore, you could not possibly have gone to the table and pinched the sapphire, as she was hanging on to your arm. I sincerely apologise to you, Gussie, and hope you'll forgive me."

"*My* arm?" said Augustus, in deep and genuine surprise, ignoring the apology, and quickly adding, "Oh, yes--er--of course. Thanks, Isobel."

We all looked at him. I had been watching him when he spoke, and to me his surprise was perfectly obvious.

"Then Aunt knows *I* didn't do it?" he said.

"Yes, Gussie," Isobel assured him, "and I'm *awfully* sorry I didn't say it, at once, last night."

"Yes--I thought you *might* have done so," replied our Augustus.

"Isobel is not so keen on exculpating herself too, you see," said I, glaring at the creature. "*If* she were holding your arm, she could not have gone to the table herself. Proving your innocence proves her own."

"Well--she might have thought of me," he grumbled.

"She has, Gussie," said Michael; "we shall all think of you, I'm sure.... Anyhow, we are all sorry we were unkind and suspicious."

"Suspicious! *You!*" said Augustus. "Huh!"

"Yes--and I'm sorry I searched you, Ghastly," put in Digby.... "I'll unsearch you by and by, if you're not careful," he added.

And then David and Burdon came in with the next course.

After lunch, feeling disgruntled and miserable, I went along to the billiard-room to knock the balls about, as one could not very well leave the house in face of Lady Brandon's request.

Augustus was before me and I turned to retreat. I was in no mood to suffer Augustus gladly.

"Police come yet?" he jeered.

"No--you're safe for the present," I replied.

"You heard what Isobel said at lunch," he squealed.

"Yes," said I, going out, "you could hardly believe your ears, could you?" and I am afraid that the anger that I felt was almost entirely due to my conviction that he was absolutely innocent. Isobel could not very well be mistaken. I supposed that Augustus must have quite forgotten the incident until Isobel mentioned it, or else had never noticed it at all. Certainly that was far more probable, than that Isobel had made a mistake as to whom she had clutched in the darkness, especially as she did not leave go until the lights came on and started us all blinking at each other.

I went up to my bedroom, feeling deadly tired after my wakeful night and all the worry, and threw myself on my bed.

I was awakened from a heavy sleep by the entrance of Digby, a couple of hours later. He held a letter in his hand.

"Hi, hog," quoth he, "wake up and listen... . Latest edition," and he sat himself down heavily on the foot of the bed.

"What's up now?" I yawned, rubbing my eyes.

"We've got to use our wits and do something to help Beau. Show the mettle of our pastures and all that... . Beau's done a bunk. Left this note with David. Says he pinched the 'Blue Water,' and isn't going to face the police."

"*What?*" I cried.

"Read it," said Digby, and passed the letter to me.

"*My dear Dig,*" it ran, "*I have told David to give you this at four o'clock, by which time I shall be well on my way to--where I am going. Will you please tell Aunt that there is no further need to chivvy any of you about the ' Blue Water.' If the police come or a mystery-merchant from Scotland Yard, tell them that you knew that I was in sore straights--or is it straits (or crookeds?) for money, but that you think that this is my first offence and I must have been led away by bad companions (you and John, of course). KEEP an eye on young John, and tell him I hope he'll be a good boy. If I send you an address later, it will be in absolute confidence, and relying wholly on your utterly refusing to give it to ANYBODY, for any reason whatsoever. I do hope that things will settle down quickly and quietly, now that the criminal is known. Sad, sad, sad! Give my love to Claudia.*

Ever thine,
Michael."

"It *can't* be true," I said. "It's impossible."

"Of course it is, fat-head," replied Digby. "He's off on the romantic tack. Taking the blame and all that... . Shielding his little brother... ."

"Which?" I asked. "You!"

"No," said Digby.

"Me?" I asked.

"Subtle mathematician," observed Digby.

"But I didn't do it," I said.

"Nor did I," said Digby, and added, "Let's say 'Taking the blame and *thinking* he's shielding his little brother' then."

"But, Dig," I expostulated, "do you think Beau seriously supposes for one moment that you or I would steal a valuable jewel--and from Aunt Patricia of all people?"

"Somebody has stolen it, haven't they?" said Digby. "And I tell you what, my lad," he added; "you say that Beau would never seriously suppose that you or I would steal it--but you yourself seriously supposed that Beau had!"

"How do you know?" I asked, aghast.

"By the way you looked at him--oh, half a dozen times."

"I had reason to suspect him," I said.

"What reason--except that you caught hold of his wrist in the dark, when he was probably doing just what you were doing, trying to catch Gussie in the act of putting it back?" asked Digby.

"I'd rather not say any more about it, Dig," I replied. "It's Beau's business after all, and ..."

"Don't be a colossal ass," interrupted Digby. "Of course it's Beau's business, and that's what we are talking about. The more we both know, the more we can both help him--either to get away, or to come back... . If we knew he is guilty, which, of course, he isn't, we could draw red herrings across his trail; and if we knew he is innocent, which he is, we could lay for the real thief and catch him out."

"Beau doesn't want him caught out, evidently," said I.

"What--not if it's the miserable Gussie?" asked my brother indignantly.

"It isn't," said I. "And Beau knows it."

"Well--let's have those reasons, and we'll get to work," said Digby. "You needn't feel as though you were giving Beau away. There is no more harm in my knowing than in your knowing, and there may be some good. I am not asking you to tell Aunt, or the police, am I, bun-head?"

This was true enough. No harm could result from Digby's knowing all that I knew.

Moreover, if, as Digby assumed, Michael were shielding somebody else, presumably he would welcome any evidence that strengthened the case against himself.

"Well," said I reluctantly, "it's like this, Dig... . Beau went down to the drawing-room last night. I met him with the key in his hand ..."

"And what were *you* doing, if one might ask?" interrupted my brother.

"Going to see if the 'Blue Water' had been returned," I replied.

"Anyhow, *Beau* hadn't returned it, had he?" grinned Digby.

"No--but at the time I, naturally enough, thought he had," said I, "and I suppose that fixed the idea in my mind. I first got the idea--naturally enough, again--when I caught his hand hovering over the glass cover in the darkness."

"Anything else?" asked Digby.

"Yes, the third reason I had for suspecting Beau--though I put my faith in him before all reason--was that I found him going to the brass box with a leather and duster to rub out the finger-prints he had made in taking and returning the key."

Digby whistled.

"Ingenious," he murmured. "As artful as our Auntie, if she had the idea... . Detectives would have the idea anyhow."

"I think she did have the idea," I said. "I believe she went straight from the drawing-room and polished all the finger-marks from the lid and front of the damned thing."

"And how do you know that Beau was on to the dodge?" asked Digby.

"He said so. He came into the hall with the cleaning-things in his hand, just as I was doing it myself."

Digby stared.

"Doing it yourself?" he said. "*Why?*"

"Oh, can't you see?" I groaned. "*If* Beau had been playing the wild ass, I didn't want his finger-prints to be found there, on top of the fact that I had been seen clutching his fist in the drawing-room."

"Yours were there as well as his," observed Digby, "if you went to the box for the key."

"Yes--they were," said I, "and they are there, alone, now."

"Stout fella," approved Digby. "I'll go and shove mine on too, and fog the Sherlocks... . But you really are a goat," he went on. "Don't you see that Beau was probably going to do precisely what *you* were doing? He was going to polish the beastly thing clean of all foot-marks, and then jab his own on."

"Why?" I asked.

"To shield the real culprit, of course," said Digby patiently.

"Yes--but *why?*" I repeated. "Why should Beau be a gratuitous ass and take the blame instead of--Gussie, for example? He'd have been more likely to nose him out and then slipper him well."

"Because he knew it wasn't Gussie," replied my brother solemnly.

"Who then?" I asked.

"He didn't know," answered Digby. "But isn't it as clear as mud, that since it wasn't Gussie or Isobel, it was you or me--or else *Claudia?*"

I was silent.

"Now look here, John," went on Digby. "'Nuff said, and time to do something instead. But first of all, do you still suspect Beau?"

"I have never suspected him," I replied. "I have only realised that I caught his hand, met him with the drawing-room key, and know he was going to rub finger-prints off the brass box."

"Plain yes or no," said Digby. "Do you suspect Beau?"

"Absolutely not," I said promptly. "No. No. *No!*"

"Very good then. Now--Did *you* do it?"

"I did not," said I.

"Nor did I. Very well! Since Isobel and Augustus mutually prove each other innocent, as she was holding his arm, yards from the table all the time--who is left?"

"*Claudia?*" said I unhappily.

"*Now* d'you get it?" smiled Digby, leaning back against the bottom of the bed, and clasping his hands round his knee.

"Good God, man," I cried, starting up. "You don't mean to tell me you suspect *Claudia* of jewel-stealing?"

"Keep calm," he replied. "I am not talking about whom I suspect. I am asking you who remains if you eliminate me and yourself as admittedly innocent, and Isobel and Augustus as proven innocent."

"Michael and Claudia!" I murmured. "Which idea is the more ridiculous?" I said aloud.

"Equally impossible," answered Digby. "Also the fact remains that it was one of those two--*if* it wasn't you. Furthermore, the fact remains that Michael has bolted for one of two reasons--because he is a frightened thief, or because he wished to shield the guilty person--you or Claudia."

A silence fell between us.

"I'm going dotty," said I at last.

"I've gone," said Digby, and we sat staring at each other. After a time he rose.

"Got to get a move on," he said.

"What are you going to do?" I asked.

"Dunno," he replied.

As he was leaving the room I said, "Do you think Michael suspects either me or you, Digby?"

"No," he replied. "He *knows* we didn't do it."

"Do you think he suspects Claudia then?"

"Er--*no*--of course not," he answered.

"Then?"

"He only *knows* that one of us three *did* do it," he replied, and went out, leaving me staring at the door.

I lay down again to think.

§ 9

Dinner that night was an extraordinary meal, at which only Isobel, Claudia, Augustus, and I appeared.

Lady Brandon, said Burdon, was dining in her own room; his Reverence the Chaplain was, by Dr. Warrender's orders, remaining in bed; Mr. Michael was not in his room when David took up his hot water; and Mr. Digby had been seen going down the drive soon after tea.

"Shocking bad form, I call it--Michael and Digby going out like this--after what Aunt said," remarked Augustus as the service-door swung to, when the servants went out for the coffee.

"You're an authority on good form, of course," I said.

"Where has Beau gone?" asked Claudia.

"He didn't tell me," I replied.

"Don't suppose he told anybody," sneered Augustus.

"Come into the drawing-room soon," said Isobel, as I held the dining-room door open for the girls to go out.

"I'm coming now," I replied. "As soon as I have had some coffee."

I did not want a *tête-à-tête* with Augustus, and I was more than a little disturbed in mind as to the meaning of Digby's absence.

What could be the reason of his defiance of Aunt Patricia's prohibition of our leaving the house? Was it possible that he knew more than he had told me?

Perhaps he had gone to the village telegraph-office to try to get into communication with Michael at one of the several places to which he might have gone.

It would be something important that would make him risk giving Aunt Patricia cause to think that he had been guilty of an ungentlemanly disobedience to her request.

I drank my coffee in silence, and in silence departed from the room. I could not forgive Gussie for being innocent and forcing Michael to suspect Claudia, Digby, or me; me to suspect Claudia, Digby, or Michael; and Digby to suspect Claudia, Michael, or me.

Most unjust of me, but most human, I fear.

In the drawing-room Isobel was at the piano, playing softly to herself, and Claudia sat staring into the fire.

I strolled over to the huge piano and sat down near it.

"Where *can* Michael be?" said Claudia.

"And Digby," added Isobel.

"I don't know," said I.

"Really and truly?" asked Claudia.

"Yes," said I. "I honestly have not the faintest idea as to where either of them is."

"I wish they'd come in," said Isobel.

"Oh, I can't bear this room," cried Claudia suddenly, and springing up, went out. As I opened the door for her, I fancied I caught a glimpse of tears on her half-averted face, though I was not prying.

As I closed the door, Isobel rose from the piano and came towards me. She looked very lovely I thought, with her misty blue eyes, misty golden hair, as fine as floss-silk, and her sweet expression. How gentle and dear she was!

"Johnny," she said, laying her hands on my chest and looking up into my eyes, "may I ask you a silly question? Just once and for all? I know the answer, but I want to hear you say it."

"Certainly, dear," said I.

"You won't be angry, Johnny!"

"Have I ever been angry with you, Isobel? Could I be?" I asked.

She looked into my eyes steadily for a few moments.

"*Did you take the 'Blue Water,' John?*" she asked.

"No, my dear, I did not," I replied, and drew her to me. And then Isobel threw her arms round my neck and I kissed her on the lips.

She burst into tears, and lifting her up in my arms, I carried her to a sofa and sat hugging her to my breast and covering her face with kisses. It had suddenly come upon me that I loved her--that I had always loved her. But hitherto it had been as a charming darling playmate and companion, and now it was as a woman.

If this knowledge between us were a result of the theft of the "Blue Water," I was glad it had been stolen.

"Darling! Darling! Darling!" I whispered as I kissed her. "Do you love me, darling Isobel?" I asked, and, for reply, she smiled starrily through her tears, put her arms round me, and pressed her lips to mine.

I thought my heart was stopping.

"*Love* you, dearest?" she asked. "You are just my life. I have loved everything you have said or done, since I was a baby!"

"Don't cry," I said, ashamed of my inarticulate inadequacy.

"I'm crying for joy," she sobbed. "Now you have told *me* you didn't do it, I know you didn't."

"What made you think I did?" I asked.

"I *didn't* think so," she replied with feminine logic; "only it was you who were against the table, John; it was you whom Michael caught; and I saw you go down in the night--to put it back, as I thought."

"Saw me?" I asked, in surprise.

"Yes, dear. I was awake and saw a light go by my door. It shone underneath it. And I came out and looked over the banisters."

"I went to see if the wretched thing had come back," I said. "And it was rather I who caught Michael than Michael who caught me, when you turned the lights out. We were both expecting to catch Gussie, and caught each other."

"And, oh, I have been so wretchedly unhappy," she went on, "thinking appearances were so against you, and yet knowing I was allowing Gussie to remain under suspicion when I knew it wasn't he... . But when it seemed the thing was actually stolen, I couldn't keep quiet any longer. It was bad enough when it was only a practical joke, as we thought... . And then I seemed to be helping to bring suspicion towards you when I cleared Gussie... ."

She wiped away a tear.

"I don't care now," she smiled. "Nothing on earth matters. So long as you love me--I don't see how I can have a care in the world... . You're *sure,* darling?"

I endeavoured to express myself without the use of halting and unfluent speech.

"When did you first love me?" asked my sweet and beautiful darling, when I released her.

"I don't know," I said. "I have always loved you, and now I worship you, and I always shall," and again she gave me a long embrace that seemed to stop the beating of my heart and lift me up and up to an incredible heaven of ecstasy and joy almost unbearable.

The sound of footsteps and a hand on the door brought us back to earth. We sprang to our feet, and when David entered, Isobel was putting away her music, and I was consulting a small pocket-book with terrific abstraction from my surroundings.

"Excuse me, sir," said David, halting before me. "Might I speak to you, sir?"

"You're doing it, David," said I.

"In private, sir, a moment," he explained.

I went to the door with him, and having closed it, he produced a note and gave it to me.

"Mr. Digby, sir. He very specially instructed me to give you this in private at ten o'clock this evening, sir, thank you, sir."

"Thank you, David," said I, and went along to the smoking-room, opening the letter as I went.

Although I felt that I ought to be filled with apprehension, anxiety, and trouble, my heart sang for glee, and I could have danced down the long corridor, to the surprise and disapproval of the various stiff and stately Brandons, male and female, who looked down from its walls.

"This is most selfish and wrong," said I, and repressed a desire to sing, whistle, and whoop, and literally jump for joy.

"Isobel! Isobel! Isobel!" sang my heart. "Isobel loves me and I love Isobel... ."

The smoking-room was empty, and I could hear the click of balls from the neighbouring billiard-room, showing why. Gussie was evidently at his favourite, somewhat aimless, evening employment.

I turned up the lights, poked up the fire, pulled up the biggest and deepest chair, and filled my pipe and lit it.

Had I come straight here from the dining-room, and here received Digby's letter, I should have snatched it, and opened it with sinking heart and trembling fingers.

Now, nothing seemed of much importance, compared with the great fact of which my heart was chanting its pæan of praise and thanks to God.

Love is very selfish I fear--but then it *is* the very selves of two people becoming one self... .

And then I read poor Digby's letter. It was as follows:--

"My dear John,

I now take up my pen to write you these few lines, hoping they find you as they won't find me. After terrific thought and mental wrestling, which cost me a trouser-button, I have come to the conclusion that I can no longer deceive you all and let the innocent suffer for my guilty sin or sinny guilt.

I go to find my noble-hearted twin, to kneel at his feet and say, 'Brother, I have sinned in thy sight' (but it was in the dark really) 'and am no more worthy to be called anything but what I am.'

No one knows the shame I feel, not even me; and, by the time you get this, I shall be well on my way to--where I am going.

Will you please tell Aunt that Michael's noble and beautiful action has wrung my heart, and I wish he had wrung my neck. I cannot let him take the blame for me, like this. I shall write to her from Town.

When you find yourself in the witness-dock or prisoner's-box tell the Beak that you have always known me to be weak but not vicious, and that my downfall has been due to smoking cigarettes and going in for newspaper competitions. Also that you are sure that, if given time, I shall redeem myself by hard work, earn thirty shillings a week at least, and return the thirty thousand pounds out of my savings.

Write and let me know how things go on, as soon as I send you an address--which you will, of course, keep to yourself. Give my love to Isobel.

Play up and don't forget you've GOT to stand by me and make people realise the truth that I actually am the thief--or suspicion still rests on Claudia (since Isobel and Gussie are out of it), if we three do not provide the criminal amongst us. And, of course, I can't let Beau suffer for me.

Directly you hear from him, let him know by wire that I have confessed and bolted, and that he can return to Brandon Abbas and admit that he was shielding the real culprit (whom he knew to be ME or YOU or CLAUDIA!). Give my love to Isobel.

Ever thine,

Digby."

For a moment this drove even Isobel from my mind.

It had never occurred to me for one moment that Digby had actually fled, as Michael had done. Could it be possible that he was speaking the truth in the letter?

Could he have stolen the "Blue Water" as he said, and had Michael's flight and shouldering of the blame forced his hand and compelled him, in very shame, to confess? ...

Or did he, in his heart of hearts, think that Michael was really guilty and had fled rather than allow three innocent people to lie under suspicion with himself? Had Digby, thinking this, fled to divert suspicion from the guilty Michael, to confuse the issue and divide the pursuit, thus giving him a better chance to get clear away! ...

Probably neither. It was much more likely that his idea was to help to shield the person whom Michael thought he was shielding, and at the same time to share with Michael the suspicion thus diverted from the guilty person.

The moment it was known that Michael had fled, the world and his wife would say, "The vile young thief!"

Directly Digby followed him they would say, "Which of them *is* the thief?" and no eye would be turned enquiringly upon those who, in their conscious innocence, had remained at home.

And whom *did* Michael and Digby suspect, if they were both innocent?

Obviously either Claudia or me.

And if they could no more suspect me than I could suspect them ... ?

It dawned on me, or rather it was stabbed into my heart suddenly, as with a knife, that it was quite as much *my* affair to help in preventing suspicion, just or unjust, from falling upon Claudia; and that if they could face obloquy, poverty, hardship, and general wrecking of their lives for Claudia and for me and for each other--why, so could I for them, and that it was my duty to go too.

Moreover, when detectives and criminal-experts got to work on the case, they would be quite capable of saying that there was nothing to prevent Isobel and Augustus from being in collusion to prove each other innocent, and would suspect one or both of them the more.

To us, who knew her, it was completely proven that Augustus was innocent, because she said so.

To a detective, it would more probably be a clue to the guilty person--the girl who produced this piece of "evidence" which incidentally proclaimed her own innocence.

Moreover, the wretched Augustus had most undoubtedly been *surprised* when Isobel said he must be innocent as she had been holding on to him all the time the light was out. If this came out, it would certainly fix the suspicion on Isobel, and if it did not, there was a strong probability that her declaration concerning Augustus would, as I have said, suggest collusion between them.

The more reason then for me to strengthen the obvious solution--that the thief was one of the Gestes.

If three people fled confessing their guilt, that was where the collusion would be--among the three rascally brothers who had plotted to rob their relative and share the spoil.

That the oldest had weakened and fled first, was to his credit, or not, according to whether you more admired courage or confession; but obviously and incontestably, the blame must lie upon these three, and not among those who remained at home and faced the music.

"*But*," said the voices of prudence, cowardice, and common sense, as well as the voice of love, "*two are enough to take the blame, surely? Let people say it was one of those two, or perhaps the two in partnership.*"

"*And why*," replied the voices of self-respect and pride, "*should those two share the blame (or the honour)? Why should they shield Isobel and* YOU, *as well as Claudia, from suspicion?*" and to the latter voice I listened.

I could not possibly sit at home and enjoy life while the Captain and the Lieutenant were in trouble, disgrace, and danger--my whole life-training, as well as instincts, forbade.

I think that within two minutes of reading Digby's letter, the question of my going was quite definitely answered, and only the minor questions of where I should go, and whether I should say anything to Isobel, remained to be settled. And one of these two problems was subconsciously solved, though I had not intentionally considered it and come to a decision.

From the moment that I had learnt of Michael's flight, I had had somewhere, just below the level of consciousness, a vague remembrance of the existence of a romantic-sounding, adventurous corps of soldiers of fortune, called the French Foreign Legion.

When thinking of Michael, and seeing mental pictures of him in the setting of Brandon Abbas, our "Prep." school, Eton and Oxford, one of the clearest of these dissolving views had been of a group of us in the Bower, at the feet of a smart and debonair young French officer, who had thrilled us with dramatic tales of Algeria, Morocco, and the Sahara; tales of Spahis, Turcos, Zouaves, Chasseurs d'Afrique, and the French Foreign Legion of Mercenaries; tales of hot life and brave death, of battle and of bivouac. At the end, Michael had said:

"I shall join the French Foreign Legion when I leave Eton... . Get a commission and go into his regiment," and Digby and I had applauded the plan.

Had Michael remembered this, and was he, even now, on his way to this life of adventure and glory, determined to win his way to soldierly renown under a *nom de guerre?* ... It would be so like Michael.

And Digby? Had he had the same idea and followed him? It would be so like Digby.

And I? Should I follow my brothers' lead, asking nothing better than to do as they did, and win their approval! ... It would be so like me.

Three romantic young asses! I can smile at them now. *Asses* without doubt; wild asses of the wildest; but still, with the imagination and the soul to be romantic asses, thank God!

§ 10

As compensation for a smaller share of the gifts of courage, cleverness, and general distinction possessed by my brilliant brothers, I have been vouchsafed a larger measure of prudence and caution--though some may think that still does not amount to much.

I have met few men to equal Michael and Digby in beauty, physical strength, courage, and intelligence; but I was, in spite of being an equally incurable romantic, "longer-headed" than they, and even more muscular and powerful. This is tremendous praise to award myself, but facts are facts.

Having decided to join them in disgrace and blame, as well as to join them in the flesh if I could--going to the Legion to look for them in the first place--I settled down to consider details, ways, and means.

I can think better in the dark, so I knocked out my pipe, burnt Digby's letter, and went up to bed.

The first fact to face, and it loomed largest and most discouraging of all, was separation from Isobel in the very moment of finding her. Paradoxically, however, the very exaltation and excitement of this wonderful thing that had happened, this finding of her, carried me along and gave me the power to leave her.

I was *tête-montée,* beside myself, and above myself, abnormal.

I would show my love that I, too, could do a fine thing, and could make a personal sacrifice to ward off from women, one of whom was mine, "the slings and arrows of outrageous fortune," outrageous suspicion and annoyance.

To leave her would be misery unspeakable--but what a beautiful misery and poignantly delightful sorrow for the heart of romantic youth to hug to itself!

Also I knew that it was quite useless for such children as ourselves--she nineteen and I twenty--at present penniless and dependent, to think of formal engagements and early marriages. Love was all and love was enough, until I should return, bronzed and decorated, successful and established, a distinguished Soldier of Fortune, to claim her hand.

I would then take my bride to be the admired and beloved Pride of the Regiment, a soldier's star and stay and queen.... (Twenty is a great age at which to be--with love in your heart and life before you....)

Should I tell her what I was going to do and have one last beautifully-terrible hour, with her in my arms, or should I write her a letter to be given to her after I had gone?

I am glad to say that I had the grace to look at it from her point of view, and to decide according to what I thought would be better for her.

In the letter I could give the impression that this was only a short separation, and that I was writing to say "*Au revoir*" rather than "Good-bye."

If I told her in an interview, my obvious wretchedness and woebegone countenance would contradict my words. I knew I should kiss and embrace her as if for the last time on earth, and look as though I were going to the scaffold rather than into hiding for a while, until the missing jewel turned up, or the thief was caught.

Yes--I had better write, being careful to avoid the suggestion that this was any more a "separation" than my going back to Oxford for the next term would have been.

That question was settled.

The next thing to consider was the problem of procedure.

I should want sufficient money and kit to enable me to get to France and subsist for a few days, probably in Paris.

Ten pounds or so, a change of underclothing, and a toothbrush, would be the sort of thing. With a very small suit-case one would be quite comfortable.

My watch, links, studs, cigarette-case, and a good gold pencil which I possessed would provide ample funds. I had more than sufficient ready money for my fare to London, and could there raise enough to carry me on to Paris and keep me for a few days.

I would breakfast with the others, and quietly walk off to catch the ten-forty to Exeter, and take the eleven-forty-five thence to London, arriving about three o'clock. I would cross to France the next day, getting there in the evening; sleep at an hotel, and, as soon as possible, become a soldier of France.

Whatever my brothers had done, I should at least have followed their example worthily, and have given a realistic and convincing imitation of the conduct of a frightened and desperate thief, fleeing from the consequences of his crime and the shame of facing his relatives and former friends.

And if Michael and Digby were actually there when I arrived--why, I should regret nothing but the separation from Isobel--a separation, albeit, during which I would qualify, in age, position, and income, for the honour of becoming her husband.

I think I had arrived at the position of Commander-in-Chief in Algeria and Grand Commander of the Legion of Honour when I fell asleep... .

I awoke in the morning in a very different frame of mind from that of the morning before. My heart was full of pride that Isobel loved me and was mine. My brain was full of schemes and plans, and my whole being tingled gloriously with a sense of high adventure.

"If youth but knew ..."

When David brought my hot water, with his inevitable, "Half-past seven, sir, and a fine morning" (when the rain stops, or the fog clears, as the case might be), I told him I should give him a letter, after breakfast, which he was to give privately to Miss Rivers at the first convenient opportunity after eleven o'clock.

I thought it better to give it to David than to a maid. He had obeyed instructions in the case of Michael's letter to Digby, and Digby's letter to me, and a maid would be more likely to chatter in the servants' hall.

I did not think that there was the slightest suspicion in that quarter, and, as Aunt Patricia had said, there was no reason why there should be any, provided the mystery of the "Blue Water" was solved without the aid of the police.

I could have posted my letter to her of course, but that would have involved delay, and an anxious night for her. It would also mean a post-mark, and I thought it would be better for her to be able to say, with perfect truth, that she had not the vaguest idea as to where I had gone.

When I had dressed, I put my brushes and shaving-tackle into an attaché-case, and crammed in a shirt, collars, and socks, and then went down to the smoking-room, and, after some unsatisfactory efforts, wrote to Isobel:

"*My darling beautiful Sweetheart,*

I had a letter from Digby last night. He has bolted because he thinks that Michael has shouldered the blame and disgrace of this theft in order to protect the innocent and shield the guilty person (who must appear to him to be Claudia, Digby, or myself, as it is not you nor Gussie). Digby told me that it was not he, and he refuses to believe that it is Michael. I don't think he suspects me either.

Now, you'll be the first to agree that I can't sit at home and let them do this, believing them to be innocent. And if either of them were guilty, I'd want, all the more, to do anything I could to help. Were it not for leaving you, for a little while, just when I have found you, I should be rather enjoying it, I am afraid.

Anyhow, I should have had to leave you in a little while, when I went up to Oxford again, and that would have been an eight weeks' separation. As it is, we are only going to be parted until this silly wretched business is cleared up. I expect the thief will return the thing anonymously as soon as he or she finds that we three are all pretending we did it, and that we will not resume our ordinary lives until restitution is made.

You know that I didn't do it, and I know that you didn't, and that's all that really matters; but you wouldn't have me hold back when the Captain and Lieutenant of the Band are out to divert suspicion from the innocent and to shame the guilty into returning Aunt's property!

I'll send you an address later on, so that you can tell me what happens--but, just at first, I want you to have no idea where I am, and to say so.

You'd despise me, really, in your heart, if I stayed at home, though I know you'll miss me and want me back. I shall come, of course, the moment you let me know that the affair is cleared up. Meanwhile, no ass of a detective will be suspecting you or Claudia, or poor innocent Gussie, since obviously one of the absconding three (or all of them) must be the thief. Aunt will go to the police about it of course, and they will soon be on our track, and trouble no one at Brandon Abbas.

And now, darling Isobel, darling Faithful Hound, I am not going to try to tell you how much I love you--I am going to do it before you get this. But everything is different since last night. The world is a perfectly glorious place, and life is a perfectly glorious thing. Nothing matters, because Isobel loves me and I love Isobel--for ever and ever. I want to sing all the time, and to tell everybody.

Isn't love absolutely WONDERFUL!

Always and always,

Your devoted, adoring, grateful

Sweetheart."

This honest, if boyish, effusion I gave to David, and repeated my instructions. He contrived to keep his face correctly expressionless, though he must have wondered how many more of us were going to give him epistles to be privately delivered after their departure to other members of the household.

Leaving the smoking-room, I met Burdon in the corridor. "Can you tell me where Mr. Michael is, sir?" he asked. "Her ladyship wishes to see him."

"No, I can't, Burdon," I replied, "for the excellent reason that I don't know."

"Mr. Digby's bed have not been slep' in either, sir," he went on. "I did not know the gentlemen were going away.... Nothing packed nor nothing."

"They didn't tell me they were going, Burdon," I said, putting on an owlish look of wonder and speculation. "They're off on some jaunt or other, I suppose.... I hope they ask me to join them."

"Racing, p'r'aps, sir?" suggested Burdon sadly.

"Shocking," said I, and left him, looking waggish to the best of my ability....

There were only the four of us at breakfast again.

Isobel's face lit up radiantly as our glances met, and we telegraphed our love to each other.

"Anyone heard how the Chaplain is?" asked Claudia.

"I went to see him last night," replied Isobel, "but the nurse said he was asleep."

"Nurse?" asked Augustus.

"Yes," said Isobel. "Dr. Warrender thought he ought to have a night-nurse, and Aunt Patricia telegraphed for one. He's going to get up to-day though, the nurse told me."

"Where's Digby?" asked Augustus.

"Why?" I said elliptically.

"Burdon asked me if I'd seen him, and said he wasn't in last night."

"I know no more than you do where he is," I honestly assured him.

"Funny--isn't it?" he sneered.

"Most humorous," I agreed.

"Perhaps Aunt will think so," countered Augustus unpleasantly... . "First Michael and then Digby, after what she said about not leaving the house!"

"Ought to have consulted you first, Gussie," said Claudia.

"Looks as though they didn't want to consult the police, if you ask me," he snarled.

"We didn't ask you, Gussie," said Isobel, and so the miserable meal dragged through.

Towards the end of it, Burdon came in.

"Her ladyship wishes to see Mr. Digby," he said to the circumambient air.

"Want a bit of doing, I should say," remarked Augustus, with a snigger.

"He's not here, Burdon," said I, looking under the table.

"No, sir," replied Burdon gravely, and departed.

"You next, my lad," Augustus stated, eyeing me severely. "I wonder if the detectives have come."

Burdon returned. "Her ladyship would like to see you in her boudoir, after breakfast, sir," said he to me.

"Told you so," remarked Augustus, as the door closed behind the butler.

"Where do you think the others have gone?" asked Claudia, turning to me. "They can't have *run away* surely? not both of them?"

"Doesn't look like it, does it?" put in Augustus.

"If they have gone away it's for an excellent reason," said Isobel.

"Best of reasons," agreed Augustus.

"Quite the best, Claudia," said I, looking at her. "*If* they have 'run away,' as you said, it is to turn suspicion away from the house and everybody in it, of course."

"Oh, of course," agreed Augustus again.

"Just what they would do," said Isobel quietly.

"It would be like Michael," said Claudia in a low voice, and getting up, went quickly out of the room.

"And Digby," added I, as she did so.

Augustus departed soon after, with a malicious "Up you go" to me, and a jerk of his thumb in the direction of Aunt Patricia's room. Our recent roughness and suspicion evidently rankled in his gentle breast.

As soon as we were alone, I turned to Isobel, who sat beside me, put my arms round her and gave and received a long kiss.

"Come out to the Bower a minute, darling," said I, and we scuttled off together. There I crushed her to my breast and kissed her lips, her cheeks, and eyes, and hair, as though I could never have enough, and never stop.

"Will you love me for ever, darling?" I asked. "Whatever may happen to us, or wherever we may be?"

She did not reply in words, but her answer was very satisfying.

"Aunt wants me," then said I, and bolted back to the house. But I had no intention of seeing Aunt Patricia.

Mine should be the more convincing rôle of the uneasy, trembling criminal, who, suddenly sent for, finds he has not the courage to face the ordeal, and flees before the ominous sound of the summons.

I was very glad this had happened, as it would appear to have given me the cue for flight.

When first sent for, I was found peacefully eating my breakfast in fancied security. When again sent for, I should be missing--obviously terrified of the command and guiltily afraid to obey it.

Going to my room, I took my attaché-case from the wardrobe, pocketed a photograph of Isobel, and went quietly down the service staircase that debouched by the luggage-lift in a passage opening into the outer hall. In a minute I was across the shrubbery and into the drive at a bend which hid it from the house.

Twenty minutes' walking brought me to the station, where I booked to Exeter. That would not tell anybody very much, for though I was perfectly well known to everybody at our local station, it would be extremely unlikely that I should be traced from so busy a junction as Exeter, in the crowd that would be booking for the morning train to Waterloo.

As I waited on our platform, I was conscious of an almost unbearable longing to go back to Brandon Abbas and Isobel. How *could* I leave her like this, now, the very day after I had found her?

I felt a bigger lump in my throat than I had ever known since I was a child. It was utterly horrible.

But for the excitement and adventure of the business, I think I should have succumbed to the longing to return. But when two loving people part, one going on a journey, it is always the departing one who suffers the less.

It is inevitable that the distractions of travel, movement, change, shall drug the pain to which the other is equally exposed without the amelioration of mental and bodily occupation.

So, between my mind and the agony of separation from Isobel came the deadening and protecting cloak of action and of the competing thoughts of other matters--journey's end, the future, money, Paris, Algeria, the probabilities of finding Michael and Digby... .

Anyhow, I conquered the yearning to go back to her, and when the local train loafed in I got into it, with a stiff upper lip and a bleeding heart, and set out on as eventful and strange a journey as ever a man took.

CHAPTER III. THE GAY ROMANTICS

"Curs'd from the cradle and awry they come
Masking their torment from a world at ease:
On eyes of dark entreaty, vague and dumb,

They bear the stigma of their souls' disease."

I remember nothing of that horrible journey from Exeter to Waterloo. It passed as a bad dream passes, and I awoke from it in London.

As has happened to others in the history of that city, I found that, in such circumstances, London was a very large place, and myself a very small and lonely atom of human dust therein.

Walking out from Waterloo Station into the unpleasing purlieus thereof, I was tempted to go to the quiet and exclusive hotel that the Brandons had patronised for very many years, and where I was well known and should feel a sense of being at home among friends.

For this very reason I resisted the temptation, and was aided to do so by the question of finance. Whatever I did, I must leave myself sufficient money for my journey to Paris and subsistence there until I should become a soldier of France, to be lodged, boarded, clothed, and paid by Madame la République.

The first thing to do was to convert my disposable property into cash, a distasteful undertaking, but essential to further progress along the path I had elected to follow. If I had to do nothing more unpleasant than that, I told myself, as I walked along down a mean street toward Westminster Bridge, the said path would be no thorny one.

And, at that moment, my eye fell upon what I took to be the very place I wanted--a pawnbroker's shop, stuffed to bursting with a most heterogeneous collection of second-hand merchandise, ranging from clothing and jewellery by way of boxing-gloves, guns, knives, meerschaum pipes and cigar-holders, cameras, umbrellas and walking-sticks, field-glasses, portmanteaux, to concertinas, cornets, and musical instruments of every description.

I entered and found a young gentleman, of markedly Hebraic appearance, behind the counter. I expected to hear him say:

"Vat d'ye vant, Mithter?" and waggle his hands, palms upwards, near his shoulders, as I remembered a song, last heard at Oxford, anent one Solomon Levi and his store at Chatham Street.

For some reason, best known to himself, he wore a bowler hat of proportions so generous that it rested upon the nape of his neck and his ears, depressing the latter well-developed organs, so that they drooped forward as droops the tired lily--though in no other way did they suggest that flower.

To compensate for the indoor wearing of this outdoor garment, he had discarded his coat, exposing shirt-sleeves that again did not suggest the lily. A very large watch-chain adorned a fancy waistcoat that was certainly worn by him at meal-times also, and his diamond tie-pin bore testimony to his financial solidity and to his taste.

I fear I looked at him for a few seconds longer than good manners could approve--but then he looked at me for precisely the same length of time, though with a difference. For I was looking with a wondering admiration, whereas he was regarding me with little of wonder and less of admiration.

It was perfectly clear that he did not regard me as a buyer, though by what instinct or experience he could tell, I know not.

"Surely," thought I, "even if I have not the appearance of one who comes to buy, I still do not look like a needy, seedy seller?"

But he knew! He knew; and his silence was eloquent.

As his bold brown eyes regarded me, his curved nostril curved a little more, and his large ripe lips, beneath the pendulous nose, ripened while I watched.

He said no word, and this fact somewhat disconcerted me, for I had hitherto regarded the Children of Israel as a decidedly chatty race.

I broke the heavy silence of the dark mysterious shop, and added strange sounds to the strange sights and stranger smells.

"I want to sell my watch and one or two things," said I to this silent son of Abraham's seed.

He did not triumph in the manifest rightness of his judgment that I was a contemptible seller and not an admirable buyer. He did not do anything at all, in fact. He did not even speak.

No word nor sigh nor sound escaped him.

I produced my watch and laid it at his feet, or rather at his stomach. It was gold and good, and it had cost twenty-five pounds. (I allude to the watch.)

"'Ow much?" said the child of the Children of Israel.

"Er--well--isn't that rather for you to say?" I replied. "I know it cost twenty-five pounds and is an excellent ..."

"'Ow much?" interrupted the swarthy Child.

"How much will you give me?" I replied... ." Suppose we split the difference and you ..."

"'Ow much?" interrupted the Child again.

"Ten pounds?" I suggested, feeling that I was being reasonable and, indeed, generous. I did not wish my necessitous condition to weigh with him and lead him to decrease his just profits.

"Two quid," said the Child promptly.

"Not a tenth of what it cost?" said I, on a note of remonstrance. "Surely that is hardly a fair and ..."

"Two quid," interrupted the Child, whose manners seemed less rich than his attire.

I was tempted to take up the watch and depart, but I felt I could not go through all this again. Perhaps two pounds was the recognised selling price of all gold watches?

Producing my cigarette-case, gold pencil, and a tiny jeweller's box containing my dress studs, I laid them before this spoiler of Egyptians, and then detached my links from my shirt-cuffs.

"'Ow much?" enquired the Child once more.

"Well," replied I, "the pencil is pretty heavy, and the studs are good. So are the links. They're all eighteen carat and the ..."

"'Ow much?" repeated the voice, which I was beginning to dislike.

"Ten pounds for the watch, pencil, and ..."

"Four quid," the Child replied, in the voice of Fate and Destiny and Doom, and seeking a toothpick in the pocket of his "gent's fancy vest," he guided it about its lawful occasions.

This would not do. I felt I must add at least five pounds to what I already had. I was a little vague as to the absolutely necessary minimum, but another five pounds seemed to me to be very desirable.

"Oh, come--make it seven," said I, in the bright tone of encouragement and optimism.

The Child regarded the point of his toothpick. It appeared to interest him far more than I, or my poor affairs, could ever do.

"Six," said I, with falsely cheerful hopefulness.

The toothpick returned to duty, and a brooding silence fell upon us.

"Five, then," I suggested, with a falsely firm finality.

The Child yawned. For some reason I thought of onions, beer, and garlic, things very well in their way and their place, and quite pleasing to those who like them.

"Then I'm afraid I've wasted your valuable time," said I, with deep wiliness, making as though to gather up my despised property.

The Child did not trouble to deny my statement. He removed his bowler hat and looked patiently into its interior, as good men do in church. The hair of the head of the Child was most copiously abundant, and wonderfully curly. I thought of oil-presses, anointed bulls of Bashan, and, with bewildered awe, of the strange preferences of Providence.

However, I would walk to the door and see whether, rather than let me go, he would offer five pounds for what had cost at least fifty.

As I did so, this representative of the Chosen People cocked an eye at my dispatch-case.

"Wotcher got there?" he growled.

Imitating his excellent economy of words, I opened the case without reply, and removing a silk shirt, vest, and socks, displayed three collars, a pair of silver-backed hair-brushes, a comb, a silver-handled shaving-brush, a razor, an ivory nailbrush, a tooth-brush, and a silver box containing soap.

"Five quid the lot and chance if you've pinched 'em," said the Child.

"You'll give me five pounds for a gold watch, links, studs, and pencil-case; a silver cigarette-case, hair-brushes, and shaving-brush; a razor, shirt, vests, socks, collars, and a leather dispatch-case?" I enquired politely.

"Yus," said the Child succinctly.

Well, I could get shaved for a few pence, and in a couple of days I should probably be in uniform.

"I'll keep the tooth-brush and a collar," I remarked, putting them in my pocket.

"Then chuck in the walkin' stick and gloves, or it's four-fifteen," was the prompt reply.

I gazed upon the Child in pained astonishment.

"I gotter *live*, ain't I?" he replied, in a piteous voice, to my cruel look.

Forbearing to observe "*Je ne vois pas la nécessité*," I laid my stick and gloves on the counter, realising that, in any case, I should shortly have no further need of them.

The Child produced a purse, handed me five pounds, and swept my late property into a big drawer.

"Thank you," said I, departing. "Good evening."

But the Child apparently did not think it was a good evening, for he vouchsafed no reply.

One should not judge a race by single specimens, of course, but--racial antipathy is a curious thing... .

Crossing Westminster Bridge, with about ten pounds in my pocket, misery in my heart, and nothing in my hand, I made my way along Whitehall to Trafalgar Square, sorely tempted by the sight and smell of food as I passed various places devoted to the provision of meals, but not of beds.

It had occurred to me that it would be cheaper to dine, sleep, and breakfast at the same place, than to have dinner somewhere, and then go in search of a bedroom for the night and breakfast in the morning.

As I walked, I thought of the hotels of which I knew--the Ritz, the Savoy, the Carlton, Claridge's, the Grosvenor, the Langham, and certain more discreet and exclusive ones in the neighbourhood of the Albany (where Uncle Hector kept a *pied-à-terre* for his use when in England).

But both their cost and their risks were almost as much against them as were those of our own family hotel. Even if I could afford to go to such hotels as these, it was quite likely that the first person I should run against, in the one I selected, would be some friend or acquaintance.

I decided to approach one of those mines of information, or towers of strength and refuge, a London policeman.

"Take a bus to Bloomsbury, and you'll find what you want. Russell Square, Bedford Square, British Museum. All round that neighbourhood," was the reply of the stalwart to whom I applied for advice, as to a cheap, quiet, and decent hotel.

I obeyed his words, and had an edible dinner, a clean and comfortable bed, and a satisfying breakfast, for a surprisingly small sum, in an hotel that looked on to the British Museum and seemed to be the favoured of the clergy--it being almost full of men of religion and their women-folk of even more religion.

The "young lady" at the bureau of this chaste hostelry did something to enhance the diminished self-respect that my Israelite had left to me, by making no comment upon the fact that I was devoid of luggage, and by refraining from asking me to produce money in advance of hospitality. Perhaps she had a more discerning eye, or perhaps merely a softer heart, than had the child of Abraham, Isaac, and Jacob; or perhaps she was merely more of a fool.

Nevertheless I was glad to get away in the morning and to seek the shop of a hairdresser, after sleeping, for the first time in my life, without pyjamas, and bathing without a sponge. I was also glad to feel that the tips which I had given, with apologies for their modesty, to the waiter and chamber-maid had seemed quite adequate in their sight, and to cover my known deficiencies both of evening wear and night-gear.

It was extraordinary how naked I felt without my links, and how dishevelled without having used a brush and comb.

Finding a desirable barber's in Oxford Street, I was shaven and shampooed and went on my way, if not rejoicing, at any rate in better case, and feeling more my own man.

§ 2

My journey to Paris was uneventful and uncomfortable, confirming me in my opinion that economy in travelling is one of the dearest economies of all.

Personally, I would always rather travel first class and miss my meals, than travel third and enjoy three good ones, on a day's journey. Nor is this in the least due to paltry exclusiveness and despicable snobbishness. It is merely that I would rather spend the money on a comfortable seat, a pleasant compartment, and freedom from crowding, than on food with cramped circumstance. Let him who, in his wisdom, would rather spend his money on good food and have the discomfort, do so by all means.

De gustibus non disputandum, as the learned say, and likewise, *Chacun à son goût.*

Anyhow, the third-class journey was by no means to my *goût* at the time, though the day quickly came when it would have seemed the height of luxury.

From Charing Cross (where I turned my pounds into francs and felt much richer) to Dover I contrasted the beautiful county of Kent with my own Devon, in favour of the latter; and, at Dover, I went on board the cross-Channel steamer, deeply and appreciatively inhaling the glorious air, after that of the dusty, stuffy, crowded compartment in which I had travelled down.

Mentally I was in a curious condition, for while one half of myself ached unbearably for Isobel, the other half rejoiced wildly at the thought of adventure, travel, novelty, spacious life, mysterious Africa, the desert, fighting, and all that appeals to the heart of romantic youth.

At Calais, the sight of a French soldier, a sentry near the Custom House, gave me a real thrill.

Was I actually going to wear that uniform myself in a day or two? A *képi,* baggy red breeches, and a long overcoat, buttoned back from the legs? How much more attractive and romantic than the familiar British uniform that seemed to suggest Hyde Park and nurse-maids, rather than palms, oases, Moorish cities, and desert warfare.

So is the unknown always better than the known, and the thing we have not, better than that we have... .

At the Gare du Nord I experienced, in an intensified form, that sense of loneliness and utter insignificance that had assailed me at Waterloo; and I went out into the bright uproar of gay Paris, feeling anything but bright, uproarious, or gay myself. I was once more faced with the problem of hotels, for I had not the least idea as to how one set about offering one's services to France as a mercenary soldier, and the first thing to do, therefore, was to find a roof and a bed to serve me while I set about the quest.

My knowledge of Paris hotels was confined to the Meurice, Crillon, the Bristol, and the Ambassadors, but I knew these to be expensive, and, moreover, places at which I might meet acquaintances. There was no great likelihood of my meeting anyone who knew me well; but there was a chance, and I wanted to behave precisely as a guilty fugitive would do.

If I were traced, and it were found that I had gone, in London and Paris, to places where I might meet friends, it would hardly look as though I were a genuine jewel-thief, anxious to cover his tracks as he fled the country.

On the other hand, I did not want to blunder into an obscure cheap hotel, without luggage, an obvious foreigner, and run the risk of a visit from a polite but inquisitive *agent de police,* as seemed to me quite possible, if I and my explanations struck the proprietor as peculiar... .

A whimsical idea struck me. Why not go to the police themselves for advice on the subject of avoiding such trouble!

Sauntering along the noisy busy thoroughfare that passes the Gare du Nord, I looked out for a gendarme.

Presently I saw one standing on an island in the middle of the road, silent, inscrutable, immobile, heavily caped, oppressed by great responsibilities. Crossing to him, I raised my hat, and in my best and politest French (which is not bad, thanks to a French governess in our youth, and the Chaplain's wisdom and care), asked him if he could direct me to a good quiet hotel.

Moving his eyes, but not his head, nor any other portion of his majestic person, he examined me from top to toe and back again.

"Monsieur is English," he pronounced.

I acknowledged the truth of his statement, wondering how he knew I was not German, Swiss, Danish, Swedish, Norwegian, nor Dutch.

"Hôtel Normandie, Rue de l'Échelle," he announced without hesitation.

"And how do I get there, *Monsieur l'Officier?*" I asked.

"*Fiacre,*" was the prompt, terse reply, and the all-seeing official eye left me and sought among the traffic. A white-gloved hand was suddenly raised, and an open cab, driven by a many-caped gentleman, who did not look like a teetotaller, approached.

"Normandie, Rue de l'Échelle," said my gendarme to the *cocher,* and gave me a military salute, as I thanked him, raised my hat, and stepped into the carriage.

I enjoyed the drive through beautiful Paris in the mingled glow of late sunset and the myriad lights of the shops and streets; but my heart sank a little as the cab drew up before a fashionable-looking hotel that stood at a busy corner, close to the Rue de Rivoli and to the Rue de la Paix.

It looked as expensive as the best. However, Fate had sent me here, and here I would stay.

Trying to look as unconcerned as a luggageless traveller may, I entered the hall, received the bow of an imposing hall-porter, and marched straight ahead, past the grand staircase and the dining-room, to where I could see the bureau, and beyond it, the palm-decked *fumoir.*

At the bureau, a very pretty girl was talking to an American in American.

This was good luck. I could make a much more convincing show in English than in my pedantic and careful French.

Standing near, and trying to look like an eccentric foreigner who habitually went about without stick or gloves in order that he might keep his hands in his pockets, I waited for the American to go.

Meanwhile, it was quite impossible to avoid hearing what was said by the keen-faced, square-shouldered, lumpy-toed, baggy-trousered, large-hatted gentleman to the lady, what time she chewed a cud of sweet recollection and Mangle's Magnificent Masticating Gum or similar enduring comestible.

When at length he took his key and went, I turned to the girl.

"So you was raised in Baltimore!" said I rapturously. "Fancy that being your home town now! Isn't it just the cutest place? Peachiest gals and bulliest cakes in America! ... Say, I reckon this gay Paree hasn't got anything on little old New York!" ...

"My!" said the young lady. "D'you know Baltimore? You don't say!" and she smiled sweetly upon me.

"*Know Baltimore!*" said I, and left it at that.... "Lots of Americans and English here, I suppose," I went on, "since the hotel folk are wise (and lucky) enough to have you in the bureau? And I suppose you speak French as well as any Parisian?"

"My, yes," she smiled. "Most as well as I speak good old U.S.... Why, yes--lots of home people and Britishers here.... Most of our waiters can help 'em out too, when they're stuck for the French of '*Yes, I'll have a highball, Bo,*'" and she tinkled a pretty little laugh.

"Guess that's fine," said I. "I want to turn in here for a day or two. All upset at my place." (Very true, indeed.) "Just to sleep and breakfast. Got a vacant location?"

"Sure," said my fair friend, and glanced at an indicator. "*Troisième*. Eighteen francs. No--breakfast only--fourteen. Going up now?" And she unhooked a key and passed it to me with a brief "*Deux cent vingt deux*. The bell-hop will show you."

"Not bringing any stuff in," I said, and drew my entire fortune from my pocket, as one who would pay whatever was desired in advance, and the more the merrier.

"Shucks," said my friendly damsel, and I gathered that I was deemed trustworthy.

In the big book that she pushed to me I wrote myself down as Smith, but clung to the "John," that there might be something remnant and stable in a whirling and dissolving universe.

"Guess I'll hike up and take possession now," said I thereafter, and with my best smile and bow I turned to the lift before she could send to the hall-porter to dispatch a supposititious suit-case to the spot.

The lift-boy piloted me to number two hundred and twenty-two, where, safe inside, I bolted the door and drew breath.

"*J'y suis, j'y reste*," said I, in tribute to my very French surroundings ..." and the less they see of me below, the less they'll notice my lack of luggage and evening kit."

It occurred to me that it might be worth the money to buy a pair of pyjamas and have them sent to Monsieur Smith, No. 222 Hôtel Normandie. If I laid them out on the flat square pillow that crowned the lace-covered bed, the chamber-maid would not be so likely to comment on the paucity of my possessions, particularly if I locked the wardrobe and pocketed the key as though to safeguard a valuable dressing-case.

If I also avoided the dining-room, where, in my lounge-suit, I should be extremely conspicuous among the fashionable evening throng, I might well hope to dwell in peaceful obscurity without rousing unwelcome interest and attention, in spite of the inadequacy of my equipment.

I decided to sally forth, buy some pyjamas, order them to be sent in at once, and then fortify myself with a two-franc dinner and a glass of *vin ordinaire*--probably *très ordinaire*--in some restaurant.

After an uncomfortable wash in the *lavabo,* I strolled nonchalantly forth, made my purchases, and enjoyed a good and satisfying meal in a cheerful place situated in a somewhat ignobler part of the Rue de Rivoli, at a little distance from the fashionable centre of Paris.

Returning to my over-furnished unhomely room, I spread out the gay pyjamas which awaited me, and wondered when the chamber-maid would come to turn down the bed. And then I realised that I need have felt no anxiety, for I had only to bolt the door and shout something when she came, and she would depart in ignorance of my complete lack of luggage and possessions.

However, I should not be able to keep her out in the morning, when I went in search of breakfast and the recruiting-office, and then the pyjamas and the locked wardrobe would play their part.

Even as I stood revolving these important trifles in my youthful breast, the door opened and in burst a hard-featured middle-aged woman. Anything less like the French chamber-maid of fiction and the drama could not well be imagined; for she was fair-haired, grey-eyed, unprepossessing, and arrayed in a shapeless black frock, plain apron, and ugly cap.

With a curt apology she flicked down a corner of the bedclothes, slapped the pyjamas down (in what is presumably the only place whence a self-respecting hotel guest can take them up), glanced at the unused washstand, and scurried from the room.

As I heard her unlock the door of the next apartment, almost before she had closed mine, I realised that she was far too busy to concern herself with my deficiencies, and ceased to worry myself on the subject.

Feeling that sleep was yet far from me, and that if I sat long in that unfriendly room I should go mad, I descended to the *fumoir,* sought a big chair in a retired nook, and, from behind a deplorable copy of *La Vie Parisienne,* watched the frequenters of this apparently popular lounge.

Here I thought long thoughts of Isobel, my brothers, and Brandon Abbas; and occasionally wondered what would happen on the morrow.

Nothing at all would happen until I had discovered the procedure for enlisting in the Foreign Legion, and the discovery of that procedure must be to-morrow's business.

Were I a romancer as well as a romantic, now would be the moment for me to announce the dramatic entry of the French officer who had fired our young imaginations, years before, and sown the seeds now bearing fruit.

As I sat there in the lounge of the Paris hotel, he would enter and call for coffee and cognac. I should go up to him and say, "*Monsieur le Capitaine* does not remember me, perhaps?" He would rise, take my hand, and say, "*Mon Dieu!* The young Englishman of Brandon Abbas!" I should tell him of my ambition to be a soldier of France, to tread in his footsteps, to rise to rank and fame in the service of his great country, and he would say, "Come with me--and all will be well... ."

Unfortunately he did not enter, and presently, finding myself the last occupant of the lounge and inclined to yawn, I crept unwillingly to bed. I fell asleep, trying to remember his name.

§ 3

The next day was Sunday, and I spent it miserably between the lounge and my bedroom.

On Monday morning, after a spongeless bath and an unsatisfying *petit déjeuner,* I sallied forth and put myself in the hands of an excellent barber, and, while enjoying his deft ministrations, had a bright idea. I would pump this chatty person.

"You don't know Algeria, I suppose?" I asked the man.

"But no, Monsieur," he replied. "Is Monsieur going there?"

"I hope to," I said. "A magnificent colony of your great country, that."

Ah, it was, indeed. Monsieur might well say so. A wonderful achievement and the world's model colony. Growing too, always growing... . This excellent *pénétration pacifique* to the South and towards Morocco... .

"They do the pacific penetration by means of the bayonets of the Foreign Legion mostly, don't they?" I asked.

The Frenchman smiled and shrugged.

"A set of German rascals," he said. "But they have their uses... ."

"How do you get them?" I asked.

Oh, they just enlisted. Made their *engagements volontaires*, like anybody else, at the head recruiting-office of the French army in the Rue St. Dominique. Simply enlisted there and were packed off to Africa... .

"But I thought service was wholly compulsory in this country?" said I. "How then do you have recruiting-offices for a conscript army?"

The worthy soul explained at length, and so far as I could follow his swift idiomatic talk, that any Frenchman could, if he liked, volunteer for service before the time came when he *must* serve, whether he liked it or not. Sometimes, for business reasons, it was very convenient to get it over and done with, instead of having it to do later, when one was established. Hence the recruiting-office for the French army. But no Frenchman could volunteer for the Legion until he had done his compulsory service... .

I let him talk on, keeping the words *Rue St. Dominique* clearly in my mind the while. I had got what I wanted, and the sooner I found this recruiting-office the better, for funds would soon be running low.

On leaving the shop I hailed a *fiacre*, said, "Rue St. Dominique," and jumped in, excusing my extravagance by my absolute ignorance of the route, and the need for haste.

Again I enjoyed the drive, feeling excited and buoyant, and filled with the sense of adventure. After a time, I found we were in what appeared to be the military quarter of Paris, and I saw the *École Militaire* and some cavalry-barracks. The streets were thronged with men in uniform, and my heart beat higher and higher as the cab turned from the Esplanade des Invalides into the Rue St. Dominique.

As the *cocher* looked round enquiringly at me, I thought it would be as well to pay him off here at the corner.

Perhaps it might not be good form to drive up, in style, to a recruiting-office, and, in any case, there was no need to let the man know where I was going... .

I found the Rue St. Dominique to be a wholly uninspiring thoroughfare, narrow, gloomy, and dingy in the extreme.

Walking along it and glancing from side to side, I soon found the building of which I was in search.

Over the door of a dirty little house was a blue-lettered notice testifying that the place was the BUREAU DE RECRUTEMENT. Below the label was the bald, laconic observation, ENGAGEMENTS VOLONTAIRES.

Well, here then was my bureau of recruitment and here would I make my "voluntary engagement," and if the Path of Glory led but to the grave, its beginning was quite in keeping with its end, for a more sepulchral-looking abode of gloom than this ugly little government-office I have never seen.

Crossing the road, I pushed open a rusty iron gate, undeterred by its agonised or warning shriek, crossed the neglected cemetery garden of this gay place, thrust back a swing door, and entered a long dark passage.

I could see no notice recommending all to abandon hope who entered here, but my drooping spirits were unraised by a strangling odour of carbolic, coal-gas, and damp.

On the wall was a big placard which, in the sacred names of Liberty, Equality, and Fraternity, offered to accept for five years the services of any applicant for admission to *La Légion Étrangère* (provided he was between the ages of eighteen and forty), and to give him a wage of a halfpenny a day.

There seemed to me to be little of Liberty about this proposal, less of Equality, and least of Fraternity.

On the other hand, it was an *engagement volontaire,* and anyone who didn't like the offer could leave it. No one was compelled to accept it, and there was no deception--on the placard at any rate.

I read the notice through again, half hoping that while I did so, someone would come and ask my business, some sound break the heavy smelly silence of Glory's cradle.

But none did, and "with well-feigned hopefulness I pushed forth into the gloom."

Venturing on, I came to a kind of booking-office ticket-window, above which were repeated the words *Engagements Volontaires.*

I looked in, and in a severe office or orderly-room, beheld an austere person in uniform, seated at a table and writing busily. The two gold stripes above his cuff inclined me to suppose that he was a non-commissioned officer, though of what rank and eminence I knew not.

He ignored me and all other insects.

How to attract his attention?

I coughed gently and apologetically. I coughed appealingly. I coughed upbraidingly, sorrowfully, suggestively, authoritatively, meekly, imperiously, agreeably, hopefully, hopelessly, despairingly, and quite vainly. Evidently I should not cough my way to glory.

"*Monsieur le Capitaine,*" I murmured ingratiatingly.

The man looked up. I liked him better when looking down.

"Monsieur would appear to have a throat-trouble," he observed.

"And Monsieur an ear-trouble," I replied, in my young ignorance and folly.

"What is Monsieur's business?" he enquired sharply.

"I wish to join the *Légion Étrangère,*" I said.

The man smiled, a little unpleasantly, I thought.

"*Eh, bien,*" he remarked, "doubtless Monsieur will have much innocent amusement at the expense of the Sergeant Major there too," and I was quite sure that his smile was unpleasant this time.

"Is Monsieur only a Sergeant-Major then?" I enquired innocently.

"I am a Sergeant-Major," was the reply, "and let me tell Monsieur, it is the most important rank in the French army."

"No?" said I, and lived to learn that this piece of information was very little short of the simple truth.

"Wait by that door, please," requested the Sergeant-Major, indicating one marked *Commandant de Recrutement,* and I felt that he had also said, "Wait, just wait, my friend, until you have enlisted."

I waited.

I should think I waited an hour.

Just as I was contemplating another visit to the buttery-hatch or ticket-office window, the door opened and my friend, or enemy, appeared.

"Be pleased to enter, Monsieur," said he suavely, and I, for some reason, or for no reason, bethought me of a poem of childhood's happy days, entitled, "The Spider and the Fly," as I entered a large, bare orderly-room.

But it was no spider that I encountered within, but a courtly and charming gentleman of the finest French type. I know nothing of his history, but I am very sure that he was of those who are "born," as the French say, and that if, in the Terror, his great-grandfather did not perish on the guillotine, it was not because he wasn't an aristocrat.

He was a white-haired, white-moustached, handsome man, dressed in a close-fitting black tunic and baggy red over-alls with a broad black stripe. His cuffs were adorned with bands of gold and of silver braid, and his sleeves with the five *galons* of a Colonel.

"A recruit for the Legion, *mon Commandant*," said the Sergeant-Major, and stood stiffly at attention.

The Colonel looked up from the desk at which he was writing, as, entering, I bared my head and bowed; he rose and extended his hand, with a friendly and charming smile.

Not thus, thought I, do British colonels welcome recruits to the ranks of their regiments.

"And you, too, wish to enlist in our Foreign Legion, do you?" he said as we shook hands. "Has England started an export trade in the best of her young men? I don't see many Englishmen here from year's end to year's end, but you, *mon enfant*, are the third this week!"

My heart gave a bound of hopeful joy... .

"Anything like me, sir?" I asked.

"*Au bout des ongles*," was the reply. "Were they your brothers by any chance? ... But I will ask no indiscreet questions."

I felt happier than I had done since I had kissed Isobel.

"Yes, *mon Commandant*," I replied. "I wish to become a soldier of France if you will have me."

"And do you understand what you are doing, Monsieur!" asked the Colonel.

"I have read the placard outside," said I.

"It is not quite all set forth there," he smiled. "The life is a very hard one. I would urge no one to adopt it, unless he were a born soldier and actually desirous of a life of discipline, adventure, and genuine hardship."

No, this certainly was not a case of the spider and the fly--or it was an entirely new one, wherein the spider discouraged flies from entering the web.

"I wish to join, sir," I said. "I have heard something of the life in the Sahara from an officer of Spahis, whom I once knew."

The Colonel smiled again.

"Ah, *mon enfant*," said he, "but you won't be an officer of Spahis, you see... . Nor an officer of the Legion either, except after some very long and lean years in the ranks and as a non-commissioned officer."

"One realises that one must begin at the bottom, *mon Commandant*," I replied.

"Well--listen then," said the Colonel, and he recited what he evidently knew by heart from frequent repetition.

"The *engagement volontaire* for *La Légion Étrangère* is for five years, in Algiers, or any other French colony, and the pay is a *sou* a day. A *légionnaire* can re-enlist at the end of the five years, and again at the end of ten years. At the end of fifteen years he is eligible for a pension varying according to his rank. A foreigner, on completion of five years' service, can claim to be naturalised as a French subject... . You understand all that, *mon enfant?*"

"Yes, I thank you, *mon Commandant*," I replied.

"Mind," continued the Colonel, "I say nothing of what is understood by the term 'service' in the Legion. It is not all pure soldiering at times.

"Nor do I say anything as to the number of men who survive to claim the pension... ."

"I am not thinking of the pension, *mon Commandant*," I replied; "nor of the alleged 'pay,' so much as of a soldier's life, fighting, adventure, experience... ."

"Ah, there is plenty of that," said the Colonel. "Plenty of that. It is a real military school and offers the good soldier great and frequent chances of distinction, glory, decoration, and promotion. Some of our most famous generals have been in the Legion, and several of the highest and most distinguished officers of the Legion began their career in its ranks... . Also, if you can show that you have been an officer in the army of your own country, you can begin as a probationary-corporal, and avoid the ranks altogether."

"Please accept me as a recruit, *mon Commandant*," said I.

"Ah, we'll see first what the doctor has to say about you--though there is little doubt about *that*, I should think," smiled the Colonel, and pulled a form towards him.

"What is your name?"

"John Smith," said I.

"Age?"

"Twenty-one years" (to be on the safe side).

"Nationality English?"

"Yes, *mon Commandant*."

"Very well. If you pass the doctor I shall see you again. *Au 'voir, Monsieur*," and with a curt nod to the Sergeant-Major, the Colonel resumed his writing.

The Sergeant-Major opened the door with a still suave "This way, if you please, Monsieur," and led me across the passage into a room already tenanted by half a dozen civilians, whom I rightly supposed to be fellow-recruits for the Foreign Legion.

I got a fleeting impression of seedy, poorer-class people, two being brush-haired, fair, fattish, and undoubtedly German, before the Sergeant-Major, opening another door in this waiting-room, motioned me to enter a small closet, from which another door led elsewhere.

"Remove *all* clothing, please," said the Sergeant-Major, and shut me in.

This was unpleasant but presumably unavoidable, and I obeyed. Before I had begun to shiver, the second door opened and I was invited to submit myself to the close and searching investigations of an undergrown but over-nourished gentleman, from beneath whose white surgical smock appeared the baggy red trousers of the French army.

This official, presumably an army-surgeon, was easily able to establish the belief in my mind that *his* ancestors had not perished on the guillotine. (Certainly not during the Terror, anyhow). More probably they danced round it, or possibly operated it.

When he had quite finished with my vile body, he bade me replace it in the closet, clothe it, and remove it with all speed. This, nothing loth, I did, and was re-conducted by the Sergeant-Major to the Colonel's office.

"Well, *mon enfant*," smiled the old officer, "you are accepted."

"And can I enlist at once, sir!" I enquired eagerly.

"Not until you have slept on it," was the reply. "Come here again to-morrow morning, if you are still of the same mind, and I will enrol you. But think well--think well. And remember that, until you sign your name on the form which I shall give you to-morrow, you are absolutely free, and have committed yourself in no way whatsoever. Think well--think well... ."

And thanking him gratefully, I went from the room, hoping that all French officers were of this stamp, as kindly and as truly gentlemanly. My hope was not fulfilled.

In the corridor, the Sergeant-Major observed, "I sincerely hope Monsieur will return," and as I assured him, with thanks, that I should do so, I fancied, rightly or wrongly, that his smile was a little mocking.

§ 4

Emerging from the stuffy gloom, I walked down the Rue St. Dominique with a light, gay step. I could have danced along, whistling and singing, for I felt practically certain that Michael and Digby were but a day or two ahead of me upon this romantic road, and that I might overtake them at any moment. Probably they were both still in France, possibly in Paris. Once I rejoined them, I should no longer feel this deadly loneliness, and should have someone to whom to talk about Isobel.

Journeys end in lovers' meetings--and but for this separation from her, there would not be the immeasurable joy of our reunion.

Really I ought to be very thankful and very happy. I was about to rejoin Michael and Digby, and to live with them again; Isobel loved me and was awaiting my return; and I was on the threshold of a great adventure in an unknown foreign land.

Knowing that I should, after to-morrow morning, live at the charges of *Madame la République* (albeit she seemed of a careful and economical turn of mind), my funds were ample, and I would take a *fiacre* back to the fashionable quarter and spend the rest of my last day of freedom in sight-seeing and idleness.

I would sit in the Tuileries Gardens, visit the Louvre, look in the shops, have an outdoor meal in the Bois, and generally behave as does the tourist who has a few hours and a few francs to spend.

I carried out my programme, whiled away the day, and crept up to my bedroom at night, too tired for anything but the blessed dreamless sleep of healthy youth.

In the morning I paid my bill and departed from the Hôtel Normandie with a curious sense of escape. I did not in the least mind becoming a halfpenny soldier and herding with all sorts and conditions of men; but I did dislike being in a first-class hotel without my dinner-kit, a change of clothes, and the small necessities of the toilet.

I again drove to the Rue St. Dominique, and, on the way, endeavoured to talk to myself as though a person of wisdom and experience were talking to another of sense and discretion. But I greatly fear that this is not what happens when I address myself.

"You have only to stop this *fiacre,* turn about, and go back," said I to me, "and there is no harm done. You will still be a free man, and can go back to Brandon Abbas as soon as you like."

But the only reply was, "Beau ... Digby... . Stand by your pals through thick and thin. Adventure: Romance: Success: Fame and Fortune: and then England, Home, and Isobel ..." and much similar youthful nonsense.

At the *Bureau de Recrutement* I was shown into a waiting-room by the Sergeant-Major, who observed:

"Ah, Monsieur has come back then! Good!" and smiled unattractively. Again I was reminded of a poem of early childhood, this time of a Lady of Riga who indulged in an unorthodox joy-ride.

In the waiting-room were some of the men I had seen on the previous day in the doctor's ante-chamber.

Among them were the Teutonic-looking pair, and I thought it probable that if I suddenly called out "*Waiter!*" or "*Garçon!*" they would both spring eagerly forward. They looked very harmless, insignificant, and unattractive--also terribly poor.

The rest were a mixed lot, Latins of sorts, apparently with nothing in common but dire poverty. They did not seem in the least ruffianly nor criminal, but just ordinary working-men, desperately poor, and as anxious and worried as hungry, homeless people always are.

It was rather curious to feel that whereas, a few minutes ago, I had been a little uncomfortable by reason of my sartorial deficiencies, I now felt uncomfortable at being so obviously a fashionably-clad and well-nourished member of a wholly different class.

My well-cut and fairly-new clothing seemed to mock the rags and general seediness of these poor fellows, my future comrades--all of whom would very probably prove much tougher soldiers than I should.

Before long, the Sergeant-Major returned and bade me follow him to the Colonel's office.

"Ah, *mon enfant*," said the old soldier, as I entered and bowed, "so you have not thought better of it, eh? Well, well, you must now do as you please."

"I wish to enlist, *mon Commandant*," I replied.

"Then read this form and sign it," he said, with a distinct sigh. "Remember though, that as soon as you have done so, you will be a soldier of France, entirely amenable to martial law, and without any appeal whatsoever. Your friends cannot possibly buy you out, and your Consul cannot help you, for five years. Nothing but death can remove you from the Legion."

I glanced over the grey printed form, a contract by which the signatory undertook to serve the French Republic for five years, as a soldier in the *Légion Étrangère*.

Five years was a long time--but Isobel would only be twenty-three at the end of it, and if Michael and Digby had done this, I could do the same... . It would be nice to return, a Colonel at twenty-five, and take Isobel to my regiment... . I signed my name.

"A little error, *mon enfant?*" smiled the Colonel, on reading my signature. "Or you prefer this *nom-de-guerre*, doubtless?"

I had written "J. Geste"!

Blushing and looking a fool, I asked to be allowed to change my mind and put my own name, and the kindly old gentleman, tearing up the form, gave me another which I signed "John Smith."

"Now, my boy, listen to me," said the Colonel. "You are a duly enlisted soldier of France and must join your regiment at once. If you do not do so, you will be treated as a deserter. You are to catch the Marseilles train from the Gare de Lyon this evening--nine-fifteen--and report yourself to the noncommissioned officer whom you will see waiting at the Marseilles terminus. Should you fail to find him, ask any *gendarme* to direct you to Fort St. Jean, and report yourself there. Don't forget. Fort St. Jean, the military depôt," and he rose and extended his hand. "I wish you good luck and quick promotion, *mon enfant*," he added. "Is there anything else I can tell you?"

"Do you always advise applicants to think better of it, sir?" I asked.

He looked at me a little sharply.

"I am not here to deter people from joining the Foreign Legion," he said... . "But some strike me as better suited to the life than others," he added, with a kindly shake of the hand. "Good-bye and good luck."

I thanked him and turned to commence my "ride on the Tiger" (along the Path of Glory).

"Come with me, recruit," said the Sergeant-Major, as he closed the door, "and move smartly."

In his office, he made out a railway-warrant for Marseilles, and a form that proclaimed the bearer to be John Smith, a soldier of the Legion, proceeding to the depôt in Algeria. He then unlocked a drawer, produced a cash-box, and doled out three francs on to the table.

"Subsistence-money, recruit," said he. "A squandering of public funds. Three *sous* would be ample."

I added two francs to them.

"Let us part friends, Sergeant-Major," said I, for I hate leaving ill-feeling behind me if I can avoid it.

"Recruit," replied he, pocketing the money, "you will get on... . *If* you respect and please all Sergeant-Majors. Good-bye."

And once more I found myself in the Rue St. Dominique, but no longer a free man. I had, with my own hand, padlocked about my ankle a chain unbreakable, the other end of which was somewhere in the desert of Sahara.

Having burnt my boats, I was quite anxious to push on, and I found myself deciding to go by the next train, instead of waiting till the evening. Had I realised that I was to sit for eighteen hours on an uncushioned wooden seat, I might have felt less eager. Eighteen hours the journey did last, however, and each hour more wearisome than the one before. I think the train must have visited every town and village in France, and the entire population have clattered noisily into my ancient, uncomfortable, unclean compartment, throughout the night. Certainly I reached Marseilles feeling ancient, uncomfortable, and unclean myself; and, unlike the compartment, very empty.

It was a wretched journey, rendered no pleasanter by the attentions of the guard, who, having seen from my railway-warrant that I was going to the Legion, behaved somewhat in the manner of a clever captor and skilful gaoler.

He was of a type of Frenchman that I do not like (there are several of them), and though he refrained from actual reproaches and abuse, he made it clear to me that I could not escape him, and to my fellow-travellers that they had a possible danger in their midst. Not precisely a convict; nor, so far as he actually *knew*, an ex-convict; but still, one who was going to join the Foreign Legion.

On arrival at the terminus, this worthy soul saved me the trouble of finding my non-commissioned officer, by himself finding the man and handing me over to him, with the air of one who has deserved well of his country and of his kind.

"There!" said he to the Sergeant. "There he is! Another little bird for your cage," and so depressed was I by hunger, sleeplessness, and aching bones that I so far departed from good manners and the equal mind as to say:

"Oh, for God's sake don't be such a funny little fat ass," but as I spoke in English he may have thought that I did but offer felicitations and regards.

I rather liked the look of the Sergeant. He was a dapper, alert person, and his bronzed face, though hard as iron, was not brutal nor vicious. He struck me as looking uncommonly like a man. He wore the usual uniform of the French infantry, but with a broad blue woollen sash round the waist, green epaulettes instead of red, and Zouave trousers.

Looking me over with a cold official stare, he asked me if I spoke French, and demanded my name, papers, and nationality.

"Another Englishman," he remarked to my intense joy. "Well--it might have been worse."

"Are you alone?" he enquired, and finding that I was, so far as I knew, bade me follow him.

Surely Michael and Digby were here, and I should see them in the next few minutes. I cheered up tremendously.

He led the way out of the station and down into the busy street and the exhilarating air and sunshine of Marseilles.

By the side of the taciturn Sergeant I walked, longing to ask him about the "other Englishmen," whose recent arrival he had implied by his exclamation, on hearing my nationality.

But his manner did not encourage polite converse, and, truth to tell, I had an even deeper longing at the moment--for the appeasement of a very healthy appetite.

I waxed diplomatic.

"A Sergeant would not share a bottle of wine with a recruit, I suppose, Monsieur?" I asked as we passed an attractive-looking café, from beneath whose gay striped awnings marble-topped tables and comfortable cane chairs shrieked an invitation to rest and refreshment.

"He would not, *bleu*," was the reply. "Not only from a natural sense of superiority, but also because it would be against the regulations. Neither is he addressed as 'Monsieur.' He has a military rank, and he is saluted by those who address him... . Some Sergeants, properly approached, might refresh themselves, perhaps, while a deserving *bleu* did the same... ."

I halted and saluted as though he were an officer. (Correct procedure in the French army, I found.)

"*Monsieur le Sergent*," said I, "will you honour me by drinking a glass of wine at this restaurant while I get some food? I am very hungry," and I produced a five-franc piece.

"Be here in quarter of an hour, *bleu*," was the reply, and taking the coin the Sergeant crossed the road to a wine-shop, as I promptly dived into the café and hungrily devoured my last civilian meal--an excellent one in every detail, down to the crisp rolls, fresh butter, and coffee worthy of the name.

I rose, feeling what Digby would call "a better and a wider man."

Sauntering out under the awning, and seeing nothing of my Sergeant, I sat me down, filled and lighted my pipe, and gazed about me. Fortified and refreshed, I felt by no means unhappy.

I had not long feasted my eyes upon the novel and interesting scene provided by the thronged thoroughfare, when the Sergeant, crossing the road, approached. I rose promptly, saluted smartly, and fell in beside him.

He eyed my clothes.

"Have you any more money, *bleu*?" he asked.

"Yes, Sergeant," I replied, feeling a little disappointed in him.

"Because if you have not, I shall return you three francs," quoth he.

I assured him that this was wholly unnecessary, though a very kindly thought--and regretted my suspicions.

"Well, I will give you some good advice instead then," said the worthy man.

I thanked him sincerely.

"Beware the Algerian wine then," he began. "The blessing and the curse of the army of Africa. I have just drunk two bottles of it. Excellent... . Beware of women, the blessing and the curse of all men. I have married three of them. Terrible... ."

I gave my solemn promise to beware, to be very ware, and neither to drink nor to marry to excess.

"Secondly, *bleu*," he went on, "when things are bad, do not make them worse, for they will be quite bad enough."

This also seemed sound advice, and I said so.

"And, thirdly--resist the decrees of Heaven if you will, but not those of your Corporal... . Of course, no one would dream of resisting the will of a Sergeant."

I agreed that no sane person would do this.

"Of course! ... But it is when you are insane that you must be careful," warned my mentor.

"Insane?" I asked.

"Yes, *bleu*," was the reply. "All good *légionnaires* go insane at times. Then they are apt to do one of *the* three horrible things. Kill themselves, kill their comrades, or defy a Sergeant."

"Why should they go insane?" I enquired in some alarm.

"They shouldn't, but they do," said my mentor. "We call it *le cafard*. The cockroach. It crawls round and round in the brain, and the greater the heat, the monotony, the hardship, the overwork, the over-marching, and the drink--the faster goes the beetle and the more it tickles... . Then the man says, '*J'ai le cafard,*' and runs amok, or commits suicide, or deserts, or defies a Sergeant... . Terrible... . And do you know what is the egg of this beetle? No? It is absinthe. Absinthe is the uncle and aunt of the grandparents of *cafard*. It is the vilest poison. Avoid it. I know what I am saying. I was brought up on it... . Terrible... . I had some just now, after my wine... ."

I promised never to look on the absinthe when it was green, nor, indeed, when it was any other colour.

"Then you will not get real *cafard*," continued the worthy man, "and you will not kill a comrade nor defy a Sergeant. You will only commit suicide, or desert and die in the desert."

"Did you ever do any of these terrible things, *Monsieur le Sergent?*" I asked.

"No, *bleu*. I did not even commit suicide," was the reply. "I merely shaved my head, painted it red, white, and blue, and was thus esteemed as a true patriot."

I began to think that two bottles of wine and an unspecified quantity of absinthe had stimulated the Sergeant's imagination, but learnt later that what he told me was absolutely true. (When engaged in repainting one of the striped sentry boxes of the barracks or the outpost where he was stationed, he had painted one side of his shaven head red and the other side blue, and separated these colours with a broad white stripe. This had drawn attention to him, and he had riveted that attention by desperate courage and resource during the operations and battle of Cinq Palmiers.)

"And what can one do to escape *le cafard?*" I asked.

"Nothing," was the discouraging reply. "Mental occupation is good, and promotion is better. But in the desert, while the Arab finds two things, the European finds three. They are there, and, therefore, there they are ... ."

I tried to look intelligent and enquiring.

"The Arab inevitably finds sun and sand--too much of both. The European inevitably finds sun, sand, and madness--too much of all three," he went on. "This madness is in the air, I suppose, or in the sun's rays. I do not know, even I, although I know so much. And now you have talked more than is seemly. Silence, *bleu*... ."

And I was silent, though inclined to ask why he addressed me as "*bleu*." I did not feel particularly blue, and I was quite sure I did not look blue in the slightest degree. (Later I learnt that it is French army-slang for a recruit, and has as much or little meaning as the English name of "rookie" for the same class of soldier.) The use of my tongue being now prohibited, I used my eyes instead, and enjoyed the marvellous panorama of the Marseilles waterside, where Arabs, Negroes, Levantines, Chinese, Moors, Annamese, Indians, and the lascars and seamen of the ships of all nations, seemed as numerous as the French themselves.

I was reminded of the story of the Tower of Babel as we made our way through the throng and round the boxes, bales, sacks, barrels, trucks, carts, trolleys, and waggons over which the gesticulating crowds swarmed and howled.

Among the sailing-ships, tramps, Oriental-looking barques, yachts, brigs, schooners, cargo-boats, and liners, moored along the quays, I kept looking for the English flag, flying at the stern; and was delighted as often as my eye fell upon it.

I had thought, at first, that all the ships must be French, as each flew the Tri-couleur at the mast, until I realised that this was complimentary to France, while the national flag flew at the stern.

My head was beginning to ache with the noise, heat, hustle, and eye-strain, when we arrived at our destination, a mediæval fort on the water's edge, obsolete and dilapidated, with an ancient lighthouse tower, and a drawbridge, leading over a moat to a great door.

One half expected to see that the sentries were halberdiers in breastplate and jerkin, trunk hose, and peaked morion... .

"Here we are, and hence--we are here," observed my Sergeant... . "Good-bye, *bleu*, and may the devil admire you."

"The same to you, Sergeant, and very many thanks," I replied.

To the Sergeant of the Guard at the gate he merely remarked, "Recruit. Legion. Poor devil!" and turning, departed, and I saw him no more.

"Follow me, you," said the Sergeant of the Guard, and led the way along prison-like stone corridors, damp, mouldering, echoing, and very depressing.

Halting at a door, he opened it, jerked his thumb in the direction of the interior, and shut the door behind me as I entered.

I was in my first French barrack-room.

Round the walls stood a score or so of cots and a number of benches, the remaining furniture of the room being a big table and a stove. Round the latter, at the table, on cots and on benches, lounged a varied assortment of men in civilian clothes--clothes ranging from well-cut lounge-suits to corduroy and rags.

Michael and Digby were not among these men, and I was sensible of a deep feeling of bitter disappointment as I realised the fact.

All these recruits looked at me, but though conscious of their regard, I was much more conscious of the poisonous foulness of the atmosphere of the room. It was horrible.

Every window was tightly shut, and every man (and the charcoal stove) was smoking, so far as I could determine with a rapid glance round the reeking place.

Presumably the men were smoking tobacco, but it was no tobacco with which I was familiar. I was reminded of gardeners' bonfires and smouldering rubbish.

Without thinking of what I was doing, I naturally and instinctively turned to the nearest window, manfully wrestled with it, and succeeded in throwing it open.

I am not in a position categorically to affirm that this was positively the first time that a window had ever been opened in Fort St. Jean, but it might well have been, to judge by the interest, not to say consternation, evoked by my simple action. What would have happened to me had a corporal or old soldier been present, I do not know.

At the table a group of three or four men who were playing cards, seemed to take umbrage at my action or my audacity. Their ejaculations sounded like those of great surprise mingled with resentment. One of them rose and turned towards me.

"You do not like the atmosphere of our little nest, perhaps?" he said, unpleasantly, and with a threatening and bullying note in his voice.

"No," I replied, and looking him carefully up and down, added, "Nor you either. What are you going to do about it?"

This was ill-mannered of me. I admit it. I was bringing my style to the level of this unpleasant-looking individual. But it seemed to me to be the best level on which to meet him. I thought it a sound plan to begin as I meant to go on, and I had not the least intention of allowing that going-on to include any undue Christian meekness. I was the last person in the world to bully anybody, and I intended to be the last person to be bullied.

I did not wish to begin by making an enemy, but still less did I wish to begin by allowing the establishment of any sort of ascendancy on the part of a fellow-recruit.

"Oho! You don't like the look of me, don't you?" said the fellow, advancing.

"Not a bit," said I, looking him over appraisingly, and then "staring him out" as we used to say in the nursery.

I could not quite "place" the individual. He certainly was not a workman and he was not a prince in disguise. A clerk, or shopman, probably, I thought, and learned later that he was a French petty official named Vogué, "rehabilitating" himself--recovering his papers and civic rights by five years' Legion service, after conviction of defalcation, and a light sentence.

"You want that window open?" he said, changing the subject.

"Monsieur is intelligent," said I.

"Suppose I want it shut?" he enquired.

"Come and shut it," said I, with disgraceful truculence.

"Suppose we all want it shut?" he hedged.

"Then there is an end of the matter," I replied. "If the majority prefer to poison themselves, they have a perfect right to do so."

"Come back and be quiet, Nosey," called one of the card-players, and he returned, grumbling.

I seated myself on the cot nearest to the open window, and put my hat on the dirty straw-stuffed pillow.... What next?

"Like the ceiling raised any?" enquired a quiet drawling voice behind me, in English.

Turning, I regarded the ceiling.

"No," I said, "it will do," and studied the speaker.

He was lying at full length on the next cot, a very small, clean-shaven man with a prominent nose and chin, a steel-trap mouth, and a look of great determination and resolution. His eyes were a very light grey, hard and penetrating, his hair straw-coloured and stubbly, his face sallow, lantern-jawed, and tanned. He looked a hard case and proved to be what he looked.

"How did you know I was English?" I asked as he stared thoughtfully at me.

"What else!" he replied, deliberately. "Pink and white.... Own the earth.... '*Haw! Who's this low fellah? Don' know him, do I?*' ... Dude.... '*Open all the windahs now I've come!*' ... British!"

I laughed.

"Are you an American?" I enquired.

"Why?" he replied.

"What else?" I drawled. "'*Sure thing, stranger.*' ... Don't care who owns the earth.... Great contempt for the effete English.... Tar and feathers.... Stars and Stripes.... '*I come from God's Own Country and I guess it licks Creation.*' ... Uneasy self-assertion...."

The American smiled. (I never heard him laugh.)

"Bo," said he, turning to the next cot, "here's a Britisher insulting of our pore country.... Handin' out the rough stuff.... Fierce, ain't it?"

A huge man slowly turned from contemplation of the ceiling, raised his head, ceased chewing, and regarded me solemnly. He then fainted with a heartrending groan.

"Killed my pard, you hev," said the little man. "He's got a weak heart.... Damn sight weaker head though, haven't you, Bo?" he added, turning to his friend, who had recovered sufficiently to continue his patient mastication either of tobacco or chewing-gum.

Lying there, Bo appeared to be some seven feet in length, four in breadth, and two in depth.

In face he greatly resembled the small man, having the same jutting chin, prominent nose, tight mouth, and hard leathery face. His eyes were of a darker grey, however, and his hair black and silky.

He also looked a hard case and a very bad enemy. Conversely though, I gained the impression that he might be a very good friend. Indeed, I liked the look of both of them, in spite of the fact that I seemed to fill them with a sort of amused contempt.

"Ses you suffers from oneasy self-insertion, Hank," went on the little man.

"Ain't inserted nawthen to-day, Buddy," replied the giant mildly. "Nary a insert. I'm oneasy in me innards, but it ain't from what you ses, Stranger. Nope. I could insert a whole hog right now, and never notice it."

"Don't go fer ter rile the Britisher, Hank, with yer silly contradicshusness," implored the other. "He don' like it, an' he don' like us. You don' want ter go gittin' inter no trouble. So shet up and go on sufferin' from oneasy self-insertion."

"Means well," continued the speaker, turning to me, "but he ain't et nawthen excep' cigarette-ends for three or four days, an' he ain't at his best."

I stared. Was it possible that they were really hungry? Certainly they looked lean and haggard enough to be starving.

I had felt quite bad enough an hour or two ago, after missing a single meal.... I should have to go carefully if I wanted to give food, and not offence.

"Would you gentlemen lunch with me?" I asked, diffidently. "Brothers-in-arms and all that...."

Two solemn faces turned and regarded me.

"He's calling you a gentleman, Hank," said the little man at length. "He don' mean no real harm though. He's talkin' English to you.... Hark! ... You listen and improve your mind."

I made another effort. "Say," quoth I, "I gotta hunch I wanta grub-stake you two hoboes to a blow-out. Guess I can cough up the dough, if yew ain't too all-fired proud to be pards with a dod-gasted Britisher." A good effort, I thought.

"Gee!" said Hank, and they rose as one man.

"Put it right there, son," said the big man, extending the largest hand I have ever seen.

I took it, and in the crushing-match that ensued, endeavoured to hold my own. It was a painful business, and when I limply took the horny fist of Buddy in turn, I was handicapped in the squeezing competition. However, I was able to give him a worthy grip, though his hand was stronger than mine.

"Where can we get something?" I asked, and Buddy said there was certain to be a canteen about. He had never yet heard of a case where a thirsty soldier, with money, was not given every encouragement to get rid of it.

"I can't drink till I've et, pard," said Hank to me. "'Twouldn't be right. If I drinks on an empty stummick, I gets unreasonable if interfered with by the bulls.... Bash a sheriff or somethin'.... When I ain't starvin', lickker on'y makes me more and more lovin' to all mankind. Yep, I gotta eat first."

"They'll have eats in the canteen," opined Buddy, "even in this God-fersaken section."

At that moment, the door of the room was thrown open by a soldier, and he entered carrying one end of a long board on which stood a row of tin bowls. Another soldier appeared at the other end, and together they bawled, "*Soupe!*"

It was invitation enough, and both the long arms of Hank shot out, and, in a moment, he was on his bed, a bowl in either hand.

Buddy followed his example.

I looked round. There appeared to me to be more bowls than there were people in the room. I snatched two, before the rush of hungry men from other parts of the room arrived with outstretched hands.

This disgusting exhibition of greed on my part cannot be excused, but may be condoned as it was not made in my own interests. I was not hungry, and the look of the stuff was not sufficiently tempting for me to eat for eating's sake. By the time I reached my cot, Hank had emptied one bowl, and was rapidly emptying the other.

"Gee! That's what I come to the Legion for," he said, with a sigh of content. When he had finished, I offered him one of my two.

"Fergit it," said he.

"I want to," said I.

He stared hard at me.

"Not hungry," I assured him.

"Honest Injun?" he asked doubtfully, but extending his hand.

"Had a big breakfast an hour ago," said I. "I never take soup in the middle of the morning. I got this for you and Mr.--er ..."

"Buddy," said the little man and took the other bowl.

Hank swallowed his third portion.

"You're shore white, pard," he said.

"Blowed-in-the-glass," agreed Buddy, and I felt I had two friends.

A large German lumbered up gesticulating, and assailed Hank.

"You eat dree!" he shouted in guttural English. "I only eat vun! Himmel! You damn dirdy tief!"

"Sure thing, Dutchy," said Buddy. "Don't yew stand fer it! You beat him up. You make him put it back."

The German shook a useful-looking fist under Hank's nose.

"I can't put it back, Dutch," said he mildly. "'Twouldn't be manners," and, as the angry German waxed more aggressive, he laid his huge and soupy hand upon the fat angry face, and pushed.

The German staggered back and fell heavily, and sat looking infinitely surprised.

"*Now,* pard," said Hank to me, "I could shore look upon the wine without no evil effecks to nobody," and we trooped out in search of the canteen.

The big gloomy quadrangle of Fort St. Jean was now crowded with soldiers of every regiment of the army of Africa, the famous Nineteenth Army Corps, and, for the first time, I saw the Spahis of whom the French officer had talked to us at Brandon Abbas.

Their trousers were voluminous enough to be called skirts, in fact one leg would have provided the material for an ample frock. Above these garments they wore sashes that appeared to be yards in length and feet in width. In these they rolled each other up, one man holding and manipulating the end, while the other spun round and round towards him, winding the sash tightly about himself as he did so.

Gaudy waistcoats, zouave jackets, fez caps, and vast scarlet cloaks completed their picturesquely barbaric costumes.

Besides the Spahis were blue-and-yellow Tirailleurs, pale blue Chasseurs d'Afrique, and red-and-blue Zouaves, blue Colonial Infantry, as well as artillerymen, sappers, and soldiers of the line, in their respective gay uniforms.

There was a babel of noise and a confusing turmoil as these leave-men rushed about in search of pay-corporals, *fourrier-sergents,* kit, papers, food, and the canteen. The place was evidently the clearing-house and military hotel for all soldiers coming from, or returning to, the army of Africa.

Following the current that flowed through this seething whirlpool, in the direction of a suggestive-looking squad of huge wine-casks that stood arrayed outside an open door, we found ourselves in the canteen and the presence of the national drink, good red wine.

"No rye-whiskey at a dollar a drink here, Bo," observed Buddy, as we made our way to a zinc-covered counter, and found that everybody was drinking claret at three-halfpence the bottle. "Drinks are on you, pard. Set 'em up."

"Gee! It's what they call 'wine,'" sighed Hank. "Gotta get used to it with the other crool de*pri*vations and hardships," and he drained the tumbler that I filled.

"It *is* lickker, Bo," replied Buddy tolerantly, and drained another.

It was, and very good liquor too. It struck me as far better wine than one paid a good deal for at Oxford, and good enough to set before one's guests anywhere.

Personally I am a poor performer with the bottle, and regard wine as something to taste and appreciate, rather than as a thirst-quenching beverage.

Also I freely confess that the sensation produced by more than enough, or by mixing drinks, is, to me, most distasteful.

I would as soon experience the giddiness caused by spinning round and round, as the giddiness caused by alcohol. More than a little makes me feel sick, silly, depressed, and uncomfortable, and I have never been able to understand the attraction that intoxication undoubtedly has for some people.

It is therefore in no way to my credit that I am a strictly sober person, and as little disposed to exceed in wine as in cheese, pancakes, or dry toast.

"Quite good wine," said I to the two Americans, "but I can't say I like it as a drink between meals."

I found that my companions were of one mind with me, though perhaps for a different reason.

"Yep," agreed Buddy. "Guess they don't allow no intoxicatin' hard lickkers in these furrin canteens."

"Nope," remarked Hank. "We gotta swaller this an' be thankful. P'r'aps we kin go out an' have a drink when we git weary-like.... Set 'em up again, Bo," and I procured them each his third bottle.

"You ain't drinkin', pard," said Buddy, eyeing my half-emptied first glass.

"Not thirsty," I replied.

"Thirsty?" said Hank. "Don' s'pose there's any water here if you was," and feeling I had said the wrong thing, covered my confusion by turning away and observing the noisy, merry throng, drinking and chattering around me. They were a devil-may-care, hard-bitten, tough-looking crowd, and I found myself positively looking forward to being in uniform and one of them.

As I watched, I saw a civilian coming from the door towards us. I had noticed him in the barrack-room. Although dressed in an ill-fitting, shoddy, shabby blue suit, a velvet tam-o'-shanter, burst shoes, and apparently nothing else, he looked like a soldier. Not that he had by any means the carriage of an English guardsman--far from it--but his face was a soldier's, bronzed, hard, disciplined, and of a family likeness to those around.

Coming straight to us, he said pleasantly, and with only the slightest foreign accent:

"Recruits for the Legion?"

"Yes," I replied.

"Would you care to exchange information for a bottle?" he asked politely, with an ingratiating smile which did not extend to his eyes.

"I should be delighted if you will drink with us," I replied, and put a two-franc piece on the counter.

He chose to think that the money was for him to accept, and not for the fat little man behind the bar to change.

"You are a true comrade," said the new-comer, "and will make a fine *légionnaire*. There are a dozen bottles here," and he spun the coin. "Now ask me anything you want to know," and he included the two stolid Americans in the graceful bow with which he concluded. He was evidently an educated and cultured person and not English.

"Sure," said Hank. "I wants ter know when we gits our next eats."

"An' if we can go out and git a drink," added Buddy.

"You'll get *soupe,* bread, and coffee at about four o'clock, and you won't be allowed to leave here for any purpose whatever until you are marched down to the boat for Oran," was the prompt reply.

His hearers pursed their lips in stolid silence.

"When will that be?" I asked.

"To-morrow by the steam-packet, unless there is a troopship going the day after," answered the new-comer. "They ship the Legion recruits in--ah--dribbles? dribblings? driblets? Yes, driblets--by every boat that goes."

"Suppose a friend of mine joined a day or two before me," I asked, "where would he be now, do you suppose?"

"He is at Fort St. Thérèse at Oran now," was the reply. "And may go on to Saida, or Sidi-bel-Abbès to-morrow or the next day. Sidi, probably, if he is a strong fellow."

"Say, you're a walking encyclopedestrian," remarked Buddy, eyeing the man speculatively, and perhaps with more criticism than approval.

"I can tell you anything about the Legion," replied the man in his excellent refined English--about which there was no accent such as that of a Londoner, north-countryman, or yokel, but only a slight foreign suggestion--"I am an old *légionnaire,* rejoining after five years' service and my discharge."

"Speaks well for the Legion," I remarked cheerfully.

"Or ill for the chance of an ex-*légionnaire* to get a crust of bread," he observed, less cheerfully.

"Been up against it, son?" asked Hank.

"Starved. Tramped my feet off. Slept in the mud. Begged myself hoarse--for work... . Driven at last to choose between gaol and the Legion... . I chose the Legion, for some reason... . Better the devils that you know than flee to the devils that you know not of... ."

"Guy seems depressed," said Hank.

"May I finish your wine!" went on the man. "It would be a sin to waste it."

"Pray do," said I, surprised; and reminded myself that I was no longer at Oxford.

"You speak wonderful English," I remarked.

"I do," was the reply; "but better Italian, Hindustani, and French. Legion French, that is."

"An' how's that, ole hoss?" enquired Buddy.

"Father an Italian pastry-cook in Bombay. Went to an English school there, run by the Jesuit Fathers. Talked Hindustani to my ayah. Mother really talked it better than anything else, being what they call a country-bred. Daughter of an English soldier and an Eurasian girl. Got my French in the Legion, of course," explained the stranger.

And then I was unfortunate, in that I partly blundered and partly was misunderstood. What I meant to say, for the sake of being conversational, was:

"And how did you come to find yourself in Africa, so very far from home?" or something chatty like that. What I actually did say was:

"Why did you join the Legion?" which sounded very bald.

"For the same reason that *you* did. For my health," was the sharp reply, accompanied by a cold stare.

I had done that which is not done.

"And did you find it--healthy?" enquired Buddy.

"Not exactly so much heal*thy* as hel*lish*," replied the Italian in brief and uncompromising style, as he drained his glass (or perhaps mine).

We all three plied him with questions, and learned much that was useful and more that was disturbing. We also gathered that the gentleman was known as Francesco Boldini to his friends, though he did not say by what name the police knew him.

I came to the conclusion that I did not like him extraordinarily much; but that in view of his previous experience he would be an exceedingly useful guide, philosopher, and friend, whose knowledge of the ropes would be well worth purchasing.

I wished I could send him on ahead for the benefit of my brothers, who had, I felt certain, come this way two or three days before me. Indeed, I refused to believe otherwise or to face the fact of my crushing disappointment and horrible position if they had not done so. I was aroused from thoughts of what might, and might not, be before me by a tremendous uproar as the artillerymen present united in roaring their regimental song:

"Si vous voulez jouir des plaisirs de la vie,
Engagez vous ici, et dans l'artillerie.
Quand l'artilleur de Metz change de garnison,
Toutes les femmes de Metz se mettent au balcon.
Artilleur, mon vieux frère,
À ta santé vidons nos verres;
Et répétons ce gai refrain:
Vivent les Artilleurs; à bas les fantassins ..."

and much more.

When they had finished and cheered themselves hoarse, a little scoundrelly-looking fellow sprang on a barrel and sang a remarkably seditious and disloyal ditty, of which the chorus, apparently known to all, was:

"Et quand il faut servir ce bon Dieu de République,
Où tout le monde est soldat malgré son consentement.
On nous envoie grossir les Bataillons d'Afrique,
À cause que les Joyeux n'aiment pas le gouvernement,
C'est nous les Joyeux,
Les petits Joyeux,
Les petits marlous Joyeux qui n'ont pas froid aux yeux... ."

At the conclusion of this song of the battalion of convicted criminals (known as the *Bataillon d'Infanterie Légère d'Afrique,* or, more familiarly, as the "*Bat d'Af*"), the men of the Colonial Infantry, known as *Marsouins,* lifted up their voices in their regimental song. These were followed by others, until I think I heard all the famous marching-songs of the French army--including that of the Legion, sung by Boldini. It was all very interesting indeed, but in time I had had enough of it... .

When we returned to the barrack-room, on the advice of Boldini, to be in time for the evening meal, I formally retained that experienced and acquisitive gentleman as guide, courier, and mentor, with the gift of ten francs and the promise of such future financial assistance as I could give and he should deserve.

"I am sorry I cannot spare more just at present," said I, in unnecessary apology for the smallness of the retaining fee; and his reply was illuminating.

"Ten francs, my dear sir," he said, "is precisely two hundred days' pay to a *légionnaire*... . Seven months' income. Think of it!" ...

And I thought of it.

Decidedly I should need considerable promotion before being in a position to marry and live in comfort on my pay... .

§ 5

"Dinner," that evening, at about five o'clock, consisted of similar "*soupe,*" good greyish bread, and unsweetened, milkless coffee. The first came, as before, in tin basins, called "*gamelles*"; the second was thrown to us from a basket; and the coffee was dipped from a pail, in tin mugs.

The *soupe* was a kind of stew, quite good and nourishing, but a little difficult to manipulate without spoon or fork. I found that my education was, in this respect, inferior to that of my comrades. After this meal--during which the German eyed our party malevolently, and Vogué, the gentleman who had objected to my opening the window, alluded to me as a "sacred *nicodème,*" whatever that may be--there was nothing to do but to adjourn once more to the canteen.

Here it was my privilege to entertain the whole band from the barrack-room, and I was interested to discover that both the German, whose name proved to be Glock, and the unpleasing Vogué, were both charmed to accept my hospitality, and to drown resentment, with everything else, in wine.

It is quite easy to be lavishly hospitable with wine at about a penny a pint.

Fun grew fast and furious, and I soon found that I was entertaining a considerable section of the French army, as well as the Legion's recruits.

I thoroughly enjoyed the evening, and was smitten upon the back, poked in the ribs, wrung by the hand, embraced about the neck, and, alas, kissed upon both cheeks by Turco, Zouave, Tirailleur, Artilleur, Marsouin, and Spahi, even before the battalion of bottles had been routed by the company of men.

I noticed that Boldini waxed more foreign, more voluble, and more unlovable, the more he drank.

If he could do anything else like a gentleman, he certainly could not carry his wine like one.

"Sah!" he hiccupped to me, with a strident laugh, "farmerly arlso there were a gross of bahtles and few men, and now arlso there are only gross men and a few bahtles!" and he smote me on the back to assist me to understand the jest. The more he went to pieces under the influence of liquor, the more inclined was I to think he had a larger proportion of Oriental strain than he pretended.

I liked him less and less as the evening wore on, and I liked him least when he climbed on the zinc-covered counter and sang an absolutely vile song, wholly devoid of humour or of anything else but offence. I am bound to admit, however, that it was very well received by the audience.

"What you t'ink of *thatt,* sah?" he enquired, when he had finished.

I replied that I preferred not to think of it, and proposed to address him in future as Cloaca Maxima.

Meanwhile, Hank and Buddy, those taciturn, observant, non-committal, and austerely-tolerant Americans, made hay while the sun of prosperity shone, drank more than any two of the others, said nothing, and seemed to wonder what all the excitement was about, and what made the "pore furriners" noisy.

"Ennybody 'ud think the boobs hed bin drinkin'," observed Buddy at last, breaking a long silence (his own silence, that is, of course). To which remark Hank replied:

"They gotta pretend thisyer wine-stuff is a hard drink, an' act like they got a whiskey-jag an' was off the water-waggon. Only way to keep their sperrits up... . Wise guys too. You'd shore think some of 'em had bin drinkin' lickker... .

"Gee! ... There's 'Taps!" he added, as the "Lights out" bugle blew in the courtyard, and the company broke up, "an' we gotta go to bed perishin' o' thirst, fer want of a drink... ."

Back to our barrack-room we reeled, singing joyously.

As I sat on my cot undressing, a little later, Buddy came over to me and said, in a low voice:

"Got 'ny money left, pard?"

"Why, yes. Certainly," I replied. "You're most welcome to ..."

"Welcome nix," was the reply. "If you got 'ny money left, shove it inside yer piller an' tie the end up--or put it inside yer little vest an' lie on it... ."

"Hardly necessary, surely?" said I. "Looks rather unkind and suspicious, you know... ."

"Please yerself, pard, o' course," replied Buddy, "and let Mister Oompara Tarara Cascara Sagrada get it," and he glanced meaningly at Boldini, who was lying, fully dressed, on his cot.

"Oh, nonsense," said I, "he's not as bad as all that... ."

Buddy shrugged his shoulders and departed.

"I gotta evil mind," he remarked as he did so.

I finished undressing, got into the dirty sheetless bed, put my money under my pillow, and then lay awake for a long time, dreaming of Isobel, of Brandon Abbas, and, with a sense of utter mystification, of the wretched "Blue Water" and its mysterious fate... .

Only last Wednesday... . Only eight people--one of whom it obviously must be... . A wretched vulgar thief... . And where were Michael and Digby now? Were they together, and only forty-eight hours ahead of me on the Path of Glory, which, according to Boldini, led to the grave with a certainty and a regularity bordering upon monotony? ... I fell asleep... .

I was awakened in the morning by the shrilling of bugles.

A corporal entered the room, bawled:

"*Levez-vous donc! Levez-vous donc!*" at the top of his voice, and departed.

I partly dressed, and then felt beneath my pillow for my money.

It was not there.

I felt savage and sick.... Robbed! ... The beastly curs....

"Here it is," said the voice of Buddy behind me. "Thought I'd better mind it when I aheered yore nose-sighs.... Shore enuff, about four a.m. this morning, over comes Mister Cascara Sagrada to see how youse agettin' on.... '*All right, Bo,*' ses I, speakin' innercent in me slumbers, '*I'm amindin' of it,*' I ses...."

"No?" said I, "not really?"

"You betcha," replied Buddy, "an' Mister Cascara Sagrada says, '*Oh, I thought somebody might try to rob him,*' he says.... '*So did I,*' I says, '*And I was right too,*' I says, an' the skunk scoots back to his hole."

"Thanks, Buddy," I said, feeling foolish, as I took the notes and coins.

"I tried to put you wise, Bo," he replied, "and now you know."

Curiously enough, it did not enter my mind to doubt the truth of what he had told me.

After a breakfast-lunch of *soupe* and bread, we were ordered by a sergeant to assemble in the courtyard.

Here he called the roll of our names, and those of a freshly-arrived draft of recruits; formed us in fours, and marched us to the *bassin*, where a steamer of the *Messageries Maritimes* line, the *Général Negrier*, awaited us.

We were herded to the fo'c'sle of this aged packet, and bidden by the corporal, who was going in charge of us, to use the ocean freely if we should chance to feel unwell, as it was entirely at our disposal.

"'We have fed our seas for a thousand years,'" thought I, and was grateful that, on this glorious day, the sea did not look at all hungry.

But if the sea were not, we soldiers of misfortune undoubtedly were. Very hungry, indeed, and as the hours passed, we grew still hungrier. Towards evening, the Château d'If and the tall lighthouse having been left far behind, murmurs on the subject of dinner began to be heard. We loafed moodily about the well-deck, between the fo'c'sle and the high midship bridge structure, talking both in sorrow and in anger, on the subject of food.

Personally I thought very regretfully of the dining-room at Brandon Abbas, and of the dinner that was even then being served therein. Tantalising odours were wafted to us from the saloon below the bridge, and our ears were not unaware of the stimulating rattle of plates and cutlery.

"When shall we get something to eat?" I asked Boldini, as he emerged from the fo'c'sle hatch.

"By regulations we should have had *soupe,* bread, and half a litre of wine at five o'clock," he replied. "Quite likely the cook is going to make a bit out of us, for these swine often do...."

However, there was activity, I observed, in the cook's galley, near the fo'c'sle--the cookhouse in which the sailors' food was prepared--so we hoped for the best while fearing the worst.

An hour later, when we were an hour hungrier and angrier, Hank's usually monumental patience had dwindled to imperceptibility.

"Here, you, Cascara," quoth he, pushing into the knot of men in the centre of which Boldini harangued them on their rights and the cause of their present wrongs, "you know the rules of this yer game. Why ain't we got no eats yet?"

"Because this thieving swine of a son of a sea-cook is going to make a bit out of us," replied Boldini.

"Thet so, now?" observed Hank mildly. "Then I allow he ain't agoin' ter live to enjy it. Nary a enjy. So he can tell himself Good-bye, for he ain't goin' to see himself no more, if I don't get no dinner. Nope... ."

I gathered from Boldini that it would be quite impossible for me to get at the corporal, as I proposed to do, since he was away in the second-class quarters, and I should be prevented from leaving the fo'c'sle if I tried to do so.

"But I can let you have a roll," he said, "if it is worth a franc to you. I don't want to starve, you know," and his pleasant smile was a little reminiscent of the Wicked Uncle in my nursery-tale book of the Babes in the Wood.

It appeared that, anticipating just what had happened, he had secreted four rolls when breakfast was served at Fort St. Jean that morning. I gave him three francs, and a roll each to Hank and Buddy.

"You have a great soul, Boldini," I remarked, on purchasing the bread, and was distressed at the unkindly guffaw emitted by Buddy at my words. An hour or so later, all signs of activity having ceased to render the cook-house attractive, it seemed but too true that food was not for us. The mob of recruits grumbled, complained, and cursed in half a dozen languages. Darkness fell, and Hank arose.

A huge greasy creature, grossly fat, filthily dirty in clothes and person, and with a face that was his misfortune, emerged from the cooking-house. He eyed us with sourest contempt.

I suggested to Boldini that the scoundrel might sell us what he ought to have given us. Boldini replied that this was precisely what would happen, on the morrow, when we were *really* hungry--provided we had money and chose to pay his prices.

Hank strode forward.

"Thet Slushy?" he enquired softly.

"That's the swine," replied Boldini.

"Come and interpretate then," requested Hank, and marched up to the cook, closely followed by Buddy.

"When do we get our doo an' lawful eats, Slush!" he asked mildly.

The cook ignored him utterly and turned to go in lofty silence, but a huge hand shot out and sank with the grip of a vice into the fat of his bulging neck, another seized his wrist, and he was run as a perambulator is run by a child, straight to the side of the ship.

"Ask the pore gink if he can swim any," requested Hank, holding the man's head over the side.

Boldini did so.

The gink kicked out viciously, but made no other reply.

"Up with it, Bud--*attaboy!*" whooped Hank, and Buddy diving at the agitated legs, gathered them in, and raised them on to the taffrail.

The crowd of recruits cheered joyously.

I thought the man was really going overboard, and begged them not to waste a perfectly good cook.

"Sure," said Hank. "He's gotta get us some grub first," and they threw the cook on the deck un-gently.

The man lumbered to his feet, and, again seizing him, Hank ran him to the galley and threw him through the door.

"*Cookez-vous, pronto!*" quoth he, and the cook seized a heavy iron saucepan and rushed out again.

But alas, it was as a weapon and not as a utensil that he wished to use it. Swinging it up with all his strength--he found it wrenched from his hand and placed ringingly upon his head.

"He's contumelious," said Hank. "He's onobedient to my signs," and became earnest. Taking the man by the throat he started to choke him.

"Tell him I'm hungry, Bo," he said to Boldini. "Tell him he can eat outer my hand when I ain't riz by hunger.... . I gotta eat outer his pots first though."

Boldini assured the cook that Hank would tear him limb from limb, and the angry crowd of recruits would see that nobody rescued him either.

The fellow ceased to struggle, and Hank hurled him into the galley.

A sort of ship's quartermaster, followed by a sailor, came up, and I feared trouble. Visions of us all in irons, awaiting a court-martial at Oran, floated before my eyes.

"Assaulting the cook?" quoth the man in uniform. "Good! Kill the thrice-accursed thieving food-spoiler, and may *le bon Dieu* assist you."

I gathered that he was not very fond of Slushy.

"His assistance will not be required, *Monsieur le Contremaître*," said the smiling Boldini, and with horrible oaths and grimaces and the worst possible grace, the cook produced a number of loaves of bread, a pail of cold stew, and some macaroni.

"We'll have that hot," announced Boldini, pointing to the stew.

With very violent curses the cook said we would not--and the crowd snarled.

On understanding this reply, Hank instructed Boldini to inform the cook that unless he did precisely as he was told, there would be great sorrow for him when we had fed. If he were obedient he would be forgiven.

The stew was put over the galley-fire in a great pan.

"Can't he rustle a few onions and sech?" enquired Buddy, pushing into the galley.

Seeing that he was a very small man, the cook gave him a violent shove in the chest, and sent him staggering.

"I'll talk to you posthumorously, Cookie," said Buddy, with ominous calm. "We wants you whole and hearty like, for the present."

"Out, little dog! Out, you indescribable pollution," snarled the cook in French.

Under Boldini's instruction and Hank's compulsion, the cook produced a string of onions and added them to the *soupe*.

"Watch him well, or he'll poison us," advised Glock, the German, who, but yesterday, had called Hank a "dirdy tief" and now appeared to love him as a brother.

We watched, very well, and gave every encouragement we could think of.

Before long, we were squatting on the deck, each man with a well-filled *gamelle* of excellent stew and a loaf of bread, feeding heartily and calling blessings on Hank, the hero of the hour. Vogué tried to kiss him.

Again the fat cook emerged from the galley in search of relaxation and repose, and with a curse turned to go.

"He ought by rights to give us each a litre of wine," said Boldini. "He's got it and means to sell it."

"Say, Bo," shouted Hank thereupon. "Don' desert us! Did you say it was wine or cawfee you was keeping fer us?"

Boldini translated.

"'*Cré bon sang!*" roared the cook, raising his hands above his head, and then shaking his big dirty fist at Boldini. "To hell with you starving gutter-scrapings! You foul swine of the slums of Europe! You ..."

"Sounds good!" remarked Buddy.

"I guess he's saying '*No*,'" opined Hank. "I'll make signs to him agin," and he rose and strode towards the gesticulating ruffian.

The cook retreated into the galley, one hand to his throat.

"Look out for a knife," called Boldini.

But the cook was cowed, and reappeared with a wooden bucket containing three or four quarts of wine. This he handed to Hank with a wish that it might choke him first and corrode his interior after.

He then requested Boldini to inform us that we were a cowardly gang of apaches and wolves, who were brave enough in a band, and slinking curs individually. He would fight and destroy every one of us--except the big one--and glad of the chance.

Boldini did so.

"I'm the smallest," remarked Buddy, and left it at that, while he finished his bread and wine.

I am a law-abiding person by nature and by training (or I was at that time), and regretted all this unseemliness. But what a loathsome blackguard a man must be to swindle hungry bewildered men (whose pay was a halfpenny a day and who had joined the army to get it!), to rob them of their meagre allowance of food in order that he might sell it to them for their last coppers, when they could hold out no longer.

According to Boldini it was this scoundrel's regular custom to pretend to each draft of ignorant browbeaten foreigners that the Government made no provision for them, and that what they wanted they must buy from him. If they were absolutely penniless they got precisely nothing at all for forty-eight hours, and the cook sold their wine and rations to other steerage passengers or to the sailors.

When they understood this, Hank and Buddy discussed the advisability of "sure eradicating" the man--its desirability being self-evident. They decided they must leave this duty, with so many others, unperformed, as the *Messageries Maritimes* Company might behave officiously and prefer French law to lynch law.

"But I'll expostulate some with the all-fired skunk--when we finished with him as a cook," observed Buddy... .

We lay on the deck propped against the hatch far into the glorious night, Hank and Buddy rolling cigarettes with my tobacco, and leaves from my pocket-book, while I enjoyed my dear old briar, as we listened to Boldini's wonderful tales of the Legion... .

The moon rose and flooded the sea with silver light.... .

By this time to-morrow, I might be with Michael and Digby... . I began to nod, fell asleep, woke cold and stiff, and retired to a very unpleasant hole in the fo'c'sle, where there were tiers of bunks and many sorrows.

I slept for about ten hours and woke feeling as fit as a fiddle and ready for anything--particularly breakfast.

§ 6According to Boldini, this should be provided at eleven o'clock, and should consist of stew and bread. At ten-thirty, by his advice, we appointed Hank as spokesman and sergeant, with Boldini as interpreter, "fell in" in front of the galley, and awaited events like a squad on parade.

"Eats at eleven, hot and plentiful, Slushy," said Hank, as the cook came to the galley-door in obvious surprise at the orderly disciplined assembly.

The cook snarled and swore.

"Do he want me to make signs to him?" asked Hank of the interpreter.

Boldini informed the cook that the draft knew precisely what its rights were, and that it was going to have them. If there was delay or shortage, or if anybody suffered any ill-effects from the food, the big man was going to beat him to a jelly.

Then, lest the cook should complain, and there be trouble at Oran, the big man was coming with a few staunch friends to see that the cook disappeared overboard, during the night! Oh, yes, we were a desperate gang, old soldiers who wouldn't be swindled, and the big man was ex-Champion Heavy Weight of America. Also, if we were well and plentifully fed, we might refrain from reporting the cook's robberies and swindles in the proper quarter... .

The cook affected immense amusement, but I thought his laughter a trifle forced, as Hank's grim leathern face creased and broke into a dental smile that held no love.

"Squad'll parade right here at eleven, *pronto,* for the hand-out, Slushy," said Hank. "Be on time--and stay healthy... . Squad--dismiss."

"*Rompez!*" shouted Boldini, and then made all clear to the cook.

At eleven, Hank's sergeant-like crisp bawl, "Recruits--*fall in,*" could be heard all over the ship; Buddy appointed himself bugler and whistled an obvious dinner-call, and Boldini roared, "*Rangez-vous, légionnaires!*"

The way in which the order was obeyed, made it clear to me that I was about the only recruit who was not an old soldier. There was nothing to be surprised at in this, however, since most continental armies are conscript, and every man is a soldier. Certainly Hank and Buddy had been in the army. Later I learned that they had together adorned the ranks of that fine and famous corps, the Texas Rangers.

Without a word, the cook filled the *gamelles* with hot stew, and Hank passed one to each man, together with a loaf. He then gave the order to dismiss, and we sat us down and fed in contentment and good-humour.

At eventide the scene was repeated, and again we ate, and then we sat and smoked and listened to the Munchausenesque tales of Boldini, who had certainly "seen life" as he said.

He was boastful and he was proud of escapades that did him little credit. If he spoke the truth, he was a brave man and a very dishonest one. He plainly revealed himself as extremely cunning, tricky, avaricious, and grasping. And yet, with all his cleverness and greed, here he was, glad to accept a *sou* a day again, to keep himself from starving.

Buddy did not like him.

"A crook," opined he. "Crooked as a snake with the belly-ache... ."

Early on the third day we sighted the African coast.

After breakfast--*soupe* and bread again--Buddy requested Boldini to ask the cook to step outside.

"What for?" asked the cook contemptuously.

Buddy requested that the man should be informed that he was a coyote, a skunk, a low-lifer, a way down ornery bindle-stiff, a plate-licking dime-pinching hobo, a dodgasted greaser, a gol-durned sneak-thief, and a gosh-dinged slush-slinging poke-out-pinching piker."

Boldini merely said:

"The little man calls you a mean lying thief and a cowardly mangy cur... . He spits on you and he wants to fight you. He is a *very* little man, *chef*."

He was, and the cook rushed out to his doom. I fancy myself as an amateur boxer. Buddy was no amateur and the cook was no boxer. I thought of a fat sluggish snake and an angry mongoose, of which Uncle Hector had once told us.

It was not a fight so much as an execution. Buddy was a dynamic ferocity, and the thieving scoundrel was very badly damaged.

When he could, or would, rise no more, Hank dragged the carcase into the galley, reverently bared his head, and softly closed the door, as one leaving a death-chamber.

"He's restin'. Hush!" he murmured.

Hank and Buddy never held official rank in the muster-roll of the Legion, but they held high rank in the hearts of the *légionnaires* who knew them. That recruit-squad would certainly have followed them anywhere, and have obeyed them blindly.

Sandstone cliffs appeared, opened out to a tiny harbour, and we approached a pier.

We were at Oran, and the Corporal, who was supposed to be in charge of us made his first appearance on our fore-deck, formed us up, and handed the squad over to a Sergeant, who came on board for the purpose.

The Sergeant called the roll of our names, ascertained that we could "form fours," "form two deep," and turn left and right correctly, and then marched us ashore.

"I am in Africa!" said I to myself, as we tramped through the wide clean streets of the European-looking little town.

Down a street of flat-roofed houses we marched, and across the broad *place,* stared at by half-naked negroes, burnous-clad Arabs, French soldiers, ordinary European civilians, and promenading ladies and officers.

On through more wide streets to narrow slums and alleys we went, till at length the town was behind us and the desert in front.

For an hour or more we marched by a fine road across the desert, up the sandstone hills on to the cliff-top, until we came in sight of an old and ugly building, another obsolete Fort St. Jean, which Boldini said was Fort St. Thérèse and our present destination.

Into the courtyard of this barrack-hostelry we marched, and here the roll of our names was again called, this time by a *sous-officier*. All were present and correct, the goods were delivered, and we were directed to break off and follow our Sergeant to a barrack-room.

As I went in behind him, with Boldini and the German, Glock, behind me, a well-known voice remarked:

"Enter the Third Robber." *It was Digby's.*

Michael and Digby were sitting side by side on a bench, their hands in their pockets, their pipes in their mouths, and consternation upon their faces!

"Good God!" exclaimed Michael. "You unutterable young fool! God help us! ..."

I fell upon them. While I shook Michael's hand, Digby shook my other one, and while I shook Digby's hand, Michael shook my head. They then threw me upon the common "bed" (about twenty feet long and six broad) and shook my feet, finally pulling me on to the ground. I arose and closed with Digby, and Michael pushed us both over. We rose and both closed with Michael, until all three fell in a heap.

We then felt better, and realised that we were objects of interest and concern, alike to our acquaintances and to the strangers within our gates.

"Gee!" said Buddy. "Fightin' already! Beat 'em up, Bo."

"Dorg-fight," observed Hank. "Chew their ears, son."

"Mad English," shrugged Vogué, the French embezzler. "They fight when civilised people embrace."

Boldini was deeply interested.

"Third *robber!*" he said on a note of mingled comment and enquiry to Glock.

"Beau and Dig," said I, "let me introduce two shore-enough blowed-in-the-glass, dyed-in-the-wool, whole-piece White Men from God's Own Country--Hank and Buddy... . My brothers, Michael and Digby."

They laughed and held out their hands.

"Americans possibly," said Digby.

"Shake," said Hank and Buddy as one man, and the four shook gravely.

"Mr. Francesco Boldini," said I. "My brothers," and neither Michael nor Digby offered his hand to the Italian, until that gentleman reached for it effusively.

"I think wine is indicated, gentlemen," he said, and eyeing us in turn, added, "'*when we three robbers meet again,*' so to speak." Michael invited Hank and Buddy to join us, and Boldini led the way and did the honours of Fort St. Thérèse.

In this canteen the wine was as good as, and even cheaper than, the wine at Fort St. Jean--cheaper than ordinary draught-beer in England.

We three sat, drinking little, and watching the others drink a good deal, for which Michael insisted on paying.

We were soon joined by some old *légionnaires,* who appeared to be stationed permanently at the place, and, from them and Boldini, heard innumerable lurid stories of the Legion, for the truth of all of which they vouched, with earnest protestations and strange oaths. I noticed that the earnestness and strangeness of the latter were in inverse proportion to the probability of the former.

"I perceive we are not about to enter '*an academy for the sons of gentlemen where religious and moral training, character-forming and development of the intelligence, are placed before examination-cramming,*' my son," observed Digby to me, quoting from the syllabus of our preparatory school, as we left the canteen.

"No," said I, "but it sounds an uncommonly good school for mercenary soldiers" (and we found that it was certainly that).

"One hopes that this is not a fair sample of our future home-life and domestic surroundings," remarked Michael as we entered the barrack-room.

It was an utterly beastly place, dark, dirty, and depressing, its sole furniture being the great wooden guard-bed before mentioned (which was simply a huge shelf, innocent of mattress or covering, on which a score or so of men could lie side by side), a heap of evil-looking brown blankets in a corner, and a couple of benches. The place would have disgraced a prison if used as a common cell.

However, Boldini assured us that things would be quite different at the depôt at Saida or Sidi-bel-Abbès--and I assumed that to be different they must be better, for they couldn't be worse.

Our evening meal was the now familiar *soupe* and bread, and Boldini told us that the unvarying African daily ration was half a pound of meat and three *sous* worth of vegetables served as stew, a pound and a half of bread, half an ounce of coffee, and half an ounce of sugar. He said it was nourishing and sufficient but deadly monotonous, and, as to the latter, I was prepared to believe him. The prospect of two meals a day, and those eternally and undeviatingly similar, seemed unexhilarating and I said so.

"One gets used to it," said Boldini, "just as one gets used to 'eternally' washing with soap and water. If you are content to wash daily with soap and water you can be content to feed daily on *soupe* and bread... . Or do you occasionally wash with champagne and a slice of cake--or hot tea and a lump of coal--as a change from the 'eternal' water and soap? ..."

"Of course," he added impudently, "if you are going to come the fine gentleman and swell mobsman ..."

"Don't be an ass, Boldini," said I, with a cold stare. "Or at any rate, try not to be an ass."

He eyed me speculatively and complied. Master Boldini struck me as a gentleman who would need keeping in his place. Whatever that might be, it was not going to be one of the offensive familiarity that breeds contempt. I was not quite certain, but I was under the impression that "swell mobsman" was a thieves'-kitchen term for a well-dressed and "gentlemanly" swindler, burglar, and general criminal, in a superior way of business.

After *soupe,* there was nothing to do but to return to the canteen, as we were not allowed to leave the Fort. We spent the evening there, and I was glad to see that Beau and Digby seemed to like Hank and Buddy as much as I did, and that the two Americans, so far as one could judge of the feelings of such taciturn people, reciprocated.

Digby constituted himself host, and everybody was quite happy and well-behaved.

With one or two exceptions, none of the recruits, whether of my own draft, or of that with which my brothers had come, struck me as interesting.

They were just a fairly representative collection of very poor men from France, Belgium, Germany (chiefly Alsace and Lorraine), Spain, Austria, and Switzerland.

They looked like labourers, artisans, soldiers in mufti, newspaper-sellers, shop-boys, clerks, and the usual sort of men of all ages whom one would see in the poorer streets of any town, or in a Rowton House.

They certainly did not look like rogues and criminals.

Two or three, out of the couple of dozen or so, were well-dressed and well-spoken, and one of them, I felt sure, was an ex-officer of the French or Belgian army.

At any rate, he had "soldier" stamped all over him, was well-dressed, smart, dapper, and *soigné;* was well-educated and had charming manners. He called himself Jean St. André, but I suspected a third name, with a *de* in front of it. He had rather attached himself to us three, and we all liked him.

It struck me that community of habits, tastes, customs, and outlook form a stronger bond of sympathy than community of race; and that men of the same social caste and different nationality were much more attracted to each other than men of the same nationality and different caste... .

When the canteen closed, Beau proposed that we should shorten the night as much as possible, and spend the minimum of time in that loathsome cell, lying packed like sardines on the bare boards of the guard-bed shelf, with a score of men and a million insects.

Digby observed that the sandy ground of the courtyard would be no harder and much cleaner; and the air, if colder, infinitely preferable to the fug of the Black Hole of St. Thérèse.

We selected an eligible corner, seated ourselves in a row propped against the wall, still warm from the day's sunshine, and prepared for a night under the wonderful African stars.

"Well, my poor, dear, idiotic, mad pup--and what the devil do you think you're doing here?" began Michael, as soon as we were settled and our pipes alight.

"Fleeing from justice, Beau," said I. "What are you?"

"Same thing," replied Michael.

"And you, Dig?" I asked.

"Who, me?" answered Digby. "Well, to tell you the truth, I, personally, am, as it were, what you might call--er--fleeing from justice... .

"*Three* fleas," he observed, breaking a long silence.

"Did you bring the 'Blue Water' with you, John?" asked Digby.

"No," I said. "No, I didn't bring it with me."

"Careless," remarked Digby.

"Did you bring it, Beau?" I asked.

"Yes," answered Michael.

"Careful," commented Digby.

"Did you bring it with you too, Dig?" I enquired.

"Never travel without it," was the reply.

"I suppose one of us three has got it," I said wearily.

"Two of us," corrected Digby.

"Oh, yes, it's here all right," said Michael. "What would be the good of our being here if it were not?

"Bring us up to date about things," he added. "How's everybody bearing up?"

I told them the details of my evasion; of how I had declined an interview with Aunt Patricia; of how the shock of somebody's disgraceful behaviour had been too much for the Chaplain's health; of the respective attitudes of Augustus, Claudia, and Isobel.

"It *is* rough on Claudia," said Michael, "and, in a different way, on the poor old Chaplain."

"And in a different way, again, on Aunt Patricia," I observed.

"Thirty thousand pounds," mused Digby. "What price dear Uncle Hector, when she breaks it to him! He'll go mad and bite her."

"Doesn't bear thinking of," said I.

"Deuced lucky for young Gussie that Isobel was able to clear him," mused Digby.

"That's what makes it so hard on Claudia--or would have done, if we hadn't bolted," said Michael. "Gussie and Isobel being out of it--it was she or one of us... ."

In the silence that followed, I was aware of a sound, close beside us, where a buttress of the wall projected. Probably a rat or some nocturnal bird; possibly a dog.

"Well--it *was* one of us," said Michael, "and we have demonstrated the fact. We've overdone it a bit, though.

"Why couldn't you have enjoyed your ill-gotten gains in peace, at home, John?" he went on. "Or left me to enjoy mine abroad? Why this wholesale emigration?"

"Yes," agreed Digby, "absolute mob. They won't be able to decide whether we were all in the job together, or whether we're chasing each other to get a share of the loot."

"No," said Michael. "Problem'll worry them like anything."

"When are we to let them know we're in the Legion, Beau?" I asked.

"We're not there yet," was the reply.

"When we are," I pursued.

"Dunno... . Think about it," said Michael.

"Don't see why we should let 'em know we're all there together," said Digby. "Better if one was at, or up, the North Pole, the other up the South Pole, and the third sitting on the Equator. More mystery about it--and they wouldn't know which to chase first."

"Something in that," agreed Michael. "If we are all together (since you two have come), we are obviously all implicated--all three thieves. If we are scattered, two of us must be innocent. There is a doubt on each of us, but not a stain on any particular one of us.... Why write at all, in fact? We are just runaway criminals. They don't write home... ."

"*My* strength is as the strength of ten, because my heart is puah," bleated Digby.

"*My* strength will be as the strength of eleven if you don't shut up," warned Michael.

"I don't see the point really, Beau," I objected. "We prove nothing at all by being scattered. We might still all be criminals. We could easily have planned to pinch the sapphire, to bolt in different directions, and to share the loot by meeting later on... . Or we could share without meeting. One of us could dispose of it in Amsterdam or somewhere, bank the money, and send a third of it to each of the others by draft or cheque, or something... ."

"Hark at the young criminal!" said Digby... . "Hasn't he got a mind?" ...

"What I mean is," I explained, "it's a bit rough on--er--those that are left at home, not to let them know where we are--alive or dead and all that... ."

"Thinking of Gussie?" asked Digby.

"Besides," I went on, "how are they to let us know if the damned thing turns up? ... And how are we to know how they are getting on? ..."

"True," agreed Michael. "We ought to let Aunt Patricia know that we are hale and hearty, and she ought to be in a position to let us know if anything happens or turns up. What we *don't* want to do meanwhile, is to spoil the impression that one of us is the thief.... I still think it would help to keep suspicion on us, and to deepen the mystery, if we don't let it be known that we are all together... . We don't want some fool saying that we three agreed to take the blame and share it, and so cleared out together to the same place ... while the thief is still at Brandon Abbas... ."

"Who *did* pinch the filthy thing?" said Digby, voicing once more the question that I had asked myself a thousand times.

"I did," said Michael.

"Then why the devil don't you put it back?" asked Digby.

"Too late now," answered Michael. "Besides, I want to lie low and then sell it for thirty thousand pounds, five years hence; invest the money in various sound things, and have the income (of fifteen hundred to two thousand a year) for life.... Live like Uncle Hector--sport, hunting, travel, big-game shooting, flat in town, clubs...."

"On Uncle Hector's money?" I said.

"Doubles the joy of it, what?" replied Michael.

"Funny thing that," put in Digby. "It's just what I'm going to do--except that I find one can't get more than about twenty thousand, and I'm going to put it into a South Sea Island plantation and an Island trading concern.... Have the best schooner in the Islands, and be my own supercargo.... Every third year, come home and live the gay life on my twenty-per-cent profits. I reckon to make about four thousand a year. Yes.... Marquesas, Apia, Honolulu, Tahiti, Papeete, Kanakas, copra, ukaleles, lava-lavas, surf-riding, Robert Louis Stevenson...."

"What are you going to do with the 'Blue Water' meanwhile?" I asked, humouring the humorists.

"Always carry it about with me," said Digby. "If I get an eye knocked out I shall wear it in the empty socket.... Blue-eyed boy.... Good idea, that...."

"Or you might put it where the monkey put the nuts--develop a pouch in your cheek. Very simple for you, I should think," I suggested.

"Both rotten ideas," objected Michael. "Marsupial is the tip. Kangaroo's custom. They carry about their young and their money and things in a sort of bag, you know... in front ... accessible. I keep it on me, night and day--wash-leather pouch in a money-belt. I thought it all out beforehand, and bought the thing in London.... Got to kill the man before you can rob him. Hatton Garden diamond-merchants wear them when they travel. Round their little tummies under their little vests...."

"What makes them all look so paunchy," corroborated Digby.

"You haven't told us what *you* are going to do, John," he went on. "Are you going to lie low for the five years and then sell it? ... What are you going to do with the money?"

"Divide it with you and Beau," I replied.

"Oh, stout fella," approved Digby. "He puts us to shame, Beau, doesn't he? Let's put him to death in return, and keep his share."

"Quite," agreed Michael. "We've got to find out what he's done with it first, though...."

And so we ragged and chatted, sitting there, three of the most incredibly foolish young fools in their folly, but perfectly care-free and leaving to the morrow what the morrow might bring forth....

Towards morning we dozed, and the dawn found us cold, stiff, and aching, but quite happy. We were together; life, the world, and adventure were before us.

§ 7 A third draft of recruits arrived after morning *soupe,* and we learnt that all were to be evacuated that day, one half going to Saida, the depôt of the Second Regiment of the Foreign Legion, and the remainder to Sidi-bel-Abbès, the depôt of the First Regiment.

The question that at once agitated our breasts was as to whether we could keep together.

We rather preferred the idea of the First Regiment to that of the Second, simply because it was the First; but we did not much care either way, provided we were not separated. To that we simply would not agree.

I was distinctly pleased to find that the two Americans wished to come with us.

They had no more intention of parting from each other than we three had, but provided that they could keep together they wanted to go where we went.

To us came Boldini as we strolled round the courtyard.

"Let's stick together, we four," quoth he. "I'm going to the First, and you'd better come too. I know all the ropes there, and can put you up to everything. Get you in right with the corporals.... Sergeant Lejaune's a friend of mine...."

"We three are certainly going together," said Michael, "and we want the two Americans to come with us, and we prefer the First, on the whole. Have we any say in the matter?"

"Ten francs would have a say," replied Boldini. "They'd talk louder than six men. Put up the ten francs, and I can work it that we six go to the First.... But why bother about the Americans? They are uncultivated people."

"We're going to cultivate them," punned Michael.

We produced the ten francs and Boldini departed to "arrange" the matter, as he said.

Whether we owed anything to his efforts or not, I never knew. He may have "squared" a corporal, or he may merely have notified our wish to go together to the *Premier Étranger*. Or, again, it may merely have been by chance that we found ourselves in the half detailed for Sidi-bel-Abbès.

As we "fell in" to march to the station, I and St. André stood behind Michael and Digby, while Boldini and an English-speaking Swiss, named Maris, stood behind Hank and Buddy, who were next to Michael and Digby. Thus, when we "formed fours," my brothers and I and St. André made one "four," and Hank, Buddy, Boldini, and Maris the "four" behind us.

This Maris seemed an excellent person. He had been a travelling valet and courier, and had all the experience, address, linguistic knowledge, and general ability to be expected of a person who could earn his living in that capacity. He attached himself to us because he liked the English, and was, as he naïvely observed, "fond of gentlemen." He was a smiling, pleasant fellow of agreeable manners and attractive appearance.

At Oran station we entrained in about the poorest and slowest conveyance ever drawn by steam. This specimen of the West Algerian Railway Company's rolling-stock made its way from Oran to Sidi-bel-Abbès at an average rate of ten miles an hour, and in spite of the novelty of the scenery and of the population of the wayside stations, we grew very weary of it.

Our two "fours" and a couple of Germans filled one compartment, and we whiled away the time by questioning Boldini concerning life in the Legion, and by listening to his innumerable stories.

It seemed somewhat dream-like to me, to be sitting in a tiny bare third-class railway-carriage, somnolently rolling across Africa in company with my brothers, two Americans, an ex-officer of a continental army, an Anglo-Indian Italian, a Swiss courier, and a pair of German workmen, listening to tales of a life as far removed from that of Europe as are the Arabian Nights.

Watching the slowly-passing scenery of the country-side, I was surprised at its difference from what one might have expected in Africa, it being neither of desert nor jungle, but a cultivated country of fields, farms, orchards, and gardens. It was not until we were approaching our destination that sand-hills and desert encroached and a note of wildness and savagery prevailed.

Negro and Arab boys and men brought fruit to our window at every station, and very fine grapes, oranges, melons, and figs could be bought extremely cheaply.

"This is all right," remarked Digby, who was always very fond of fruit, "if one can get fruit at this price in Sidi-bel-Abbès."

"Yes," said Boldini drily, "if you devote your entire income entirely to fruit, you'll be able to get a little every day of your life."

A halfpenny a day for fruit does not sound much, but the devotion of one's total income to it seems excessive.

"No income tax?" asked Digby, and we were relieved, if surprised, to hear that there was none.

We reached Sidi-bel-Abbès Station in the evening, and were received by a sergeant and corporals, were lined up and marched off, in fours, along a broad road. At the station gate I noticed a picket of non-commissioned officers, who sharply scrutinised all who passed it.

As we marched along, I got a somewhat Spanish impression of the town, probably because I heard the tinkling of a guitar and saw some women with high combs and mantillas, among the nondescript Europeans who were strolling between the yellow houses. Entering the town itself, through a great gate in the huge ramparts, we were in a curiously hybrid Oriental-European atmosphere in which moved stately Arabs, smart French ladies, omnibuses, camels, half-naked negroes, dapper officers, crowds of poor Jewish-looking working-folk, soldiers by the hundred, negroes, grisettes, black newspaper boys selling the *Écho d'Oran,* pig-tailed European girls, Spaniards, Frenchmen, Algerian Jews, Levantines, men and women straight from the Bible, and others straight from the Boulevards, Arab policemen, Spahis, Turcos, Zouaves, and Chasseurs d'Afrique.

No less hybrid was the architecture, and the eye passed from white gleaming mosque with glorious minaret to gaudy café with garish lights; from showy shops to shuttered Oriental houses; from carved balconies and coloured tiles to municipal clock-towers and enamel advertisements; from Moorish domes and arches to French newspaper kiosks and lamp-posts; from Eastern bazaars to Western hotels and clubs and Government offices and secretariats.

And almost everywhere were beautiful avenues of palms and groves of olives, ably seconding the efforts of Moorish mosque and Arab architecture in the unequal struggle between artistic Oriental romance and vulgar Occidental utilitarianism. Hybridism insisted through other senses too, for the ear saught now the "*Allah Akbar! Lah illah il Allah! Ya Saidna Mohammed rais ul Allah!*"of the muezzin on the minaret; the shouting of an angry Spanish woman; the warning cries in *sabir* of a negro driver; snatches of French conversation from passing soldiers; the loud wrangling in Arabic of a police *goumier* and some camelmen; and a strange haunting chorus from behind a wall, of:

"***Travaja la muqueir***
Travaja bono
Bono bezef la muqueir
Travaja bono."

And to the nostrils were wafted scents of Eastern food and Western drink, camel-dung fires and Parisian patchouli; Eastern spices and Western cooking; now the odour of unwashen Eastern men, now of perfumed Western women.

"Kind of 'Algeria at Olympia,' this," observed Digby. "Good spot. Reminds one of Widdicombe."

Turning from a main thoroughfare we entered a lane that ran between the barracks of the Spahi cavalry and those of the Foreign Legion.

Through the railings of great iron gates we could see a colossal three-story yellow building, at the far side of a vast expanse of parade ground.

"Our College," remarked Digby.

On either side of the gates were guard-house and prison. A small door was opened beside the gates, and we filed through. The guard, seated on a long bench outside the guard-house, observed us without enthusiasm. The Sergeant of the Guard emerged and looked us over, and then closed his eyes, while he slowly shook his head.

A knot of men, clad in white uniform with wide blue sashes round their waists, gathered and regarded us.

"*Mon Dieu!*" said one, "there's that blackguard Boldini back again. As big a fool as he is a knave, evidently!"

Boldini affected deafness.

And then appeared upon the scene the only man I have ever met who seemed to me to be bad, wholly bad, evil all through, without a single redeeming virtue save courage.

He came from the regimental offices, a fierce-looking, thick-set, dark man, with the face and figure of a prize-fighter; glaring and staring of eye, swarthily handsome, with the neck and jowl of a bull-dog. He also had the curious teeth-baring, chin-protruding jaw-thrust of a bull-dog, and there were two deep lines between the heavy beetling brows.

A digression: This was Colour-Sergeant Lejaune, a terrible and terrifying man, who had made his way in the Legion (and who made it further still) by distinguishing himself among distinguished martinets as a relentlessly harsh and meticulous disciplinarian, a savagely violent taskmaster, and a punishing non-com. of tremendous energy, ability, and courage.

To his admiring superiors he was invaluable; to his despairing subordinates he was unspeakable. He was a reincarnation and lineal descendant of the overseers who lashed the dying galley-slaves of the Roman triremes, and as different from the officers as were the overseers from the Roman centurions.

He would have made a splendid wild-beast tamer, for he had all the courage, strength, forceful personality, hardy overbearing consciousness of superiority, and contemptuous, callous brutality required in that bold, ignoble profession. And it pleased him to regard himself as one, and to treat his legionaries as wild beasts; as dangerous, evil, savage, criminal brutes, instead of as what they were--fairly representative specimens of the average population of the countries from which they came.

Nor should it be supposed that Colour-Sergeant Lejaune was himself a typical representative specimen of his class, the Legion non-com. Though these men are usually harsh and somewhat tyrannical martinets, they are not villainous brutes.

Lejaune was. He took an actual delight in punishing, and nothing angered him more than to be unable to find a reason for doing it.

Probably he began by punishing (to the fullest extent of his powers and opportunity), in order to secure the most perfect discipline and to display his zeal, efficiency, and worth as a strong non-com.; and, from that, came to punish as a habit, until the habit became a taste, and then a lust and an obsession.

And later, through the coming to the Legion of a deserter from the Belgian army, we learnt a sinister, significant, and explanatory fact.

Lejaune had been dismissed from the Belgian Congo service for brutalities and atrocities exceeding even the limit fixed by good King Leopold's merry men.

There had been an exposure engineered by foreign missionaries, a world-wide scandal, and some white-washing--in the course of which Lejaune had been washed out.

From being a sergeant of the Belgian army, and a Congo rubber-station factor, autocratic, well-paid, and with absolute power, he had become a legionary, and by forcefulness, energy, and courage had made good.

Once more he had scope for the brutality, violence, and ferocious arrogance that had been his assets in the Belgian Congo, of terrible memory.

At times he was undoubtedly mad, and his madness took the form of sadistic savagery.

Upon this man, Boldini certainly had some claim, or between them there was some bond, for Lejaune never punished Boldini, and they were at times seen in private confabulation, though, of course, no non-commissioned officer ever walked out, nor drank, with a private soldier.

The Belgian deserter, one Vaerren, declared that Boldini had been a civilian subordinate in the Congo, and in Lejaune's district, and had been imprisoned for peculation and falsifying his trade returns. Of the truth of this I know nothing, but I do know that Lejaune favoured the man and procured his promotion to Corporal, when he himself became Sergeant-Major.

And it was into the hands of this Lejaune that we were now delivered.

To resume: Colour-Sergeant Lejaune called the roll of our names and looked us over.

Noting the insignificant stature of Buddy, a pocket Hercules, his face set in a contemptuous sneer.

"An undersized cur," he remarked to the Sergeant of the Guard.

"Guess I've seen better things than you dead on a sticky fly-paper, anyhow," replied Buddy promptly.

Mercifully Lejaune knew no English--but he knew that a wretched recruit had dared to open his miserable mouth.

"Silence, dog!" he roared. "Open your foul lips again, and I'll close them for a month with my boot.... Speak again, you hound, and I'll kick your teeth down your throat."

Buddy had not understood a word. He had seen a sneer, and heard contemptuous words; and he had dared to presume upon being an ignorant recruit, not even in uniform. Now he heard an angry roar, and was too old a soldier to do anything but stiffen to attention.

It was borne in upon him that there was *some* pep to Legion sergeants, and they were *some* roosters, on their own dung-hill. Better argue with a New York cop on Broadway at midnight, than to donate back-chat to the rough-neck.

But the mischief was done, and Buddy was a marked man. More, any friend of Buddy was a marked man, and any friend of his friend's, unto the third and fourth generation.

When the bloodshot eye of Colour-Sergeant Lejaune fell upon Boldini, it halted, and a long look passed between the two men. Neither spoke.

Upon us three Gestes he looked with disfavour.

"Runaway pimps," he said. "Show me your hands."

We held them out.

"Going to tell our fortunes.... Beware of a dark ugly man," whispered Digby to me.

The Colour-Sergeant regarded our decently kept hands and snorted:

"I'll harden those for you, by God... . Never done a stroke of work in your lives... . I'll manicure you before you die... . I'll make you wish you had gone to gaol instead."

He looked Hank over.

"A lazy hulk, I'll take my oath," he observed. "I'll teach you to move quickly, in a way that'll surprise you," he promised.

"Shore, Bo," replied Hank mildly, wishing to be polite, though ignorant of what had been said to him. "Spill another mouthful," he added encouragingly.

"Silence, you chattering ape from the trees!" roared Lejaune. "Speak again and I'll tie your wrists to your ankles in the small of your back for a week. By God, I'll cripple you for life, you two-legged talking camel."

And Hank also grasped that silence is frequently more than gold and speech much less than silver.

Having duly impressed the draft, Colour-Sergeant Lejaune announced that the Seventh Company would be afflicted with the lot of us, and serve it right. He then suddenly roared:

"*Garde à vous! Pour défiler! Par files de quatre, à droit,*" and looked eagerly and anxiously for a victim. His face clouded with chagrin and disappointment. The draft had moved like guardsmen. Those who understood French had sprung to attention and turned like machines, and those who did not understand the actual words had moved with them.

"*En avant... . Marche!*" he concluded, and we stepped off like the old soldiers most of us were.

Across the drill-ground we marched to the storeroom of the *fourrier-sergent* of the Seventh Company, and received our kit which, in addition to two cloth uniforms, included white fatigue uniforms, linen spats, underclothing, the blue woollen sash or cummerbund, cleaning materials, soap and towels, but no socks, for the Legion does not wear them.

We were then inspected by the *adjudant-major,* who corresponds to the English adjutant (whereas the *adjudant* is a non-commissioned officer), and marched by a corporal to our *casernes,* or barrack-rooms.

Going up staircases and along corridors, a squad of ten of us, including Boldini, St. André, Vogué, Maris, Glock, Buddy, Hank, my brothers, and myself, were directed to our room--a huge, clean, well-ventilated bare chamber, in which were thirty beds. Here we were handed over to some *légionnaires,* who were polishing their belts, cartridge-pouches, and accoutrements.

"*Bleus,*" said Corporal Dupré to these men. "Show them what to do, Schwartz, Colonna, Brandt, Haff, and Delarey... . Kit, bedding, *paquetage, astiquage,* everything. Don't go *en promenade* before they know their boots from their *képis.*"

"All right, Corporal," said one of the men, and when the Corporal had gone out, changed his tone as he went on:

"The devil damn all *bleus*. Why couldn't you go to hell, instead of coming here to waste our time? ... However, you shall repay us in the canteen. Come on, get to work now, and the sooner we can get to the bottles ..."

But Boldini had a word to say.

"Wriggle back into the cheese you crawled out of, you one-year, half-baked imitation of a soldier," he snapped. "I was a legionary and fought in Madagascar, Morocco, and the Soudan when you were in the foundling orphanage."

"Name of a name of a name of a name!" gabbled one of the men, "if it isn't old Boldini come back!" and he roared with laughter and threw himself on a bed.

"Wait till I'm a corporal, friend Brandt," said Boldini. "I'll make you laugh louder than that."

He did not have to wait, however, as the man redoubled his yells of laughter.

The return of Boldini, for some reason, struck him as a most priceless joke.

"Here, you Colonna, Schwartz, and Haff, take those five and I'll attend to these," said Boldini; and proceeded to direct us to appropriate beds and put our kit on them.

He then gave us a clever exhibition of clothes-folding, and built up a secure and neat little *paquetage* of uniform and kit on the shelf above his bed.

"There you are--do that first," said he. "Everything in elbow-to-finger-tip lengths, piled so," and we set about folding coats, trousers, overcoats, and kit, as he had done, and putting the pile on the shelf at the head of the bed as there was no kit-bag or box of any sort.

Having done this, we had our first lesson in *astiquage,* the polishing of belts, and cartridge-pouches, with wax and rags; and then in rifle-cleaning.

We were next conducted downstairs and out to the concrete open-air *lavabo,* and shown where to wash our white canvas fatigue-uniforms. We were then hurried to the canteen, that we might do our duty to our comrades of the *escouade* and pay our footing.

The scene here resembled that in the canteens of Forts St. Jean and St. Thérèse, save that the men were all *légionnaires,* of course, and the person behind the bar was a woman--a veritable French *vivandière* and *fille du regiment.*

Here again, a few francs procured an incredible quantity of wine and all was harmony, noise, and hectic gaiety of the kind induced by alcohol. Returning to our barrack-room at the call of the "Lights out" bugle, we completed our preparations for the morrow by the meagre light of the *caserne* night-lamp.

We gathered that we should be aroused by the *garde-chambre* at five-fifteen in the morning, and should have to be on recruit-parade at five-thirty in white uniform and sash, with knapsack, rifle, belts, and bayonet, and that everything must be immaculate and shining. Also that, before quitting the room, the blankets and mattresses of the bed must be folded and piled, and arranged to a hairbreadth accuracy, and the floor beneath the bed swept clean.

Apparently this cleanliness need not extend to the person, for there were no washing facilities of any sort in the room, nor on the whole of that floor of the barracks, nor on the one below. An eccentric, in search of a morning wash, had to make his way down four flights of stairs to a rude and crude kind of lavatory on the ground-floor.

As the *garde-chambre* saw no reason to arouse himself more than a quarter of an hour before he was himself due for parade, and then had to fetch the coffee-pail before arousing the others, this was apt to be a crowded quarter of an hour of inglorious life.

So, with the conscientious fears of the ignorant novice, at least one recruit endeavoured to have everything right and ready before he went to bed, and secretly determined to wake himself at half-past four next morning, to make a good beginning.

Michael's bed was in the corner by the huge window, Boldini's was next, Digby's next, and then that of an Italian calling himself Colonna. Mine came next, then Brandt's, then Buddy's, then Haff's, and then Hank's--always an old *légionnaire* next to a recruit, and so on throughout the room.

In the corner by the door, was the bed of Corporal Dupré, who was in command of the *escouade* and in charge of the room.

He was an active, noisy, bustling person, humorous and not unkindly when sober; when overfull of canteen wine he was sullen, suspicious, and dangerous. Being very fond of wine he was easily approachable by anyone who chose to provide it--or rather the means of purchasing it.

While we three and the Americans were gathered in a group, putting the last touches to our kit and extracting information and advice from Boldini, he came into the room, undressed and went to bed.

As he lay down he bawled:

"Silence! If any man makes a sound, between now and sunrise, he'll make the next sound in hospital," and fell asleep.

We got into our beds in a silence that could be felt.

I remained awake, because I was anxious to go to sleep; and lay thinking of Isobel, of what was happening at Brandon Abbas, of our strange position, and of the "Blue Water."

When I thought of what now lay before me, I was unutterably thankful that my guess, or instinct, had been right, and that I was with Michael and Digby.

It would have been rather terrible to find myself in this galley alone. With Beau and Digby here, it would be just adventure--hard, rough, and dangerous, no doubt--but no easy flowery path leads to any place worth arriving at.

And what of Michael and Digby? They each still pretended to be the culprit, which was doubly as absurd an idea as that either one of them should be.

Michael's look had been one of sheer horror and consternation when he had caught sight of me at Port St. Thérèse, and he had seemed to feel that my flight was a complication and a catastrophe on which he had never reckoned.

Had he felt the same about Digby, or had Digby known more than he told me? I must try to find out... .

I fell asleep and was awakened, apparently a minute later, by the *garde-chambre* shouting something as he lit a big central lamp that hung from the ceiling.

Men sat up in bed; each took a tin mug from a hook below the shelf above his head, and held it out to the *garde-chambre,* who went round with a great jug, giving everybody about half a pint of coffee. It was hot, strong, and good.

The Corporal shouted:

"*Levez-vous! Levez-vous!*" and then, as on the Eve of Waterloo, "there was hurrying to and fro--and sudden partings," if not "tremblings of distress and cheeks all pale... ."

Michael, Digby, and I rushed to the far-off lavatory, dashed our heads into water and fled back towelling.

I found my bed "made," my kit laid out neatly, my boots brushed, everything put ready as by a valet, and Brandt sweeping under my bed.

I stared in astonishment.

"A couple of *sous,* comrade!" said Brandt, and I understood. An income of a halfpenny a day is one that will stand a good deal of augmenting.

Turning to see if I could do anything for Michael or Digby, I found that Boldini and Colonna were before me, each earning in a few minutes, as a valet, what it took them two days to earn as a soldier.

In a surprisingly short time, all were dressed and ready, the *garde-chambre* had swept up the dust and dirt that the men had brushed out from under the beds, and Corporal Dupré had been round to see that the beds were properly made and everything tidy. Then, following upon a shout of "*Garde à vous,*" the Colour-Sergeant of the Company entered and inspected the room and the men.

All prayed that he might find no fault, for if he did, he would punish the Corporal, and the Corporal would punish the offenders tenfold.

In the French army, non-commissioned officers can, like prefects in our public schools, award punishments without reference to officers. They give the punishment, enter it in the *livre de punitions,* and there is an end of the matter--unless the officer, inspecting the book, increases the punishment by way of punishing the offender for getting punished.

The system enhances the power and position of the non-com. enormously, and undoubtedly makes for tremendous discipline--and some injustice and tyranny.

All was well this morning, however, and the great man's iron face remained impassive, and his hard mouth unopened.

We took our Lebel rifles from the rack, put our bayonets in their frogs, and clattered down to the parade-ground at five-thirty, on that glorious cold morning.

The battalion marched away to field-exercises, and the recruits were formed up, told off by *escouades,* each under a corporal, and taken out to the "plateau," a vast drill-ground near the *village nègre,* for physical training, which to-day was simply steady running. It was nothing much for young athletes like us three, but a little cruel for half-starved or out-of-condition men, who had not run for some time.

On other mornings the physical culture took the form of gymnastics, boxing, or a long route-march.

On our return to barracks, wet and warm, we had our morning meal of *soupe* and bread, and a quarter-litre of good wine. Tin plates and *gamelles* were rattled out of hanging-cupboards, and we sat at the long tables that occupied the centre of the big room. There was meat as well as vegetables in my excellent stew, and the bread, though grey, was palatable, and more than sufficient in quantity.

After a rest, the recruits had a lecture, and after that, squad and company drill, while the battalion did attack-formation exercise on the plateau.

After this we were set to work with brooms and wheel-barrows at tidying up around the barracks, and were then free to go to the *lavabo* to wash and dry our white uniforms.

At five o'clock we got our second meal, exactly like the first, and were then finished for the day, save in so far as we had to prepare for the next, in the way of cleaning and polishing the leather and metal of our arms and equipment--no small task, especially with stuff fresh from store.

Here the poverty of the Legion again helped us, for no man need do a stroke more than he wishes of this kind of work, while he has a halfpenny to spare.

We soon found that it was a real and genuine kindness to let a comrade have a go at our leather and brass, our rifles and bayonets, our dirty fatigue suits and underclothing; for, to him, a job meant the means of getting a packet of *caporal* cigarettes, a bottle of wine, a postage-stamp, a change of diet, a piece of much-needed soap, or a chance to replenish his cleaning materials.

We three did not shirk our work, by any means, but very often, when weary to death, or anxious to go out of barracks, we gave our *astiquage* work to one of the many who begged to be allowed to do it.

The recruits progressed with astonishing speed, being practically all trained soldiers before they joined, and picked up the necessary Legion-French remarkably rapidly.

We three very soon became good soldiers, aided by our intelligence, strength, sobriety, athletic training, sense of discipline, knowledge of French, and a genuine desire to make good.

More fortunate than most, we were well-educated and had "background"; a little money (thanks to Michael's forethought), which was wealth in the Legion; good habits, self-control, and a public-school training; and we were inoffensive by reason of possessing the consideration, courtesy, and self-respecting respect for others proper to gentlemen.

Less fortunate than most, we were accustomed to varied food, comfortable surroundings, leisure, a great deal of mental and physical recreation, spaciousness of life, and above all, *privacy*.

But at first, everything was new and strange, remarkable and romantic; we were Soldiers of Fortune, we were together, and we were by no means unhappy. But oh, how I longed to see Isobel!

And gradually, wondering thoughts as to the "Blue Water" and its whereabouts, retired to the back of my mind, for the world was too much with us altogether, for there to be time available for introspection or day-dreaming. Our days were too full and busy and our nights all too short for thought. They were scarce long enough for the deep dreamless sleep necessary to men who were worked as we were.

And how we blessed Sundays--those glorious life-saving days of complete rest.

On our first Sunday morning in the Legion, we three sat on Michael's bed and held a "Council of War," as we had so often done, in the days of the Band, at Brandon Abbas.

It was decided that I should write to Isobel, telling her where I was, and saying that I knew where Michael and Digby were, and could send them any messages or news.

Isobel was to use her discretion as to admitting that she knew where I was, but if she did admit it, she was to add--the simple truth--that she had not the slightest idea as to where the others were.

This plan was Michael's, and as he seemed keen on it, and neither Digby nor I saw anything against it, we adopted it, and I wrote a letter which she could show to Aunt Patricia, or not, as she liked.

I wrote as follows:--

"*Légionnaire John Smith, No. 18896,*

7th Company, Premier Étranger,

Sidi-bel-Abbès, Algeria.

Dear Isobel,

A letter to the above address will find me. Michael and Digby know it also. I can send them any messages, or news, from Brandon Abbas. Neither of them is in England. Either of them will let me know if he changes his present address. I am in excellent health. I shall write again if I hear from you. I am so anxious to know what is happening at home.

John."

Michael and Digby approved of this, as it opened up a line of communication with Brandon Abbas, but made no change in the situation.

From what we had learnt, after discreet enquiries of Boldini, we had quite come to the conclusion that the English police would take no steps in pursuit of the legionary, John Smith, so long as he remained in the Legion, even though there were strong reasons for suspecting him to be John Geste who had disappeared at the time of the jewel-robbery.

But I privately inserted a scrap of paper on which was a message of undying and unalterable love to my sweetheart. This she could destroy, and the letter she could produce for Aunt Patricia's information or not, as might seem best to her in whatever circumstances arose... .

On a Saturday night, a fortnight later, I got a private and personal love-letter that made me wildly happy and as proud as a peacock; and, with it, a long letter that I could send to Michael and Digby if I wished to do so.

This latter said that things were going on at Brandon Abbas exactly as before.

Aunt Patricia had, so far, communicated neither with the police nor with anybody else, and had taken no steps, whatsoever, in the matter.

Apparently she had accepted the fact that one of the three Gestes had stolen the "Blue Water"--and, extraordinarily and incredibly, she was just doing nothing at all about it, but simply awaiting Uncle Hector's return.

She had released Augustus, Claudia, and Isobel herself, from the prohibition as to leaving the house, and had asked no questions of any of them since the day that I had disappeared. On that day, she had accepted the solemn assurance of Augustus, Claudia, and Isobel, that they knew *absolutely nothing* as to where the Gestes had gone, which of them was the thief, or whether they were in league.

"I cannot understand her," she wrote, "nor get at what she thinks and feels. She fully accepts, apparently, my exculpation of Gussie (and incidentally of myself at the same time) and scorns to suspect Claudia. She has told us that we are absolutely free from suspicion, and she wishes us to make no further reference to the matter at all. Gussie is, of course, unbearable. He has '*known all along that you would come to a bad end--the three of you,*' but while certain that you are all in it together, he believes that you, John, are the actual thief. I told him that I had a belief too, and when he asked what it was, I said, '*I believe that if you gave your whole soul to it, Gussie, you might possibly, some day, be fit to clean John's boots--or those of any other Geste...* .' I also said that if he ever uttered another word on the subject I would discover, when the police came, that I had made a mistake in thinking that it was *his* arm I had held when the light failed! ... Am I not a beast? But he does make me so angry with his sneers and conscious rectitude, the mean little rascal.

However, as I have said, the police have not come yet, and absolutely nothing is being done. The servants haven't a ghost of an idea that anything is wrong, and life goes on just as if you three had merely gone up to Oxford for this term. Burdon must wonder that you all went so suddenly and with so little kit, but I don't suppose it interests him much.

I don't know *what* Uncle Hector will say about the delay in going to Scotland Yard! It almost looks as though Aunt wants the culprit to escape, or else feels that Uncle Hector would prefer that there should be no public scandal if it could possibly be avoided, and the sapphire recovered privately. Somehow I can't think that Aunt would have any mercy on the thief, though--and I really don't think she'd suppose Uncle Hector would prefer this delay to scandal. Surely he is not the person to care twopence about scandal, and he certainly is not the person to approve a delay that may make recovery impossible. I can't make it out *at all.*

Fancy Uncle Hector robbed of thirty thousand pounds! He'll go raving mad and kill people!

Oh, John, where *is* the wretched thing? And how long will it be before you can all come back? I shall wire to you at once if it turns up, and I shall certainly come and see you if you don't come soon--for it's my private opinion that you are all three together! ..."

I produced this letter for Michael and Digby to read, at our Sunday "Council of War" next morning.

Michael read it without a word of comment, and with an inscrutable face.

Digby said, "The little darling! I bet she comes out to Sidi if the thing doesn't turn up!" and he bounced on the bed, with glee, at the idea.

"Wonder what Uncle Hector will do?" said Michael. "Poor Aunt Patricia will get a thin time... ."

"For not preventing us from pinching it?" jeered Digby.

"No--for not calling in the police at once," said Michael.

"I wonder why she didn't," I remarked.

"Yes," said Michael. "Funny, isn't it?"

And yawning and turning round from the window, out of which we had been looking, I noticed that Boldini was asleep on his bed behind us. It was curious how quietly that man could move about, with his cat-like steps and silent ways.

§ 8Recruit-days passed swiftly away, and we were too busy and too tired to be wretched.

From five in the morning till five in the evening we were hard at it, and after that we had plenty to do in preparing our kit and accoutrements for the morrow.

That done, or given to a needy comrade to do, we dressed in our walking-out uniforms, according to the particular *ordre du jour,* and went for a walk in tawdry hybrid Sidi, or to hear the Legion's magnificent band in the Place Sadi Carnot, or the Jardin Publique. Usually we three went together, but sometimes the two Americans and St. André would accompany us, and Boldini whenever we could not shake him off.

He stuck to us closer than a brother sticketh, and after his first usefulness was over (and paid for), as we gained experience and learnt the ropes, we certainly did not desire his society for himself alone.

But apparently he desired ours, and ardently.

The more we saw of the two Americans, the better we liked them, and the same applied to St. André--but precisely the converse was true of Boldini.

However, we were not troubled by his presence when Buddy went out with us, for the American would have none of him, and scrupled not to say so with painful definiteness.

"Get to hell outa this, Cascara Sagrada," he would say truculently. "Don' wantcha. Go gnaw circles in the meadow and keep away from me with both feet... . Skoot, son," or some equally discouraging address.

Painful as this was, we were glad to profit by it, for Boldini waxed more and more offensively familiar. Put into words, the message of his manner to us three (his implications, and the general atmosphere he endeavoured to create) was:

"Come--we're all scoundrels together! Why this silly pretence of innocence and superiority? Let's be a united gang and share all loot" kind of idea.

I did not understand Buddy's virulent detestation of the man, though; and when I asked him about it one day, when he flatly refused to let Boldini join us in the canteen, all he could reply was:

"He's a rattlesnake with a silent rattle, and he's Lejaune's spy. You wanta watch out. He's on your trail fer somethin'," and Hank had confirmed this with a drawled, "Shore, Bo, watch the critter."

The first time that Boldini showed objection to Buddy's rudeness, the latter promptly invited him to come below and bring his fists--an invitation which Boldini declined (and was for ever the admitted inferior, in consequence).

Another person who most certainly watched us, and with a baleful boding eye, was Colour-Sergeant Lejaune himself, now, alas, Sergeant-Major.

We were, however, far too keen, careful, and capable to give him the opportunity he obviously desired.

When he came in for room-inspection, he made no pretence of not giving us and our kit, accoutrements, and bedding, a longer and more searching inspection than he gave to anybody else except Buddy.

When I met the long hard stare of his hot and cruel eyes, I thought of a panther or some other feral beast whose sole mental content was hate... .

"We're sure *for* it, pard," said Buddy to me, after one of these inspections. "Our name's mud. That section-boss makes me feel like when I butted into a grizzly-b'ar. On'y I liked the b'ar better."

"Yep," agreed Hank. "He's a grizzly-b'ar... . But I've shot a grizzly-b'ar, I hev."

"They ain't immortal," he added mildly.

It was also quite clear that Corporal Dupré had found that he had said the wrong thing when he replied to Lejaune's enquiry as to what sort of unspecified animals we were, by declaring that we were model recruits whose sole object appeared to be the meriting of his approval.

Corporal Dupré was not a bad fellow at heart, but "he had got to live," and it grew clearer and clearer, as the weeks went by, that we three could do nothing right and Boldini nothing wrong.

Our chief offence was that we would commit no offence, but we felt we walked on very thin ice... .

In less than a couple of months we were dismissed recruit-drills and became full-blown *légionnaires*.

Above the head of my bed appeared a printed paste-board card, bearing the legend, *John Smith, No. 18896, Soldat* 2ème *Classe,* and I was a (second-class) Soldier of Fortune, taking my place in the ranks of my battalion. In time I should be a *Soldat* 1ère *Classe*, if I were good.

Michael, Digby, the two Americans, Maris, and St. André came to the battalion at the same time, and our little party kept together.

We now learned what marching really is, and why the Legion is known in the Nineteenth Army Corps as the *cavalerie à pied*. The route-marches were of appalling length at an unvarying five kilometres an hour. Over English roads, in the English climate, and with the English soldier's kit, they would have been incredible. Over sand and desert stones, under the African sun, and with the much heavier kit of the legionary (which includes tent-canvas, firewood, a blanket, and a spare uniform), they were infinitely more so.

On one occasion we took a stroll of five hundred miles, marching continuously at thirty miles a day, as the Colonel thought we wanted "airing."

In addition to these marches, we had admirable training in skirmishing and scouting, plenty of company and battalion drill, first-aid, field engineering, varied rifle-range work, and the theory of infantry warfare.

By the time we three felt ourselves old soldiers, we also began to feel we were stagnating mentally, and becoming mechanical, bored, and stale. Night after night of strolling about Sidi-bel-Abbès was not good enough, and our brains were demanding exercise.

Michael decreed that we should study Arabic, both for the good of our souls and with a view to future usefulness at such time as we should be generals entrusted with diplomatic missions or military governorships.

Our Arabic proved useful before then.

We got books from the library, engaged a half-caste clerk, who worked in the *Bureau Arabe,* to meet us for an hour, four evenings a week, for conversation; and took to haunting Arab cafés instead of French ones.

We distinctly liked the dignified and courteous men with whom we talked over the wonderful coffee.

We made rapid progress and, after a time, made a point of talking Arabic to each other. It is an easy language to learn, especially in a country where it is spoken.

And still Boldini haunted us like our shadow, Corporal Dupré waited for a chance to report us, and Lejaune bided his time.

But we were wary and we were unexceptionable soldiers. Even these skilful fault-finders and fault-makers could not get an opportunity, and we were favourably noticed by our Lieutenant (Debussy) and Captain (Renouf), of whom we saw all too little. Theirs to lead us in manœuvres and war, the non-commissioned officers' to prepare us to be led. And in this the officers assisted them only by their authority. In every possible way, and some impossible ways, they upheld the power of the non-coms., backed them up on every occasion, took their word for everything, and supported them blindly.

There was no appeal. What the non-commissioned officer said, was true; and what he did, was right, as against the private soldier. The resulting discipline was wonderful-- and so was the bitterness, hatred, and despair of some of the victims of injustice and personal spite.

A sergeant had only to continue punishing a victim, for the latter to earn the unfavourable notice of the officer, when the latter read the punishment book, and to find his punishment doubled--with a warning to beware lest something really serious happened to him.

The Americans were not as lucky, or not as careful, as we three. For one thing, they sometimes drank the appalling maddening filth sold in the low-class wine-shops of the Spanish quarter or the Ghetto. Crude alcohol made from figs, rice, or wood, and known as *bapédi, tchum-tchum,* and *genièvre,* would make Buddy's temper explosive and uncertain, while it rendered Hank indiscriminatingly affectionate and apt to fall heavily upon the neck of the Sergeant of the Guard, when the latter admitted him, singing joyously, in the watches of the night.

Then was Lejaune happy, and reminded them of how they had opened their mouths in his presence, upon the evening of their entry into the Legion.

When they were confined to barracks, he would have the defaulters' roll called at odd times, in the hope of their missing it, and, when they were in the *salle de police,* would see that the Sergeant of the Guard turned them out hourly, under pretence of suspecting that they had tobacco or drink.

Sometimes he would go himself to their cells, in the middle of the night, rouse them with a sudden roar, and give a swift, harsh order, in the hope that it would be disobeyed through resentment or drunken stupidity.

I think he would have given a month's pay to have succeeded in goading one of them into striking him. It was my constant fear that Buddy would do so. And daily we dinned this into their ears, and prayed that something of the sort would not happen. However, they were old soldiers and wily Americans... .

And so the months passed, and every week I heard from my darling. Nothing happened at Brandon Abbas.

Gussie had gone to Sandhurst, the Chaplain was about again, and Uncle Hector had postponed his home-coming after all, and had gone to Kashmir to shoot bear, as he had had poor sport with tiger in the Central Provinces.

No reference was ever made to the missing "Blue Water," no questions had been asked of Isobel, and she had volunteered no information as to our whereabouts and her being in communication with me.

Also she would "come into" her money on her next birthday, and she was then going to do a little travelling, and intended to wander in Algeria!

"Hope she comes before we go--or that we don't go before she comes," said Digby, on learning this last piece of information--for we were full of hope that we should be among those selected for the big special draft that was going south before long.

Everyone knew that a battalion, a thousand strong, was going to "demonstrate" on the border shortly, and "demonstrating" meant further peaceful penetration with the bayonet, active service, and chances of distinction, decoration, and promotion.

If we did not go we should be bitterly disappointed, and lapse into mere bored and disillusioned victims of a monotonous soul-killing routine, daily doing the drill in which we were perfect; cursing the guard-mounting, sentry-go, and endless "fatigues"; learning the things we knew by heart; performing the exercises and operations we could do blindfold; and dragging ourselves through the killing route-marches that we hated.

But what a cruel thing if we were selected and sent off just as Isobel was coming!

On the other hand, if we were not taken (and we were still very junior soldiers), we should at any rate have Isobel's visit to Sidi-bel-Abbès to look forward to.

So great was my longing to see her that, had I been alone, I really think that I should, at times, have toyed with the idea of "going on pump," "making the promenade," which all *légionnaires* continually discuss and frequently attempt. This "going on pump," whatever that may mean, is the Legion name for deserting, and generally consists in slow preparation and swift capture, or a few days' thirst-agony in the desert, and ignominious return, or else in unspeakable torture and mutilation at the hands of the Arabs.

Less than one in a hundred succeed in escaping, for, in addition to the patrols, the desert, and the Arabs, the native armed-police *goumiers* receive a reward of twenty-five francs a head for the return of deserters, dead or alive.

Being matchless trackers, well-armed, good shots, and brave men, they are very successful bloodhounds.

However, the attempt is frequently made by maddened victims of injustice or of sheer monotony and hardship, and their punishment, when caught, varies from leniency to cruel severity, according to the degree of *cafard* from which they were suffering, and to the amount of uniform and kit they may have lost.

One man, whom I knew personally, when under sentence to appear before the supreme court-martial of Oran, which in his case meant certain death, got clean away, and was known to have escaped from the country.

Several, whom I knew, went off into the desert and were either found dead and mutilated, or never heard of more; and many either escaped and surrendered again, or were brought back running, or dragging on the ground, at the end of a cord tied to the saddle of an Arab police *goum*... .

However, we had come here to make careers for ourselves as Soldiers of Fortune, and to become Generals in the Army of France, as other foreigners had done, from the ranks of the Legion. And we did our utmost to achieve selection for the picked battalion that was to march south for the next forward leap of the apostles of pacific penetration (or pacification of the newly-penetrated areas) of the Sahara of the Soudan.

§ 9

One evening, at about this period of our depôt life, Maris, the Swiss ex-courier, came to me as I lay on my cot, resting and awaiting the return of Michael and Digby from *corvée*. Said he:

"I have something to tell you, Monsieur Smith. You have done me many a good turn, and you saved me from prison when my tunic was stolen and I could not have replaced it in time for the *adjudant's* inspection... . Will you and your brothers meet me at Mustapha's at six to-night? It will be worth your while. We shall be safe enough there, especially if we talk in English ..." and he glanced apprehensively round the busy room, and jerked his head towards Colonna and an Italian named Guantaio, who were working together at the table.

I thanked him and said that I would tell my brothers, and that if they returned in time, from the "fatigue" on which they were engaged, we would look in at Mustapha's.

When Michael and Digby came in from the job of sweeping and weeding, for which they had been seized by a sergeant, I told them what Maris had said.

"Better go," remarked Michael. "Maris is the clean potato, I think. No harm in hearing it anyhow."

Mustapha's was an Arab café, where we got splendid coffee very cheaply--thick, black, and sweet, with a drop of vanilla, a drop of hashish oil, or of opium, a drop of orange-essence, and other flavourings.

Here we rested ourselves on a big and very low divan, with a solid wall behind us, and awaited Maris, who came a few minutes later.

"It's like this, my friends," said he, in his excellent English, when we had got our little clay cups of coffee steaming on the floor in front of us. "I don't want to make what you call the mare's nest, isn't it? But Boldini is up to his tricks again... . I have heard a lot about him from Vaerren and from old *légionnaires* who served with him before... . He is the bad hat, that one. They say that Lejaune will get him made a corporal soon... . Well, I have noticed things, I.

"Yes. And last night I was sitting in the Tlemcen Gardens. It was getting dark. Behind the seat were bushes, and another path ran by the other side. Some *légionnaires* came along it, and sat down on a seat that must have been just behind mine. They were talking Italian. I know Italian well, and I always listen to foreign languages... . Yes, I shall be a courier again when the little trouble has blown over about the man I taught not to steal my fiancée, while I travel. Yes... ."

He paused dramatically, and with much eye-rolling and gesticulation continued:

"Boldini it was, and Colonna and Guantaio. He had been trying to get them to do something and they were afraid. Boldini, for some reason, also wanted Colonna to change beds with him, to make this something easier to do.

"'*Yes, and what if I am caught?*' said Colonna.

"'*You're as good a man as he is,*' said Boldini.

"'*And what about his brothers? Yes--and his friends the Americans?*' asked Colonna.

"'*And what about YOUR friends--me and Guantaio and Vogué and Gotto? WHAT ABOUT SERGEANT-MAJOR LEJAUNE, if someone makes a row, and Corporal Dupré reports the man to him and I give my humble evidence as an eye-witness--in private? Eh? ... "Brothers," you say! Aren't Lejaune and I like brothers?*'

"'*Why not do it yourself then?*' said Guantaio.

"'*Because I'm going to be made corporal soon,*' replied Boldini, 'and I mustn't be in any rows... . Ah, when I'm corporal, I shall be able to look after my friends, eh?*' Then he went on to remind them of what they could do with a thousand francs--more than fifty years of their pay, for a two-minute job.

"Then Guantaio, who seems to be a pluckier dog than Colonna, said:

"'*How do you know he has got it?*' and Boldini replied, '*Because I heard them say so. They are a gang. Swell thieves. They have asked me if thieves in the Legion are given up to the police. When the third one joined at Oran, I guessed it from what they said. And they were flash with their money. They got together at night, out in the courtyard, and I crept up behind a buttress close to them and listened. I could not hear everything, but they spoke of a jewel-robbery and thirty thousand pounds. The one they call "Le Beau" said he kept it like the* CANGURO ... *the kangaroo ... keeps its young! I heard him plainly.*

"'*And where does the* CANGURO *keep its young! In a pouch on its stomach, and that is where this thief, Légionnaire Guillaume Brown, keeps this jewel. In a pouch... . He wears it day and night.*

"'*And it's a thousand francs for the man that gets me the pouch. And I'll take the chance and risk of getting the jewel sold in the Ghetto for more than a thousand... . Some of those Ghetto Jews are millionaires... . I'd put the lamp out. One man could gag and hold him, while the other got it, and they could run to their beds in the dark.*' ...

"And much more of the same sort he talked, egging them on, and then they went away, but with nothing settled," continued Maris.

Digby and I burst into laughter at mention of the kangaroo, and Michael turned, smiling to Maris.

When the latter stopped, Digby asked if Boldini had not also divulged that he wore a sapphire eye, and I enquired if the wily Italian had not observed a lump in Digby's cheek, where a simian pouch concealed a big jewel.

"The fool overheard an elaborate joke," said Michael to Maris; "but we're very much obliged to you."

"Oh, he is the fool all right," said Maris; "but he is also the knave.

"Knave of diamonds!" he added, with a grin. "I just tell you because I like you English gentlemen, and it is just possible that they may try to steal your money-belt, if they think there is a chance of getting something valuable."

We filled the worthy Maris up with *cous-cous* and *galettes* (pancakes and honey), and strolled back to barracks.

When we were alone, I said to Michael:

"You *do* wear a money-belt, Beau. Let me have it at night for a bit--in case these gentle Italians have been persuaded, and something happens in the dark."

"Why?" asked Michael.

"Well," replied I, "you could favour them with your full personal attention, untroubled with grosser cares, if you had no property to protect. Also you could establish the fact that you don't wear a money-belt at night."

"I'd sooner establish despondency and alarm in the thief, thanks," said Michael.

"What a lark!" chuckled Digby, "I'm going to wear a brick under my sash and swear it's a ruby. Anyone that can pinch it while I slumber, can have it for keeps.... I must find this Boldini lad." ...

But, personally, I did not regard the matter as precisely a lark.

I had heard of Italian knives, and it seemed to me that a man might well be found dead in his bed, with a knife--or his own bayonet--through his heart, and nobody be any the wiser.... And even if justice could be done, which was doubtful, that would not bring the dead man back to life.

We had been long enough in the Legion to know its queer code of morals, and on the subject of theft the law was very peculiar, very strict, and very savage.

One might steal any article of uniform, and be no thief. It was a case of "robbery no stealing." To take another man's uniform or kit was merely " to decorate oneself," and decorating oneself was a blameless pastime, regarded universally as profitable, amusing, and honourable. Public opinion was not in the slightest degree against the time-honoured practice, and the act was concealed from none save the owner of the sequestrated property.

This was all very silly, for it was a most serious matter, involving very heavy punishment, for a man to be found to be short of so much as a strap when "showing-down" kit for inspection by the *adjudant*. Nevertheless, you might "decorate yourself" with a tunic, a sash, an overcoat, a pair of boots, a pair of trousers, or the whole of a man's "washing" from the line in the *lavabo,* and no one thought one penny the worse of you, save the unfortunate whom you had robbed.

The idea was, that if you were short of an article of equipment (after all, the property of *Madame la République,* and not of the individual), you must help yourself where you could, your victim must help himself where he could, his victim must do likewise, and so on. And whoever was caught out, in the end, as short of kit, was the fool and the loser in this childish game of "beggar my neighbour" (of his uniform).

Of his uniform, public property--but of nothing else.

Anything else was private property and sacred. To steal private property was not self-"decoration" at all, but theft; and theft, in that collection of the poorest of poor men, was the ultimate horrible crime, infinitely worse than murder. The legionary did not value his life much, but he valued his few tiny possessions beyond estimation.

With the abomination of theft, the Legion itself dealt, and dealt most drastically, for it could not be tolerated where everything private was so valuable, and so easily stolen if a thief should arise in the midst.

There was no thought of appeal to Authority in a case of theft; nor was there either enquiry or comment on the part of Authority when a case occurred and was punished by the men themselves, according to Legion law and custom.

And we were soon to see the law in operation and to behold an example of the custom...

Since Michael absolutely refused to let me wear his money-belt for him at night, I decided that I must think of some other plan--in view of this story told by Maris. I did not doubt its truth for one moment, as it merely confirmed, in particular, what I had thought and Buddy had voiced, in general--that Boldini's interest in our comings and goings, our conversation and habits, our antecedents and private affairs, had a sinister cause and object.

At first I thought of arranging with Digby that he and I should take turns to keep watch, but I discarded this plan as impossible. Nobody who worked as long and as hard as we did, could possibly lie awake in bed, and Michael would soon have "put an end to our nonsense" if we had sat up to guard him.

I then thought of going to Boldini and saying:

"Kangaroos have a horrible kick, my friend," or, "Better not let me see you putting the light out, Boldini," or even frankly and plainly promising to kill him, if anybody attempted to rob my brother.

After pondering the matter and consulting Digby, who did not take as serious a view of it as I did, I had the bright idea of getting the advice of an older, worldly-wiser, and far cleverer person than myself--and appealed to Buddy.

What he did not know about crooks and the best ways of defeating them was not worth knowing, and his experiences in the Texas Rangers had been those of detective, policeman, watch-dog, and soldier combined.

I accordingly walked out one evening with Hank and Buddy, "set the drinks up" at the Bar de Madagascar off the Rue de Daya, and told them that I had excellent reason to believe that Boldini was arranging with Colonna and Guantaio to rob my brother, one night.

"My brother can look after himself, of course," said I; "but these curs have got hold of the idea that he has a marvellous jewel which we three have stolen... . What I'm wondering is whether Guantaio, who looks like a *pucca* Sicilian bandit, would stick a knife into him, to make sure of getting his belt. That's the only thing that worries me."

"Fergit it, son," was Buddy's prompt reply. "Those slobs would never do that. Don't trust each other enough, for one thing. Far too risky, for another. That sort of poor thieving boob wouldn't dare. Why, one drop of blood on his hands or shirt, or one yell outa your brother, an' he'd be taken red-handed."

"Shore," agreed Hank. "Not in barracks they wouldn't. Git him up a side-street and bash him on the head, more like. Anybody mighta done it there. Lots o' guys git done in fer their sash an' bayonet in the *village nègre,* an' them low dives an' hash-joints in the Spanish quarter... . Don't let him go around alone, an' he's safe enough."

This was reassuring, and it was common sense. It would, of course, take a very cool, skilful, and courageous murderer to kill a man sleeping in a room with thirty others.

"I don't know so much," I said, arguing against myself and for the sake of complete reassurance. "Suppose Guantaio or Colonna simply crept to the bed and drove a bayonet through the blankets and through his heart. There'd be no bloodstains on the murderer ..."

"Not when he started monkeying with the belt?" put in Buddy. "And wouldn't there be no sound from your brother? Not a cheep outa him? Fergit it, I say."

"Look at here, Bo," argued Hank. "Figger it was you agoin' to stick me. How'd you know where my heart was, me curled up under the blankets, and nearly dark an' all? How'd you know as everybody was asleep all right? How'd you know there wouldn't be noise? ... Shucks! 'Tain't horse-sense... . Nope. These legendaries don't stand fer murder in the barrack-room, still less fer robbery, and least of all fer bein' woke up at night outa their due and lawful sleep." ...

"See, boy," interrupted Buddy at this point, "that barrack-room is just your brother's plumb safest place. As fer his kohinoor di'mond, I allow he can sure look after that himself."

"Shore thing," agreed Hank.

"Absolutely," said I. "If there's no fear of his being murdered in his sleep, there's an end of the matter. I'd rather like Boldini to go and try to rob him."

"I wouldn't go fer to say as much as that, Bo," demurred Buddy. "I'd undertake to clear your brother out every night of his life--every cent outa his belt--and the belt likewise also, too... . P'r'aps Mister Cascara Sagrada could do as much," and we smiled, both thinking of the occasion upon which Buddy had "minded" my money for me.

"Look at here, Bo," said Hank at this. "I gotta little idee. Surpose I goes to Cascara an' ses to him, '*Pari*' I ses, '*if that English legendary, Willyerm Brown, No. 18897, gits robbed, I'm sure agwine ter do you an onjustice. I'm agwine ter beat you up most ugly. So's yer own father, if you had one, wouldn't know yer, an' yer mother'd disown yer,*' or something discouragin' like that."

I thanked this large slow person, but declined, assuring him that we could take excellent care of ourselves, and I had only wanted to know if murder were a possible contingency.

"Not inside the barracks. Not till hell pops," said Buddy.

"Sure thing," agreed Hank. "But don't let him prowl around no boweries nor hootch-joints, on his lonesome. Nope."

"An' tell him from me that I'll mind his money-belt an' be responserble, if he likes," offered Buddy. "Then he can sleep free and easy like, an' also deal faithful with any guy as comes snooping around in the night, without having to waste time feeling if his gold-dust is there all right... ."

I again thanked him, changed the subject, and soon afterwards got them back to barracks, "a-settin' sober on the water-waggon, a credit to all men," as Hank observed. And, this very night, there happened that which must have given certain gentlemen of our barrack-room to think, and to think seriously, of abandoning any schemes for their quick enrichment, had they been entertaining them.

I was awakened by a crash and a shout... . Springing up, instantly awake, I saw two men struggling on the floor near Michael's bed. The one on top, pinning the other down with a hand on his throat, was Michael. As I leapt from my bed, I was aware that the room was alive and that men were running with angry shouts to see what, and who, had broken their sacred sleep--a horrible violation of strictest Legion law.

"Wring the sneakin' coyote's neck, Bo," shouted Buddy.

"'*Learn him to be a toad*,' Beau," quoted Digby, and with cries of "Thief! Thief!" the wave of shouting, gesticulating men swept over the two and bore one of them to the surface. It was neither Guantaio nor Colonna, neither Gotto nor Vogué--one of whom I had fully expected to see.

White-faced, struggling, imploring, in the grip of a dozen indignantly outraged and savagely ferocious *légionnaires,* was a man from the next room.

I looked round for Boldini.

He was sound asleep in his bed! And so was Corporal Dupré in his, and with his face to the wall--both of them men whom the squeak of a mouse would awaken.

"What are you doing here, *scélérat?*" shouted half a score of fierce voices as the man was pulled hither and thither, buffeted, shaken, and savagely struck.

"Speak up, you Brown! What about it?" roared Schwartz, who had got the man by the throat. "Was he stealing?"

"On the table with him," yelled Brandt.

"Yes, come on. Crucify the swine," bawled the huge bearded Schwartz, shaking his victim as a terrier shakes a rat.

Hank, followed by Buddy, barged into the middle of the scrum, throwing men right and left. "'Tain't one of Boldini's outfit," I heard Buddy say.

"Give the guy a fair trial," shouted Hank. "Lynchin' fer hoss-thieves an' sich--but give him a trial," and he seized the man himself. "Cough it up quick," he said to the terrified wretch, who seemed about to faint.

"Wait a minute," shouted Michael, in French. "He belongs to me... . He's had enough... ."

The crowd snarled. Several had bayonets in their hands.

"I lost my way," screamed the prisoner.

"And found it to the bed of a man who has money," laughed a voice. "Legion law! On the table with him!"

Michael jumped on the table.

"Silence, you fools!" he shouted. "Listen!" and the crowd listened. "I woke up and found the man feeling under my pillow. I thought he was somebody belonging to the room. Somebody I have been waiting for. Well--he isn't. Let him go--he won't come again... ."

At that there was a perfect yell of derision and execration, and Michael was sent flying by a rush of angry men. While he, Digby, and I were struggling to get to the table, the thief was flung on to it and held down; a bayonet was driven through each of his hands, another through each of his ears, and he lay moaning and begging for mercy. As I got to the table, sick with disgust, with some idea of rescuing the poor beast, I was seized from behind and flung away again.

"Lie there and think about it, you thieving cur," shouted Schwartz to the thief.

"Stop your snivelling--or I'll put another through your throat," growled Brandt.

Hank seized me as I knocked Haff down. "Let be, Johnny," he said, enveloping me in a bear's hug. "It's the salootary custom of the country. They discourages thievin' in these parts. But I wish it was Boldini they was lynchin'... ."

I tried to shake him off, as I saw Michael spring on Schwartz like a tiger.

There was a sudden cry of "*Guard!*" a swift rush in all directions, and the guard tramped in, to find a silent room--full of sleeping men--in the midst of which were we three pulling bayonets out of a white wooden table, and a whiter whimpering man.

"What's this?" said the Corporal of the Guard... .

"An accident," he answered himself, and, completely ignoring me, he turned to the stolid guard, gave the curt order:

"To the hospital," and the guard partly led, and partly carried, the wretched creature away.

What his name was, whether he was incited by Boldini, or whether he was merely trying to rob a man known to have money, I did not know. As Michael caught him feeling under the pillow, it seemed quite likely he was merely looking for a purse or coins. On the other hand, he may have tried the shelf and *paquetage,* and then under the pillow, in the hope of finding the alleged belt and jewel, before essaying the far more risky business of rifling the pouch and money-belt.

Talking the affair over the next day, none of us could remember having seen Guantaio or Colonna in the fray, so I concluded that, like Boldini, they had decided not to be awakened by the noise.

As all the old *légionnaires* prophesied would be the case, we heard nothing whatever from the authorities about the riot and the assault upon the thief. Clearly it was considered best to let the men enforce their own laws as they thought fit, provided those laws were reasonable and in the public interest.

When the injured man came out of hospital, we took an interest in his movements. He proved to be a Portuguese named Bolidar, a wharf-rat docker from Lisbon, and quite probably an amateur of petty crime. He stuck to his absurd tale that he had mistaken the room and was feeling his way into what he thought was his own bed.

We came to the conclusion that he was either staunch to his confederates, or else afraid to implicate them. We saw more of him later at Zinderneuf.

"Leave him to me," said Buddy. "I'll loosen his tongue--the miserable hoodlum. One night that dago swine is agwine to tell me an' Hank the secrets of his lovin' heart... ."

"He'll sure sob 'em out," opined Hank. But whether he was to do this under the influence of wine or of terror, I did not gather.

What we did gather, a week or two later, was that we were the most famous gang of international crooks and jewel-thieves in Europe, and had got away with a diamond worth over a million francs. With this we had sought safety in the Legion, that we might lie low until the affair was forgotten, and then sell the diamond whole, or have it cut up, as might seem best.

We were Germans pretending to be English, and we had stolen the diamond, in London, from Sir Smith, a great English general, to whom it had been presented by the Prince of Wales, who was in love with his sister. Buddy solemnly informed me that Bolidar knew all this "for certain." Bolidar had got it from a friend of ours. No--no names--but if Hank and Buddy could get the diamond--"rescue" it from the rascals--he, Bolidar, was in a position to promise them a thousand francs, *and* the protection of--someone who was in a position to protect them.

"So there you are, pard," concluded Buddy, with an amused grin. And there we were. But only for another month. At the end of that time we found ourselves in the selected draft under orders for the south, and our chance had come of winning that distinction, decoration, and promotion which was to be our first step on the Path of Glory--which was to lead not to the grave but to fame and fortune.

CHAPTER IV. THE DESERT

We left the depot of Sidi-bel-Abbès in the spirit in which boys leave school at the end of the half. The thought of escape from that deadly crushing monotony and weariness, to active service, change, and adventure, was inexpressibly delightful. The bitterness in my cup of joy was the knowledge that I was going before Isobel could visit Algeria, and that if we were sent to the far south, and were constantly on the move, I could only hear from her at long and irregular intervals.

I poured out my heart to her in a long letter, the night before we marched; told her I was absolutely certain I should see her again; and begged her not to waste her youth in thinking of me if a year passed without news, as I should be dead.

Having had my hour of self-pity, and having waxed magnificently sentimental, I became severely practical, made all preparations, tallowed my feet, and, laden like a beast of burden, fell in, for the last time, on the parade-ground of the Legion's barracks at Sidi-bel-Abbès.

With a hundred rounds of ammunition in our pouches, joy in our hearts, and a terrific load upon our backs, we swung out of the gates to the music of our magnificent band, playing the March of the Legion, never heard save when the Legion goes on active service.

Where we were going, we neither knew nor cared. That it would be a gruelling murderous march, we knew and did not care. We should march and fight as a battalion, or we should be broken up into companies and sections, and garrison desert-outposts where we should be in touch with our enemies--be they raiding Touaregs, rebellious Arab tribes, *jehad*-preaching Moors, or fanatical Senussi--and in a state of constant active-service.

Possibly we were going to take part in some comprehensive scheme of conquest, extending French dominion to Lake Tchad or Timbuktu. Possibly we were about to invade and conquer Morocco once and for all.

Our ideas were vague and our ignorance abysmal, but what we did know was, that we were on the road, we carried "sharp" ammunition, we were a self-contained, self-supporting unit of selected men, that the barracks and their killing routine were behind us, and the freedom and movement of active service were before us, with adventure, change, fighting, and the chance of decoration and promotion.

Merrily we sang as we tramped, passing gaily from "*Voilà du Boudin*" to "*La casquette de Père Bougeaud,*" "*Pan, pan, l'Arbi,*" "*Des marches d'Afrique,*" "*Père Brabançon,*" and "*Soldats de la Légion,*" and other old favourites of the march.

Michael, Digby, and I were in one "four" with Maris, and behind us were Hank, Buddy, St. André, and Schwartz. At night, we shared the little tent, which we could build in a minute and a quarter, with the canvas and jointed tent-poles that we carried. We slept on our overcoats with our knapsacks for pillows, our rifles chained together and the chain handcuffed to a man's wrist.

We were keen, we were picked men, and nobody went sick or fell out. Had he done so, he would have died an unpleasant death, in which thirst, Arabs, and hyenas would have been involved.

We cheerfully did our utmost like men, cheerfully grumbled like fiends, cheerfully dropped like logs at the end of a forty-kilometre march, and cheerfully arose like automata, at the sound of the 2 a.m. réveillé bugle.

We had insufficient water, insufficient rice and macaroni, no meat nor vegetables, and insufficient bread, and were perfectly fit and healthy. We had no helmets and no spine-pads, we wore heavy overcoats, we had only a linen flap hanging from our caps to protect our necks, and we had no cases of sunstroke nor heat apoplexy.

And, in time, we reached Ain-Sefra and rested to recoup and refit, the *fourrier-sergents* having a busy time, chiefly in the matter of boots.

Here we learnt that the whole of the Sahara was fermenting in one of its periodic states of unrest, simply asking for peaceful penetration, what with Touareg raids on protected villages, Senussi propaganda, tribal revolts, and sporadic outbursts of mutiny and murder.

There was also much talk of a serious concentration in the south-east, engineered from Kufra, and a "sympathetic strike" on the part of the numerous and warlike tribes along the Moroccan border.

When this materialised, it would be found that they had struck simultaneously at every French outpost, fort, and settlement, on the Saharan border from Morocco to Tripoli.

The programme, then, was to carry fire and sword northward to the sea, and sweep the surviving *Roumis* into it, freeing the land for ever from the polluting presence of these unbelieving dogs.

Let Morocco, Tunisia, Tripoli, and Egypt join hands, and under the green banner of a purified faith and the spiritual leadership of Our Lord the Mahdi el Senussi, carry on the good work in the name of Allah the All-Merciful, the Compassionate, and Mahomet his Prophet, until Islam was again free, triumphant, and conqueror of all... .

This we gathered by talking to Arab *goumiers,* marabouts, camel-drivers, and villagers, in their own tongue; as well as from orderlies and officers' servants who overheard the conversation of their masters at mess... .

From Ain-Sefra we marched to Douargala, where a large force of all arms was concentrating, and from this place we proceeded south, either to trail the French coat in the sight of the Arab, or as a reconnaissance in force and a protective screen behind which the brigade could make its preparations at leisure and in security.

And, in the fullness of time, after endless desert marching, the battalion found itself strung out along a chain of oases between which communication was maintained by camel-patrols, which met half-way and exchanged reports, orders, information, cigarettes, and bad language.

It was at El Rasa, the last of this chain of oases (which must have marked the course of one of those subterranean rivers which are common in Northern Africa) that our half-company came in contact with the Arabs and we had our first taste of desert warfare.

Arab *goumiers* came in at dawn one day, riding in haste, with the news that they had seen the camp-fires of a big Touareg *harka* about twenty miles to the south, where an ancient well marked the "cross-roads" of two caravan routes, as old as civilisation; routes charted by the bones of countless thousands of camels and of men who had trodden them until they died of thirst, starvation, heat, disease, or murder at the hands of Bedouin and Touareg nomads.

These are the oldest roads in the world and the grim relics that line them are those of yesterday and those of centuries ago. They were ancient when Joseph came to Egypt, and the men and beasts that venture upon them have not changed in fifty centuries.

§ 2

We were in touch with the enemy at last. At any moment we might be fighting for our lives. We were delirious with excitement.

At once our little force in the oasis and this Arab *harka* became a microcosm of the whole war, and our Lieutenant Debussy sent out a small reconnoitring force under Sergeant-Major Lejaune, which should be to the strung-out battalion what the battalion was to the brigade at Douargala.

It was the good luck of our *escouade* to be selected for this duty, and within half an hour of the arrival of the *goumiers*, we were advancing *en tirailleur* in the direction from which they had come. Over the loose, hot sand we plodded, our scouts far in advance and our flankers far out to left and right.

"Are we the bait of a trap? Or would you call us the point of a spear?" said Michael, marching between Digby and me.

"Both," replied Digby, "a bit of meat on the end of a spear, say."

And I wondered how many of us would be bits of meat before nightfall.

Not that I felt in the least degree apprehensive or depressed. If I had to analyse and describe my feelings, I should say that beneath a strong sensation of pleasurable excitement was that undercurrent of slight nervous anxiety which one experiences before going in to bat, or when seated in a corner of the ring, awaiting the word "*Time*" at the beginning of a boxing contest.

I would not have been elsewhere for worlds, but at the same time I wondered what the smack of a bullet felt like, and how much chance a bayonet stood against the heavy sword or the lance of a charging Arab... .

There was no doubt about it that Sergeant-Major Lejaune knew his job, and I found myself wishing that he were not such a wholly hateful person.

I should have liked to admire him as much as I admired his military skill, and ability as a commander, and I began to understand how soldiers love a good leader when it is possible to do so.

One felt that nobody could have handled the situation with more grasp and certainty than he did, and that if any kind of catastrophe or disaster ensued, it would be owing to no fault in the ability, courage, and promptitude of Sergeant-Major Lejaune.

To watch him conducting operations that day, was to watch a highly skilled artisan using his tools with the deftness and certainty of genius.

On a low, flat-topped rocky hill, we halted and rested, all except Lejaune himself and the scouts whom he sent to various distant sand-hills and low rocky eminences which, while visible from the detachment, gave a wide range of vision in the supposed direction of the enemy.

Among others set to similar tasks, I was ordered to watch one particular man and to report any movement on his part. I watched the tiny distant figure through the shimmering heat haze, which danced over the sand and stones, until my eyes ached and I was forced, from time to time, to close them and cover them with my hand.

Upon opening them after one of these brief rests, which were absolutely necessary, I saw that he was crawling back from his position. When below the skyline, he rose and ran, stooping for a short distance. He then halted and signalled "*Enemy in sight.*"

The moment that I had pointed him out to Corporal Boldini, Lejaune was notified, and he sent a man named Rastignac running to an eminence, well to our left rear, and a minute later we were lining the edge of our plateau on the side to which this man had disappeared.

Here we lay concealed, and waited.

A few minutes later, the man who had been sent off, fired a shot and exposed himself on the highest point of his rocky hillock.

To my surprise, I saw our scouts retiring and running--not back to us, but to him; and, a minute or two later, I saw a flutter of white on a distant sand-hill.

Rallying on the man who was firing from the top of the rock, the scouts opened fire at distant camel-mounted figures who began to appear over the sand-hills. We received no orders, save to the effect that we should lie as flat and still as the hot stones that concealed us.

Between two of these I watched the scattered fringe of Arabs increase to lines, and the lines to masses of swiftly-moving camel-riders, and soon their deep menacing cry of "*Ul-ul-ul-ul-ul-ullah Akbar,*" came to our ears like the growing roar of an advancing sea.

As they came on, the little party of our scouts fired rapidly, and after about the thousand-yard range, a camel would occasionally sprawl headlong to the ground, or a white-clad figure fall like a sack and lie motionless on the sand.

On swept the Arab *harka* at the top pace of their swift camels, the men in front firing from the saddle, the others brandishing their long, straight swords and waving their lances aloft.

Rapidly and steadily the little band of scouts fired into the brown of them, and, by now, every bullet was hitting man or beast in the closely-packed irregular ranks of the swiftly-advancing horde.

It was thrilling. I felt I must get a grip upon myself, or I should be shaking with excitement, and unable to shoot steadily when our turn came to take part in the fight.

And then, to my amazement, I saw that our scouts were retreating. One by one, they sprang up from behind rocks and fled to their right rear, each man dropping and firing as his neighbour rose to retreat in his turn. Before long, the little band was again in position, nearer to us and still further behind us. With increased yells, the Arabs swerved to their left and bore down upon them, men and camels falling beneath the magazine-fire of their rifles.

I could scarcely keep still. How long was this unequal fight to continue? None of the scouts had been hit by the wild fire of the camel-riders, but in a couple of minutes they would be overwhelmed by this wave of mounted men, and, outnumbered by fifty to one, would have as much chance as has a fox beneath a pack of hounds.

And as I held my breath, the tiny handful again rose to their feet, turned their backs upon the Arabs, and fled as one man toward a sand-hill in our rear. With a simultaneous yell of mingled execration and triumph, the Arab *harka* swerved again, seemed to redouble their speed, and bore down upon their prey.

And then, Sergeant-Major Lejaune stood up on a rock, gave a crisp order, coolly as on parade, and, at less than fifty yards, the Arab masses received the withering blast of our magazine-fire. Swiftly as our hands could move the bolts of our rifles and our fingers press the trigger, we fired and fired again into the surging, shrieking, struggling mob, that halted, charged, retired, and then fled, leaving quite half their number behind.

But of those who were left behind, by no means all were killed or even wounded, and our orgy of slaughter rapidly turned to a desperate hand-to-hand fight with dismounted and unwounded Arabs, who, knowing they must die, had but the one idea of gaining Paradise and the remission of sins, in the slaying of an infidel.

With a shout of "*Baïonnettes au canon,*" Lejaune had us to our feet, and launched us in a fierce bayonet-charge down the slope of our plateau upon the Arab swordsmen, who were rallying to the attack, on foot. Our disciplined rush swept them back, they broke and fled, and, still keeping us in hand, Lejaune quickly had a double rank of kneeling and standing men shooting down the fleeing or still defiant foot-men, and making practice at the remains of the mounted *harka* disappearing over the skyline.

Within half an hour of the first signalling of the approach of the enemy, the only Arabs in sight were those that lay singly and in little bloodstained heaps, in the shallow valley into which they had been decoyed by our scouts.

It was a neat little action, reflecting the highest credit on Lejaune and on the man who was the senior in charge of the scouts. The latter, one Gontran, was promoted corporal, in orders next day, and Sergeant-Major Lejaune made *adjudant*.

The Arabs must have lost over a hundred men in this fight, as against our three killed and five wounded.

Such was my first experience of war, my first "smelling of powder" and my blooding. I had killed a man with cold steel and I think at least three with my rifle.

Reflecting on this I was glad to remember that these Touaregs are human wolves, professional murderers, whose livelihood is robbery with violence, which commonly takes the form of indescribable and unmentionable tortures.

Nor is the *Roumi,* the infidel dog, the favourite object of their treacherous attack, save in so far as he is a more rewarding object of attention. They are as much the scourge and terror of the Arab villager, the nomad herdsman, or the defenceless negro, as they are of the wealthy caravan or their peaceful co-religionists of the town, the *douar,* and the oasis.

The man whom I had killed with my bayonet, had made it necessary to my continued existence, for he rushed at me with a great, heavy, straight-bladed sword, exactly like those used by our Crusaders of old.

Whirling this round his head, he aimed a blow at me that would have split my skull had I not promptly side-stepped, drawing back my bayonet as I did so. As the sword missed my head, I drove at his chest with all my strength, and the curved hilt of my Lebel bayonet touched his breast-bone as he fell staggering back, nearly pulling the rifle out of my hands.

I found afterwards that Digby had had his coat torn under the armpit by a spear, which, as he remarked, was not fair wear, but tear, on a good coat. He had shot his assailant at a range which he estimated as being a good half-inch, and he was troubled with doubts as to whether this would be considered quite sporting in the best Arab circles.

"Of course," he said, "the bird wasn't actually 'sitting'--though he's sitting now... ."

Michael, being particularly good with the bayonet, and a noted winner of bayonet *v.* bayonet competitions, had used the butt of his rifle in the mêlée, and seemed to think it unfair of the Arab to wear a turban, that diminishes the neat effectiveness of this form of fighting! However, neither of them was hurt, nor were any of our more immediate friends.

Having buried our dead and obliterated their graves, we retired slowly toward El Rasa, weary to death and thoroughly pleased with ourselves, to make our report... .

§ 3

The pitched battle of El Rasa was fought next day, our battalion holding the oasis against tremendous odds until supports came from the brigade, and the Arabs learnt what quick-firing little mule-guns can do, when given such a target as a huge mob of horse and camel-men advancing *en masse* over a level plain.

As my part in this battle was confined to lying behind the bole of a palm-tree and shooting whenever I had something to shoot at, I have no adventures to relate. I might as well have spent the day on a rifle-range.

But I saw a magnificent charge of a couple of squadrons of Spahis upon a vastly superior number of Arab cavalry, which, shaken by artillery fire, appeared to be hanging in doubt as to whether to make one of their fierce rushes, overwhelming and desperate, upon the infantry lining the edge of the oasis. It was a thrilling and unforgettable sight... .

After the signal victory of El Rasa, the brigade moved on southward and we preceded it, the weeks that followed being a nightmare of marching that ended in the worse nightmare of garrison duty in the ultimate, furthermost, desert outpost of Zinderneuf, where we had the initial misfortune of losing Digby and many of our friends, including Hank and Buddy.

They departed to the mounted-infantry school at Tanout-Azzal, where the gentle art of mule-handling was taught, and the speed of the swift-marching legionary increased by mounting him on a mule. A company of such men was thus rendered as mobile as a squadron.

It was a cruel blow to Michael and me, this separation from our brother and from those best of friends, Hank and Buddy.

However, we were certain to be reunited sooner or later, and there was nothing to do but to make the best of this and the other drawbacks and miseries of Zinderneuf.

CHAPTER V. THE FORT AT ZINDERNEUF

"They learn that they are not as others are,
Till some go mad, and some sink prone to earth,
And some push stumbling on without a star."

Things began badly and rapidly grew worse in this ill-omened mud fort, isolated in the illimitable desert like a tiny island in the midst of a vast ocean.

Cafard broke out early, and in a very virulent form, both suicidal and homicidal in its nature.

It took this terrible form, I verily believe, largely by reason of the fact that Captain Renouf, our Commandant, shot himself after a month of life in this dreadful oven of a place.

I do not, of course, know his reason for doing this, but it was rumoured that he found he had contracted a horrible disease. This tragedy cast a deeper gloom over a place and a community already gloomy beyond description.

Within a week of this disaster, for a disaster it was to all of us, a most unusual manifestation of *cafard* was exhibited, when a corporal killed a sergeant and then committed suicide. What Corporal Gontran's grievance against the sergeant was, I do not know, but this again was an exceedingly unfortunate affair, as, like Captain Renouf himself, both these men were on the side of the angels, inasmuch as they were decent, fair-minded, and reasonable people.

But the Fates and the Furies had one more disaster in store for the unhappy garrison before they were ready to launch upon our luckless heads the final torrent of destruction.

Lieutenant Debussy, the new Commandant, sickened and died, and his place was taken by none other than Adjudant Lejaune.

From the moment in which it was known that the Lieutenant was dead, the atmosphere of Zinderneuf changed from bad to worse and rapidly from worse to the worst possible.

The lion-tamer had entered the cage, and the lions, sullen, infuriated, and desperate, knew that he held in one hand the whip that should drive them to revolt, and in the other the revolver that should instantly punish the first sign of it.

§ 2

Life at Zinderneuf was not really life so much as the avoidance of death--death from sunstroke, heat-stroke, monotony, madness, or Adjudant Lejaune.

Cafard was rampant; everybody was more or less abnormal and "queer" from frayed nerves, resultant upon the terrific heat and the monotony, hardship, and confinement to a little mud oven of a fort; many men were a little mad, and Adjudant Lejaune, in the hollow of whose hand were our lives and destinies, was a great deal more than a little mad.

From the point of view of the authorities, he was sane enough, for he could maintain an iron discipline; make all reports and returns, to the minute and to the letter; and, if attacked, he could be trusted to keep the Tri-couleur flying while there was a man alive in the Fort.

From the point of view of his subordinates, he was nevertheless a madman, and a very dangerous one.

At times, I was almost glad that Digby was not with us, much as I missed him; and at those times I almost wished that Michael was not, much as I depended on him.

Danger to oneself is unpleasant enough, when it is that of being murdered by a lunatic. When to it is added the danger, and constant fear, of a similar fate overtaking people whom one loves, it becomes ten times worse.

Michael and I both begged each other not to be so foolish as to play into Lejaune's hands, by giving him the faintest chance to accuse us of any breach of duty or discipline, or of so much as an insubordinate look, even under the greatest provocation. But we felt that the time would come when Lejaune would cease to wait for an excuse, and that all we could do was to put off the evil day... .

"I'm positively glad, now, that Dig isn't here," said Michael to me, one terrible afternoon, as we lay gasping on our burning cots during siesta hours, in our stifling *caserne*.

"Hank and Buddy too," he added. "One word of back-chat to Lejaune would have been fatal.... And Dig might have done it. Buddy more so.... Or if Hank once lost control he'd lay Lejaune out like a pole-axed ox...."

"Somebody'll do for him one of these days, if we don't soon get a new commanding officer," said I. "And a good job too."

"Not it," contradicted Michael. "It would be one degree worse than letting him live.... These asses would give three loud cheers, march off into the desert, and survive about three days of it--if the Arabs didn't get them before they died of thirst."

"It'll happen," prophesied I. "Schwartz is getting very mysterious and important these days. Oh, it'll happen all right."

"That's what I think," said Michael, "and it's about the worst thing that *could* happen. And if no one goes and does it spontaneously, there'll be a plot to murder him--if there isn't one already, which I believe there is, as you say--and we should have the choice of fighting for Lejaune--(for *Lejaune!*)--or being two of a gang of silly, murdering mutineers with nothing but a choice of beastly deaths--thirst and Arabs in the desert, or court martial and a firing party at dawn.... Rotten."

"If he's promoted Lieutenant and kept in command here, he won't last a week," said I.... "What's going to happen if they make a plot to mutiny and we're the only two that refuse to join them?"

"We should join Lejaune instead, where dead men tell no tales, I expect," answered Michael.

"What would Sergeant Dupré and Corporal Boldini do?" I speculated.

"If it were a case of saving their skins they'd join the mutineers, I should say--if they were given the option," replied Michael. "They probably loathe Lejaune as much as we do, and neither of them is exactly the man to die for a principle.... If they woke to find a gang of bad men, with rifles, round their beds, they'd '*take the cash and let the discredit go*,'-- '*Nor heed the rumble of a distant drum*' from Tokotu," he added.

"I doubt if they'd be given the option," I said.

"So do I," agreed Michael. "They're not loved. They've been whips and scorpions in Lejaune's hands too long and too willingly."

"And if we were 'approached' on the subject of a mutiny and did our miserable duty in warning Lejaune and the others?" I asked.

"We should promptly get thirty days' cells from Lejaune for currying favour with horrible lies, and short shrift from the mutineers for being *escrocs*," said Michael....

"Let us give thanks unto the Lord and count our many blessings, my brethren," he yawned, and, at that moment, Schwartz, Haff, Brandt, Bolidar, Delarey, and Vogué entered the room and joined Guantaio, Colonna, and Gotto at the other end of it. Here they conversed in low voices, with occasional glances at us.

§3

And to me, one night, came Schwartz, as I sat in a corner of the little courtyard, trying to imagine that the night was cooler than the day, and this spot, which faced north, less hot than the others.

He was a huge, powerful, hairy ruffian, who would have made a great pirate-captain, for he had brains, courage, and determination, quite unhampered by over-fine scruples of honour or mercy. He was further endowed with a magnetic personality and power of command.

"Are you enjoying life, Smith?" he asked, seating himself beside me.

"Quite as much as you are, Schwartz," I replied.

"Would you like a change?" he enquired.

"I am fond of change," said I.

A brief silence ensued.

"Have you ever seen a pig die?" he asked suddenly.

"No," I replied.

"Well, you soon will," he assured me.

"Feeling ill?" I enquired rudely. I did not like the gross Schwartz.

"You are going to see a big pig die," he went on, ignoring my vulgarity. "A sacred pig. An anointed pig. A striped pig. A promoted pig. Oh, an *adjudant* pig."

"So?" I murmured.

"Yes. *Monsieur le Cochon* is going to become *Monsieur Porc.*"

"And are you going to become *Monsieur Charcutier*, 'Mr. Pork-butcher,' so to speak?" I enquired. There could be no harm in knowing all there was to know about this business.

"Aha! my friend," growled the German, "that remains to be seen. So many want a *côtelette de porc* or a *savouret de porc*. We shall have to cast lots."

He was silent for a minute and sat beside me, gnawing his knuckles. He was shaking from head to foot with fever, excitement, or diseased nerves.

"Do you want a chance to be *charcutier?*" he asked.

"I have had no experience of pig-killing," I answered.

"Look you," he growled, seizing my arm, "you will have the experience shortly, *either as pig or as butcher,* for all here will be *cochon* or *charcutier*--in a day or two. See? Choose whether you will be a pig or a butcher.... And tell your brother to choose.... Meantime, if any man comes to you and says '*porc*,' you reply '*cochon*.' Then he will know that I have spoken to you, and you will know that he is one of us. See? And you and your brother make up your minds quickly. We don't care either way. There are enough of us--oh, enough...." And as somebody approached, he got up and slouched off.

That night I told Michael what I had heard.

The next day it was Guantaio. I was sitting in the same place and he crept towards me purposefully.

"Who's that?" he asked, and, hearing my name, came and sat down beside me, as Schwartz had done.

"It's hot," he said, removing his *képi* and puffing.

"It is," I agreed.

"Are you fond of hot ... *porc?*" he enquired.

"*Cochon!*" said I playfully.

"Ah!" he replied at once. "What do you think of it all?"

"I never think," said I.

This silenced him for a minute.

"They are ten to one," he said suddenly. "Ten butchers to a pig. What chance has the big pig and one or two biggish pigs against a score of butchers?"

"Ah!" I said imitatively. "What do you think of it all?"

"I never think," said Guantaio, with a malevolent smile. I yawned and stretched and affected to settle myself to slumber.

"How would you and your brother like to be *pigs* if I could find two or three other pigs to join the big pig, and the one or two biggish pigs?" he enquired, nudging me.

I belied my statement that I never thought, and did some rapid thinking.

Had it been arranged that he should sound me as soon as Schwartz had hinted at the assassination of Lejaune? Was it his task to find out whether my name was to be put on the "butcher" list or on the "pig" list? Were all those who did not wholeheartedly join the "butchers" to be shot in their beds on the night of the mutiny?

Or, again, was the rogue trying to find out which was likely to be the stronger party, and did he intend to betray his friends to the non-commissioned officers, if he thought them likely to win?

"How should we like to become *pigs,* you say?" I temporised... . "I should hate to be butchered--shouldn't you?"

"Very much," he replied... . "But do you know," he went on, "I have heard of pigs attacking men. *Taking them unawares* and eating them up... ."

"I should hate to be eaten up by a pig--shouldn't you?" I observed.

"Very much," he agreed again. "One does not want to be slaughtered by butchers nor eaten by pigs."

"No," said I. "Need either happen?"

"Not if one is a wise pig--forewarned and forearmed--who attacks the butchers, *taking them unawares,*" he replied.

"Has the big pig got his eye on the butchers?" I asked.

"No," replied Guantaio. "Nor have the biggish pigs."

"And are you going to open the eyes of the blind pigs?" I enquired.

"I don't know," answered Guantaio. And I had a very strong conviction that he was speaking the truth, for there was a ring of genuine doubt and puzzlement in his voice. At any rate, if he were lying when he said it, he was lying extraordinarily well.

No--he did not know what to do, I decided, and he was simply trying to find out where his private interests lay. Would it pay him better to stand in with his friends, and assist in the mutiny and the murder of Lejaune and the non-commissioned officers? Or would he do better for himself if he betrayed his friends, warned his superiors, and assisted them to defeat the mutineers?

That he was one of the ringleaders of the plot was obvious, since he was the bosom friend of Colonna, Gotto, Vogué, and the rest of Schwartz's band, and had always been one of the circle in their recent confabulations and mutterings together.

I followed the excellent, if difficult, plan of trying to put myself in Guantaio's place, and to think with his mind.

On the one hand, if I were Guantaio, I should see the great dangers attendant on the mutiny. It might fail, and if it succeeded, it could only be the prelude to a terrible march into the desert--a march of doomed men, hunted by the Arabs and by the French alike, and certain to die of thirst and starvation if not killed by enemies.

On the other hand, if I were the excellent Guantaio, I should see the advantages attendant upon playing the part of the saviour of the situation. Reward and promotion were certain for the man who saved the lives of his superiors and the honour of the flag, and who preserved the Fort of Zinderneuf for France. And, of course, it would be the simplest thing in the world for Lejaune, Dupré, Boldini, Guantaio, and a few loyal supporters to defeat the conspirators and secure the mutineers. It would only be a matter of entering the barrack-room at night, seizing the arms, and covering the suspects with the rifles of the loyalists, while the guard arrested them. Anyone resisting, could be shot as soon as he raised a hand.

Lejaune alone could do the business with his revolver, if he entered the room while all were asleep, and shot any man who did not instantly obey any order that he gave.

In fact, I began to wonder why Guantaio should be hesitating like this. Surely it was to his interest to betray his friends?

Certainly he would not allow any ridiculous scruples to hinder him from committing any treacherous villainy, and certainly it was far less dangerous, in the long run, to be on the side of authority--for the mutineers' real danger only *began* with the mutiny, and it steadily increased from the moment when they set forth into the desert to escape.

More and more I wondered at his hesitation.

And then a light began to dawn upon my brain. This Guantaio was the henchman of his compatriot, Corporal Boldini. Boldini might be killed when the mutineers killed Lejaune; for hate and vengeance were the mainsprings of the plot, and Boldini was hated second only to Lejaune himself. He might not be given the option of joining the mutineers when Lejaune was murdered. Suppose the Italians, Boldini, Guantaio, Colonna, and Gotto, were a united party, led by Boldini, with some sinister end of their own in view? And might not Guantaio be doubtful as to whether the rôle allotted to him were not too much that of the cat's-paw?

Suppose the Boldini party intended to fish in troubled waters--for a pearl of great price? In other words, suppose they hoped to do what they had certainly tried, and failed, to do in Sidi-bel-Abbès, when they had induced Bolidar to attempt to rob my brother?

Most undoubtedly these rogues believed Boldini's story that we were a gang of jewel-thieves and that Michael carried about with him a priceless gem--to which they had at least as much right as he had. No--I decided--Guantaio spoke the truth when he said he did not know what to do. He was a knave all through. He would betray anybody and everybody. He was afraid that his share in the mutiny would be death, whether it failed or not, and what he really wanted to do was to follow the course most likely to lead him to the possession of two things--a whole skin and a share in the jewel--unless indeed he could get the jewel itself.

"It's a difficult problem, my friend," mused I sententiously. "One does not know which side to take... . One would like to be a pig, if the pigs are going to catch the butchers napping... . On the other hand, one would like to be a *charcutier,* if the butchers are going to act first... ."

We sat silent awhile, the excellent Guantaio making a perfect meal of his nails.

"And--that is a point!" I went on. "When *are* the butchers going to kill?"

"*Monsieur le Grand Charcutier*" (by whom, I supposed, he meant Schwartz) "talks of waiting till full moon," was the reply. "If a new Commandant has not come by then, or if *Monsieur le Grand Cochon* has been promoted and given command before then, it would be a good date... . Do it at night and have full moon for a long march... . Rest in the heat of the day, and then another big moonlight march, and so on... ."

"So one has three or four days in which to make up one's mind?" I observed.

"Yes," replied Guantaio. "But I don't advise your waiting three or four days before doing it.... Schwartz will want to know in good time.... So as to arrange some butchers for each pig, you see...."

"And what about Lejaune?" I asked, since we were to use names and not fantastic titles. "Suppose somebody warned him? What then?"

"Who *would?*" asked Guantaio. "Who loves that mad dog enough to be crucified, and have his throat cut, on his behalf? Why *should* anyone warn him? Wouldn't his death be a benefaction and a blessing to all?"

"Not if things went wrong," I replied. "Nor if it ended in our all dying in the desert."

"No," agreed Guantaio, gnawing away at his nails. "No ... I hate the desert ... I fear it ... I fear it...."

Yes--that was the truth of the matter. He feared being involved in a successful mutiny almost as much as in an unsuccessful one.

"Suppose, *par exemple,* I went and warned Lejaune?" I asked.

"Huh! He'd give you sixty days' *cellule,* and take damned good care you never came out alive," replied Guantaio, "and he would know what he knows already--that everybody hates him and would be delighted to kill him, given a good opportunity.... And what would your comrades do to you?"

He laughed most unpleasantly.

No--I decided--friend Guantaio would not like me to warn Lejaune. If Lejaune were to be warned, Guantaio would prefer to do the warning himself.

"How would they know that I was the informer?" I asked.

"Because I should tell them," was the reply. "If Lejaune gets to know--then you and nobody else will have told him."

So that was it? Guantaio could turn informer, having sworn that I was going to do so! Not only would he save his own skin, but Michael would soon have a friend and brother the less, when Schwartz and his merry men heard who had betrayed them.

"Of course, you and your brother would be held to have acted together, as you always do," said Guantaio.

So that was it again? Michael and I being denounced to the mutineers as traitors, Guantaio might well be moved to murder and rob Michael--secure in his honourable rôle of executioner of justice upon a cowardly traitor.

The Legion knew no punishment too severe for infliction upon any man who acted contrary to the interests of his comrades. Guantaio need not fear the fate of Bolidar in such circumstances.

"What would you do if you were me?" I asked.

"Join the butchers," was the prompt reply. "You and your brother must follow Schwartz. Better the enmity of Lejaune than of half the barrack-room led by Schwartz. Lejaune couldn't come straight to your bed and murder you, anyhow. Schwartz could, and would. And he *will,* unless you join him...."

Yes, undoubtedly the filthy creature was in grave doubt about the best course to pursue, and spoke from minute to minute as new ideas and fresh views occurred to him, and as his fears and hopes swayed him.

At present he saw the desirability of me and Michael being mutineers. Just now, he had seen some advantage in our not being of their party....

Probably the most puzzling and baffling thing to a tortuous mind is simple truth. It is often the subtlest diplomacy, when dealing with such people as this. So I decided to speak the plain truth, and leave him to make what he could of it.

"I shall talk the matter over with my brother," I said, "and we will decide to-night. Probably we shall warn Lejaune. You can tell Schwartz that. And I can give him a definite answer to-morrow. Then he can do as he pleases."

"You won't warn Lejaune until you have told Schwartz you are going to do so, of course?" asked Guantaio, and I had seen his eyes light up as I announced the probability of our defying Schwartz. That seemed to suit him finely.

"No, I won't," I assured him. "Neither will my brother... . Provided, of course, that nothing will be done to-night? No mutinying, I mean... ."

"Oh, no," said Guantaio. "They're not ready yet. A few haven't joined. Schwartz would like to get everybody, of course; but failing that, he wants to know exactly *who* is to be killed before they start. It will prevent unfortunate accidents... . Also they want the full moon... ."

"Well--I shall decide to-night," I said. "And now please go away. I want to think--and also I'm not extraordinarily fond of you, Guantaio, really... ."

§ 4

The first thing to do now was to find Michael and decide as to what line we were going to take.

He was on sentry-go, and I must wait.

Meantime, I might find St. André, Maris, Glock, and one or two others who were fundamentally decent honest men of brains and character, and less likely than some of the rest to be driven by blind hatred of Lejaune, or the dominance of Schwartz, into murderous folly that was also suicidal.

St. André was lying on his cot in the barrack-room. He looked at me as I entered. Taking my belt and a polishing-rag, I strolled in the direction of his bed, and came to a halt near him, rubbing industriously.

"Are you fond of pork, *mon ami?*" I enquired softly, without looking away from my work.

"I am something of a *cochon* about it," he replied in a low voice, and added, "Anyhow, I would rather be that than a butcher."

So he had been approached, too.

"Follow me outside when I go," I said.

A few minutes later he found me in the courtyard, and I learned that Schwartz had sounded him that day; told him that he must choose between being a pig or a butcher; and had given him a couple of days in which to make up his mind. Schwartz had concluded by informing St. André that all who were not *for* him would be treated as being *against* him, and that eighty per cent of the men had willingly taken the oath to follow him and to obey him absolutely... .

"What are you going to do, St. André?" I asked.

"What you and your brother do," was the immediate reply.

He went on to say that he had thought of nothing else from the moment he had learnt of the plot, and that he had come to the conclusion that he would join with Michael and me, to do what seemed the best thing.

"You see, my friend," he concluded, "one, of course, cannot join in with these poor madmen--one has been an officer and a gentleman. Even if one *had* sunk low enough to do such a thing, and one eased one's conscience by saying that Lejaune deserves death, the fact remains that these lunatics can but step from the frying-pan into the fire."

"Exactly," I agreed.

"Here we live--in hell, I admit--but we do *live,* and we are not here for ever," he went on. "Out in the desert we shall not live. Those who do not die of thirst, will die by slow torture under the knives of the Arab women."

"They will," said I.

"Besides," he continued, "I would not join them if we could march straight into the service of the Sultan of Morocco and be welcomed and rewarded with high rank in his army.... I am a Frenchman and have been an officer and a gentleman.... I am here through no fault of my own. St. André is my real name. My brother is a Lieutenant in a Senegalese battalion.... But you and your brother are not Frenchmen, and if you could get to Morocco, each of you could be another Kaid McLean.... But you could not get to Morocco on foot from here.... You would be hunted like mad dogs, apart from all question of food and water.... You could not do it...."

"We are not Frenchmen and we have not been officers, St. André," I replied; "but we are gentlemen--and we do not murder nor join murder-gangs.... And as you say--we could not do it and would not if we could."

"No, I knew you would not join them," said St. André, seizing my hand, "and I told myself I should do just what you and your brother did."

"Well--I'll talk it over with him as soon as he comes off duty, and we will let you know what we decide," I said, "but certainly it will not be to join them.

"Meanwhile," I added, "you get hold of Maris--he's a decent good chap, and see what he has got to say. You might try Glock, Dobroff, Marigny, Blanc, and Cordier, too, if you get a chance.... They are among the least mad in this lunatic asylum."

"Yes," agreed St. André, "if we can form a party of our own, we may be able to save the situation," and he went off.

I waited for Michael, sitting on a native bed, of string plaited across a wooden frame, that stood by the courtyard wall near the guard-room.

Seated here in the stifling dark, I listened to the gibberings, groans, yells, and mad laughter that came from the *cellules,* where some of Lejaune's victims were being driven more and more insane by solitary confinement and starvation.

When Michael was relieved, I followed him as he went to the barrack-room to put his rifle in the rack and throw off his kit.

"I'll be sitting on the *angareb,*" I said. "More developments."

"I'll be with you in five minutes," he replied.

When he joined me, I told him what Guantaio had said, and I added my own views on the situation, together with those of St. André.

Michael listened in silence.

"Position's this, I think," he said, when I had finished. "Schwartz and his band of lunatics proposing to murder Lejaune and anybody who stands by him, Guantaio has given the show away to Corporal Boldini because he thinks the mutiny too risky. Boldini wants to join the mutineers if they're likely to be successful--but not otherwise. Probably he, Guantaio, Colonna, Gotto, and Bolidar are in league to get the mighty 'diamond'--one way or the other--out of this mutiny. If we join the mutineers, Boldini and Co. will join, too, with the idea of killing me and robbing me in the desert and getting to Morocco with the Cullinan-Kohinoor... . Or to put it more truly, Boldini would get the 'Co.' to do the murdering and stealing, and then kill or rob whichever of his gang brought it off. If we refuse to join the mutineers, Boldini's plan would then be to get Guantaio to murder me in my bed--ostensibly for being a traitor to the noble cause of mutiny--and pinch the Great Diamond from my belt... . Failing that, Boldini would use us in helping to suppress the mutiny, hoping that, in the scrap, I might get done in, and he could rob my corpse. He could do more than hope it. He could arrange it... ."

"On the other hand," said I, "Boldini may know nothing whatever about the plot, and Guantaio may be wondering whether to let the mutiny go on, or whether to warn his old pal Boldini and give the show away."

"Quite so," agreed Michael. "We're absolutely in the dark in dealing with hopeless congenital bred-in-the-bone liars like Guantaio. We can only go on probabilities, and, on the whole, the swine seemed to be egging you on to join the plot... . Well, that means he has some definite personal interest in our joining it. Obviously if he hadn't, he wouldn't care a damn whether we joined it or not."

"What's to be done, Beau?" I asked.

"Get together an opposition-gang of non-mutineers, and then tell Schwartz plainly that we are going to warn Lejaune and also going to obey Lejaune's orders on the subject," was the prompt reply.

"Exactly," said I. "Just about what I told Guantaio... . And St. André will stand in with us, whatever we decide to do.

"But suppose we can get no one else," I pondered.

"Then we and St. André will warn Lejaune and tell him he can count on us three to be true to our salt," said Michael.

"Without warning Schwartz?" I asked.

"Certainly not," replied Michael. "We can't sneak like that."

"Of course, Schwartz and Co. will do us in, as traitors," I observed.

"Probably," agreed Michael. "Try to, anyhow.

"If we can get up a strongish party, Schwartz's lot may chuck the idea of mutiny," he went on. "If they don't, it will be a case of who strikes first. We must warn Lejaune the moment we've made it quite clear to Schwartz that we're going to do so then and there, unless he gives up the whole idea... . Whether he gives it up, or not, will depend on the number we can get to back us."

We sat silent for a minute or two, pondering this cheerful position.

"Tell you what," he said suddenly, "we'll call a meeting. The Briton's panacea. Tomorrow evening at six, the other side of the oasis, and we'll invite St. André, Blanc, Cordier, Marigny, and any other Frenchmen who'd be likely to follow St. André. Then there's Maris, Dobroff, Glock, and Ramon, among the foreigners, who might join us... . I wish to God that Digby, Hank, and Buddy were here."

"They'd make all the difference," said I.

"Well--if that lot will join us, we can probably turn Schwartz's murder-party into a mere gang of ordinary deserters, if go they must... ."

Shortly afterwards, St. André, looking for us, came to where we were sitting.

"I've spoken to Maris," said he, "and he's with you two, heart and soul. I also sounded Marigny, but he takes the line that we can't possibly be such curs as to warn the unspeakable Lejaune and betray our own comrades."

"We can't be such curs as not to do so," said Michael.

"Precisely what I tried to make him see," replied St. André. "It's a question of the point of view and of the degree of mental and moral development.... To us it is unthinkable that we should stand by and see murder done, the regiment disgraced, the Flag betrayed, and the fort imperilled.... We are soldiers of France...."

He stood up and saluted dramatically, but not self-consciously, in the direction of the flagstaff.

"To Marigny and his kind," he went on, "it is just as unthinkable that, having been entrusted with a secret by a comrade, they should betray this secret and thwart and endanger the friends who have put their faith in them."

"The point of view, as you say," agreed Michael. "Personally, though, I've not been entrusted with a secret by a comrade. I have merely had a threatening and impudent message from a ruffianly blackguard named Schwartz. He tells me he is going to commit a murder. I reply that he is not going to commit a murder, and that unless he abandons the intention, I am going to warn his victim. That seems a clear issue to me."

"And to me," said St. André.

"I also found Blanc to be much of the same mind as Marigny," he went on. "Averse from promoting or even condoning murder, but even more averse from 'betraying' his comrades.... I've only spoken to those three so far...."

"Well, look here," said Michael. "To-morrow at six, beyond the oasis. All our friends and all who are not actually of Schwartz's gang. You get Marigny, Blanc, and Cordier, and any other Frenchman you think might join us, and we'll bring Maris, Ramon, Dobroff, and Glock, and possibly one or two more. They'll come.... They'll come, because, obviously, it's a life-or-death matter for all of us. We must try to see that none of Schwartz's gang know about the meeting, at any rate until it's over--but if they do, we can't help it. I suppose we have as much right to lay plans as they have?"

"It's a good idea," agreed St. André. "I'll be there and bring whom I can. About six o'clock."

§ 5

Next evening, a handful of the better sort assembled near the *shaduf* in the shade of the palm-grove, out of sight of the fort. Besides Michael, St. André, Maris, and myself, there were Cordier, Blanc, Marigny, Ramon, Dobroff, Glock, Vaerren, and one or two others-- fifteen or sixteen of us altogether--enough, as Michael remarked to me, to control events, provided a united party, with a common policy, could be formed.

But this proved impossible. Ideas of right and wrong, honour and dishonour, fair dealing and vile dealing, were too discrepant and probably tinctured by other thoughts and motives, such as those of fear, hatred, ennui, vengeance, and despair.

Michael addressed the meeting first.

"As you all very well know," said he, "there is a plot to murder Lejaune and the non-coms., to desert and to abandon the fort. Schwartz is the ringleader and says that those who do not declare themselves supporters will be considered as enemies--and treated as such. Personally, I do not do things because Schwartz says I must, nor do I approve of shooting men in their beds. Supposing I did, I still should disapprove of being led out into the desert by Schwartz, to die of thirst. Therefore I am against his plot--and I invite you all to join with me and tell Schwartz so. We'll tell him plainly that unless he gives up this mad scheme of murder and mutiny, we shall warn Lejaune... ."

Here a growl of disapproval from Marigny and Blanc, and some vigorous head-shaking, interrupted Michael's speech.

"I swear I will warn Lejaune," put in St. André, "but I will warn Schwartz first--and if he likes to drop the murder part of the scheme, he can do what else he likes. Any sacred imbecile who wants to die in the desert can go and do it, but I have nothing to do with mutinies... ."

"*No treachery!*" roared Marigny, a typical old soldier, grizzled and wrinkled; an honest, brainless, dogged creature who admired Schwartz and loathed Lejaune.

"Don't bray like that, my good ass," said Michael turning to him, "and try not to be a bigger fool than God meant you to. Where is the treachery in our replying to Schwartz, '*Thank you, we do not choose to join your murder-gang. Moreover, we intend to prevent the murder--so drop the idea at once.*' Will you kindly explain how the gentle Schwartz is thus 'betrayed'?"

"I say it *is* betrayal of comrades--to tell an anointed, accursed, nameless-named dog's-tail like Lejaune that they are plotting against him. Treachery, I say," replied Marigny.

Michael sighed patiently.

"Well--what are you going to do, Marigny--since you must either be against Schwartz or for him?" asked Maris.

"I'm *for* him," replied Marigny promptly.

"A slinking, skulking murderer?" asked Michael contemptuously. "I thought you were a soldier--of sorts."

"I'm for Schwartz," said Marigny.

"Then go to him," snapped Michael. "Go on... . Get out... . We should prefer it--being neither cowards afraid of Schwartz, nor creeping murderers."

Marigny flushed, clenched his fists and, with an oath, put his hand to his bayonet and made as though to spring at my brother; but he evidently thought better of it as Michael closed his right hand and regarded the point of Marigny's chin.

With a snarl of "Dirty traitors!" the old soldier turned and strode away.

"Anybody else think as he does?" asked Michael.

"I can't agree to betraying old Schwartz," said Blanc, a Marseilles seaman, noisy, jolly, brave, and debonair; a rotund, black-eyed, bluff Provençal.

"Well--say what you are going to do then," said Michael sharply: "Join Schwartz's murderers or else join us."

"I can't join Lejaune's boot-lickers," said Blanc.

"Then join Schwartz's gang of assassins. You may perhaps be safer there," said Michael, and Blanc departed grumbling.

"I must join my compatriots, I'm afraid," said Glock.

"You are 'afraid'!" mocked Michael. "You have said it! It is Schwartz you are afraid of. You needn't be. You'll be safer outside that gang of murderers."

"I can't betray my compatriots," repeated Glock.

"Well--can you go to them and say--(what is the truth)--'*I don't believe in murder and I am certain this business will end in the deaths of* ALL *of us. Drop it or I and my friends will make you.*' Can you do that?" asked Michael.

Big, simple Glock, with his blue eyes and silly face, could only scratch his head and shuffle awkwardly from one foot to another.

"They'd kill me," he said.

"They certainly will kill you of thirst, if you let them lead you out there," argued Michael, with a wave of his arm to the encompassing desert.

"It seems we've all got to die, either way," said Glock.

"It's what I am trying to prevent, isn't it, fat-head?" answered Michael. "If the decent men of this garrison would act together and tell Schwartz to stop his silly tricks, no one need die."

"Except those whom *Lejaune* is killing," said Cordier, a clever and agreeable Frenchman who had certainly been a doctor, and whose prescriptions and treatment his comrades infinitely preferred to those of any army surgeon. "If that pariah cur of the gutters of Sodom and Gomorrah could be shot with safety to the rest of us--I'd do it myself to-night, and write my name among those of the benefactors of the human race."

"Oh? Where do *you* stand then?" asked Michael.

"I come in with you and St. André," replied Cordier, "though I admit my sympathies are wholly with Schwartz. Still ... one's been a gentleman... ."

And in the end we found that only Cordier could really be depended upon to join Michael, St. André, Maris, and myself as a staunch and reliable party of anti-Schwartz, pro-duty-and-discipline non-murderers, prepared to tell the mutineers that they must drop their assassination plot, or Lejaune would be warned.

One by one, the others went off, some apologetic and regretful, some blustering, some honestly anxious to support what they considered Schwartz's brave blow for their rights, some merely afraid to do what they would have liked to do.

When we five were at length alone, Michael said, "Well, I'm afraid we're not going to scare Schwartz off his scheme."

"No," agreed Cordier. "It looks more as though we are only going to provide him with some extra labour. More little pigs... ."

"There won't be any pigs if Lejaune acts promptly," said St. André.

"None," agreed Maris, "and I'm almost tempted to vote for warning Lejaune *before* saying anything to Schwartz. It would give us more chance..."

"No. No. We can't do that," said Cordier. "We must give old Schwartz a fair show. If he'll cut out the murder items from his programme, we'll say nothing, of course, and he can carry on. If he won't, we'll do our duty as decent folk, and give Lejaune his chance."

"Will he take it?" I asked. "Will he listen?"

"Not to one of us alone," said St. André. "But he'd have to take notice of a deputation, consisting of the five of us, all telling the same tale."

"A deputation consisting of ourselves, coming from ourselves?" smiled Cordier.

"After all, though," asked Maris, "does it matter if he believes or not? Suppose one of us goes and tells him the truth--isn't that enough? If he likes to punish the man and ignore his warning, that's his affair."

"Quite," agreed Michael. "But it's ours too! We don't want to be shot in our beds because Lejaune won't listen to us... . If Schwartz isn't forestalled, every man in this fort who hasn't joined his gang by the day after to-morrow will share Lejaune's fate."

"That means us five, Boldini, Dupré, and Lejaune," said Cordier.

"Unless Boldini is in with them,--which is quite likely," put in St. André.

"Yes, seven of us," mused Michael, "even without Boldini. If Lejaune listens to our tale of woe and acts promptly, we five and the two non-coms. are a most ample force for him to work with... . Simply a matter of acting a night before they do--and there need be no bloodshed either."

"Fancy fighting to protect *Lejaune!*" smiled Cordier. "Enough to make *le bon Dieu* giggle."

"We're fighting to protect the Flag," said St. André. "Lejaune is incidental. We're going to fight a murderous mutiny--and another incidental is that we are probably going to save our own lives thereby... ."

"Who'll tell Schwartz?" interrupted Cordier.

"I will," said Michael.

"We all will," said I. "Let us five just go to him together and warn him. We won't emphasise the fact that we speak for ourselves only."

"That's it," agreed St. André. "We'll tell Schwartz that we're a 'deputation' to him--and do the same when we go on to interview Lejaune--if that's necessary."

And so the five of us agreed to go in search of Schwartz then and there, to tell him that we would take no part in mutiny and murder, and to warn him that we should report the matter at once, unless he agreed to abandon the part of his scheme that included the slaughter of superiors and the coercion of comrades.

§ 6

As we left the oasis and strolled towards the fort, we met a man carrying pails, for water. As he passed, I saw it was the Portuguese, Bolidar, the man who had been so roughly handled for attempted theft in our barrack-room at Sidi-bel-Abbès. He had always pretended that, on that melancholy occasion, he had strayed, under the influence of liquor, into the wrong room, and that, when caught, he was merely getting into what he thought was his own bed!

Warned by Hank and Buddy, however, we, on the other hand, regarded the gentleman as the miserable tool of Boldini, who had taken him up when Guantaio, Colonna, and Gotto had declined to do his stealing for him.

As he passed Michael, he half stopped, winked, made as though to speak, and then went on. Looking back, I saw that he had halted, put his pails down, and was staring after us.

Seeing me turn round, he signalled to me to come to him, and began walking towards me.

Here was a man with whom a quiet talk might be very useful, particularly as he had made the first overtures.

"I want to speak to your brother and you," he whispered. "Privately. I daren't be seen doing it. I am in Hell--and yet I am going to Hell. Yes, I am going to Hell--and yet I am in Hell now."

He was evidently in a very unbalanced state of mind. He was trembling, and he looked terribly ill.

"Go into the oasis and wait," said I. "I'll bring my brother along soon."

"I must hide ... I must hide ... I must hide," he kept repeating.

"All right," I agreed. "You hide. I'll stroll along whistling '*Père Bougeaud*' when I bring my brother."

"Lejaune will tear my throat out... . He'll eat my heart... . So will Schwartz... . So will Boldini... ."

"Well, you won't feel the second two," I comforted him, "and you haven't got three hearts... . You tell us all about it," I added soothingly. "We'll look after you. Pull yourself together now," for I thought he was going to burst into tears.

"You won't bring anybody else? You won't tell anybody else? Not a word?" he begged.

"Not a soul. Not a word," I replied. "You wait for us in the far clump of palms beyond the well," and I went after Michael.

As soon as I could speak to him alone, I told him about Bolidar.

"Good," said Michael. "We'll hear what the merchant's got to say before we tackle Schwartz. The bold Bolidar evidently wants to hedge a bit, for some reason... . 'When rogues fall out.' ... Let's go straight back before he changes what he calls his mind."

Michael ran on and asked St. André and the others to wait a little while and do nothing until he returned.

We then went back to the oasis, and as we passed near the well, I whistling "*Avez-vous vu la casquette de Père Bougeaud?*" Bolidar joined us, trembling with fear and fever.

We went and sat down together with a high sand-hill between us and the oasis.

At first, Bolidar was incoherent and almost incomprehensible, but soon it was quite clear that the wretched creature was turning to us as a last hope and last resort in his extremity of anxiety, suspense, and terror.

Realising what it was that drove him to unburden himself to us--sheer cowardly fear for his own wretched skin--we never for one instant doubted the truth of what he said.

He oozed truth as he did abject funk, from every pore, and he showed it in every gleam of his bloodshot rolling yellow eyes, and in every gesticulation of his trembling dirty yellow hands.

"My friends," he gabbled, "I must confess to you and I must save you. I can bear it no longer. My conscience... . My rectitude... . My soul... . My sense of gratitude... ."

Michael winked at me. We did not value Bolidar's conscience and gratitude as highly as we did his state of trembling fright, when estimating his motives for "confession." ...

"On that terrible night when I was so cruelly misjudged and so cruelly treated, you tried to save me... . Yes, even though it was you whom I was supposed to be trying to rob... . An absurd idea, of course ..." and he laughed nervously.

There was no doubting the fact that the gentle dago was in a rare state of terror. His convulsive swallowings, drawn yellow features, tremblings and twitchings, clenched hands and wild eyes, were really distressing.

"Most absurd idea, of course," murmured Michael. "What is it you want to tell us?"

"Your diamond! Your diamond!" whispered Bolidar hoarsely, gripping Michael's wrist and staring into his eyes.

"Ah--my diamond. And what about it?" said Michael gently.

"Lejaune! Lejaune means to get it," he hissed. "And he'll kill me! He'll kill me! If he doesn't, Schwartz will.... Or Boldini.... What *shall* I do? What *can* I do?" he screamed.

Michael patted the poor rascal's shoulder.

"There! There! Never mind. No one's going to kill you," he soothed him, almost as though he had been a baby. "Now tell us all about it and we'll see what can be done.... You join our party and you'll be safe enough."

"*Your* party?" asked Bolidar. "What is *your* party? And what are you going to do?"

"Oh--we are a party all right. The stoutest fellows in the garrison--and we're going to *warn* Lejaune--if Schwartz doesn't agree to give up the murder part of the plot," replied Michael.

"You're going to do *what?*" asked Bolidar, open-eyed and open-mouthed.

"Going to warn Lejaune," repeated Michael.

Bolidar threw his hands up and shook with mirthless laughter.

"*But he* KNOWS!--*He* KNOWS! *He* KNOWS ALL ABOUT IT, *and who's in it--and when it's to be--and every word that's said in the place!*" cackled Bolidar in a kind of broken, hoarse voice.

Michael and I stared at each other aghast.

"Who tells him?" asked Michael.

"*I do,*" was the proud reply of this shameless animal. "And when he has got your diamond, he will kill me," he snivelled.

I was absolutely staggered. If Lejaune knew all about it, what of our precious threat to Schwartz? And what was our position now?

"Why doesn't Lejaune do something then?" asked Michael.

"Oh, he'll *do* something all right," said Bolidar. "He'll do a good deal, the night before Schwartz and his fools intend to strike."

"Why does he wait?" we asked simultaneously.

"To see what you two are going to do," was the reply. "If you join Schwartz you'll be killed *with* Schwartz, the night before the mutiny is due--and I'm to secure the diamond. It is not really supposed that you'll join him though. And if you don't join Schwartz you are to be killed in the attack *on* him instead."

"By whom?" asked Michael.

"*By me,*" replied Bolidar. "You see, if you should join Schwartz, I am to be loyal and enter the barrack-room with Lejaune and the others on the night. As we cover the mutineers with our rifles, mine is to go off and kill you.... If you don't join Schwartz, I am to be a mutineer, and when *you* enter the barrack-room with Lejaune and the loyal party, in the night, I am to shoot you from my bed.... Either way you are to die--and I am perfectly sure that I shall die too.... Oh, God! Oh, Jesus Christ! Oh, Holy Virgin! Oh, Saints in Heaven!" he blubbered.

"And suppose I refuse to give Schwartz any answer, and remain perfectly neutral?" asked Michael.

"Then I am to harangue the mutineers and urge them to kill you as a non-supporter! You *and* any others that won't join them, so that it will not look as though I have any personal motive or feeling with regard to you specially. Then I am to offer to 'execute' you... . Having done it, I am to get the diamond and give it to Lejaune... . Yes," he added with another whispering gasp, "Lejaune is going to shoot me if you are killed without my securing the jewel for him ..." and he rocked his body to and fro in despair.

"He ought to have an apron to throw over his head and cry into--like an old peasant woman whose cow has died," said Michael in English.

"Yes," I agreed. "Let's get all we can out of the brute before we let him go."

"Is Boldini in this?" Michael asked Bolidar. "I mean, are he and Lejaune working together?"

"Well--Boldini knows that Lejaune knows," was the reply. "And those two are going to use Dupré and St. André and Cordier and Maris and you two, for the arrest of the unarmed mutineers in the middle of the night. That is, if you refuse to join Schwartz as they anticipate... . But I doubt if Boldini and Lejaune quite trust each other. Guantaio says they don't. He thinks that Boldini intends to get the diamond for himself, and that Lejaune suspects as much. At least that is what Guantaio tells me--but I don't wholly trust him... ."

"Don't you really?" said Michael.

"No. I don't think he's absolutely honest," said Bolidar doubtfully.

"You surprise me," admitted Michael. "The dirty dog!"

"He has made proposals to me which I have rejected with contempt," said Bolidar.

"Dangerous?" asked Michael.

"Absurdly," replied Bolidar. "Besides, how was I to know that I should get my share? It's bad enough to *have* to trust Lejaune as one is compelled to do--without risking things with a rascal like Guantaio."

"Has Boldini made--er--proposals which you rejected with contempt?" Michael enquired.

"Oh, yes. But as I pointed out to him--Lejaune is *adjudant* while Boldini is only *caporal*."

"And what did he say to that?" asked Michael.

"That a live *caporal* is better than a dead *adjudant*," was the interesting reply.

"Sounds sinister," I observed in English.

"Nice little crowd," said Michael in the same language. "One really doesn't know where one is, nor where to start on the job of making head or tail of the business.

"Let's get this clear now," he said to Bolidar. "You are Lejaune's--er--man. You warned him of Schwartz's plot to mutiny and kill him, while acting as though you were a ringleader. You have told every detail to Lejaune and kept him up to date with every development. Lejaune has given you the job of killing me. If I join Schwartz, you are to turn loyal, go over to Lejaune, and shoot me in my bed when we are arrested.

"If I refuse to join Schwartz you are to continue as a mutineer and shoot me, from your bed, when I come in with the loyal party to arrest you.

"If I decline to declare myself you are to be my executioner, self-appointed, on behalf of the worthy mutineers--who will have no neutrals about. And all this in order that Lejaune may get a diamond that is supposed to be in my possession... ."

Bolidar was sunk in a lethargy of miserable thought. He slowly nodded in affirmation.

"And probably Boldini has a plan of his own which involves a dead *adjudant* and leaves a live *caporal*--also in pursuit of a diamond! And Boldini's plan, I suppose, is to support Lejaune until he has got the diamond, and then withdraw the support--and the diamond? ..."

Bolidar came out of his fit of brooding abstraction.

"That is what Guantaio said," he replied. "He wanted me to join Boldini, Colonna, Gotto, and himself. We were to plot, and kill Lejaune *and* those who stood by him against the mutineers, after those poor fools had been arrested and either shot (in 'self-defence,' of course) or put in the cells. When we had got the diamond we could decide whether to liberate the mutineers and use them in fighting our way to Morocco, or whether their mouths had better be closed... . We could set fire to the fort and clear out--and everything would be put down to the account of the Arabs... ."

"And why did you not fall in with this pretty scheme!" asked Michael.

"Well--who could trust Boldini? Or Guantaio? Or any of them, for that matter? They are not *honest* men. Once Boldini had the diamond, what would be the worth of the life of the man who had a claim on a share of it? To have the diamond would, of course, be death! To be one of a syndicate owning it would, of course, be death! Even to know who had got it would be death, for the man who had it would kill you lest you robbed him or demanded your share... . How *can* one work with such dishonest people?" and the speaker's voice broke with righteous indignation.

"And has Guantaio made any other proposals which you have rejected with contempt?" asked Michael.

"Oh--any number," replied Bolidar. "He seems to think I'm a fool. He actually proposed that I should rob you, and he and I should desert together, before all this mutiny business takes place. I was almost tempted--but--but--"

"Quite," said Michael. "It must be a great handicap."

"It is," agreed Bolidar. "And besides," he added, "how could two men walk across two thousand miles of desert, apart from the question of *goums* and the Touaregs? ... And wouldn't Guantaio murder me directly we got to Morocco?"

"Unless you murdered him first," said Michael.

"Yes," agreed Bolidar, "but one might leave it too late ..." and he meandered on about the untrustworthiness of Italians.

"Well, now. Let's get down to business," Michael interrupted. "What have you told us all this for? What do you want us to do?"

"Why," said Bolidar, "I felt I must deal with honest men and I must get away. It is certain death for me. If I get the diamond I shall be killed for it, or for knowing that Lejaune has got it. If I don't get it, Lejaune will kill me for failing him, or else for knowing too much when there is a court martial about the mutiny... ."

"Well?" Michael encouraged him.

"I thought that if I told you two all about it--the real truth to honest men--you would save my life and your own, and give me a share in the diamond."

"How save our lives?" Michael asked.

"All desert together before the mutiny, and you give me a third-part share in the diamond when we are safe."

"How do you know we should keep our promise?" asked Michael.

"Because you are English... . In Brazil, we say, '*Word of an Englishman!*' and '*Word of an American!*' when we are swearing to keep faith. If you promise, I know you will perform."

"This is very touching," said Michael. "But suppose I give you my word that I haven't got a diamond and never possessed a diamond in my life?"

Bolidar smiled greasily, as at one who must have his little jest.

"Oh, *Señor!*" he murmured, waggling his head and his hands idiotically.

"One knows of the little parcel in your belt-pouch," he said.

"Oh, one does, does one?" smiled Michael. "Fancy that now!"

Silence fell.

"Well--as you just said, two or three people can't march off into the desert and expect to live for more than a day or two," observed Michael after a while.

"We might make a party," suggested Bolidar. "It is known that St. André, Maris, Cordier, and one or two more refuse to listen to Schwartz's plan to kill Lejaune."

"Nor are they deserters," said Michael.

"No--but when they know that they are to be killed by the mutineers if they don't join them, or to be killed by Lejaune if they do--what then? ... Tell them the truth--that Lejaune is going to have no survivors of this mutiny--whichever side they may be on. No. He's going to have the diamond and the credit and glory of suppressing the mutiny and saving the fort single-handed. He'll teach *les légionnaires* to mutiny! Their mutiny shall end in death for the lot of them--and in wealth and promotion for Lejaune. He sees himself an officer and a rich man on the strength of this fine mutiny.... And what happens to the men who told him about the diamond--the men who helped him and risked their lives for him? What, I ask you? ... Death, I tell you. *Death! Death! Death!*" he screamed, trembling and slavering like a trapped beast.

"And who *did* tell him about this wonderful diamond!" asked Michael.

"Boldini," replied Bolidar. "As soon as he rejoined, he told him of the gang of famous London jewel-thieves who had fled from the English police to the Legion. He and Guantaio and Gotto were to get it and give it to Lejaune, who would protect them and who would either place it and share with them, or keep it until they had all served their time.... I don't know."

"And they put you up to steal it in Sidi, eh?" asked Michael. "Why you?"

But Bolidar spurned such an unworthy suggestion.

"Anyhow, we're getting away from the point," Michael interrupted him. "What's to be done? We're certainly not going to desert. I wonder if one could possibly persuade the gentle Lejaune that there's no such thing as a diamond in Zinderneuf?"

"What--pretend you hid it and left it--at Sidi-bel-Abbès?" said Bolidar. "That's an idea! ..."

Michael laughed.

"Did you leave it at Sidi?" asked Bolidar.

"I most certainly have not got a diamond here," replied Michael.

"Do you swear it by the name of God? By your faith in Christ? By your love of the Blessed Virgin? And by your hope for the intercession of the Holy Saints?" asked Bolidar.

"Not in the least," replied Michael. "I merely say it. I have not got a diamond--'*Word of an Englishman.*'"

"It's a chance," whispered Bolidar. "Dear Christ! It's a chance. Oh, lovely Christ, help me! ... I'll tell Lejaune you left it at Sidi."

"Tell him what you like," said Michael.

Bolidar pondered.

"Huh! Anyhow, he'll *make sure* you haven't got it," he said darkly, and rose to his feet. "But I'll try it. I'll try it. There is a small hope... . I'll tell you what he says," he added.

"You'll tell us *something,* I've no doubt," replied Michael, as the heroic Portuguese took up his pails and slunk off.

§ 7

"Well, my son--a bit involved, what?" smiled my brother as we were left in solitude.

"What *can* one do?" I asked feebly.

"Nothing," replied Michael promptly and cheerfully. "Just await events and do the straight thing. I'm not going to bunk. And I'm not going to join any beastly conspiracy. But I think I'm going to 'beat Bolidar to the draw' as Hank and Buddy would say--when he tries to cover me with his rifle."

"In other words, you're going to shoot friend Bolidar before friend Bolidar shoots you?" I said.

"That's it, my son. If he's cur enough to do a dirty murder like that, just because Lejaune tells him to, he must take his little risks," replied Michael.

"And if that happens--I mean if I see him cover you and you shoot him--Lejaune is going with him. It is as much Lejaune's murder as it is Bolidar's," I said.

"You're going to shoot Lejaune, eh?" asked Michael.

"I am," said I, "if Bolidar covers you. Why should he cover *you,* in particular, out of a score or so of men, unless he has been told to shoot you?"

"Well--we'll tell Bolidar just what's going to happen, and we'll invite him to tell Lejaune too. It would be fairer, perhaps," said Michael.

"Golly," I observed. "Won't it make the lad gibber! One more slayer on his track!"

"Yes," smiled Michael. "Then he'll know that if neither Lejaune nor Boldini nor Schwartz kills him, *I* shall. Poor old Bolidar... ."

"What about poor old us?" I asked.

"We're for it, I should say," replied Michael. "Of course, Lejaune won't believe that this wonderful diamond they are talking about has been left at Sidi, and he'll carry on."

"I'm muddled," I groaned. "Let's get it clear now:

"*One:* We tell Schwartz we won't join his gang, and that we will warn Lejaune of the plot to murder him ..."

"Or shall we tell Schwartz that *Lejaune knows all about it?*" Michael interrupted.

"Good Lord, I'd forgotten that," I said. "I suppose we'd better."

"Then they'll crucify poor old Bolidar for good, this time," grinned Michael. "Serve him right too. Teach him not to go about murdering to order... ."

"We need not say who told us that Lejaune knows," I observed.

"And then they *will* know that you and I are beastly traitors!" said Michael. "Of course, they will at once think that we told him ourselves."

"Probably Guantaio has told them that, and done it himself, meanwhile," I suggested.

"Oh, damn it all--let's talk about something else," groaned Michael. "I'm sick of their silly games."

"Yes, old chap. But it's pretty serious," I said. "Let me just go over it again:

"*One:* We tell Schwartz that we won't join his gang. And that Lejaune knows all about his plot.

"*Two:* Lejaune acts before Schwartz does, and he raids the barrack-room the night before the mutiny. We shall either be in bed as though mutineers, or we shall be ordered to join the guard of loyal men who are to arrest the mutineers.

"*Three:* In either case, Bolidar is to shoot you. But directly he raises his rifle in your direction, you are going to shoot him. (You'll have to take your rifle to bed with you if Lejaune is going to pretend that you are a mutineer.)

"*Four:* If I see that Bolidar is out to murder you, I shall shoot Lejaune myself. (I shall take my rifle to bed too, if we are left with the mutineers.)

"*Five:* If ..."

"Five: The fat *will* be in the fire, nicely, then," interrupted Michael. "What can we do but bolt into the desert with the rest, if you kill Lejaune? You'd be the most badly-wanted of all the badly-wanted mutineers, after that... . They'd get us too, if they had to turn out a desert-column of all arms... ."

We pondered the delightful situation.

"Besides," Michael went on, "you couldn't do it. Of course you couldn't. It would be a different thing if Lejaune were raising a rifle to shoot you, as Bolidar will be doing to me, if I shoot Bolidar. You couldn't just blow Lejaune's head off, in cold blood. That is exactly what Schwartz is going to do... . And what we object to."

And it was so, of course. I might just as well go to Schwartz and offer to be the butcher.

"Well," said I, "suppose I cover Lejaune with my rifle and tell him I'll blow his head off the moment he moves--and then I tell him to ..."

"Consider himself under arrest?" jeered Michael. "And what are you then, but the rankest mutineer of the lot? Besides, it's quite likely that Lejaune won't be there. He's brave enough--but he'd like to survive the show. In fact, he intends to be the sole survivor, I should say."

"Looks as though we've simply *got* to join Schwartz then," I said.

"Damned if I do," replied Michael. "I'm certainly going bald-headed for anyone who goes for me, but I'm not going to join any mutineers, nor commit any murders."

"Nor are you," he added, as I stared glumly out into the desert.

"What *is* to be done then?" I asked once again.

"*Nothing,* I tell you," repeated Michael. "We've got to 'jump lively when we do jump,' as Buddy says; but we can only wait on events and do what's best, as they arise. Meanwhile, let's hold polite converse with the merry Schwartz... . Come on."

And we got up and strolled through the starlit darkness to the Fort.

"I suppose we can take it that Sergeant Dupré knows all about the plot?" I said, as we passed into the stifling courtyard.

"No doubt of it," replied Michael. "I am inclined to think Lejaune would try to keep a nice compact 'loyal party' to deal with the mutineers, and hope they'd be like the Kilkenny cats, mutually destructive... . Say, Dupré, Boldini, and five or six *légionnaires*... . Some of whom would be killed in the scrap... . Of course, one doesn't know *what* his plans really are--except that he means to get a diamond, a lot of kudos, and a nice little vengeance on his would-be murderers... ."

As we entered the barrack-room, we saw that a committee-meeting of the "butcher" party was in session. They stared in hostile fashion at Michael and me as we went to our cots and got out our cleaning-rags from the little bags.

I sat down on my bed and began melting wax on to my belt and pouches, preparatory to *astiquage* labours.

The conspirators' heads drew together again.

Michael went over to where they were grouped at the end of the long table.

"Have you come with your answer to a question I asked you about some *cochons?*" growled Schwartz, scowling at him.

"I have come with some news about a *cochon,* my friend," replied Michael.

Half a dozen pairs of eyes glared at him, and I strolled over. So did St. André from his cot. Just then Maris and Cordier entered, and I beckoned to them.

"He knows *all* about it," said Michael.

Schwartz sprang to his feet, his eyes blazing, his beard seeming to bristle, and his teeth gleaming as he bared them. He was a dangerous savage-looking ruffian.

"*You* have told him!" he shouted, pointing in Michael's face. "You treacherous filthy cur, you have betrayed us!" and he glanced to where a bayonet hung at the head of his bed.

"And come straight here and told you?" sneered Michael coldly. "If you were as clever as you are noisy, you might see I should hardly do that. You're a pretty leader of a gang of desperate mutineers, aren't you?"

Schwartz stared in amazement, struck dumb by the cool daring of the person who had the courage and effrontery to taunt and insult *him.*

Michael turned to Brandt, Haff, Delarey, Guantaio, Vogué, and the rest of Schwartz's familiars.

"A remarkable leader," he said. "Here you are, the gang of you, making your wonderful plans, *and Lejaune knows every word you say,* and precisely what you are going to do--almost as soon as you know it yourselves! ... *Join* you? No, thanks. You have talked cleverly about 'pigs' and 'butchers'--but what about a lot of silly *sheep?* You make me tired," and Michael produced a most convincing and creditable yawn.

"Well, what are you going to do?" he asked as they sat open-mouthed. "Whatever it is, Lejaune will do it first," he added, "so you'd better do nothing."

"And Lejaune will do it first," I put in.

Michael's coolness, bitter contempt for them, and his obvious sincerity, had won. They knew he spoke the truth, and they knew he had not betrayed them to Lejaune.

I watched Guantaio, and decided that save perhaps for a little courage, he was another Bolidar. Certainly Boldini would hear of Michael's action, if Lejaune did not, as soon as Guantaio could get away from his dupes.

"What to do!" murmured Schwartz. "What to do! If Lejaune knows everything! ..."

"Declare the whole thing off," said Michael, "and then the noble soul who has told Lejaune so much, can tell him that too," and Michael's eye rested on Guantaio.

It rested so long upon Guantaio, that that gentleman felt constrained to leap to his feet and bluster.

"Do you *dare* to suggest ..." he shouted and stopped. *(Qui s'excuse s'accuse.)*

"I did not know I had suggested anything," said Michael softly. "Why *should* I suggest anything, my friend?"

"If it were you--I'd hang you to the wall with bayonets through your ears, you yellow dog," growled Schwartz, glaring at Guantaio.

"He lies! He lies!" screamed Guantaio.

"How do you know?" asked Michael. "How do *you* know what Lejaune knows?"

"I meant that you lie if you say that I betrayed the plot," blustered Guantaio.

"I haven't said it," replied Michael. "It is only you who have said it... . You seem to be another of the clever ones... ."

Michael's coolness and superiority were establishing a kind of supremacy for him over these stupid creatures, driven and bedevilled as they were by *cafard* and by Lejaune.

They stared at each other and at us.

"What's to be done?" said Schwartz... . "By God! When I catch the traitor ..." he roared and shook his great fists above his shaggy head.

"Nothing's to be done," replied Michael again, "because you can *do* nothing. You are in Lejaune's hands absolutely. Take my advice and drop this lunacy, and you may hear nothing more of it... . There may be a new Commandant here in a week or two ..."

"Yes--and his name may be Lejaune," answered Schwartz.

"Anyhow--he *knows,* and he's got us," put in Brandt. "I vote we all join in the plot and then all vote it abandoned. Then he can't punish one more than another. He can't put the whole blasted garrison in his cursed cells, can he?"

"You're right," said Haff. "That's it. Abandon the whole scheme, I say. *And* find out the traitor and give him a night that he'll remember through eternity in Hell... ."

But the ferocious Schwartz was of a different fibre, and in his dogged and savage brain the murder of Lejaune was an *idée fixe.*

"Abandon nothing!" he roared, springing to his feet. "I tell you I ..." And then Michael laid his hand on his arm.

"Silence, you noisy fool," he said quietly. "Don't you understand *yet* that whatever you say now will go straight to Lejaune?"

Schwartz, foaming, swung round on Guantaio.

"Get out of this," he growled menacingly, and pointed to the door.

"I swear I ..." began Guantaio indignantly.

"Get out, I say!" bawled Schwartz, "and when the time comes for us to strike our blow--be careful. Let me only *suspect* you, and I'll hang you to the flagstaff by one foot... . By God, I will... . *Go!*"

Guantaio slunk off.

"Now listen to me again," said Michael. "As I told you, Lejaune knows all about your plot to murder him and desert at full moon. I did not tell him. But I was going to tell him, if, after I had warned you, you refused to abandon the scheme."

Schwartz growled and rose to his feet again.

"Oh yes," Michael went on, "I was going to warn you first, to give you a chance to think better of it--in which case I should have said nothing, of course... . But now get this clear. If I know of any *new* scheme, or any change of date or method, or anything that Lejaune does not already know--I shall tell him... . Do you understand? ..."

"You cursed spy! You filthy, treacherous hound! You ..." roared Schwartz. "Why should *you* ..."

"Oh, don't be such a noisy nuisance, Schwartz," interrupted Michael. "I and a party of my friends don't choose *to give Lejaune the chance he wants,* and we don't really like murder either... . We have as much right to live as you, haven't we?"

"*Live,*" snarled Brandt. "D'you call *this* living?"

"We aren't dying of thirst, anyhow," replied Michael. "And if we are chivvied and hunted and hounded by Lejaune, it's better than being hunted to our deaths by a camel-company of *goums* or by the Touaregs, isn't it?"

"And who *are* your precious friends?" asked Haff.

"There are five of them here, for a start," said St. André.

"And how many more?" asked Schwartz.

"You'll find that out when you start mutinying, my friend," said Maris. "Don't fancy that all your band mean all they say."

"In fact," put in Cordier, "you aren't the only conspirators. There is also a plot *not* to mutiny, d'you see? ... And some good 'friends' of yours are in it too."

"So you'd better drop it, Schwartz," I added. "None of us is a spy, and none of us will report anything to Lejaune without telling you first and inviting you to give it up. And if you refuse--Lejaune is going to know all about it. You are simply surrounded by *real* spies, too, mind."

"You cowardly hounds!" growled Schwartz. "There isn't a *man* in the place... . *Cowards,* I say."

"Oh, quite," agreed Michael. "But we've enough pluck to stick things out while Lejaune is in command, if *you* haven't... . Anyhow--you know how things stand now," and he strolled off, followed by St. André, Maris, Cordier, and myself.

"This is a *maison de fous,*" observed St. André.

"A corner of the lunatic asylum of Hell," said Cordier.

"Some of us had better keep awake to-night, I think," observed Maris.

"Especially if Bolidar is not in his bed," I added.

Michael drew me aside.

"We'll have another word with that sportsman," he said. "I think he'll have the latest tip from the stable, and I fancy he'll believe any promise we make him."

§ 8

After completing our *astiquage* and other preparations for the morrow, Michael and I strolled in the courtyard.

"What'll Schwartz do now?" I asked.

"Probably act to-night," said Michael, "unless he swallowed our bluff that our party consists of more than us five. He may be wondering as to how many of his supposed adherents will really follow him if he starts the show... ."

"He may see how many will take a solemn oath to stand by him and see it through, if he gives the word for to-night," I suggested.

"Quite likely," agreed Michael. "And if neither Guantaio nor Bolidar knows about it, Schwartz may pull it off all right."

"I don't somehow see Lejaune taken by surprise, when he knows what's brewing," I said.

"No," replied Michael. "But he may be relying on Bolidar giving him the tip."

"What are we going to do if we wake up and find that the show has begun?" I asked.

"Stand by Lejaune," replied Michael. "France expects that every halfpenny legionary this day will do his dooty."

"It'll be too late to save Lejaune if we're awakened by rifle-shots and 'alarums and excursions without,' won't it?" I observed.

"That won't be our fault," said Michael. "If they murder Lejaune and the others, all we can do is to decline to join the mutineers."

"If we survive and they desert, I suppose the senior soldier will carry on as Commandant of the fort," I mused. That will take some deciding if only St. André, Maris, Cordier, you, and I are left... ."

"St. André has been a French officer," observed Michael.

"Yes--but they'll select you, old chap," I said.

"Then I'll use my powers to appoint St. André," smiled my brother.

Someone passed and repassed us in the dark, and then waited near the lantern by the quarter-guard, to identify us by its light.

It was Schwartz.

"See here, you," he said as he recognised us. "Come with me... . Now... . What are you going to do if someone kills Lejaune without doing himself the honour of consulting your lordships?"

"Nothing," replied Michael, as we walked away from the light. "We shall continue in our duty as soldiers. We shall obey the orders of the senior person remaining true to his salt and the Flag."

"The devil burn their filthy Flag!" snarled Schwartz. "I spit on it."

"A pity you came under it, if that's what you think," said Michael.

"Then you and your gang of cowards and blacklegs will not interfere?" asked Schwartz.

"If you will desert, you will desert," replied my brother. "That is not our affair. If we know what you are going to do, we shall report it, if we can't stop it. If we can prevent mutiny and murder we shall... . As for deserting--I should say the Legion would be well rid of you."

"Oh, you do, do you, Mr. Preacher?" replied Schwartz, who was evidently putting great and unwonted restraint upon himself. "What I want to know is whether you are going to fight us or not?"

"Certainly--if ordered to," replied Michael.

"And if there is no one to order you?" sneered Schwartz.

"Then obviously we shall not be ordered to, my good ass," was the unsoothing reply. "And we certainly shan't hinder your departure... . Far from it," he added.

Schwartz turned to go.

"Look to yourselves! I warn you! Look to yourselves," he growled.

"Oh, we shall. Don't you worry," replied Michael.

"They'll do it to-night," he added, as we watched Schwartz disappear. "We must secure our rifles and we must keep awake."

I wondered how much longer we should be able to stand this intolerable strain, in addition to the terrific heat and monotony of hardship.

"Go and look for Bolidar," said my brother after a brief silence. "I'll hunt round too. Bring him here if you find him. We'll ask him what's likely to happen if they mutiny to-night. Then we can fix up a plan of action with St. André and the others."

I went back to the barrack-room.

Bolidar was deep in conclave with Schwartz, Brandt, Haff, Vogué, Delarey, and one or two others, round Schwartz's bed.

I pretended to go to my *paquetage* for something, and then retired and reported to Michael.

"That's all right then," he said. "Whatever the fools fix up for to-night will be reported to Lejaune to-night, and he will know what to do.

"We'll have a word with Bolidar though, by and by," he added. "Nothing like knowing what's going to happen."

Half an hour later, we returned to the reeking, stifling room. Most of the men were lying on their cots. Bolidar was sitting on a bench, polishing his bayonet.

"Will you polish mine too?" I said, going over to him. "Follow me out," I whispered, as I gave him my bayonet.

I strolled back to my cot, began to undress, and then, taking my mug, went out of the room as though for water.

Watching the lighted doorway I waited in the darkness.

Ten minutes or so later, Bolidar came out.

"Well?" I asked.

"Lejaune does not believe a word about the diamond not being here," he said, "and the mutineers are going to shoot him and all the non-coms. on morning parade to-morrow instead of at night. They think he will be expecting it at night, as some informer must have told him that is the plan.... He'll be off his guard.... They are going to kill Dupré and Boldini simultaneously with Lejaune.... If your party is a big one they are going to leave you alone, if you leave them alone. They will load themselves up with water, wine, food, and ammunition, and march out at sunset.

"Blanc, who has been a sailor, is going to lead them straight over the desert to Morocco, by Lejaune's compass.... Schwartz is to be Captain; Brandt and Haff, Lieutenants; Delarey and Vogué, Sergeants; and Glock and Hartz, Corporals.... There will be twenty privates....

"They are going to court martial Guantaio, and if he is found guilty they are going to hang him.... *I* know enough to get him hung, the dirty traitor...."

"And you?" I asked.

"I am to shoot Lejaune," he replied, "to prove my sincerity and good faith. If I don't, I am to be shot myself.... Guantaio has been maligning me to Schwartz."

"Have you told Lejaune this?" I asked this astonishing creature.

"*I am just going to do so now,*" he replied, and I gasped.

"And I suppose he'll arrest them to-night?" I asked.

"Probably. *If he believes me,*" was the interesting answer.

"What if he doesn't?" I enquired, and, at that, the wretch had another "nerve-storm" or hysterical fit of trembling, with demented gesticulations and mutterings.

"What *shall* I do? What *shall* I do?" he kept on. "What *will* become of me? God help me! Help me! Help me!"

"Look here," said I. "You tell me and my brother everything--the absolute truth, mind--and we'll save you all right, provided you do nothing against us. No covering with your rifle, mind!"

He clutched my hand in his hot shaking fists.

"You stand in honestly with our party, and you'll be safe," I went on. "We'll prevent the mutiny, and nobody will be killed. Neither you nor anybody else."

I hoped I spoke the truth. Perhaps if I now told Schwartz that I knew about the new morning scheme, and assured him that Lejaune knew it too, he'd own himself defeated and give it all up. On the other hand, he might run amok, yelling to his gang to follow him... . Lejaune's prearranged plans would probably settle their business promptly. Would Lejaune then go and shoot whomsoever else he thought might be better dead?

Bolidar slunk off, and I went back to the barrack-room.

Taking my Arabic copy of the Q'ran from the shelf above my bed, I winked at Michael, and opening the book, seated myself beside him, and began to read in Arabic, as we often did.

Having read a verse, I went on in the same monotone, as though still reading, and said in Arabic:

"To-morrow. Morning. They will kill. One now goes to give information," and then went on with the next verse. I then gave the book to Michael, who followed the same plan. Soon I heard between actual verses:

"We have warned them. Say nothing. He will strike to-night. Do not sleep. I will tell our friends," and then another verse of the wisdom of the Prophet, before closing the book.

Soon after this, Bolidar entered the room and began to undress.

"What about my bayonet, you, Bolidar?" I called across to him.

"Oh--half a minute, Smith," he replied, and began polishing it.

A little later he brought it over, and as he bent over my bed to hang the weapon on its hook, whispered:

"I have not told him... . To-morrow," and went back to his place.

Under cover of the "Lights out" bugle, I repeated this to Michael.

"That's all right then," said he. "We shall have a quiet night."

And then perfect silence descended on the room as usual.

§ 9

It was an unpleasant night for me, nevertheless, for I by no means shared Michael's faith in its quiet.

What more likely, I thought, than that Lejaune should choose to-night for his anticipatory counter-stroke? He must have an iron nerve or very great faith in his spies, otherwise he could hardly continue thus to sit on the powder-barrel when the fuse was alight.

Or had he other and surer sources of information, than the tales of Bolidar, and Guantaio's reports to Boldini? Was one of Schwartz's most trusted lieutenants merely Lejaune's *agent provocateur?*

Could Schwartz himself be Lejaune's jackal? No, that was nonsense, and this horrible atmosphere of treachery and suspicion was poisoning my mind. Whereas Lejaune himself was wholly evil and was probably after Michael's fabulous jewel--patiently and remorselessly creeping towards it along a path that led through quagmires of treachery and rivers of blood--Schwartz was a comparatively honest and honourable brute, madly thirsting for vengeance upon a savage beast-tamer who had driven him to utter desperation by injustice and savage cruelty. And, save for Bolidar and Guantaio, his followers were like him, brave men of average character, de-humanised by an inhuman system and the more inhuman monster who applied it.

And why did not the monster strike! For what was he waiting, when every hour increased his danger? Surely it could not be merely the love of the fearless man for prolonging a terribly menacing and precarious situation?

Could it be that, before taking action, he really wished to know absolutely for certain what Michael and I were going to do when the mutineers rose?

Or was he waiting to be surer of Boldini or Dupré?

Of course, if he felt that in the presence of the "diamond" no reliance could be placed on either of these two colleagues, and if, as a shrewd and experienced judge of men, he estimated Bolidar and Guantaio at their true worth, or worthlessness--perhaps it was quite impossible for him to act at all. If practically every one in the garrison belonged to one of two parties--the "honest" mutineers determined to desert, or the rascally thieves determined to steal the great jewel and get away with it--what could the man do?

Was he hoping to use the thieves to fight the mutineers and to deal with the surviving party himself? Hardly that, for the mutineers greatly outnumbered the thieves.

On the other hand, could he not quite easily secure the arms of the mutineers, and arrest the men in their beds by employing the thieves? He could--but what then? The thieves would murder him and escape with the jewel--probably releasing the mutineers and organising them as the "diamond's" unsuspecting escort to Morocco. And each man of the thief-party (Boldini, Guantaio, Colonna, Gotto, and quite probably Vogué and Dupré) would hope that by good luck or more likely by good management--he would be sole survivor of the thief-party.

I tried to put myself in Lejaune's place.

What should I do if I were he, in such circumstances? If I wished first to save my life, and secondly to secure a gem of great price which I believed to be reposing in the pouch of one of the two or three men upon whom I could depend in time of trouble?

And I found it easier to ask the question than to answer it, since one party wanted my life and the other party wanted the jewel.

Having tried to put myself in Lejaune's place, I began to understand his delay in acting. He did nothing because he *could* do nothing.

I almost began to pity the man as I realised his position. He had not a soul to turn to in his loneliness and danger. Well--he was now reaping the reward of his consistent brutality to all who were his subordinates, as well as of his beastly avarice.

Hitherto he had always been backed by the immeasurable power and authority of his superiors, and could inevitably rely upon their inalienable support and unswerving approval. Now he had no superiors, and, face to face with the men whom he had so long outraged, bedevilled, and wronged, he must stand or fall alone.

And it looked as though he must fall.

Then an idea occurred to me. *Had he sent for outside help?* Was a column already on its way from Tokotu, where there were Senegalese as well as a mule-mounted company of the Legion? Was that what he was waiting for?

No. In the first place he would sooner, I felt absolutely certain, lose his life than send out an appeal for help against the very men he was supposed to command, the very men whose trembling disciplined fear of him was his chief pride and loudest boast. It would certainly be the end of all promotion for Adjudant Lejaune if he had to do such a thing as that. In the second place it might also destroy this chance of getting the fabulous gem. It was only in very troubled waters that he, in his position, could fish for that.

I decided that there had been no S.O.S. appeal from Zinderneuf to Tokotu.

I tossed and turned in my hot and uncomfortable bed as the problem tossed and turned in my hot uncomfortable brain; and my attempt to decide what I should do in Lejaune's place ended in my deciding that I simply did not know what I *could* do.

It almost seemed best for Lejaune to put himself at the head of the "honest" mutineers, arrest the thief-party, and then appeal to the others with promises of amendment in his conduct and reform of their condition... . But arrest the thieves for what? ... And suppose the mutineers laughed at the promised amelioration of their lot?

It was a hopeless *impasse*. I gave it up and turned once more on to my other side. This brought my face toward the door and there, in the doorway, stood--Lejaune.

There stood Lejaune--looking from bed to bed. He was quite alone and he held a revolver in his hand... . Whom was he going to shoot?

Was this the beginning of the end?

Without thinking, I raised myself on my elbow.

He saw me at once, and, first placing a finger to his lips, beckoned to me.

I stared in amazement.

Frowning savagely, he beckoned again, with a swift and imperious movement of his arm.

What was the idea? Was he going to murder me outside? Or was he going to tell me to fetch Michael out? In that case, had I better refuse or just spring on him, get the revolver, and ... and what? Neither murder nor mutiny was going to improve our precarious position.

As these thoughts flashed through my mind, I seized my trousers and tunic, struggled into them, and tiptoed to the door.

"Follow me," said Lejaune, and led the way to his quarters.

Closing the door of his bare, comfortless little room, and seating himself at the table, Lejaune stared at me in silence, his hot arrogant eyes glaring beneath heavy eyebrows contracted in a fierce evil-tempered frown.

"Do you and your miserable brother want to live?" he suddenly growled. "Answer me, you dog."

"On the whole, I think so, *mon Adjudant*," I replied, trying to strike a note between defiant impudence and cringing servility.

"Oh--on the whole, you do, do you?" sneered Lejaune, and again stared in silence. "Well--if you do, you'd better listen carefully to what I say, for only I can save you. D'you understand? Answer me, you swine."

"Yes, *mon Adjudant*," I replied.

"See here then, you infection," he went on, "there's some talk among those dogs, of a jewel. A diamond your gang of jewel-thieves got away with, in London. Also there is a plot among them to murder you both and steal it, and desert with it."

"Is that so, *mon Adjudant?*" said I, as he stopped.

"Don't you answer me! God smite you, you unspeakable corruption!" he roared. "Yes, it is so," he went on, mimicking me savagely, "and I know all about it, as I know everything else that is done, and said, and thought too--*thought*, I say--in this place... . Now I don't care a curse what you stole, and I don't care a curse what becomes of you and that anointed thief, your brother; but I won't have plots and plans and murders in any force under *my* command. Understand *that!* D'you hear me, sacred animal? Answer me."

"I hear you, *mon Adjudant,*" I admitted.

"Very well then," he growled. "I am going to teach these sacred curs to attend to their duty and leave diamonds and plots alone. By God, I am! To that end, I am going to detail you and your brother and a few more--say, Légionnaires St. André, Cordier, and Maris, as a Corporal's guard to arrest the ringleaders among those impudent swine. And I myself am going to attend to the business. You'll act at my personal orders, under my personal command, and you'll shoot down any man whom I tell you to shoot--as mutineering mad dogs *should* be shot. D'you hear me, you fish-faced, cod-eyed, bug-eating, dumb *crétin!* Answer me!"

"I hear you, *mon Adjudant,*" I replied.

"Well--say so then, grinning imbecile. And to put an end to this thrice-accursed nonsense, and prevent any more disturbances of this sort, your brother will hand over this diamond to me. I'll put it where no plots and plans will trouble it... . You and your cursed jewels! Wrecking discipline and causing trouble! You ought to be doing twenty years in gaol, the pair of you... . D'you hear me, blast your soul? Answer me, damn you."

"I hear you, *mon Adjudant,*" I replied.

"Very well. To-morrow morning, you and your brother and the others will have duties assigned you. You'll be given ammunition. You or your brother or both, will be put over the magazine, and will shoot anyone, except myself, who approaches it. *Anyone,* you understand, whether non-commissioned officer or *légionnaire*... . I'll teach the swine--by God, I'll teach them! ... Now then ... it was your brother I wanted, but you happened to be awake and I saw no point in entering that cage of treacherous hyenas--go and tell your brother what I have said, and as soon as I have that diamond locked for safety in the Company treasure-chest, I'll give you a chance to save your worthless lives... .

"Listen carefully now. Creep back and wake your brother, St. André, Maris, and Cordier, and tell them to get up and steal silently from the room with their rifles... . I shall be at the door with that revolver and I'll shoot *anybody*--on the first movement that I don't like... . Go! ..."

I saluted and turned about.

So the hour had come! And Lejaune was about to act! Moreover he was going to act on Bolidar's information that Michael, Maris, St. André, Cordier, and I had refused to join the mutineers, and so belonged to neither party. He was going to make us five loyal soldiers the executioners of the rebels.

He had a perfect right to order us to seize any mutineer and to shoot the man if he resisted arrest. Also it was our plain duty to obey him... .

But Michael? What would happen when Michael denied any knowledge of a diamond? How would he fare at Lejaune's hands when the mutiny had been suppressed? Lejaune's bare word was sufficient to send him to join the defeated mutineers--whether they were in the next world or in that antechamber of the next world, the Penal Battalion... .

"Make a sound--or a false move, and you'll be the first that dies--the first of many, I hope," growled Lejaune, as I crept down the passage between thick mud walls, and I felt the muzzle of his revolver jabbed into the small of my back.

The blood surged to my head, and I all but sprang round. One second's space of time for a drive at the point of his jaw--and I asked no more.

But he wouldn't give me that second, and I couldn't do much for Michael with my spine shattered by a ·450 expanding bullet. Lejaune would think as much of shooting me as he would of putting his foot on a scorpion... . And if, by any wild chance, I succeeded, and knocked him out and secured the revolver--how should we be any the better off? Boldini and his gang, and probably Dupré too, were after the "diamond," and would kill Michael to get it... .

With Lejaune following, I reached the door of our barrack-room. Here the *adjudant* halted, his revolver raised, and whispered:

"Your brother, Maris, Cordier, St. André--quick... ." I crept to Michael's bed.

What would happen if he sprang up with a shout, and roused the snoring sleepers around him? Could Lejaune overawe the lot, or would they, empty-handed, have the courage to rush him? Probably they would not. Everybody waits for a lead in a case like that.

I began whispering in Michael's ear.

"Beau, old chap! ... It's John... . Don't make a noise... . Beau, old chap! ... It's John... . Hush! Don't make a noise... ."

He woke, and was instantly alert.

"What's up?" he whispered.

"Take your tunic and trousers and boots, get your rifle, and go out. Lejaune is relying on our party. Take your bayonet... ."

He saw Lejaune in the doorway, near which was the night-lamp, and got off his cot.

I crept to St. André, and woke him in the same way.

"The *adjudant* wants us," I whispered. "He's at the door."

"Good!" said St. André. "It is time he did something."

Maris also woke quietly, and soon grasped what was wanted of him.

By the time I had roused Cordier, Michael was creeping from the room, dressed, his rifle in his hand. I saw Lejaune give him some cartridges from his bulging side-pockets. I crept out too, taking my rifle and bayonet, and Lejaune gave me ten cartridges.

"Go outside and load," he whispered. "Quick... . Then shoot any man, at once, if he sets his foot on the floor, after a warning."

We charged our magazines and stood behind Lejaune in the doorway, rifles at the ready. St. André joined us and received the same orders. Lejaune shook his fist at Maris and Cordier, and beckoned to them angrily. Not one of the sleepers stirred.

When the other two joined us, Lejaune said:

"St. André and Cordier--remain here until relieved. If any man wakes, order *silence,* cover him with your rifle, and say you'll shoot him if he leaves his bed. *Do* it at once, to any man and every man, who disobeys. Fail, and I'll shoot you myself... . Follow me, you others," and he quietly returned to his quarters.

"Guard the door, you," he said to Maris, "and shoot *anybody* who approaches. *Anybody,* I say."

"Now you, *quick*," he said, entering the room and closing the door. "Give me this wretched diamond that is the cause of all this trouble."

He glared at Michael.

"You jewel-thieves have corrupted the whole of this garrison, and are a menace to discipline. I'll take charge of it now; and then I'll take charge of some of those swine who think they can plot murder and robbery and desertion in *my* Company, by God! ... Out with it, you thieving gaolbird... . *Quick*... . Unless you want your throat cut by those mad dogs of mutineers who've fixed *your* business for this morning, at parade... . Oh yes, I know all about it... . *Quick,* I say--the Devil blast your dirty soul ..." and he shook his fist.

Michael stared back, as one lost in astonishment and wonder.

"'Diamond,' *Monsieur l'Adjudant?*" he murmured.

Lejaune's swarthy face was suffused, his eyes bulged and blazed.

"You try any tricks with me and I'll blow your filthy head off--here and now!" he roared, picking up his revolver from the table where he had laid it.

"Give me that diamond, you scurvy hound, and I'll keep it until I know whose property it is. D'you think I'm going to have the discipline of this fort spoiled by every cursed runaway jewel-thief that chooses to hide here with his swag, and tempt honest men? ... Out with it, you gallows-cheating gaol-breaker, before I put you where you belong... .*Quick!*"

"I have no diamond, *mon Adjudant,*" replied Michael quietly, and giving back look for look.

"As I could have told you, *mon Adjudant,*" I put in, "my brother has never had a diamond in his life and neither have I."

Words failed Lejaune.

I thought (and hoped) that he was going to have an apoplectic fit. His red face went purple and his eyes bulged yet more. He drew back his lips, baring his cruel-looking teeth and causing his moustache to bristle.

He raised and pointed the revolver, and I was just about to bring up my rifle, but had the presence of mind to realise that he could shoot twice with the lifted revolver, before I could even bring my rifle up to cover him. Michael did not turn a hair, and I was thankful that I, too, had sufficient restraint to stand motionless at attention. A movement would have been mutiny, and probably--death.

I felt certain that Lejaune would have shot us both, then and there (and would have searched Michael's body), but for the precarious position in which he himself stood, and the fact that he needed us alive--for the present.

At any moment we might hear the rifles of St. André and Cordier, as the mutineers rushed them. Or, at any moment, for all that Lejaune knew, the mutineers might burst into the room, headed by St. André, Cordier, and Maris, to kill him. He believed that, like Michael and me, these three were faithful--but he did not *know* they were.

He was a brave man. Situated as he was, his life hanging by a thread, he still attended to the business in hand. He turned his heavy glare from Michael to me.

"Oh? You would talk, would you?" he said, in a quiet and most sinister tone of terrible self-repression. "Well! Well! You haven't *much* more time for talking. Not *many* more words to say... . Would you like to make another remark or two before I shoot you? ... No? ... Won't you speak again, gaol-bird? A little prayer, perhaps? ..." and the scoundrel turned the revolver from Michael's face to mine, and back again to Michael's.

It was most unpleasant, the twitching finger of an infuriated homicidal maniac on the hair trigger of a loaded revolver, a yard from one's face--a maniac who longed for our deaths that he might enrich himself beyond the dreams of his own avarice!

He began to swear blasphemously, horribly, foully. All that he had learnt of vileness among the vile with whom he had consorted, he poured over us. He literally and actually foamed.

We stood like statues. He put the revolver down in front of him, the better to tear his hair with both hands.

I thought of the aborigines of the Congo over whom his power had been absolute, and whose lives and deaths were in his hand and mere questions of his profit and loss ...

And then suddenly, a thought which had been clamouring for attention for some minutes suddenly occupied my mind and brought comfort and a curious sense of security.

Of course, Lejaune would do nothing to us until the mutiny was quelled, and he was again unthreatened and supreme.

We five were his only defence, the sole support of his authority, his one chance of saving not only his life, but his reputation and career. Obviously he would not kill two-fifths nor one-fifth of his loyal troops at the moment of his greatest need. It was absurd.

And then, without thought, I did what would have been the bravest thing of my life if it had been done consciously, and with intent. I defied, insulted, and outfaced Lejaune!

"Look here, Lejaune," said I coolly, and in the manner of an Oxford undergraduate addressing an extortionate cabman or an impudent servant. "Look here, Lejaune, don't be a silly fool. Can't you understand that in about two minutes you may be hanging on that wall with bayonets through your hands--and *left* there, in a burning fort, to die? Or pinned out on the roof with the sun in your face! Don't be such an ass. We've got no diamond and you've got five good men to fight for you, more's the pity! Stop gibbering about jewels and be thankful that we five know our duty if you don't... ."

"*Very* Stout Fella," murmured my brother. "*Order of Michael* for you, John."

What would happen if the meanest slave in his palace went up to the Emperor of Abyssinia and smacked his face? ... I don't know. Nor did Lejaune, or he would have done it, I think.

Probably the Emperor would begin by gasping and feeling faint. Lejaune gasped and looked faint.

Then he sprang to his feet with a sound that was a mixture of a roar, howl, and scream. As he did so, Michael's left hand made a swift, circling swoop, passed under Lejaune's hand, and swept the revolver to the floor.

Almost as it clattered to the ground, my bayonet was at Lejaune's throat and my finger was round my trigger.

Whether Lejaune had been going to shoot or not, I do not know, but he certainly looked as though rage had destroyed the last of his sanity, and our death was all he cared about.

Anyhow, he couldn't shoot now.

"Move--and I'll kill you," I hissed dramatically, feeling like a cinema star and an ass.

Michael picked up the revolver.

"So you *are* mutineers, you beautiful loyal lying grandsons of Gadarene swine, are you?" panted Lejaune, moving his head from side to side, and drawing deep breaths as though choking.

"Not at all," said Michael calmly. "We're decent soldiers wishing to do our duty properly--not to babble about diamonds two minutes before a mutiny breaks out... . Man, don't you know the fort will be burnt, the garrison gone, and you dead (if you are lucky), in an hour's time--unless you do your job while you've a chance? ..."

"*Cré bon sang de bon jour de bon malheur de bon Dieu de Dieu de sort,*" swore Lejaune, "and I'll deal with you after this *chien d'une révolte*. But wait! You wait, my clever little friends. Hell's bells! I'll teach you one of my little lessons... . If you don't both die *en crapaudine,* by God, you shall live *en crapaudine*... ."

"Reward for saving your valuable life, I suppose," said Michael.

"You'll do that as your simple duty, my little friend. Oh, you love your duty. You are '*decent soldiers wishing to do your duty properly and not babble about diamonds,*' I believe? ... Good! Come and do your duty then. We'll see what you'll babble about afterwards, with your mouths full of salt and sand, *en crapaudine,* eh? Perhaps you'll prefer drops of water to diamonds then, eh! ... You wait... ."

He turned to me.

"And you talked about hanging on walls. And being pinned out in the sun, my little friend, eh? Will you kindly wait until I have you strapped up in a cell, *of which I alone have the key?* Perhaps it will not be I who '*jabbers about jewels*' then, eh? ... You wait... ."

"Your turn to jabber now, anyhow, Lejaune," said I wearily. "You're a fatiguing fellow. What about doing something *now,* and less of this 'waiting' business?"

The man pulled himself together, exerted his undeniably powerful will, and got the better of his immediate impulse.

"Come with me," he said quietly, and with a certain dignity. "Our real conversation is postponed until I have dealt with a few other unspeakables. We will then see what happens to those that threaten officers and point rifles at them... . Put that revolver down... ."

"Open the door, John," said Michael. I lowered my rifle and did so.

Maris, on guard outside, looked at me enquiringly. Presumably he had heard Lejaune's roars of rage.

Michael put the revolver on the table.

Lejaune took it up and strode to the open door.

"Follow me, you three," he said, and led the way to the barrack-room, without hesitating to turn his back to us.

Apparently he had complete faith in our loyalty to duty, and knew that he could depend upon us to obey any proper military order. At the door of the barrack-room stood St. André and Cordier, *faisant sentinelle.*

"Any trouble?" growled Lejaune, as they silently sprang to attention.

"No one has moved, *mon Adjudant,*" replied St. André.

"Put down your rifles," said Lejaune to us three, "and bring all arms out of this room, quickly and silently. You other two will shoot any man who leaves his bed."

We set to work, emptying the arms-rack of the Lebel rifles first, and then going from bed to bed and removing the bayonet from its hook at the head of each.

A steel bayonet-scabbard struck a tin mug, and a man sat up. It was Vogué.

"Cover him," said Lejaune, and the two rifles turned toward the startled man. He looked in the direction of the voice.

"Lie down, man," I whispered. Vogué fell back instantly and closed his eyes.

It was remarkable with what speed slumber claimed him.

On my last journey to the door, with a double armful of bayonets, the inevitable happened. One slipped and fell. As it did so, I shot out my foot. The bayonet struck it and made little noise, but my foot knocked against a cot and its occupant sprang up, blinking.

"*Himmel!* What's that?" he said.

It was Glock.

"Lie down, Glock," I whispered. "Look," and I nodded my head toward the door.

"Shoot him if he moves," said Lejaune calmly.

Glock lay down again, staring at Lejaune, as a hypnotised rabbit at a snake.

I passed on, and in another minute there was not a weapon in the room, nor was there a sound. None slept so deeply as Corporal Boldini, who was nearest to the door.

Lejaune took a key from his pocket. "Into the armoury with them, St. André, Cordier, and Maris, quick!" he said. "You, St. André, mount guard. Send the key back to me with Cordier and Maris, and shoot *instantly* any living soul that approaches the place, other than one of these four men.

"Now then," he continued to Michael and me, as the others crept off, laden with rifles, "some of these swine are awake, so keep your eyes open... . If several jump at once, shoot Schwartz and Brandt. Then Haff and Delarey. If only one man moves, leave him to me... ."

A very, very faint lightening of the darkness outside the windows showed that the false dawn was breaking. As I stared into the room, I found myself trying to recall a verse about "Dawn's left hand" being in the sky and,

> ***"Awake! for morning in the bowl of night***
>   ***Has flung the stone that puts the stars to flight;***
> ***And lo! the Hunter of the East has caught***
>   ***The Sultan's turrets in a noose of light."***

I tried to put it into Arabic, and wondered how the original sounded in the liquid Persian... . Was it "turrets" or "terrace"? ...

What sort of a stone was Lejaune about to fling into the bowl of night? ...

Would he order the four of us, when the other two returned, to open fire and begin a massacre of sleeping men!--an indiscriminate slaughter? ...

He was quite capable of it. These were mutineers who had threatened his life, and, worse still, his sacred authority and discipline.

Why should he wait, he would argue, for a court martial to do it? Besides, if he waited, there would never be a court martial. He could not permanently arrest the whole lot with only five men, and guard his prisoners, garrison his fort, carry on all the work of the place, and mount sentries, with five men. What would happen when the five slept, ate, cooked, mounted guard on the roof? It couldn't be done. It was their lives or his, and the very existence of the fort.

Perhaps he'd only shoot the ringleaders?

What should I do if Lejaune ordered me to open fire on unarmed men in their beds? What would Michael do?

What was my duty in such a case, with orders from such an officer? Private conscience said, "Absolutely impossible! Sheer murder! You are not an executioner... . Not the public hangman."

Military conscience said, "Absolutely necessary. These men are guilty of the greatest military crime. It is Lejaune'e duty to save the fort at any coat. *Your* duty is to obey your officer implicitly. If you refuse, you are a mutineer, as criminal as they."

The windows grew lighter.

Maris and Cordier crept back, their work completed. Maris gave Lejaune the key of the armoury.

"St. André is on guard over the magazine, *mon Adjudant*," whispered he, saluting.

"Good!" said Lejaune. "Maris, Brown, and Cordier, remain here. Shoot instantly any man who puts his foot to the ground. If there's a rush, shoot Schwartz first. Your own lives depend on your smartness. They're all unarmed, remember... . Come with me, you, Smith, and I'll disarm the guard and sentries... . Use your wits if you want to see daylight again."

He glared round the room.

"Aha, my little birds in a trap," he growled. "You'd plot against *me*. Me, l'Adjudant Lejaune, would you? ... Ah! ..."

I followed him down the passage.

"I'll clear that dog of a sentry off the roof first," he said. "Then there'll be no shooting down on us when I disarm the guard... ."

Leading the way, he went up the stairs that opened on to the flat roof, round which ran a thick, low, crenellated wall, embrasured for rifle-fire.

A sentry patrolled this roof at night, though the high lookout platform was not occupied, for obvious reasons, during the hours of darkness.

Lejaune relieved the sentry and posted me. He then took the man's rifle from him and ordered him to go below to the guard-room and request Sergeant Dupré to come up to the roof.

"Now," said he to me as the man went, "come here. Look," and he pointed down into the courtyard to the open door of the guard-room. "I shall order Sergeant Dupré to take the rifles of the guard and sentries, and then to send one man out of the guard-house with the lot. If any man comes out with only one rifle, shoot him at once. Shoot anybody who comes through that doorway, except a man with half a dozen rifles. And shoot to kill too."

I raised my rifle and covered the lighted doorway below me, at the other side of the courtyard.

"You understand," growled Lejaune. "The moment Sergeant Dupré enters that guard-room, after I've spoken to him, you shoot anybody who carries one rifle. A man with a rifle is a proclaimed and confessed mutineer... ."

I felt that he was right, and that it was my duty to obey him, little as I relished the idea of shooting comrades like bolting rabbits.

Should I shout, "*Drop that rifle!*" before I fired, and shoot if the man did not do it? I wondered if Lejaune would kill me if I did so.

I saw the relieved sentry cross the courtyard and enter the guard-room, and a moment later Sergeant Dupré came out.

"Watch!" growled Lejaune. "That sentry will talk, and they may make a rush."

Nothing stirred below.

Sergeant Dupré came up the stairs, out on to the roof, and saluted Lejaune.

"I want the rifles of the guard and sentries, Sergeant Dupré," said Lejaune. "Send one man, and only one, to me here, with the lot. Shoot instantly any man who hesitates for a second. No man is to leave the guard-room (except the one who carries all the rifles), or he'll be shot as he does so... ." And he pointed at me, standing with my rifle resting in an embrasure and covering the doorway below.

Sergeant Dupré saluted and turned about with a quiet, "Very good, *mon Adjudant*."

He descended the stairs and emerged into the courtyard, crossed it to the gate beneath the gate-house, and took the rifle from the sentry there. The man preceded him to the guard-room. Dupré visited the other sentries, repeating the procedure.

A minute after the Sergeant's last visit to the guard-room, a man came out. I was greatly relieved to see that he carried three or four rifles over each shoulder, the muzzles in his hands.

"Watch," growled Lejaune. "They may all rush out together now. Open rapid fire if they do," and he himself also covered the doorway with the rifle he had taken from the sentry.

The man with the rifles, one Gronau, a big stupid Alsatian, came up the stairs. I did not look round, but kept my eyes fixed on the doorway through which a yellow light (from "where the great guard-lantern guttered") struggled with that of the dawn.

I heard a clattering crash behind me and then I did look round, fully expecting to see that the man had felled Lejaune from behind.

Gronau had released the muzzles of the rifles, they had crashed down on the roof, and he was standing pointing, staring, his silly eyes goggling and his silly mouth wide open.

So obviously was he stricken by some strange vision, that Lejaune, instead of knocking him down, turned to look in the direction of his pointing hand.

I did the same.

The oasis was swarming with Arabs, swiftly and silently advancing to attack!

Even as I looked, a huge horde of camel-riders swept out to the left, another to the right, to make a detour and surround the fort on all sides. There were hundreds and hundreds of them already in sight, even in that poor light of early dawn.

Lejaune showed his mettle instantly.

"Run like Hell," he barked at Gronau. "Back with those rifles," and sent him staggering with a push. "Send Sergeant Dupré here, quick."

"Down to the barrack-room," he snapped at me. "Give the alarm. Take this key to St. André and issue the rifles. Send me the bugler. Jump, or I'll ..."

I jumped.

Even as I went, Lejaune's rifle opened rapid fire into the advancing hordes.

Rushing down the stairs and along the passage, I threw the key to St. André, who was standing like a graven image at the door of the magazine.

"*Arabs!*" I yelled. "Out with the rifles and ammunition!"

Dashing on, I came to the door of the barrack-room.

Michael was pointing his rifle at Boldini's head. Maris was covering Schwartz, and Cordier was wavering the muzzle of his rifle over the room generally. Everybody was awake, and there was a kind of whispered babel, over which rose Michael's clear and cheerful:

"Show a foot anybody who wants to die... ."

Nobody showed a foot, though all seemed to show resentment, especially Boldini, with a loaded rifle a yard from his ear.

Taking this in at a glance, I halted, drew breath and then bawled, "*Aux armes! Aux armes! Les Arbis! Les Arbis!*" and, with a shout to Michael and the other two, of:

"*Up with you--we're surrounded,*" I turned to dash back, conscious of a surge of unclad men from the beds, as their gaolers rushed after me. Whoops and yells of joy pursued us, and gleeful howls of:

"*Aux armes! Les Arbis!*" as the delighted men snatched at their clothes.

St. André staggered towards us beneath a huge bundle of rifles.

Dupré and the guard were clattering up the stairs.

As we rushed out on to the roof, Lejaune roared:

"Stand to! Stand to! Open fire at once! Rapid fire! Give them Hell, you devils! Give them Hell!" and, ordering Dupré to take command of the roof, he rushed below.

A couple of minutes later, a constant trickle of men flowed up from below, men in shirt-sleeves, men bareheaded and barefooted, men in nothing but their trousers--but every man with a full cartridge-pouch and his rifle and bayonet.

Lejaune must have worked like a fiend, for within a few minutes of Gronau's dropping of the rifles, every man in the fort was on the roof, and from every embrasure rifles poured their magazine-fire upon the yelling, swarming Arabs.

It had been a very near thing. A very close shave indeed.

But for Gronau's coming up and diverting attention from the inside of the fort to the outside, there probably would not have been a man of the garrison alive in the place by now--except those of the wounded sufficiently alive to be worth keeping for torture.

One wild swift rush in the half-light, and they would have been into the place--to find what? A disarmed garrison!

As I charged my magazine and fired, loaded and fired, loaded and fired, I wondered if these things were "chance," and Gronau's arrival and idle glance round, at the last moment that gave a chance of safety, pure accidental coincidence.

A near thing indeed--and the issue yet in doubt, for it was a surprise attack. They had got terribly close, the oasis was in their hands, and there were many hundreds of them to our little half-company.

And they were brave. There was no denying that, as they swarmed up to the walls under our well-directed rapid-fire, an Arab falling almost as often as a legionary pulled the trigger.

While hundreds, along each side, fired at our embrasures at a few score yards' range, a large band attacked the gate with stones, axes, heavy swords, and bundles of kindling-wood to burn it down.

Here Lejaune, exposing himself fearlessly, led the defence, controlling a rapid volley-fire that had terrible effect, both physical and moral, until the whole attack ceased as suddenly as it had begun, and the Touaregs, as the sun rose, completely vanished from sight, to turn the assault into a siege and to pick us off, in safety, from behind the crests of the sand-hills.

I suppose this whirlwind dawn attack lasted no more than ten minutes from the moment that the first shot was fired by Lejaune, but it had seemed like hours to me.

I had shot at least a score of men, I thought. My rifle was hot and sweating grease, and several bullets had struck the deep embrasure in which I leaned to fire.

Below, the plain was dotted over with little heaps of white or blue clothing, looking more like scattered bundles of "washing" than dead ferocious men who, a minute before, had thirsted and yelled for the blood of the infidel, and had fearlessly charged to drink it.

Our bugler blew the "Cease fire," and on the order, "Unload! Stand easy," I looked round as I straightened myself up, unloaded my rifle, and stood at ease.

It was a strange sight.

At every embrasure there was a caricature of a soldier--in some cases almost naked--at his feet a litter of spent cartridges, and, in one or two instances, a pool of blood. As I looked, one of these wild figures, wearing nothing but a shirt and trousers, slowly sank to the ground, sat a moment and then collapsed, his head striking with a heavy thud. It was Blanc, the sailor.

Lejaune strode over from his place in the middle of the roof.

"Here," he shouted. "No room nor time, yet, for shirkers," and putting his arms round the man, dragged him from the ground and jerked him heavily into the embrasure.

There he posed the body, for Blanc appeared to be dead. Into the embrasure it leaned, chest on the upward sloping parapet, and elbows wedged against the outer edges of the massive uprights of the crenellation.

Lejaune placed the rifle on the flat top of the embrasure, a dead hand under it, a dead hand clasped round the small of the butt, the heel-plate against the dead shoulder, a dead cheek leaning against the butt.

"Continue to look useful, my friend, if you can't *be* useful," he jeered; and as he turned away, he added:

"Perhaps you'll see that route to Morocco if you stare hard enough."

"Now then, Corporal Boldini," he called, "take every third man below, get them fed and properly dressed, and double back here if you hear a shot, or the 'Assembly' blown. If there's no attack, take below one-half of the rest.... Then the remainder.... Have all *klim-bim* and standing-to again in thirty minutes.... You, St. André, and Maris, more ammunition. A hundred rounds per man.... Cordier, pails of water. Fill all water-flasks and then put filled pails there above the gate.... They may try another bonfire against it.... Sergeant Dupré, no wounded whatsoever will go below. Bring up the medical panniers.... Are all prisoners out of the cells?" ...

He glared around, a competent, energetic, courageous soldier. "And where's the excellent Schwartz?" he went on. "Here, you dog, up on to that look-out platform and watch those palm trees--till the Arabs get you.... Watch that oasis, I say.... You'll have a little while up there for the thinking out of some more plots...." And he laid his hand on the butt of his revolver, as he scowled menacingly at the big German.

Schwartz sprang up the ladder leading to the high look-out platform that towered far above the roof of the fort. It was the post of danger.

"Now use your eyes, all of you," bawled Lejaune, "and shoot as soon as you see anything to shoot at."

Ten minutes or so later, Boldini returned with the men whom he had taken below, now all dressed as for morning parade. They took their places and the Corporal hurried round the roof, touching each alternate man on the shoulder.

"Fall out, and go below," he ordered.

Ten minutes or so later they were back, fed, clothed, and in their right minds. Gone like magic were all signs of *cafard,* mutiny, and madness. These were eager, happy soldiers, revelling in a fight.

With the third batch I went, hoping to be back before anything happened. Not a rifle-shot broke the stillness, as we hastily swallowed *soupe* and coffee, and tore at our bread.

"Talk about 'They came to curse and remained to pray,'" murmured Michael, with bulging cheeks. "These jolly old Arabs removed our curse and remained for us to slay. There'll be no more talk of mutiny for a while."

"Nor of anything else, old bean," I replied, "if they remain to prey."

"Never get in here," said Michael. "They couldn't take this place without guns."

"Wonder what they're doing?" I mused.

"Diggin' themselves in on the crests of the sand-hills," said Michael. "They can't rush us, so they're going to do some fancy shooting."

"Yes. What about a regular siege?" I asked. "And killing only one of us to a score of them that we kill! We should be too few to man the four walls eventually."

"What about relief from Tokotu?" suggested Michael.

"Over a hundred miles away!" I replied, "and no wires. Nor any chance to heliograph across a level desert, even if they could see so far."

"Chance for the *médaille militaire,*" grinned Michael. "Go to Lejaune and say, '*Fear not! Alone I will walk through the encircling foe and bring you relief.*' Then you walk straight through them, what?"

"Might be done at night," I mused.

"I *don't* think," said Michael. "These merry men will sit round the place in a circle like a spiritualists' *séance,* holding hands, rather than let anyone slip through them."

"Full moon too," I observed. "Anyhow, I'm very grateful to the lads for rolling up... ."

"Shame to shoot 'em," agreed Michael, and then Boldini hounded us all back to the roof, and we resumed our stations.

All was ready, and the Arabs could come again as soon as they liked.

Lejaune paced round and round the roof like a tiger in a cage.

"Hi you, there!" he called up to Schwartz. "Can you see nothing?"

"Nothing moving, *mon Adjudant,*" replied Schwartz.

A moment later he shouted something, and his voice was drowned in the rattle and crash of a sudden outbreak of rifle fire in a complete circle all round the fort. The Arabs had lined the nearest sand-hills on all sides of us, and lying flat below the crests, poured in a steady independent fire.

This was a very different thing from their first mad rush up to the very walls, when they hoped to surprise a sleeping fort and swarm up over the walls from each other's shoulders.

They were now difficult to see, and a man firing from his embrasure was as much exposed as an Arab lying flat behind a stone or in a trench scooped in the sand.

There was a man opposite to me, about a hundred yards distant, who merely appeared as a small black blob every few minutes. He must have been lying on a slope or in a shallow sand trench, and he only showed his head for a few seconds when he fired. I felt that either he or I would get hurt, sooner or later, for he, among others, was potting at my embrasure.

It was certainly "fancy shooting" as Michael had said, waiting for the small object, a man's head, to appear for five seconds at a hundred yards' range, and get a shot at it. It was certainly interesting too, and more difficult than rifle-range work, for one's nerves are not steadied nor one's aim improved by the knowledge that one is also being shot at oneself, and by several people.

With unpleasant frequency there was a sharp blow on the wall near my embrasure and sometimes the high wailing song of a ricochet, as the deflected and distorted bullet continued its flight at an angle to the line of its arrival.

The morning wore on and the sun gained rapidly in power.

Unreasonably and unreasoningly I did not expect to be hit, and I was not hit, but I was increasingly conscious of the terrific heat and of a severe headache. I wondered if high nervous tension made one more susceptible, or whether the day was really hotter than usual... .

Suddenly, the man on my right leapt back, shouted, spun round and fell to the ground, his rifle clattering at my feet.

I turned and stooped over him. It was the wretched Guantaio, shot through the middle of his face.

As I bent down, I was suddenly sent crashing against the wall, as Lejaune literally sprang at me.

"By God!" he roared. "You turn from your place again and I'll blow your head off! *Duty*, you dog! Get to your duty! What have you to do with this carrion, you cursed, slinking, cowering, hiding shirker ..." and as I turned back into my embrasure, he picked up the choking, moaning Guantaio and flung him into the place from where he had fallen.

"Stay there, you rotten dog," he shouted, "and if you slide out of it, I'll *pin* you up with bayonets through you," and he forced the dying wretch into the embrasure so that he was wedged in position, with his head and shoulders showing through the aperture between the crenellations on either side of him.

"I'll have no skulking malingerers here," he roared. "You'll all stay in those embrasures alive or *dead*, while there's an Arab in sight... ."

Suddenly the Arab fire dwindled and slackened and then ceased. Either they had had enough of our heavy and accurate fire, or else some new tactics were going to be introduced. I imagined that a camel-man had ridden all round the sand-hills, out of sight, calling the leaders to colloquy with the Emir in command.

Our bugles sounded the "Cease fire."

"Stand easy! ... Wounded lie down where they are," rang out Lejaune's voice, and some half-dozen men sank to the ground in their own blood. I was thankful to see that Michael was not among them.

Sergeant Dupré with Cordier, who had been a doctor, went to each in turn, with bandages and stimulants.

"Corporal Boldini," barked Lejaune, "take the men down in three batches. Ten minutes for *soupe* and a half-litre of wine each. Come back at the '*pas gymnastique*' if you hear the 'Assembly' blown... . St. André, replenish ammunition. Each man to have a hundred... . Stop that bandaging, Cordier, and stir yourself... ."

When my turn came, later, to go below, I was more thankful for the comparative darkness and coolness of the *caserne* than for the *soupe* and wine even, for my head was splitting.

"'*Moriturus te saluto*,'" said Cordier, as he raised his mug of wine.

"Don't talk rot," said I. "You're no more *moriturus* than--*Madame la République*."

"I shall be dead before sunset," replied Cordier. "This place will be a silent grave shortly ... ' *Madame la République--morituri te salutant!*' ..." and he drank again.

"He's fey," said Michael. "Anyhow, better to die fighting than to be done in by Lejaune afterwards.... If I go, I'd like to take that gentle *adjudant* with me... ."

"He's a topping soldier," I said.

"Great," agreed Michael. "Let's forgive him."

"We will, if he dies," said I. "I am afraid that he'll see to it that he *needs* some forgiving, if he and we survive this show, and he gets control again... ."

"Yes," said Michael. "Do you know, I believe he's torn both ways when a man's hit. The brute in him says, '*That's one for you, you damned mutineer,*' and the soldier in him says, '*One more of a tiny garrison gone.*'"

"He's a foul brute," I agreed. "He absolutely *flung* two wounded, suffering men back into their embrasures--and enjoyed doing it."

"Partly enjoyment and partly tactics," said Michael wiping his lips, and lighting a cigarette. "He's going to give the Arabs the idea that not a man has been killed. Or else that he has so many men in the fort that another takes the place of each one that falls... . The Touaregs have no field-glasses, and to them a man in an embrasure is a man... ."

"What about when there are too few to keep up any volume of fire?" I asked.

"He may hope for relief before then," hazarded Michael.

"He does," put in St. André, who had just joined us and taken a seat at the table. "Dupré told me so. The wily beggar has kept the two *goums* outside every night lately--presumably ever since he knew of the conspiracy. They had orders to go, hell for leather, to Tokotu, and say the fort was *attacked,* the moment they heard a rifle fired, *inside or out.*"

"By Jove!" I exclaimed. "Of course! He wouldn't send to Tokotu to ask for help in quelling a mutiny of his own men, before it happened--but he wouldn't mind a column arriving because a *goum* had erroneously reported an attack on the fort."

"Cunning lad!" agreed Michael. "And he knew that when the conspiracy was about to bloom and he nipped it in the bud, he'd be pretty shorthanded after it, if he should be attacked--even by a small raiding party out for a lark!"

"Yes," said Cordier. "He saved his face and he saved the fort too. If a shot had been fired at the mutineers, the *goums* would have scuttled off as ordered, and the relief-column from Tokotu would have found an heroic Lejaune cowing and guarding a gang of mutineers.... As it is, they'll know to-morrow morning, at Tokotu, that the place is invested, and they'll be here the next day."

"Question is--where shall *we* be by then!" I observed.

"In Hell, dear friends," smiled Cordier.

"Suppose the *goums* were chopped in the oasis!" said Michael. "Taken by surprise, as we were."

"What I said to Dupré!" replied Cordier. "But Lejaune was too old a bird. They camped in the oasis by day, but were ordered to be out at night, and patrol separately, one north to south on the east and the other on the west, a half-circle each, from sunset to sunrise, Dupré says ... Likely they'd have been chopped in the oasis in the daytime all right, sound asleep--but they wouldn't be caught at dawn. They were well outside the enveloping movement from the oasis when the Arabs surrounded the place, and the *goums* would be off to Tokotu at the first shot or sooner.... By the time ..."

"Up with you," shouted Boldini, and we hurried back to the roof and resumed our stations. The wounded were again in their places, one or two lying very still in them, others able to stand.

On either side of me, a dead man stood wedged into his embrasure, his rifle projecting before him, his elbows and the slope of the parapet keeping him in position.

I could see no sign of life from my side of the fort. Nothing but sand and stones over which danced the blinding aching heat-haze.

Suddenly there was a cry from Schwartz on the look-out platform.

"The palms," he shouted and pointed. "They're climbing them." He raised his rifle and fired.

Those were his last words. A volley rang out a minute later, and he fell.

Bullets were striking the wall against which I stood, upon its *inner* face. Arab marksmen had climbed to the tops of the palms of the oasis, and were firing down upon the roof. From all the sand-hills round, the circle of fire broke out again.

"Rapid fire at the palms," shouted Lejaune. "Sergeant Dupré, take half the men from the other three sides to that one. Bring those birds down from their trees quickly.... Brandt, up with you on to the look-out platform. Quick...."

I glanced round as I charged my magazine afresh. Brandt looked at the platform and then at Lejaune. Lejaune's hand went to the revolver in the holster at his belt, and Brandt climbed the ladder, and started firing as quickly as he could work the bolt of his rifle.

Michael was still on his feet, but, as I turned back, I saw his neighbour spin round and crash down, clutching with both streaming hands at his throat.

When I took another swift glance later, the man had been wedged into the embrasure and posed by Lejaune as a living defender of the fort.

Soon afterwards I heard a shout from above, and turning, saw Brandt stagger backwards on the high platform. He struck the railing, toppled over, and came with a horrible crash to the roof.

"Find a good place for that carrion, Sergeant Dupré," shouted Lejaune. "Make him ornamental if he can't be useful."

I then heard him call the name of Haff.

"Up you go, Haff," he shouted. "You're another of these brave *risque touts*. Up you go!"

Schwartz, Brandt, Haff! Doubtless the next would be Delarey and Vogué.... And then Colonna, Gotto, and Bolidar.... Guantaio was dead.... Why didn't he send Michael up there? Presumably he hoped to keep him, St. André, Cordier, Maris, and me alive until the mutineer ringleaders and the diamond-stealers were dead.... He wouldn't want to be left victorious over the Arabs, only to find himself defenceless in the hands of the mutineers and the thieves.

I glanced up at Haff and saw that he was lying behind Schwartz's body, and firing over it as though it were a parapet along the edge of the platform.

I wondered how long this second phase of the fight had lasted, and whether we could hold out till night fell and the Arabs could not see to shoot.... Would they shoot by moonlight? It was unlikely, the Arab being, as a rule, averse from any sort of night work except peaceful travelling. A dawn rush is his favourite manœuvre....

It was agony to fire my rifle, for my head ached with one of those terrible eye-strain heat-stroke pains that give the feeling that the head is opening and shutting, exposing the brain. Every explosion of my rifle was like a blow on the head with a heavy hammer. I had almost come to the end of my tether when once again the fire of the Arabs slackened and dwindled and died away.

On the "Cease fire" bugle being ordered by Lejaune, I straightened up. I looked round as the words, "Unload! Stand easy!" rang out.

Michael was all right, but a good half of the garrison was dead or dying, for quite half the men remained partly standing, partly lying, wedged into their embrasures as the others obeyed the orders shouted by Lejaune.

Among the dead were both Sergeant Dupré and Corporal Boldini, and both had been stuck up to simulate living men. Haff must be dead too, for Delarey had been sent up to the platform, and was lying flat behind a little pile of bodies.

St. André was alive, for Lejaune called out:

"St. André, take rank as Corporal. One half the men to go below for *soupe* and coffee. Double back quick if you hear the 'Assembly' blown ..." and St. André passed round the roof, touching each alternate man of those who were standing up, and saying, "Fall out, and go below."

In many embrasures was a man whom he did not touch.

Poor Cordier had spoken truly as concerned his own fate, for he remained at his post, staring out with dead eyes across the desert.

Maris was dead too. There were left three men--St. André, Michael, and myself, upon whom Lejaune could rely if the Arabs now drew off and abandoned the siege of the fort.

But this, the Arabs did not do.

Leaving a circle of what were presumably their best marksmen, to pick off any of the defenders of the fort who showed themselves, the bulk of them retired out of sight behind the oasis and sand-hills beyond it.

By Lejaune's orders, the embrasures were occupied only by the dead, the living being ordered below in small parties, for rest and food.

St. André was told to see that every man left his bed and *paquetage* as tidy as for inspection, and that the room was in perfect order. Lejaune himself never left the roof, but had *soupe,* coffee, and wine brought up to him.

To the look-out platform he sent Vogué to join the bodies of his fellow-conspirators, Schwartz, Haff, and Delarey.

Except for a crouching sentry in the middle of each wall of the roof, those who were not below, feeding and resting, sat with their backs to the wall, each beside his embrasure.

The fire of the Arab sharpshooters did no harm, and they wasted their ammunition on dead men.

And so the evening came and wore away and the moon rose.

Where we were, we lay, with permission to sleep, St. André having the duty of seeing that two sentries patrolled each wall and were changed every two hours.

By Lejaune's orders, Vogué, in the dusk before moonrise, pushed the bodies of Schwartz, Haff, and Delarey from the look-out platform to fall down to the roof. They were then posed in embrasures, as though living defenders of the fort. It seemed to give Lejaune special pleasure to thrust his half-smoked cigarette between Schwartz's teeth, and pull the dead man's *képi* rakishly to one side.

"There, my fine conspirator," said he when the body was arranged to his liking. "Stand there and do your duty satisfactorily for the first time in your life, now you're dead. Much more useful now than ever you were before."

"He's a devil! He's a devil! He's mad--*mad!* ..." groaned Vogué as he dragged the body of Delarey past me.

"Up with him! Put him over there," growled Lejaune, when Vogué had got the body in his arms. "I'll allot your corpse the place next to his, and your pipe shall be stuck between your teeth. You are fond of a pipe, friend Vogué! Helps you to think out plots, eh? ... Up with him, you dog ..." and he kept his hand on the butt of his revolver as he baited the man. He then sent him back to the look-out platform, to be a target for the Touaregs when the moon rose, or the sun, if he lived to see it... .

I had a talk with Michael when our turn came to go below for a rest and food.

"Looks like a thin time to-morrow," said Michael. "If they pot a few of us and then rush, they should get in."

"Yes," I agreed. "They ought to keep up a heavy fire while their ammunition lasts, and then charge on camels in one fell swoop. And then climb up from the backs of the camels. A lot would be killed but a bigger lot would get in."

"Don't give them the tip, anyhow," grinned Michael. "Two or three hundred of the devils inside the place, and it would be a short life and a merry for the half-dozen or so of us who were left by that time... ."

"If we can stand them off to-morrow, the relief from Tokotu ought to roll up the next morning," I said.

"If either of those *goums* got away and played the game," agreed Michael. "They may have been pinched though... . The relief will find a thin house here, if they do come... . It'll mean a commission for Lejaune all right."

"Nice if he's confirmed in command here, and we survive!" I remarked.

"Yes," said Michael, "and talking of which, look here, old son. If I take the knock and you don't, I want you to do something for me... . Something *most* important ... what?"

"You can rely on me, Beau," I said.

"I know I can, John," he replied. "There's some letters. A funny *public* sort of letter, a letter for Claudia, and one for you, and one for Digby, in my belt--and there's a letter and a tiny packet for Aunt Patricia. If you possibly can, old chap, get that letter and packet to Aunt. No hurry about it--*but get it to her*. See? *Especially the letter*. The packet doesn't much matter, and it contains nothing of any value, but I'd die a lot more comfortable if I knew that Aunt Patricia was going to get that letter after my death... ."

"Oh, shut it, Beau," I said roughly. "Your number's not up yet. Don't talk rot."

"I'm only asking you to do something *if* I'm pipped," said Michael.

"And, of course, I'll do it if I'm alive," I replied... . "But suppose we're both killed?"

"Well--the things are addressed and stamped, and it's usual to forward such letters and packets found on dead soldiers, as you know. Depends on what happens... . If we die and Lejaune survives, I doubt their being dispatched. Or rather, I don't doubt at all... . Or if the Arabs get in, there's not much chance of anything surviving... . But if we're both killed and the relief gets in here before the Arabs do, the officer in charge would do the usual thing... . Anyhow, we can only hope for the best... .

"Anything I can do for you if it's the other way round, John?" he added.

"Well, love to Dig, you know, and there's a letter for Isobel, and you might write to her if ever you get back to civilisation and say we babbled of her, and sang, '*Just before the battle, Mother,*' and '*Bring a flower from Maggie's grave*' and all that... ."

Michael grinned.

"I'll say the right things about you to Isobel, old son," he said, "and if otherwise, you'll see that Aunt gets my letter, eh? Be sure I'm dead though... . I mean if I were captured alive by Arabs, or anything humorous like that, I don't want her to get it while I'm alive... . Of course, all five of the letters are important, but I *do* want Aunt to get hers... ."

And then St. André ordered our little party up to the roof, and brought down the other one.

The Arabs had ceased their desultory firing, and might have been a hundred miles away. Only the sight of a little smoke from their camp-fires and the occasional scent of the burning camel-dung and wood betrayed their presence, for none were in sight, and they made no sound. No one doubted, however, that a very complete chain of watchful sentries ringed us round, and made it utterly impossible for anyone to leave the fort and bring help to his besieged comrades.

The fact that Lejaune sent no one to make the attempt seemed to confirm the story that Dupré had told Cordier as they bandaged the wounded, and to show that Lejaune believed that the *goums* had got away.

It would be a wellnigh hopeless enterprise, but there was just a chance in a thousand that a daring and skilful scout might be able to crawl to where their camels were, and get away on one. Nor was Lejaune the man to take any count of the fact that it was almost certain torture and death for the man who attempted it.

I decided that, on the one hand, he felt pretty sure the *goums* had got away to Tokotu directly the Arabs appeared, and that, on the other hand, the two or three men whom he could trust were just the men whom he could not spare.

Unless St. André, Michael, and I were with him, his fate would be the same whether he drove the Arabs off or not, and doubtless he would rather go down fighting Arabs, than be murdered by his own men.

I was ordered on duty as sentry, and, for two hours, patrolled my side of the roof with my eyes on the moonlit desert, where nothing moved and whence no sound came.

When relieved, I had a little chat with St. André after he had posted my relief.

"Dawn will be the dangerous time; they'll rush us then," he said, "and it will want quick shooting to keep them down if they come all together and on all four sides at once. They must be a hundred to one... . I wonder if they'll bring ropes and poles, or ride their camels right up to the walls... ."

"If they don't count the cost, I don't see how we can keep them out," I said.

"Nothing could keep them out," replied St. André. "But if they fail at dawn they won't try again until the next dawn. They'll just pepper us all day and tire us out... . They think they have all the time they want."

"Haven't they?" I asked.

"No," replied St. André. "Lejaune is certain that one of the *goums* got away. The Arabs couldn't get them *both,* he says, as they were at opposite sides of the fort, and half a mile apart always, at night."

"What about their ammunition!" I asked. "The Touaregs', I mean."

"The more they spend the more determined they'll be to get ours, and the more likely to put their money on a swift dawn-rush with cold steel... ."

I lay down and fell asleep, to be awakened by the bugle and Lejaune's shout of "*Stand to!*"

There was no sign of dawn and none of the Arabs.

From the centre of the roof, Lejaune addressed the diminished garrison of Fort Zinderneuf.

"Now, my merry birds," said he, "you're going to *sing,* and sing like the happy joyous larks you are. We'll let our Arab friends know that we're not only awake, but also merry and bright. Now then--the *Marching Song of the Legion* first. All together, you warbling water-rats--*Now.*" And led by his powerful bellow, we sang at the tops of our voices.

Through the Legion's extensive repertoire he took us, and between songs the bugler blew every call that he knew.

"Now *laugh,* you merry, happy, jolly, care-free, humorous swine. *Laugh....* You, Vogué, up there--roar with laughter, or I'll make you roar with pain, by God... . Out with it. *Now...* ."

A wretched laugh, like that of a hungry hyena, came down from the look-out platform.

It was so mirthless a miserable cackle, and so ludicrous, that we laughed genuinely.

"Again, you grinning dog," roared Lejaune. "Laugh till your sides ache, you gibbering jackal. Laugh till the tears run down your horrible face, you shivering she-ass. Laugh! ... *Now...* ."

Again the hideous quavering travesty of a laugh rang out, and the men below roared heartily at the ridiculous noise.

"Now then, you twittering sniggering *soupe*-snatchers, laugh in turn," shouted Lejaune. "From the right you start, Gotto."

Gotto put up a pretty good roar.

"Now beat *that,* next. Out with it, or, by God, I'll give you something to laugh at," Lejaune continued.

And so round that circle of doomed men, among the dead men, ran the crazy laughter, the doomed howling noisily, the dead smiling secretly out to the illuminated silent desert.

"Now all together with me," roared Lejaune, and great guffaws rang out, desecrating the silence and the beauty of the moonlit scene.

It was the maddest, most incredible business--that horrible laughter among the dead, from men about to die.

Certainly the Arabs must have thought us mad and certainly they were not far wrong. Anyhow, they knew we were awake and must have gathered that we were cheerful and defiant.

For Lejaune was justified of his madness, and no dawn attack came.

Whether the Touaregs regarded us as "The afflicted of Allah," and feared to rush the place, or whether they realised that there could be no element of surprise in the attack, I do not know, but it was never made.

And when the sun rose and they again lined the sand-hills and opened their heavy fire upon the fort, every embrasure was occupied by an apparently unkillable man, and every Arab who exposed himself paid the penalty.

But not all those who lined the walls of Zinderneuf were beyond scathe by Arab bullets. Now and then there would be a cry, an oath, a gurgling grunt or cough, and a man would stagger back and fall, or die where he crouched, a bullet through his brain.

And, in every case, Lejaune would prop and pose and arrange the body, dead or dying, in the embrasure whence it had fallen, and to the distant Arab eyes it must have seemed that the number of the defenders was undiminished.

As the morning wore on, Lejaune took a rifle, and, crouching beside each dead man in turn, fired several shots from each embrasure, adding to the illusion that the dead were alive, as well as to the volume of fire.

Later still, he set one man to each wall to do the same thing, to pass continually up and down, firing from behind the dead.

When the Arab fire again slackened and then ceased, toward midday, and our bugle blew the "*Cease fire,*" I hardly dared to turn round.

With a sigh of relief, I saw Michael among the few who rose from their embrasures at the order "*Stand easy.*"

It was a terribly tiny band. Of all those who had sprung from their beds with cries of joy, at the shout of "*Aux armes!*" yesterday morning, only Lejaune, St. André, Michael, Colonna, Marigny, Vogué, Moscowski, Gotto, Vaerren, and I were still alive.

The end was inevitable, unless relief came from Tokotu before the Arabs assaulted the place. All they had to do now, was to run in and climb. Ten men cannot hold back a thousand.

If we survived to see the arrival of a relieving force it would be the dead who saved us, these dead who gave the impression of a numerous, fearless, ever-watchful garrison, who would cause an attack across open ground to wither beneath the blast of their rifles like grass beneath a flame.

"Half the men below, for *soupe* and coffee and half a litre of wine, Corporal St. André," ordered Lejaune. "Back as soon as you can--or if the '*Assembly*' is blown ..." and St. André took each alternate man.

Soon coffee and *soupe* were ready, although the cook was dead, and we sat at table as though in a dream, surrounded by the tidy beds of dead men.

"Last lap!" said Michael, as I gave him a cigarette. "Last cigarette! Last bowl of *soupe!* Last mug of coffee! Last swig of wine! Well, well! It's as good an end as any--if a bit early... . Look out for the letter, Johnny," and he patted the front of his sash.

"Oh, come off it," I growled. "Last nothing. The relief is half-way here by now."

"Hope so," replied Michael. "But I don't greatly care, old son. So long as you see about the letter for me."

"Why *I*, rather than you, Beau?" I asked. "Just as likely that you do my posting for me."

"Don't know, Johnny. Just feel it in my bones," he replied. "I feel I'm in for it and you're not, and thank the Lord for the latter, old chap," and he gave my arm a little squeeze above the elbow. (His little grip of my arm, and squeeze, had been one of my greatest rewards and pleasures, all my life.)

As we returned to the roof at the end of our meal, Michael held out his hand to me.

"Well, good-bye, dear old Johnny," he said. "I wish to God I hadn't dragged you into this--but I think you'll come out all right. Give my love to Dig."

I wrung his hand.

"Good-bye, Beau," I replied. "Or rather, *au 'voir*... . Of course, you didn't 'drag' me into this. I had as much right to assume the blame for the theft of the 'Blue Water' as you and Dig had... . And it's been a great lark... ."

He patted my shoulder as we clattered up the stairs.

Lejaune assigned one side of the roof to Michael and the opposite one to me. Vogué and Vaerren respectively were sent to the other two. Our orders were to patrol the wall and shoot from behind a dead man, if we saw an Arab.

St. André took Colonna, Marigny, Moscowski, and Gotto below.

Lejaune himself went up to the look-out platform with his field-glasses and swept the horizon in the direction of Tokotu. Apparently he saw no sign of help.

Nothing moved on the sand-hills on my side of the fort, and I watched them over the heads of my dead comrades... .

How much longer could this last?

Would the Touaregs draw off from this fort-with-an-inexhaustible-garrison?

Would the relief come in time! If not, would they be in time to avenge us? It would be amusing if the Arabs, having got into the fort, were caught in it by the Senegalese and mounted troops from Tokotu--a poetic justice--for not a man of them would escape!

Where *did* all the flies come from? ... Horrible! ...

St. André and his party returned to the roof, and now two men were posted to each wall, St. André and Lejaune remaining in the centre of the roof to support whichever side of the fort should need it most when the attack came.

When it did come, it was a repetition of the siege-tactics and attrition warfare, a desultory fire of sharpshooters, and most of it aimed at the dead.

Up and down his half of the wall, each of the defenders hurried, firing from a different embrasure each time.

The Arabs must have been completely deceived, for they came no nearer, and fired impartially at the silent corpse-guarded embrasures and at those from which our eight rifles cracked.

Glancing round, as I darted from one embrasure to another, I saw that both Lejaune and St. André were in the firing-line now, and that Lejaune had one wall of the fort to himself. There were only seven of us left. Michael was among them.

The Arab fire died down.

Lejaune himself picked up the bugle and sounded the "*Cease fire.*" I saw that Vogué, Moscowski, and Marigny were dead and propped up in their places. St. André was dabbing his face with a rag, where a bullet had torn his cheek and ear.

Colonna, Gotto, and I were sent below to get food, and we spoke not a single word. When we returned, Michael, Vaerren, and St. André went down in their turn.

Lejaune walked up and down the roof, humming "*C'est la reine Pomaré,*" to all appearance cool and unconcerned.

Not an Arab was to be seen, and not a shot was fired.

I wondered whether they withdrew for meals or for prayers--or whether they fired so many rounds per man from their trenches on the sand-hills, and then awaited their reliefs from the oasis.

Certainly it was a leisurely little war--on their side; and no doubt they were well advised to conduct it so. They must have lost terribly in their first attack, and they had learnt wisdom.

A shot rang out.

"*Stand to!*" shouted Lejaune, and blew the "*Assembly*" two or three times, as though calling up reserves from below to the already well-manned walls.

That fort and its garrison must have been a sore puzzle to the gentle Touareg.

The firing recommenced and grew hotter, and an ominous change took place in the Arab tactics.

While a heavy fire was maintained from the crests of the sand-hills, men crawled forward *en tirailleur* and scratched shallow holes in the sand, behind stones.... Nearer and nearer they came.... They were going to assault again.

I rushed from embrasure to embrasure, up and down my side of the roof, pausing only just long enough to bring my fore-sight on to an Arab. Time after time I saw that I hit one of the running or crouching crawling figures drawing ever closer to the wall.

Lejaune was like a man possessed, loading and firing, dashing from place to place, and rushing from one side of the fort to the other, to empty the magazine of his rifle....

Why from one side to the other? ... As I loaded and fired, emptied and recharged my magazine, I found myself asking this question.

Glancing round, I saw the reason. There was no one defending the two walls that ran to left and right of mine.

Lejaune was firing a burst from one, and then dashing across to the other--defending two walls at once.

Only one man was defending the wall behind me. Swiftly I looked across.

It was not Michael....

Only Lejaune, St. André, and I were on our feet.

This was the end....

Michael was gone--but I should follow him in a minute.

Cramming another clip of cartridges into my hot rifle, I looked across again.

The opposite wall was now undefended.

Rushing across the roof from left to right, Lejaune shouted:

"Both walls, damn you! To and fro, curse you! Shoot like hell, blast you!" and I dashed across and emptied my magazine from that side, a shot from a different embrasure each time.

Back again I ran, and got off a burst of fire along the opposite wall.

And so Lejaune and I *(Lejaune and I!)* held Fort Zinderneuf for a while, two against a thousand.

And when I was nearly spent, panting like a hunted fox, dripping with sweat, and nearly blind with eye-strain and headache, the Arab fire again dwindled and died, and there was perfect silence--an incredible dreadful silence, after those hours of deafening racket.

"Go below, you, quick!" shouted Lejaune, pointing to the stairs. "Boil coffee and *soupe,* and bring them here. Double back, quick, the moment a shot is fired. They may be at us again in a few minutes.... If we keep them off till dark, we're saved...."

"Hurry, you swine," he roared, as I stood staring at where Michael lay on his face in a pool of blood.

I dragged myself to the stairs as Lejaune cursed me.

As I went down them I heard him merrily blowing the "*Cease fire,*" and bawling fierce orders to imaginary defenders of the fort.

I stumbled to the cook-house.

"*Keep them off till dark and we're saved,*" did he say?

I hadn't the very faintest desire to be saved. Why should I be saved when Michael lay there so still?

As I struck a match to light the oil-stove, I thought I heard a shot. Rushing back up the stairs, I saw that Lejaune was posing a corpse in an embrasure. One body still lay where it had fallen.

It was Michael's.

I must have been mistaken as to hearing the sound of a shot. At any rate all was silent now, and Lejaune, his back to me, was fitting the dead man's rifle to his shoulder and clasping the dead left hand round the barrel.

I turned and crept back to my duties as cook, placed twigs and wood beneath the *soupe*-kettle, and turned up the wick of the oil-stove... .

And as I watched the fire burn up, I imagined Lejaune posing Michael's body--perhaps long before life was out of it... . The thought was unbearable.

He might be in agony.

He might be so wounded that his life could be saved if he lay flat. Not all the killed had been killed outright--though many of them had died immediately, as only their heads were exposed and their wounds were in the brain or throat.

There was really no more reason why Michael should be spared than any of the others should be--but he was my dearly-loved brother, and I simply could not bear it. I could not have his poor wounded body flung about like a sack of potatoes, and stuck up by the jeering Lejaune with indignities and insults.

He might not yet be dead, and his life might depend on what I did now! I turned to run upstairs.

Was I then going to mutiny after all? Was I going to defy my superior officer and tell him what he should, and what he should not, do in the fort that he commanded?

Was I going to tell him that Michael was of superior clay and not to be treated as all the others had been treated?

I was.

And as I ran up the stairs, another thought struck me.

Michael's last request and instructions! I must get those letters and the little packet that he had spoken about. I must say to Lejaune:

"I'll fight till I drop, and I'll obey you implicitly--but leave my brother's body alone--leave it to me... ."

After all, things were a little different now.

Lejaune and I were the only survivors. We had passed through Hell unscathed, and, at the last, two against a thousand, had kept the Flag flying.

Surely he could be decent now, unbend a little, and behave as a man and a comrade... .

As I came out on to the roof, Lejaune was bending over Michael.

He had unfastened my brother's tunic, torn the lining out of his *képi*, removed his sash, and opened the flat pouch that formed part of the money-belt that Michael wore.

Lying beside Lejaune, were three or four letters, and a torn envelope. In his hands were a tiny packet, bound up in string and sealing-wax, and an opened letter.

I sprang toward him, seeing red, my whole soul ablaze with indignant rage that this foul vulturous thief should rob the dead, rob a soldier who had fought beside him thus--a brave man who had probably saved his life, before the fight began.

"So he '*had no diamond*,' had he? Didn't know what I meant, didn't he?" the ruffian jeered, holding up the packet and the letter in his left hand.

"You damned thief! You foul pariah-dog!" I shouted, and, in a second, his revolver was at my face.

"Stand back, you swine," he growled. "Back further. Back, I say... ."

One movement, and I should be dead.

And a good thing too, but I had a word or two to say first. As I stepped back, he lowered the revolver and smiled horribly... .

"I didn't know that *men* crept round robbing the dead, after a fight, Lejaune," I said. "I thought that was left to Arab women--of the vilest sort... . You dirty thieving cur--you should be picking over dust-bins in the Paris gutters, not defiling an honourable uniform--*chiffonnier!* ..."

Lejaune bared his teeth and laughed unpleasantly.

"A fine funeral oration from a jewel-thief!" he snarled. "Any more grand sentiments before I blow out what brains you have? No? Well, I think I promised you that I would attend to you, all in good time. Now I'm going to do it... . I am going to shoot you now, where you stand. Half a dozen through the stomach, shall we say? I don't want to hurry you unduly out of this pleasant world... . Oh no, don't think I want you any longer. The Arabs won't attack again to-day, and they've settled all my mutineers nicely for me... . And a relief-column will arrive at dawn... . Then you and the rest of these cursed dogs will be given a hole in the sand for the lot of you--and I shall get the Cross of the Legion of Honour, a Captain's commission, and a trip to Paris to receive thanks and decoration... . And at Paris, my chatty little friend, I shall dispose of this trifle that your gang so kindly brought to the Legion for me!" and he again held up the little packet in his left hand.

"A rich man, thanks to you--and to *this* ..." and as he said the last word, he actually kicked Michael's body!

Even as I snatched at my sword-bayonet, and leapt forward--in the instant that my dazed and weary mind took in the incredible fact of this brutal kick--it also took in another fact even more incredible--*Michael's eyes were open, and turned to me.*

Michael was alive! ... I would live too, if possible... . My hand, still grasping my bayonet, fell to my side.

"Good!" said Lejaune. "Armed attack on a superior officer--and in the face of the enemy! ... Excellent! I court martial you myself. I find you guilty and I sentence you to *death*... . I also carry out the sentence myself... . *Thus* ..." and the revolver travelled slowly from my face to the pit of my stomach.

"*There!* ..."

As Lejaune had spoken, Michael's right hand had moved. As the last word was uttered, the hand seized Lejaune's foot, jerking him from his balance, as he pulled the trigger in the act of looking down and of stumbling.

Blinded, deafened, and dazed, I leapt and lunged with all my strength and drove my bayonet through Lejaune. I stumbled, and it was torn from my hand. When I could see again (for I must have ducked straight at the revolver as he fired it, or else he must have raised it as his foot was pulled from under him), he was lying on his back, twitching, the handle of the bayonet protruding from his chest, the blade through his heart.

Lejaune was dead, and *I* was the mutineer and murderer after all! *I* was the "butcher" and *Lejaune* the "pig."

CHAPTER VI. A "VIKING'S FUNERAL"

"All night long, in a dream untroubled of hope,
He brooded, clasping his knees."

I stooped over Michael, whose eyes were closed again. Was he dead--his last act the saving of my life?

I don't think I felt very much, at the moment. My mind was numb or blank, and I wasn't certain that the whole affair was not a nightmare... .

Michael opened his eyes.

"Stout Fella," he whispered. "Got the letters?"

I told him that he would deliver them in person. That we were the sole survivors. That the relief would come soon and we should be promoted and decorated.

"For stabbing Lejaune!" he smiled. "Listen, Johnny... . I'm for it, all right. Bled white... . Listen... . I never stole anything in my life... . Tell Dig I said so, and *do* get the letter to Aunt Patricia... . You mustn't wait for the relief... . Lejaune's body... . They'd shoot you... . Get a camel and save yourself... . In the dark to-night... . If you can't get away, say I killed Lejaune... . I helped to, anyhow ..."

I do not know what I said.

"No. Listen... . Those letters... . You are to leave one on me... . Leave it in my hand... . Confession... . Do the thing thoroughly... . No need for you and Dig to carry on with the game now... . You must get the confession published or it's all spoilt... ."

"You've nothing to confess, Beau, old chap," I said... . "Half a minute, I'm going to get some brandy... ."

His fingers closed weakly on my sleeve.

"Don't be an ass, Johnny," he whispered. "Confession's the whole thing... . Leave it where it'll be found or I'll haunt you... . Gnaw your neck and go '*Boo*' in the dark... . No, don't go... . Promise... . God! *I'm going blind...* . John ... John... . Where are you? ... Promise... . Confession... . John ... John ..."

Within two minutes of his seizing Lejaune's foot and saving my life, my brother was dead... . My splendid, noble, great-hearted Beau... .

I have not the gift of tears. I have not cried since I was a baby, and the relief of tears was denied me now.

No. I could not weep. But I looked at the revolver, still clutched in Lejaune's right hand... . It was only a momentary temptation, for I had something to do for Michael. His last words had laid a charge on me, and I would no more fail Michael dead, than I would have failed him when he lived.

Michael's affairs first--and if the Touaregs rushed the place while I attended to them, I would just take Lejaune's revolver and make a good end. I ought to get five of them, and perhaps might grab one of their heavy straight swords and show them something.... .

I turned to the letters.

One of them was addressed to Lady Brandon. She should get it, if I had the ingenuity, courage, and skill to keep myself alive long enough. One was addressed to Claudia. That too... . There was one for me, and one for Digby. And there was another, crushed up in Lejaune's left hand. The envelope from which he had torn it lay near. It was addressed to *The Commissioner of Police, Scotland Yard, London, England*. Poor Michael's "confession" of something he had never done! I was sorely tempted to destroy it, but his words were still in my ears, urgent and beseeching. *I was to see that the "confession" was published.*

Well--let it remain where it was. It would get a wide-enough publicity if it were found in the dead hand of the murdered Commandant of a beleaguered fort.... . I picked up the packet that Lejaune had dropped when I struck him, and put it with the three letters into my pocket. I then opened the one addressed to me. It ran as follows:--

"*My dear John,*

When you get this, take the letters that are with it to Brandon Abbas, as soon as you can. Send them if you can't take them. The one for Aunt Patricia solves the Mystery of the 'Blue Water,' at any rate to HER *satisfaction, and she can publish the solution or not, as she thinks fit, later on.... . After Uncle Hector's death, for example.... . Meanwhile, I beg and beseech and instruct and order you, to see that the letter addressed to the Chief of Police is not burked. It is exactly what we all bolted for--this averting suspicion from innocent people (including your Isobel, don't forget, Johnny boy!). We took the blame between us, and the first of us to die should shoulder the lot, of course, so that the other two can go home again. You or Dig would do this for his brothers, and so will I, if I pip first. So off with the home letters--*HOME, *and see that the other one gets into the papers and into the hands of the police and all that. I have written an absolutely identical letter to this for Digby too, so I am sure that one or both of you will see that my wishes are carried out. No nonsense about* 'DE MORTUIS NIL NISI BONUM,' *mind. It is the living we have to think about, so do exactly as I tell you. You'll be doing the best for me, as a matter of fact, as well as for the living, if you carry out what I ask--so* GO TO IT, PUP.

If I outlive you, I shall do the same by you or Dig, SO GO TO IT.

You spoilt my plans by your balmy quixotic conduct in bunking from home--now put them right by doing exactly as I say.

Good-bye, dear old stoutest of Stout Fellas. See you in the Happy Hunting Grounds.

Beau.

P.S.--Don't come near me there, though, if you destroy that confession."

I put the letter down and looked at his face. Peaceful, strong, dignified, and etherealised beyond its usual fineness and beauty.... . I closed his eyes and folded his hands upon his chest.... .

How *could* I let this thing happen--let the world have confirmation of the suspicion that Michael was a despicable mean thief? Or rather, how could I publish to a world that knew little or nothing about the affair, that Michael had done such a miserable deed?

I looked at his face again.

How could I disobey his last instructions, refuse his last request?

Nor was it a request made impulsively, on the spur of the moment. He had thought it all out, and written it down long ago, in case of just such an event as had happened--his predeceasing us... .

What would Digby do in my position? Would he take that paper from Lejaune's hand and destroy it? I felt he would not. He *could* not, had he been present at Michael's death, and heard his dying words... . Not having done so, would he blame me if I left that confession there, to be found by the relieving force?

Well--if he did, he must, and I must act according to my own light--if I could find any... .

And suppose the Arabs assaulted again, before the relief arrived?

That would settle the problem quite finally, for they would loot the place, mutilate the dead, and then make the fort the funeral pyre of the mangled corpses... .

I found myself wishing they would do so, and then saw the cowardice of my wish.

No, it was my affair now to--to--to ... I actually found that I was nodding, and had all but fallen backwards as I sat!

In fact, a heavy faintness, an unspeakable weariness, formed the only sensation of which my mind or body was now conscious. I had seen too much, done too much, suffered too much, felt too much, in the last few hours, to have any other feeling left, save that of utter exhaustion. I felt that I could die, but could not sleep.

In the very act of pulling myself together and saying that *this* would not do, I must have fallen into a state of semicoma that was not sleep.

I shook it off, to find that a new day was dawning, and, for a minute, I gazed around at the extraordinary sight that met my eyes--the bloodstained roof, the mounds of cartridge-cases, the stiff figures crouching in the embrasures, the body of Lejaune with the handle of my bayonet protruding from his chest; and Michael's calm smiling face, as noble in death as in life... .

"I must go, Beau, old chap," I said aloud, "if I am to get your letter and parcel to Aunt Patricia and tell them of your heroic death."

I knelt and kissed him, for the first time since babyhood.

And only then, actually not till then, I remembered the Arabs!

There was no sign of them whatsoever, alive or dead, which may partly account for my having completely forgotten their existence... .

I should not be doing much toward carrying out Michael's wishes if I walked straight into their hands. Nor was death any less certain if I remained in the fort till relief came, and Lejaune's body was found with my bayonet in it.

Idly I supposed that I might remove it and replace it by that of another man, and blame him for the murder. I had not the faintest intention of doing so, of course, nor would my tale have been very convincing, since I was alive and everybody else neatly disposed and arranged, *after* death. It did occur to me that perhaps I could pretend that I was the hero of the whole defence, and had posed all these corpses myself, including that of the man who had murdered Lejaune, but, of course, I did not seriously consider the idea.

No. Unless I wanted to die, I must evade both the Arabs and the relieving force from Tokotu. If I could do that, I must, thereafter, evade the entire population of the desert between Zinderneuf and safety, as well as evading any avenging search-party that might be sent out after me. There were also the little matters of thirst, starvation, and exposure. All I could do in the way of preparation in that direction would be to load myself with food, water, spare boots, and ammunition.

Rising to my feet, I wearily dragged myself down the stairs and filled and relit the oil-stove. While the kettle was boiling for coffee, I foraged round, filled my water-bottle with water and three big wine-bottles with the same liquid. Water was going to be infinitely more precious than any wine, before I was much older. I also emptied my knapsack and haversack of everything but a pair of boots, and filled them to bursting, with bread, coffee, and the bottles of water.

I thought my best plan would be to load myself up to the weight I was accustomed to, but to let my burden consist of food and water. This would grow lighter as I grew weaker--or I should grow weaker as it grew lighter. Anyhow, it seemed the best thing to do, but how I longed for a camel! The thought occurred to me that if the relief did not arrive that day, I could remain in the fort till night, and then try to get one of the Arabs' camels when it was dark. A moment's reflection, however, made it clear that if the relief did not enter the fort pretty soon, the Arabs would.

The sooner I got away, the better chance I should have of doing it successfully.

I ate and drank all I could, shouldered my burdens and returned to the roof for a last look round. If I could see anything of the Arabs in one direction I could, at least, try to get away in the opposite quarter. If not, I must simply trust to luck, and crawl off in the direction opposite to the oasis, as being the likeliest one to offer a chance of escape.

I gazed round in all directions. There still was no sign of an Arab, though, of course, there might have been any number beyond the oasis, or behind the sand-hills that surrounded the fort.

I glanced at Lejaune. Should I remove my bayonet from its place in his evil heart?

No. My whole soul revolted from the idea... . And as for any hope of concealing the manner of his death, it would still be perfectly obvious that he had been stabbed by a comrade and not shot by the enemy.

Besides, I had killed him in self-defence--self-defence from as cold-blooded, dastardly, and criminal a murder as a man could commit.

No. Let the righteously-used bayonet stay where it was--and incidentally I had quite enough to carry without the now useless thing... .

"Good-bye, Beau," I said, crossing to where he lay--and, as I spoke, I almost jumped, for the brooding silence was broken by a shot, followed by several others... .

The Arabs? ... No--these were neither rifle shots nor fired towards the fort. The sound of them made that quite evident.

Crouching, I ran to the side of the roof and looked.

On a distant sand-hill was a man on a camel, a man in uniform, waving his arm above his head and firing his revolver in the air.

It was a French officer.

The relief had arrived from Tokotu, and I must escape or be tried, and shot, for the murder of my superior officer in the very presence of the enemy... .

Yes--but what about this same enemy? Where were they? Was that fine fellow riding to death and torture? Straight into an ambush, a trap of which the uncaptured fort with its flying flag was the bait? That might well be the explanation of there having been no dawn-assault that morning, while I slept. They might, with Arab cunning, have decided that it would be a much better plan to maintain the siege, unseen and unheard, and lure the relieving force, by an appearance of peace and safety, into marching gaily into an oasis covered by hundreds of rifles lining neighbouring sand-hills. They could massacre the relief-column and then turn to the fort again. If no relief-force came, they could still assault the fort whenever they thought fit... .

As these thoughts flashed through my mind, I decided that I must warn that man, riding gaily to his death, deceived by the peaceful quiet of the scene, and the floating Tri-couleur at the flagstaff top. Seeing the walls lined, as they were, with soldiers, the Flag floating above them, and no sign of any enemy, he would at once conclude that we had long since driven them off.

Obviously this must be the case, or he would have heard sounds of rifle-fire, miles away, he would think.

I must warn him, for I had no doubt, in my own mind, that hundreds of Arab eyes were watching him.

Nor was it this man alone, rejoicing there in our safety. A whole column must be close behind him. Comrades of ours who had marched day and night to our relief. Of course, I could not let them walk into the trap, deceived by the very ruse that had deceived the Arabs... .

This officer was no fool, doubtless, but how was he to know that the fort was a whited sepulchre, tenanted by the dead, unable to signal to him that he was walking into an ambush with his column? Naturally he would assume, that since the apparently crowded fort gave him no warning of danger, there *was* no danger, and he and his column could come gaily marching into the fort from which its foes had fled.

This being so, I must warn him myself. I was certain that Michael would approve, and that he would have done so himself had he been in my place. It might mean death instead of escape, but death was certainly preferable to sneaking off while a whole column of one's comrades marched to a destruction one had the power to avert.

What to do? Should I lower the Flag? Run it up and down a few times? Wave my arms and dance about, up on the look-out platform? ...

As likely as not, he would take any such signals as signs of joy and welcome. If I were he, approaching a fully-manned fort over whose crowded walls floated the Flag, I should certainly see nothing of warning about such demonstrations as those.

Until I was actually fired upon, I should certainly suppose I was safe and being welcomed to the fort by those whom I had been too late to assist in their victory over some impudent little raiding-party.

Exactly! *Until fired upon!* That would surely give him something to think about--and, moreover, would give me a chance of escape, even yet... . Long before he came within shouting-distance he would be rushed by the Arabs. I would do the firing.

Kneeling down and resting my rifle in an embrasure, I aimed as though my life depended on hitting him. I then raised my fore-sight half an inch, and fired. Rushing to another embrasure, I took another shot, this time aiming to hit the ground, well in front of him.

He halted.

That was enough.

If he walked into an ambush now, he was no officer of the Nineteenth Army Corps of Africa... .

Rushing across to the side of the roof furthest from his line of approach, I dropped my rifle over, climbed the parapet, hung by my hands and then dropped, thanking God that my feet would encounter sand... . Snatching up my rifle, I ran as hard as I could go, to the nearest sand-hill. If this were occupied I would die fighting, and the sounds of rifle-fire would further warn the relief-column. If it were not occupied, I would hide and see what happened. Possibly I might be able to make a very timely diversion upon the Arab flank if there were a fight, and, in any case, I might hope to escape under cover of darkness... . The sand-hill was not occupied, I was safely out of the fort, and a chance of getting safely away existed, whether the Arabs attacked the column or not.

I crept into an Arab trench and set to work to make a hole in it, that I might be as inconspicuous as possible should anybody come, or look, in my direction.

From between two stones on the edge of the parapet of my trench, I could watch the fort and the oasis. I was conscious of an uneasy sensation as I watched, that I myself might be under the observation of enemies in my rear... .

As soon as I saw what the Arabs and the approaching column were going to do, I would consider the possibilities of a safe retreat in the most likely direction... .

I began to wish something would happen, for the situation was a little trying, and there was too strong a suggestion of leaving an Arab frying-pan on the one hand, to step into the French fire on the other ... an Arab torture by frying ... a French firing-party at dawn.

While I lay gazing to my front and wondering what might be happening behind me, I was astonished to see the French officer come round the corner of the fort, alone, and proceeding as unconcernedly as if he were riding in the streets of Sidi-bel-Abbès! ...

Well! I had done my best for him and his column. I had risked my own safety to warn him that things were not what they seemed--and if the Arabs got him and his men, it was not my fault.

He could hardly call *being shot at* a welcome from the fort? ... Round the walls he rode, staring up at the dead defenders.

I wondered if the shade thrown by the peaks of their caps would so hide and disguise their faces that, from below, it would be impossible to see that the men were dead... .

What were the Arabs doing? ... Leaving him as further bait for the trap, and waiting for the whole column to walk into it?

Ought I to warn them again? Surely once was enough? It would mean almost certain capture for me, by one side or the other, if I fired again... . Apparently this officer was unwarnable, moreover, and it would be nothing but a vain sacrifice to proclaim my existence and my position, by firing again... . And while I argued the matter with my conscience, I saw that all was well--the relieving force was approaching *en tirailleur,* preceded by scouts and guarded by flankers.

Slowly and carefully the French force advanced, well handled by somebody more prudent than the officer who had arrived first, and by no means disposed to walk into an Arab ambush.

A few minutes later, I heard the trumpeter summoning the fort, blowing his calls to dead ears.

I could imagine the bewilderment of the officer standing before those closed gates, waiting for them to open, while the dead stared at him and nothing stirred.

As I waited for him to climb up into the fort or to send somebody in, to open the gates for him, I came to the conclusion that the Arabs must have abandoned the siege and departed altogether. I wondered whether this had been due to Lejaune's ruse and the fort's apparently undiminished garrison, or to news, from their scouts, of the approach of a strong relief force. Anyhow, gone they were, and very probably they had raised the siege and vanished after moon-rise the previous night... .

The officer, his *sous-officier,* the trumpeter, and a fourth man, stood in a little group beneath the wall, some three hundred yards or so from where I lay... . I gathered that the fourth man was refusing to climb into the fort. There was pointing, there were gesticulations, and the officer drew his revolver and presented it at the face of the man who had shaken his head when the officer pointed up at the wall.

The trumpeter, his trumpet dangling as he swung himself up, climbed from the back of his camel to a projecting waterspout, and through an embrasure into the fort.

I expected to see him reappear a minute later at the gate, and admit the others.

He never reappeared at all, and, about a quarter of an hour later, the officer himself climbed up and entered the fort in the same way.

As before, I expected to see the gates opened a minute later--but nothing happened. There was silence and stillness. The minutes dragged by, and the men of the relief-column stood still as statues, staring at the enigmatical fort.

Presently I heard the officer bawling to the trumpeter, the men outside the fort began to move towards it in attack-formation, another squadron of the relief-column arrived on mules, the gates were thrown open from within, and the officer came out alone.

He gave some orders, and re-entered the fort with his second-in-command. No one else went in.

A few minutes later, the officer's companion reappeared, called up a sergeant, and gave orders, evidently for camping in the oasis.

It occurred to me that my situation was about to become an unwholesome one, as, before long, there would be vedettes posted on all four sides of the fort in a big circle, to say nothing of patrols.

I must be going, if I wished to go at all, before I was within a ring of sentries... .

After a good look round, I crawled painfully and slowly to the next sand-hill, trusting that the two in the fort would find too much of interest, within its walls, to have time to look over them and see me on my brief journey from cover to cover. Apparently this was the case, for when I reached the next sand-hill and looked back from behind its crest, there was no sign that I had been seen.

I rested, regained my breath, and then made another bolt to the sand-hill behind me, keeping the fort between the oasis and my line of retreat, and a good look-out for the vedette which, sooner or later, was certain to come more or less in this direction.

My best plan would be to creep from cover to cover, between the sand-hills, as I was doing, until beyond the vedette-circle, and then hide and rest till night fell. A good night's forced marching and I should be thirty miles away before the sun gained full strength, on the morrow. As though for a prize--and, of course, my life *was* the prize--I carried out this careful scouting retirement until I was half a mile from the fort and among the big stones that crowned a little hill of rock and sand. Here I was safe enough for the present. I could lie hidden and see where the vedettes were posted; sleep in what shade there was; eat, drink, rest, and gather strength; and set forth, when the moon rose, on my fairly hopeless journey... . Fairly hopeless? ... Absolutely hopeless--unless I could secure a camel... . And then and there, I firmly rejected the idea that entered my mind--of killing a vedette to get his beast. That I could regard as nothing better than cold-blooded murder.

A more acceptable notion was that of trying to creep into the oasis, during the night, and stealing a camel from there. It would be an extremely difficult thing to do successfully, for there would be brilliant moonlight, a very sharp look-out for Arabs, and a horrible row from the camel when one disturbed it... . Yes, very difficult and dangerous, but just possible, inasmuch as I was in uniform and might be believed if, challenged by the camel-guard, I pretended I was an orderly in search of his camel, for duty. Or if I walked up boldly and announced that I had been ordered to take a camel and ride back to Tokotu with a dispatch... . Distinctly possible, I considered. With really good luck and a really good bluff, it might be done. The good luck would lie in the camel-guard being unaware that I wasn't a member of the relief-force at all.

If I were not recognised, if my bluff were convincing, if I were not caught in the act by the very officer whom I should be pretending to have sent me for a camel; or if, on the other hand, there were a chance of simply stealing the camel unseen--I might get away with it. But there seemed to be a good many *ifs*... .

However, after thinking the matter over from all points of view, and weighing the chances impartially, I came to the conclusion that there was more likelihood of Michael's letter reaching Aunt Patricia if I had a shot at getting a camel, than if I did not. A thousand-mile stroll across the Soudanese Sahara did not strike me as one that would lead me home, in view of the fact that it takes a good man to do it under the somewhat more favourable conditions of preparation, organisation, and the protection of numbers and of the law (such as it is).

I decided to wait until night, see what happened, and reconnoitre the oasis with a view to deciding whether theft, bluff, or a combination of the two, offered the greater possibilities of success in securing a mount.

And the more I could concentrate my thoughts upon problems and considerations of this sort, the longer could I postpone and evade the on-rushing realisation of my loss ... the longer could I keep myself numb and insensate beneath the hammer-blows of the terrible Fact that lurked and struck, lurked and struck; the longer deafen myself to the waxing Voice with its ... *Michael is dead ... Michael is dead... . Listen and heed--Michael is dead... .*

In spite of the terrific heat and my unutterable misery and wretchedness, I fell asleep, and slept soundly until towards evening.

§ 2

When I awoke, I realised that I had been lucky. The nearest vedette was quite a thousand yards to my right, and so placed that there was no fear of my being seen, so long as I exercised reasonable precaution.

The sun was setting, the appalling heat of the day was waning in fierceness, and the fort and oasis presented a scene of normal military activity--or rather inactivity--for nothing whatever moved in or around the fort, and there was but little coming and going about the oasis. Here and there, a sentry's bayonet gleamed, a man led a mule or camel; a little column of smoke rose from among the palms, as a cooking-fire was lighted or replenished.

So far as I could see, the fort had not been taken over by a new garrison, nor to my surprise, had the dead been removed from the walls. Those motionless figures could not be living soldiers, for no Commandant would have kept his whole force on duty like that--particularly after a day-and-night march such as this one had just made.

I should have expected to see that the dead had been buried, the fort occupied, the look-out platform manned, and the sentry-posts occupied. However, it didn't matter to me what they did, so long as they left their camels in the oasis... .

As I watched, a small party, preceded by an officer on a mule, crossed from the oasis and entered the fort. I expected to see them remove the dead from the embrasures, but they did not do so. From where I was, I could not see on to the roof, but I should have seen them at work, had they come to the wall and begun their labours as a burial fatigue-party... .

Before long, the party returned to the oasis, the officer remaining in the fort. I wondered what they made of the *adjudant* with a French bayonet in him, of the dead *légionnaire* with his eyes closed and his hands crossed upon his breast, of the men dead upon their feet, of the complete absence of life in the uncaptured fort from which two warning shots had come... . Some of the superstitious old legionaries would have wonderful ideas and theories about it all!

The evening wore on, the sun set, and the great moon rose. In the brief dusk, I crept nearer to the fort and oasis, crouching and crawling from sand-hill to sand-hill. I would wait until everybody who was not on duty would be asleep; and then work round and enter the oasis, walking up boldly as though sent from the fort with a message. If challenged, I would act precisely as I should have done if dispatched by an officer to get my camel and hasten back to Tokotu... .

I imagined myself saying to a sentry who was disposed to doubt me, "All right, you fool, you hinder me--go on... . Don't blame me, though, when I say what delayed me! ..." and generally showing a perfect willingness to be hindered, provided I was not the one to get the blame... .

From the crest of the next sand-hill, I saw that the men of the relieving-column were parading outside the oasis, and I wondered what this portended.

As I watched, they marched towards the fort, halted, faced into line, with their backs towards me, and stood easy. I concluded that their officer had given them an "off" day after their long march, and was now going to work them all night at clearing up the fort, burying the dead, and generally re-establishing Zinderneuf as a going concern among the military outposts of Empire-according-to-a-Republic.

This might be very favourable to my plans. If I marched boldly up to the oasis, as though coming from the fort, when everybody was very busy, and demanded a camel, I should probably get one... .

The Commandant rode out from the oasis on a mule, and the men were called to attention. He was evidently going to address them--probably to congratulate them on the excellence of their forced march and refer to the marvellous defence put up by the garrison of the fort, who had died to a man in defence of the Flag of their adopted country.

Suddenly, the man standing beside him cried out and pointed to the fort. Instinctively I looked in the direction of his pointing finger--and very nearly sprang to my feet at what I saw.

The fort was on fire!

It was very much on fire too, obviously set alight in several places and with the help of oil or some other almost explosive combustible.... And what might *this* mean? Surely it was not "by order"? Not the result of official decision?

Of course not.... Could it be the work of some superstitious legionary left alone in the place as watchman? No. If there were anybody at all on duty there, he would have been up on the look-out platform, the emptiness of which had puzzled me....

How was this going to affect my chance of escape? Ought I to make a dash for the oasis while all hands were engaged in an attempt to put the fire out?

And, as I stared, in doubt and wonder, I was aware of a movement on the roof of the fort!

Carefully keeping the gate-tower between himself and the paraded troops, a man was doing precisely what I myself had done! I saw his cap as he crept crouching along below the parapet, I saw his arm and rifle come through an embrasure, I saw the rifle fall, and a minute or so later, as a column of smoke shot up, I saw him crawl through the embrasure and drop to the ground. By good luck or by skill, he had chosen a spot at which he was hidden from the vedette that had been a thousand yards to my right....

And who could he be, this legionary who had set fire to the fort of Zinderneuf? He certainly had my sympathy and should have my assistance. I must see that he did not crawl in the direction of the vedette. He might not know that he was there. I began creeping in a direction that would bring me on to his line of retreat in time to warn him.

A few minutes later he saw me, and hitched his rifle forward. Evidently he did not intend to be taken alive. Very naturally, after setting fire to one of *Madame la République's* perfectly good forts.... I drew out what had been a handkerchief, and from the safe obscurity of a sand-valley, waved it. I then laid my rifle down and crawled towards him. I noticed that he was wearing a trumpet, slung behind him.

As I came closer to the man, I was conscious of that strange contraction of the scalp-muscles which has given rise to the expression "his hair stood on end with fright."

I was not frightened and my hair did not stand on end, but I grew cold with a kind of horrified wonder as I saw what I took to be the ghost or astral form *of my brother* there before me, looking perfectly normal, alive, and natural.

It *was* my brother--my brother Digby--Michael's twin....

"Hullo, John," said Digby, as I stared open-mouthed and incredulous, "I thought you'd be knocking about somewhere round here. Let's get off to a healthier spot, shall us?"

For all his casual manner and debonair bearing, he looked white and drawn, sick to death, his hands shaking, his face a ghastly mask of pain.

"Wounded?" I asked, seeing the state he was in.

"Er--not physically.... I have just been giving Michael a '*Viking's Funeral*,'" he replied, biting his lip.

Poor, poor Digby! He loved Michael as much as I did (he could not love him more), and he was further bound to him by those strange ties that unite twins--psychic spiritual bonds, that make them more like one soul in two bodies than separate individuals. Poor, poor Digby!

I put my arm across his shoulders as we lay on the sand between two hillocks.

"Poor old John!" he said at length, mastering his grief. "It was you who laid him out, of course. You, who saw him die.... Poor Johnny boy! ..."

"He died trying to save my life," I said. "He died quite happily and in no pain.... He left a job for us to do.... I've got a letter for you. Here it is.... Let's get well off to the flank of that vedette and lie low till there's a chance to pinch a camel and clear out ..." and I led the way in a direction to bring us clear of the vedettes and nearer to the oasis.

A couple of minutes after our meeting, we were snugly ensconced behind the crest of a sand-hill, overlooking the parade of our comrades, the oasis, and the burning fort. A higher hillock behind us, and to our right, screened us from the nearest vedette.

"*And,*" said Digby, in a voice that trembled slightly, "they're not going to spoil Michael's funeral. Nor are they going to secure any evidence of your neat job on the foul Lejaune.... They're going to be attacked by Arabs ..." and he raised his rifle.

"Don't shoot anybody, Dig," I said. It seemed to me there had been enough bloodshed, and if these people were now technically our enemies and might soon be our executioners, they were still our comrades, and innocent of offence.

"Not going to--unless it's myself," replied Digby. "Come on, play Arabs with me ..." and he fired his rifle, aiming high.

I followed his example, shooting above the head of the officer as I had done once before that day.

Again and again we fired, vedettes to left and right of us joining in, and showing their zeal and watchfulness by firing briskly at nothing at all--unless it was at each other.

It was a sight worth seeing, the retreat of that company of legionaries. At a cool order from the officer, they faced about, opened out, doubled to the oasis, and went to ground, turning to the enemy and taking cover so that, within a couple of minutes of our first shots, there was nothing to be seen but a dark and menacing oasis, to approach which was death....

"Good work!" said Digby. "And they can jolly well stop there until the fort is burnt out.... We'll go in and get camels, as vedettes whose camels have been shot by these attacking Arabs, later on.... If we swagger up to the sentry on the camels, and pitch a bold yarn, it ought to be all right...."

"Yes--better if one of us goes," said I. "Then, if he doesn't return, the other can clear off on foot, or try some other dodge."

"That's it," agreed Digby. "I'll have first go."

"Now tell me all that happened," he added, "and then I'll bring you up to date."

I did so, giving him a full account of all our doings, from the time he had left us to go to the mounted company.

"Now tell me a few things, Dig," I said, when I had finished, and he knew as much as I did.

He then told me of how his *escouade* had suddenly been ordered from Tanout-Azzal to Tokotu. Here they had found, of all people on this earth, the Spahi officer who had once visited Brandon Abbas, now Major de Beaujolais, seconded from his regiment for duty with mounted units in the *Territoire Militaire* of the Soudan, where the mobile Touaregs were presenting a difficult problem to the peaceful penetrators towards Timbuktu and Lake Tchad.

The Major had not recognised Digby, of course, nor Digby him, until he heard his name and that he was a Spahi.

(And it was at him that I had been shooting that day, or rather it was he at whom I had not been shooting. It was this very friend of boyhood's days whom I had been trying to warn against what I thought was an ambush! ... Time's whirligig! ...)

At Tokotu, news had been received that Zinderneuf was besieged by a huge force of Touaregs, and de Beaujolais had set off at once.

The rest I knew until the moment when I had seen Digby, who was de Beaujolais' trumpeter, climb into the fort... .

"Well--you know what I saw as I got on to the roof," said Digby, "and you can imagine (can you, I wonder?) what I felt when I saw Beau lying there... . I dashed down below and rushed round to see if you were among the wounded, and then realised that there *were* no wounded, and that the entire garrison was on that awful roof... . That meant that you had cleared out, and that it was your bayonet ornamenting Lejaune's chest, and that it was you who had disposed Michael's body and closed his eyes. *Someone* must have done it, and it wasn't one of those dead men... . Who else but you would have treated Michael's body differently from the others? As I have told you, I was mighty anxious, coming along, as to how you and Michael were getting on, and whether we should be in time, and I had been itching to get up on to the roof while de Beaujolais was being dramatic with Rastignac... . You can guess how anxious I was *now*... . What with Michael's death and your disappearance... .

"I could almost *see* you killing Lejaune, and felt certain it was because he had killed Michael and tried to kill you for that cursed 'diamond' ... I tell you I went dotty... .

"'*Anyhow--he shall have a "Viking's Funeral,"*' I swore, and I believe I yelled the words at the top of my voice, '*and then I must find John.*' ... You know, it was always Beau's constant worry that harm would come to you. It was the regret of his life, that he was responsible for your bolting from home... . You young ass... .

"Anyhow, my one idea was to give him a proper funeral and then to follow you up. I guessed that you had stuck there, the sole survivor, until you saw de Beaujolais, and then slipped over the wall... .

"Then I heard someone scrambling and scraping at the wall, climbing up, and I crept off and rushed down below, with the idea of hiding till I got a chance to set fire to the beastly place, if I could do nothing better for Beau... . I saw the door of the punishment-cell standing open, and I slipped in there and hid behind the door. There was just room for me, and I should never be seen until someone came in and closed the door of the cell--which wasn't likely to happen for a long while... .

"Soon I heard de Beaujolais bawling out for me, and by the sound of his voice he wasn't much happier than I was... . The sight upstairs was enough to shake *anybody's* nerve, let alone the puzzle of it all... . By and by I heard him and the Sergeant-Major talking and hunting for me. They actually looked into the cell once, but it was obviously empty--besides being a most unlikely place for a soldier to shut himself in voluntarily! ... I gathered that old Dufour was even less happy than de Beaujolais, who certainly wasn't enjoying himself... . Presently they went away, and the place became as silent as the grave. It occurred to me that whatever else they made of it they must be certain that Lejaune had been killed by one of his own men and that the man must have bolted. If I could also vanish in this mysterious place, it would give them something more to puzzle over; and if I could absolutely destroy it, there would be no evidence for them to lay before a court martial... . Mind, I had been marching for twenty-four hours and was all but sleeping on my feet, so I wasn't at my brightest and best, by a long way--apart from what I had just seen... .

"When I felt pretty certain that there was no one about, I crept up on to the roof again and took a look round.

"There was a sentry at the gate, and the company was evidently going to camp in the oasis, and have a sleep before entering the fort.

"I pulled myself together, crawled over to where Beau lay, heaved him up in my arms and carried him below to his own bed in the barrack-room. All round his cot I laid piles of wood from the cook-house and drenched it with lamp oil. I did my best to make it a real '*Viking's Funeral*' for him, just like we used to have at home. Just like he used to want it. My chief regret was that I had no Union Jack to drape over him... .

"However, I did the best I could, and covered the whole pyre with sheets of canvas and things... . All white, more or less... . There was no sign of the wood and oil... . He looked splendid... . Then, after thinking it over, I took the spare Tri-couleur and laid that over all... . It wasn't what I would have liked, but he had fought and died under it, so it served... . It served... . Served... ."

Digby's head was nodding as he talked. He was like a somnambulist. I tried to stop him.

"Shut up, John... . I must get it clear... . *Oh, Beau! Beau!* ... I did my best for you, old chap... . There was no horse, nor spear, nor shield to lay beside you... . But I put a dog at your feet though... . And your rifle and bayonet were for sword and spear... ."

He must be going mad, I feared.

"A dog, old chap?" I said, trying to get him back to realities. "You are not getting it right, you know... ."

"Yes, a dog... . A dog at his feet... . A dog lying crouching with its head beneath his heels... ."

This was getting dreadful.

"I did not carry it down, as I carried Beau. I took it by one foot and dragged it down... ."

"*Lejaune?*" I whispered.

"Yes, John. Lejaune--with your bayonet through his heart. *He* won't give dumb evidence against you--and Beau had his '*Viking's Funeral*' with a dog at his feet... ."

I think I felt worse then than I had felt since Michael died. I gave Digby a sharp nudge in the ribs with my elbow.

"Get on with it and don't drivel," I said as though in anger.

"Where was I?" said Digby, in the tone of a man waking from a nap.

"Oh, yes. And when all was ready, John, I sat and talked to Beau and told him I hadn't the faintest idea as to what he'd been up to in this 'Blue Water' business, but what I *did* know was that, far from being anything shady, it was something quixotic and noble... . And then what do you think I did, John? ... I *fell asleep*--and slept till the evening... .

"I was a bit more my own man when I woke up. I went up on the roof to see what was doing... . Creeping to the wall and peeping over, I saw that the Company was parading, and that I had cut it very fine. I thanked God that I had awakened in time, for in a few minutes they would be marching in, to clean up and take over.

"I crept back and set fire to Beau's funeral pyre. Then I rushed off and poured a can of oil over the pile of benches and furniture that I had heaped up in the next room. I set light to that and knocked another can over at the foot of the stairs. I lit it and bolted up to the stair of the look-out platform. At the bottom of this, I did the same, and by that time it would have taken more water than there is in the Sahara to put the fire out... . I decided that Beau's funeral was all right, the evidence against you destroyed, and the time arrived for me to clear out... ."

He yawned prodigiously.

"So I came to look for you, John... . To look for ... for ..."

Digby was asleep.

Should I go to sleep too? The temptation was sore. But I felt that if we were to save ourselves, we must do it at once. We could hardly hope to lie there all night and escape detection in the morning, when the place would be swarming with scouts and skirmishers.

I decided to watch for an hour or two, while poor Digby slept. At the end of that time I would wake him and say that I was going to make the attempt to get a camel... .

It was extraordinarily silent... . It seemed impossible that the oasis, lying there so black and still, was alive with armed men. Even the camels and mules were behaving as though aware that the night was unusual. Not a grunting gurgle from the one or a whinnying bray from the other broke the brooding stillness of the night. I wondered if every man had been made responsible for the silence of his own animal, and had muzzled and gagged it. I smiled at the idea.

Not a light showed. Was the idea to make the smouldering fort a bait for the Arabs whom de Beaujolais would suppose to be in the neighbourhood--a bait to attract them to his lead-and-steel-fanged trap? ...

How would it be possible, after all, for me to approach that silvered black oasis, across the moonlit sands, without being challenged, seized, and exposed for what I was? I had anticipated approaching a normal, somnolent camp--not a tensely watchful look-out post, such as the oasis had become from the time Digby and I had fired our rifles.

Would it be better, after all, to sleep all night and try to bluff the camel-guard on the morrow, when the whole place would be buzzing with life and activity? It seemed a poor look-out anyway. And how bitterly one would regret not having made the attempt on foot, if one were seized in the effort to take a camel... .

Having decided that Digby had slept for about a couple of hours, I woke him up.

"What about it, Dig?" I said. "Are we going to have a shot at getting a camel, or are we going to march? We must do one or the other, unless you think we might do any good here by daylight... ."

"Oh, quite," replied Digby. "I'm sure you're right, John," and went to sleep again, in the act of speaking.

This was not exactly helpful, and I was trying to make up my mind as to whether I should give him another hour, or knock him up again at once, when I saw two camel-riders leave the oasis. I rubbed my eyes.

No. There was no doubt about it. A patrol was going out, or dispatches were being sent to Tokotu.

Here were two camels. Two well-fed, well-watered camels were coming towards us.

I did not for one moment entertain the thought of shooting their riders, but I certainly toyed for a moment with the idea of offering to fight them, fair and square, for their beasts! If we won, we should ride off and they would tramp back to the oasis. If they won, they'd continue about their business and we should be where we were... . A silly notion... . About two seconds after revealing ourselves, we should be looking into the muzzles of their rifles, and have the option of death or ignominious capture... . Why *should* they fight us? ... I must really pull myself together and remember who I was and where I was... .

The camels drew nearer and I decided, from their direction, they were on the way to Tokotu.

I crawled down the reverse slope of my sand-hill and ran along the valley at its base. Climbing another hillock, I saw that a repetition of the manœuvre would bring me on to their line. I did not know what I was going to do when I got there, but I felt there would be no harm in trying to find out who they were and where they were going. If we followed them and got a chance to steal their camels while they were not too far from the oasis to return on foot, I had an idea that we might take that chance. The temptation would be very strong, as it was a matter of life and death to us, while to them it would be merely a matter of a long day's march and a fearful tale of terrific combat with the horde of Arabs who had shot their camels... .

Suddenly a well-known voice remarked conversationally:

"We sure gotta put them nigs wise, Buddy... . We don' want nawthen to eventooate to the pore boobs through us not taking 'em by the hand... ."

"Hank!" I yelped in glee and thankfulness, and he and Buddy turned their camels towards me.

"Here's *one* of the mystery boys, anyhow," went on Hank. "I allowed as how you'd be around somewheres when we see you all three gone missin' from the old home... ."

In a valley between two sand-hills, Hank and Buddy brought their camels to their knees and dismounted. Both wrung my hand in a painful and most delightful manner.

"No offence, and excusin' a personal and dellikit question, Bo," said Buddy, "but was it you as had the accident with the cigar-lighter an' kinder caused arsonical proceedins? ..."

"Sort of 'arson about' with matches like?" put in Hank solemnly.

"No," I said. "It was Digby set fire to the fort."

"Then I would shore like to shake him by the hand, some," said Hank. "Is he around?"

"Having a nap over there," I replied.

"The other bright boy too?" asked Buddy. "An' where's Lejaune? Havin' set fire to the home, hev you taken Poppa by the ear an' led him out into the garden for to admire? ..."

As quickly as possible I told him what had happened--of Michael's death and "funeral."

"He was a shore white man, pard. 'Nuff said," commented Hank.

"He was all-wool-an'-a-yard-wide, Bo," said Buddy, and I felt that Michael might have had worse epitaphs.

A brief silence fell upon us.

"Gee!" said Hank after a while. "Wouldn't it jar you? It shore beats the band. Such nice quiet boys too--always behavin' like they was at a party, an' perlite as Hell--an' one of 'em kills the Big Noise an' the other sets the whole gosh-dinged outfit afire an' burns out the dod-gasted burg... . *Some* boys, I allow... ."

I greatly feared that our deeds of homicide and arson had raised us higher in the estimation of these good men than any number of pious acts and gentle words could ever have done.

As I led the way to where I had left Digby sleeping, I asked the Americans where they were going.

"Wal--we was sorta sent lookin' fer some nigs from Tokotu," replied Hank. "Ole Man Bojolly allows they'll run into an Injun ambush if they ain't put wise. We gotta warn them there's Injuns about, fer all the location's so quiet an' peaceful-lookin' ..."

"I wonder they didn't git you two boys when they shot us up," he added.

"We *were* the Arabs," I confessed with modest pride.

"Gee!" admired Buddy. "Can you beat it! ... I shore thought there was thousands come gunnin' fer us.... Oh, *boy!* You quiet perlite young guys.... *Mother!* ..."

"How many guns did you shoot then?" enquired Hank.

"Two," I replied. "Rapid fire. And then the vedettes obligingly joined in."

Buddy gave a brief hard bark, which may, or may not, have been meant for laughter.

"Sunday pants of Holy Moses!" he observed. "And that lyin' son of a skunk of a Schneider swore he shot seven of you himself--and the rest of you carried away their bodies as he retired in good order! Thinks he oughta get the *médaille militaire* or somethin'... ."

"Yep," confirmed Hank, "an' Ole Man Dupanloup estimates the lot that was agwine ter rush the parade, when he held 'em up, at from a hunderd to a hunderd an' fifty. He lost count of the number he killed--after a score or so... . Gee! At them north outposts there was *some* bloody battle, son... ."

"*And* some bloody liars," observed Buddy, who had sojourned in London.

I had difficulty in awaking poor Digby, but when he realised that Hank and Buddy were actually present in the flesh, he was soon very much awake and on the spot.

"Say, boys," he went on, after greeting them and hearing their tale of the Battle of the Vedettes, "it's a lot to ask, I know. But *do* you think you could be attacked, like Dupanloup, by about a hundred and fifty of us, and lose your camels? ... They'd be shot beneath you, or on top of you, if you like,--while you fought desperately--one to seventy-five, isn't it? ... You would have peace with honour, and we'd have a chance to save our lives. We don't pretend that they're very valuable, but we've got something we really must do for our brother... . And I promised Mother I'd bring the Baby home," he added, indicating me.

"Fergit it, son," replied Hank to Digby, but he looked at Buddy.

"Couldn't you possibly let us have them?" I said. "If we went a mile or two further on, we could kick up a fearful row with our four rifles, and you could go back and collect a medal when old Dupanloup gets his... . Stroll home doing a rear-guard stunt, and we'd pepper the scenery in your direction before we rode off... . The Senegalese are safe enough. There are no Arabs and no ambush... . And we simply shan't have a little dog's chance without camels."

"*We* want 'em, Bo," replied Hank with quiet finality.

"Shore," agreed Buddy, eyeing him.

I was surprised and disappointed. Even more disappointed at the attitude of my friends than at the loss of the camels.

"Well--all right then! We won't *fight* you for them," said Digby, "but I wish it had been someone else."

"I don't get your drift. Snow again, Bo," said Buddy, who seemed pained.

"Why someone else? Don't you admire our low and vulgar ways, pard?" asked Hank. "Don't you like us?"

"Yes, but to be honest, at the moment I like your camels better," replied Digby.

"Well, then--you got the lot, ain't you?" asked Hank. "What's bitin' you now, Bo?"

"Do you mean *you're coming with us?*" I asked, a great light dawning upon me, a light that so dazzled my eyes that I was afraid to look upon it.

"You shore said a mouthful, Bo," replied Hank. "Why, what did you figger? That we'd leave you two innercent children to wander about this yer sinful world all on your lone? ..."

"After you bin and killed their Big Noise? And obliterised their nice little block-house?" put in Buddy. "'Twouldn't be right, boy. '*Course* we're comin' along."

I really had to swallow hard as I took their horny hands.

"But look here, boys," Digby remonstrated, after following my example and trying to express thanks without words, "there's no need for that. Give us your camels and anything else you can safely spare, and go back in modest glory. There's nothing against *you*. If you're caught escaping with us and helping us, you'll be shot with us. It will be 'desertion in the face of the enemy when sent on reconnaissance' when it comes to the court martial."

"Go back nawthen," said Buddy. "Look at here. This is what Hank wants to say... . Is there any Injuns around? Nope. Is those nigs from Tokotu in any danger? Nope. Hev you had a square deal in this Madam Lar Republic-house stunt? Nope. Didn't you and your brother stand by your dooty in this mutiny game? Yep. Wasn't you two scrapping all the time and doing your damnedest till everybody else had handed in their checks! Yep. And then didn't this Lejaune guy start in to shoot you up? Shore. And what'll happen to you now if they get you? Shoot you up some more. Shore. 'Tain't a square deal... .

"Well, we figger that these nigs from Tokotu aren't on the chutes fer the bow-wows. Nope. They're marchin' on right now fer Zinderneuf--like John Brown's body--or was it his soul?--safe enough... . We allow you ain't got no chance on a lone trail. Not a doggoned smell of one. You're two way-up gay cats an' bright boys, but you're no road-kids. You don't know chaparral from an arroyo nor alkali sage-brush from frijoles. You couldn't tell mesquite from a pinto-hoss. Therefore Hank says we gotta come along... ."

"Shore thing," agreed Hank, "and time we vamoosed too, or we'll hev these nigs a-treadin' on us. They'll go fer a walk on empty stummicks--ours... ."

A minute later each of the camels bore two riders, and we were padding off at a steady eight miles an hour.

"Any pertickler direction like?" said Hank, behind whom I was riding. "London? N'York? Morocker? Egyp'? Cape Town? All the same ter me."

Buddy drove his camel up beside ours.

"What about it, Dig?" said I to my brother. "We've got to get out of French territory... . Morocco's north-west; Nigeria's south-east... ."

"And where's water?" replied Digby. "I should say the nearest oasis would be a sound objective."

"If there's a pursuit, they'd take the line for Morocco for certain, I should say," I pointed out. "I vote for the opposite direction and a beady eye on our fellow-man, if we can see him. Where there are Arabs there'll be water somewhere about, I suppose."

"Shore," said Hank. "We'll pursoo the pore Injun. What's good enough fer him is bad enough for us. You say wheer you wants ter go, an' I allow *we'll see you there*--but it may take a few years. What we gotta do first is turn Injun, see? ... Git Injun glad rags, and live like they does. We're well-armed and got our health an' strength an' hoss-sense. When in the desert do as the deserters does... . Yep. We gotta turn Injun."

From which I gathered that Hank the Wise firmly advocated our early metamorphosis into Arabs, and the adoption of Arab methods of subsistence in waterless places.

"Injuns lives by lettin' other folks *pro*-juce an' then collectin'," put in Buddy.

"We gotta collect," said Hank.

"From the collectors," added Buddy.

From which I gathered further that our friends were proposing not only that we should turn Arab, but super-Arab, and should prey upon the Touareg as the Touareg preyed upon the ordinary desert-dweller. It seemed a sound plan, if a little difficult of application. However, I had infinite faith in the resourcefulness, experience, staunchness, and courage of the two Americans, and reflected that if anybody could escape from this predicament, it was these men, familiar with the almost equally terrible American deserts.

"I vote we go south-west," said Digby. "We're bound to strike British territory sooner or later and then we're absolutely safe, and can easily get away by sea. We're bound to fetch up in Nigeria if we go steadily south-west. If we could hit the Niger somewhere east of Timbuktu--it would lead us straight to it."

"Plenty o' drinkin' water in the Niger, I allow," observed Buddy. "But there don't seem ter be no sign-posts to it. It shore is a backward state, this Sahara... ."

"Anyhow it's south-west of us now, and so's Nigeria," Digby insisted.

"Starboard yer hellum," observed Hank. "Nigeria on the port bow--about one thousand miles."

And that night we did some fifty or sixty of them without stopping, by way of a good start--a forced march while the camels were fresh and strong.

As we padded steadily along, we took stock of our resources.

With my bottles of water, and the regulation water-bottles, we had enough for two or three days, with careful rationing.

Similarly with food. I had a haversack full of bread, and the other three had each an emergency ration as well as army biscuits.

Of ammunition we had plenty, and we hoped to shoot dorcas gazelle, bustard, and hare, if nothing else.

Had Michael been with us, I should have been happy. As it was, the excitement, the mental and physical activity, the hopes and fears attendant on our precarious situation and the companionship of my brother and these two fine Americans combined to help me to postpone my defeat by the giants of misery, pain, and grief that were surely only biding their time, lurking to spring when I could no longer maintain my defences.

Digby, I think, was in much the same mental condition as myself, and I wondered if I, too, had aged ten years in a night.

As we jogged steadily on, the monotony of movement, of scene, and of sound, sent me to sleep, and every now and then I only saved myself from falling by a wild clutch at Hank, behind whom I was sitting.

No one spoke, and it is probable that all of us slept in brief snatches--though they must have been very brief for those who were driving the camels. I came fully awake as the sun peered over the far-distant edge of the desert to our left. I longed for a hot bath and hotter coffee, for I ached in every nerve and muscle.

""*They'll have fleet steeds that follow,*" quoth young Lochinvar,'" said Digby.

"They've got 'em," replied Buddy, looking behind as we topped a ridge of rock.

On we drove, south-west, throughout what was, very comparatively speaking, the cool of the morning, until Hank thought we should be making more haste than speed by continuing without resting the camels.

"I don' perfess ter know much about these doggoned *shammos,* as they call 'em," observed Hank, "but I allow you can't go very far wrong if you treats 'em as hosses."

"Shore," agreed Buddy, "'cept that they got more control of their passions like.... Fer eats, and fer settin' up the drinks, anyhow.... They can live on nawthen. An' as that's just what we pervided for 'em, they oughta thrive."

"We'll have to find *something* for them," said Digby, "if it's only newspaper or the thatch of a nigger's hut."

"I hev heard of 'em eatin' people's hats at dime shows and meenageries," said Hank. "My Aunt 'Mandy went to Ole Man Barnum's show on her golden weddin' day, an' a camel browsed her hat and all her back hair, an' she never knowed it until she felt a draught.... Yep. They kin hev our *képis* if they wait till we got some Injun shappos an' pants an' things...."

I was aware that camels had meagre appetites and queer, limited tastes, embracing a narrow selection ranging from bran to the twigs of dead thorn-bush, but I agreed with Digby that we should have to give them something, and something other than our caps. Our lives depended upon these two ugly, unfriendly beasts, for without them we should either be quickly recaptured or else we should die of thirst and starvation, long before we could reach any oasis. In the rapidly narrowing shadow of a providential great rock in this thirsty land, we lay stretched on our backs, after an ascetic meal of bread and water.

"What's the programme of sports, Hank?" I asked, as we settled ourselves to sleep.

"Another forced march ter git outta the onhealthy location o' Zinderneuf," he replied. "Then we gotta scout fer Injuns or an oasis. Spread out in a four-mile line an' peek over every rock and hill.... We'll shore fix it ..." and he went to sleep.

Personally I slept till evening without moving, and I was only then awakened by the grumbling, gurgling roar of the camel that Hank was girthing up, one of his feet pressed against its side and all his weight and strength on the girth-rope.

Having put the camel-blanket on the other animal, lifted the wooden framework regulation saddle on to it, girthed it up, taken the nose-reins over the beast's head and looped them round the pommel, he bawled "All aboard," and stood with his foot on the kneeling camel's near fore-knee, while I climbed into the rear part of the saddle. He then vaulted into the front seat and the camel, lurching heavily, came to its feet with an angry hungry roar.

Buddy and Digby mounted the other beast, and once more we were off, not to stop until we estimated that there were at least a hundred miles between us and Zinderneuf.

This was, of course, too good to last--or too bad, from the camels' point of view. At the end of this second ride they must have food and a day's rest, if not water.

Again I slept spasmodically, towards morning, especially after Hank had insisted upon my embracing him round the body and leaning against him.

I was awakened from a semi-slumbrous state of coma by an exclamation from Buddy, to realise that it was day again, the camels were standing still, and their riders gazing at what Buddy was indicating with outstretched arm.

Over the level stretch of unblown sand which we were crossing, ran a broad and recent trail of camel footprints.

This trail crossed ours, though not at right angles. If we were going south-west I should think the riders were going south--or north.

Hank and Buddy brought the camels to their knees, with the gentle insistent "*Oosha, baba, oosha; adar-ya-yan!*" which is about the only order that a camel obeys without cavil or protest.

Following the footmarks and regarding them carefully, they decided that there were about twenty camels in the party, that they were going south, and that they had passed quite recently.

"What we bin lookin' for!" observed Hank with grim satisfaction, as he swung himself back into the saddle. "The nearer we kin git to them Injuns, the quicker--but we don' wanta tread on 'em. Keep yer eyes skinned, boys." And the others having remounted, on we went.

I should think we followed this trail for three or four hours, without seeing anything but the eternal desert of sand and rock.

For some time I had been wondering how much longer we were to go on without resting the camels, when a grunt of satisfaction from Hank renewed my waning interest in life. He brought the camel to a halt and pointed, as Buddy ranged up beside us.

We had come to the bank of a very wide and rather shallow dry river-bed, whose shelving sides led down to gravel and stones which at one time must have been subject to the action of running water. The place looked as though a river had flowed along it ten thousand years ago.

But what Hank was pointing to was the spot to which the footprints led.

Beneath a huge high rock, that rose from the middle of the river-bed, was a dark inviting shadow around which were dry-looking tufts of coarse grass, stunted dwarf acacias, and low thorn-bushes.

The camels were perceptibly eager to get to this spot.

"Water," said Hank. "May have to dig."

But there was no need to dig. Beneath and around the rock was a pool, fed presumably from a subterranean source. It wasn't the sparkling water of an English spring, bubbling up among green hills, by any means. The green was rather in the water, but we were not fastidious, and certainly the camels were not. On the contrary, we were delighted and deeply thankful.

Here were shade, water, and camel-food, giving us a new lease of life, and encouragement on our way. It was evident that a party of travellers had recently halted here.

"Good old Touaregs," said Digby, as we dismounted in the glorious shade. "Obliging lads. We'll follow them up just as long as they are going our way home."

"We gotta do more'n foller 'em up," said Hank. "We gotta *catch* 'em up. They gotta lend us some correc' desert-wear striped gents' suitings. Likewise grub-stake us some."

"Shore," agreed Buddy. "An' we ain't no hoss-thieves neither, but I allow they gotta lend us a couple o' good camels too."

From the first, the Americans had been anxious to secure Arab dress, both on account of possible pursuit from Zinderneuf, and as being less conspicuous and less likely to bring every wandering Arab band down upon us, directly they caught sight of us and recognised us for hated *Roumis*.

They were doubly anxious to procure the disguise on learning that, in the south, towards Nigeria, there were numerous forts and outposts of the French Niger Territory, garrisoned by Senegalese, and that between these posts, numerous patrols would carefully watch the caravan-routes, and visit such Arab towns and settlements as existed.

It would certainly be better to encounter a patrol in the rôle of Arabs than in that of runaway soldiers from the Foreign Legion.

Accordingly Hank decreed that we must push on, only enough time being spent here for the camels to eat and drink their fill. He was of opinion that the party we were following was an offshoot of the big band that had attacked Zinderneuf and was on its way to "gather in" some village which they visited periodically.

Here they would appropriate its harvest of dates or grain, such camels as might be worthy, those of its sons and daughters who might be suitable for slaves, and any goats, clothing, money, and useful odds-and-ends that they might fancy.

These Touareg bands make an annual tour and visit the villages of an enormous area, in the spirit of somewhat arbitrary and undiscriminating tax-collectors. What they want, by way of tax, is everything the villagers possess that is portable, including their young men and maidens.

If the villagers are reasonable and relinquish everything with a good grace, there need not be any bloodshed--or very little, just in the way of fun and sportive merriment.

The Touaregs do not wish to destroy the village and slaughter the inhabitants, because they prefer to find a peaceful and prosperous community here, again, next year.

All they wish to do, is to clean them out absolutely and leave them alone to amass some more. But if the villagers choose to be uppish and truculent, giving their visitors trouble-- they must take the consequences--which are fire and sword and torture.

Or, if the band is off its regular beat and not likely to come that way again, it combines sport with business, and leaves no living thing behind it, nor any roofed dwelling in what was a village--scarcely one stone upon another of what was a little town.

After about three hours' rest, we pushed on again, and rode for the remainder of the day and right through the night. The fact that we did not come up with our quarry seemed to confirm the theory that they were a war-party on raiding business. Peaceful caravans and travellers would never go at such a pace, and we should have overtaken such a party easily... .

On this side of the river, or rather river-bed, the scenery began to change. The earth grew greyer in colour, cactus and acacia began to appear, and there were numerous great rock *kopjes*. The change was from utterly lifeless sand-desert to rock-desert, having a sparse vegetation.

Suddenly we heard distant rifle-fire to our front--a few scattered shots. Simultaneously, Hank and Buddy brought the camels to their knees among the rocks, and we dismounted, unslinging our rifles as we did so.

"Mustn't get the *shammos* shot up," said Hank to me. "You hold 'em, Bo, while we rubber around some," and they skirmished forward.

Nothing further being heard and nothing seen, they returned, and we rode on again.

Rounding a great rock, a mile or two further on, a rock that reminded one of a Dartmoor tor, we saw an ugly sight.

A woman had been tied to an acacia tree and horribly mutilated. I need say no more about the sight and its effect upon us, although I might say a good deal.

It was evident that she had been herding a flock of goats... .

"Village near," said Hank, and he and Buddy again simultaneously wheeled the camels round, and we retired behind the tor and dismounted.

"We'll corral the hosses here, and scout some," said Hank. "It'll be worth dollars to see these darned coyotes before they see us."

This time the camels were tied with their *agals,* and left. We advanced *en tirailleur,* as though to the attack of an Arab *douar,* a manœuvre with which our training had made us only too familiar.

Gradually we approached what appeared to be a completely deserted village by an oasis at the edge of a deep ravine. I should think there had been a village on this spot for thousands of years, though the present buildings were wretched mud huts crowning the basements of ancient stone houses of great strength. It was as though a tribe of gipsies, encamped permanently on an Ancient British hut-circle site on Dartmoor, had used the prehistoric stones in the construction of their rude dwellings.

Into this village, evidently very recently abandoned, we made our way with due precaution.

In one of the huts, on a rough *angareb,* lay a wounded man. As we entered, he drew a curved dagger from his belt and feebly struck at us.

"We are friends," said I in Arabic. "Tell us what has happened. We want to help... ."

Digby also aired his Arabic, and the man was convinced.

He appeared to understand all we said, and I understood him about as well as an English-speaking Frenchman would understand a Devonshire yokel.

I gathered that the usual village tragedy had developed as follows:

A woman, minding goats, had seen a band of Touaregs approaching (this man called them "The Veiled Ones, the Forgotten of God"), and had foolishly, or bravely, got up on a rock and screamed the news to a youth, who was working nearer the village. They had both then started running, but the Touaregs had caught the woman. The youth had roused the village and the men had rushed out with their rifles to some rocks near by, ready to fire on the Touaregs, and hoping to give the impression of a large and well-armed force, fully prepared to give them a warm reception. The women and children had scuttled to the big ravine behind the village, down which they would make their way to their usual hiding-place.

A couple of lads had been sent off to warn the men who had taken the camels out to graze.

The speaker had been one of these men, and while he and one or two others were collecting the camels and driving them to the ravine, a Targui scout had come upon them and shot him. The rest of the Touaregs had come straight to the spot, circled round, fired a volley, and closed in on the camels.

He himself had been left for dead. When he came to his senses he was alone with the corpses of the other camel-guards, and he had slowly crawled to his hut to die.

The Touaregs had camped and were calmly enjoying a well-earned rest. Apparently the village men were still watching events from their place among the rocks, the women and children were in hiding down the ravine, and the camels were captured.

I gathered that it would have been less calamitous had the camels been in hiding down the ravine, and the women and children captured.

We explained the situation to Hank and Buddy.

"Sport without danger, and business with pleasure," was their view, but we must give the Touaregs the shock of their lives.

We held a council of war, and it was decided that the wounded man should get in touch with the villagers and tell them that we were friends of theirs. More, we were deadly enemies of the Touaregs, and (most) we'd get the camels back and give them those of the Touaregs too--if they'd play the man and do as we bade them.

Having told his tale and grasped that we really wished to befriend him, the wounded man seemed to be farther from death than he had thought. He was shot through the chest, but I did not think that his lungs had suffered, as there was no hæmorrhage from the mouth.

After a drink of water and a pill, which Digby gave him with the assurance that it would do *wonders* for him (though I doubted whether they were wonders suitable to the situation), he got off the *angareb* and staggered to the doorway of the hut. From here he peered beneath his hand for a while, and then tottered out and did some signalling.

Very pluckily he stuck to it until an answering movement among the rocks, unseen by us, satisfied him, and he returned to the hut.

Shortly afterwards, a hail brought him to the door again, and this time he walked off fairly steadily, and disappeared into the ravine.

He returned with a big, dirty squint-eyed Arab, who, he said, was the headman of the village, which was called Azzigig (or sounds to that effect).

The headman was in the mental condition of one who sees men as trees walking, when he found himself in the presence of four armed and uniformed *Roumis,* two of whom spoke Arabic to him, and all of whom wished him to put up a fight for Azzigig, Home, and Beauty.

His own idea was to thank Allah that things were no worse, and to lie low until the Touaregs chose to depart, praying meanwhile that they would do so in peace, without troubling to hunt out the villagers, burn the houses, slaughter the goats, and have a little torture-party before doing so.

When I asked if he felt no particular resentment about the mutilated woman and the slaughtered camel-guards, to say nothing of the loss of the entire stock of camels, he replied that it was doubtless the will of Allah, and who should dispute that?

When I pointed out that it was obviously the will of Allah that we should arrive in the nick of time, and that the Touaregs should camp and rest instead of riding off, he said he would go and talk with his brethren.

This he did, and returned with a deputation of very dirty, suspicious, evil-looking Arabs, who evidently did not believe what he had told them, and had come to see for themselves.

"Gee!" observed Buddy. "Watta ugly bunch o' low-lifer hoboes."

"*Some* stiffs," agreed Hank.

However, I harangued the stiffs, offering them a chance of recovering their camels and teaching the Touaregs a lesson. I fumbled for the Arabic for "catching a Tartar" as I tried to get these fatalists to see they had as much "right to life, liberty, and the pursuit of happiness" as Touaregs, and that the latter had no God-given privilege to torture, murder, and rob. As for the "Will of Allah," let them follow us and show a little pluck, and they'd soon see what was the will of Allah in the matter.

In support Digby said, "Anyhow, we're going to attack them, whether you do or not. Those who help us will share the loot."

As the loot would include excellent rifles and incomparable camels, this gave the poor wretches something to think about. In the end, they agreed that if we would really fight for them, and with them, and give them all the loot, except a couple of camels, as we had promised, they would fight their hardest.

We began by reconnoitring the Touareg camp.

Absolutely certain of their complete security, the robbers had merely lighted fires and lain down to rest, leaving one of their number to guard their own camels and two to guard those stolen from the villagers.

Presumably these guards were more herdsmen than sentries, as the Touaregs had nothing to fear. Villagers do not attack victorious Hoggar robbers. It simply is not done. All that was necessary was to prevent the camels from straying, and to have a rest before proceeding on the tax-gathering journey--with or without a little sport in the village before starting... .

Our plan was simple for our job was easy.

Half a dozen selected heroes of Azzigig were to deal with the somnolent loafing camel-guards--silently if possible. Every rifle that Azzigig could boast was then to be discharged into the Touareg camp, from as close a range as it was possible to wriggle to.

When the Touaregs bolted to the ravine, as they certainly would do, to take cover from this blast and organise their defence--they would find their way blocked by the entire French army, in uniform, with a bugler blowing calls to bring up thousands more! ...

I must say that the villagers behaved very well. They were, of course, born desert fighters, and we had put heart into them.

After a tremendous volley, at about forty yards' range, they charged like fiends, and when we four arose from behind rocks and the Touaregs recoiled in astounded terror, they surrounded them like a pack of wolves.

In a brief, mad, happy minute of hacking, stabbing, and shooting, they worked off a good deal of the personal and ancestral grudge of centuries. As they outnumbered the Touaregs by five or six to one, had them at a complete disadvantage, and knew we were behind them, they made a short job of it and a clean one.

From another point of view it was not a clean one.

At any rate, we prevented torture even if we could not save life. For once it was the under-dog's turn, and he used his teeth... .

Digby, not unreasonably, claimed that the bugle really won the battle.

The upshot of the business was that we left Azzigig, each riding a splendid *mehari* camel, and each clad in the complete outfit of a Touareg raider--newly washed for us by the grateful dames of the village. Nor could the lads-of-the-village do enough for us. What they could, and did, do, was to provide us with a guide and a spare camel laden with food and water, to help us on our way to the next village and oasis in the direction of our goal.

A desperate band of ruffians we looked, Touareg to the last detail of dress, weapons, and accoutrement.

Lean and leathery hawk-faced Hank and Buddy made splendid Arabs, and seemed to enjoy "playing Injun" like a pair of boys.

They soon learned the uses and arrangings of the *serd* and *jubba* vests, the *kaftan* inner coat, the *hezaam* sash, the *jelabia* overall, the *sirwal* baggy trousers, the *ma-araka* skull cap with the *kafiya* head-dress bound round with the *agals,* ropes of camel-hair. The blue veils which the Touaregs wear, were the chief trouble, but in time we grew accustomed to them.

I do not know whether these veils are a centuries-old relic of the days when the Touaregs were a white race and took care of their complexions; whether they were a sudden bright idea for keeping the sand from the lungs in windy weather; whether they were invented for purposes of mystery and playing bogey with their enemies and victims; or whether they simply evolved as useful desert-wear for people always on the move, against cutting sand-filled winds and a burning glare that smites upward as well as downward. Anyway, it is curious that only the Touaregs evolved them.

On our camels we carried *zemzimayas* full of water, and *jaafas,* or leather sacks, which our hosts filled with *hubz,* or native bread, and *asida,* horrible masses of dough mixed with oil and onions, flavoured with *fil-fil,* a sort of red pepper.

On the spare camel were huge *khoorgs,* or saddle-bags, filled with *alafs* of fodder for the camels, as well as *girbas* full of water.

We discarded our two military saddles and replaced them with Arab *sergs,* and, in fact, "went native" altogether, retaining nothing European but our rifles and Digby's bugle.

And in doing this, even, we were not guilty of any anomaly. I had been interested to note that, along with heavy swords of Crusader pattern, and lances and knives of a type unchanged since the days of Abraham, the Touaregs carried splendid magazine-rifles of the latest pattern.

Both these and their ammunition were of Italian make, and I wondered whether they had been captured in Tripoli, or smuggled by the Chambaa rifle-runners of Algeria. As two men had Turkish rifles and cartridges of ·450 calibre, I thought it likely that the former was the source. The useful bugle was, of course, concealed.

Before we departed, the village pulled itself together, and, evidently trying to show us "what Todgers' could do" in the way of a *diffa,* or feast, regaled us upon *fatta,* a mess of carrots, bread, and eggs, and a quite decent *cous-cous* of goat.

For wassail, the headman brought up from the "cellar" (under his bed) a magnum (leather) of *laghbi,* a rare old vintage palm-juice, which had lain mellowing and maturing in bottle for quite a week.

I found that my names for things of this sort were not always the same as the names I had learned in Algeria, but by any other name they smelled as remarkable.

I asked Hank what he thought of the "liquor."

"Fierce, ain't it?" replied he, and left me to apply mine own evaluation to the word.

"Guess we could stop here to be the Big Noise of the tribe," remarked Buddy, endeavouring to feed himself gracefully with his fingers--not an easy thing to do when a spoon is the indicated instrument.

"Yep. Shakers and emus," agreed Hank, with hazy memories of sheikhs and emirs perhaps.

"And a harem-scarum," added Buddy.

"Why don' the gals jine the hash-party?" he enquired, looking round to where the women, in their long *barracans,* sat afar off and admired the prandial performances of their lords.

"Shut up. Take no notice of the women-folk," said Digby. "Sound plan among Mussulmans of any kind."

"No doubt yore right, pard," agreed Buddy, "but there shore is a real little peach over there jest give me the glad eye like a Christian gal as knowed a hill o' beans from a heap o' bananas. Cute an cunnin'.... Still, we don't want no rough stuff from the Injuns.... My, but it was a cinch ..." and he sighed heavily... .

CHAPTER VII. ISHMAELITES

"Greater love hath no man than this,
That a man lay down his life for his friends."

I could fill a large volume with the account of our adventures, as Touaregs of the Sahara, on this ride that began at Azzigig, in the French Soudan, and ended (for some of us) at Kano in Nigeria, in British West Africa.

It was perhaps the longest and most arduous ride ever achieved by Europeans in the Sahara--few of whom have ever crossed the desert from north to south without an organised caravan.

We rode south-west when we could, and we rode north-east when we must, as when, north of Aïr, we were captured by Touaregs on their way to their own country on the borders of Morocco.

During one terrible year we made an almost complete circle, being at one time at El Hilli, within two hundred miles of Timbuktu, and, at another, at Agadem, within the same distance of Lake Tchad--and then later finding ourselves at Bilma, five hundred miles to the north.

Sometimes thirst and hunger drove us to join salt-caravans, and sometimes slave-caravans (and we learnt that slavery is still a very active pursuit and a flourishing business in Central Africa). Generally these caravans were going in the direction opposite to ours, but we had to join them or perish in the waterless desert.

Sometimes we were hunted by gangs larger than our own; sometimes we were met at villages with volleys of rifle-fire (being taken, naturally, for what we pretended to be); sometimes we reached an oasis only to find it occupied by a patrol of French Senegalese troops--far more dangerous to us than the nomadic robbers for whom we were a match when not hopelessly outnumbered.

Whether we did what no Europeans have ever done before, I do not know, but we certainly went to places where Europeans had never been before, and "discovered" desert cities which were probably prehistoric ruins before a stone of Damascus was laid.

We encountered no Queens of Atlantis and found no white races of Greek origin, ruled by ladies of tempestuous petticoat, to whom it turned out we were distantly related.

Alas, no. We found only extremely poor, primitive, and dirty people, with whom we sojourned precisely as long as untoward circumstance compelled.

Of course, we could never have survived for a single month of those years, but for the desert-skill, the courage, resourcefulness, and experience of Hank and Buddy.

On the other hand, the ready wits of Digby, and our knowledge of Arabic, saved the situation, time after time, when we were in contact with our fellow-man.

On these occasions we became frightfully holy. Hank and Buddy were *marabouts* under a vow of silence, and we were Senussi on a mysterious errand, travelling from Kufra in the Libyan desert to Timbuktu, and visiting all sorts of holy places on the way.

Luckily for us, there were no genuine Senussi about; and the infinite variety of sects, with their different kinds of dervishes, and the even greater variety of people who spoke widely differing dialects of Arabic, made our task comparatively easy.

Probably our rifles, our poverty, and our obvious truculence did still more in that direction.

We suffered from fever, terrific heat, poisonous water, bad and insufficient food, and the hardships of what was one long campaign of active warfare to live.

At times we were very near the end, when our camels died, when a long journey ended at a dried-up well, when we were surrounded by a pack of the human wolves of the desert, and when we were fairly captured by a *harka* of Touaregs, suspicious of our *bona fides*... .

As I have said, an account of our *katabasis* would fill a volume, but the description of a few typical incidents will suffice to give an idea of it, without rendering the story as wearisome as was the journey.

For example, our discovery of the place where there certainly ought to have been "*a strange fair people of a civilisation older, and in some ways higher, than our own; ruled over by a woman, so incredibly beautiful, so marvellously ...*" etc.

One day we rode over the crest of a long ridge of sand-covered rock--straight into a band of armed men who outnumbered us by ten to one, at least, and who were ready and waiting for us with levelled rifles.

We did as we had done before, on similar exciting occasions. The Holy Ones, Hank and Buddy, fell dumb, and Digby became the emissary of the Senussi Mahdi; I, his lieutenant.

Digby rode forward.

"*Salamoune aleikoumi Esseleme, ekhwan*" (Peace be unto you, brothers), said he, in solemn, sonorous greeting, to which a fine-looking old man replied, to my great relief, "*Aselamu, alaikum, marhaba, marhaba*" (Greetings to you and welcome), in a different-sounding Arabic from ours. It turned out later that the old gentleman took us for an advance-party of a big band of Touaregs who were near, and was only too charmed to find us so charming.

Digby then proceeded with the appropriate account of ourselves, alluding to the dumb forbidding Hank and Buddy, as most holy men, *khouans, hadjis, marabouts,* under a strict vow of silence that it would be ill work for any man to attempt to break. Himself and me he described as *m'rabets,* men hereditarily holy and prominent in faith and virtue.

How much of this our hearers understood, and how much of what they understood, they believed, I could not tell, but they were obviously relieved to find us friendly and not part of a larger force.

We were promptly invited to come along, and thought it best to comply, there being little reason against doing so and much against refusing. In any case they had "got us," from the moment we came upon their levelled rifles, our own slung behind us; and we were at their mercy. As we rode along, nominally guests, but feeling we were prisoners, I was interested to hear Digby assuring the old sheikh that though we were as holy as it is given to mere men to be, we were nevertheless good hefty proselytisers who carried the Q'ran in one hand and the sword in the other, fighting-men who would be pleased to chip in, if the Touaregs attacked his band.

The old gentleman returned thanks and said that, once home, they did not fear all the Touaregs in the Sahara, as the place was quite impregnable. This sounded attractive, and proved to be perfectly true.

What did trouble them, was the fact that when they set off with a caravan of camels for sale at Tanout, it was more than likely that they would, for months, have to fight a series of pitched battles or lose the whole of the wherewithal to purchase grain for their subsistence, for there was nothing a Touareg robber desired more than camels.

"It is the only wealth that carries itself," observed Digby sententiously.

After riding for some three or four hours towards some low rocky mountains, we reached them and approached a narrow and lofty pass. This we threaded in single file, and, coming to the top, saw before us an endless plain out of which arose a *gara*, an abrupt and isolated plateau looking like a gigantic cheese placed in the middle of the level expanse of desert.

Toward this we rode for another hour or two, and discovered it to be a precipitous mountain, sheer, cliff-sided, with a flat top; the whole, I suppose, about a square mile in area.

Apparently it was quite inaccessible and untrodden by the foot of man, or even of mountain sheep or goat. Only an eagle, I imagined, had ever looked upon the top of that isolated square mile of rock.

I was wrong, however, the place proving to be a gigantic fort--a fort of the most perfect kind, but which owed nothing whatever to the hand of man.

Circling the cliff-like precipitous base of the mountain, we came to a crack in the thousand-foot wall, a crack that was invisible at a hundred yards.

Into this narrow fissure the sheikh led us in single file, and, squeezing our way between gigantic cactus, we rode along the upward-sloping bottom of a winding chasm that was not six feet wide.

Suddenly our path was cut by a deep ravine, some three yards wide, a great crack across the crack in which we were entombed. Bridging this was laid a number of trunks of the *dom* palm, and over these a matting of palm-leaf and sand made a narrow but safe path for camels.

Obviously this bridge could easily be removed if necessary, and the place defended with the greatest ease, if any enemy were foolish enough to attempt to bridge the abyss while the defenders dropped boulders from terrific heights, and fired their rifles at point-blank range from behind the strong stone wall that faced the chasm.

Having crossed the bridge, we rode on upward to where this narrow slit in the mountain opened out into a big rock-enclosed square like a landing on a staircase--beyond which camels could not go.

In this natural *serai* we dismounted and left our beasts, continuing our climb on foot.

It was, indeed, an impregnable place, and I did not see how the best troops in the world could capture it, so long as there remained a stout-hearted defender in any one of the invisible places that commanded the path up which two men could nowhere climb abreast, and where, in many places, only one could squeeze with difficulty.

And on the plateau was a walled city, a city built of blocks of dressed stone, blocks larger than any I have ever seen put to such purpose, and obviously of such an age in this use as must have left them old there when the world, as we know of it, was young.

It was a great and melancholy place, containing, I should think, at least three times as many dwelling-places as there were dwellers. Personally, I lost any sense of our precarious position and all feeling of danger and anxiety, in interest and wonderment at this "walled city set upon a hill," and such a hill.

But, as I have said, there was no wonderful white race here for us to restore to touch with modern civilisation. Nor was there any wonderful black race either. The inhabitants of this strange city were just ordinary Arabs, I believe, though I am no ethnologist, and, so far as they knew, they had "always" lived there.

Nevertheless, I felt perfectly certain that no ancestor of theirs had placed those incredible monoliths in position, nor made for themselves doorways twelve and fifteen feet in height, leading into chambers ten feet higher.

These people were undoubtedly the long-established dwellers in this city, but none the less were they dwellers in someone else's city, and merely camping in it at that, even if for a few thousand years.

However, they were very interesting people, living simply and austerely under the benign sway of their patriarchal sheikh, and quite hospitable and friendly. They knew but little of the outside world, though they realised that there were *Roumis* and infidels of all kinds, other cities than their own, holy places besides Mecca and Medina, and greater sheikhs, sultans, and emperors than their own. They apparently regarded the world, or at any rate their world, as divided up into Touareg robbers on the one hand, and the enemies and victims of Touaregs on the other.

In their marvellous rock fastness they were safe, but out on the desert they were at the mercy of any nomadic robber-band stronger than themselves.

Water they had in plenty, as their mountain contained an apparently inexhaustible well and spring, and they had goat-flesh and a little grain, vegetables, and dates, but were compelled to make the six months' caravan journey to Tanout for the grain that formed the staple of their food, as well as for ammunition, salt, and cooking-vessels--for which commodities they exchanged their camels as well as dressed goatskins, and garments beautifully woven and embroidered by their women-folk.

With these good folk we stayed for some days, a pleasant restful oasis in the weary desert of our lives, receiving genuine Arab hospitality, and repaying it with such small gifts as were of more value to them than to us, and by offering to scout for, and fight with, their caravan then about to set out across a notoriously dangerous tract of country to the east.

We must have puzzled the simple souls of this inbred dying people, for though we were obviously of strict piety, and observed the same hours of prayer as themselves from the *fedjer* at dawn to the *asha* at night, we would not pray in company with them, nor, as we sat and *faddhled* (or gossiped) round the sheikh's fire at night, would we say one word on religious subjects. We ran no unnecessary risks. A dignified "*Allahou akbar*" or "*In châh Allah*," showed our agreement with the speaker and our pious orthodoxy, and it had to suffice. As puritanical protestant reforming Senussi, we had a higher and purer brand of Islamism than theirs, but refrained from hurting their feelings by any parade of it... .

Digby was great, and his descriptions of Mecca and Medina, Baghdad, Constantinople, and Cairo, Fez, Timbuktu, and Kufra, held his hearers spellbound and left them little time for questions.

Hank and Buddy were equally great, in what they did not say and the manner in which they did not say it.

Nevertheless, it was well we could make the departure of the caravan our opportunity for going, and it was well that our hosts were what they were, and even then the ice, at times, was very thin.

We descended from this extraordinary and apparently absolutely unknown prehistoric city, and set off with the caravan, rested and in better case than we had been in for months.

We were going in the right direction, we were approaching Aïr, we should then be near a caravan-route on which were wells; and if our danger from our fellow-men, Arab and French, was likely to increase, our danger from the far more terrible enemy, the desert, would decrease.

With luck, we might parallel the caravan-route and make dashes for water when opposite the oases on the route, trusting that we should be able to evade French patrols (of Senegalese infantry and Arab *goumiers)* and Touareg raiding-parties alike.

We said our "*Abka ala Kheir*" (good-byes) to our late hosts and heard their "*Imshi besselema*" (Go in peace) with real regret, at the last oasis on our common route, pressed on in good heart and high hopes, did very well for a month, and then fell straight into the hands of the rascally and treacherous Tegama, Sultan of Agades, when we were only four hundred miles from the frontier of Nigeria and safety.

§ 2

Our visit to Agades was a very different affair from that to the impregnable city on the hill. In the latter place we felt no real fear and little anxiety. In Agades we walked very warily, our hearts in our mouths and our heads loose upon our necks. To the old sheikh we had been objects of wonder and interest. To the Sultan Tegama we were objects of the most intense suspicion.

There was nothing of the simple out-of-the-world dweller-apart, about the swashbuckling ruffians of this City of the Plain, nor about the arch-ruffian Tegama, their leader (executed later by the French for treachery), nor would the pose of pious Senussi emissaries have been of any avail in these circumstances. In the idiom of Buddy, there was no moss upon the teeth of the Sultan Tegama and his gang. In the idiom of Digby there were no flies upon these gentlemen.

We owed our lives to the fact that we escaped before the worthy Tegama had quite placed us, and was quite certain that we were not what we pretended to be--seditious mischief-makers from the north, bent upon raising the desert tribes of the centre and south against the French in a great pan-Islamic *jehad*.

Not that Tegama had the slightest objection to being so "raised"; far from it. Nothing would have suited him better, for there was nothing he enjoyed more; and if to rapine and slaughter, fire and sword, robbery and massacre, he could add the heaven-gaining merit of the destruction of the Unbeliever and the overthrow of his empire in Africa, the cup of his happiness would be full... .

But we puzzled him undoubtedly. Our accent, manners, habits, ignorance, eyes, complexions, faces, and everything about us puzzled him.

Certainly we spoke Arabic fluently and knew men and cities; we seemed to be *hadjis* all right; we inveighed with convincing bitterness against the French; we were upstanding desert fighting-men with nothing whatsoever European about our clothing and accoutrements; we were too small a party to be dangerous, and there was no earthly reason why we should be French spies (for the emissaries of France came perfectly openly in the shape of extremely well-equipped military expeditions, pursuing the well-worn way of all peaceful penetrators, and were a source of fear and bitter hatred to the Sultan)--*but,* we had no credentials; we gave absolutely no information whatsoever about the strength, disposition, and movements of the French forces; we had no cut-and-dried play for an on-fall; and the dumbness of two of us did not seem to mark them out as born emissaries of sedition, unrest, and rebellion!

When Tegama voiced these suspicions, Digby, with fine courage, took the high hand and, as tactfully as possible, hinted that there might be things in the minds of the Great Ones, our masters, that were not to be comprehended by every petty desert chieftain, and that one thing about their minds was the certainty of a powerful and dangerous resentment against anybody who hindered the free movements of their messengers, or behaved as though they were the friends of the very Infidels from whom these Great Ones were endeavouring to free Islam... .

And the gentle Tegama halted long between two opinions, whether to impale us out of hand, or whether to put off till to-morrow what he would like to do to-day, in case we were what we said we were.

It was an unpleasant time, and though we were not ill-treated nor imprisoned, our rifles and camels were "minded" for us, and we never found ourselves alone--particularly when we walked abroad, although it was obvious that no one could escape from Agades on foot.

We felt that at any moment Tegama might decide that we were genuine delegates and emissaries from those who were then so busily stirring the fermenting brew of pan-Islamic discontent in northern Africa--and let us go; and also that at any moment we might so betray ourselves that he would decide we were impostors--and forthwith impale us, living, on the sharpened stump of a young tree... .

We had been caught at dawn, in an oasis south west of the Baguezan mountains, by a *harka* of Tegama's that had evidently been raiding and robbing to the north, and, for a week or so, we rode south as the prisoner-guests of the emir in command, a magnificent specimen of the best type of desert Arab.

Him Digby had told the same tale that he had told to the old sheikh and many another inquisitive wayfarer, but he had decided to alter his tale for the private ear of the Sultan as soon as we learnt that it was to so important and well-informed a person that we were to be taken.

Whispering together at night, we decided that Hank and Buddy must of course remain dumb, and that we must put up a terrific bluff of mystery. It would be worse than hopeless to pretend to be Senussi from Kufra, in a place like Agades, where it was quite probable there were specimens of the genuine article, and where our stories would rapidly be tested and found wanting.

And so we took the high hand with Tegama, so far as we dared; told him that we had no definite message for him *yet,* but that on our return journey he would hear things that would surprise him, and so forth... .

Agades proved to be a very ancient, clay-built, sand-buried walled town, containing a remarkable mosque with a tower like a church spire, and although so utterly lost in the very heart of the Sahara, still in touch with the outside world by reason of being on the pilgrim-route to Mecca, and on the great caravan-route that crosses Africa.

The only other building that was not insignificant was the Sultan's palace, a big two-storied building of baked clay, surrounded by a high thick clay wall, the gateway through which was practically a short tunnel.

Through this tunnel, and past very strong gates made of palm-trunks nailed solidly together upon cross-pieces, we were led into a dirty square of desert sand and stones, two sides of which were formed by mud huts that backed against the high enclosing wall.

One side of the square was occupied by the palace and another by a mosque. Camels, goats, chickens, and dirty men ornamented this palace courtyard or back-yard.

We were invited to enter the palace, and through another small tunnel came into a big windowless hall, with unornamented clay walls, clay ceiling, and clay floor.

Here we were kept waiting with our escort, and stood in haughty silence until conducted across a small inner courtyard to the presence-chamber of the Sultan of Agades.

This was another windowless clay room with great arched ceiling beams and a door, ten feet from the ground, up to which ran a clay staircase. In the middle of the wall opposite the door by which we entered, was a throne, also of clay--a base material for so exalted a symbol, but at least it was of honest clay, which its occupant was not.

Cross-legged on this bed-like throne, in dirty white robes, sat Tegama, who carried on his face the stamp of his ruling passions, greed, cruelty, lust, savagery, and treachery. Around him stood a small group of wazirs, sheikhs, soldiers, and what I uncomfortably took to be executioners.

The Sultan glared at us and I felt sorrowful to the tips of my toes. I knew by now all the ways that such gentlemen have of putting to death those of whom they do not approve, and I liked none of them at all. Impaling, a favourite one, I liked, perhaps, the least... .

Digby took the bull by the horns, greeted Tegama politely, hoped he was well, professed pleasure at seeing him, and said he had a good deal to say to him later on, when he had made some arrangements further south and had taken the political temperature of one or two places in Damerghou and Damergrim.

Digby took it for granted that we were honoured guests, and that nothing so silly as the idea of molesting us would ever occur to so wise and great a ruler as the good Tegama of Agades.

The good Tegama of Agades continued to eye us coldly.

"And who might *you* be, with your talk of El Senussi?" he enquired contemptuously.

"That is for your ear alone," replied Digby. "I have told the sheikh whom we--er--*met,* in the Baguezan oasis, such things as are fitting to be told to underlings. I come from those whose business is not shouted in every *douar* and *quasr* and chattered about to every wayfarer."

And here I boomed:

"No, indeed! Allah forbid!" and smiled at the idea.

"Oh, you can talk, can you?" sneered Tegama, who had evidently been told that some of us were dumb.

"*Salaam aleikum wa Rahmab Allah,*" I intoned piously. "Our Master in the north--*Rahmat ullahi Allahim*--(and he may be in Morocco, and he may be in Algiers, and he may be near here with a mighty army of the Faithful)--is not one of whose affairs his messengers babble, nor is he one whose messengers are delayed."

"And what is his message?" asked Tegama, with, I thought, less sneer in his voice.

"That comes not here *yet,*" replied Digby. "The word comes to the great and good Sultan of Agades later, when the time is ripe ..." and much more of bluff and mystification that sufficiently impressed Tegama to lead him to wait and see.

He waited but he did not see, for we escaped--this time, I must admit, thanks to Buddy's irrepressible interest in "squaws."

What he could have achieved had he had the free use of his tongue I cannot say. In this case, although love was not only blind, but dumb as well, it contrived to laugh at locksmiths, and we other three benefited by the laughter.

We got away and on good camels, but we had not a rifle among us, nor any other weapon of any sort whatever.

I am tempted to tell, in full, the story of this evasion, for it was a most romantic business, with all the accessories of fiction and melodrama. I have said that the story of this journey alone would fill a large volume, and it would be small exaggeration to say that a complete account of our sojourn in Agades would fill another.

I wish I had space in which to tell of the incredible things we saw in this place, whose atmosphere and ways and deeds were those of a thousand years ago.

I have read that the first Europeans to set foot in Agades were the members of the French Military Mission (which came with the great annual salt-caravan from the south in 1904), but I could tell of a fair-bearded man who stared at us with blazing *grey* eyes, a man whose tongue had been cut out, whose ears and fingers had been cut off, and who was employed as a beast of burden.

I could also tell of a Thing that sat always in the Sôk, mechanically swaying its body to and fro as it crooned. Its lips, eyelids, ears, hands, and feet had been cut off, it was blind, and it crooned in *German*.

I could tell of such scenes as that of the last hours of a very brave man, who was bound face downwards on a plank that was thrust over the edge of an enormously deep dry well. At the other end of the plank was a big stone and a jar of water that slowly leaked, either by reason of a crack or its porosity. When the water had leaked away to such an extent that the weight of the jar and stone was less than that of the man, he and the plank would go headlong down into the dark depths from which he would never return.

There he lay staring down into the horrible place, while round about sat citizens of leisure who told him to hurry with his last prayers, for the water was nearly gone, while others bade him to heed them not, for he had hours longer to wait... .

I should like to tell of Tegama's executioners, four negroes who were the most animal creatures I ever saw in human form, and not one of whom was less than seven feet in height. The speciality of their leader was the clean, neat flicking-off of a head or any required limb, from a finger to a leg, with one stroke of a great sword; while that of another was the infliction of the maximum number of wounds and injuries without causing the death of the victim.

They were skilled labourers and their work was their hobby... .

I could tell of some very remarkable adventures, risks, dangers, and escapes in Agades, and of some very strange doings in that horrible "palace" with its plots and intrigues, jealousies and hatreds, factions and parties, if space permitted.

And when our time and opportunity came (and we were led one dark night to where four camels, with water and food for two or three days, awaited us) we would not have taken advantage of the chance, being weaponless, had we not felt that we ran a greater danger by remaining.

Tegama was growing more suspicious and more truculent, and I rather think that the dumb Hank and Buddy had been overheard in fluent converse. Probably we gave ourselves away too (whenever we ate, drank, prayed, sat, stood, sneezed, or did anything else whatsoever), as the weirdest kind of weird Mussulmans who ever said, "*Bismillah arahman arahmim... .*"

It was time to go and we went, aided by a young person of magnificent physique, magnificent courage, and negroid ancestry--probably the daughter of some negro slave-woman from Lake Tchad... .

Unfortunately it was utterly impossible for her to get us weapons.

§ 3

We escaped from Tegama, but not from the consequences of our encounter with him. He did not destroy us, but it was to him that we owed our destruction.

Riding as hard as we could, we followed the tactics of our escape from Zinderneuf, feeling sure that if Tegama pursued and recaptured us, our fate would be sealed and our deaths lingering and unpleasant.

We therefore avoided the caravan-route that runs from Agades, and struck out into the desert, hoping that, as hitherto, we should, sooner or later, discover someone or something that would lead us to water.

After three days of painful wandering, we chanced upon the wretched encampment of some aboriginal Beri-Beri bushmen, black, almost naked, and armed only with bows and arrows. They apparently lived by trapping ostriches by means of tethered foot-traps concealed beneath the bushes and trees, thorns and acacias, on which the birds feed.

These primitive people were camped beside an inexplicable pool of water among colossal boulders as big as cathedrals.

Here we rested ourselves and our camels for a day or two, and then again set out, with our leather water-skins filled and our food-bags nearly empty.

A couple of days later we were riding in a long line, just within sight of each other, and scouting for signs of human beings or water.

Hank was on the right of the line, I next to him and half a mile away, having Buddy on my left, with Digby at the far end.

Looking to my right, I saw Hank, topping a little undulation, suddenly wheel towards me, urging his camel to its topmost speed.

As I looked, a crowd of riders swarmed over the skyline, and, two or three of them, halting their camels, opened fire on us.

Buddy rode at full speed toward me and Hank. Digby was cut off from view by a tor of rocks.

"Dismount and form sqar'," yelled Hank, riding up.

I knew what he meant. We brought our camels to their knees, made a pretence of getting out rifles from under the saddles, crouched behind the camels, and levelled our sticks as though they were guns, across the backs of the animals, and awaited death.

"This is whar we gits what's comin' to us," said Buddy.

"The durned galoots may not call our bluff," growled Hank.

The band, Hoggar or Tebu robbers by the look of them, bore down upon us with yells of "*Ul-ul-ul-ul-ul-ullah Akbar,*" on pleasure and profit bent--the pleasure of slaughtering us and the profit of taking our camels--brandishing swords, lances, and rifles as they swept along.

I could have wept that we had no rifles. Steady magazine fire from three marksmen like ourselves, would have brought the yelling fiends crashing to earth in such numbers as might have saved us and provided us with much that we sorely needed.

The feeling of utter impotence was horrible, and like the impotence of nightmare.... To be butchered like sheep without striking a blow.... Could Digby possibly escape? ... Or would they see his tracks and follow him after slaughtering us? ... There was an excellent chance that they would pass straight on without crossing his trail.... Would they swerve from our apparently levelled rifles? No. On they came.... Digby might be well away by now....

And then from somewhere, there rang out loud, clear, and (to these Arabs) terrible, *a bugle-call*--that portentous bugle-call, menacing and fateful, that had been almost the last thing so many desert tribesmen had heard, the bugle-call that announced the closing of the trap and preluded the hail of bullets against which no Arab charge could prevail.

The effect was instant and magical. The band swerved to their right, wheeled, and fled--fled to avoid what they thought a terrible trap, so neatly baited and into which they had so nearly fallen!

As the bugle-calls died away, Hank roared orders in French at the top of his enormous voice, and away to the left a man was apparently signalling back with excited energy, to the French forces behind him, "*enemy in sight.*"

Evidently the panic-stricken mob of raiders thought that the danger was behind the spot on which they had first seen Hank, for they fled in a direction to the right of the rocks behind which Digby had blown his bugle....

Suddenly my heart leapt into my throat, as one of the robbers, perhaps their leader or a candidate for leadership, swerved to the left from the ruck of the fleeing band, and, either in a spirit of savage vengeance, or the desire, not uncommon with these people, for single combat in the presence of many onlookers, rode at the man who had exposed himself to signal back to the French force of which he was evidently the scout....

"Quick!" I shouted. "He'll get him," and I found myself yelling Digby's name.

We scrambled on to our camels, Hank bawling commands in French, and Buddy yelling devilish war-whoops.

Digby stooped and then poised himself in the attitude of a javelin-thrower. As the Arab raised his great sword, Digby's arm shot forward and the Arab reeled, receiving the stone full in his face, and jerking the camel's head round as he did so. Digby sprang at the man's leg and pulled him down, the two falling together.

They rose simultaneously, the Arab's sword went up, Digby's fist shot out, and we heard the smack as the man reeled backwards and fell, his sword dropping from his hand. Digby seized it and stood over the half-stunned robber, who was twitching and clawing at the sand....

And then we heard another sound.

A rifle was fired, and Digby swayed and fell.

An Arab had wheeled from the tail of the fleeing band, fired this shot at thirty yards' range, and fled again, we three on our galloping camels being not a hundred yards from him.

* * * * * * *

Digby was dead before I got to him, shot through the back of the head with an expanding bullet....

We tied the Arab's feet, and I blew bugle-calls to the best of my ability.

I am going to say nothing at all about my feelings.

Digby was dead. Michael was dead. I felt that the essential me was dead too.

I lived on like an automaton, and--like a creature sentenced to death--I waited for the blow to fall, the moment of collapse to come.

§ 4

We buried Digby there, although we expected the return of the Arabs at any moment.

"He shore gave his life for ourn," said Hank, chewing his lips.

"'*Greater love hath no man,*'" I was able to reply.

Buddy said nothing, but Buddy wept. He then untied the completely-recovered Arab, a huge, powerful young fellow, twice his size, and without weapons on either side, fought him and beat him insensible.

Discussing the question of this robber's future, I suggested we should bind his hands, put him on his camel, and make him our guide--bidding him lead us first to the oasis from which the band had come.

"Lead us not into temptation," said Buddy. "He'd shore lead us where he wanted us."

Speaking to the man in his own tongue, when he had recovered from Buddy's handling of him, I asked him what he was prepared to do to save his life... . Could he lead us south, parallel with the caravan route, from one oasis or water-hole to another, if we agreed to set him free as soon as we were in the Kano territory?

He replied that he would willingly lead us to Hell and cheerfully abide there himself, so long as he got us there too. He was undoubtedly a brave man.

I told him that in that case we should take his camel and weapons (unfortunately for us he had no rifle), and leave him where he was, to die of thirst.

"*El Mektub Mektub*" (What is written is written), he replied, with a shrug, and that was all we could get out of him.

In the end we took him with us, bound, on his camel, which was tied to Buddy's, and left him at the first water-hole to which we came. This we found by following the track made by his friends as they had come northward.

From here we rode on with filled water-skins and half the food-supply of the Arab whom we had abandoned... .

Digby's death proved to be the first tragic catastrophe of a series of disasters that now overtook us.

First we encountered a terrible sand-storm that nearly killed us, and quite obliterated all tracks.

Then we missed the caravan-route when we reluctantly decided to return to it, either crossing it in ignorance, where the ground was too rocky for there to be any footprints, or else riding over the road itself at a spot where all traces of it had been wiped out, or buried, by the sand-storm.

Next, nearly dead with thirst, we reached a water-hole, and found it dried up!

Here our starving camels ate some poisonous shrub or other, speedily sickened, and within thirty-six hours were all dead.

We thus found ourselves stranded in the desert, not knowing whether the caravan-route was to the east or to the west of us, without rifles, without food, without camels, and with one goat-skin containing about a pint of water.

This we decided not to drink until we must literally drink or die, though it seemed that we must surely do that in any case.

For a day we struggled on, incredibly, without water, and at the end of the day wondered whether we were a day's march further from the caravan-road on which were oases, wells, water-holes, and villages.

Once we found it (if ever), we would risk the French patrols until we could again get camels. On the caravan-route, death was probable, here in the desert, on foot, it was certain.

Night found us unable to speak, our lips black, and cracked in great fissures, our tongues swollen horribly, our throats closed, and our mouths *dry*. (It is an incredibly horrible thing to have one's mouth literally and really *dry*, like hard leather.)

I pointed at the precious water-skin and raised my eyebrows interrogatively.

Hank shook his head and pointed at the setting sun and then at the zenith. We must drink to-morrow when we should, if possible, be in worse case than now.

We reeled on through the night, for our lives depended on reaching the "road."

Towards morning, I could go no further and sank down without meaning to do so. I tried to rise and failed. Seeing that I could do no more, the other two lay down beside me, and we fell asleep.

The sun woke me to see Buddy, with a face like death, staring at a scrap of paper torn from a pocket-book.

He passed it to me. On it was scrawled:

"*Pards,*

Drink up the water slow and push on quick. Good old Buddy, we bin good pards. Hank.

Hank was gone... .

Buddy untied the neck of the goat-skin and filled his mouth with water. He held the water in his mouth for a minute and then swallowed it slowly.

"Take a mouthful like that and then swaller," he croaked hoarsely.

"We gotta do what Hank ses," he added, as I shook my head. I could not drink the water.

"We gotta hike," wheezed Buddy. "We don' wanta make what he done all for nix. All no good, like. He won't come back an' drink it... . Yew ain't goin' to *waste* his life, pard? ... He done it fer *you*... ."

I filled my mouth and swallowed--but I could not swallow the lump in my throat... .

We staggered on through that day and the next, moistening our mouths at intervals, and just before sunset, on the second day, saw a mirage of palm trees, a village, a little white mosque, and--the mirage was real.

We stayed at this village for months, scouring the desert for Hank, working as cultivators, water-carriers, watchmen, camelmen, and at any other job that offered, and we were never both asleep at the same time.

When French patrols visited the place, we hid, or fled into the desert, with the entire sympathy of the villagers. We could have joined more than one south-bound caravan, but I would not urge Buddy to leave the place.

He had such faith in the indestructibility of Hank, that he hoped against hope, until hope deferred made his heart sick.

At first it was:

"He'll come mushin' in here ter-morrer, a-throwin' his feet like the Big Buck Hobo, rollin' his tail like a high-fed hoss, an' grinnin' fit ter bust... ."

Then it was:

"Nobody couldn't kill Hank... . He's what you call ondestructible... . Why, back in Colorado, he shore chased a man over the Panamint Mountains an' right across Death Valley once, an' inter the Funeral Mountains t'other side. A hoss-rustler, he was, and when ole Hank got him, he was stone dead with heat an' thirst, an' Hank turned right round an' hiked back and come out alive! ..."

And at last, when a caravan came from the north actually going south to Zinder (the military headquarters of the *Territoire Militaire)* and comparative civilisation, he proposed that we should join it as camelmen and guards.

"You can't stop here fer keeps, pard," he said. "I reckon I bin selfish. But I couldn't leave ole Hank while there was a chance... ."

But for Michael's letter (and my longing to see Isobel), I would have urged Buddy to stay, for that was what he really wanted to do.

Nothing could destroy his faith in his friend's superiority to the desert and to death. We joined the caravan as fighting-men, one dumb, and later (as we neared Zinder) we left it though we had little fear of getting into trouble there. Still, it was just possible that some non-com. of the big garrison there might know and recognise us, and possible that a well-equipped desert-party of *goumiers* might have come along the caravan-road from Zinderneuf.

Our adventures between Zinder and the British border at Barbera, where we first saw Haussas in the uniform of the West African Field Force, were numerous, and our hardships great; but Fate seemed to have done its worst--and now that I had lost Digby, and Buddy had lost Hank, and neither of us cared very much what happened, our luck changed and all went fairly well.

And one day we rode, on miserable donkeys, into the great city of Kano, and I revealed myself to an astounded Englishman as a compatriot.

He was kindness itself, and put me in communication with a friend, or rather a friend of Aunt Patricia's, a Mr. Lawrence of the Nigerian Civil Service. This gentleman sent me money and an invitation to come and stay with him at his headquarters and to bring Buddy with me.

And when I told Buddy that on the morrow he was actually going to ride in a train once more--I found that he was not.

He had only come to Kano to see me safe, and, having done so, he was going straight back to look for Hank!

Nothing would shake his determination, and it was waste of words to try. Nor was it pleasant to strive to persuade him that his friend was dead.

"Would *you* go if it was yore brother that was lost, pard?" he said.

"Nope... . Hank give his life fer us... ."

All I could do was to see him fitted out with everything procurable in Kano--a fine camel, a spare one for food, water, ammunition, and a small tent, and a Haussa ex-soldier as servant and guide, recommended by the Kano Englishman, an official named Mordaunt.

The latter made it clear to the Haussa that he was to go north with this American "explorer," obey him in all things, receive half his pay before starting, and the other half, with a bonus depending in value upon his merit, when he returned to Kano with his master, or honourably discharged.

Mordaunt was good enough to accept my word that if he would be my banker in this matter, I would adjust things as soon as I saw Mr. Lawrence, who was an old friend of his.

I hated parting with the staunch, brave, great-hearted little Buddy, and I felt that he would never return to Kano unless it was with Hank, and I had no hope whatever of his doing that... .

I wondered if I should ever have had the cold iron courage to go voluntarily back into that Hell, after escaping it by a miracle, on such a ghost of a chance of finding a friend... .

§ 5

I took the train at Kano to some place of which I have forgotten the name, and Lawrence met me on the platform. I remembered his face as soon as I saw it, as that of the quiet, rather dour and repellent man who had been to Brandon Abbas two or three times when we were there.

He came nearer to showing excitement, while he listened to my story, than I thought was his wont. When I had finished he said:

"I should like to know when fiction was much stranger than this piece of truth! ... And you *still* do not know the rights of this 'Blue Water' mystery?"

"No," I said. "I only know that my brother Michael never stole anything in his life."

"Quite so," he replied. "Of course... . And now I have something to tell *you*. Your Major de Beaujolais was sent down to Zinder and from there he went home on leave *via* Kano-- and on Kano railway-station platform I met him, and he told me the whole of the story of Zinderneuf Fort from *his* side of the business, and about finding your brother's 'confession.' I went on to Brandon Abbas and told Lady Brandon what he told me--and it really did not seem to interest her enormously!"

It was my turn to feel excited now.

It was incredible to sit there in a hammock-chair under the African stars, outside this man's tents, a whiskey-and-soda in my hand and a cheroot in my mouth, and hear him tell how *he* had taken our Zinderneuf story to *Brandon Abbas!*

I think I was soon past wonder and all power to feel astonishment.

What did strike me and what did give me endless food for speculation, from then until I saw her, was his account of how Aunt Patricia had received his incredible news. Apparently she did not seem even to *want* to get the wretched jewel back. Her attitude had puzzled Lawrence, and it puzzled me as he described it... .

When Lawrence had finished his tale he gave me much Brandon Abbas news.

Sir Hector Brandon was dead. He had died miserably, alone in Kashmir, of cholera--his servants and coolies having fled as soon as the disease was recognised for what it was.

The Chaplain had died of what was apparently a paralytic stroke. Claudia had married one of the richest men in England, nearly old enough to be her grandfather.

Augustus, always a poor horseman, had fallen off his hunter and been dragged until he was very dead indeed.

Isobel was quite well. No, she had not married. How long was it since Mr. Lawrence had heard from Lady Brandon? Oh, quite recently, only a month or so ago. She wrote more frequently nowadays. Seemed to have no one to turn to for advice, now the Chaplain was dead... .

Isobel was well and unmarried! (I was conscious that I was breathing more freely and my heart functioning more regularly than it had done since this grave austere official had mentioned Claudia's marriage.) ...

Did she feel towards me as she had done that morning when I did not say good-bye to her--that morning that seemed so long ago that it might have been in a previous existence, that morning that *was* so long ago?

And so Aunt Patricia knew! Yet what did she know after all? Merely that Michael professed and confessed to be the single-handed thief of the "Blue Water," and that he, and he alone, was to blame... .

Did she yet know *the truth* as to the theft?

§ 6

I had been feeling horribly ill for some time, and now I collapsed altogether with a combination of malarial fever and dysentery--that ill-omened union after whose attack a man is never quite the same again.

Had I been Lawrence's own son, he could not have done more for me, and the Government doctor, who came post-haste by rail and horse, was splendid. It was a close call and a long, slow recovery, but the day came at last when I found myself weak, shaky, and emaciated on Maidobi platform *en route* for Lagos and home.

George Lawrence was with me, having sworn not to let me out of his sight until he had delivered me safe and sound at Brandon Abbas. I put aside the unworthy thought which occurred to me--that it was himself he yearned to see safe and sound at that house! The idea occurred to me when I found that whatever I said about Michael interested him to the extent that it bore upon Michael's relations to Aunt Patricia, and that his interest in the mystery of the "Blue Water" was limited to its bearing upon Aunt Patricia's affairs.

And so, one day, I found myself on the deck of a steamer, breathing glorious sea-air, and looking back upon the receding coast of horrible Africa, and almost too weak to keep my eyes from watering and my throat from swelling, as I realised that I was leaving behind me all that was mortal of two of the best and finest men that ever lived--my brothers, Michael and Digby. Also two more of the finest men of a different kind, Hank and Buddy, possibly alive, probably dead (for no word had come to Kano)--and, but for Isobel, I should have wished that I were dead too.

But I was glad to be alive, and in my selfishness let my joy lay balm upon my grief for my brothers and my friends--for in my pocket were cables from Isobel, cables dispatched as soon as Lawrence's letter reached Brandon Abbas, announcing my appearance in Nigeria, and the deaths of Michael and Digby.

§ 7

I will not write of my meeting with her. Those who love, or ever have loved, can imagine something of what I felt as I walked to the Bower, which she had elected to be our meeting-place rather than a railway-platform, or a steamer's deck.

There was my darling, more beautiful than ever, and, if possible, more sweet and loving... .

Well, joy does not kill, or I should not have survived that hour. Aunt Patricia was coldly kind, at first.

I was made to feel that she had sent for me one day, and I had refused to come, and had further disobeyed her by leaving the house, against her expressed desires!

After lunch, in the drawing-room, the room from which the "Blue Water" had disappeared, I gave her, in the presence of Isobel and George Lawrence, the letter and packet that had been Michael's charge to me.

She opened the letter first and read it, and then read aloud in a clear and steady voice:

"My most dear and admired Aunt Patricia,

When you get this, I shall be dead, and when you have read it I shall be forgiven, I hope, for I did what I thought was best, and what would, in a small measure, repay you for some of your great goodness to me and my brothers.

My dear Aunt, I knew you had sold the 'Blue Water' to the Maharajah (for the benefit of the tenants and the estate), and I knew you must dread the return of Sir Hector, and his discovery of the fact, sooner or later.

I was inside one of the suits of armour when you handed the 'Blue Water' over to the vizier or agent of the Maharajah. I heard everything, and when once you had said what you said and I had heard it--it was pointless for me to confess that I knew--but when I found that you had had a duplicate made, I thought what a splendid thing it would be if only we had a burglary and the 'Blue Water' substitute were stolen! The thieves would be nicely done in the eye, and your sale of the stone would never be discovered by Sir Hector.

Had I known how to get into the Priests' Hole and open the safe, I would have burgled it for you.

Then Sir Hector's letter came, announcing his return, and I knew that things were desperate and the matter urgent. So I spirited away that clever piece of glass or quartz or whatever it is, and I herewith return it (with apologies). I nearly put it back after all, the same night, but I'm glad I didn't. (Tell John this.)

Now I do beg and pray you to let Sir Hector go on thinking that I am a common thief and stole the 'Blue Water'--or all this bother that everybody has had will be all for nothing, and I shall have failed to shield you from trouble and annoyance.

If it is not impertinent, may I say that I think you were absolutely right to sell it, and that the value is a jolly sight better applied to the health and happiness of the tenants and villagers and to the productiveness of the farms, than locked up in a safe in the form of a shining stone that is of no earthly benefit to anyone.

It nearly made me regret what I had done, when those asses, Digby and John, had the cheek to bolt too. Honestly, it never occurred to me that they would do anything so silly. But I suppose it is selfish of me to want all the blame and all the fun and pleasure of doing a little job for you.

I do so hope that all has gone well and turned out as I planned. I bet Uncle Hector was sick!

Well, my dear Aunt, I can only pray that I have helped you a little.

With sincerest gratitude for all you have done for us,

Your loving and admiring nephew,

'Beau' Geste."

* * * * * * *

"A *beau geste,* indeed," said Aunt Patricia, and for the only time in my life, I saw her put her handkerchief to her eyes.

* * * * * * *

Extract from a letter from George Lawrence, Esq., C.M.G. of His Majesty's Nigerian Civil Service, to Colonel Henri de Beaujolais, Colonel of Spahis, XIXth (African) Army Corps:

* * * * * * *

"... *And so that is the other side of the story, my friend. Alas, for those two splendid boys, Michael and Digby Geste... .*

And the remaining piece of news is that I do most sincerely hope that you will be able to come over to England in June.

You are the best man I know, Jolly, and I want you to be my Best Man, a desire heartily shared by Lady Brandon.

Fancy, old cabbage, after more than thirty years of devotion! ... I feel like a boy!

And that fine boy, John, is going to marry the 'so beautiful child' whom you remembered. Lady Brandon is being a fairy godmother to them, indeed. I think she feels she is somehow doing something for Michael by smoothing their path so... ."

THE END

BOOK TWO

BEAU SABREUR

"A man may escape from his enemies or even from his friends, but how shall a man escape from his own nature?"

TO "NOBBY."
TRUE COMRADE,
TO WHOM THIS BOOK OWES MUCH.

NOTE

The Author would like to anticipate certain of the objections which may be raised by some of the kindly critics and reviewers who gave so friendly and encouraging a chorus of praise to *Beau Geste, The Wages of Virtue,* and *The Stepsons of France.*

Certain of the events chronicled in these books were objected to, as being impossible.

They were impossible.

The only defence that the Author can offer is that, although perfectly impossible, they actually happened.

In reviewing *The Wages of Virtue,* for example, a very distinguished literary critic remarked that the incident of a girl being found in the French Foreign Legion was absurd, and merely added an impossibility to a number of improbabilities.

The Author admitted the justice of the criticism, and then, as now, put forth the same feeble defence that, although perfectly impossible, it was the simple truth. He further offered to accompany the critic (at the latter's expense) to the merry town of Figuig in Northern Africa, and there to show him the tombstone (with its official epitaph) of a girl who served for many years, *in the Spahis, as a cavalry trooper,* rose to the rank of Sergeant, and remained, until her death in battle, quite unsuspected of being what she was--a European woman.

And in this book, nothing is set forth as having happened which has not happened--including the adoption of two ex-Legionaries by an Arab tribe, and their rising to Sheikdom and to such power that they were signatories to a treaty with the Republic.

One of them, indeed, was conducted over a French troopship, and his simple wonder at the marvels of the *Roumi* was rather touching, and of pleasing interest to all who witnessed it ...

The reader may rest assured that the deeds narrated, and the scenes and personalities pictured, in this book, are not the vain outpourings of a film-fed imagination, but the re-arrangement of actual happenings and the assembling of real people who have actually lived, loved, fought and suffered--and some of whom, indeed, live, love, fight and suffer to this day.

Truth *is* stranger than fiction.

PART I

FAILURE

(OUT OF THE UNFINISHED MEMOIRS OF
MAJOR HENRI DE BEAUJOLAIS
of the Spahis and the French Secret Service)

"To set the cause above renown,
To love the game beyond the prize,
To honour, while you strike him down,
The foe that comes with fearless eyes;
To count the life of battle good,
And clear the land that gave you birth,
Bring nearer yet the brotherhood
That binds the brave of all the earth... ."
--Sir Henry Newbolt.

THE MAKING OF A BEAU SABREUR

CHAPTER I. "OUT OF THE DEPTHS I RISE"

I will start at the very nadir of my fortunes, at the very lowest depths, and you shall see them rise to their zenith, that highest point where they are crowned by Failure.

Behold me, then, clad in a dirty canvas stable-suit and wooden clogs, stretched upon a broad sloping shelf; my head, near the wall, resting on a wooden ledge, a foot wide and two inches thick, meant for a pillow; and my feet near the ledge that terminates this beautiful bed, which is some thirty feet long and seven feet wide. It is as long as the room, in fact, and about two feet from the filthy brick floor.

Between my pampered person and the wooden bed, polished by the rubbing of many vile bodies, is nothing. Covering me is a canvas "bread-bag," four feet long and two wide, a sack used for the carrying of army loaves. As a substitute for sheets, blankets and eider-down quilt, it is inadequate.

The night is bitterly cold, and, beneath my canvas stable-suit, I am wearing my entire wardrobe of underclothes, in spite of which, my teeth are chattering and I shiver from head to foot as though stricken with ague.

I am not allowed to wear my warm regimentals and cloak or overcoat, for, alas! I am in prison.

There is nothing else in the prison but myself and a noisy, *nouveau riche,* assertive kind of odour.

I am wrong--and I wish to be strictly accurate and perfectly truthful--there are hungry and insidious insects, number unknown, industrious, ambitious, and successful.

Some of my fellow troopers pride themselves on being men of intelligence and reason, and therefore believe only in what they can see. I cannot see the insects, but I, intelligent or not, believe in them firmly.

Hullo! there is something else... . A rat has run across my face... . I am glad so rude a beast is in prison. Serve him right... . On the whole, though, I wish he were not in prison, for he is nibbling at my ambrosial locks... . If I smite at him wildly I shall administer a severe blow to the brick wall, with my knuckles... .

The door, of six-inch oak, is flung open, and by the light of the lantern in the hand of the Sergeant of the Guard, I see a man and a brother flung into my retreat. He falls heavily and lies where he falls, in peaceful slumber. He has been worshipping at the shrine of Bacchus, a false god. The door clangs shut and leaves the world to darkness and to me, and the drunken trooper, and the rat, and the insects.

I shiver and wriggle and scratch and wonder whether the assertive odour will conquer, or my proud stomach rise victorious over ... Yes, it is rising ... Victorious? ... No ...

Again the door opens and a trooper enters, thanking the Sergeant of the Guard, in the politest terms, for all his care and kindness. The Sergeant of the Guard, in the impolitest terms, bids the trooper remove his canvas trousers.

He does so, and confirms what the Sergeant had feared--that he is wearing his uniform trousers beneath them. The Sergeant of the Guard confiscates the nethermost garments, consigns the prisoner to the nethermost regions, gives him two extra days in this particular region, and goes out.

As the door clangs, the new-comer strikes a match, produces half a candle, lights it, and politely greets me and the happy sleeper on the floor.

"Let us put this one to bed," he suggests, sticking his candle on the pillow-shelf; and I arise, and we lift the bibulous one from the hard floor to the harder, but less damp and filthy, "bed."

Evidently a humane and kindly soul this. I stand rebuked for my callousness in leaving the drunkard on the ground.

But he does not carry these virtues to excess, for, observing that the Bacchanal has been cast into prison in his walking-out uniform (in which he was evidently brought helpless into barracks), he removes the man's tunic, and puts it on over his own canvas stable-jacket.

"The drunk feel nothing," he observes sententiously. "Why should the sober feel cold?"

I no longer stand rebuked.

By the light of his candle, I study the pleasing black hole in which we lie, its walls decorated by drawings, poems, aphorisms, and *obiter dicta* which do not repay study.

It is a reeking, damp and verminous cellar, some thirty feet square, ventilated only by a single grated aperture, high up in one of the walls, and is an unfit habitation for a horse or dog.

In fact, Colonel du Plessis, our Commanding Officer, would not have one of the horses here for an hour. But I am here for fifteen days (save when doing punishment-drill) and serve me jolly well right.

For I have *tirée une bordée*--absented myself, without leave, for five days--the longest period that one can be absent without becoming a deserter and getting three years' hard labour as such.

Mind, I am not complaining in the very least. I knew the penalty and accepted it. But there was a lady in the case, the very one who had amused us with her remark to de Lannec, anent a stingy Jew politician of her acquaintance--"When a man with a Future visits a lady with a Past, he should be thoughtful of the Present, that it be acceptable--and expensive." She had written to me, beseeching me in the name of old kindnesses, to come quickly to Paris, and saying that she knew nothing but Death would keep me from helping her in her terrible need.... .

And Death stayed his hand until I had justified this brave and witty little lady's faith; and now, after the event, sends his fleas, and odours, and hideous cold too late.... . Dear little Véronique Vaux! ...

There is a great commotion without, and the candle is instantly extinguished by its owner, who pinches the wick.

Evidently one foolishly and futilely rebels against Fate, and more foolishly and futilely resists the Guard.

The door opens and the victim is flung into the cell with a tremendous crash. The Sergeant of the Guard makes promises. The prisoner makes sounds and the sounds drown the promises. He must be raging mad, fighting-drunk, and full of vile cheap canteen-brandy.

The humane man re-lights his candle, and we see a huge and powerful trooper gibbering in the corner.

What *he* sees is, apparently, a gathering of his deadliest foes, for he draws a long and nasty knife from the back of his trouser-belt, and, with a wild yell, makes a rush for us.

The humane man promptly knocks the candle flying, and leaps off the bed. I spring like a--well, *flea* is the most appropriate simile, just here and now--in the opposite direction, and take up an attitude of offensive defence, and to anybody who steps in my direction I will give of my best--where I think it will do most good... .

Apparently the furious one has missed the humane one and the Bacchanalian one, and has struck with such terrific force as to drive his knife so deeply into the wood that he cannot get it out again.

I am glad that my proud stomach, annoyed as I am with it, was not between the knife and the bed... .

And I had always supposed that life in prison was so dull and full of *ennui*... .

The violent one now weeps, the humane one snores, the Bacchanalian one grunts chokingly, and I lie down again, this time without my bread-bag.

Soon the cruel cold, the clammy damp, the wicked flea, the furtive rat, the noisy odour, and the proud stomach combine with the hard bench and aching bones to make me wish that I were not a sick and dirty man starving in prison.

And a few months ago I was at Eton! ... It is all very amusing... .

CHAPTER II. UNCLE

Doubtless you wonder how a man may be an Etonian one year and a trooper in a French Hussar Regiment the next.

I am a Frenchman, I am proud to say; but my dear mother, God rest her soul, was an Englishwoman; and my father, like myself, was a great admirer of England and of English institutions. Hence my being sent to school at Eton.

On my father's death, soon after I had left school, my uncle sent for me.

He was even then a General, the youngest in the French Army, and his wife is the sister of an extremely prominent and powerful politician, at that time--and again since--Minister of State for War.

My uncle is fantastically patriotic, and *La France* is his goddess. For her he would love to die, and for her he would see everybody else die--even so agreeable a person as myself. When his last moments come, he will be frightfully sick if circumstances are not appropriate for him to say, "*I die--that France may live*"--a difficult statement to make convincingly, if you are sitting in a Bath chair at ninety, and at Vichy or Aix.

He is also a really great soldier and a man of vision. He has a mind that plans broadly, grasps tenaciously, sees clearly.

Well, he sent for me, and, leaving my mother in Devonshire, I hurried to Paris and, without even stopping for *déjeûner,* to his room at the War Office.

Although I had spent all my holidays in France, I had never seen him before, as he had been on foreign service, and I found him to be my *beau idea l*of a French General--tall, spare, hawk-like, a fierce dynamic person.

He eyed me keenly, greeted me coldly, and observed--"Since your father is spilt milk, as the English say, it is useless to cry over him."

"Now," continued he, after this brief exordium, "you are a Frenchman, the son of a Frenchman. Are you going to renounce your glorious birth-right and live in England, or are you going to be worthy of your honoured name?"

I replied that I was born a Frenchman, and that I should live and die a Frenchman.

"Good," said my uncle. "In that case you will have to do your military service... . Do it at once, and do it as I shall direct... .

"Someday I am going to be the master-builder in consolidating an African Empire for France, and I shall need tools *that will not turn in my hand...* .Tools on which I can rely *absolutely...* . If you have ambition, if you are a *man,* obey me and follow me. Help me, and I will make you... . Fail me, and I will break you... ."

I stared and gaped like the imbecile that I sometimes choose to appear.

My uncle rose from his desk and paced the room. Soon I was forgotten, I think, as he gazed upon his splendid Vision of the future, rather than on his splendid Nephew of the present.

"France ... France ..." he murmured. "A mighty Empire ... Triumphant over her jealous greedy foes... . "England dominates all the east of Africa, but what of the rest--from Egypt to the Atlantic, from Tangier to the Gulf? ... Morocco, the Sahara, the Soudan, all the vast teeming West ...

"Algeria we have, Tunisia, and corners here and there... . It is not enough... . It is nothing... ."

I coughed and looked more imbecile.

"Menaced France," he continued, "with declining birthrate and failing man-power ... Germany only awaiting *The Day...* . Africa, an inexhaustible reservoir of the finest fighting material in the world. The Sahara--with irrigation, an inexhaustible reservoir of food... ."

It was lunch-time, and I realized that I too needed irrigation and would like to approach an inexhaustible reservoir of food. If he were going to send me to the Sahara, I would go at once. I looked intelligent, and murmured:

"Oh, *rather,* Uncle!"

"France must expand or die," he continued. And I felt that I was just like France in that respect.

"The Soudan," he went on, "could be made a very Argentine of corn and cattle, a very Egypt of cotton--and ah! those Soudanese! What soldiers for France! ...

"The Bedouin must be tamed, the Touareg broken, the Senussi won over... . *There* is where we want trained emissaries--France's secret ambassadors at work among the tribes ...

"Shall the West come beneath the Tri-couleur of France, or the Green Banner of Pan-Islamism? ..."

At the moment I did not greatly care. The schemes of irrigation and food-supply interested me more. Corn and cattle ... suitably prepared, and perhaps a little soup, fish and chicken too... .

"We must have safe Trans-Saharan Routes; and then Engineering and Agricultural Science shall turn the desert to a garden--France's great kitchen-garden. France's orchard and cornfield. And the sun's very rays shall be harnessed that their heat may provide France with the greatest power-station in the world... ."

"Oh, yes, Uncle," I said. Certainly France should have the sun's rays if I might have lunch.

"But conquest first! Conquest by diplomacy... . Divide and rule--that Earth's poorest and emptiest place may become its richest and fullest--and that France may triumph... ."

Selfishly I thought that if my poorest and emptiest place could soon become the richest and fullest, *I* should triumph... .

"Now, Boy," concluded my uncle, ceasing his swift pacing, and impaling me with a penetrating stare, "I will try you, and I will give you such a chance to become a Marshal of France as falls to few... . Listen. Go to the Headquarters of the military division of the *arrondissement* in which you were born, show your papers, and enlist as a *Volontaire*. You will then have to serve for only one year instead of the three compulsory for the ordinary conscript--because you are the son of a widow, have voluntarily enlisted before your time, and can pay the *Volontaire's* fee of 1,500 francs... . I will see that you are posted to the Blue Hussars, and you will do a year in the ranks. You will never mention my name to a soul, and you will be treated precisely as any other private soldier... .

"If you pass out with high marks at the end of the period, come to me, and I will see that you go to Africa with a commission in the Spahis, and your foot will be on the ladder... . There, learn Arabic until you know it better than your mother-tongue; and learn to know the Arab better than you know yourself... . *Then* I can use you!"

"Oh, *yes,* Uncle," I dutifully responded, as he paused.

"And some day--some day--I swear it--you will be one of France's most valuable and valued servants, leading a life of the deepest interest, highest usefulness and greatest danger... . You will be tried as a cavalryman, tried as a Spahi officer, tried as my aide-de-camp, tried as an emissary, a negotiator, a Secret-Service officer, and will get such a training as shall fit you to succeed me--and *I* shall be a Marshal of France--and Commander-in-Chief and Governor-General of the great African Empire of France... .

"But--fail in any way, at any one step or stage of your career, and I have done with you... . Be worthy of my trust, and I will make you one of France's greatest servants... . And, mind, Boy--you will have to *ride alone,* on the road that I shall open to you... ." He fell silent.

His fierce and fanatical face relaxed, a sweet smile changed it wholly, and he held out his hand.

"Would you care to lunch with me, my boy?" he said kindly.

"Er--*lunch,* Uncle?" I replied. "Thank you--yes, I think I could manage a little lunch perhaps... ."

CHAPTER III. THE BLUE HUSSAR

Excellent! I would be worthy of this uncle of mine, and I would devote my life to my country. (Incidentally I had no objection to being made a Marshal of France, in due course.)

I regarded myself as a most fortunate young man, for all I had to do was my best. And I *was* lucky, beyond belief--not only in having such an uncle behind me, but in having an English education and an English training in sports and games. I had won the Public Schools Championship for boxing (Middle-weight) and for fencing as well. I was a fine gymnast, I had ridden from childhood, and I possessed perfect health and strength.

Being blessed with a cavalry figure, excellent spirits, a perfect digestion, a love of adventure, and an intense zest for Life, I felt that all was for the best in the best of all possible worlds. As for "riding alone"--excellent ... *I* was not going to be the sort of man that allows his career to be hampered by a woman!

§ 2

A few weeks after applying at the proper military headquarters, I received orders to appear before the *Conseil de Revision* with my papers, at the Town Hall of my native district; and, with a hundred or so other young men of every social class and kind, was duly examined, physically and mentally.

Soon after this, I received a notice directing me to present myself at the cavalry barracks, to be examined in equitation. If I failed in the test, I could not enter a cavalry regiment as a one-year *Volontaire*.

I passed all right, of course, and, a little later, received my *feuille de route* and notification that I was posted to the Blue Hussars and was to proceed forthwith to their barracks at St. Denis, and report myself.

I had spent the interval, partly with my mother and her people, the Carys; and partly in Paris with a Lieutenant de Lannec, appointed my guide, philosopher and friend by my uncle, under whom de Lannec was then working at the War Office. To this gentleman I was indebted for much good advice and innumerable hints and tips that proved invaluable. Also for the friendship of the dear clever little Véronique Vaux, and, most of all, for that of Raoul d'Auray de Redon, at a later date.

To de Lannec I owed it that if in my raw-recruit days I was a fool, I was not a sanguinary fool; and that I escaped most of the pit-falls digged for the feet of the unwary by those who had themselves only become wary by painful experience therein.

Thanks to him, I also knew enough to engage permanently a private room for myself at a hotel in St. Denis, where I could have meals and a bath; to have my cavalry boots and uniform privately made for me; and to equip myself with a spare complete outfit of all those articles of clothing and of use, the loss or lack of which brings the private soldier to so much trouble and punishment.

§ 3

And one fine morning I presented myself at the great gates of the barracks of the famous Blue Hussars, trying to look happier than I felt.

I beheld an enormous parade ground, about a quarter of a mile square, with the Riding School in the middle of it, and beyond it a huge barracks for men and horses. The horses occupied the ground-floor and the men the floors above--not a nice arrangement I thought. (I continued to think it, when I lived just above the horses, in a room that held a hundred and twenty unwashed men, a hundred and twenty pairs of stable-boots, a hundred and twenty pairs of never-cleaned blankets--and windows that had been kept shut for a hundred and twenty years, to exclude the exhalations from the stable (because more than enough came up through the floor).

I passed through the gates, and a Sergeant came out from the Guard-Room, which was just beside them.

"Hi, there! Where d'ye think you're going?" he shouted.

"I have come to report myself, Sergeant," I replied meekly, and produced my *feuille de route*.

He looked at it.

"One of those anointed *Volontaires*, are you?" he growled. "Well, my fine gentleman, I don't like them, d'you understand? ... And I don't like you... . I don't like your face, nor your voice, nor your clothes, nor anything about you. D'you see? ..."

Mindful of de Lannec's advice, I held my tongue. It is the one thing of his own that the soldier may hold. But a good Sergeant is not to be defeated.

"Don't you dare to stand there and sulk, you dumb image of a dead fish," he shouted.

"No, Sergeant," I replied.

"And don't you back-answer me either, you chattering baboon," he roared.

"You have made a bad beginning," he went on menacingly, before I could be either silent or responsive, "and I'll see you make a bad end too, you pimply *pékin!* ... Get out of this-- go on--before I ..."

"But, Sergeant," I murmured, "I have come to join ..."

"You *will* interrupt me, will you?" he yelled. "That's settled it! Wait till you're in uniform--and I'll show you the inside of a little stone box I know of. That'll teach you to contradict Sergeants... . Get out of this, you insubordinate rascal--and take your *feuille de route* to the Paymaster's Office in the *Rue des Enfants Abandonnés*... . I'll deal with you when you come back. Name of an Anointed Poodle, I will! ..."

In silence I turned about and went in search of the *Rue des Enfants Abandonnés*, and the Paymaster's Office, feeling that I was indeed going to begin at the bottom of a fairly steep ladder, and to receive some valuable discipline and training in self-control.

I believe that, for the fraction of a second, I was tempted to seek the train for Calais and England, instead of the Street of the Abandoned Children and the Office of the Paymaster. (Were they Children of Abandoned Character, or Children who had Been Abandoned by Others? Alas, I knew not; but feeling something of a poor Abandoned Child myself, I decided that it was the latter.)

Expecting otherwise, I found the non-commissioned officer who was the Paymaster's Clerk, a courteous person. He asked me which Squadron I would like to join, and I replied that I should like to join any Squadron to which the present Sergeant of the Guard did not belong.

"Who's he?" asked the clerk.

I described the Sergeant as a ruffianly brute with a bristly moustache, bristly eyebrows, bristly hair, and bristly manners. A bullying blackguard in fact.

"Any private to any Sergeant," smiled the clerk; "but it sounds like Blüm. Did he swear by the name of an Anointed Poodle, by any chance?"

"That's the man," said I.

"Third Squadron. I'll put you down for the Second... . Take this paper and ask for the Sergeant-Major of the Second Squadron. And don't forget that if you can stand well with the S.S.M. and the *Adjudant* of your Squadron, you'll be all right... ."

§ 4

On my return to the Barracks, I again encountered the engaging Sergeant Blüm at the Guard-Room by the gates.

"To what Squadron are you drafted?" he asked.

"To the Second, Sergeant," I replied innocently.

"And that's the worst news I have heard this year," was the reply. "I hoped you would be in the Third. I'd have had you put in my own *peloton*. I have a way with aristocrats and *Volontaires,* and *macquereaux*... ."

"I did my best, Sergeant," I replied truthfully.

"*Tais donc ta sale gueule,*" he roared, and turning into the Guard-Room, bade a trooper do some scavenging work by removing me and taking me to the Office of the Sergeant-Major of the Second Squadron.

I followed the trooper, a tall fair Norman, across the great parade-ground, now alive with men in stable-kit, carrying brooms or buckets, wheeling barrows, leading horses, pumping water into great drinking-troughs, and generally fulfilling the law of their being, as cavalrymen.

"Come along, you gaping pig," said my guide, as I gazed around the pleasing purlieus of my new home.

I came along.

"Hurry yourself, or I'll chuck you into the manure-heap, after the S.S.M. has seen you," added my conducting Virgil.

"Friend and brother-in-arms," said I, "let us go to the manure-heap at once, and we'll see who goes on it... . I don't know why you ever left it... ."

"Oh--you're one of those beastly *bullies,* are you?" replied the trooper, and knocked at the door of a small bare room which contained four beds, some military accoutrements, a table, a chair, and the Squadron Sergeant-Major, a small grey-haired man with an ascetic lean face, and moustache of grey wire, neatly clipped.

This was a person of a type different altogether from Sergeant Blüm's. A dog that never barked, but bit hard, Sergeant-Major Martin was a cold stern man, forceful and fierce, but in manner quiet, distant, and almost polite.

"A *Volontaire!*" he said. "A pity. One does not like them, but such things must be... ."

He took my papers, asked me questions, and recorded the answers in the *livret* or regimental-book, which every French soldier must cherish. He then bade the trooper conduct me to Sergeant de Poncey with the bad news that I was to be in his *peloton*.

"Follow me, bully," said the trooper after he had saluted the Sergeant-Major and wheeled from the room... .

Sergeant de Poncey was discovered in the exercise of his duty, giving painful sword-drill to a punishment-squad, outside the Riding School. He was a handsome man who looked as though life held nothing for him but pain. His voice was that of an educated man.

The troopers, clad in canvas uniform and clogs, looked desperately miserable.

They had cause, since they had spent the night in prison, had had no breakfast, and were undergoing a kind of torture. The Sergeant would give an order, the squad would obey it, and there the matter would rest--until some poor devil, sick and half-starved, would be unable to keep his arm, and heavy sword, extended any longer. At the first quiver and sinking down of the blade, the monotonous voice would announce:

"Trooper Ponthieu, two more days *salle de police,* for not keeping still," and a new order would be given for a fresh form of grief, and another punishment to the weakest.

Well--they were there for punishment, and they were certainly getting it.

When the squad had been marched back to prison, Sergeant de Poncey attended to me. He looked me over from head to foot.

"A gentleman," said he. "Good! I was one myself, once. Come with me," and he led the way to the *quartiers* of the Second Squadron, and the part of the room in which his *peloton* slept.

Two partitions, some eight feet in height, divided the room into three, and along partitions and walls were rows of beds. Each bed was so narrow that there was no discomfort in eating one's meals as one sat astride the bed, as though seated on a horse, with a basin of *soupe* before one. It was thus that, for a year, I took all meals that I did not have at my hotel.

At the head of each bed hung a cavalry-sword and bag of stable-brushes and cleaning-kit; while above each were a couple of shelves bearing folded uniforms covered with a canvas bag on which was painted their owner's *matricule* number. Crowning each edifice was a *shako* and two pairs of boots. Cavalry carbines stood in racks in the corners of the room.... As I stared round, the Sergeant put his hand on my arm.

"You'll have a rough time here," he said. "Your only chance will be to be rougher than the time."

"I am going to be a real rough, Sergeant," I smiled. I liked this Sergeant de Poncey from the first.

"The worst of it is that it *stays,* my son," replied Sergeant de Poncey. "Habit becomes second nature--and then first nature. As I told you, I was a gentleman once; and now I am going to ask you to lend me twenty francs, for I am in serious trouble.... Will you?"

"No, Sergeant," I said, and his unhappy face darkened with pain and annoyance. "I am going to give you a hundred, if I may.... Will you?"

"You'll have a friend in me," was the reply, and the poor fellow positively flushed--I supposed with mingled emotions of gratitude, relief and discomfort.

And a good friend Sergeant de Poncey proved, and particularly valuable after he became Sergeant-Major; for though a Sergeant-Major may not have power to permit certain doings, he has complete power to prevent Higher Authority from knowing that they have been done....

A Corporal entering the room at that minute, Sergeant de Poncey called him and handed me over to him with the words:

"A recruit for your *escouade,* Lepage. A *Volontaire*--but a good fellow. Old friend of mine.... See?"

The Corporal saw. He had good eyesight; for the moment Sergeant de Poncey was out of earshot, he added:

"Come and be an 'old friend' of mine too," and led the way out of the *quartiers,* across the great barrack-square, to the canteen.

Cheaply and greasily handsome, the swarthy Corporal Lepage was a very wicked little man indeed, but likeable, by reason of an unfailing sense of humour and a paradoxical trustworthiness. He had every vice and would do any evil thing--except betray a trust or fail a friend. Half educated, he was a clerk by profession, and an ornament of the city of Paris. Small, dissipated and drunken, he yet had remarkable strength and agility, and was never ill.

In the canteen he drank neat cognac at my expense, and frankly said that his goodwill and kind offices could be purchased for ten francs. I purchased them, and, having pouched the gold piece and swallowed his seventh cognac, the worthy man inquired whether I intended to jabber there the *entire* day, or go to the medical inspection to which he was endeavouring to conduct me.

"This is the first I have heard of it, Corporal," I protested.

"Well, it won't be the last, Mr. Snipe, unless you obey my orders and cease this taverning, chambering and wantonness," replied the good Lepage. "Hurry, you idle apprentice and worthless *Volontaire*."

I hurried.

Pulling himself together, Corporal Lepage marched me from the canteen to the dispensary near by.

The place was empty save for an Orderly.

"Surgeon-Major not come yet, Corporal," said the man.

Lepage turned upon me.

"Perhaps you'll let me finish my coffee in peace another time," he said, in apparent wrath, and displaying sharp little teeth beneath his waxed moustache. "Come back and do your duty."

And promising the Orderly that *I* would give him a cognac if he came and called the Corporal from the canteen as soon as the Surgeon-Major returned, he led the way back.

In the end, I left Corporal Lepage drunk in the canteen, passed the medical examination, and made myself a friend for life by returning and getting the uplifted warrior safely back to the barrack-room and bed.

An amusing morning.

§ 5

I shall never forget being tailored by the *Sergent-Fourrier* that afternoon. His store was a kind of mighty shop in which the Regimental Sergeant-Tailor, Sergeant-Bootmaker Sergeant-Saddler and Sergeant-Storekeeper were his shop-assistants.

Here I was given a pair of red trousers to try on--"for size." They were as stiff, as heavy, and nearly as big, as a diver's suit and clogs, and from the knees downwards were of solid leather.

They were not riding-breeches, but huge trousers, the legs being each as big round as my waist. As in the case of an axiom of Euclid, no demonstration was needed, but since the Sergeant-Tailor bade me get into them--I got.

When the heavy leather ends of them rested on the ground, the top cut me under the arm-pits. The top of that inch-thick, red felt garment, hard and stiff as a board, literally cut me.

I looked over the edge and smiled at the Sergeant-Tailor.

"Yes," he agreed, "*excellent*," and handed me a blue tunic to try on, "for size." The only faults in this case were that my hands were invisible within the sleeves, and that I could put my chin inside the collar after it had been hooked. I flapped my wings at the Sergeant-Tailor.

"Yes, you go into that nicely, too," he said, and he was quite right. That there was room for him, as well, did not seem to be of importance.

The difficulty now was to move, as the trousers seemed to be like jointless armour, but I struggled across the store to where sat the Sergeant-Bootmaker, with an entire range of boots of all sizes awaiting me. The "entire range" consisted of four pairs, and of these the smallest was two inches too long, but would not permit the passage of my instep.

They were curious leather buildings, these alleged boots. They were as wide as they were long, were perfectly square at both ends, had a leg a foot high, heels two and a half inches thick, and great rusty spurs nailed on to them. The idea was to put them on under the trousers. "You've got deformed feet, oh, *espèce d'imbécile*," said the Sergeant-Bootmaker, when his complete range of four sizes had produced nothing suitable. "You ought not to be in the army. The likes of you are a curse and an undeserved punishment to good Sergeants, you orphaned Misfortune of God.... . Put on the biggest pair... ."

"But, Sergeant," I protested, "they are exactly five inches longer than my feet!"

"And is straw so dear in a cavalry regiment that you cannot stuff the toes with it, Most Complete Idiot?" inquired the man of ideas.

"But they'd simply fall off my feet if I tried to walk in them," I pointed out.

"And will not the straps of your trousers, that go underneath the boots, keep the boots on your feet, Most Polished and Perfected Idiot?" replied this prince of bootmakers. "And the trousers will hide the fact that the boots are a little large."

As all I had to do was to get from the barracks to my hotel, where I had everything awaiting me, it did not so much matter. But what of the poor devil who had to accept such things without alternative?

When I was standing precariously balanced inside these boots and garments, the *Sergent-Fourrier* gave me a Hussar shako which my ears insecurely supported; wound a blue scarf round my neck, inside the collar of the tunic, and bade me go and show myself to the Captain of the Week--who was incidentally *Capitaine en Second* of my Squadron.

Dressed as I was, I would not willingly have shown myself to a mule, lest the poor animal laugh itself into a state of dangerous hysteria.

Walking as a diver walks along the deck of a ship, I plunged heavily forward, lifting and dropping a huge boot, that hung at the end of a huge trouser-leg, at each step.

It was more like the progression of a hobbled clown-elephant over the tan of a circus, than the marching of a smart Hussar. I felt very foolish, humiliated and angry.

Guided by a storeroom Orderly, I eventually reached the door of the Captain's office, and burst upon his sight.

I do not know what I expected him to do. He did not faint, nor call upon Heaven for strength.

He eyed me as one does a horse offered for sale. He was of the younger school--smart, cool and efficient; a handsome, spare man, pink and white above a shaven blueness. In manner he was of a suavely sinister politeness that thinly covered real cruelty.

"Take off that tunic," he said.

I obeyed with alacrity.

"Yes, the trousers are too short," he observed, and added: "Are you a natural fool, that you come before me with trousers that are too short?"

"*Oui, mon Capitaine,*" I replied. I felt I *was* a natural fool, to be there in those, or in any other, trousers.

"And look at your boots. Each is big enough to contain both your feet. Are you an *un*natural fool to come before me in such boots?"

"*Oui, mon Capitaine,*" I replied. I felt I *was* an unnatural fool, to be there in those, or in any other, boots.

"I will make a note of it, recruit," said the officer, and I felt he had said more than any roaring Sergeant, shouting definite promises of definite punishments.

"Have the goodness to go," he continued in his silky-steely voice, "and return in trousers twice as large and boots half as big. You may tell the *Sergent-Fourrier* that he will shortly hear something to his disadvantage... . It will interest him in you... ."

It did. It interested all the denizens of that horrible storeroom, that stank of stale leather, stale fustian, stale brass, and stale people.

("I would get them into trouble, would I? ... I would bring reprimands and punishments upon senior Sergeants, would I? ... Oh, Ho! and Ah, Ha! Let me but wait until I was in their hands ... !")

A little later, I was sent back to the Captain's room, in the identical clothes that I had worn on the first visit. My trousers were braced to my chin, the leather ends of the legs were pulled further forward over the boots, a piece of cloth was folded and pushed up the back of my tunic, my sleeves were pulled back, and a fold or tuck of the cloth was made inside each elbow. A crushed-up ball of brown paper relieved my ears of some of the weight of my shako.

"You come back here again, unpassed by the Captain, and I swear I'll have you in prison within the week," promised the *Sergent-Fourrier*.

I thanked him and shuffled back.

My Captain eyed me blandly across the table, as I saluted.

"Trousers are now too big," he observed, "and the tunic too small. Are you *really* determined to annoy me, recruit?" he added. "If so, I must take steps to protect myself... . Kindly return and inform the *Sergent-Fourrier* that I will interview him later... ."

Pending that time, the *Sergent-Fourrier* and his myrmidons interviewed *me*. They also sent me back in precisely the same garments; this time with trousers braced only to my breast and with the sleeves of my tunic as they had been at first.

My Captain was not in his room, and I promptly returned and told the truth--that he had found no fault in me this time... .

Eventually I dragged my leaden-footed, swaddled, creaking carcase from the store, burdened with an extra tunic, an extra pair of incredible trousers, an extra pair of impossible boots, a drill-jacket, a *képi*, two canvas stable-suits, an overcoat, a huge cape, two pairs of thick white leather gauntlets big enough for Goliath of Gath, two terrible shirts, two pairs of pants, a huge pair of clogs, and no socks at all.

Much of this impedimenta was stuffed into a big canvas bag.

With this on my back, and looking like Bunyan's *Christian* and feeling like no kind of Christian, I staggered to my room.

Here, Corporal Lepage, in a discourse punctuated with brandified hiccups, informed me that I must mark each article with my *matricule* number, using for that purpose stencils supplied by the *Sergent-Fourrier*.

Feeling that more than stencils would be supplied by that choleric and unsocial person, if I again encountered him ere the sun had gone down upon his wrath, I bethought me of certain advice given me in Paris by my friend de Lannec--and cast about for one in search of lucrative employment.

Seated on the next bed to mine, and polishing his sword, was a likely-looking lad. He had a strong and pleasing face, calm and thoughtful in expression, and with a nice fresh air of countrified health.

"Here, comrade," said I, "do you want a job and a franc or two?"

"Yes, sir," he replied, "or two jobs and a franc or three ... I am badly broke, and I am also in peculiar and particular need to square Corporal Lepage."

I found that his name was Dufour, that he was the son of a horse-dealer, and had had to do with both horses and gentlemen to a considerable extent.

From that hour he became my friend and servant, to the day when he gave his life for France and for me, nearly twenty years later. He was very clever, honest and extremely brave; a faithful, loyal, noble soul.

I engaged him then and there; and his first job in my service was to get my kit stencilled, cleaned and arranged *en paquetage* on the shelves.

He then helped me to make myself as presentable as was possible in the appalling uniform that had been issued to me, for I had to pass the Guard (and in full dress, as it was now noon) in order to get out to my hotel where my other uniforms, well cut by my own tailor, were awaiting me, together with boots of regulation pattern, made for me in Paris.

To this day I do not know how I managed to waddle past the Sergeant of the Guard, my sword held in a gloved hand that felt as though cased in cast iron, my big shako wobbling on my head, and the clumsy spurs of my vast and uncontrollable boots catching in the leather ends of my vaster trousers.

I did it however, with Dufour's help; and, a few minutes later, was in my own private room and tearing the vile things from my outraged person.

As I sat over my coffee, at a quarter to nine that evening, after a tolerable dinner and a bottle of *Mouton Rothschild,* dreaming great dreams, I was brought back to hard facts by the sudden sound of the trumpeters of the Blue Hussars playing the *retraite* in the *Place*.

That meant that, within a quarter of an hour, they would march thence back to Barracks, blowing their instant summons to all soldiers who had not a late pass--and that I must hurry.

My return journey was a very different one from my last, for my uniform, boots, and shako fitted me perfectly; my gauntlets enabled me to carry my sword easily ("*in left hand; hilt turned downwards and six inches behind hip; tip of scabbard in front of left foot,*" etc.), and feeling that I could salute any officer or non-commissioned officer otherwise than by flapping a half-empty sleeve at him.

Once more I felt like a man and almost like a soldier. My spirits rose nearly to the old Eton level.

They sank to the new Barrack level, however, when I entered the room in which I was to live for a year, and its terrific and terrible stench took me by the throat. As I stood at the foot of my bed, as everybody else did, awaiting the evening roll-call, I began to think I should be violently unwell; and by the time the Sergeant of the Week had made his round and received the Corporal's report as to absentees (stables, guard, leave, etc.) I was feeling certain that I must publicly disgrace myself.

However, I am a good sailor, and when the roll-call (which has no "calling" whatever) was finished, and all were free to do as they liked until ten o'clock, when the "*Lights out*" trumpet would be blown, I fled to the outer air, and saved my honour and my dinner.

I had to return, of course, but not to stand to attention like a statue while my head swam; and I soon found that I could support life with the help of a handkerchief which I had had the fore-thought to perfume.

While I was sitting on my bed (which consisted of two trestles supporting two narrow planks, and a sausage-like roll of straw-mattress and blankets, the whole being only two feet six inches wide), gazing blankly around upon the specimen of my fellow-man in bulk, and wondering if and when and where he washed, I was aware of a party approaching me, headed by the fair trooper who had been my guide to the office of the Squadron Sergeant-Major that morning.

"That is it," said their leader, pointing to me. "It is a *Volontaire*. It is dangerous too. A dreadful bully. Tried to throw me into the muck-heap when I wasn't looking ..."

"Behold it," said a short, square, swarthy man, who looked, in spite of much fat, very powerful. "Regard it. It uses a scented handkerchief so as not to smell us."

"Well, we are not roses. Why *should* he smell us?" put in a little rat-like villain, edging forward.

He and the fat man were pushed aside by a typical hard-case fighting-man, such as one sees in boxing-booths, fencing-schools and gymnasia.

"See, *Volontaire*," he said, "you have insulted the Blue Hussars in the person of Trooper Mornec and by using a handkerchief in our presence. I am the champion swordsman of the Regiment, and I say that such insults can only be washed out in ..."

"Blood," said I, reaching for my sword.

"No--*wine*," roared the gang as one man, and, rising, I put one arm through that of the champion swordsman and the other through that of Trooper Mornec, and we three headed a joyous procession to the canteen, where we solemnly danced the *can-can* with spirit and abandon.

I should think that the whole of my *peloton* (three *escouades* of ten men each) was present by the time we reached the bar, and it was there quickly enriched by the presence of the rest of the Squadron.

However, brandy was only a shilling a quart, and red wine fourpence, so it was no very serious matter to entertain these good fellows, nor was there any fear that their capacity to pour in would exceed mine to pay out.

But, upon my word, I think the combined smells of the canteen--rank tobacco-smoke, garlic, spirits, cooking, frying onions, wine, burning fat and packed humanity--were worse than those of the barrack-room; and it was borne in upon me that not only must the soldier's heart be in the right place, but his stomach also... .

The "*Lights out*" trumpet saved me from death in the canteen, and I returned to die in the barrack-room, if I must.

Apparently I returned a highly popular person, for none of the usual tricks was played upon me, such as the jerking away (by means of a rope) of one of the trestles supporting the bed, as soon as the recruit has forgotten his sorrows in sleep.

De Lannec had told me what to expect, and I had decided to submit to most of the inflictions with a good grace and cheerful spirit, while certain possible indignities I was determined to resist to the point of serious bloodshed.

With Dufour's help, I inserted my person into the sausage precariously balanced on the planks, and fell asleep in spite of sharp-pointed straws, the impossibility of turning in my cocoon, the noisy illness of several gentlemen who had spent the evening unwisely, the stamping and chain-rattling of horses, the cavalry-trumpet snoring of a hundred cavalry noses, and the firm belief that I should in the morning be found dead from poisoning and asphyxiation.

All very amusing... .

CHAPTER IV. A PERFECT DAY

I found myself quite alive, however, at five o'clock the next morning, when the Corporal of the Week passed through the room bawling, "Anyone sick here?"

I was about to reply that although I was not being sick at the moment, I feared I shortly should be, when I realized that the Corporal was collecting names for the Sergeant-Major's morning report, and not making polite inquiries as to how we were feeling after a night spent in the most mephitic atmosphere that human beings could possibly breathe, and live.

There is no morning roll-call in the Cavalry, but the Sergeant-Major gets the names of those who apply for medical attention, and removes them from the duty-list of each *peloton*.

For half an hour I lay awake wondering what would happen if I sprang from my bed and opened a window--or broke a window if they were not made for opening. I was on the point of making this interesting discovery when the *reveillé* trumpets rang out, in the square below, and I was free to leave my bed--at five-thirty of a bitter cold morning.

Corporal Lepage came to me as I repressed my first yawn (fearing to inhale the poison-gas unnecessarily) and bade me endue my form with canvas and clogs, and hie me to the stables.

Hastily I put on the garb of a gutter-scavenger and guided by Dufour, hurried through the rain to my pleasing task.

In the stable was a different smell, but it was homogeneous and, on the whole, I preferred the smell of the horses to that of their riders. (You see, we clean the horses thoroughly, daily. In the Regulations it is so ordered. But as to the horsemen, it says, "*A Corporal must sleep in the same room with the troopers of his escouade and must see that his troopers wash their heads, faces, hands and feet*." This much would be something, at any rate, if only he carried out the Regulations.)

At the stables I received my first military order.

"Clean the straw under those four horses," said the Sergeant on stable-duty.

An unpleasing but necessary work.

Some one had to do it, and why not I? Doubtless the study of the art of separation of filthy straw from filthier straw, and the removal of manure, is part of a sound military training.

I looked round for implements. I believed that a pitchfork and shovel were the appropriate and provided tools for the craftsman in this line of business.

"What the hell are you gaping at? You ..." inquired the Sergeant, with more liberty of speech than fraternity or equality.

"What shall I do it with, Sergeant?" I inquired.

"Heaven help me from killing it!" he moaned, and then roared: "Have you no *hands,* Village Idiot? D'you suppose you do it with your toe-nails, or the back of your neck?"

And it was so. With my lily-white hands I laboured well and truly, and loaded barrows until they were piled high. I took an artistic interest in my work, patting a shapely pyramid upon the barrow, until:

"Dufour," I said, "I am going to be so *very* sick. What's the punishment? ..."

The good Dufour glanced hastily around.

"Run to the canteen," he whispered. "I can do the eight stalls easy. Have a hot coffee and cognac."

I picked up a bucket and rushed forth across the barrack-square, trying to look like one fulfilling a high and honourable function. If anybody stopped me, I would say I was going to get the Colonel a bucket of champagne for his bath... .

At the canteen I found a man following a new profession. He called himself a Saviour-from-Selfish-Sin, and explained to me that the basest thing a soldier could do was to *faire Suisse,* to drink alone.

No one need drink alone when *he* was there, he said, and he gave up his valuable time and energy to frequenting the canteen at such hours as it might be empty, and a man might come and fall into sin.

I drank my coffee and cognac and then went outside, inhaled deeply for some minutes, and soon felt better. Catching up my bucket, I returned to the stables, trying to look like one who has, by prompt and determined effort, saved the Republic.

Dufour finished our work and told me we must now return to the barrack-room in time to get our bags of grooming-implements before the trumpets sounded "*Stables*" at six o'clock.

"You begin on the horse that's given you, sir," said Dufour, "and as soon as the Sergeant's back is turned, clear out again, and I'll finish for you."

"Not a bit of it," I replied. "I shall be able to groom a horse all right. It was loading those barrows with my bare hands that made me feel so sea-sick."

"You'll get used to it," Dufour assured me.

But I doubted it. "Use is second nature," as de Poncey said, but I did not think it would become my second nature to scavenge with my bare hands... . Nor my third... .

At six o'clock we returned to the stables, and the Lieutenant of the Week allotted me my horse and ordered me to set about grooming him.

Now I have the horse-gift. I love and understand horses, and horses love and understand me. I was not, therefore, depressed when the horse laid his ears back, showed me a white eye, and lashed out viciously as I approached the stall. It merely meant that the poor brute had been mishandled by a bigger brute, and that fear, instead of love, had been the motive appealed to.

However, I had got to make friends with him before he could be friendly, and the first step was to enter his stall--a thing he seemed determined to prevent. I accordingly slipped into the next one, climbed over, and dropped down beside him. In a minute I was grooming him, talking to him, handling him, making much of him, and winning his confidence.

I swore to myself I would never touch him with whip nor spur: for whip and spur had been his trouble. He was a well-bred beast, and I felt certain from his colour, socks, head, eye and general "feel" that he was not really vicious. I don't know how I know what a horse thinks and feels and *is,* but I do know it.

I groomed him thoroughly for nearly an hour, and then fondled him and got him used to my voice, hands and smell. I rather expected trouble when I took him to water, as Dufour had put his head round the partition and warned me that *Le Boucher* was a dangerous brute who had sent more than one man on a stretcher to hospital.

At seven o'clock the order was given for the horses to be taken to the water-troughs, and I led *Le Boucher* out of his stall. Seizing a lock of his mane, I vaulted on to his bare back and prepared for trouble.

He reared until I thought he would fall; he put down his head and threw up his heels until I thought that *I* should; and then he bucked and bounded in a way that enabled me to give an exhibition of riding.

But it was all half-hearted. I felt that he was going through the performance mechanically, and, at worst, finding out what sort of rider I was.

After this brief period of protest he trotted off to the watering-tank, and I never again had the slightest trouble with *Le Boucher.* I soon changed the stupid name of "The Butcher," to "Angelique," partly in tribute to one of the nicest of girls, and partly in recognition of the horse's real temper and disposition... .

After "Stables," I was sent to get the rest of my kit, and was endowed with carbine, saddle, sword-belt, cartridge-box and all sorts of straps and trappings. I found my saddle to be of English make and with a high straight back, behind which was strapped the cylindrical blue portmanteau, with the regimental crest at each end.

I also found that the bridle was of the English model, not the "9th Lancer" pattern, but with bit and snaffle so made that the head-stall remained on the horse when the bit-straps were taken off.

It was ten o'clock by the time that I had received the whole of the kit for myself and horse, and that is the hour of breakfast. Our trumpets sang "*Soupe*" and the bucket was lowered from the hand of the soldier who crossed the wide plain--of the barrack-square.

Everybody rushed to put away whatever he held in his hand, and to join the throng that poured into the Regimental kitchen and out by another door, each man bearing a *gamelle* (or saucepan-shaped tin pot), of *soupe* and a loaf of bread. Having washed my hands, without soap, at the horse-trough, I followed.

Holding my own, I proceeded to my room, placed it on my bed, sat astride the bed with the *gamelle* before me, and fell to.

It wasn't at all bad, and I was very hungry in spite of my previous nausea.

The meal finished, the Orderly of the *Caporal d'Ordinaire* collected the pots and took them back to the kitchen.

My immediate desire now was a hot-and-cold-water lavatory and a good barber. It was the first day of my life that had found me, at eleven o'clock, unwashen and uncombed, to say nothing of unbathed. At the moment I wanted a shave more ardently than I wanted eternal salvation.

"And now, where is the lavatory, Dufour?" I asked, as that youth stowed away his spare bread behind his *paquetage*.

"Beside the forage-store, sir," he replied, "and it is a grain-store itself. There is an old Sergeant-pensioner at the hospital, who remembers the day, before the Franco-Prussian War, when it was used as a lavatory, but no one else has ever seen anything in it but sacks of corn."

"Isn't washing compulsory, then?" I asked.

"Yes. In the summer, all have to go, once a fortnight, to the swimming-baths," was the interesting reply.

"Do people ever wash voluntarily?" I asked.

"Oh, yes," said Dufour. "Men going on guard, or on parade, often wash their faces, and there are many who wash their hands and necks as well, on Sundays, or when they go out with their girls.... You must not think we are dirty people...."

"No," said I. "And where can this be done?"

"Oh, under the pump, whenever you like," was the reply, and I found that it was the unsullied truth.

No one was hindered from washing under the pump, if he wished to do such a thing....

At twelve o'clock, Corporal Lepage sent me to join the Medical-Inspection Squad, as I must be vaccinated.

After that operation, dubiously beneficial by reason of the probability of one's contracting tetanus or other sorrows as well as immunity from smallpox, I returned to my bright home to deal with the chaos of kit that adorned my bed-side; and with Dufour's help had it reduced to order and cleanliness by three in the afternoon, when "*Stables*" was again the pursuit in being.

After "Stables" we stood in solemn circles around our respective *Caporaux-fourriers* to hear the Regimental Orders of the Day read out, while Squadron Sergeant-Majors eyed everybody with profound suspicion and sure conviction of their state of sin.

So far as I could make out, the Regimental Orders of that particular day consisted of a list of punishments inflicted upon all and sundry (for every conceivable, and many an inconceivable, military offence), including the officers themselves--which surprised me.

So far as I remember, the sort of thing was:

"*Chef d'Escadron* de Montreson, fifteen days' *arrêts de rigueur* for being drunk and disorderly in the town last night.

"*Capitaine Instructeur* Robert, eight days' *arrêts simples* for over-staying leave and returning with uniform in untidy condition.

"*Adjudant* Petit, four days' confinement to room for allowing that room to be untidy.

"*Trooper* Leduc, eight days' *salle de police* for looking resentful when given four days' *salle de police*.

"*Trooper* Blanc, eight days' *salle de police* for possessing and reading a newspaper in *quartiers*.

"*Trooper* Delamer, thirty days' extra *salle de police* from the Colonel for having received sixteen days' extra *salle de police* from his Captain because he had received four days' extra *salle de police* from Sergeant Blüm, who caught him sleeping in the stables when he should have been sleeping in the *salle de police*.

"*Trooper* Mangeur, eight days' confinement to Barracks for smiling when given four days' Inspection with the Guard Parade."

And so on.

When the joyous parade was finished, I was free, and having cleaned and beautified myself, I passed the Sergeant of the Guard in full-dress uniform, and sought mine inn for dinner, peace, and privacy.

But oh! how my heart ached for any poor soul who, being gently nurtured, had to remain in that horrible place for three years, and without the privilege, even if he could afford it, of a private place to which he could retire to bathe and eat, to rest and be alone.

CHAPTER V. BECQUE--AND RAOUL D'AURAY DE REDON

I settled into the routine of my new life very quickly, and it was not long before I felt it was as though I had known no other.

At times I came near to desperation, but not so near as I should have come had it not been for my private room at the hotel, the fact that I did much of my work with other *Volontaires* in a special class, and the one great certainty, in a world of uncertainty, that there are only twelve months in a year.

From 6.30 to 8 we *Volontaires* were in "school"; from 8 to 10 we drilled on foot; from 10 to 11 we breakfasted; from 11 to 12 we were at school again; from 12 to 1 we had gymnastics; from 1 to 2 *voltige* (as though we were going to be circus riders); from 2.30 to 5 "school" once more; from 5 to 6 dinner; from 6 to 8 mounted drill--and, after that, kit-cleaning!

It was some time before my days grew monotonous, and shortly after they had begun to do so, I contrived to brighten the tedium of life by pretending to kill a man, deliberately, in cold blood, and with cold steel. I fear I give the impression of being a bloodthirsty and murderous youth, and I contend that at the time I had good reason.

It happened like this.

Dufour came to me one night as I was undressing for bed, and asked me whether I would care to spend an interesting evening on the morrow.

Upon inquiry it turned out that he had been approached by a certain Trooper Becque, a few days earlier, and invited to spend a jolly evening with him and some other good fellows.

Having accepted the invitation, Dufour found that Becque and the good fellows were a kind of club or society that met in a room above a little wine-shop in the Rue de Salm.

Becque seemed to have plenty of money and plenty of ideas--of an interesting and curious kind. Gradually it dawned upon the intrigued Dufour that Becque was an "agent," a Man with a Message, a propagandist, and an agitator.

Apparently his object was to "agitate" the Regiment, and his Message was that Law and Order were invented by knaves for the enslavement of fools.

Dufour, I gathered, had played the country bumpkin that he looked; had gathered all the wisdom and wine that he could get; and had replied to Becque's eloquence with no more than profound looks, profounder nods, and profoundest hiccups as the evening progressed; tongues were loosened, and, through a roseate, vinous glow, the good Becque was seen for the noble friend of poor troopers that he professed to be.

Guided by a proper love of sound political philosophy and sound free wine, Dufour had attended the next meeting of this brave brotherhood, and had so far fallen beneath the spell of Becque's eloquence as to cheer it to the echo, to embrace him warmly and then to collapse, very drunk, upon a bench; and to listen with both his ears.

After his third or fourth visit, he had asked the good Becque if he might formally join his society, and bring a friend for whom he could vouch as one who would listen to Becque's sentiments with the deepest interest.... . Would I come?

I would--though I feared that if Becque knew I was a *Volontaire,* it would be difficult to persuade him that I was promising anarchistic material. However, I could but try, and if I failed on my own account, I could still take what action I thought fit, on the word of Dufour.

On the following evening, having arrayed myself in the uniform that had been issued to me by the *Sergent-Fourrier* when I joined, I accompanied Dufour to the rendezvous. Becque I did not know, nor he me, and I received a hearty welcome. Watching the man, I decided that he was a half-educated "intelligent." He had an evil, fanatical face and a most powerful muscular frame.

I played the gullible brainless trooper and took stock of Becque and his gang. The latter consisted of three classes, I decided: First, the malcontent dregs of the Regiment--men with grievances, real or imaginary, of the kind known as "hard cases" and "King's hard bargains," in England; secondly, men who in private life were violent and dangerous "politicians"; and thirdly, men who would go anywhere, agree with anything, and applaud anybody--for a bottle of wine.

Becque's talk interested me.

He was clearly a monomaniac whose whole mental content was *hate*--hate of France; hate of all who had what he had not; hate of control, discipline and government; hate of whatsoever and whomsoever did not meet with his approval. I put him down as one of those sane lunatics, afflicted with a destruction-complex; a diseased egoist, and a treacherous, dangerous mad dog. Also a very clever man indeed, an eloquent, plausible and forceful personality.... . The perfect *agent-provocateur,* in fact.

After a certain amount of noisy good fellowship in the bar of this low wine-shop, part of the company adjourned to the room above, the door was locked, and the business of the evening began.

It appeared that Dufour had not taken the Oath of Initiation, and it was forthwith administered to him and to me. We were given the choice of immediate departure or swearing upon the Bible, with terrific oaths and solemnities, that we would never divulge the secret of the Society nor give any account whatsoever of its proceedings.

The penalty for the infringement of this oath was certain death.

We took the oath, and settled ourselves to endure an address from Becque on the subject of The Rights of Man--always meaning unwashen, uneducated, unpatriotic and wholly worthless Man, *bien entendu.*

Coming from the general to the particular, Becque inveighed eloquently against all forms and manifestations of Militarism, and our folly in aiding and abetting it by conducting ourselves as disciplined soldiers. What we ought to do was to "demonstrate," to be insubordinate, to be lazy, dirty, inefficient, and, for a start, to be passively mutinous. By the time we had spread his views throughout the Regiment and each man in the Regiment had written unsigned letters to a man in another Regiment, with a request that these might again be forwarded to other Regiments, the day would be in sight when passive mutiny could become active.

Who were a handful of miserable officers, and more miserable N.C.O.'s, to oppose the will of eight hundred united and determined men? ...

After the address, as proper to an ignorant but inquiring disciple, I humbly propounded the question:

"And what happens to France when her army has disbanded itself? What about Germany?"

The reply was enlightening as to the man's honesty, and his opinion of our intelligence.

"The German Army will do the same, my young friend," answered Becque. "Our German brothers will join hands with us. So will our Italian and Austrian and Russian brothers, and we will form a Great Republic of the Free Proletariat of Europe. All shall own all, and none shall oppress any. There shall be no rich, no police, no prisons, no law, no poor... ."

"And no *Work,*" hiccupped a drunken man, torn from the arms of Morpheus by these stirring promises.

As the meeting broke up, I buttonholed the good Becque, and, in manner mysterious, earnestly besought him to meet me *alone* outside the Hôtel Coq d'Or to-morrow evening at eight-fifteen. I assured him that great things would result from this meeting, and he promised to come. Whereupon, taking my sword, I dragged my mighty boots and creaking uniform from his foul presence, lest I be tempted to take him by the throat and kill him.

§ 2

At eight-fifteen the next evening I was awaiting Becque outside my hotel, and when he arrived I led him, to his great mystification, to my private room.

"So you are a *Volontaire,* are you?" he began. "Are you a spy--or--"

"Or what?" I asked.

He made what I took to be a secret sign.

With my left hand I patted my right elbow, each knee, the top of my head, the back of my neck and the tip of my nose.

Becque glared at me angrily.

I raised my eyebrows inquiringly, and with my right hand twice patted my left shin, my heart, my stomach, and the seat of my trousers... . I also could make "secret signs"! I then rang for a bottle of wine wherewith I might return his hospitality of the previous night-- before I dealt with him.

When the waiter retired I became serious, and got down to business promptly.

"Are you a Frenchman?" I asked.

"I am, I suppose," replied Becque. "My mother was of Alsace, my father a Parisian--God curse him! ... Yes ... I am a Frenchman... ."

"Good," said I. "Have you ever been wrongfully imprisoned, or in any way injured or punished by the State?"

"*Me? ... Prison? ... No!* What d'you mean? ... Except that we're *all* injured by the State, aren't we? There didn't ought to be any State."

"And you hold your tenets of revolution, anarchy, murder, mutiny, and the overthrow and destruction of France and the Republic, firmly, and with all your heart and soul, do you?" I asked.

"With all my heart and soul," replied Becque, and added, "What's the game? Are you fooling--or are you from the Third Central? Or--or--"

"Never mind," I replied. "Are you prepared to die for your faith? That's what I want to know."

"I am," answered Becque.

"*You shall*," said I, and arose to signify that the conversation was ended.

Opening the door, I motioned to the creature to remove itself.

§ 3

At that time, you must know, duelling was not merely permitted but, under certain conditions, was compulsory, in the French Army, for officers and troopers alike.

It was considered, rightly or wrongly, that the knowledge that a challenge to a duel would follow insulting conduct, must tend to prevent such conduct, and to ensure propriety of behaviour among people of the same rank.

(Unfortunately, no one was allowed to fight a duel with any person of a rank superior to his own. There would otherwise have been a heavy mortality among Sergeants, for example!)

I do not know whether it may be the result or the cause of this duelling system, but the use of fists is regarded, in the French cavalry, as vulgar, ruffianly and low. Under no circumstances would two soldiers "come down and settle it behind the Riding School," in the good old Anglo-Saxon way. If they fought at all, they would fight with swords, under supervision, with seconds and surgeons present, and "by order."

A little careful management, and I should have friend Becque where I wanted him, give him the fright of his life, and perhaps put him out of the "agitating" business for a time.

I told Dufour exactly what I had in mind, and, on the following evening, instead of dining at my hotel, I went in search of the scoundrel.

He was no good to me in the canteen, on the parade-ground, nor in the street. I needed him where the eye of authority would be quickly turned upon any unseemly *fracas*.

Dufour discovered him doing a scavenging *corvée* in the Riding School, under the eye of Sergeant Blüm. This would do excellently... .

As the fatigue-party was dismissed by the Sergeant, Dufour and I strolled by, passing one on either side of Becque, who carried a broom. Lurching slightly, Dufour pushed Becque against me, and I gave him a shove that sent him sprawling.

Springing up, he rushed at me, using the filthy broom as though it had been a bayonet. This I seized with one hand, and, with the other, smacked the face of friend Becque right heartily. Like any other member of the snake tribe, Becque spat, and then, being annoyed, I really hit him.

As he went head-over-heels, Sergeant Blüm rushed forth from the Riding School, attracted by the scuffling and the shouts of the fatigue-party and of Dufour, who had certainly made noise enough for six.

"What's this?" he roared. "Are you street curs, snapping and snarling and scrapping in the gutter, or soldiers of France? ... Take eight days' *salle de police* both of you... . Who began it, and what happened?"

The excellent Dufour gabbled a most untruthful version of the affair, and Sergeant Blüm took notes. Trooper Becque had publicly spat upon *Volontaire* de Beaujolais, who had then knocked him down... .

The next evening's orders, read out to the troopers by the *Caporaux-Fourriers*, contained the paragraph, by order of the Colonel:

"The Troopers Becque and de Beaujolais will fight a duel on Monday morning at ten o'clock, with cavalry-swords, in the Riding School, in the presence of the Major of the Week, the Captain of the Week, and of the Second Captains of their respective Squadrons, of Surgeon-Major Philippe and Surgeon-Major Patti-Reville, and of the Fencing-Master, in accordance with Army Regulation 869:--*If a soldier has been gravely insulted by one of his comrades, and the insult has taken place in public, he must not hesitate to claim reparation for it by a duel. He should address his demand to his Captain Commanding, who should transmit it to the Colonel. But it must not be forgotten that a good soldier ought to avoid quarrels*... .

"The successful combatant in this duel will receive fifteen days' imprisonment, and the loser will receive thirty days'."

On hearing the order, I was of opinion that the loser would disappear from human ken for more than thirty days.

§ 4

On entering the Riding School with Dufour on the Monday morning, I was delighted to see Sergeant Blüm in the place of the Fencing-Master, who was ill in hospital.

This was doubly excellent, as my task was rendered easier and Sergeant Blüm was placed in an unpleasant and risky situation. For it was the Fencing-Master's job, while acting as Master of Ceremonies and referee, to stand close by, with a steel scabbard in his hand, and prevent either of the combatants from killing, or even dangerously wounding the other!

Severe punishment would follow his failing to do his duty in this respect--and the noisy, swaggering Blüm was no *maitre d'armes*.

As instructed, we were "in stable kit, with any footwear preferred," so I had tucked my canvas trousers into socks, and put on a pair of gymnasium shoes.

Scrutinizing Becque carefully, I came to the conclusion that he would show the fierce and desperate courage of a cornered rat, and that if he had paid as much attention to fencing as to physical culture and anarchistic sedition, he would put up a pretty useful fight. I wondered what sort of a swordsman he was, and whether he was in the habit, like myself and a good many troopers, of voluntarily supplementing the compulsory attendance at fencing-school for instruction in "foils and sabres." ...

When all the officers and official spectators were present, we were ordered to strip to the waist, were given heavy cavalry-swords, and put face to face, by Sergeant Blüm, who vehemently impressed upon us the imperative duty of instantly stopping when he cried "*Halt!*"

Blüm then gave the order "*On guard,*" and stood with his steel scabbard beneath our crossed swords. Throughout the fight he held this ready to parry any head-cuts, or to strike down a dangerous thrust. (And they called this a *duel*!)

My great fear was, that with the clumsy lout sticking his scabbard into the fight and deflecting cuts and thrusts, I should scratch Becque or Becque would scratch me. This would end the preposterous fight at once, as these glorious affairs were "first-blood" duels--and my object was to incapacitate Becque, and both frighten and punish a viperous and treacherous enemy of my beloved country.

I stared hard into Becque's shifty eyes. Blüm gave the word--"*Go!*" and Becque rushed at me, making a hurricane attack and showing himself to be a very good and determined fighter.

I parried for dear life, and allowed him to tire his arm and exhaust his lungs. Blüm worried me nearly as much as Becque, for he leapt around yelling to us to be "careful," and swiping at both our swords. He made me laugh, and that made me angry (and him furious), for it was no laughing matter.

"*Halt*!" he cried, and I sprang back, Becque aiming another cut at my head, after the order had been given.

"You, Becque," he shouted, "be more careful, will you? D'you think you are beating carpets, or fighting a duel, you ..."

Becque was pale and puffing like a porpoise. He had not attempted a single thrust or feint, but had merely slashed with tremendous speed, force and orthodoxy. He was a strong, plain swordsman, but not a really good and pretty fencer.

Provided neither of us scratched the other's arm, nor drew blood prematurely, I could put Becque where I wanted him--unless the fool Blüm foiled me. It was like fighting two men at once... .

"*On guard*!" cried Blüm. "*Go!*" ...

Becque instantly cut, with a *coup de flanc,* and, as I parried, struck at my head. He was fighting even more quickly than in the first round, but with less violence and ferocity. He was tiring, and my chance was coming... . I could have touched him a dozen times, but that was not my object... . I was sorely tempted, a moment later, when he missed my head, and the heavy sword was carried out of guard, but the wretched Blüm's scabbard was between us in a second... .

Becque was breathing heavily, and it was my turn to attack... . *Now!* ... Suddenly Becque sprang backward and thrust the point of his sword into the ground. Quite unnecessarily, Blüm struck my sword down, and stepped between us.

"What's the matter, you?" snapped Major de Montreson.

"I am satisfied," panted Becque. This was a trick to get a much-needed breathing-space.

"Well, I'm not," replied the Major sourly. "Are you?" he asked, pointing to me.

"It is a duel *au premier sang,* Monsieur le Majeur," I replied, "and there is no blood yet."

"Quite so," agreed the Major. "The duel will continue at once. And if you, Becque, retreat again like that, you shall fight with your back to a corner... ."

"*On guard!*" cried Sergeant Blüm, and we crossed swords again. "*Go!*" ... Becque made another most violent assault. I parried until I judged that his arm was again tired, and then feinted at his head. Up went his sword and Blum's scabbard, and my feint became a thrust--beneath the pair of them, and through Becque's right breast... .

France, my beautiful France, my second Mother, had one active enemy the less for quite a good while.

"I'll do that for you again, when you come out of hospital, friend Becque," said I, as he staggered back.

§ 5

There was a most tremendous row, ending in a *Conseil de discipline,* with myself in the dock, Becque being in the Infirmary. As all was in order, however, and nothing had been irregular (except that the duellists had really fought), I was not sent, as my comrades had cheerfully prophesied, to three years' hard labour in the *Compagnies de discipline* in Algeria. I was merely given fifteen days' prison, to teach me not to fight when duelling another time; and, joy of joys, Sergeant Blüm was given *retrogradation*--reduction in rank.

I walked most warily in the presence of Corporal Blüm, until, as the result of my being second in the April examination (in Riding, Drill and Command, Topography, *Voltige,* Hippology and Gymnastics) for *Volontaires,* I became a Corporal myself.

Life, after that promotion, became a little less complex, and improved still further when I headed the list of *Volontaires* at the October examination, and became a Sergeant.

§ 6

After hanging between life and death for several weeks, Becque began to mend, and Surgeon-Major Patti-Reville pronounced him to be out of danger.

That same day I received an order through Sergeant de Poncey to visit the junior officer of our squadron, *Sous-Lieutenant* Raoul d'Auray de Redon, in his quarters, after stables.

"And what the devil does that mean, Sergeant?" I asked.

"I know no more than you," was the reply, "but I do know that Sub-Lieutenant d'Auray de Redon is one of the very finest gentlemen God ever made... . He has often saved me from suicide--simply by a kind word and his splendid smile... . If only our officers were all like him!"

I, too, had noticed the young gentleman, and had been struck by his beauty. I do not mean prettiness nor handsomeness, but *beauty.* It shone from within him, and illuminated a perfectly formed face. A light of truth, strength, courage and gentleness burned like a flame within the glorious lamp of his body. He radiated friendliness, kindness, helpfulness, and was yet the best disciplinarian in the Regiment--because he had no need to "keep" discipline. It kept itself, where he was concerned. And with all his gentle goodness of heart he was a strong man. Nay, he was a lion of strength and courage. He had the noble *élan* of the French and the cool forceful determination and bulldog tenacity of the Anglo-Saxon.

After a wash and some valeting by Dufour, I made my way to Sub-Lieutenant d'Auray de Redon's quarters... .

He was seated at a table, and looked up with a long appraising stare, as I saluted and stood at attention. "You sent for me, *mon Lieutenant*," I murmured.

"I did," replied de Redon, and the brilliant brown eyes smiled, although the strong handsome face did not.

"Why did you want to fight this Becque?" he suddenly shot at me.

I was somewhat taken aback.

"Er--he--ah--he has dirty finger-nails, *mon Lieutenant*," I replied.

"Quite probably," observed de Redon. "Quite... . And are you going to start a Clean Finger-nail Crusade in the Blue Hussars, and fight all those who do not join it and live up to its excellent tenets?"

"No, *mon Lieutenant*," I admitted.

"Then why Becque in particular, out of a few hundreds?" continued de Redon.

"Oh!--he eats garlic--and sometimes has a cast in his eye--and he jerks at his horse's mouth--and had a German mother--and wipes his nose with the back of his hand--and grins sideways exposing a long yellow dog-tooth, *mon Lieutenant*," I replied.

"Ah--you supply one with interesting information," observed my officer dryly. "Now I will supply you with some, though it won't be so interesting--because you already know it... . In addition to his garlic, cast, jerks, German mother, nose-wiping and dog-tooth, he is a seditious scoundrel and a hireling spy and agitator, and is trying to seduce and corrupt foolish troopers... . You have attended his meetings, taken the oath of secrecy and fidelity to his Society, and you have been closeted with him in private at your hotel."

I stared at de Redon in astonishment, and said what is frequently an excellent thing to say--nothing.

"Now," continued my interlocutor, "perhaps you will answer my questions a little more fully... . Why did you challenge Becque, after you had joined his little Society for engineering a mutiny in the Regiment, for achieving the destruction of the State, and for encompassing the ruin of France?"

"Because of the things I have already mentioned, *mon officier,* and because I thought he would be the better for a rest," I replied. "I considered it a good way to end his little activities. My idea was to threaten him with a duel for every meeting that he held... ."

"Ah--you did, eh?" smiled de Redon. "And now I want you to tell me just what happened at these meetings, just what was said, and the names of the troopers who were present."

"I cannot do that, sir," I replied... . "As you seem to be aware, I took a solemn oath to reveal nothing whatsoever."

Sub-Lieutenant Raoul d'Auray de Redon rose from his chair, and came round to where I was standing. Was he--a gentleman--going to demand with threats and menaces that I break my word--even to such a rat as Becque?

"Stand at ease, Trooper Henri de Beaujolais," he said, "and shake hands with a brother of the Service! ... Oh, yes, I know all about you, old chap... . From de Lannec--though I don't know whether your uncle is aware of the fact... ."

I took the proffered hand and stammered my thanks at this honour from my superior officer.

"Oh, nonsense, my dear boy. You'll be *my* 'superior officer' some day, I have no doubt... . I must say I admire your pluck in coming to *Us* by way of the ranks... . How soon will you come to Africa? ... I am off next month ... Spahis ... until I am perfect in languages and disguises... . Isn't it a glorious honour to be one of your uncle's picked men? ... And now about this Becque. You needn't pursue him any more. I have been giving myself a little Secret Service practice and experiment. Much easier here in France than it will be in Africa, by Jove! ... Well, we know all about Becque, and when he leaves hospital he will go where there will be nothing to distract his great mind from his great thoughts for two or three years... . He may be a mad dog, as you say, but I fancy that the mad dog has some pretty sane owners and employers."

"Some one has denounced him, then?" I said.

"No, my dear de Beaujolais, not yet. But some one is going to do so. Some one who attended his last meeting--and who was too drunk to take any oaths... . So drunk that he could only giggle helplessly when invited to swear!"

"*You*?" I asked.

"Me," replied Sub-Lieutenant d'Auray de Redon. "'And no *Work*'! You may remember my valuable contribution to the great ideas of the evening... ."

Such was my first encounter with this brilliant and splendid man, whom I came to love as a brother is rarely loved. I will tell in due course of my last encounter with him.

§ 7

A letter from de Lannec apprised me of the fact that my uncle had heard of the duel, and seemed amused and far from displeased with me... .

Poor old de Lannec! He wrote that his very soul was dead within him, and his life "but dust and ashes, a vale of woe and mourning, a desert of grief and despair in which was no oasis of joy or hope." ...

For he had lost his adored Véronique Vaux... . She had transferred her affections to a colonel of Chasseurs d'Afrique, and departed with him to Fez! ...

CHAPTER VI. AFRICA

At the end of the year, my uncle was pleased grimly to express himself as satisfied, and to send me forthwith to the Military School of Saumur, where selected Cavalry-Sergeants of good family and superior education are made into officers.

Here nothing amusing occurred, and I was glad when, once more, wires were pulled and I was instructed to betake myself and my new commission to Algeria and present myself at the *Quartier des Spahis* at Sidi-bel-Abbès.

I shall never forget my first glimpse of my new home. It is indelibly etched upon the tablets of my memory.

I stood at the great gates in the lane that separates the Spahis' barracks from those of the Foreign Legion, and thought of the day--so recently passed--when I had stood, a wretched civilian, at those of the Blue Hussars in St. Denis... .

Outside the red-white-and-blue-striped sentry-box stood a bearded dusky giant, a huge red turban crowning the snowy linen *kafiya* that framed his face; a scarlet be-medalled Zouave jacket covering a gaudy waistcoat and tremendous red sash; and the most voluminous skirt-like white baggy trousers almost concealing his great spurred cavalry-boots. A huge curved cavalry-sabre hung at his left side, and in his right hand he bore a carbine.

"And so this is the type of warrior I am to lead in cavalry-charges!" thought I, and wondered if there were any to equal it in the world.

He saluted me with faultless smartness and precision, and little guessed how I was thrilled to the marrow of my bones as I returned the first salute I had received from a man of my own Regiment.

Standing at the big open window of the *Salle de Rapport* in the regimental offices near the gate, was a strikingly smart and masculine figure--that of an officer in a gold-frogged white tunic (that must surely have covered a pair of corsets), which fitted his wide shoulders and narrow waist as paper fits the walls of a room.

Beneath a high red *tarbush* smiled one of the handsomest faces I have ever seen. So charming was the smile, so really beautiful the whole man, that it could be none other than Raoul d'Auray de Redon, here a couple of years before me.

I know now that one man *can* really love another with the love that is described as existing between David and Jonathan... . I do not believe in love "at first sight," but tremendous attraction, and the strongest liking at first sight, soon came, in this case, to be a case of love at second sight... . To this day I can never look upon the portrait of Raoul d'Auray de Redon, of whom more anon, without a pang of bitter-sweet pain and a half-conscious prayer... .

By the Guard-Room stood a group that I can see now--a statuesque *sous-officier* in spotless white drill tunic and trousers, white shoes and a *tarbush*(miscalled a fez cap)--*l'Adjudant* Lescault; an elderly French Sergeant-Major in scarlet patrol-jacket, white riding-breeches with a double black stripe down the sides, and a red *képi* with a gold band; an Arab Sergeant, dressed like the sentry, save for his chevrons; and the Guard, who seemed to me to be a mixture of Arabs and Frenchmen--for some of them were as fair in complexion as myself.

Beyond this group stood a Lieutenant, examining a horse held by an Arab groom, and I was constrained to stare at this gentleman, for beneath a red tunic he wore a pair of the colossal Spahi white skirt-trousers, and these were gathered in at the ankle to reveal a pair of tiny pointed-toed patent shoes. His other extremity was adorned by a rakish peaked *képi* in scarlet and gold.

My future brothers-in-arms these... .

I glanced beyond them to the Oriental garden, tree-embowered, which lay between the gates and the distant low-colonnaded stables that housed the magnificent grey Arab horses of the Regiment; and feeling that I could embrace all men, I stepped forward and entered upon my heritage... .

§ 2

Nevertheless, it was not very long before life at the depôt in Sidi-bel-Abbès grew very boring indeed. One quickly grew tired of the mild dissipations of our club, the *Cercle Militaire,* and of the more sordid ones of the alleged haunts of pleasure boasted by that dull provincial garrison-town.

Work saved me from weariness, however, for I worked like a blinded well-camel--at Arabic--in addition to the ordinary duties of a cavalry-officer.

To the Spahis came Dufour, sent by my uncle at my request, and together we pursued our studies in the language and in disguises. Nor was I sorry when, at the earliest possible moment, my uncle again pulled wires, and I was ordered to Morocco.

In that fascinating country I was extremely lucky--lucky enough, after weary garrison-duty at Casa Blanca, or rather Ain Bourdja, outside its walls, Rabat, Mequinez, Fez, Dar-Debibagh and elsewhere--to be at the gory fight of R'fakha and to charge at the head of a squadron; and to play my little part in the Chaiova campaigns at Settat, M'koun, Sidi el Mekhi and the M'karto.

After the heavy fighting round, and in, Fez, I was a Captain, and had two pretty little pieces of metal and ribbon to hang on my tunic; and in the nasty little business with the Zarhoun tribe (who took it upon them to close the roads between Fez and Tangier and between Meknes and Rabat) I was given command of the squadron that formed part of the composite battalion entrusted with the job.... .

With this squadron was my good Dufour, of course, a non-commissioned officer already wearing the *medaille militaire* for valour. Of its winning I must briefly tell the tale, because the memory of it was so cruelly and poignantly before my mind in the awful hour when I had to leave him to his death, instead of dying with him as I longed to do.... .

On that black day I saw again, in clear and glowing colours, this picture:

I am charging a great *harka* of very brave and fanatical Moors, at the head of my squadron.... . We do not charge in line as the English do, but every man for himself, hell-for-leather, at the most tremendous pace to which he can spur his horse.... . Being the best mounted, I am naturally well ahead.... . The earth seems to tremble beneath the thundering onrush of the finest squadron in the world.... . I am wildly happy.... . I wave my sabre and shout for joy.... . As we are about to close with the enemy, I lower my point and straighten my arm. (Always use the point until you are brought to a standstill, and then use the edge with the speed and force of lightning.) The Moors are as cunning as they are brave. Hundreds of infantry drop behind rocks and big stones and into nullahs, level their long guns and European rifles, and blaze into the brown of us. Hundreds of cavalry swerve off to right and left, to take us in flank and surround us, when the shock of our impact upon the main body has broken our charge and brought us to a halt. They do not know that we shall go through them like a knife through cheese, re-form and charge back again--and even if we do not scatter them like chaff, will effectually prevent their charging and capturing our silent and almost defenceless little mountain-guns.... .

We thunder on, an irresistible avalanche of men and horses, and, like a swimmer diving from a cliff into the sea--I am into them with a mighty crash.... . A big Moor and his Barbary stallion go head-over-heels, as my good horse and I strike them amidships, like a single projectile; and, but for the sword-knot whose cord is round my wrist, I should have lost my sabre, pulled from my hand as I withdrew it from beneath the Moor's right arm.... .

I spur my horse; he bounds over the prostrate horse and man; I give another big Moslem my point--right in the middle of his long black beard as I charge past him--and then run full tilt into a solid mass of men and horses. I cut and parry; slash, parry and cut; thrust and strike, and rise in my stirrups and hack and hew--until I am through and spurring again to a gallop.... . And then I know that my horse is hit and going down, and I am flying over his head and that the earth rises up and smashes my face, and strikes my chest so cruel a blow that the breath is driven from my body, and I am a living pain.... .

Oh! the agony of that struggle for breath, after the smashing crash that has broken half my ribs, my right arm and my jaw-bone... . And, oh! the torture of my dead horse's weight on my broken leg and ankle... .

And why was my throat not being cut? Why no spears being driven through my back? Why was my skull not being battered in? ...

I got my dripping face from out of the dust, wiped it with my left sleeve, and got on to my left elbow... .

I was the centre of a terrific "dog-fight," and, standing across me, leaping over me, whirling round and round, jumping from side to side like a fiend and a madman, a grand athlete and a great hero--was Dufour... . Sick and shattered as I was, I could still admire his wonderful swordsmanship, and marvel at his extraordinary agility, strength, and skill... . Soon I realized that I could do more than admire him. I could help, although pinned to the ground by my horse and feeling sick, shattered, and smashed... . With infinite pain I dragged my revolver from its holster, and rejoiced that I had made myself as good a shot with my left hand as with my right.

Then, lying on my right side, and sighting as well and quickly as I could in so awkward a position, I fired at a man whose spear was driving at Dufour's back; at another whose great sword was swung up to cleave him; at a third, whose long gun was presented at him; and then, after a wave of death-like faintness had passed, into the very face of one who had sprung past him and was in the act of driving his big curved dagger into my breast... .

As I aimed my last shot--at the man whose sword was clashing on Dufour's sabre--the squadron came thundering back, headed by Lieutenant d'Auray de Redon, and never was I more glad to see the face of my beloved Raoul... .

He and several of the Spahis drew rein, scattered our assailants and pursued them, while Dufour caught a riderless troop-horse and--I am told--lifted me across the saddle, jumped on its back, behind the saddle, and galloped back to our position.

It seems that he had been behind me when my horse came down, had deliberately reined up, dismounted, and run to rescue me--when he was attacked. Nor had he striven to cut his way out from among the few who were surrounding him, but had stood his ground, defending me until he was the centre of the mob of wild fanatics from which Raoul's charge saved us in the nick of time. He was bleeding from half a dozen sword-cuts by the time he got me away, though not one of them was severe... .

Yes--this was the picture that burned before my eyes on the dreadful day of which I shall tell you.

Duty is a stern and jealous God... .

§ 3

I made a quick recovery, and thanked Heaven and our splendid surgeons when I found that I was not, as I had feared, to be lame for life.

I got back to work, and when my uncle, punctual to his life's programme, came out to Africa, I was able to join his Staff as an officer who knew more than a little about the country and its fascinating towns and people; an officer who could speak Arabic and its Moorish variant like a native; and who could wander through *sūq* and street and bazaar as a beggar; a pedlar; a swaggering Riffian *askri* of the *bled;* a nervous, cringing Jew of the *mellah;* a fanatic of Mulai Idris; a camel-man, or donkey-driver--without the least fear of discovery.

And I believe I could tell him things that no other officer in all Morocco could tell him of subterranean tribal politics; gutter intrigues of the fanatical mobs of towns that mattered (such as Meknes, for example, where I relieved my friend Captain de Lannec and where I was soon playing the Jew pedlar, and sending out messengers up to the day of its rising and the great massacre); and the respective attitudes, at different times, of various parts of the country and various classes of the people towards the Sultan Abd-el-Aziz; the would-be Sultan, Mulai Hafid; the Pretender Mulai Zine, his brother; or the great powerful *marabout* Ibn Nualla.

My uncle was pleased with the tool of his fashioning--the tool that would *never* "turn in his hand," and my name was writ large in the books of the *Bureau des Affaires Indigènes* at Rabat... .

Nor do I think that there was any jealousy or grumbling when I became the youngest Major in the French Army, and disappeared from human ken to watch affairs in Zaguig and in the disguise of a native of that mean city... . I entered it on foot, in the guise of a hill-man from the north, and as I passed through the tunnel of the great gate in the mighty ramparts, a camel-driver rose from where he squatted beside his beast and accosted me.

We gave what I think was an unexceptionable rendering of the meeting of two Arab friends who had not seen each other for a long time.

"Let me be the proud means of giving your honoured legs a rest, my brother," said the man loudly, as he again embraced me and patted my back with both hands. "Let my camel bear you to the lodging you honour with your shining presence... . God make you strong... . God give you many sons... . God send rain upon your barley crops... ." And he led me to where his kneeling camel snarled.

And may I be believed when I say that it was not until he had patted my back (three right hand, two left, one right, one left) that I knew that this dirty, bearded, shaggy camel-man was Raoul d'Auray de Redon, whom I was to relieve here! I was to do this that he might make a long, long journey with a caravan of a certain Sidi Ibrahim Maghruf, a Europeanized Arab merchant whom our Secret Service trusted--to a certain extent.

Raoul it was however, and, at Sidi Ibrahim Maghruf's house, he told me all he could of local politics, intrigues, under-currents and native affairs in general.

"It's high time we made a plain gesture and took a firm forward step," he concluded. "It is known, of course, that we are coming and that the Military Mission will be a strong one--and it is anticipated that it will be followed by a column that will eventually remark *J'y suis--J'y reste*... . Well, the brutes have asked for it, and they'll get it--but I think it is a case of the sooner the quicker... .

"I'll tell you a curious thing, my friend. I have been attending some very interesting gatherings, and at one or two of them was a heavily-bearded fanatic who harangued the audience volubly and eloquently--but methought his Arabic had an accent... . I got Sidi Ibrahim Maghruf to let me take his trusted old factotum, Ali Mansur, with me to a little fruit-party which the eloquent one was giving.

"When old Ali Mansur had gobbled all the fruit he could hold and we sat replete, listening to our host's harangue upon the greatness of Islam and the littleness (and nastiness) of Unbelievers--especially the *Franzawi* Unbelievers who have conquered Algeria and penetrated Tunisia and Morocco and intended to come to Zaguig--I asked old Ali if he thought the man spoke curious Arabic and was a foreigner himself.

"'He is an Egyptian or a Moor or a Turk or something else, doubtless,' grunted Ali. 'But he is a true son of Islam and a father of the poor and the oppressed. *Wallahi,* but those melons and figs and dates were good--Allah reward him.'

"So I decided that I was right and that this fellow's Arabic *was* a little queer.... Well, I followed him about, and, one evening, saw him meet another man, evidently by appointment, in the Zaouia Gardens.... And the other man made a much quicker job of tucking his legs up under him on the stone seat, and squatting cross-legged like a true native, than my suspect did. He was a little slow and clumsy about it, and I fancied that he would have sat on the seat in *European* fashion, if he had been alone and unobserved.... Whereupon I became a wicked cut-purse robber of a mountaineer, crept up behind those two, in barefooted silence, and suddenly fetched our eloquent friend a very sharp crack on the head with my heavy *matrack* stick.... He let out one word and sprang to his feet. The hood of my dirty *burnous* was well over my ingenuous countenance and the evening was growing dark, but I got a clear glimpse of his face, and then fled for my life.... I am a good runner, as you know, and I had learned what I wanted--or most of it."

I waited, deeply interested, while Raoul paused and smiled at me.

"When a man has an exclamation fairly *knocked* out of him, so to speak, that exclamation will be in his mother-tongue," continued Raoul. "And if a man has, at times, a very slight cast in his eye, that cast is much enhanced and emphasized in a moment of sudden shock, fright, anger or other violent emotion."

" True," I agreed.

"My friend," said Raoul, "that man's exclamation, when I hit him, was '*Himmel*!' and, as he turned round, there was a most pronounced cast in his left eye. He almost squinted, in fact...."

"The former point is highly interesting," I observed. "What of the other?"

"Henri," replied Raoul. "Do you remember a man who--let me see--had dirty finger-nails, ate garlic, jerked his horse's mouth, had a German mother, wiped his nose with the back of his hand, revealed a long dog-tooth when he grinned sideways, and had a cast in his eye? ... A man in the Blue Hussars, a dozen years and more ago? ... Eh, *do* you?"

"*Becque!*" I exclaimed.

"Becque, I verily believe," said Raoul.

"But wouldn't he exclaim in French, under such sudden and violent shock?" I demurred.

"Not if he had been bred and born speaking the German of his German mother in Alsace," replied my friend. "German would be literally his mother-tongue. He would learn from his French father to speak perfect French, and we know that his parents were of the two nationalities."

"It *may* be Becque, of course," I said doubtfully.

"I believe it is he," replied Raoul, "and I also believe you're the man to make certain.... What about continuing that little duel--with no Sergeant Blüm to interrupt, eh?"

"If it is he, and I can manage it, the duel will be taken up at the point where it was stopped owing to circumstances beyond Monsieur Becque's control," I remarked.

"Yes. I think *ce bon* Becque ought to die," smiled Raoul, "as a traitor, a renegade and a spy.... For those things he is--as the French-born son of a Frenchman, and as a soldier who has worn the uniform of France and taken the oath of true and faithful service to the Republic."

"Where was he born?" I asked.

"Paris," replied Raoul. "Bred and born in Paris. He was known to the police as a criminal and an anarchist from his youth, and it appears that he got into the Blue Hussars by means of stolen or forged papers in this name of Becque... . They lost sight of him after he had served his sentence for incitement to mutiny in the Blue Hussars... ."

And we talked on far into the night in Sidi Ibrahim Maghruf's great moonlit garden.

Next day, Raoul departed on his journey of terrible hardships--a camel-man in the employ of Sidi Ibrahim Maghruf, to Lake Tchad and Timbuktu, with his life in his hands and all his notes and observations to be kept in his head.

§ 4

Of the man who might or might not be Becque, I saw nothing whatever in Zaguig. He may have taken fright at Raoul's sudden and inexplicable assault upon him, and thought that his secret was discovered, or he may have departed by reason of the approach of the French forces. On the other hand he may merely have gone away to report upon the situation in Zaguig, or again, he may have been in the place the whole time.

Anyhow, I got no news nor trace of him, and soon dismissed him from my mind. In due course I was relieved in turn by Captain de Lannec and returned to Morocco, and was sent thence into the far south, ostensibly to organize Mounted Infantry companies out of mules and the Foreign Legion, but really to do a little finding-out and a little intelligence-organizing in the direction of the territories of our various southern neighbours, and to travel from Senegal to Wadai, with peeps into Nigeria and the Cameroons. I was in the Soudan a long while.

Here I had some very instructive experiences, and a very weird one at a place called Zinderneuf, whence I went on leave *via* Nigeria, actually travelling home with a most excellent Briton named George Lawrence, who had been my very senior and revered fag-master at Eton!

It is a queer little world, and very amusing.

And everywhere I went, the good Dufour, brave, staunch and an extraordinarily clever mimic of any kind of native, went also, "seconded for special service in the Intelligence Department"--and invaluable service it was. At disguise and dialect he was as good as, if not better than, myself; and it delighted me to get him still further decorated and promoted as he deserved.

And so Fate, my uncle, and my own hard, dangerous and exciting work, brought me to the great adventure of my life, and to the supreme failure that rewarded my labours at the crisis of my career.

Little did I dream what awaited me when I got the laconic message from my uncle (now Commander-in-Chief and Governor-General):

"*Return forthwith to Zaguig and wait instructions.*"

Zaguig, as I knew to my sorrow, was a "holy" city, and like most holy cities, was tenanted by some of the unholiest scum of mankind that pollute the earth.

Does not the Arab proverb itself say, "*The holier the city, the wickeder its citizens*"?

CHAPTER VII. ZAGUIG

After the cities of Morocco, the Enchantress, I hated going back to Zaguig, the last-won and least-subdued of our Saharan outposts of civilization; and after the bold Moor I hated the secretive, furtive, evil Zaguigans, who reminded me of the fat, fair and false Fezai.

Not that Zaguig could compare with Fez or Marrakesh, of course, that bright jewel sunk in its green ocean of palms, with its wonderful gardens, Moorish architecture, cool marble, bright tiles, fountains and charming hidden *patios*.

This Zaguig (now occupied by French troops) was an ash-heap populated with vermin, and very dangerous vermin, too.

I did not like the position of affairs at all. I did not like the careless over-confident attitude of Colonel Levasseur; I did not like the extremely scattered disposition of the small garrison, a mere advance-guard; and I did not like the fact that Miss Mary Hankinson Vanbrugh was, with her brother, the guest of the said Colonel Levasseur.

You see, I *knew* what was going on beneath the surface, and what I did not know from personal observation, Dufour could tell me.

(When I was not Major de Beaujolais, I was a water-carrier, and when Dufour was not Adjudant Dufour of the Spahis, he was a seller of dates and melons in the *sūq*. When I was here before, I had been a blind leper--when not a coolie in the garden of Sidi Ibrahim Maghruf, the friend of France.)

Nor could I do more than lay my information before Colonel Levasseur. He was Commanding Officer of the troops and Governor of the town, and I was merely a detached officer of the Intelligence Department, sent to Zaguig to make arrangements for pushing off "into the blue" (on *very* Secret Service) as soon as word came that the moment was ripe... .

Extracts from a letter, written by my uncle at Algiers, and which I found awaiting me at Zaguig, will tell you nearly as much as I knew myself.

"... and so, my dear Henri, comes your chance--the work for which the tool has been fashioned... . Succeed and you will have struck a mighty blow for France (and you will not find France ungrateful). But mind--you will have to be as swift and as silent as you will have to be clever, and you must stand or fall absolutely alone. If they fillet you and boil you in oil--you will have to boil unavenged. A desert column operating in that direction would rouse such a howl in the German Press (and in one or two others) as would do infinite harm at home, and would hamper and hinder my work out here for years. The Government is none too firmly seated, and has powerful enemies, and you must not provide the stick wherewith to beat the dog.

"On the other hand, I am expecting, and only waiting for, the dispatch which will sanction a subsidy of a million francs, so long as this Federation remains in alliance with France and rejects all overtures to Pan-Islamism. That is the fear and the danger, the one great menace to our young and growing African Empire.

"God grant that you are successful and that you are before Bartels, Wassmuss or any Senussi emissaries.

"What makes me anxious, is the possibility of this new and remarkable Emir el Hamel el Kebir announcing himself to be that very Mahdi whom the Bedouin tribes of that part are always expecting--a sort of Messiah.

"As you know, the Senussi Sidi el Mahdi, the holiest prophet since Mahommet, is supposed to be still alive. He disappeared at Garu on the way to Wadai, and an empty coffin was buried with tremendous pomp and religious fervour at holy Kufara. He reappears from time to time, in the desert, and makes oracular pronouncements--and then there is a sort of 'revival' hysteria where he is supposed to have manifested himself.

"If this Emir el Hamel el Kebir takes it into his head to announce that he is the Mahdi, we shall get precisely what the British got from their Mahdi at Khartoum--(and that son of a Dongola carpenter conquered 2,000,000 square miles in two years)--for he has got the strongest tribal confederation yet known... .

"Well--I hope you won't be a Gordon, nor I a Wolseley-Kitchener, for it's peace we want now, peace--that we may consolidate our Empire and then start making the desert to bloom like the rose... .

"You get a treaty made with this Emir--whereby he guarantees the trade routes, and guarantees the friendship of his tributary tribes to us, and a 'hostile neutrality' towards the Senussi and any European power in Africa, and you will have created a buffer-state, just where France needs it most.

"Incidentally you will have earned my undying gratitude and approbation--and what you like to ask by way of recognition of such invaluable work... . We must have peace in the East in view of the fact that the Riffs will always give trouble in the West... .

"... Sanction for the subsidy may come any day, but you will have plenty of time for your preparations. (When you get word, be gone in the same hour, and let nothing whatsoever delay you for a minute.) ... d'Auray de Redon came through from Kufara with one of Ibrahim Maghruf's caravans and saw this Mahdi or Prophet himself... . He also takes a very serious view, and thinks it means a jehad sooner or later... . And, mind you, he maybe Abd el Kadir (grandson of the Great Abd el Kadir, himself), though I believe that devil is still in Syria.

"The fellow is already a very noted miracle-monger and has a tremendous reputation as a warrior. He is to the Emir Mohammed Bishari bin Mustafha Korayim abd Rahu what the eagle is to the hawk--a dead hawk too, according to an Arab who fell in with Ibrahim Maghruf's caravan, when fleeing from a great slaughter at the Pass of Bab-el-Haggar, where this new 'Prophet' obliterated the Emir Mohammed Bishari... . The said Arab was so bitter about the 'Prophet,' and had such a personal grudge, that d'Auray de Redon cultivated him with talk of revenge and gold, and we may be able to make great use of him... . I shall send him to you at Zaguig with d'Auray de Redon who will bring you word to start, and any orders that I do not care to write... .

"In conclusion--regard this as THE most important thing in the world--to yourself, to me, and to France... ."

Attached to this letter was a sheet of notepaper on which was written that which, later, gave me furiously to think, and at the time, saddened and depressed me. I wondered if it were intended as a warning and "*pour encourager les autres*," for it was not like my uncle to write me mere Service news.

"*By the way, I have broken Captain de Lannec, as I promised him (and you too) that I would do to anyone who, in any way, failed me....* A woman, of course.... *He had my most strict and stringent orders to go absolutely straight and instantly to Mulai Idris, the Holy City, and establish himself there, relieving Captain St. André, with whom it was vitally important that I should have a personal interview within the month.*

"*Passing through the Zarhoun, de Lannec got word from one of our friendlies that a missing Frenchwoman was in a village among the mountains. She was the* amie *of a French officer, and had been carried off during the last massacre, and was in the* hareem *of the big man of the place.... It seems de Lannec had known her in Paris.... One Véronique Vaux.... Loved her, perhaps.... He turned aside from his duty; he wasted a week in getting the woman; another in placing her in safety; and then was so good as to attend to the affairs of his General, his Service and his Country!* ...

"*Exit de Lannec....*"

Serve him right, of course! ... Yes--of course... .

A little hard? ... Very, very sad--for he was a most promising officer, a tiger in battle, and a fox on Secret Service; no braver, cleverer, finer fellow in the French Army... . But yes, it served him right, certainly... . He had acted very wrongly--putting personal feelings and the fate of *a woman* before the welfare of France, before the orders of his Commander, before the selfless, self-effacing tradition of the Service... . Before his *God*--Duty, in short.

He deserved his punishment... . Yes... . He had actually put a mere woman before *Duty*... . "*Exit de Lannec.*" ... Serve him right, poor devil... .

And then the Imp that dwells at the Back of my Mind said to the Angel that dwells at the Front of my Mind:

"*Suppose the captured woman, dwelling in that unthinkable slavery of pollution and torture, had been that beautiful, queenly and adored lady, the noble wife of the stern General Bertrand de Beaujolais himself?*"

Silence, vile Imp! *No one* comes before Duty.

Duty is a Jealous God... .

I was to think more about de Lannec ere long.

§ 2

I confess to beginning with a distinct dislike for the extremely beautiful Miss Vanbrugh, when I met her at dinner, at Colonel Levasseur's, with her brother. Her brother, by the way, was an honorary ornament of the American Embassy at Paris, and was spending his leave with his adventurous sister and her maid-companion in "doing" Algeria, and seeing something of the desert. The Colonel had rather foolishly consented to their coming to Zaguig "to see something of the *real* desert and of Empire in the making," as Otis Hankinson Vanbrugh had written to him.

I rather fancy that the *beaux yeux* of Miss Mary, whom Colonel Levasseur had met in Paris and at Mustapha Supérieur, had more to do with it than a desire to return the Paris hospitality of her brother.

Anyhow, a young girl had no business to be there at that time... .

Probably my initial lack of liking for Mary Vanbrugh was prompted by her curious attitude towards myself, and my utter inability to fathom and understand her. The said attitude was one of faintly mocking mild amusement, and I have not been accustomed to regarding myself as an unintentionally amusing person. In fact, I have generally found people rather chary of laughing at me.

But not so Mary Vanbrugh. And for some obscure reason she affected to suppose that my name was "*Ivan.*" Even at dinner that first evening, when she sat on Levasseur's right and my left, she addressed me as "*Major Ivan.*"

To my stiff query, "Why *Ivan,* Miss Vanbrugh?" her half-suppressed provoking smile would dimple her very beautiful cheeks as she replied:

"But surely? ... You *are* really *Ivan What's-his-name* in disguise, aren't you? ... Colonel Levasseur told me you are a most distinguished Intelligence Officer on Secret Service, and I think that must be one of the Secrets... ."

I was puzzled and piqued. Certainly I have played many parts in the course of an adventurous career, but my duties have never brought me in contact with Russians, nor have I ever adopted a Russian disguise and name. Who was this "*Ivan What's-his-name*"? ... However, if the joke amused her ... and I shrugged my shoulders.

"Oh, *do* do that again, Major Ivan," she said. "It *was* so delightfully French and expressive. You dear people can talk with your shoulders and eyebrows as eloquently as we barbarous Americans can with our tongues."

"Yes--we are amusing little funny foreigners, Mademoiselle," I observed. "And if, as Ivan What's-his-name, I have made you smile, I have not lived wholly in vain... ."

"No. You have not, Major Ivan," she agreed. A cooler, calmer creature I have never encountered... . A man might murder her, but he would never fluster nor discompose her serenity while she lived.

Level-eyed, slow-spoken, unhurried, she was something new and strange to me, and she intrigued me in spite of myself.

Before that evening finished and I had to leave that wide moonlit verandah, her low rich voice, extreme self-possession, poise, grace, and perfection almost conquered my dislike of her, in spite of her annoying air of ironic mockery, her mildly contemptuous amusement at me, my sayings and my doings.

As I made my way back to my quarters by the Bab-el-Souq, I found myself saying, "Who the devil *is* this *Ivan What's-his-name?*" and trying to re-capture an air that she had hummed once or twice as I sat coldly silent after some piece of slightly mocking irony. How did it go?

Yes, that was it.

§ 3

Miss Vanbrugh's curiosity and interest in native life were insatiable. She was a living interrogation-mark, and to me she turned, on the advice of the over-worked Levasseur, for information--as it was supposed that what I did not know about the Arab, in all his moods and tenses, was not worth knowing.

I was able to bring that sparkling dancing flash of pleasure to her eyes, that seemed literally to light them up, although already as bright as stars, by promising to take her to dinner with my old friend Sidi Ibrahim Maghruf.

At his house she would have a real Arab dinner in real Arab fashion, be able to see exactly how a wealthy native lived, and to penetrate into the innermost arcana of a real *hareem.*

I had absolute faith in old Ibrahim Maghruf, and I had known him for many years and in many places.

Not only was he patently and provenly honest and reliable in himself--but his son and heir was in France, and much of his money in French banks and companies. He was a most lovable old chap, and most interesting too--but still he was a *native*, when all is said, and his heart was Arab.

It was difficult to realize, seeing him seated cross-legged upon his cushions and rugs in the marble-tiled French-Oriental reception-room of his luxurious villa, that he was a self-made man who had led his caravans from Siwa to Timbuctu, from Wadai to Algiers, and had fought in a hundred fights for his property and life against the Tebu, Zouaia, Chambaa, Bedouin, and Touareg robbers of the desert. He had indeed fulfilled the Arab saying, "*A man should not sleep on silk until he has walked on sand.*"

Now he exported dates to France, imported cotton goods from Manchester, and was a merchant-prince in Islam. And I had the pleasant feeling that old Ibrahim Maghruf loved me for myself, without *arrière pensée,* and apart from the value of my reports to Government on the subject of his services, his loyalty, and his influence.

In his house I was safe, and in his hands my secret (that I was a French Intelligence-Officer) was safe; so if in the maximum of gossip, inquiry and research, I told him the minimum of truth, I told him no untruth whatsoever. He, I believe, responded with the maximum of truth and the minimum of untruth, as between a good Mussulman and a polite, friendly, and useful Hell-doomed Infidel.

Anyhow, my disguise, my *hejin* camels--of the finest breed, brindled, grey-and-white, bluish-eyed, lean, slender greyhounds of the desert, good for a steady ten kilometres an hour--and my carefully selected outfit of necessities, watched night and day by my Soudanese orderly, Djikki, were safe in his charge.

§ 4

It was on calling at the Vanbrughs' quarters in the big house occupied by Colonel Levasseur, to take Miss Vanbrugh to Sidi Maghruf's, that I first encountered the pretty and piquant "Maudie," an artless and refreshing soul. She met me in the verandah, showed me into the drawing-room, and said that Miss Vanbrugh would be ready in half a minute. I wondered if she were as flirtatious as she looked... .

Maudie Atkinson, I learned later, was a London girl,--a trained parlour-maid who had attracted Miss Vanbrugh's notice and liking by her great courage, coolness and resource on the occasion of a disastrous fire in the English country-house at which Miss Vanbrugh was visiting. Maudie had been badly burnt in going to the rescue of a fellow-servant, and had then broken an arm in jumping out of a window.

Visiting the girl in the cottage-hospital, and finding that she would be homeless and workless when she left the hospital, Miss Vanbrugh had offered her the post of maid-companion, and in her democratic American way, treated her much more as companion than maid... .

When asked in Paris, by Miss Vanbrugh, if she were willing to accompany her to Africa, Maudie had replied,

"Oh, Miss! That's where *the Sheikhs* live, isn't it?" And on being assured that she need not be afraid of falling into the hands of Arabs, had replied,

"Oh, Miss! I'd give anything in the world to be carried off by a Sheikh! They *are* such lovely men. I *adores* Sheikhs!"

Further inquiry established the fact of Maudie's belief that Sheikhs were wealthy persons, clad in silken robes, exhaling an odour of attar of roses, residing on the backs of wondrous Arab steeds when not in more wondrous silken tents--slightly sunburnt Young Lochinvars in fact, and, like that gentleman, of most amazingly oncoming disposition; and, albeit deft and delightful, amorous beyond all telling.

"Oh, *Miss*," had Maudie added, "they catches you up into their saddles and gallops off with you into the sunset! No good smacking their faces neither, for they don't take 'No' for an answer, when they're looking out for a wife... ."

"Or wives," Miss Vanbrugh had observed.

"Not if you're the first, Miss. They're true to you... . And they fair *burn* your lips with hot kisses, Miss."

"You can do that much for yourself, with hot tea, Maudie... . Where did you learn so much about Sheikhs?"

"Oh--I've got a book all about a Sheikh, Miss. By a lady ..."

"Wonder whether the fair sob-sister ever left her native shores--or saw all her Sheikhs on the movies, Maudie?" was Miss Vanbrugh's damping reply.

And when she told me all this, I could almost have wished that Maudie's authoress could herself have been carried off by one of the dirty, smelly desert-thieves; lousy, ruffianly and vile, who are much nearer the average "Sheikh" of fact than are those of the false and vain imaginings of her fiction... .

Some Fiction is much stranger than Truth... .

The dinner was a huge success, and I am not sure which of the two, Sidi Ibrahim Maghruf or Miss Mary Vanbrugh, enjoyed the other the more.

On my translating Ibrahim's courteous and sonorous, "*Keif halak,* Sitt Miriyam! All that is in this house is yours," and she had replied,

"What a bright old gentleman! Isn't he too cute and sweet? I certainly should like to kiss him," and I had translated this as,

"The Sitt admires all that you have and prays that God may make you strong to enjoy it," we got down to it, and old Ibrahim did his best to do us to death with the noblest and hugest feast by which I was ever defeated... .

A gazelle stalked solemnly in from the garden and pattered over the marble floor.

"Major Ivan, it isn't gazelles that Grandpapa Maghruf should pet. It's boa-constrictors ..." groaned Miss Vanbrugh, as the thirty-seventh high-piled dish was laid on the red cloth at our feet... .

The feast ended at long last and we got away, surprised at our power to carry our burden, and staggered home through the silent moonlit night, preceded by Dufour and followed by Achmet (my splendid faithful servant, loving and beloved, Allah rest his brave soul!)--and Djikki, for I was taking no chances.

§ 5

For next day, at an hour before sunset, the good Colonel Levasseur, in his wisdom, had decreed a formal and full-dress parade of the entire garrison, to salute the Flag, and "to impress the populace." It seemed to me that he would certainly impress the populace with the fact of the utter inadequacy of his force, and I told him so.

He replied by officiously ordering me to be present, and "thereby render the garrison adequate to anything."

The good Levasseur did not like me and I wondered whether it was on account of Miss Vanbrugh or the fact that he was twenty years my senior and but one grade my superior in rank... . Nor did I myself greatly love the good Levasseur, a man very much *du peuple,* with his stubble hair, goggle-eyes, bulbous nose, purple face and enormous moustache, like the curling horns of a buffalo.

But I must be just to the brave Colonel--for he died in Zaguig with a reddened sword in one hand and an emptied revolver in the other, at the head of his splendid Zouaves; and he gave me, thanks to this officious command of his, some of the best minutes of my life... .

Cursing *ce bon* Levasseur, I clattered down the wooden stairs of my billet, in full fig, spurred cavalry-boots and sword and all, out into a narrow stinking lane, turned to the right--and began running as I believe I have never run before or since, not even when I won the senior quarter-mile at Eton--in somewhat more suitable running-kit.

For I had seen a sight which made the blood run cold throughout my body and yet boil in my head.

A woman in white riding-kit, on a big horse, followed by a gang of men, was galloping across an open space.

One of the men, racing level with her and apparently holding to her stirrup with one hand, drove a great knife into her horse's heart with the other, just as she smashed him across the head with her riding-crop.

As the horse lurched and fell, the woman sprang clear and dashed through the open gate of a compound.

It all happened in less time than it takes to tell, and by the time she was through the gate, followed by the Arabs, I was not twenty yards behind.

Mon Dieu! How I ran--and blessed Levasseur's officiousness as I ran--for there was only one woman in Zaguig who rode astride officers' chargers; only one who wore boots and breeches, long coat and white solar-topi.

By the mercy of God I was just in time to see the last of her pursuers vanish up a wooden outside stair that led to the flat roof of a building in this compound--a sort of fire-wood-and-hay store, now locked up and entirely deserted, like the streets, by reason of the Review.

When I reached the roof, with bursting lungs and dry mouth, I saw Miss Vanbrugh in a corner, her raised riding-crop reversed in her hand, as, with set mouth and protruding chin, she faced the bloodthirsty and bestial fanatics, whom, to my horror, I saw to be armed with swords as well as long knives.

In view of the stringent regulations of the Arms Act, this meant that the inevitable rising and massacre was about to begin, or had already begun.

It was no moment for kid-gloved warfare, nor for the niceties of chivalrous fighting, and I drove my sword through the back of one man who was in the very act of yelling, "Hack the ... in pieces and throw her to the dogs," and I cut half-way through the neck of another before it was realized that the flying feet behind them had not been those of a brother.

My rush carried me through to Miss Vanbrugh, and as I wheeled about, I laid one black throat open to the bone and sent my point through another filthy and ragged *jellabia* in the region of its owner's fifth rib.

And then the rest were on me, and it was parry, and parry, and parry, for dear life, with no chance to do anything else--until suddenly a heavy crop fell crashing on an Arab wrist and I could thrust home as the stricken hand swerved.

Only two remained, and, as I took on my hilt a smashing blow aimed at my head, dropped my point into the brute's face and thrust hard--the while I expected the other man's sword in my side--I was aware, with the tail of my eye, of a pair of white-clad arms flung round a black neck from behind. As the great sword of the disconcerted Arab went wildly up, I sprang sideways, and thrust beneath his arm-pit... .

Then I sat me down, panting like a dog, and fought for breath--while from among seven bodies, some yet twitching in the pool of blood, a spouting Thing dragged itself by its fingers and toes towards the stairs... . Had I been a true Hero of Romance, I should have struck an attitude, leaning on my dripping sword, and awaited applause. In point of actual fact, I felt sick and shaky.

"The boys seem a little--er--*fresh*," complained a cool quiet voice, and I looked up from my labours of breath-getting. She was pale, but calm and collected, though splashed with blood from head to foot.

"*Some* dog-fight, Major Ivan," she said. "Are you hurt?"

"No, Miss Vanbrugh," I answered. "Scratched and chipped a bit, that's all.... . Are you all right? ... You are the coolest and bravest woman I have ever met... . You saved my life... ."

"Nonsense!" was the reply. "What about mine? I certainly was in some trouble when you strolled in... . And I was *mad* that I couldn't explain to these beauties that this was the first time I had ever come out without my little gun! ... I could have wept at myself... .

"Major, I'm going to be just a bit sick... . I've got to go home right now... . Steward! *Basin* ..."

I wiped my sword (and almost kissed it), sheathed it, picked the girl up, and carried her like a baby, straight to my quarters... . That I had heard no rifle-fire nor mob-howling, showed that the revolt had not begun... .

Achmet was on guard at my door, but Dufour had taken his place at the Review as I had told him.

I laid her on my bed, brought cognac and water, and said, "Listen, Miss Vanbrugh. I am going to bring your maid here. Don't you dare go out of this room till I return with her--in fact Achmet won't let you. There's going to be Hell to-night--or sooner--and you'll be safer here than at the Governor's house, until I can get *burkahs* and *barracans* for you and the maid, and smuggle you down to Ibrahim Maghruf's... ."

"But what about all the pretty soldier-boys, won't they deal with the Arabs?" interrupted the girl.

"Yes, while they're alive to do it," I replied, and ran off... .

§ 6

Not a soul in the streets! A very bad sign, though fortunate for my immediate purpose of getting Maudie to my quarters unseen.

I had not far to go, and was thankful to find she was at home. Otis Vanbrugh had gone out. I noted that the maid was exhilarated and thrilled rather than frightened and anxious, when I explained that there was likely to be trouble.

"Just like Jenny What's-her-name, the Scotch girl in the Indian Mutiny... . You know, sir, the Siege of Lucknow and the bagpipes and all that... . I know a bit of po'try about it... . Gimme half a mo', sir, and I'll put some things together for Miss Mary... . *Lumme!* What a lark!" and as the droll, brave little soul bustled off, I swear she murmured "*Sheikhs!*"

Sheikhs! A lark! *Une escapade!* ... And suppose the house of Sidi Ibrahim Maghruf was the first that was looted and burnt by a victorious blood-mad mob, as being the house of a rich, renegade friend of the Hell-doomed Infidel? ...

"Hurry, Maudie," I shouted, and out she came--her pretty face alight and alive at the anticipation of her "lark"--with a big portmanteau or suit-case. Taking this, I hurried her at top speed back to the Bab-el-Souq.

"Oh, my *Gord*! Look!" ejaculated poor Maudie as we came to where the slaughtered horse lay in its blackening pool, and a Thing still edged along with toes and fingers, leaving a trail. It must have rolled down those stairs... .

Some of the bloom was gone from the "lark" for the gay little Cockney, and from her bright cheeks too... .

For me a stiff cognac and off again, this time to the house of Sidi Ibrahim Maghruf. It was useless to go to Colonel Levasseur yet. I had said all I could say, and he had got all his men--for the moment--precisely where they ought to be, all in one place, under one command; and if the rising came while they were there, so much the better.

I would see Sidi Ibrahim Maghruf, and then, borrowing a horse, ride to Levasseur, tell him of the attack on Miss Vanbrugh, assure him that the rising would be that night, and beg him to act accordingly.

Sidi Ibrahim Maghruf's house, as usual, appeared to be deserted, empty and dead. From behind high blind walls rose a high blind house, and from neither of the lanes that passed the place could a window be seen.

My private and particular knock with my sword-hilt--two heavy, two light, and two heavy--brought a trembling ancient to the iron-plated wicket in the tremendously heavy door. It was good old Ali Mansur.

I stepped inside and the old mummy, whose eye was still bright and wits keen, gave me a message which I doubt not was word for word as his master and owner had delivered it to him.

"Ya, Sidi, the Protection of the Prophet and the Favour of Allah upon Your Honour's head. My Master has been suddenly called away upon a journey to a far place, and this slave is alone here with Djikki, the Soudanese soldier. This slave is to render faithful account to your Excellency of his property in the camel-sacks; and Djikki, the Soudanese, is ready with the beautiful camels. The house of my Master, and all that is in it, is at the disposal of the Sidi, and these words of my Master are for the Sidi's ear. '*Jackals and hyenas enter the cave of the absent lion to steal his meat!*'"...

Quite so. The wily Ibrahim knew more than he had said. He had cleared out in time, taking his family and money, until after the massacre of the tiny garrison and the subsequent looting was over, the town had been recaptured, a sharp lesson taught it, and an adequate garrison installed.... . There is a time to run like the hare and a time to hunt with the hounds.

No--this would be no place to which to bring the two women.

I ordered the ancient Ali to tell Djikki to saddle me a horse quickly, and then to fetch me any women's clothing he could find--*tobhs, aabaias, foutas, guenaders, haiks, lougas, melah'af, mendilat, roba, sederiya, hezaam, barracan*--any mortal thing he could produce, of female attire.

My big Soudanese, Private Djikki, grinning all over his hideous face, brought the horse from the huge stables in the big compound, reserved for camels, asses, mules, well-bullocks, milch-cows and goats, and I once again gave him the strictest orders to have everything absolutely ready for a desert journey, at ten minutes' notice.

"It always is, Sidi," he grinned. "On my head and my life be it."

There are times when I love these huge, fierce, staunch Soudanese, childish and lazy as they are. (I had particular reason to love this one.) They are like coal-black English bull-dogs--if there are such things.... .

I again told him where to take the camels and baggage, by way of the other gate, if the mob attacked the house.

The ancient returning with the bundle of clothing, I bade Djikki run with it to my quarters and give it to his old pal Achmet, and to come back at once.

I then mounted and rode off through the strangely silent town, to where Colonel Levasseur was holding his futile parade in the vast market-square--a poor handful consisting of his 3rd Zouaves, a company of *Tirailleurs Algériens*--possibly none too loyal when the Cry of the Faith went up and the Mullahs poured forth from the mosques to head a Holy War--and a half-squadron of *Chasseurs d'Afrique*. What were these against a hundred thousand fanatics, each anxious to attain remission of sins, and Paradise, by the slaying of an Infidel, a *giaour*, a *meleccha*, a dog whose mere existence was an affront and an offence to the One God?

There should have been a strong brigade and a battery of artillery in the place.... .

The old story of the work of the soldier ruined by the hand of the politician--not to mention the subject of mere lives of men.... .

A dense and silent throng watched the review, every house-top crowded, every balcony filled, though no women were visible, and you could have walked on the heads of the people in the Square and in every street and lane leading to the Square, save four, at the ends of which Levasseur had placed pickets--for the easier scattering of his little force after the parade finished!

By one of these empty streets I rode, and, through an ocean of sullen faces, to where the Governor sat his horse, his *officier d'ordonnance* behind him, with a bugler and a four of Zouave drummers.

The band of the 3rd Zouaves was playing the *Marseillaise,* and I wondered if its wild strains bore any message to the silent thousands who watched motionless, save when their eyes turned expectantly to the minaret of the principal mosque... . To the minaret... . Expectantly? ... Of course!

It was from there that the signal would come. On to that high-perched balcony, like a swallow's nest on that lofty tower, the muezzin would step at sunset. The deep diapason of his wonderful voice would boom forth the *shehada,* the Moslem profession of faith, "*Ash hadu illa illaha ill Allah, wa ash hadu inna Mohammed an rasul Allah*"; he would recite the *mogh'reb* prayer, and *then*--then he would raise his arms to Allah and call curses on the Infidel; his voice would break into a scream of "*Kill! Kill!*" and from beneath every dirty *jellabia* would come sword and knife, from every house-top a blast of musketry... . I could see it all... .

"You are late, Major," growled the Governor, accusingly and offensively, as I rode up.

"I am, Colonel," I agreed, "but I am alive. Which none of us will be in a few hours unless you'll take my advice and expect to be attacked at odds of a hundred to one, in an hour's time." And I told him of Miss Vanbrugh's experience.

"Oh, you Intelligence people and your mares'-nests! A gang of rude little street-boys I expect!" laughed this wise man; and ten minutes later he dismissed the parade--the men marching off in five detachments, to the four chief gates of the city and to the Colonel's own headquarters respectively.

As the troops left the Square, the mob, still silent, closed in, and every eye was turned unwaveringly to the minaret of the mosque... .

§ 7

I rode back towards my quarters, cudgelling my brains as to the best thing to do with the two girls. The Governor's house would be in the thick of the fighting, and it was more than probable that Ibrahim Maghruf's house would be looted and burnt... .

Yes, they would perhaps be safest in my quarters, in Arab dress, with Achmet to defend them with tongue and weapons... . I had better send for Otis Vanbrugh too, and give him a chance to save himself--if he'd listen to reason--and to look after his sister... . But my house was known as the habitation of a *Franzawi* officer... .

And I myself would be in an awkward dilemma, for it was no part of my duty to get killed in the gutters of Zaguig when my uncle was relying on me to be setting off on the job of my life--that should crown the work of *his.* Nor was it any part of my inclination to sit cowering in an upper back room with two women and a civilian, while my comrades fought their last fight... . Hell! ...

As I swung myself down from my horse, by the door in the lane at the back of my house, I was conscious of a very filthy and ragged Arab, squatting against the wall on a piece of foul old horse-blanket, his staff, begging-bowl, and rosary beside him. He begged and held out his hand, quavering for alms in the name of Allah, the Merciful, the Compassionate-- "*Bismillah arahman arahmim!*" in Arabic--and in French, "*Start at once!*" ...

The creature's eyes were bloodshot and red-rimmed, his mangily-bearded cheeks were gaunt and hollow, his ribs showed separate and ridged through the rents in his foul *jellabia,* and a wisp of rag failed to cover his dusty shaggy hair. And at the third stare I saw that it was my friend, the beautiful and smart Captain Raoul d'Auray de Redon.

I winked at him, led my horse to the stable on the other side of the courtyard, and ran up the wooden stair at the back of the house... . So it had come! I thought of my uncle's letter and the underlined words--"*begone in the same hour.*"

I tore off my uniform, pulled on my Arab kit, the dress of a good-class Bedouin, complete from *agal*-bound *kafiyeh* to red-leather *fil-fil* boots--and, as I did this and rubbed dye into my face and hands, I thought of a dozen things at once--and chiefly of the fate of the girls.

I could not leave them alone in this empty house, and it would be delivering them to death to take them back to the Governor's villa... .

I shouted for Achmet and learned that he had given the Arab clothing to Miss Vanbrugh.

"Run to the house of His Excellency the Governor, and tell the Roumi Americani lord, Vanbrugh, the brother of the Sitt Miriyam Vanbrugh, to come here in greatest haste. Tell him the Sitt is in danger here. Go on the horse that is below, and give it to the Americani... ."

This was ghastly! I should be *escaping in disguise* from Zaguig, at the very time my brothers-in-arms were fighting for their lives... . I should be leaving Mary Vanbrugh to death or worse than death... .

I ran down the stairs again and glanced round the courtyard, beckoning to Raoul who was now sitting just inside the gate. Turning back, I snatched up a cold chicken and a loaf from my larder and, followed by Raoul, hurried back to my room to make a bundle of my uniform. Wringing Raoul's hand, I told him to talk while he ate and I worked. He told me all about the Emir upstart and about the guide, as he drew a route on my map.

"The tribes are up, all round the north-west of here," he said later, "and hurrying in. It's for sunset this evening--as I suppose you have found out... ."

"Yes--and warned Levasseur... . He's besotted... . Says they'd never dare do anything while *he* and his Zouaves are here! And he's got them scattered in small detachments--and, Raoul, there are two *white* girls here... ."

"Where?" interrupted my friend.

"In the next room," I answered, and hurriedly told him about them.

"God help them," he said. "They'll be *alone* in an hour... ."

"What are you going to do?" I asked. "Are you to come with me?"

"No--the General doesn't want us both killed by this Emir lad, he says. And he thinks you're the man to pull it off, now that poor de Lannec's gone... . I confess I begged him to let me go, as it was I who brought him confirmation of the news... . He said it was your right to have the chance, Henri, on your seniority as well as your record, apart from the fact that you'd handle the situation better than I... . Said it was such almost-certain death too, that he'd prefer to send his own nephew! ... I nearly wept, old chap, but he was absolutely right. You are the man... ."

Noble loyal soul! Steel-true and generous--knowing not the very name of jealousy. He gave me every ounce of help, information and guidance that it lay in his power to do.

"No--I'm not even to come with you, Henri... . I shall join the mob here and lead them all over the shop on false scents. Confuse their councils and start rumours that there's a big French army at the gates, and so on... . Then I'll get back with the news of what's happened here... . There's one thing--it'll strengthen the General's hand and get more troops into Africa, so poor Levasseur and his men won't have ..."

There came a bang at the door, Raoul crouched in a dark corner and Otis Vanbrugh burst in, followed by Achmet.

"Where's my sister!" he shouted, looking wildly round and seeing two Arabs, as he thought.

"I am Major de Beaujolais, Mr. Vanbrugh," said I. "Your sister and her maid are in the next room--putting on Arab dress. There will be a rising this evening and a massacre... . The worst place for you and your sister will be the Governor's house. Will you hide here until it's over--and try to keep alive somehow until the French troops arrive? Levasseur will start telegraphing the moment fighting begins, but it'll be a matter of days before they can get here--even if the wires aren't cut already--and you and the two girls will be the sole living white people in the city... . If you don't starve and aren't discovered... . Anyhow, your only chance is to hide here with the girls... ."

"Hide nothing, sir!" burst out Vanbrugh. "I shall fight alongside my host and his men."

"And your sister?" I asked.

"She'll fight too. Good as a man, with a gun."

"And when the end comes?" I said gently.

"Isn't there a chance?" he asked.

"Not the shadow of a ghost of a chance," I said. "Five little scattered detachments--each against ten thousand! They'll be smothered by sheer numbers... . And you haven't seen an African mob out for massacre and loot... ."

"Let's talk to my sister," he answered, and dashed out of the room.

"*Un brave*," said Raoul as we followed.

He was--and yet he was a gentle, refined and scholarly person, an ascetic-looking bookman and ornament of Chancelleries. I had thought of James Lane Allen and "Kentucky Cardinals," for some reason, when I first met him. He had the eyes and forehead of a dreaming philosopher--but he had the mouth and chin of a *man*... .

In the next room were two convincing Arab females each peering at us through the muslin-covered slit in the all-enveloping *bourkah* that covered her from head to foot.

"Say, Otis, what d'you know about *that*," said one of the figures, and spun round on her heel.

"Oh, *sir*," said the other, "*isn't* it a lark! Oh, *Sheikhs!*"

"Oh, Shucks! you mean," replied Vanbrugh, and hastily laid the situation before his sister.

"And what does Major Ivan say?" inquired she. "I think we'd better go with him... . Doesn't he look cunning in his Arab glad rags?"

I think I should have turned pale but for my Arab dye.

"I'm leaving Zaguig at once," I said.

"Not *escaping?*" she asked.

"I am leaving Zaguig at once," I repeated.

"Major de Beaujolais has just received dispatches," said Raoul in English, "and has to go."

"How *very* convenient for the Major!" replied Mary Vanbrugh... . "And who's *this* nobleman, anyway, might one ask?"

"Let me present Captain Raoul d'Auray de Redon," said I, indicating the filthy beggar.

"Well, don't present him too close... . Pleased to meet you, Captain. You *escaping* too?"

"No, Mademoiselle, I am not escaping," said Raoul, and added, "Neither is Major de Beaujolais. He is going on duty, infinitely against his will at such a time. But he's also going to dangers quite as great as those in Zaguig at this moment... ."

I could have embraced my friend.

Miss Vanbrugh considered this.

"Then, I think perhaps I'll go with him," she said. "Come on, Maudie. Grab the grip... . I suppose you'll stay and fight, Otis? Good-bye, dear old boy, take care of yourself ..." and she threw her arms round her brother's neck.

"*Mon Dieu,* what a girl!" Raoul laughed.

"You have heard of the frying-pan and the fire, Miss Vanbrugh?" I began.

"Yes, and of pots and pans and cabbages and kings. I'm quite tired of this gay city, anyway, and I'm coming along to see this Where-is-it place... ."

Vanbrugh turned to me.

"For God's sake take her," he said, "and Maudie too."

"Oh, *yes,* sir," said Maudie, thinking doubtless of Sheikhs.

"Why--surely," chimed in Miss Vanbrugh. "Think of Major Ivan's good name... . He *must* be chaperoned."

"I'm sorry, Vanbrugh," I said. "I can't take your sister ... I'm going on a Secret Service mission--of the greatest importance and the greatest danger... . My instructions are to go as nearly alone as is possible--and I'm only taking three natives and a white subordinate as guide, camel-man and cook and so forth... . It's *impossible* ..."

(No *de Lannec* follies for Henri de Beaujolais!)

But he drew me aside and whispered, "Good God, man, I'm her brother! I *can't* shoot her at the last. You are a stranger... . There is a *chance* for her, surely, with you--"

"Impossible," I replied.

Some one came up the stair and to the door. It was Dufour in Arab dress. He had hurried back and changed, in his quarters.

"We should be out of this in a few minutes, sir, I think," he said. "They are only waiting for the muezzin. Hundreds followed each detachment to the gates... ."

"We *shall* be out of it in a few minutes, Dufour," I answered. "Get on down to Ibrahim Maghruf's. Take Achmet. Don't forget anything--food, water, rifles, ammunition, compasses. See that Achmet takes my uniform... . I'll be there in ten minutes."

"Let the gentle Achmet take the grip, then," said Miss Vanbrugh, indicating her portmanteau.

Raoul touched my arm.

"Take the two girls in a *bassourab*," he whispered. "It would add to your plausibility, in a way, to have a *hareem* with you... . You might be able to hand them over to a north-bound caravan too, with promise of a tremendous reward if they're taken safe to a French outpost."

"Look here, couldn't Vanbrugh ride north-west with them himself?" I suggested. "He's a plucky chap and ..."

"And can't speak a word of Arabic. Not a ghost of a chance--the country's swarming, I tell you. They wouldn't get a mile. Too late ..."

"Wouldn't *you* ...?" I began.

"Stop it, Henri," he answered. "I'm not de Lannec ... My job's here, and you know it... . I may be able to do a lot of good when they get going. Mobs always follow anybody who's got a definite plan and a loud voice and bloody-minded urgings... ."

"De Beaujolais--what can I say--I *implore* you ..." began Vanbrugh.

"Very well," I said. "On the distinct understanding that I take *no* responsibility for Miss Vanbrugh, that she realizes what she is doing, and that I shall not deviate a hair's breadth from what I consider my duty... . Not to save her from death or torture... ."

There could be no harm in my taking her out of the massacre--but neither was *I* a de Lannec!

"Oh, Major! you *are* so pressing... . Come on, Maudie, we're going from certain death to sure destruction, so cheer up, child, and let's get busy ..." said the girl.

I turned away as Vanbrugh crushed his sister to his breast, and with a last look round my room, I led the way down the stairs, and out into the deserted silent street, my ears tingling for the first mob-howl, the first rifle-shot.

* * * * *

That poor unworthy fool, de Lannec! ...

CHAPTER VIII. FEMME SOUVENT VARIE

"Somewhere upon that trackless wide, it may be we shall meet
The Ancient Prophet's caravan, and glimpse his camel fleet."
A. FARQUHAR.

We were quite an ordinary party. Two sturdy desert Bedouins, Dufour and I, followed by two heavily shrouded females and trailed by a whining beggar--Raoul.

I had refused to let Vanbrugh come to Ibrahim Maghruf's house with us, partly because his only chance of not being torn to pieces in the streets was to get quickly back to the Governor's, where he could use a rifle with the rest; partly because I wanted him to take a last message and appeal to the Governor; and partly because I did not want a European to be seen going into Ibrahim's, should the place be watched.

I had taken farewell of him in the compound of my quarters, repeating my regrets that I could take *no* responsibility for his sister, and feeling that I was saying goodbye to a heroic man, already as good as dead.

He would not listen to a word about escaping from the town and taking his chance with my party until we were well away, and then shifting for himself.

He didn't desert friends in danger, he said; and with a silent hand-grip and nod, we parted, he to hurry to his death, and I to take his sister out into the savage desert and the power of more savage fanatics--if she were not killed or captured on the way... .

All was ordered confusion and swift achievement at Ibrahim Maghruf's house, as the splendid riding-camels were saddled and the special trotting baggage-camels were loaded with the long-prepared necessities of the journey.

Here Raoul presented to me a big, powerful and surly Arab, apparently, named "Suleiman the Strong," who was to be my guide. He was the man who had escaped from one of this new Mahdi's slaughters, and been picked up by the caravan in which Raoul had been carrying on his work, disguised as a camel-driver.... .

This Suleiman the Strong actually knew the Mahdi, having had the honour of being tortured by him personally; and apparently he only lived for his revenge. I thought he should be an extremely useful person, as he knew the wells and water-holes on the route, though I did not like his face and did not intend to trust him an inch farther than was necessary. Anyhow, he would lead me to the Great Oasis all right, for he had much to gain in the French Service--pay, promotion and pension--and nothing to lose.

Luckily there were spare camels, left behind by Ibrahim Maghruf, as well as my own: and Djikki and Achmet soon had a *bassourab* (a striped hooped tent--shaped something like a balloon) on to a riding-camel for the girls, and another baggage-camel loaded with extra sacks of dates, *girbas* of water, and bags of rice, tea, coffee, sugar and salt, as well as tinned provisions.

As I was helping the girls into the *bassourab,* showing them how to sit most comfortably--or least uncomfortably--and giving them strictest injunctions against parting the curtains until I gave permission, Raoul touched my arm.

"Better go, Major," he said. "*It's begun*--hark! ..."

As he spoke, a growing murmur, of which I had been subconsciously aware for some minutes--a murmur like the sound of a distant sea breaking on a pebble beach--rose swiftly to a roar, menacing and dreadful, a roar above which individual yells leapt clear like leaping spray above the waves. Rifles banged irregularly and then came crash after crash of steady volley-firing.... .

"*En avant--marche!*" said I; the old mummy opened the compound gate; and I rode out first, on my giant camel, followed by Djikki leading the one that bore the two girls. After them rode Suleiman, in charge of the baggage-camels, behind which came Achmet. Last of all rode Dufour.

For a minute, Raoul ran along the narrow lane in front of us. As we turned into the street that led to the southeastern gate--luckily not one of the four at which poor Levasseur had stationed detachments--a mob of country-dwelling tribesmen came running along it, waving swords, spears, long guns and good rifles above their heads, and yelling "*Kill! Kill!*"

"Halt! ... Back! ..." I shouted to Djikki, and brought my little caravan to a stand-still at the mouth of the lane, wondering if our journey was to end here in Zaguig. I had my rifle ready, and Dufour, Djikki, Achmet and Suleiman pushed up beside me with theirs.... .

The mob drew level.

"*Good-bye, Henri,*" said a voice from below me, and out in front of them bounded Captain Raoul d'Auray de Redon--a filthy dancing-dervish--span round and round, and then, with his great staff raised in one hand and his rosary in the other, yelled:

"*The Faith! The Faith! The Faith! ... Kill! Kill! ...* This way, my brothers! ... Quick! Quick! ... I can show you where there are infidel dogs! ... *White women! ... Loot!*" and he dashed off, followed by the mob, down a turning opposite to ours, across the main street. That was the last I ever saw of Raoul.

It was the last ever seen of him in life by any Frenchman, save for the glimpses that Levasseur and his comrades got, by the light of burning houses, of a wild dervish that harangued the mob just when it was about to charge--or led great sections of it off from where it could do most harm to where it could do least.

One cannot blame poor Levasseur that he supposed the man to be a blood-mad fanatical ring-leader of the mob--and himself ordered and directed the volley that riddled the breast of my heroic friend and stilled for ever the noblest heart that ever beat for France.

§ 2

As the mob streamed off after their self-constituted leader, I gave the word to resume the order of march, and led the way at a fast camel-trot toward and through the gate, and out into the open country.

I breathed more freely outside that accursed City of the Plain... . Another small mob came running along the road, and I swerved off across some irrigated market-gardens to make a chord across the arc of the winding road.

A few scoundrels detached themselves from the mob and ran towards us, headed by a big brute with a six-foot gun in one hand and a great sword in the other. I did not see how he could use both. He showed me.

As they drew nearer, I raised my rifle.

"Get your *own* loot," I snarled. "There's plenty more in Zaguig... ." There was a laugh, and half of them turned back.

The leader however stuck his sword in the ground, knelt, and aimed his long gun at my camel. Evidently his simple system was to shoot the beasts of mounted men and then hack the head off the rider as he came to earth.

However, rifles are quicker than *jezails,* blunderbusses, snap-haunces or arquebusses, and without reluctance I shot the gentleman through the head.

My followers, who, with a disciplined restraint that delighted me, had refrained from shooting without orders, now made up for lost time, and the remainder of the tribesmen fled, doubtless under the impression that they had stirred up a hornets' nest of loot-laden Touareg... .

I again pushed forward quickly, smiling to myself as I remembered the small voice that had issued from the *bassourab* after I had fired, remarking, "A bell-ringer for Major Ivan!"

Evidently those *bassourab* curtains had been opened in spite of what I had said... .

A red glare lit the sky. The mob-howl--that most terrible and soul-shaking of all dreadful sounds--rose higher and louder, and the crashing volleys of disciplined fire-control answered the myriad hangings of the guns and rifles of the mob.

At a bend of the road, I found myself right into another hurrying crowd, and I visualized the northern roads as covered with them. There was no time to swerve, and into them we rode.

"Hurry, brothers, or you'll be too late," I shouted, and behind me my four followers yelled "*Kill! Kill!*" and we were through the lot, either before they realized that we were so few, or because they took us for what we were--a well-armed band from whom loot would only be snatched with the maximum of bloodshed.

And to these wild hill-tribesmen, the glare of the burning city was a magnet that would have drawn them almost from their graves.

On once again, and, but for a straggler here and there, we were clear of the danger-zone.

In a couple of hours we were as much in the lonely uninhabited desert as if we had been a hundred miles from the town.

I held the pace however, and as we drove on into the moonlit silence, I tried to put from me the thoughts of what was happening in Zaguig, and of the fate of my beloved friend and of my comrades whom harsh Duty had made me desert in their last agony.... I yearned to flee from my very self.... I could have wept....

§ 3

It was after midnight when I drew rein and gave the word to *barrak* the camels and to camp.

Before I could interfere, Djikki had brought the girls' camel to its knees, with a guttural "*Adar-ya-yan,*" and with such suddenness that poor Maudie was shot head foremost out of the *bassourab* on to the sand, as a tired voice within said,

"What is it *now*? Earthquakes? ..."

Maudie laughed, and Miss Vanbrugh crawled out of the *bassourab*. "Major," she observed, "I'm through with the cabin of the Ship of the Desert.... The deck for me. I don't ride any more in that wobbling wig-wam after to-night.... And there isn't real *room* for two. Not to be sea-sick in solid comfort."

"You'll ride exactly where and how I direct, Miss Vanbrugh," I replied, "until I can dispose of you somehow."

"*Dear* Major Ivan," she smiled. "I *love* to hear him say his little piece," and weary as she was, she hummed a bar of that eternal irritating air.

In a surprisingly short time we had the little *tentes d'arbri,* which should have been mine and Dufour's, up and occupied by the girls; fires lighted; water on to boil for tea; a pot issuing savoury odours, as its contents of lamb, rice, butter, vegetables and spice simmered beneath the eye of Achmet, who turned a roasting chicken on a stick.

Maudie wanted to "wait" on Miss Vanbrugh and myself, but was told by her kind employer and friend to want something different. So the two girls, Dufour, and I made a *partie-carrée* at one fire, while Achmet ministered to us; and Djikki and Suleiman fed the camels, and afterwards did what Miss Vanbrugh described as their "chores," about another.

After we had eaten, I made certain things clear to Miss Vanbrugh and Maudie, including the matter of the strictest economy of water for their ablutions, when we were away from oases; and the absolute necessity of the promptest and exactest obedience to my orders.

After supper the girls retired to the stick-and-canvas camp-beds belonging to Dufour and myself; and I allotted two-hour watches to Djikki, Achmet, and Suleiman, with "rounds" for Dufour and myself at alternate hours.

Visiting the camels and stacked loads, I saw that all was well--as I expected from such experienced desert-men as my followers....

None of the water-*girbas* appeared to be leaking.... I rolled myself in a rug and lay down to count the stars....

§ 4

"Good-morning, Major Ivan," said a cool voice, at daybreak next morning, as I issued stores and water for breakfast. "Anything in the papers this morning?"

"I hope you and Maudie slept well, Miss Vanbrugh," I replied. "Have you everything you want?"

"No, Kind Sir, she said," was the reply. "I want a hot bath and some tea, and a chafing-dish--and then I'll show you some *real* cookery."

She looked as fresh as the glorious morning, and as sweet in Arab dress as in one of her own frocks.

"You may perhaps get a bath in a week or two," I replied.

"A *hot* bath?" she asked.

"Yes. In a saucepan," I promised.

"And to-day we're going to make a forced march," I added, "with you and Maudie safe in the *bassourab*. After that it will have to be the natural pace of the baggage-camels and we'll travel mostly by night--and you can ride as you please,--until we bid you farewell."

"Why at night?" asked the girl. "Not just for my whims?"

"No.... Cooler travelling," I replied, "and the camels go better. They can't see to graze--and our enemies can't see *us*."

"Of course. I was afraid you were thinking of what I said about the *bassourab*, Major, and planning to save the women and children...."

"How's Maudie?" I asked.

"All in, but cheerful," she replied. "She's not used to riding, and her poor back's breaking."

"And yours?" I asked.

"Oh, I grew up on a horse," she laughed, "and can grow old on a camel.... Let me dye my face and dress like a man, and carry a rifle, Major. Maudie could have the *bassourab* to herself then, with the curtains open."

"I'll think about it," I replied.

All that day we marched, Suleiman riding far ahead, as scout and guide....

After going my rounds that night, I had a talk with this fellow, and a very interesting and illuminating talk it was.

I learned, in the first place, that the Emir el Hamel el Kebir was a desert "foundling," of whom no one knew anything whatsoever.

This looked bad, and suggested one of the "miraculous" appearances of the Mahdi el Senussi or an imitation of it.

Also, from Suleiman's grudging admissions, and allowing for his obvious hatred, the Emir appeared to be a mighty worker of miracles in the sight of all men--an Invincible Commander of the Faithful in battle, and a man of great ability and power.

He was evidently adored by his own tribe--or the tribe of his adoption, to whom he had appeared in the desert--and apparently they regarded their present importance, success and wealth, as their direct reward from Allah for their hospitable acceptance of this "Prophet" when he had appeared to them.

I reflected upon my earlier studies of the British campaigns in Egypt against Osman Digna, and Mohammed Ahmed the Mahdi, and the Khalifa--and upon the fate of any Englishman who had ridden--with two white women--into the camp of any of these savage and fanatical warriors.

On my trying to get some idea of the personality and character of the Emir, Suleiman could only growl:

"He is a treacherous Son of Satan. He poisoned the old Sheikh whose salt he had eaten, and he tortured me. *Me,* who should have succeeded the good old man--to whom I was as a son... ."

This sounded bad, but there are two sides to every story, and I could well imagine our Suleiman handsomely earning a little torture.

"I fled from the Tribe," continued Suleiman, "and went to the Emir Mohammed Bishari bin Mustapha Korayim abd Rabu, who took me in and poured oil and wine into my wounds... .

"Him also this *Emir* el Hamel el Kebir slew, falling upon him treacherously in the Pass of Bab-el-Haggar, and again I had to flee for my life. A caravan found me weeks later, at the point of death in the desert, and they took me with them... .

"The man who brought me to you befriended me from the first, and showed me how to make a living as well as how to get my revenge on this foul pretender and usurper. This '*Emir*' el Hamel"--and the gentle Suleiman spat vigorously.

"Are you a *Franzawi*, Sidi?" he asked, after a brief silence.

"Like you, I work for them," I replied. "They pay, splendidly, those who serve them well; but their vengeance is terrible upon those who betray them--and their arm is long," I added.

"Allah smite them," he growled; and asked, "Will they send an army and wipe out this el Hamel?"

"What do I know?" I replied. "It is now for us to spy upon him and report to them, anyhow."

"Let him beware my knife," he grunted, and I bethought me that were I a Borgia, or my country another that I could mention, here would be one way of solving the problem of the new Mahdi menace.

"The *Franzawi* hire no assassins, nor allow assassination," I replied coldly... ." Keep good watch ..." and left him, pondering many things in my heart... .

Oh for a friendly north-bound caravan to whose leader I might give these two girls, with a reasonably easy mind, and every hope that they would be safe... .

Poor old de Lannec... . None of that nonsense for *me!*

§ 5

Day followed lazy day and night followed active night, as weeks became a month and we steadily marched southeast; but no caravan gladdened my eyes, nor sight of any human being, away from the few oases, save once a lonely Targui scout, motionless on his *mehara* camel on a high sand-hill at evening.

After seeing this disturbing sight, I made a forced march all through the night and far into the next day, and hoped that we had escaped unseen and unfollowed.

I was very troubled in mind during these days.

Not only was my anxiety as to the fate of the two girls constant, but I was annoyed to find that I thought rather more about Mary Vanbrugh than about the tremendously important work that lay before me.

My mind was becoming more occupied by this slip of a girl, and less by my mission, upon which might depend the issues of Peace and War, the lives of thousands of men, the loss or gain of an Empire perhaps--certainly of milliards of francs and years of the labour of soldiers and statesmen... .

I could not sleep at night for thinking of this woman, and for thinking of her fate; and again for thinking of how she was disturbing my thoughts which should have been concentrated on Duty... .

And she was adding to my trouble by her behaviour toward me personally.

At times she appeared positively to loathe me, and again at times she was so kind that I could scarcely forbear to take her in my arms--when she called me "*Nice Major Ivan*," and showed her gratitude--though for what, God knows, for life was hard for her and for poor Maudie, the brave uncomplaining souls.

For the fact that her brother's fate must be a terrible grief to her I made allowance, and ascribed to it her changeful and capricious attitude toward me.

Never shall I forget one perfect night of full moon, by a glorious palm-shaded desert pool, one of those little oases that seem like Paradise and make the desert seem even more like Hell.

It was an evening that began badly, too.

While fires were being lighted, camels fed, and tents pitched, the two girls went to bathe.

Strolling, I met Maudie returning, and she looked so fresh and sweet, and my troubled soul was so full of admiration of her, for her courage and her cheerfulness, that, as she stopped and, with a delightful smile, said:

"Excuse me, sir, but is that Mr. Dufour a *married* man?" I laughed and, putting a brotherly arm about her, kissed her warmly.

With remarkable speed and violence she smacked my face.

"*Maudie!*" said I aghast, "you misunderstood me entirely!"

"Well, you won't misunderstand *me* again, sir, anyhow!" replied Maudie, with a toss of her pretty head, and marched off, chin in air.

As she did so, a tinkling laugh from among the palms apprised me of the fact that Miss Vanbrugh had been an interested witness of this romantic little episode!

Nothing was said at dinner that evening, however, and after it, I sat apart with Mary Vanbrugh and had one of the delightfullest hours of my life.

She began by speaking of her brother Otis, and the possibilities of his being yet alive, and then of her parents and of her other brother and sister.

Papa was what she called "a bold bad beef-baron," and I gathered that he owned millions of acres of land and hundreds of thousands of cattle in Western America.

A widower, and, I gathered, a man the warmth of whose temper was only exceeded by the warmth of his heart. The other girl, in giving birth to whom his beloved wife had died, was, strangely enough, the very apple of his eye, and she it was who kept house for him while Mary wandered.

The older brother had apparently been too like his father to agree with him.

"Dad surely was hard on Noel," she told me, "and Noel certainly riled Dad... . Would he go to school or college? Not he! He rode ranch with the cow-boys and was just one of them. Slept down in their bunk-house too. Ran away from school as often as he was sent--and there Dad would find him, hidden by the cow-boys, when he thought the boy was 'way East.

"Dad was all for education, having had none himself. Noel was all for avoiding it, having had some himself... .

"One merry morn he got so fresh with Dad, that when he rode off, Dad pulled himself together and lassoed him--just roped him like a steer--pulled him off his pony and laid into him with his quirt!

"Noel jumped up and pulled his gun. Then he threw it on the ground and just said, '*Good-bye, Dad. I'm through*,' and that was the last we saw of brother Noel... . How I did cry! I worshipped Noel, although he was so much older than I. So did Dad--although Otis never gave him a minute's trouble, and took to education like a duck... . He's a Harvard graduate and Noel's a 'roughneck,' if he's alive... ."

"And you never saw Noel again?" I said. I wanted to keep her talking, to listen to that beautiful voice and watch that lovely face.

"Never. Nor heard from him. We heard *of* him though once--that after hoboing all over the States he was an enlisted man in a cavalry regiment, and then that a broncho-buster, whom our overseer knew, had seen him on a cattle-ship bound for Liverpool."

"And now you roam the wide world o'er, searching for the beloved playmate of your youth?" I remarked, perhaps fatuously.

"Rubbish!" was the reply. "I've almost forgotten what he looked like, and might not know him if I met him... . I'd just love to see him again though--dear old Noel. He never had an enemy but himself and never did a mean thing... . And now tell me all about *you*, Major Ivan, you stern, harsh, terrible man!" ...

I talked about myself, as a man will do--to the right woman. And by-and-by I took her hand and she did not withdraw it--rather clasped it as I said:

"Do you know, the devil tried to tempt me last night to give the order to saddle up and ride north, and put you in a place of safety... ."

"Did you fall, Major?" she asked quietly--and yes, she did return my pressure of her strong little hand.

"I did not even listen to the tempter," I replied promptly. "But I'm feeling horribly worried and frightened and anxious about you... ."

"Business down yonder urgent, Major?" she asked.

"Very."

"And your chief's trusting you to put it through quick, neat and clean?"

"Yes."

"Then defy the devil and all his works, Major," she said, "and don't let my welfare interfere with yours... ."

"I shan't, Miss Vanbrugh," I replied. "But if we could only meet a caravan ..."

"Nonsense! You don't play Joseph's Brethren with *me*, Major."

"How can I take you into the power of a man who, for all I know, may be a devil incarnate.... . I should do better to shoot you myself... ."

"I was going to say, 'Make a camp near the oasis and ride in alone,' but I shan't let you do that, Major."

"It is what I had thought of--but a man like this Emir would know all about us and our movements, long before we were near his territory... . And what happens to you, if I am made a prisoner or killed? Dufour would not go without me--nor would Achmet and Djikki for that matter."

"You are going to carry on, just as if I were not here, my friend," she said, "and I'm coming right there with you--to share and share alike. I can always shoot myself when I'm bored with things... . So can Maudie. She's got a little gun all right ... I wouldn't be a drag on you, Major, for anything in the world ... Duty before pleasure--of course... ."

And as she said those words, and rubbed her shoulder nestlingly against mine, I took her other hand ... I drew her towards me ... I nearly kissed her smiling lips ... when she snatched her hand away, and, springing up, pointed in excitement towards the oasis.

"What is it?" I cried in some alarm, for my nerves were frayed with sleeplessness.

"I thought I saw a kind of winged elephant cavorting above the trees. You know--like a flying shrimp or whistling water-rat of the upper air, Major Ivan... ."

And as I raged, she laughed and sang that cursed air again, *with* words this time--and the words were:

"There are heroes in plenty, and well known to fame
  In the ranks that are led by the Czar;
But among the most reckless of name or of fame
  Was *Ivan* Petruski Skivah.
He could imitate Irving, play euchre, or pool,
  And perform on the Spanish guitar:--
In fact, quite the cream of the Muscovite team
  Was *Ivan* Petruski Skivah."

Damn the girl, she had been laughing at me the whole time!

I gave the order to saddle up and did a double march, on towards the south of the rising sun--when it did rise--to punish her for her impertinence and to remind her that she was only with me on sufferance... . She should see who was the one to laugh last in *my* caravan...

And, *mon Dieu!* What a fool de Lannec was!

CHAPTER IX. THE TOUAREG--AND "DEAR IVAN"

One or two days later, as we jogged along in the "cool" of the evening, Dufour, the trusty rearguard of my little caravan, rode up to me.

"We're followed, sir," said he. "Touareg, I think. I have sent Djikki back to scout."

"If they're Touareg they'll surround our next camp and rush us suddenly," I said. "Our night-travelling has upset them, as there has been no chance for the surprise-at-dawn that they're so fond of."

"They'll follow us all night and attack when they think we are busy making camp tomorrow morning," said Dufour.

"We'll try to shake them off by zig-zagging and circling," I replied. "If it weren't for the women, it would be amusing to ride right round behind them and attack... . They may be only a small gang and not a *harka*."

Mary Vanbrugh closed up. I had been riding ahead in haughty displeasure, until Dufour came to me.

I had done with Mary Vanbrugh. "What is it, Major?" she asked.

"Nothing, Miss Vanbrugh," I replied.

"What men-folk usually wag their heads and their tongues about," she agreed.

Maudie's *bassourab*-adorned camel overtook us as we dropped into a walk and then halted.

"What is it, Mr. Dufour?" I heard her ask.

"*Sheikhs!*" replied Dufour maliciously, and I wondered if his face had also been slapped.

I looked at Maudie. Methought she beamed joyously.

Half an hour later, Djikki of the wonderful eye-sight came riding up at top-speed.

"Veiled Touareg," he said. "The Forgotten of God. About five hands of fingers. Like the crescent moon--" from which I knew that we were being followed by about five and twenty Touareg, and that they were riding in a curved line--the horns of which would encircle us at the right time.

There was nothing for it but to ride on. We were five rifles--six counting Mary Vanbrugh--and shooting from behind our camels we should give a good account of ourselves against mounted men advancing over open country.

Nor would so small a gang resolutely push home an attack upon so straight-shooting and determined a band as ourselves.

But what if they managed to kill our camels?

"Ride after Suleiman as fast as you can, Miss Vanbrugh, with Maudie. Achmet will ride behind you," said I. "You and I and Djikki will do rear-guard, Dufour... ."

"Don't be alarmed if you hear firing," I added to the girls.

"Oh, Major, I shall jibber with fright, and look foolish in the face," drawled Mary Vanbrugh, and I was under the impression that Maudie's lips parted to breathe the word "*Sheikhs!*"

We rode in this order for an hour, and I then left Djikki on a sand-dune, with orders to watch while the light lasted. I thought he would get our pursuers silhouetted against the sunset and see if their numbers had increased, their formation or direction changed, and judge whether their pace had quickened or slackened.

"As soon as it is dark, we'll turn sharp-right, for a couple of hours, and then left again," I said to Dufour.

"Yes, sir," said he. "They won't be able to follow tracks in the dark. Not above a walking pace."

He had hardly spoken when a rifle cracked... . Again twice... . Aimed from us, by the sound... . Djikki! ... We wheeled round together and rode back along our tracks. We passed Djikki's *barraked* camel and saw the Soudanese lying behind the crest of a sand-hill. He stood up and came down to us.

"Three," he said. "Swift scouts in advance of the rest. I hit one man and one camel. The others fled. Four hundred metres."

For a Soudanese it was very fine marksmanship.

"It'll show them we're awake, anyhow," said Dufour; and we rode off quickly, to overtake the others.

As soon as it was as dark as it ever is in the star-lit desert, I took the lead, and turned sharply from our line as we were riding over a rocky stony patch that would show no prints of the soft feet of camels.

For an hour or two I followed the line, and then turned sharply to the left, parallel with our original track.

Thereafter I dropped to the rear, leaving Dufour to lead. I preferred to rely upon his acquired scientific skill rather than upon Suleiman's desert sense of direction, when I left the head of the caravan at night. Dropping back, I halted until I could only just see the outline of the last rider, Achmet, sometimes as a blur of white in the star-shine, sometimes as a silhouette against the blue-black starry sky... .

Vast, vast emptiness... . Universes beyond universes... . Rhythmic fall of soft feet on sand... . Rhythmic swaying of the great camel's warm body... . World swaying... . Stars swaying... .

I will not falsely accuse myself of having fallen asleep, for I do not believe I slept--though I have done such a thing on the back of a camel. But I was certainly slightly hypnotized by star-staring and the perfect rhythm of my camel's tireless changeless trot... . And I had been very short of sleep for weeks... . Perhaps I did sleep for a few seconds? ...

Anyhow, I came quite gradually from a general inattentiveness toward the phenomena of reality, to an interest therein, and then to an awareness that gripped my heart like the clutch of a cold hand.

First I noted dully that I had drawn level with Achmet and was some yards to his right... . Then that Djikki, or Suleiman perhaps, was riding a few yards to my right... . And then that some one else was close behind me.

I must have got right into the middle of the caravan. Curious... . *Why, what was this?* ... I rubbed my eyes... . None of *us* carried a lance or spear of any kind!

It was then that my blood ran cold, for I knew I was *riding with the Touareg!*

I pulled myself together and did some quick thinking. Did each of them take me for some other member of their band who had ridden to the front and been overtaken again? Or were they chuckling to themselves at the poor fool whom they had outwitted, and who was now in their power? ...

Was it their object to ride on with me, silently, until the Touareg band and the caravan were one body--and then each robber select his victim and slay him?

What should I do? My rifle was across my thighs. No; I could not have been asleep or I should have dropped it.

I slowly turned my head and looked behind me. I could see no others--but it was very dark and others might be near, besides the three whom I could distinguish clearly.

Achmet was not in sight. What *should* I do? ...

Work, poor brain, work! Her life depends on it... .

Could I draw ahead of them sufficiently fast to overtake the caravan, give a swift order, and have my men wheeled about and ready to meet our pursuers with a sudden volley and then rapid fire?

I could try, anyhow. I raised the long camel-stick that dangled from my wrist, and my camel quickened its pace instantly. There is never any need to strike a well-trained *mehara*... . The ghostly riders to right and left of me kept their positions... . I had gained nothing... .

I must not appear to be trying to escape... . With faint pressure on the left nose-rein of my camel, I endeavoured to edge imperceptibly toward the shadow on my left. I would speak to him as though I were a brother Targui, as soon as I was close enough to shoot with certainty if he attacked me.

The result showed me that the raiders had not taken me for one of themselves--I could get no nearer to the man, nor draw further from the rider on my right... .

Wits against wits--and Mary Vanbrugh's life in the balance... .

Gently I drew rein, and slowed down very gradually. My silent nightmare companions did the same.

This would let the caravan draw ahead of us, and give my men more time for action, when the time for action came.

Slower and slower grew my pace, and I drooped forward, nodding like a man asleep, my eyes straining beneath my *haik* to watch these devils who shepherded me along.

My camel dropped into a walk, and very gradually the two shadows converged upon me to do a silent job with sword or spear... .

And what of the man behind me? The muscles of my shoulder-blades writhed as I thought of the cold steel that even then might be within a yard of my back... .

Suddenly I pulled up, raised my rifle, and fired carefully, and with the speed that has no haste, at the rider on my right. I aimed where, if I missed his thigh, I should hit his camel, and hoped to hit both. As my rifle roared in the deep silence of the night, I swung left for the easier shot, fired again, and drove my camel bounding forward. I crouched low, as I worked the bolt of my rifle, in the hope of evading spear-thrust or sword-stroke from behind.

As I did so a rifle banged behind me, at a few yards range, and I felt as though my left arm had been struck with a red-hot axe.

With the right hand that held the rifle, I wheeled my camel round in a flash, steadied the beast and myself and, one-handed, fired from my hip at a camel that suddenly loomed up before me. Then I wheeled about again and sent my good beast forward at racing speed.

My left arm swung useless, and I could feel the blood pouring down over my hand, in a stream... .

This would not do... .

I shoved my rifle under my thigh, and with my right hand raised my left and got the arm up so that I could hold it by the elbow, with the left hand beneath my chin.

I fought off the feeling of faintness caused by shock and the loss of blood--and wondered if Suleiman, Djikki, Achmet and Dufour would shoot first and challenge afterwards, as I rode into them... .

Evidently I had brought down the three camels at which I had aimed--not a difficult thing to do, save in darkness, and when firing from the back of a camel, whose very breathing sways one's rifle... .

I was getting faint again... . It would soon pass off... . If I could only plug the holes and improvise a sling... . As the numbness of the arm wore off and I worried at it, I began to hope and believe that the bone was not broken... . Fancy a shattered elbow-joint, in the desert, and with the need to ride hard and constantly... .

I was aware of three dark masses in line... .

"Major! *Shout!*" cried a voice, and with great promptitude I shouted--and three rifles came down from the firing position.

"Where is she?" I asked.

"I made her ride on with Achmet, hell-for-leather," replied Dufour. "I swore she'd help us more that way, till we can see what's doing... . What happened, sir?"

I told him.

"They'll trail us all right," said Dufour. "Those were scouts and there would be a line of connecting-links between them and the main body. Shall we wait, and get them one by one?"

"No," I replied. "They'd circle us and they'd get the others while we waited here. It'll be daylight soon... ."

It was in the dim daylight of the false dawn that we sighted the baggage-camels of the caravan.

"Those baggage-camels will have to be left," said Dufour.

"You can't ride away from Touareg," I answered.

"It's hopeless. We've got to fight, if they attack. They may not do so, having been badly stung already. But the Targui is a vengeful beast. It isn't as though they were ordinary Bedouin... ."

The light grew stronger, and we drew near to the others. I told Djikki to drop back and to fire directly he saw anything of the robbers--thus warning us, and standing them off while we made what preparations we could.

I suddenly felt extremely giddy, sick, and faint. My white *burnous* made a ghastly show. I was wet through, from my waist to my left foot, with blood. I must have lost a frightful lot ... artery... .

Help! ...

The next thing that I knew was that I was lying with my head on Maudie's lap, while Mary Vanbrugh, white of face but deft of hand, bandaged my arm and strapped it across my chest. She had evidently torn up some linen garment for this purpose. Mary's eyes were fixed on her work, and Maudie's on the horizon. The men were crouched each behind his kneeling camel.

"*Dear* Major Ivan," murmured Mary as she worked.

I shut my eyes again, quickly and without shame. It was heavenly to rest thus for a few minutes.

"Oh, is he *dead*, Miss?" quavered poor Maudie.

"We shall all be dead in a few minutes, I expect, child," replied Mary. "Have you a safety-pin? ... Dead as cold mutton... . *Sheikhs,* my dear! ... Shall I shoot you at the last, Maudie, or would you rather do it yourself?"

"Well--if you wouldn't *mind*, Miss? Thank you very much, if it's not troubling you."

Silence.

"*Dear* Major Ivan," came a sweet whisper. "Oh, I *have* been a beast to him, Maudie... . Yes, I'll shoot you with pleasure, child... . How *could* I be such a wretch as to treat him like that... . He is the bravest, nicest, sternest ..."

I felt a cad, and opened my eyes--almost into those of Mary, whose lips were just ... were they ... *were* they? ...

"Yes, Miss," said Maudie, her eyes and thoughts afar off. "He is a beautiful gentleman... ."

"Hallo! the patient has woken up!" cried Mary, drawing back quickly. "Had a nice nap, Major? How do you feel? ... Here, have a look into the cup that cheers and inebriates"; and she lifted a mug, containing cognac and water, to my lips.

I drank the lot and felt better.

"My heart come into my mouth it did, sir, when I saw you fall head-first off that camel. You fair *splashed* blood, sir," said Maudie. "Clean into me mouth me heart come, sir."

"Hope you swallowed the little thing again, Maud. Such a sweet *garden* of romance as it is! ... '*Come into the maud, Garden!*' for a change... . That's the way, Major... . Drinks it up like milk and looks round for more. Got a nice clean flesh wound and no bones touched, the clever man... ."

I sat up.

"Get those camels further apart, Dufour," I shouted. "Absolute focal point to draw concentrated fire bunched like that ..."

Nobody must think that I was down and out, and that the reins were slipping from a sick man's grasp.

The men were eating dates as they watched, and Mary had opened a tin of biscuits and one of sardines.

"Hark at the Major saying his piece," a voice murmured from beneath a flowing *kafiyeh* beside me. "Isn't he fierce this morning!"

I got to my feet and pulled myself together... . Splendid... . Either the brandy, or the idea of a kiss I foolishly fancied that I had nearly received, had gone to my head. I ate ravenously for the next ten minutes, and drank cold tea from a water-bottle.

"There's many a slip between the kiss and the lip," I murmured anon, in a voice to match the one that had last spoken.

I was unwise.

"Wrong again, Major Ivan Petruski Ski*vah*! I was just going to blow a smut off your grubby little nose," was the prompt reply, and I seemed to hear thereafter a crooning of:

"But among the most reckless of name and of fame

Was Ivan Petruski Skivah

....

... and perform on the Spanish guitar

In fact, quite the cream of 'Intelligence' team

Was Ivan Petruski Skivah... ."

as Miss Vanbrugh cleaned her hands with sand and then re-packed iodine and boric lint in the little medicine-chest.

I managed to get on to my camel, and soon began to feel a great deal better, perhaps helped by my ferocious anger at myself for collapsing. Still, blood is blood, and one misses it when too much is gone.

"Hide on with Achmet again," I called to Miss Vanbrugh, and bade the rest mount. "We'll keep on now, just as long as we can," I said to Dufour, and ordered Djikki to hang as far behind us as was safe. In a matter of that sort, Djikki's judgment was as good as anybody's... .

Dufour then told me a piece of news.

A few miles to the south-east of us was, according to Suleiman, a *shott,* a salt-lake or marsh that extended to the base of a chain of mountains. The strip of country between the two was very narrow.

We could camp there.

If the Touareg attacked us, they could only do so on a narrow front, and could not possibly surround us. To go north round the lake, or south round the mountains, would be several days' journey.

"That will be the place for us, sir," concluded Dufour.

"Yes," I agreed, "if the Touareg are not there before us."

CHAPTER X. MY ABANDONED CHILDREN

That would have been one of the worst days of my life, and that is saying a good deal, had it not been for a certain exaltation and joy that bubbled up in my heart as I thought of the look in Miss Vanbrugh's eyes when I had opened mine... .

What made it so terrible was not merely the maddening ache in my arm that seemed to throb in unison with the movement of my camel, but the thought of what I must do if this pass was what I pictured it to be, and if the Touareg attacked us in strength.

It would be a very miserable and heart-breaking duty--to ride on and leave my men to hold that pass--that I might escape and fulfil my mission. How could I leave Dufour to die that I might live? How could I desert Achmet and Djikki, my servants and my friends? ...

However--it is useless to attempt to serve one's country in the Secret Service, if one's private feelings, desires, loves, sorrows, likes and dislikes are to be allowed to come between one and one's country's good... . Poor de Lannec! How weak and unworthy he had been... .

There was one grain of comfort--nothing would be gained by my staying and dying with my followers... . It would profit them nothing at all... . They would die just the same... .

If the Touareg could, by dint of numbers, overcome four, they could overcome five. I could not save them by staying with them... .

But oh, the misery, the agony, of ordering them to hold that pass while I rode to safety!

How could I give the order: "Die, but do not retire--until *I* have had time to get well away"?

And the girls? Would they be a hindrance to me on two of the fleetest camels... . And perhaps any of my little band who did not understand my desertion of them would think they were fighting to save the women, whom I was taking to safety--*if I decided to take them.*

But it would be ten times worse than leaving my comrades in Zaguig... .

How could I leave *Mary Vanbrugh*--perhaps to fall, living, into the hands of those bestial devils?

The place proved an ideal spot for a rearguard action, and the Touareg were not before us.

Lofty and forbidding rocks rose high, sheer from the edge of a malodorous swamp, from whose salt-caked edge grew dry bents that rattled in the wind.

Between the swamp and the stone cliffs was a tract of boulder-strewn sand, averaging a hundred yards in width.

Here we camped, lit fires, and prepared to have a long and thorough rest--unless the Touareg attacked--until night.

Achmet quickly pitched the little *tentes d'abri,* fixed the camp-beds for the girls, and unrolled the "flea-bags" and thin mattresses, while his kettle boiled. It was a strangely peaceful and domestic scene--in view of the fact that sudden death--or slow torture--loomed so large and near.

Dufour himself ungirthed and fed the camels while Suleiman stood upon a rock and stared out into the desert. He could probably see twice as far as Dufour or I... .

"*Into* that tent, Major," said the cool sweet voice that I was beginning to like again. "I have made the bed as comfy as I can. Have Achmet pull your boots off. I'll come in ten minutes or so, and dress your arm again."

"And what about *you?*" I replied. "I'm not going to take your tent. I am quite all right now, thanks."

"Maudie and I are going to take turns on the other bed," she replied. "And you *are* going to take 'my' tent, and lie down too. What's going to happen to the show if you get ill? Suppose you get fever? Suppose your arm mortifies and falls into the soup? ... Let's get the wound fixed again, before those low-brow Touareg shoot us up again... . You'll find a cold water compress very soothing... . Go along, Major... ."

I thought of something more soothing than that--the touch of cool deft fingers.

"I'd be shot daily if you were there to bind me up, Miss Vanbrugh," I said as I gave in to her urgency, and went to the tent.

"Well--perhaps they'll oblige after breakfast, Major, and plug your other arm," observed this most unsentimental young woman.

"But, my dear!" I expostulated. "If I had no arms at all, how could I ...?"

"Just what *I* was thinking, Major," was the reply, as, to hide a smile, she stooped over the big suit-case and extracted the medicine chest... .

As we hastily swallowed our meal of dates, rice, biscuits and tinned milk, I gave my last orders to Dufour... .

"You'll hold this pass while there is a man of you alive," I said.

"*Oui, mon Commandant,*" replied the brave man, with the same quiet nonchalance that would have marked his acknowledgment of an order to have the camels saddled.

"Should the Touareg abandon the attempt (which they will not do), any survivor is to ride due south-east until he reaches the Great Oasis."

"*Oui, mon Commandant.*"

"Even if Suleiman is killed, there will be no difficulty in finding the place, but we'll hear what he has to say about wells and water-holes--while he is still hale and hearty."

"*Oui, mon Commandant.*"

"But I fear there won't be any survivors--four against a *harka*--say, a hundred to one... . But you must hold them up until I am well away... . They won't charge while your shooting is quick and accurate... . When they do, they'll get you, of course... . Don't ride for it at the last moment... . See it through here, to give the impression that you are the whole party. I must not be pursued... . Die here... ."

"*Oui, mon Commandant.*"

"Excuse me, Major de Beaujolais," cut in the voice of Miss Vanbrugh, icily cold and most incisive, "is it possible that you are talking about *deserting your men?* ... Leaving them to die here while you escape? ... *Ordering* them to remain here to increase your own chance of safety, in fact... ."

"I was giving instructions to my subordinate, who will remain here with the others, Miss Vanbrugh," I replied coldly. "Would you be good enough to refrain from interrupting... ."

My uncle's words burned before my eyes!--"*A woman, of course! ... He turned aside from his duty... . Exit de Lannec... .*"

Miss Vanbrugh put her hand on Dufour's arm.

"If you'll be so kind as to enrol me, Mr. Dufour--I am a very good rifle shot," she said. "I shall dislike perishing with you intensely, but I should dislike deserting you infinitely more," and she smiled very sweetly on my brave Dufour.

He kissed her hand respectfully and looked inquiringly at me.

"And Maudie?" I asked Miss Vanbrugh. "Is she to be a romantic heroine, too? I hope she can throw stones better than most girls, for I understand she has never fired a rifle or pistol in her life... ."

"I think you really are the most insufferable and detestable creature I have *ever* met," replied Miss Vanbrugh.

"Interesting, but hardly germane to the discussion," I replied.

"Listen, Miss Vanbrugh," I continued. "If the Touareg are upon us, as I have no doubt they are, I am going to ride straight for the Great Oasis. Dufour, Achmet, Djikki and Suleiman will stand the Touareg off as long as possible. Eventually my men will be rushed and slaughtered. If sufficiently alive, when overcome and seized, they will be tortured unbelievably. The Touareg may or may not then follow me, but they will have no chance of overtaking me as I shall have a long start. I shall have the best of the riding camels, and I shall make forced marches... . Now--I see no reason why you and Maudie should not accompany me *for just as long as you can stand the pace... .*"

"Oh, Major--we might conceivably hinder you and so imperil your most precious life, endanger your safety--so essential to France and the world in general... ."

"I'll take good care you don't do that, Miss Vanbrugh," I replied. "But, as I say, there is no reason why you and your maid should not ride off with me--though, I give you fair warning, I shall probably ride for twenty-four hours without stopping--and you will be most welcome. In fact, I pray you to do so... . Trust me to see to it that you are no hindrance nor source of danger to the success of my mission... ."

"Oh--I fully trust you for *that,* Major de Beaujolais," she replied bitterly.

"Then be ready to start as soon as we get word from Djikki that they are coming," I said. "Once again, there is no reason why you should not come with me..."

"Thank you--but there is a very strong reason. I would sooner die twice over... . I remain here," was the girl's reply. "I can think of only one thing worse than falling alive into the hands of these beasts—and that is deserting my *friends,* Mr. Dufour, Achmet and Djikki.... Why, I wouldn't desert even that evil-looking Suleiman after he had served me faithfully.... I wouldn't desert a dog...."

"And Maudie?" I asked.

"She shall do exactly as she pleases," answered the girl.

Turning to Maudie, who was listening open-mouthed, she said:

"Will you ride off with Major de Beaujolais, my child, or will you stay with me? You may get to safety with this gallant gentleman—if you can keep him in sight.... It is death to stay here, apparently, but I will take care that it *is* death and not torture for you, my dear."

"Wouldn't the Sheikhs treat us well, Miss?" asked Maudie.

"Oh, *Sheikhs!*" snapped Miss Vanbrugh. "These are two-legged *beasts,* my good idiot. They are human wolves, torturing *devils,* merciless *brutes*....What is the worst thing you've got in your country?"

"Burglars, Miss," replied Maudie promptly.

"Well, the ugliest cut-throat burglar that ever hid under your bed or came in at your window in the middle of the night, is just a dear little woolly lambkin, compared with the best of these murderous savages...."

Maudie's face fell.

"I thought perhaps these was Sheikhs, Miss.... Like in the book.... But, anyhow, I was going to do what you do, Miss, and go where you go—of course, please, Miss."

"I am afraid you are another of those ordinary queer creatures that think faithfulness to friends and loyalty to comrades come first, dear," said Miss Vanbrugh, and gave Maudie's hand a squeeze. "But you'll do what I tell you, Maudie, won't you?"

"That's what I'm here for, please, Miss, thank you," replied the girl.

"Well, you're going with Major de Beaujolais," said Miss Vanbrugh. "I hate sending you off with a gentleman of his advanced views and superior standards—but I should hate shooting you, even more."

"Yes, Miss, thank you," answered Maudie, and I rose and strolled to my tent.

Ours is not an easy service. Duty is a *very* jealous God....

Miss Vanbrugh came and dressed my arm, and we spoke no word to each other during the process. How I *hated* her! ... The unfair, illogical little vixen! ... The *woman!* ...

A few minutes later Suleiman uttered a shout. He could see a rider on the horizon. I hurried towards him.

"It is Djikki, the black slave," he said.

"Djikki, the French Soudanese soldier, you dog," I growled at him, and at any other time would have fittingly rewarded the ugly scowl with which he regarded me.

"They are coming," shouted Djikki as his swift camel drew near; and we all rushed to work like fiends at packing-up and making preparations, for flight and fight respectively.

"They are more than ten hands of five fingers now," said Djikki, as he dismounted.... "More than a battalion of soldiers in numbers.... They are riding along our track.... Here in an hour."

"Miss Vanbrugh," said I, "I have got to go. If you stay here I shall go on and do my work. When that is successfully completed, I shall come back to this spot and shoot myself....

Think of Maudie, too--if you won't think of yourself or me. Do you want the girl to meet some of her 'Desert Sheikhs' at last?"

"*Can* you leave Dufour and the Brown Brothers, Major de Beaujolais? ... I love that little Djikki-bird... ."

"I can, Miss Vanbrugh, because I *must*. And if I, a soldier, can do such a thing, a girl can. What could you do by stopping to die here?"

"Shoot," she replied, "as fast and as straight as any of them."

"My dear lady," I said, "if four rifles won't keep off a hundred, five won't. If five can, four can... . And I must slink off... ."

I could have wept. We stood silent, staring at each other.

"Your say goes, Major. I suppose you are right," answered the girl, and my heart leapt up again. "But I *hate* myself--and I *loathe* you... ."

All worked like slaves to get the four swiftest camels saddled and loaded with light and indispensable things. The fourth one, although a *mehara,* had to carry one *tente d'abri* and bed, water, and food.

I could hardly trust myself to speak as I wrung Dufour's hand, nor when I patted the shoulder of my splendid Achmet. Djikki put my hand to his forehead and his heart, and then knelt to kiss my feet.

The drop of comfort in the bitter suffering of that moment was my knowledge that these splendid colleagues of mine--white man, brown man, and black--knew that what I was doing was my Duty and that what they were about to do was theirs... .

I bade Suleiman fight for his life; he was too new a recruit to the Service to be expected to fight for an ideal... .

Miss Vanbrugh and Maudie mounted their *mehari*--Maudie still as cheerful and plucky as ever, and, I am certain, thrilled, and still hopeful of tender adventure.

I should be surprised if her novelette-turned brain and rubbish-fed imagination did not even yet picture the villainous desert wolves, who were so close on our trail, as the brave band of a "lovely" Desert Sheikh in hot pursuit of one Maudie Atkinson, of whose beauty and desirability he had somehow heard... .

There was a shout from Suleiman again. Something moving on the horizon.

I gave the word to start, and took a last look round.

My men's camels were *barraked* out of danger. Each man had a hundred rounds of ammunition, a *girba* of water, a little heap of dates, and an impregnable position behind a convenient rock... .

Four against scores--perhaps hundreds... . But in a narrow pass... . If only the Touareg would content themselves with shooting, and lack the courage to charge. "Say, Major," called Mary, "let those desert dead-beats hear six rifles for a bit! They may remember an urgent date back in their home-town, to see a man about a dog or something... . Think we're a regular sheriff's posse of *vigilantes* or a big, bold band of Bad Men... ."

Dare I? It would take a tiny trifle of the load of misery from my shoulders... .

I would!

We brought our camels to their knees again, and re-joined the garrison of the pass, the men of this little African Thermopylæ... .

Miss Vanbrugh chose her rock, rested her rifle on it, sighted, raised the slide of her back-sight a little--all in a most business-like manner.

Maudie crouched at my feet, behind my rock, and I showed her how to work the bolt of my rifle, after each shot. I was one-handed, and Maudie had, of course, never handled a rifle in her life.

I waited until we could distinguish human and animal forms in the approaching cloud of dust, and then gave the range at 2,000 metres. "*Fixe!*" I cried coolly thereafter, for the benefit of my native soldiers. "*Feux de salve... . En Joue! ... Feu!*"

It was an admirable volley, even Suleiman firing exactly on my word, "*Feu,*"although he knew no word of French.

Three times I repeated the volley, and then gave the order for a rapid *feu de joie* as it were, at 1,500 metres, so that the advancing Touareg should hear at least six rifles, and suppose that there were probably many more.

I then ordered my men, in succession, to fire two shots as quickly as possible, each firing as soon as the man on his left had got his two shots off. This should create doubt and anxiety as to our numbers.

I then ordered rapid independent fire.

The Touareg had deployed wildly, dismounted, and opened fire. This rejoiced me, for I had conceived the quite unlikely possibility of their charging in one headlong overwhelming wave... .

It was time to go.

"Run to your camel, Maudie. Come on, Miss Vanbrugh," I shouted; and called to Dufour, "God watch over you, my dear friend."

I had to go to the American girl and drag her from the rock behind which she stood, firing steadily and methodically, changing her sights occasionally, a handful of empty cartridge-cases on the ground to her right, a handful of cartridges ready to her hand on the rock... .

I shall never forget that picture of Mary Vanbrugh--dressed as an Arab girl and fighting like a trained soldier... .

"*I'm not coming!*" she cried.

I shook her as hard as I could and then literally dragged her to her camel.

"Good-bye, my children," I cried as I abandoned them.

§ 2

"We rode for the rest of that day, and I thanked God when I could no longer hear the sounds of rifle-fire, glad though I was that they had only died away as distance weakened them, and not with the suddenness that would have meant a charge, massacre and pursuit.

I was a bitter, miserable and savage man when at last I was compelled to draw rein, and Miss Vanbrugh bore my evil temper with a gentle womanly sweetness of which I had not thought her capable.

She dressed my arm again (and I almost hoped that it might never heal while she was near) and absolutely insisted that she and Maudie should share watches with me. When I refused this, she said:

"Very well, Major, then instead of one watching while two sleep, we'll both watch, and Maudie shall chaperone us--and that's the sort of thing Euclid calls *reductio ad absurdum,* or plumb-silly." And nothing would shake her, although I could have done so willingly.

What with the wound in my arm and the wound in my soul, I was near the end of my tether... .

We took a two-hour watch in turn, poor Maudie nursing a rifle of which she was mortally afraid.

CHAPTER XI. THE CROSS OF DUTY

We rode hard all the next day, and the two girls, thanks to the hard training of the previous weeks, stood the strain well.

It was for the sake of the camels and not for that of the two brave women that I at length drew rein and halted for a four-hour rest at a water-hole.

As I strode up and down, in misery and grief at the thoughts that filled my mind--thoughts of those splendid men whom I had left to die, Mary Vanbrugh came from the little *tente d'abri* which I had insisted that she and Maudie should use.

"Go and lie down," she said. "You'll get fever and make that arm worse... . You must rest *sometimes,* if you are to carry on at all."

"I can't," I said. "They were like brothers to me and I *loved* each one of them."

"Talk then, if you can't rest," replied the wise woman. "Tell me about them... ."

"Go and lie down yourself," I said.

"It's Maudie's turn for the bed," she answered. "Tell me about them... . Sit down here... ."

I told her about Dufour and his faithful service of nearly twenty years; of how he had offered his life for mine, and had saved it, more than once.

"And Djikki?" she asked.

"He, too," I replied. "He is a Senegalese soldier, and I took him for my orderly because of his great strength and endurance, his courage, fidelity and patience... . He was with me when I was doing some risky work down Dahomey way... . There was a certain king who was giving trouble and threatening worse trouble--and it was believed that he was actually getting Krupp guns from a German trading-post on the coast... .

"We were ambushed in that unspeakable jungle, and only Djikki and I survived the fight... . We were driven along for days, thrashed with sticks, prodded with spears, tied to trees at night, and bound so tightly that our limbs swelled and turned blue.

"We were given entrails to eat and carefully defiled water to drink... . And one morning, as they untied us, that we might stagger on--towards the king's capital--Djikki snatched a *machete,* a kind of heavy hiltless sword, from a man's hand, and put up such a noble fight as has rarely been fought by one man against a crowd. In spite of what we had been through, he fought like a fiend incarnate... . It was Homeric... . It was like a gorilla fighting baboons, a tiger fighting dogs.

That heavy razor-edged blade rose and fell like lightning, and every time it descended, a head or an arm was almost severed from a body--and he whirled and sprang and slashed and struck until the whole gang of them gave ground, and as he bellowed and charged and then smote their leader's head clean from his shoulders, they broke and ran.... And Djikki--dripping blood, a mass of gashes and gaping wounds--ran too.... With me in his arms....

"And when he could run no longer, he laid me down and cut the hide things that bound my wrists and elbows behind me, and those that cut into the flesh of my knees and ankles. Then he fainted from loss of blood....

"I collapsed next day with fever, dysentery, and blood-poisoning, and Djikki--that black ex-cannibal--carried me in his arms, like a mother her baby, day after day, for five weeks, and got food for the two of us as well....

"During that time I tasted the warm blood of monkeys and the cold flesh of lizards.... And when, at last, we were found, by pure good luck, near a French post on the Great River, he had not, as I discovered later, eaten for three days (although I had) and he had not slept for four nights.... But he had not left me and saved himself, as he could so easily have done....

"Instead of doing thirty miles a day and eating all he got, he did ten miles a day with me in his arms, and gave me the food--pretending he had eaten.... The doctor at the Fort said he had never seen anyone so starved and emaciated, and yet able to keep his feet.... No, he never left me...."

"And *you* have left *him*," said Miss Vanbrugh.

"I have left him," I replied....

"And Achmet?" she asked.

"The most faithful servant a man ever had," I said. "He has nursed me through fever, dysentery, blindness, wounds, and all sorts of illnesses, as gently and tirelessly as any woman could have done.

"He is a Spahi and a brave soldier.... Once I was getting my squadron across a deep crocodile-infested river, swollen and swift, very difficult and dangerous work if you have not had plenty of practice in handling a swimming horse.... I crossed first and then returned. Finally, I came over last, and a huge crocodile took my horse--the noise and splashing of the crossing squadron having subsided--and I went down with the pair of them, heavily weighted too.... It was my Achmet who spurred his horse back into the water, swam to the spot and dived for me, regardless of crocodiles and the swift current.... We were both pretty well dead by the time he managed to grab an overhanging branch, and they dragged us out...."

A silence fell between us....

"Another time, too," I went on, "Achmet and Dufour undoubtedly saved my life--and not only at the risk of their own, but at the cost of horrible suffering.

"We were besieged in a tiny entrenched bivouac, starving and nearly dead with thirst. All that came into that little hell was a hail of tribesmen's bullets by day and a gentle rain of snipers' bullets by night....

"Had we been of the kind that surrenders--which we were not--we should only have exchanged the tortures of thirst for the almost unimaginable tortures of the knives and red-hot irons of the tribesmen and their women.... Day by day our sufferings increased and our numbers diminished as men died of starvation, thirst, dysentery, fever, heat-stroke, wounds--or the merciful bullet....

"The day temperature was rarely much above 120° and never below it, and from the sun we had no shelter. Generally a sirocco was blowing at fifty miles an hour, as hot as the blast from the open door of a furnace, and the sun was hidden in the black clouds of its dust....

Often it was as though night fell ere noon; and men, whose ration of water was a teacupful a day, had to breathe this dust. Our mouths, nostrils, eyes, ears were filled with it... . And, on dark nights, those devils would place fat *girbas* of water where, at dawn, they would be in full view of men dying of thirst ... in the hope of luring them from the shelter of rocks and sand-trenches to certain death ... and in the certainty of adding to their tortures... . But my men were Spahis, and not one of them complained, or grumbled, or cast off discipline to make a dash for a *girba* and death... .

"Dufour asked to be allowed to crawl out at night and try to get one of those skins--in which there might still remain a few drops of water--or possibly catch one of the fiends placing a *girba*--and I would not allow it... . I would not weigh Dufour's life against the ghost of a chance of getting a little water--and that poisoned, perhaps... . Nor did I feel that I had any right to go myself, nor to send any of my few remaining men... .

"Then Achmet volunteered to try... .

"But I am wandering ... what I started to say was this... . Three days before we were relieved I was shot in the head, and for those three days Dufour not only maintained the defence of that post, garrisoned by dying men, but *devoted half his own tiny ration of water to me and my wound*... .Achmet threatened to knife him when Dufour tried to prevent him from contributing *the whole* of his! ...

"And when the relief-column arrived there was not a man on his feet, except Dufour, though there were several lying, still alive, gripping their rifles and facing their foes... .

"Dufour could give no information to the Colonel commanding the relief-column, because he could not speak, and when he sat down to write an answer to a question, he collapsed, and the surgeons took him over... ."

"You *accepted* half Dufour's and the whole of Achmet's water-ration?" asked Miss Vanbrugh.

"I was unconscious from the time I was hit until the day after the relief," I replied. "I should never have recovered consciousness at all had not the excellent Surgeon-Major arrived--nor should I have lived until he did arrive, but for Achmet's bathing my head and keeping it clean and 'cool'--in a temperature of 120° and a howling dust-storm... . I learnt all about it afterwards from a Spahi Sergeant who was one of the survivors... . Achmet did not sleep during those three days... . Nor did he taste water... ."

"And I have left *him* too," I added.

Mary Vanbrugh was silent for a while.

"Major de Beaujolais," she said at length, "suppose there had been only one camel, when you--er--departed from the pass. Suppose the Touareg had contrived to shoot the rest... . Would you have taken that camel and gone off alone?"

"Yes," I replied.

"Leaving Maudie--and me?"

"Unhesitatingly," I replied.

She regarded me long and thoughtfully, and then, without speaking, returned to the tent where Maudie slept, dreaming, doubtless, of Sheikhs.

Of course I would have left them. Was I to be another de Lannec and turn aside from the service of my country, imperil the interests and welfare of my Motherland, be false to the traditions of my great and noble Service, stultify the arduous and painful training of a lifetime, fail the trust reposed in me, and betray my General--*for a woman?*

But, oh, the thought of that woman struggling and shrieking in the vile hands of those inhuman lustful devils!

And, oh, my splendid, brave Dufour; simple, unswerving, inflexible devotee of Duty--who loved me.... Oh, my great-hearted faithful Djikki, who had done for me what few white men could or would have done; Djikki, who loved me....

Oh, my beloved Achmet, strong, gentle soul, soldier, nurse, servant and friend ... who loved me....

Yes--*of course* I would have taken the last camel, and with only one rider, too, to give it every chance of reaching the Great Oasis by forced marches.

And, *of course,* I would leave those three to die alone, to-morrow, if they survived to-day....

Hard? ...

Indeed, and indeed, ours is a hard service, a Service for hard men, but a noble Service. And--Duty is indeed a jealous God.

§ 2

And, one weary day, as we topped a long hill, we saw a sight that made me rub my eyes and say, "This is fever and madness!"

For, a few hundred yards from us, rode a Camel Corps--a drilled and disciplined unit that, even as we crossed their skyline, deployed from column to line, at a signal from their leader, as though they had been Spahis, *barraked* their camels, in perfect line and with perfect intervals, and sank from sight behind them, with levelled rifles.

Surely none but European officers or drill-sergeants had wrought that wonder?

I raised my hands above my head and rode toward their leader, as it was equally absurd to think of flight or of fight....

Caught! ... Trapped! ...

The commander was a misshapen dwarf with huge hunched shoulders and big head.

"*Aselamu, Aleikum,*" I called pleasantly and coolly. "Greeting to you."

"*Salaam aleikum wa Rahmat Allah,*" growled the Bedouin gutturally, and staring fiercely from me to the *bourkah*-covered women. "Greeting to you, and the peace of Allah."

"*Keif halak?*" I went on. "How do you do?" and wondered if this were the end.... Would Mary shoot herself in time? ... Did my mission end here? ...

No--discipline like this did not go hand-in-hand with foul savagery. There was a hope....

"*Taiyib,*" replied the dwarf. "Well"--and proceeded to ask if we were alone.

"Quite," I assured him, swiftly rejecting the idea of saying there was an army of my friends close behind, and asked in turn, with flowery compliments upon the drill and discipline of his squadron, who he was.

"Commander of a hundred in the army of my Lord *the Emir el Hamel el Kebir,* Leader of the Faithful, and Shadow of the Prophet of God," was the sonorous reply; and with a falsely cheerful ejaculation of surprise and joy, I announced that I was the emissary of a Great Power to the Court of the Emir....

We rode on, prisoner-guests of this fierce, rough, but fairly courteous Arab, in a hollow-square of riflemen whose equipment, bearing and discipline I could not but admire....

And what if this Emir had an army of such--and chose to preach a *jehad,* a Holy War for the establishment of a Pan-Islamic Empire and the overthrow of the power of the Infidel in Africa?

CHAPTER XII. THE EMIR AND THE VIZIER

"And all around, God's mantle of illimitable space ..."
A. FARQUHAR.

In a few hours we reached the Great Oasis, an astounding forest of palm-trees, roughly square in shape, with a ten-mile side.

My first glimpse of the Bedouin inhabitants of this area showed me that here was a people as different in spirit from those of Zaguig as it was possible to be.

There was nothing here of the furtively evil, lowering suspicious fanaticism that makes "holy" places so utterly damnable.

Practically no notice was taken of our passage through the tent-villages and the more permanent little *qsars* of sand-brick and baked mud. The clean orderliness, prevalent everywhere, made me rub my eyes and stare again.

At the "capital" we were, after a long and anxious waiting, handed over to a person of some importance, a *hadji* by his green turban, and, after a brief explanation of us by our captor--addressed as Marbruk ben Hassan by the *hadji*--we were conducted to the Guest-tents.

To my enormous relief, the girls were to be beneath the same roof as myself, and to occupy the *anderun* or *hareem* part of a great tent, which was divided from the rest by a heavy partition of felt. Presumably it was supposed that they were my wives.

This Guest-tent stood apart from the big village and near to a group of the largest and finest tents I ever saw in use by Arabs. They were not of the low black Bedouin type, spreading and squat, but rather of the pavilion type, such as the great Kaids of Morocco, or the Sultan himself, uses.

Not very far away was a neat row of the usual kind of low goatskin tent, which was evidently the "lines" of the soldiers of the bodyguard.

Flags, flying from spears stuck in the ground, showed that the pavilions were those of the Emir--and a Soudanese soldier who came on sentry-go near the Guest-tent, that we were his prisoners.

The *hadji* (a man whom I was to know later as the Hadji Abdul Salam, a *marabout* or *mullah* and a *hakim* or doctor), returned from announcing our arrival to the Emir.

"Our Lord the Emir el Hamel el Kebir offers you the three days' hospitality, due by Koranic Law--and by the generosity of his heart--to all travellers. He will see you when you have rested. All that he has is yours," said he.

"Including the edge of his sword," I said to myself.

But this was really excellent. I thought of poor Rohlfs and contrasted my reception at the Great Oasis with his at Kufara, near where he was foully betrayed and evilly treated.

Not long afterwards, two black slave-women bore pots of steaming water to the *anderun,* and a boy brought me my share, less picturesquely, in kerosene-oil tins.

"Can I come in, Major?" called Miss Vanbrugh. "I've knocked at the felt door... . More felt than heard... . I want to dress your arm."

I told her that I was feeling happier about her than I had done since we started, for I was beginning to hope and to believe that we were in the hands of an enlightened and merciful despot, instead of those of the truculent and destructive savage I had expected to find.

"How do you like this hotel?" I inquired as she pinned the bandage.

"Nothing like it in N'York," she replied. "Maudie's sitting on cushions and feeling she's half a Sheikhess already... ."

"I'm going to put on my uniform," I announced. "Will you and she help a one-armed cripple?"

They did. And when the Hadji Abdul Salam, and a dear old gentleman named Dawad Fetata, came with one or two more *ekhwan* to conduct me to the presence of the Emir, I was a French Field-Officer again, bathed, shaven, and not looking wholly unworthy of the part I had to play.

§ 2

Seated on dyed camel-hair rugs piled on a carpet, were the Emir el Hamel el Kebir and his Vizier, the Sheikh el Habibka, stately men in fine raiment.

I saw at a glance that the Emir, whatever he might claim to be, was no member of the family of Es Sayed Yussuf Haroun es Sayed es Mahdi es Senussi, and that if he pretended to be the expected "Messiah," Sidi Sayed el Mahdi el Senussi, he was an impostor.

For he was most unmistakably of Touareg stock, and from nowhere else could he have got the grey eyes of Vandal origin, which are fairly common among the Touareg, many of whom are blue-eyed and ruddy-haired.

I liked his face immediately. This black-bearded, black-browed, hawk-faced Arab was a man of character, force and power. But I wished I could see the mouth hidden beneath the mass of moustache and beard. Dignified, calm, courteous, strong, this was no ruffianly and swashbuckling fanatic.

My hopes rose high.

The Vizier, whose favour might be most important, I took to be of Touareg or Berber-Bedouin stock, he too being somewhat fair for a desert-Arab. He was obviously a distaff blood-relation of the Emir.

These two men removed the mouth-pieces of their long-stemmed *narghilehs* from their lips and stared *and* stared *and* stared at me, in petrified astonishment--to which they were too stoical or too well-bred to give other expression.

I suppose the last person they expected to see was a French officer in uniform, and they sat in stupefied silence.

Had not the idea been too absurd, I could almost have thought that I saw a look of fear in their eyes. Perhaps they thought for a moment that I was the herald of a French army that was even then getting into position round the oasis!

Fear is the father of cruelty, so I hoped that my fleeting impression was a false one. I would have disabused their minds by plunging straight *in medias res,* and announcing my business forthwith, but that this is not the way to handle Arabs.

Only by devious paths can the goal be reached, and much meaningless *faddhling* (gossip) must precede the real matter on which the mind is fixed.

I greeted the Emir with the correct honorifics and in the Arabic of the educated.

He replied in an accent with which I was not familiar, that of the classical Arabic of the *Hejaz,* I supposed, called "the Tongue of the Angels" by the Arabs.

Having exchanged compliments and inquired after each other's health, with repeated "*Kief halaks?*" and "*Taiyibs,*" I told the Emir of the attack upon us by the Touareg at the Salt Lake, and of my fears as to the fate of my followers.

"The Sons of Shaitan and the Forgotten of God! May they burn in Eblis eternally! Do they dare come within seven days of *me*!" growled the Emir, and clapped his hands. A black youth came running.

"Send me Marbruk ben Hassan, the Commander of a Hundred," said the Emir, and when the deformed but powerful cripple came, and humbly saluted his Lord, the latter gave a prompt order.

"A hundred men. Ten days' rations. Ride to the Pass of the Salt Lake. A band of the Forgotten of God were there three days ago. Start within the hour ..." He then whispered with him apart for a moment, and the man was gone.

The Vizier had not ceased to stare unwaveringly at me, but he uttered no word.

The Emir and I maintained a desultory and pointless conversation which concluded with an invitation to feast with him that night.

"I hear that you are accompanied by two Nazrani ladies. I am informed that wives of *Roumis* eat with their Lords and in the presence of other men. I shall be honoured if the Sitts--your wives doubtless?--will grace my poor tent... ."

One thing I liked about the Emir was the gentlemanly way in which he had forborne to question me on the subject of the astounding presence of two white women. I accordingly told him the plain truth at once, thinking it wisest and safest.

"You will receive no such treatment here as they of Zaguig meted unto you," said the Emir, when I had finished my story. "They who come in peace may remain in peace. They who come in war remain in peace also--the peace of Death.

" His voice was steely if not menacing. "Do you come in peace or in war, *Roumi?*" he then asked, and as I replied,

"On my head and my life, I come in peace, bearing a great and peaceful message," I fancied that both he and the Vizier looked relieved--and I again wondered if they imagined the presence or approach of a French army.

§ 3

Whatever I may forget, I shall remember that night's *diffa* of *cous-cous;* a lamb stuffed with almonds and raisins, and roasted whole; *bamia,* a favourite vegetable of the Arabs; stewed chicken; a *pillau* of rice, nuts, raisins and chopped meat; *kaibabs* of kid; camel-milk curds; a paste-like macaroni cooked in butter, and heavy shortbread fried in oil and eaten with sugar. Between the courses, we drank bowls of lemon-juice to aid our appetites, and they needed aid as the hours wore on.

When we were full to bursting, distended, comatose, came the ceremonial drinking of mint tea. After that, coffee. Finally we were offered very large cakes of very hard plain sugar.

Only five were present, the Emir, the Vizier, Mary, Maudie, and myself. We sat cross-legged on a carpet round a red cotton cloth upon which was a vast brass tray, laden with blue bowls filled to overflowing, and we ate with our fingers.

As I entered with Miss Vanbrugh and Maudie, and they dropped their *barracans,* thus exposing the two Paris frocks which the latter had put in the portmanteau at Zaguig, the effect upon the two Arabs was electrical. They were as men dreaming dreams and seeing visions.

I thought the Emir was going to collapse as he looked at Mary; and I watched the Vizier devouring her with hungry eyes. I grew a little nervous.

"The Lady Sitt Miriyam Hankinson el Vanbrugh," said I, to make an imposing and sonorous mouthful of title, "and the Sitt Moad el Atkinson."

I suppose they were the first white women the Arabs had seen, and they were struck dumb and senseless by their beauty.

Nor was the effect of their hosts much less upon the girls. Miss Vanbrugh stared, fascinated, at the gorgeous figure of the Emir, while poor Maudie did not know whether she was on her head or her heels.

"*Sheikhs!*" she murmured. "*Real* Sheikhs! Oh, sir, *isn't* the big one a lovely man! ..." The Emir, dragging his eyes from Mary, smiled graciously at the other fair woman, and murmured:

"*Bismillah! Sitt Moad. Oua Aleikoume Esselema, 'lhamdoula!*" and to me in his classic Arabic, "Sweet as the dates of Buseima is her presence," which I duly, translated.

And then Mary found her voice.

"Well! Well! Major," she observed. "Aren't they sure-enough genuine Parlour Sheikhs of song and story!" and before I could stop her, she offered her hand to the Emir, her eyes dancing with delight.

Probably neither the Emir nor the Vizier had ever "shaken hands" before, but Mary's smile, gesture and "*Very* pleased to meet you, Sheikh," were self-explanatory, and both the Arabs made a good showing at this new ceremonial of the strange *Roumis* and their somewhat brazen, unveiled females.

Indeed the Vizier seemed to know more about holding Mary's hand than releasing it, and again I grew nervous.

When the Emir said to me, "Let the other Lady, the Sitt Moadi, lay her hand upon my hands also," and I translated, I thought Maudie would have swooned with pleasure and confusion. Not only did the Emir "shake hands"--he stroked hands, and I grew less and less happy.

An amorous Arab is something very amorous indeed. With these desert despots, to desire is to take, and if I were an obstacle it would be very easy to remove me. And what of the girls *then?* ... As the meal progressed and the sense of strangeness and shyness wore off, I was glad that the Sheikh and his Vizier could not possibly know a word of English, for Miss Vanbrugh's criticisms were pungent and Maudie's admiration fulsome.

I was kept busy translating the Emir's remarks to the girls, and mistranslating the girls' remarks concerning the appearance, manners, and probable customs of their hosts.

At times I was in a cold perspiration of fear, as I thought of how utterly these two women were in the power of these men, and again at times, watching their faces, I saw no evil in them. Hard they were, perhaps relentless and ruthless, but not cruel, sensual nor debauched.

"Major," Miss Vanbrugh remarked, "d'you think these Parlour Sheikhs would like to hear a little song? ... Tell them it's grace after meat," and before I could offer my views on the propriety of thus entertaining our hosts, or translating her remark, I once more heard the familiar air, but this time to the words:

"The Sons of the Prophet are hardy and bold,
  And quite unaccustomed to fear;
But of all--the most reckless of life and of limb,
  Was Abdul the Bul-bul Emir! ...
When they wanted a man to encourage the van.
  Or to shout 'Attaboy!' in the rear,
    Or to storm a redoubt,
    They always sent out
For Abdul the Bul-bul Emir!
For Abdul the Bul-bul Emir!"

The Arabs stared, almost open-mouthed, and I explained that after-dinner singing was a custom with the *Roumis* and that the song, out of compliment to our hosts, described the greatness, wisdom, virtue, and courage of another famous Emir.

When we were at last permitted to cease from eating, and white-clad servants removed the remains of the *diffa*, the Emir bade me request Mary Vanbrugh to talk of her country and her home, that I might translate her words to him.

He then asked many questions through me.

Thereafter he directed that Maudie should talk.

But having almost realized the ambition of her life, Maudie was shy and could only stammer incoherently while gazing bright-eyed, flushed, with parted lips and quickened breathing, at the huge, handsome, and gorgeously arrayed Emir.

The Vizier, the Sheikh el Habibka, scarcely uttered a word the whole evening, but he hardly took his eyes from Miss Vanbrugh's face.

In the bad moments to which I have alluded, I felt that if the worst came to the worst, Maudie would be imprisoned in the Emir's *hareem,* and Mary in that of this Sheikh el Habibka--unless the Emir took them both... .

The sooner I could dangle before their eyes the million francs and the enormous advantages of an *entente* and an alliance with France, the better it would be; and the less they saw of the girls the better it would be also... .

"Well, Major, it's time you went to bed," said Mary. "Remember you're a sick man!"

"We can't move till the Emir gives the hint," I replied.

"Well, I wish he'd do it, the great old coot. Tell him what I'm saying, Major--that he fancies he's some punkins, but he's not the perfect little gentleman he thinks he is, or he'd see I'm tired to death," and she yawned heavily... .

Luckily the Emir shortly afterwards suggested that we might be weary, and though I told him that no one could be weary in his presence, he hinted that *he* was so in mine.

The leave-taking made it clear that Maudie's hand delighted the Emir, while that of Mary was precious in the sight of the Sheikh el Habibka. There was a look of determination in that man's eye... .

As we entered the Guest-tent I said to Miss Vanbrugh, "Scream if there's any trouble in the night."

"Scream? I shall *shoot*. Let the 'trouble' do the screaming. Good night, Major," was this independent and courageous young lady's reply.

§ 4

The next day I had an interview with the Emir, in the presence, as always, of the Vizier, and, after infinite meanderings around all subjects but the real one, we came to it at last.

I made it clear that what I offered him was the friendship of a most powerful protector, great wealth, and all the advantages that would ensue if a caravan-road were made and guarded from the Great Oasis to Zaguig, and trade-relations opened up between his people and the North.

I glanced at the possibility of our supplying him with arms, including machine-guns and, possibly, light artillery--later on.

I grew eloquent in showing him how the friendship of France could raise him to a safe independence, and how, in the rôle of protégé of France, he could benefit his people and give them the blessings of civilization.

The Emir repeated my phrase, but with a peculiar intonation.

"The blessings of civilization!" he mused. "Drink... . Disease... . Unrest... . Machine-guns... . Has the civilization of the *Roumis* always proved such a blessing to the darker races who have come in contact with it?"

The two stroked their beards, and eyed me long and thoughtfully. I assured the Emir that it would be in his power to pick and choose. Isolated as his people were, there need be no "contact." All France wanted was his friendship.

Provided he were loyal and kept the terms of the treaty exactly, he could use the subsidy as he pleased, and could discriminate between the curses and the real blessings of western civilization.

Surely he could see to it that only good ensued? Nothing was farther from the thoughts of the French Government than interference--much less conquest, or even "peaceful penetration." All we asked was that the Confederation which he ruled should be a source of strength and not of weakness to us--that the Great Oasis should be an outpost of France in the hands of the Emir el Hamel el Kebir... . And I hinted at his own danger from others who would not come to him thus, with offers of gold and protection, but with armies... .

"We will talk of these matters again," said the Emir at length. "*Khallas!* It is finished... ."

That evening, a riding-party was arranged, and, mounted on beautiful horses, the Sheikh el Habibka and Miss Vanbrugh rode together; the Emir, on a white camel, rode with Maudie--who, very wisely, would not get on a horse; and I rode with a party of fine courteous Arabs who were minor sheikhs, officers of the soldiery, councillors, friends and hangers-on of the Emir and the Vizier.

We rode through the oasis out into the desert.

I did not enjoy my ride, for, before very long, I lost sight of the two girls, and could only hope for the best while fearing the worst.... Women are so attracted by externals and so easily deceived by a courteous and gallant manner.

One comfort was that neither girl could speak a word of Arabic, so there was nothing to fear from plausible tongues.

Any love-making would have to be done in dumb-show, and I was beginning to feel that there was no likelihood of *force majeure*--both men giving me the impression of innate gentlemanliness and decency.

Still--Arabs are Arabs and this was the Sahara--and, as I noted that the Emir returned with Miss Vanbrugh and the Vizier with Maud, I wanted nothing so much as to get safely away with my women-folk and a signed treaty of alliance.

But this was just what I could not do.

Time after time, I sought audience with the Emir, only to find that he was engaged or sleeping or busy or absent from the Oasis.

Time after time, when his guest at meat, riding, or *faddhling* with him on the rug-strewn carpet before the pavilions, I tried to get him to discuss the object of my visit--but in vain.

Always it was, "We will talk of it to-morrow, *Inshallah*."

His eternal "*Bokra! Bokra!*" was as bad as the *mañana* of the Spaniards. And "to-morrow" never came... .

The return of Marbruk ben Hassan and his camel-squadron brought me news that depressed me to the depths and darkened my life for days. I was given understanding of the expression "a broken heart." ...

Evidently my heroes had fought to their last cartridge and had then been overwhelmed. Beneath a great cairn of stones, Marbruk and his men had buried the tortured, defiled, mangled remains of Dufour, Achmet and Djikki.

It was plain to me that Suleiman had deserted, for the parts of only three corpses were found, and the track of a single camel fleeing south-eastward from the spot.

That he had not fought to the last, and then escaped or been captured alive by the Touareg, was shown by the fact that, where he had lain, there were but few empty cartridge-cases, compared with the number lying where my men had died; and by the fact of the track of the fleeing camel.

I retired to my tent, saying I wished to see no one for a day, and that I wanted no food.

It was a black and dreadful day for me, the man for whom those humble heroes had fought and died; and, for hours, I was hard put to it to contain myself.

I did see some one however--for Miss Vanbrugh entered silently, dressed my rapidly healing wound, and then stroked my hair and brow and cheek so kindly, so gently, and with such deep understanding sympathy that I broke down.

I could almost have taken her in my arms, but that I would not trade on my misery and her sympathy--and without a word spoken between us she went back to the *anderun* ... the blessed, beautiful, glorious woman.

Did she understand at last? ... Duty... . My duty to my General, my Service, and my Country.

That evening she was visited by the future Sheikh of the tribe that had first accepted the Emir, a charming and delightful little boy, dressed exactly like a grown man.

With him came his sister, a most lovely girl, the Sitt Leila Nakhla.

Her, the two girls found haughty, distant, disapproving, and I gathered that the visit was not a success--apart from the question of the language difficulty.

Bedouin women do not go veiled in their own villages and camps, and I saw this Arab "princess" at a feast given by her guardian, the white-bearded, delightful old gentleman, Sidi Dawad Fetata.

It was soon very clear to me that the Sitt Leila Nakhla worshipped the Emir; that the grandson of old Sidi Dawad Fetata worshipped the Sitt Leila Nakhla; and that the latter detested our Maudie, from whose face the Emir's eye roved but seldom.

The little London sparrow was the hated rival of a princess, for the hand of a powerful ruler! Oh, Songs of Araby and Tales of fair Kashmir! What a world it is!

But what troubled me more than hate was love--the love that I could see dawning in the eyes of the Sheikh el Habibka as he sat beside Miss Vanbrugh and plied her with tit-bits from the bowls.

I watched him like a lynx, and he me. How he *hated* me! ...

Time after time I saw him open his lips to speak, sigh heavily, and say nothing. But if he said nothing he did a good deal--including frequent repetitions of the *Roumi* "shake-hands" custom, which he misinterpreted as a hold-hands habit.

He had learnt the words, and would say, "*Shakand, Mees*," from time to time, in what he thought was English.

And Mary? She was infinitely amused. Amused beyond all cause that I could see; and I was really angry when she glanced from me to the Sheikh el Habibka--he holding her hand warmly clasped in both of his--and quietly hummed, in a conversational sort of voice:

"Said the Bul-bul, 'Young man, is your life then so dull
  That you're anxious to end your career?
For Infidel, know--that you've trod on the toe
  Of Abdul, the Bul-bul Emir!'
The Bul-bul then drew out his trusty chibouque,
  And shouting out 'Allah Akbar!'
Being also intent on slaughter, he went
  For Ivan Petruski Skivah!" ...

This interested the Sitt Leila Nakhla not at all. She watched Maudie, while young Yussuf Latif Fetata watched Leila. To me this girl was most charming, but became a little troublesome in her demands that I should translate every remark that Maudie made. I believe the Sitt's position in the Tribe was unique, owing to her relationship to the future Sheikh, and the kind indulgence of the Emir, who treated her as a child.

The chief result of this feast was to increase my anxiety and to add to my determination to bring my business to an issue and depart.

CHAPTER XIII. "CHOOSE"

But now, alas! the attitude of the Emir, and of his all-important and powerful Vizier toward me began to change. They grew less friendly and my position less that of guest than prisoner-guest, if not prisoner.

The most foolish proverb of the most foolish nation in the world is, "When you get near women you get near trouble," but in this instance it seemed to apply.

Mary and Maudie were the trouble; for the Emir was undoubtedly falling in love with Maudie, and the Vizier with Mary.

I wondered what would have happened if they had both fallen in love with the same girl. I suppose one of them would have died suddenly, in spite of the fact that they appeared to be more like brothers than master and servant.

And there was no hope in me for Maudie. Maudie blossomed and Maudie bloomed. If ever I saw a wildly-quietly, composedly-distractedly, madly-sanely happy woman, it was our Maudie.

She grew almost lovely. How many of us have an incredibly impossible beautiful dream--and find it come impossibly true? Maudie had dreamed of attar-scented, silk-clad, compelling but courtly Sheikhs, ever since she had read some idiotic trash; and now an attar-scented, silk-clad, compelling but courtly Sheikh *was* (in Maudie's words) "after" Maudie!

And Miss Vanbrugh? She, too, seemed happy as the day was long, albeit capricious; and though she did not apparently encourage the Sheikh el Habibka, nor "flirt" exactly, she undoubtedly enjoyed his society, as well as that of the Emir, and rode alone with either of them, without fear. They must have been silent rides--with a strange dumb alphabet! Nor would she listen to my words of warning.

"Don't you worry, Major de Beaujolais," she would say, "I tell you they are *all right*. Yes, *both* of them. I am just as safe with them as I am with you... . And I'm *awfully* safe with you, Major, am I not?"

Women always know better than men--until they find they know nothing about the matter at all.

The next thing that I did not like, was the giving of feasts to which the girls alone were invited; and then feasts at which Mary alone, or Maudie alone, was the guest.

However, such invitations were commands, of course; the feasts were held in the Emir's pavilion, which was but a few yards from our tent; I took care that the girls had their pistols, and I always sat ready for instant action if I should hear a scream when either of them was there alone.

Nor was there any great privacy observed, for servants were in and out with dishes, and unless there was a strong *gibli* blowing, the pavilion entrance was open.

But more and more I became a prisoner, and now when I took my daily ride it was with Marbruk ben Hassan and an escort--for my "protection."

One night, as I lay awake, the horrible thought occurred to me of using Miss Vanbrugh and Maudie to further my ends--and I was almost sick at the bare idea. Whence come these devilish thoughts into clean minds?

No. At that I drew the line. My life for France, but not a girl's honour.... I thrust the vile thought from me.

Soon afterwards I fell asleep and had a curious dream....

I was in a vast hall, greater than any built by mortal hands. At the end to which I faced were vast black velvet curtains. As I stood gazing at these, expectant, they parted and rolled away, revealing a huge pair of golden scales, in each great cup of which was seated a most beautiful woman.

One, a noble and commanding figure, wore the Cap of Liberty and I knew her to be the Genius and Goddess and Embodiment of France.... The other, a beautiful and beseeching figure, I saw to be Mary Vanbrugh.

Each of these lovely creatures gave me a smile of ineffable sweetness and extended a welcoming hand.... A great voice cried "*Choose,*" and, as I strode forward, the great curtains fell--and the dream became a nightmare in which a colossal brazen god stretched a vast hand from a brazen sky to destroy me where I stood in the midst of an illimitable arid desert....

§ 2

Then to me, one night, came the Emir and the Vizier, clearly on business bent. There was no *faddhling*. As soon as I had offered them seats upon the rugs and produced my last Turkish cigarettes, the Emir got to business.

"Touching the treaty with your Excellency's great country," he began, and my heart leapt with hope. "I will sign it--on terms.... On terms further than those named hitherto."

He stopped and appeared to be enjoying the Turkish cigarette intensely.

"And they are, Commander of the Faithful and Shadow of the Prophet?" I inquired.

"That you take the treaty, signed and sealed by me, and witnessed by my Vizier and twelve ekhwan--*and leave the two Sitts whom you brought here.*"

So it had come! I was faced with the decision of a lifetime!

"*That is impossible,* Emir el Hamel el Kebir," I seemed to hear myself reply, after a minute of acute agony, which bathed me in perspiration from head to foot.

The Emir raised his big black eyebrows and gave me a supercilious, penetrating hawk-stare of surprise and anger.

"And why?" he inquired quietly.

"Because they put themselves under my protection," I replied, "and I have put myself and them under yours...."

"And I am merely suggesting that they remain there," interrupted the Emir.

"For how long?" I sneered.

"That is for *them* to say," was the reply.

"Then let them say it," I answered. "Emir, I have treated you as a Bedouin Chief, a true Arab of the Desert, a man of chivalry, honour, hospitality, and greatness. Would you, in return, speak to me of trafficking in women? ..."

To Hell with their treaty and their tribes... .--and then the face of my uncle, the words of his letters, and memories of my life-work rose before my eyes.... Neither of these girls was a Frenchwoman.... I had not asked them to come here.... I had warned them *against* coming.... . I had told them plainly that I was going on a mission of national importance.... . And de Lannec.... . "*Exit de Lannec*"! ...

I strode up and down the tent, the two Arabs, calm, imperturbable, stroking their beards and watching me.... . I reasoned with myself, as a Frenchman should, *logically.*

Glorious logic--the foe of sloppiness, emotionalism, sentimentality.

I can but hope, looking back upon this crucial moment of my life, that such matters as my utter ruin and disgrace; my loss of all that made life good; my fall from a place of honour, dignity, and opportunity, to the very gutters of life; my renunciation of ambition, reward and success--weighed with me not at all, and were but as dust in the balance.... .

I can but hope that, coolly and without bias, I answered the question as to whether the interests of France, the lives of thousands of men, the loss of incalculable treasure should, or should not, out-weigh the interests of two foreign women.

Should thousands of French soldiers suffer wounds and death--or should these two girls enter the *hareems* of Arab Sheikhs? ...

Should I fulfil the trust reposed in me or betray it?

"*I want tools that will not turn in my hand... . Tools on which I can absolutely rely,*" my uncle--my General, the representative of my Country--had said to me; and I had willingly offered myself as a tool that would *not* turn in his hand ... that would *not* fail him... .

And if "it is expedient that one man shall die for the people," was it not expedient that two foreign women should be sacrificed to prevent a war, to save an Empire? ... Two lives instead of two thousand, twenty thousand, two hundred thousand.... .

If, as my uncle said, there would always be danger in Morocco to the French African Empire, and if, whenever that danger arose, this great Tribal Confederation became a source of even greater danger ... ?

"And for what was I *here?* For what had I been fashioned and made, taught and trained, hammered on the hard anvil of experience? ... Why was I in *my Service--but to do the very thing that it now lay to my hand to do?*"

As an honest and honourable man, I must put the orders of my General, the honour and tradition of my Service, and, above all, the welfare of my Country, before everything-- and *everybody.*

Logic showed me the truth--and, suddenly, I stopped in my stride, turned and shook my fist in the Emir's very face and shouted: "*Damn your black face and blacker soul, you filthy hound! Get out of my tent before I throw you out, you bestial swine! ...* WHITE WOMEN! *You black dogs and sons of dogs ... !*" and, shaking with rage, I pointed to the doorway of my tent.

They rose and went--and, with them, went all my hopes of success. What had I done? What *had* I done? ... But Mary--sweet, lovely, brave, fascinating Mary ... *and that black-bearded dog!*

Let France sink beneath the sea first... .

But what *had* I done? ... What had I *done?* ... What is 'Right' and what is 'Wrong'? What voice had I obeyed?

Anyhow, I was unfit, utterly unfit, for my great Service--and I would break my sword and burn my uniform, go back to my uncle, confess what I had done and enlist in the Foreign Legion... .

Oh, *splendid de Lannec!* ... *He was right, of course*... .

But this was ruin and the end of Henri de Beaujolais.

Then a voice through the felt wall that cut off my part of the tent from the *anderun* said,

"Your language certainly sounded bad, Major! I am glad I don't understand Arabic!"

I was not very sure that *I* was glad she did not.

And as little as she understood Arabic did I understand whether I had done right or wrong.

But one thing I understood. I was a Failure... . I had failed my General, my Service, and my Country--but yet I somehow felt I had not failed my higher Self... .

§ 3

It was the next morning that Miss Vanbrugh greeted me with the words:

"Major, you haven't congratulated me yet. I had an honest-to-God offer of marriage from a leading citizen of this burg yesterday... . I'm blushing still... . Inwardly... ."

I was horrified... . What next?

"From whom?" I asked.

"The Sheikh el Habibka el Wazir."

"Good God!" I groaned. "Miss Vanbrugh, we shall have to walk very very delicately... ."

"So'll the Sheikh-lad," observed Mary grimly.

"But how did he make the proposal?" I inquired, knowing that no one in the place could translate and interpret except myself.

"By signs and wonders," answered the girl. "*Some* wonders! He certainly made himself clear ... !"

"Was he? ... Did he? ..." I stammered, hardly knowing how to ask if the ruffian had seized her in his hot, amorous embrace and made fierce love to her... . My blood boiled, though my heart sank, and I knew that depth of trembling apprehension that is the true Fear--the fear for another whom we--whom we--esteem.

"Now don't you go prying heavy-hoofed into a young thing's first love affair, Major--because I shan't stand for it," replied Miss Vanbrugh.

"Had you your pistol with you?" I asked.

"I had, Major," was the reply. "I don't get caught that way twice."

And I reflected that if the Sheikh el Habibka el Wazir was still alive, he had not been violent.

That day I was not allowed to ride out for exercise, and a big Soudanese sentry was posted closer to my tent-door.

Hitherto I had felt myself under strict surveillance; now I was under actual arrest.

The girls were invited, or ordered, to go riding as usual, and my frame of mind can be imagined.

Nothing could save them... . Nothing could now bring about the success of my mission--unless it were the fierce greed of these Arabs for gold... . I was a wretchedly impotent puppet in their hands... .

Now that I had mortally insulted and antagonized these fierce despots, what could I do to protect the woman ... the women ... whom I had brought here, and whose sole hope and trust was in me? ...

I realized that a mighty change had been slowly taking place in my mind, and that it had been completed in the moment that the Emir had offered to sell me the treaty for the bodies of these girls... . I knew now that--instead of the fate of Mary Vanbrugh being an extra anxiety at the back of a mind filled with care concerning the treaty--the fate of the treaty was an extra anxiety at the back of a mind filled with care concerning the fate of Mary Vanbrugh!

Why should this be?

I had begun by disliking her... . At times I had hated her ... and certainly there were times when she appeared to loathe me utterly... . Why should life, success, duty, France herself, all weigh as nothing in the balance against her safety? ...

De Lannec? Fool, trifler, infirm of purpose, devoid of sense of proportion, broken reed and betrayer of his Service and his Motherland--*or unselfish hero and gallant gentleman?*

And what mattered the answer to that question, if I was an impotent prisoner, absolutely helpless in the power of this outraged Emir--and she was riding with him, alone... .

CHAPTER XIV. A SECOND STRING

That night I was honoured by a visit from the Hadji Abdul Salam, the chief *marabout* and *hakim* of this particular tribe, and a man whose immense influence and power seemed disproportionate to his virtues and merits. (One of the things the Occidental mind can never grasp, is the way in which the Oriental mind can divorce Faith from Works, the office from its holder, and yield unstinted veneration to the holy *priest,* knowing him to be, at the same time, a worthless and scoundrelly *man.*) ...

The good Hadji crept silently into my tent, in the dead of night, and very nearly got a bullet through his scheming brain.

Seeing that he was alone and apparently unarmed, I put my pistol under my pillow again, and asked him what he wanted.

The Reverend Father-in-Islam wanted to talk--in whispers--if I would take a most solemn oath to reveal nothing that he said. I was more than ready, and we talked of Cabbages and Kings, and also of Sealing-Wax and Whether Pigs have Wings... . And, after a while, we talked of Murder--or rather the Holy One did so... . He either trusted my keeping faith with him or knew he could repudiate anything I might say against him later.

I had a touch of fever again, and I was still in the state of mental turmoil natural to one who has just seen the edifice of a life's labour go crashing to the earth, and yet sits rejoicing among the ruins--thanking God for failure; his mind moaning a funeral dirge over the grave of all his hopes and strivings--his heart chanting a pæan of praise and thanksgiving over the saving of his Self... .

"Come, let us sit upon the ground
And tell sad stories of the death of Kings,
How some have been deposed, some sleeping killed,"

I quoted, from Etonian memories of Shakespeare's *Richard the Second*.

The Reverend Father looked surprised, and said he had a proposal to make.

This was that he should contrive to effect my escape, and that I should return with an army, defeat the Emir, and make the Hadji Abdul Salam ruler in his place.

An alternative idea was suggested by the probable assassination of the Emir by one Suleiman the Strong, "of whom I knew," and who was even now somewhere in the Great Oasis, *and had visited the tents of the Holy Hadji!*

Would I, on the death of the Emir, help the Hadji to seize the Seat of Power? He could easily poison Suleiman the Strong when he had fulfilled his vengeance--and his usefulness--or denounce him to the Tribe as the murderer of the Emir, and have him impaled alive... .

The pious man swore he would be a true and faithful friend to France.

"As you are to your master, the Emir?" I asked.

The Hadji replied that the Emir was a usurper, and that no one owed fealty to a usurper.

Moreover this was positively my only chance, as I was to be put to death shortly... . The Emir might then send a deputation to the Governor-General of French Africa, offering to make an alliance on receipt of a subsidy of a million francs and other advantages, and swearing that no emissary of the Governor-General's had ever reached him.

Or he might just let the matter rest--merely keeping the women, killing me, and washing his hands of French affairs, or, rather, declining to dirty his hands with them... . Or, of course, Suleiman might get him--and then the Wazir could be eliminated, and the good Hadji, with French support, could become the Emir and the Friend of France... .

"Supposing you could enable me to escape," I said when the good Hadji had finished. "I should not do so without the women. Could you effect their escape with me?"

He could not and would not. Here the Holy One spat and quoted the unkind words of the great Arab poet, Imr el Kais:

"One said to me, '*Marry!*'
I replied, 'I am *happy*--
Why take to my breast
A sackful of serpents?
May Allah curse all woman-kind!'"

Two faithful slave-women always slept across the entrance to the *anderun,* where the girls were. Even if the slaves could be killed silently, it would be impossible to get so big a party away from the place--many camels, much food, *girbas* of water... . No, he could only manage it for me alone.

He could visit me at night and I could leave the tent in his *burnous* and green turban... . He could easily bribe or terrify a certain Arab soldier, now on sentry-go outside, and who was bound to be on duty at my tent again sooner or later. I could simply ride for dear life, with two good camels, and take my chance.

But the women--*no*. Besides, if it ever came out that he had helped *me* to escape, it would not be so bad.... But as for getting the women away, he simply would not consider it....

No--if I were so extremely anxious about the fate of my two women ("and, Merciful Allah! what are women, that serious men should bother about them?"), the best thing I could do was to consider his firm and generous offer--the heads of the Emir and his Vizier on a charger, and the faithful friendship to France of their successor in power, the Hadji Abdul Salam.... The Emir had announced his intention of making the boy-Sheikh not only Sheikh of his Tribe, but eventually Emir of the Confederation also. The Hadji would be the young prince's Spiritual Guide, Tutor, Guardian and Regent--until the time came to cut the lad's throat....

"So Suleiman the Strong is here--and is going to assassinate the Emir, is he?" I said, after we had sat eyeing each other, warily and in silence, for some minutes.

(*I must warn the Emir as soon as possible.*)

"Yes," replied the Hadji. "And where will you be *then,* if I am your enemy?"

"Where I am now, I expect," I replied, yawning with a nonchalance wholly affected.

"*And* your women?" asked the good man.

I ground my teeth, and my fingers itched to seize this scoundrel's throat.

"Take my advice and *go*," he continued. "Go in the certainty that you will have done what you came for--made an indissoluble and everlasting treaty of alliance between the *Franzawi* and the Great Confederation, through their real ruler, the Hadji Abdul Salam, Regent for the young Emir after the assassination of the Emir el Hamel el Kebir, impostor and usurper.... And if he is not assassinated, no matter--come with an army--and a million francs, of course--kill him, and make the boy nominal Emir.... I swear by the Sacred names of God that France shall be as my father and my mother, and I will be France's most obedient child.... *Go,* Sidi, while you can...."

"Get two facts clearly and firmly into your noble mind, Holy One," I replied. "The first is that I do not leave this place without the lady Sitts; and the second is that France has no dealings whatsoever in assassination--nor with assassins!"

Then the reverend gentleman played his trump card.

"You are in even greater danger than you think, Sidi," he murmured, smiling wryly with his mouth and scowling fiercely with his eyes. "And our honourable, gracious and fair-dealing Lord, the Emir el Hamil el Kebir, is but playing with you as the cat with the mouse.... *For you are not the only mouse in his trap*--oh, no! Not by any means.... What are *Roumi* brains against those of the Arabs, the most wise, learned, subtle and ancient of all the races of the earth? ... Why, you poor fool, *there are other messengers from another Power, here, in the Great Oasis*--and our fair-spoken Lord gives them audience daily in their camp...."

I sprang to my feet.... Could this scoundrel be speaking the truth.... A cold fear settled on my heart.... What likelihood was there of my leaving this place alive, if this were true and my own folly and madness had driven the Emir into the arms of these agents of some other Power?

My life was nothing--but what of the fate of Mary Vanbrugh, when my throat was cut? ... I broke out into a cold perspiration, and the fever left me.... My brain grew clearer and began to act more quickly. I smiled derisively and shook an incredulous head.

"And supposing I showed you their camp, Sidi?" sneered the Hadji. "Suppose I gave you the opportunity to *see* a disguised *Roumi* and *to speak to him?*"

"Why--then I should be convinced," I replied, and added--"And that would certainly change my--er--attitude toward you and your proposal.... . When I have seen these men, and spoken with them--you may visit me again, with advantage to your purse... ." I must play this foul-feeding fish on a long line, and match his tricks with tricks of my own. If it was to be *Roumi* brains against Arab brains here also--well, we would see what we should see... .

"What manner of man is the leader of these emissaries of another Power?" I asked. "How many of them are there? ... What is the Emir's attitude ... ? Tell me all you can... . I can buy true information at a high price... ."

"So can these others," grinned the pious Hadji. "The leader has already shaken a bag of good fat Turkish *medjidies* before my eyes, and promised it in return for my help."

"I could shake a bag of something better than that dirty depreciated Turkish rubbish before your eyes, Hadji," I replied, "and pour it into your lap too... . Fine new coins of pure gold! French twenty-franc pieces! Beautiful for women's chains and bangles, and even more beautiful to spend on fine raiment, tents, camels, weapons, food, servants, rugs, horses ..."

The rascal's eyes glittered.

"How many, Sidi?" he asked.

"As many as you earn... . As many as your help is worth... . Now talk... ."

"It is a small caravan, Sidi," began this saintly *marabout,* "but very well equipped. There is plenty of money behind it... . I never saw better camels nor weapons, and their hired camel-men are well-paid and content... . I do not know from whom they really come, but they have the blessing of the Father of the Faithful, God's Vicar upon Earth, who rules at Stamboul, and of the Great Sheikh of the Senussi. They say this openly in *mejliss*--and prove it with documents, passes, *firmans* and letters--but they talk privately, at night, with the Emir and the Wazir... ."

"What do they offer, openly?" I asked.

"The friendship and protection of the King of Kings, the Sultan of the Ottoman Empire, Father of the Faithful, who dwells at Stamboul; and the friendship and alliance of the powerful Sheikh el Senussi... . A great Pan-Islamic Alliance is being formed, in readiness for a certain Day of *Jehad*...."

"And in private?" I asked.

"That I do not know," was the reply. "Only that dog of a Wazir--may swine defile the graves of his ancestors--knoweth the mind of the Emir; and he alone accompanies him to the tents of the *Roumi.*"

"But this I *do* know," he continued, "*they will give me wealth untold if I will poison you and the two Sitts,* whom they declare to be female spies of the French--sent to debauch and beguile the Emir with their charms... ."

"How do they know of our presence here?" I asked quietly, though my blood boiled.

"Oh, I visit them! ... I visit them! ... And we talk... . We talk... ." replied this treacherous reptile. "They say I might, if I preferred, kill you and seize the Sitts for my *hareem* for a while, before I either slay them or cut out their tongues... . Dumb women are the only discreet ones ..." and the Hadji laughed merrily.

I managed to smile coldly, while I burned hotly with fierce rage, and changed the subject.

"Are they Great Men, Lords, Sidis, Nobles, Officers, Born Leaders, these emissaries?" I asked.

"No," replied the Hadji. "They are low men on high horses. They do not walk, speak, look, give, ride, eat nor act as men of noble birth... ."

Through a narrow aperture at the entrance to my tent I could see that the stars were paling.

"You shall take me to their camp--now--Hadji," I said, and pulled on *burnous, haik, kafiyeh,* and *fil-fil* boots.

The Hadji seemed a little startled.

"It would not look well for me to be seen visiting their camp now," he said. "It will soon be light... ."

"You need not visit their camp," I replied. "Take me to where I can see it, and then disappear."

The good man sat awhile in thought.

"How much, Sidi?" he asked.

"I am not like those others," I replied. "I do not shake bags of money in the faces of pious and honest men, nor haggle and bargain. I richly reward those who serve me well-- very richly--when their service is completed... . Now do as I say, or go away, and let me sleep in peace, for this chatter wearies me ..." and I yawned.

The Hadji went to the doorway and collogued with the soldier without.

Returning, he said that he had dispatched my sentry to inform the guard at the camp of the emissaries that a man would shortly visit the latter, and must not be challenged, as he came from the Emir on secret business. The countersign was "Stamboul."

"This fellow, one Gharibeel Zarrug, is entirely faithful to me, Sidi," he added. "You can always send me messages by his mouth. I can arrange that he is very frequently on guard over your tent."

We sat in silence for a few minutes, a silence broken by the Hadji's request for a taste of the *sharab* of the Infidels. I gave the good man a nip of cognac and I believe this bound him to my interests (until they clashed with his) more strongly than gold would have done. He had all the stigmata of the secret drunkard, and his tongue continually flickered at his lips like that of a snake.

The soldier returned and whispered.

"Come, Sidi," said the Hadji, "I will take you as far as is safe."

"Safe for me or for you?" I asked.

"Nowhere is safe for *you*, Sidi," was the reply. "Take my advice and flee for your life--to return with an army, and a treaty which I will sign as Regent... ."

I did my best by careful noting of direction, the stars, clumps of trees, tents, water-runnels and stones, to ensure my being able to make the return journey... .

After we had walked for about a mile, the Hadji stopped in the black shadow of some palms and pointed to an orderly cluster of tents, just visible from where we stood.

"That is their camp, Sidi," said the Hadji, "and beyond those palms are their camel-lines and servants' quarters and the bivouac of a Camel Corps section--provided for the--ah-- protection of the party ..." and without another word the Reverend Father vanished.

§2

I walked boldly across to the principal tent, ignored the distant sentry, and entered.

Two men slept on rugs, one an obvious Oriental, the other slightly fairer of complexion and with heavy moustache and huge beard.

I studied his face by the light of the lantern that hung from the tent-pole, and learned nothing from it--but I suspected a disguised European. The man's hands were larger than those of an Arab and there was more colour, in what I could see of his cheeks, than I should expect in those of a native.

Turning to the lamp, I unhooked it and held it to his face, so that the light fell upon it while mine was in the shadow thrown by the back of the lamp--a common bazaar affair of European make, such as hangs on the walls of the cheap hotels of Algeria and Tunis. I then drew a bow at a venture.

I struck the sleeper heavily on the chest, and, as he opened his eyes and sat up, said coolly:

"*Bon jour, mon cher Monsieur Becque!*"

My shaft winged true.

"*Himmel!*" he exclaimed, half awake and startled into unguarded speech. And then, collecting his scattered wits, said in French--"*What is it? Who are you?*" and his hand went under his pillow.

"Keep still!" I said sternly, and my revolver came from under my *burnous,* and he looked into the muzzle of it.

And, as he looked, the cast in his left eye was obvious.

"Who *are* you?" he said again in French.

And then a third voice added, in the same tongue, "Whoever you are, drop that pistol. *Quick*--I have you covered."

Like a fool, I had absolutely forgotten the second man in my excitement at discovering that it was indeed *Becque,* the man whom Raoul d'Auray de Redon had seen in Zaguig before its occupation by the French... . My old friend, *Becque!* ...

An awkward dilemma! ... If I dropped my revolver I should be at their mercy, and if I did not I should probably be shot in the back and buried in the sand beneath their tent--for even if they did not know who I was, they knew (thanks to the triple traitor, Abdul Salam) that I was a rival and an enemy... . Who else would speak French in that place?

How neatly should I be removed from their path!

None but the rogue Abdul Salam knew that I was aware of their existence--much less that I had actually entered their tent... . The sentry of course did not know me, in my disguise, and the sound of the pistol-shot could easily be explained, if it were heard and inquiries were made... . An accident... . A shot at a prowling pariah cur or jackal that had entered the tent and alarmed one of them, suddenly awakened... .

I should simply *disappear,* and my disappearance would be a soon-forgotten mystery, and probably ascribed to sudden flight prompted by fear--for had I not abused the Emir with unforgettable and unforgiveable insults? ... And then what of Mary Vanbrugh and Maudie--the French female spies sent to beguile and debauch the Emir and win his consent to the treaty? ... *Mary Vanbrugh would think I had fled, deserting her--in the name of Duty!*

All this flashed through my mind like lightning. What should I do? ... What about a shot into Becque's vile heart and a swift wheel about and a shot at the Arab?

No--he would fire in the same second that I shot Becque, and he could not miss me at a range of six feet.... Nor could I, even in such a situation, shoot a defenceless man in his bed....

Perhaps I could have done so in the days before Mary Vanbrugh had made me see Life and Honour and true Duty in so different a light....

Then I should have said, "What would France have me do?" Now I said, "What would Mary Vanbrugh have me do?"

And I somehow felt that Mary would say: "Live if you can, and die if you must--but not with this defenceless man's blood on your hands, his murder on your conscience ..." even if she knew what he had plotted and proposed concerning her and her maid.

Perhaps a couple of seconds had passed--and then the voice behind me spoke again with sharp menace.

"*Quick*--I am going to shoot! ..."

"*So am I,*" said yet a fourth voice coolly, in Arabic, and even, in that moment, I marvelled that the Arab speaker should so aptly have gathered the import of the French words--though actions, of course, speak louder than words.

I recognized the voice of the Emir.

"Everybody shooting everybody this morning," added the Vizier--inevitable shadow of his master.

Keeping Becque covered I turned my head. Two excellent European revolvers threatened the fellow who, green with fright, put his automatic on the ground.

I put my own back into the holster beneath my *burnous*. Evidently the Emir was making one of his unobtrusive visits to the excellent Becque--and he had come in the nick of time. Or was he so well served that he had known of my visit here, and come to catch me and Becque together?

"*Kief halak,* Emir el Hamel el Kebir," I said coolly. "The sound of thy voice is sweet in my ears and the sight of thy face as the first gleam of the rising sun."

"In the circumstances, I do not doubt it, *Roumi,*" was the reply, "for you stood at the Gates of Death.... What do you here?"

"I am visiting an old friend, Sidi Emir," I replied, "and my purpose is to resume a discussion, interrupted, owing to circumstances beyond his control, many years ago."

The Emir and the Vizier, their inscrutable, penetrating eyes fixed on mine, stared in thoughtful silence.

"Explain," said the Emir at length.

"Lord Emir of Many Tents and Ruler of many Tribes, Leader of the Faithful and Shadow of the Prophet," I said, "you are a person of honour, a warrior, a man of your hands as well as a man of your word.... Like me, you are a soldier.... Now, I once honoured this dog--for an excellent reason--by crossing swords with him. For an even better and greater reason I would cross swords with him again--and finish, utterly and completely, the duel begun so long ago.... I tell you, a lover of your People, that this cur would betray his People. I tell you, a respecter of women, that this white reptile is trying to achieve the dishonour and death of two white women.... You may think I wish merely to kill one who is a rival for your favour and alliance. Were that all he is, I would not try to defeat him thus. I would meet a fair adversary with fair attempts to out-bid and out-manœuvre him.... But as he has secretly plotted most foully against my country (and his own), against the lives and honour of the lady Sitts, and against my life--I ask you to let me meet him face to face and foot to foot and sword to sword--that I may punish him and rid my country of a matricidal renegade... ."

The two Sheikhs stared in silence, stroking their beards, their hard unreadable eyes, enigmatic, faintly mocking, watching my face unwaveringly.

"Swords are sharp and final arguments--and some quarrels can only be settled with them," mused the Emir. "What says our other honoured guest ... ?"

"Oh, I'll fight him!" spoke up Becque. "It will give me real pleasure to kill this chatter-box... ."

He turned to me with a smile that lifted one corner of his mouth and showed a gleaming dog-tooth.

"And so you are the bright *de Beaujolais,* are you?" he marvelled. "Well, well, well! Think of that now! ... De Beaujolais--the Beau Sabreur of the Blue Hussars! ... De Beaujolais, the Beau Sabreur of the Spahis and the Secret Service! ... De Beaujolais, the Hero of Zinderneuf! ... Well, my friend, I'll make you de Beaujolais of a little hole in the sand, shortly, and see you where the birds won't trouble you--and you won't trouble *me!* ... The great and clever de Beaujolais! ... Ha! Ha! Ha!" And the brave, brazen rogue roared with laughter.

(But how in the name of his father the Devil did he know anything of the affair at Zinderneuf?)

"You shall fight as soon as the light is good," said the Emir. "And you shall fight with Arab swords--a strange weapon to each of you, and therefore fair for both"; and, calling to Yussuf Fetata, he bade him send for two swords of equal length and weight and of exactly similar shape.

CHAPTER XV. "MEN HAVE THEIR EXITS ..."

Half an hour later, Becque and I stood face to face in the shadow, cast by the rising sun, of a great clump of palms.

We were stripped to the waist, and wore only baggy Arab trousers and soft boots.

Each held a noble two-edged sword, pliant as cane, sharp as a razor, exact model of those brought to the country by Louis the Good and his Crusaders. I verily believe they *were* Crusaders' swords, for there are many such in that dry desert where nothing rusts and a good sword is more prized, cared for, and treasured, than a good woman.

I looked for a knightly crest on the blade of mine. Had there been one, and had it been the very crest of the de Beaujolais family (for I have ancestors who went on Crusade)--what an omen! What a glorious and wonderful coincidence! What a tale to tell!

But I will be truthful and admit that there was no private mark whatever. Such things do not happen in real life--though it is stark fact that a venerable friend of mine killed a Dahomeyan warrior in Dodd's advance on Dahomey, and took from him the *very Gras rifle that he himself had carried as a private in* 1870! (He knew it both by its number and by a bullet-hole in the butt. It had evidently been sold to these people by some dealer in condemned army stores.)

The only fault I had to find with my beautiful Crusader- sword was that it had no hand-guard, nothing between handle and blade but a thin straight cross-piece. However, the same applied to Becque's weapon.

I looked at Becque. He "peeled well" as English boxers say, was finely muscled, and in splendid condition.

Whether the strangeness of our weapons would be in his favour as a stronger if less finished swordsman, or in mine, remained to be seen.

He spat upon his right hand--coarse and vulgar as ever--and swung his sword mightily, trying its weight and balance.

In a little group under the trees stood the Emir, the Vizier; young Yussuf Fetata (to whose family the swords belonged); the powerful dwarf who had first captured me, Marbruk ben Hassan; the Emir's body-servant, El R'Orab the Crow; the Egyptian-Arab colleague of Becque, and a few soldiers.

"Hear my words," said the Emir, and his hawk-like stare was turned to Becque, "for the least attempt at foul play, I will shoot you dead... . When I say '*Begin*'--do so. When I say '*Stop*,' do so instantly... . I shall not say '*Stop*' while both of you are on your feet, unless one of you does anything unbecoming a chivalrous warrior... ."

I bowed and gave the Emir the sword-salute... .

"*Begin!*" he said a moment later, and Becque repeated the very tactics of our previous duel.

He rushed at me like a tiger, his sword moving like forked lightning, and I gave my whole mind and body to parry and defence. I was not in the best of health and strength, thanks to my wound, my sleepless nights of anxiety, and my confinement to the tent--and if Becque chose to force the pace and tire himself, I was content.

All critics of my "form" have praised my foot-work, and I used my feet and brain to save my arm, for the swords were heavy.

At the end of his first wild whirling attack, when his sword ceased for a moment to rise and fall like a flail in the hands of a madman, I feinted for his head, and, as his sword went up, I lunged as though I held a sabre. He sprang back like a cat, and then made a Maltese-cross pattern with his sword--as though he were a Highlander wielding a light claymore--when I pursued.

Nothing could pass that guard--but it was expensive work, costly in strength and breath, and he was very welcome to make that impressive display--and I kept him at it by light and rapid feints... .

Suddenly his sword went up and back, as to smite straight down upon my skull, and, judging that I had time for the manœuvre, I did not parry--but sprang to my left and slashed in a smart *coup de flanc* that took him across the ribs beneath the raised right arm. A little higher and he would never have lifted his arm again; but, as it was, I gave him a gash that would mean a nice little blood-letting. In the same second, his sword fell perpendicularly on my right thigh, merely slicing off an inconsiderable--shall I say "rasher"--and touching no artery nor vein of importance.

I had drawn first blood--first by a fraction of a second--and I had inflicted a wound and received a graze.

"*Mary Vanbrugh*," I whispered.

I saw momentary fear in Becque's eyes, but knew it was only fear that I had wounded him too severely for him to continue the fight.

He began to retreat; he retreated quickly; he almost ran backward for a few paces--and, as I swiftly followed, he ducked, most cleverly and swiftly, below my sword--as it cut sideways at his neck--and lunged splendidly at my breast. A side step only just saved me, for his point and edge ploughed along the flesh of my left side and the other edge cut my upper arm as it rested for the moment against my body.... But the quick *riposte* has always been my strong point, and before his sword returned on guard, I cut him heavily across the head.

Unfortunately it was only a back-handed blow delivered as my sword returned to guard, and it was almost the hilt that struck him. Had it been the middle of the edge--even at such close quarters and back-handed--the cut would have been more worthy of the occasion. As it was, it did friend Becque no good at all.

"*Mary Vanbrugh,*" I whispered, a second time.

And then my opponent changed his tactics and used his sword two-handed.

One successful stroke delivered thus would lop off a limb or sever a head from a body--but though the force of every blow is doubled in value, the quickness of every parry is halved, and, since my opponent chose to turn his weapon into a mace, I turned mine into a foil, instead of obediently following his tactics.

It was rhinoceros against leopard now, strong dog against quick cat--possibly Goliath against David....

Hitherto we had crossed swords point downward, as in "sabres," now I held mine point upward as in "foils," and dodged and danced on my toes, feinting for a thrust.

Cut or thrust? ...

A cut from Becque would be death for de Beaujolais--and I was very sure a thrust from de Beaujolais would be death for Becque....

My foe forced the pace again.... He rushed like a bull, and I dodged like a matador. A hundred times his sword swept past my head like a mighty scythe, and so swift was he that never had I a chance for the matador's stroke--the *coup de grâce*. We were both panting, our breath whistling through parched throats and mouths, our bare chests heaving like bellows.... We were streaming with sweat and blood--and, with glaring glassy eye, Becque was fiercely scowling, and he was hoarsely croaking:

"*Curse you!* you damned dancing-master! *God smite you!* ... *Blast you,* you jumping monkey!" with each terrific stroke; and de Beaujolais was smiling and whispering "*Mary Vanbrugh ... Mary ... Mary ...*" but, believe me, de Beaujolais was weakening, for he had lost a lot of blood, his left arm was a useless weight of lead, he was growing giddy and sick and faint--and suddenly Becque, with a look of devilish hate and rage upon his contorted face, swept his sword once more above his head, and this time swept it up too far!

It was well above his head--and pointing downward behind him--for a stroke that should cleave me to the chin, when I dropped my point and lunged with all my strength and speed.... "*Mary Vanbrugh!*" ...

I had won. My sword stood out a foot behind him....

He tottered and fell.... My knees turned to water and I collapsed across his body.

"*Exit Becque!*" thought I, as I went down--"and perhaps de Beaujolais too! ..."

I recovered in a few minutes, to find that the Emir himself was holding my head and pouring glorious cold water on my face, chest and hands... . The Vizier was washing my cuts... .

Becque was not dead--but, far from surgeons and hospitals, no man could long survive the driving of that huge sword through his body... .

Poor devil!--but he *was* a devil!

"The Sitt has bandages and cordials," I said to the Emir, as I rose to my feet, and he at once despatched R'Orab the Crow to bid the slave-girls of the *anderun* to ask the lady Sitt to send what was needed for a wounded man.

I did what I could for the unconscious Becque and then I resumed my *jelabia, haik, kafiyeh* and *burnous,* after drinking deeply of the cool water, and dabbing my bleeding wounds.

The congratulatory Arabs crowded round me, filled with admiration of the victor. Would they have done the same with Becque, if he had won? ... Nothing succeeds like success... . To him that hath shall be given... . *Væ victis*... . Thumbs down for the loser... .

"Do you send for medicaments for yourself or for your enemy, Sidi?" asked the Emir.

"For my enemy, Emir," I replied. "It is the Christian custom."

"But he *is* your enemy," said the Emir.

"Anyone can help an injured *friend*," I replied. "If that is held to be a virtue, how much more is it a virtue to help a fallen foe?"

Sententious--but suitable to the company and the occasion.

The Emir smiled and shook my hand in European fashion, and the Vizier followed his example.

I was in high favour and regard--for the moment--as the winner of a good stout fight... . *For the moment!* ... What of the morrow, when their chivalrous fighting blood had cooled--and my foul insults and abuse were remembered? ...

§ 2

And then appeared Mary Vanbrugh, following El R'Orab, who carried the medicine chest and a bottle and some white stuff--lint or cotton-wool and bandages.

I might have known that she would not merely send the necessary things, when she heard of wounds and injuries.

She glanced at the semi-conscious Becque, a hideous gory spectacle, and then at me. I suppose I looked haggard and dishevelled and there was a little blood on my clothes--also I held the good sword, that had perhaps saved her life and honour, in my hand.

"*Your* work?" she said in a voice of ice and steel.

I did not deny it.

"More *Duty?*" she asked most bitterly, and her voice was scathing. "Oh, you *Killer,* you professional paid hireling *Slayer*... . Oh, you *Murderer* in the sacred name of your noble *Duty!* ... Tell these men to bring me a lot more water--and to make a stretcher with spears or tent-poles and some rugs ..." and she got to work like a trained nurse.

"Tear up a clean *burnous,* or something, in long strips," she said as I knelt to help her ..." and then get out of my sight--you *sicken* me... ."

"Are you hurt, too?" she asked a moment later, as more blood oozed through from my thigh, ribs and arm.

"A little," I replied.

"I am glad you *are*," said Miss Vanbrugh; "it serves you right"--and then ..." Suppose it had been *you* lying here dying ... ?"

I supposed it, and thanked the good God that it was not--for her sake.

When she had cleaned, sterilized and bandaged Becque's ghastly wound, she bade me tell the Arabs to have him carried to the Guest-tents and laid on my bed, that she might nurse him! Her orders were obeyed, and, under her superintendence, the wounded man was carried away with all possible care.

I noticed that the Emir bade Yussuf Fetata conduct the Egyptian-Arab back to his tent, and see that he did not leave it.

When everything possible had been done for Becque, and he lay on my bed motionless and only imperceptibly breathing, Mary Vanbrugh turned to me.

"I'll attend to *you* now, Killer," said she.

"Thank you, Miss Vanbrugh," I replied, "I can attend to what scratches I have quite well."

She looked at me, as in doubt. Her instinctive love of mothering and succouring the injured seemed to be at war with her instinctive hatred of those who cause the injury.

"Let me see the wound in your side," she said. "If you can look after your leg yourself, you cannot dress and bandage a wound in the ribs properly."

"I wouldn't trouble you for worlds, Miss Vanbrugh," I replied. "Doubtless the noted Doctor Hadji Abdul Salam will treat me... . These Arab specialists have some quite remarkable methods, such as making one swallow an appropriate quotation from the *Q'ran,* written on paper or rag, correctly blessed and suitably sanctified... . Do me a lot of good, I should think... . And possibly Maudie would lend a hand if the Doctor thinks a bandage ..." And then loss of blood, following a terrific fight (on an empty stomach) had its humiliating effect on my already enfeebled body, and down I went in a heap... .

When I recovered consciousness, Mary Vanbrugh and a very white-faced Maudie were in the tent, and I was lying, bandaged, on some rugs.

Dear Becque and I--side by side!

"Brandy," said Mary Vanbrugh to Maudie, as I opened my eyes. Maudie poured some out, and gave it to me. I drank the cognac, and was very soon my own man again. How often was this drama to be repeated? ... First the Touareg bullet; now Becque's sword. What would the third be?

I was soon to know.

I sat up, got to my feet, stiff, sore, bruised and giddy, but by no means a "cot-case."

"Lie down again at once, Killer," said Mary Vanbrugh sharply.

"Thank you, Miss Vanbrugh," I replied. "I am all right again now, and very greatly regret the trouble I have given you. I am most grateful... ."

"I do not desire your gratitude, Killer," interrupted the pale, competent, angry girl.

"... To Becque--I was going to say--for being so tender with me," I continued. And then I said a thing that I have regretted ever since--and when I think of it, I have to find some peace in the excuse that I was a little off my balance.

"It is not so long since you were fairly glad of the killing-powers of a Killer, Miss Vanbrugh," I went on, and felt myself a cad as I said it... . "On a certain roof in Zaguig, the Killer against eight, and your life in the balance... . I apologize for reminding you... . I am ashamed ..."

"*I* am ashamed ... *I* apologize--humbly, Major de Beaujolais," she replied, and her eyes were slightly suffused as I took her hand and pressed it to my lips... . "But oh! why *do* you ... why *must* you ... all these fine men ... that Mr. Dufour, Achmet, Djikki, and now this poor mangled, butchered creature... . Can you find *no* Duty that is help and kindness and love, instead of this Duty of killing, maiming, hurting ... ?"

Yes--I was beginning to think that I could find a Duty that was Love... .

§ 3

Becque rallied that night, incredibly. His strong spirit flickered, flared up, and then burnt clearly.

I was getting myself a drink, being consumed with thirst, when he spoke:

"So you win, de Beaujolais," he said quietly.

"I win, Becque," I replied.

I would not rejoice over a fallen foe, and I would not express regret to a villainous renegade and a treacherous cur--who, moreover, had plotted the death, mutilation and dishonour of two white girls (and one of them *Mary Vanbrugh).*

"It's a queer world," he mused. "You all but shot me that day, and I all but got you hanged... . The merest chance saved me, and luck saved you... ."

I supposed this to be the semi-delirious wanderings of a fevered mind... . But the brave evil Becque did not look, nor sound, delirious.

"What do you mean?" I said, more for the sake of saying something than seriously to ask a question.

"Ah--the brilliant de Beaujolais--Beau Sabreur of the Blue Hussars and the Spahis! ... Bright particular star of the *Bureau Arabe,* the Secret Service, the Intelligence Department of the French Army in Africa! ... You think you know a lot, don't you, and you're very pleased with your beautiful self--but you don't know who it was that turned your own men from down-trodden slaves into bloodthirsty mutineers, do you? ... And you were never nearer death in all your days... . Do you know, my clever friend, that if those cursed Arabs had not attacked at that moment, nothing could have saved you--thanks to me? ... Do you know that your own men were going to hang you to the flag-staff and then burn the place and march off? ... '*Another mutiny in the discontented and rotten French Army*'! ... Headlines in the foreign Press! ... Encouragement to the enemies of France! ... That would have been splendid, eh?"

I thought hard, and cast back in my memory... .

Most certainly I had never attempted to shoot Becque, and still more certainly I had never been in danger of hanging, at the hands of the gentleman.

In spite of his apparent command of his faculties, he must be wandering in his mind-- indeed, a place of devious and tortuous paths in which to wander.

Silence fell, disturbed only by the droning of the flies which I whisked from his face.

A few minutes later the closed eyes opened and glared at me like those of a serpent.

"Beautiful, brainy de Beaujolais," the hateful voice began again. "How nearly I got you that day and how I have cursed those Arabs ever since--those black devils from Hell that saved you... ."

Delirium, undoubtedly... . I brushed the flies again from the sticky lips and moistened them with a corner of a handkerchief dipped in lemon-juice.

"And when and where was that, Becque?" I asked conversationally.

"I suppose the mighty warrior, the Beau Sabreur, the brain of the French Army, has forgotten the little episode of Zinderneuf? ..."

Zinderneuf! ...

What *could* this Becque know of Zinderneuf? ...

Was yet another mystery to be added to those that clustered round the name of that ill-omened shambles?[1]

[1] *Vide "Beau Geste"*.

Zinderneuf! ... Mutiny ...

What was it Dufour had said to me when I ordered the parade before entering that silent fort, garrisoned by the Dead, every man on his feet and at his post... . ("The Dead forbidden to die. The Fallen who were not allowed to fall?")... . He had said "*There is going to be trouble... . They are rotten with* cafard *and over-fatigue... . They will shoot you and desert* en masse! ..."

Could this Becque have been there? ... Utterly impossible... .

Again I thought hard, cast back in my memory, and concentrated my whole mind upon the events of that terrible day... .

Dufour was there, of course... .

Yes, and that excellent Sergeant Lebaudy, I remembered, the man who was said to have the biggest voice in the French Army... .

And that punishing Corporal Brille whom I once threatened with a taste of the *crapaudine*, when I found him administering it unlawfully... . I could see their faces... . Yes... . And that trumpeter who volunteered to enter that House of the Dead... . Of course ... he was one of the three Gestes, as I learned when I went to Brandon Abbas in England to be best man at George Lawrence's wedding... . Lady Brandon was their aunt... .

Yes, and I remembered two fine American soldiers with whom I spoke in English--men whom I had, alas, sent to their deaths by thirst or Arabs, in an attempt to warn St. André and his Senegalese, that awful night.

I could recall no one else... . No one at all... .

"And what do *you* know about Zinderneuf, Becque?" I asked.

His bitter sneering laugh was unpleasant to hear. "Oh, you poor fool," he replied. "I know this much about Zinderneuf--that you nearly stepped into your grave there... . Into the grave that *I* dug for you there... . However, this place will do equally well."

With my mind back in Zinderneuf, I absently replied:

"You think I shall find my grave *here,* do you, Becque?"

"I most earnestly hope so," replied Becque, "I truly hope, and firmly believe, this Emir will do to you and your women what I have urged him--and tried to bribe him--to do."

I kept silent, for the man was dying.

"You are not out of the wood yet, Beautiful de Beaujolais, Beau Sabreur," the cruel, bitter voice went on... . "My colleague has a brain--if he hasn't much guts--and he has money too. And the power to put down franc for franc against you or anybody else, and then double it... . Oh, we shall win... . And I'd give my soul to survive to see the hour of success--and you impaled living on a sharpened palm-trunk and *your Secret Service women given to the Soudanese soldiers... .*"

I bit my lips and kept silence, for the man was surely dying.

§ 4

In spite of the considered opinion of which Miss Vanbrugh had delivered herself, I am a humane man, and if I fight my foe as a soldier should fight him, I try to be *sans rancune* when the fight is over.

While Becque was awake and conscious, I would sit with him, bear with his vileness, and do what I could to assuage the sufferings of his last hours... . Sometimes men change and relent and repent on their death-beds... . I am not a religious man, but I hold tenaciously to what is good and right, and if approaching death brought a better frame of mind to Becque, I would do everything in my power to encourage and develop it... . I would meet him more than half-way, and if his change of heart were real, I would readily forgive him, in the name of France and of Mary Vanbrugh... .

"Well, Becque," I said, "I shall do my best against your colleague--and *I* would give a great deal to survive to see the hour of success, and you, not impaled living, but speeded on your way, with a safe conduct, back to whence you came."

"You mealy-mouthed liar," replied my gentleman. "You have killed me, and there you sit and *gloat... .*"

"Nonsense, Becque," I replied. "I am glad I won the fight--but I'd do anything I could to help or ease or comfort you, poor chap... ."

"Another lie, you canting hypocrite and swine," Becque answered me.

"No," I said. "The simple truth."

"Prove it, then," was the quick answer.

"Well?" I asked, and rose to get him anything he wanted or to do anything that he might desire.

"Look you, de Beaujolais," he said, "you are a soldier... . So am I... . We have both lived hard--and my time has come... . Nothing can possibly save me--here in the desert without surgeons, anæsthetics, oxygen, antiseptics--and I may linger for days--wounded as I am... . I *know* that nothing on God's earth can save me--so do you... . Then let me die now and like a soldier... . Not like a sick cow in the straw... . Shoot me, de Beaujolais... ."

"I can't," I replied.

"No--as I said--you are a mealy-mouthed liar, and a canting hypocrite, full of words and words ..." answered Becque; and then in bitter mockery he mimicked my "*I'd do anything I could for you, poor chap! ...*"

"I can't murder you, Becque," I said.

"You *have*," he replied. "Can't you complete your job? ... No... . The Bold-and-Beautiful de Beaujolais couldn't do that--he could only gloat upon his handiwork and spin out the last hours of the man he had killed... . You and your Arab-debauching women from the stews of Paris... ." And he spat.

"One of those women worked over you like a nurse or a mother, Becque," I said. "She lavished her tiny store of cognac, *eau-de-Cologne,* antiseptics and surgery stuff on you--"

"As I said," he interrupted, "to keep me alive and gloat... ."

Silence fell in that hot, dimly-lighted tent, and I sat and watched this Becque.

After a while he spoke again.

"De Beaujolais," he said, "I make a last appeal as a soldier to a soldier... . Don't keep me alive, in agony, for days--knowing that I shall be a mortifying mass of gangrene and corruption before I die... . Knowing that nothing can save me... . I appeal to you, to you on whose head my blood is, to spare me *that*... . Put your pistol near me--and let Becque die as he has lived, with a weapon in his hand... ."

I thought rapidly.

"... Come, come, de Beaujolais, it is not *much* to ask, surely. It leaves your lily-white hands clean and saves your conscience the reproach that you let me suffer tortures that the Arabs themselves would spare me... ."

I came to a decision.

"De Beaujolais--if I have the ghost of a chance of life, refuse my request... . If I have no chance, and you *know* I have none--as surely as you know the sun will rise--then, if you are a man, a human creature with a spark of humane feeling in you--put your pistol by my hand... . You can turn your back if you are squeamish... . Do it, de Beaujolais, and I will die forgiving you and repenting my sins... ."

His voice broke, and I swallowed a lump in my throat as I rose and went to where my revolver hung to the tent-pole. My sword had passed below his lungs and had penetrated the liver and stomach and probably the spinal cord. He would never leave that bed, nothing upon earth could save him, and his long lingering death would be a ghastly thing... . It *was* the one thing I could do for him.

I put the pistol beside his right hand.

"Good-bye, Becque," I said. "In the name of France and Mary Vanbrugh I forgive the evil you tried to do to them both... . Personally I feel no hate whatsoever... . Good-bye, brave man--good-bye, old chap... ." And I touched his hand and turned my back.

The bullet cut my ear.

I sprang round and knocked the pistol from Becque's hand.

"You treacherous *devil*!" I cried.

"You poor gullible *fool*!" he answered, with the wry smile that showed the gleaming fang.

The sentry raised the door flap and looked in, and Mary Vanbrugh rushed from the *anderun* half of the tent, as I picked up my revolver.

"*Oh! What is it?*" she asked breathlessly.

"An accident," replied Becque. "One of the most deplorable that ever happened... . I shall regret it all my life... ." And he laughed.

There was no denying the gameness and stout heart of this dear Becque.

"More Duty, I thought, perhaps, Major de Beaujolais," observed the girl.

"It was. As I conceived it, Miss Vanbrugh," I replied.

After looking at Becque's bandages and giving him a sip of hot *soupe*, made with our compressed meat-tablets and a little cognac, she returned to the *anderun*, bidding me drink the *soupe*, for Becque could do little more than taste it.

"You win again, you dog!" said Becque, as soon as we were alone. "What a fool I was to aim at your head--with a shaking hand! ... But I did so want to see those poor brains you are so proud of.... *Now*, will you kill me?"

"No," I answered.

"*I know you won't!*" he replied. "You haven't the guts.... *And I know I shall recover...* . Why, you fool, I breathe almost without pain.... My lungs are absolutely sound.... You only gave me a flesh wound and I heal splendidly. Always have done...."

The poor wretch evidently did not know that the bandages hid as surely mortal a wound as ever man received. His talk of fatal injuries and certain death, which he had supposed to be a ruse that would gull and fool me, was but the simple truth.

"I'll be on my feet in a week, you witless ape," he continued, "and I'll get you yet! ... Believe me, Beautiful de Beaujolais, I won't miss you next time I shoot.... But I hope it won't come to that.... I want to see you die quite otherwise--and then I'll deal with your Arab-debauching harlots.... But I'll get you somehow! I'll *get* you, my Beau Sabreur! ..."

He raised himself on one elbow, pointed a shaking hand at my face, spat, and fell back dead....

CHAPTER XVI. FOR MY LADY

"The worldly hopes men set their hearts upon,
Turn ashes--or they prosper;
Anon, like snow upon the desert's dusty face,
Lighting a little hour or two--are gone...."

Becque's body having been borne away at dawn for burial, I soon began to wonder if the events of the previous day and night had really occurred, or whether they were the nightmare imaginings of a delirious fever-victim.

My wounds were real enough, however, and though slight, were painful in the extreme, throbbing almost unbearably and making movement a torture.

I would not have been without them though, for three times that day Mary Vanbrugh dressed them, and if I scarcely heard her voice, I felt the blessed touch of her fingers.

But she attended me as impersonally and coldly as a queen washing the feet of beggars, or as a certain type of army-surgeon doctoring a sick negro soldier.

As she left the tent on the last of her almost silent visits, she paused at the door-curtain and turned to me.

"What exactly *was* that shot in the night, Major de Beaujolais?" she asked.

"It was Becque shooting at me," I replied. "You did not suppose that it was me shooting at Becque, did you, Miss Vanbrugh?"

"I really did not know, Major de Beaujolais," answered the girl. "I should not be so foolish as to set *any* limit to what you might do in the name of *Duty!* ... Nothing *whatever* would surprise me in that direction, now, I think... ."

"A man's duty *is* his duty," I replied.

"Oh, quite," she answered. "I would not have you deviate a hair's breadth from your splendid path... . But since the day you informed me that you would have left me to the mercies of the Touareg--had there been but one camel--I have been thinking ... a good deal... . Yes, '*A man's duty is his duty,*' and--if I might venture to speak so presumptuously--a woman's duty is *her* duty, too... ."

"Surely," I agreed.

"And so I find it *my* duty to hinder you no further, and to remain in the Oasis with these fine Arabs--*under the protection of the Emir el Hamel el Kebir*... ."

"*What!*" I shouted, startled out of my habitual calm and courtesy. "You find it your '*duty*' to do *what?*"

I felt actually faint--and began to tremble with horror, fear, and a deadly sickness of soul.

"I think you heard what I said," the girl replied coldly, "and I think you know that I always mean what I say, and say what I mean... . Oh, believe me, Major de Beaujolais--I have some notions of my own on *duty*--and it is no part of mine to hinder yours... ."

I drank some water, and my trembling hand spilt more than my dry throat swallowed.

"So I shall remain here," she went on, "and I think too that I prefer the standards and ideals of this Emir... . Somehow I do not think that *anything* would have induced *him* to leave a woman to certain death or worse... . Not even a *treaty!*" and the bitter scorn of her accents, as she said that word, was terrible.

Her voice seared and scorched me... . I tried to speak and could not.

"Nor do I feel that I shall incur any greater danger here than I should in setting off into the Desert again with a gentleman of your pronounced views on the subject of the relative importance of a woman and a piece of paper... . Nor shall my maid go with you... . I prefer to trust her, as well as myself, to these people of a less-developed singleness of purpose ... and I *like* this Emir--enormously."

I found my voice... . Clumsily, owing to my wounds, I knelt before her... .

"Miss Vanbrugh ... *Mary* ..." I cried. "This is inhuman cruelty... . This is *madness!* ... Think! ... A girl like yourself--a lovely fascinating woman--here ... alone... . You must be insane... . Think... . A *hareem*--these Arabs... . I would sooner shoot you here and now... . This is sheer incredible *madness*... ."

"Yes--like yourself, Major de Beaujolais," she replied, drawing back from me. "*I* am now 'mad' on the subject of *Duty*... . It has become an obsession with *me* too--(an example of the influence of one's companions upon one's character!)--and I find it my duty to leave you entirely free to give the whole of your mind to more important matters--to leave you entirely free to depart alone as soon as your business is completed--for I will be no further hindrance to you... . Good-bye, and--as I do not think I shall see you again--many thanks for bringing me here in safety, and for setting me so high a standard and so glorious an example... ."

I do not know what I replied--nor what I did. I was *all* French in that moment, and gave full rein to my terrible emotion.

But I know that Mary Vanbrugh left the tent with the cold words:

"Duty, Major de Beaujolais--before *everything!* We will *both* do our Duty... . I shall tell the Emir el Hamel el Kebir that I intend to remain here indefinitely, under his protection, and that I hope he will give you your precious treaty, and send you off at once... . My conscience--awakened by you--will approve my doing what *I* now see to be *my* duty... . Good-bye, Major de Beaujolais... ."

I sat for hours with my pistol in my hand, and I think I may now claim to know what suffering *is*... . Never since that hour have I had a word of blame for the poor soul who blows his brains out... .

§ 2

I saw no one else that day, but during the night I was awakened from a fitful and nightmare-ridden doze by the Hadji Abdul Salam.

Once more he rehearsed his proposals and warnings, modified now by the elimination of Becque.

ONE: Would I, by his help, escape alone, immediately, and return with a strong French force and make him France's faithful (well-paid) vassal Emir Regent of the Great Confederation? Or

TWO: Would I promise him a great bag of gold and my help in his obtaining the Regency of the Confederation, if he procured the death of the Emir at the hands of Suleiman the Strong, and solemnly swore to poison the said Suleiman at as early a date thereafter as convenient? (He could not poison the Emir, for that distrustful man took all precautions against such accidents.)

He fully warned me that by rejecting both his proposals I should most certainly come to a painful and untimely end, and my two women become *hareem* slaves. He was in a position to state with certainty and truth that the Emir had decided to kill me and the Arab-Egyptian, keep the money, camels, weapons and other effects of both of us, and then accept the earlier offer of the Great Sheikh el Senussi and make an offensive and defensive alliance with him.

I heard him out, on the chance that I might glean something new.

When he had finished and I had replied with some terseness, I pointed to the doorway and remarked:

"And now, Holy One, depart in peace, before I commit an impiety. In other words--get out, you villainous, filthy, treacherous dog, before I shoot you... ."

The Hadji went, and as he crept from my tent, he ran into the arms of the Sheikh el Habibka el Wazir--and I saw him no more in this life, and do not expect to see him in the next.

I heard that he fell ill and died shortly after. People are apt to do so if they obstruct the ways of desert Emirs.

I lay awake till dawn, probably the most anxious, distracted, troubled man in Africa... .

Mary Vanbrugh... . France... . My Service... . My uncle... . My Duty... . An outraged, unforgivably insulted despot, a fierce, untrammelled tyrant whose "honour" was his life--and in whose hands lay the fate of the two women for whose safety I was responsible.

§ 3

Things came to a head the next night.

The Emir el Hamel el Kebir and the Sheikh el Habibka el Wazir entered my tent, and, as though nothing had happened to disturb the friendliest relationship, were cordially pleasant.

Much too friendly methought, and, knowing Arabs as I do, I could not suppress the feeling that their visit boded me no good. I grew certain of it--and I was right.

After formal courtesies and the refusal of such hospitalities as I could offer, the Emir said:

"Your Excellency has the successful accomplishment of this mission much at heart?"

"It would be a fine thing for your people and pleasing to mine," I replied. "Yes, I have it much at heart."

"Your Excellency has the welfare and happiness of the Sitt Miriyam much at heart?" went on the sonorous voice.

Was there a mocking note in it?

"So much so that I value it more than the Treaty," I replied.

"And the other night Your Excellency called me *dog* and *swine,* and *filthy black devil,* I think," was the Emir's next utterance.

"Yes," he went on, as I was silent. "Yes. And Your Excellency has these matters much at heart. He admires this fair woman greatly. Perhaps he loves her? *Possibly he would even die for her?* ..."

The Vizier watched the Emir, stroked his beard, and smiled.

"Your Excellency would achieve a great deed for France? ... But perhaps he loves France not so much that he would die for her? Perhaps this woman is as his Faith, since he is an Infidel? ... Yes, perchance she *is* his Faith? ..."

The two men now stared at me with enigmatic eyes, cruel, hard and unfathomable, the unreadable alien eyes of the Oriental... .

There was a brief silence, a contest of wills, a dramatic struggle of personalities.

"*Are you prepared to die for your Faith?*" asked the Emir--and I started as though stung. Where had I heard those words before? Who had said them?

I had. I had used those identical words to Becque' himself at St. Denis, years ago... . Well, perhaps I could make a better showing than Becque had then done--as much better as my cause was nobler.

"*I am,*" I replied in the words of the dead man.

"*You shall,*" said the Emir, as I had said to Becque--and I swear that as he said it, the Vizier's face fell, and he smote his thigh in anger... . Was he my friend?

"Listen," said the Emir. "These two women shall go free, in honour and safety, on the day after Death has wiped out the insults you have put upon me. After those words '*dog*' '*son of a dog,*' '*swine,*' '*black-faced devil,*' I think that we may not both live... . Nor would I slay with mine own hand the man who comes in peace and eats my salt... . Speak *Roumi*... ."

"What proof and assurance have I that you would keep your word, Emir?" I asked.

"None whatever--save that I have given it," was the reply. "It is known to all men who know me, that I have never broken faith; never failed in promise or in threat... . *If you die by your own hand to-night, your white women are as free as air.* I, the Emir el Hamel el Kebir, swear upon the Holy Q'ran and by the Beard of the Prophet and the Sacred Names of God that I will deliver the two Sitts, in perfect safety, wheresoever they would be."

"And if I decline your kind suggestion that I should commit suicide?" I sneered in my fear, misery and rage.

"Then you can slink away in safety; the signed Treaty goes with you; the Sitt Miriyam enters the *hareem* of the Sheikh el Habibka el Wazir; and the Sitt Moadi enters mine... ."

"You Son of Satan! You devilish dog--" I began.

"*Choose*--do not chatter," said the Emir.

Now my revolver was in its holster and my sword leant against the tent-pole... .

Let me think... . Kind God, let me think... . If I could shoot both these dogs and the sentry who would rush in--could I get the girls out of their beds and on to camels and away--I, single-handed, against the bodyguard of Soudanese, whose lines were not a hundred yards away, and against the whole mob that would come running? Such things were done in the kind of books that Maudie read, no doubt.

No. I was utterly and hopelessly in the power of these men. And what of the Treaty, if it *were* possible for us to escape?

"Since you give your word that the Treaty shall be signed and loyally kept, or, on the other hand, that the two Sitts shall be escorted to safety--why not do these wise and noble actions without sullying them with murder?" I asked.

"Do you not punish those who mortally insult *you*?" asked the Emir.

"I fight them," I replied, and my heart gave a little bound of hope as an idea occurred to me. "I fight them--I do not murder them. Fight me to-morrow, Emir--and if I die, let the Sitts go, taking the Treaty with them."

"And if *I* die?" asked the Emir.

"It will be the Hand of Allah," I replied. "It will be a sign that you have done wrong. The Vizier must have orders to see that we all go in safety, bearing the Treaty with us."

The Emir smiled and shook his head.

"A *brave* man would fight me with the condition that the Sitts go in any case and take the Treaty with them--and that I go if I win," said I.

"I do not fight those who come to me in peace and receive my hospitality," answered the Emir with his mocking smile.

He was but playing with me, as the cat plays with the mouse it is about to kill.

"No? You only murder them?" I asked.

"Never," replied the Emir. "But I cannot prevent their taking their own lives if they are bent upon it... . If you die to-night, the Sitts leave here to-morrow. You *know* I speak the truth... ."

I did. I rose, and my hand went slowly and reluctantly to my holster. Life was very sweet--with Mary so near and dear.

I grasped the butt of the weapon--and almost drew and fired it, with one motion, into the smiling face of the Emir. But that could lead to nothing but the worst. There was no shadow of possibility of any appeal to force doing anything but harm.

I drew my revolver, and the hands of the two Arabs moved beneath their robes.

"Your pistol is unloaded," said the Sheikh, "but ours are not."

I opened the breech of the weapon, and saw that the cartridges had been extracted... .

"Get on with the murder, noble Emir--true pattern of chivalry and model of hospitality," I said, and added: "But remember, if evil befalls the Sitts, never again shall you fall asleep without my cold hand clutching you by the throat--you disgrace to the name of man, Mussulman and Arab... . You defiler of the Koran and enemy of God."

"If you mean that you wish to die that the Sitts may go free, and my honour may be cleansed of insult ..." replied the Emir, and he softly clapped his hands, as the Vizier angrily growled an oath in his beard... . *Was* he my friend? ...

The slave who was the Emir's constant attendant and whom he called El R'Orab the Crow, stooped into the tent.

"Bring the cur and some water," said the Emir.

El R'Orab the Crow left the tent and soon returned, leading a pariah-dog on a string, and carrying an earthenware bowl of water.

Producing a phial from beneath his sash, the Vizier poured what looked like milk into the bowl. The slave set it before the dog, and retired from the tent. Evidently the matter had been arranged beforehand... .

As such dogs invariably do, this one gulped the water greedily.

The imperturbable Arabs, chin on hand, watched.

Scarcely had the dog swallowed the last of the water, when it sneezed, gave a kind of choking howl, staggered, and fell.

In less than a minute it was dead. I admit that it seemed to die fairly painlessly.

I rose again, quickly produced the Treaty from the back of my map-case, and got sealing-wax and matches from my bag... .

"*Sign the Treaty,*" I said, "*and let me go.*" ...

The Emir, smiling scornfully, signed with my fountain-pen, and sealed with a great old ring that bore cabalistic designs and ancient Arabic lettering.

The Vizier, grinning cheerfully, witnessed the signature--both making a jumbled mass of Arabic scratchings which were their "marks" rather than legible signatures... . I could understand the Emir's contempt, but not the obvious joy of the Vizier.

Again the Emir clapped his hands. R'Orab the Crow entered, and the dog and the bowl were removed.

"Bring us tea," said the Emir; and, returning, the slave brought four steaming cups of mint tea, inevitable accompaniment of any "ceremony."

Into one the Emir poured the remainder of the contents of the phial and passed it to me.

"We would have drunk together," he said, "you drinking that cup--and we would have wished prosperity and happiness to the Sitts. '*May each marry the man she loves,*' we would have said, and you would have died like a brave man... . Now cast the poison on the ground, O Seller of Women, and take this other cup. Drink tea with us--to the prosperity of our alliance with France instead."

And beneath the smiling eyes of the Emir and the fierce stare of the Vizier, I said in Arabic: "*The Treaty is signed and witnessed, Emir!*" and in my own mother-tongue I cried: "*Happiness to my Lady, and success to my Country,*"and, rising to my feet, I drank off the poisoned cup--clutched at my throat--tried to speak and choked ... remembered Suleiman the Strong and tried to tell the Emir of his presence and his threat ... choked ... choked ... saw the tent, the lamp, the men, whirl round me and dissolve--and knew I was falling,

falling--falling through interstellar space into Eternity--and, as I did so, was aware that the two Arabs sprang to their feet.... Blind, and dying, I heard a woman scream.... I ...

NOTE

Thus abruptly ends the autobiography of Major Henri de Beaujolais--which he began long after leaving the Great Oasis and the society of the Emir el Hamel el Kebir and his Wazir (or Vizier).

The abrupt ending of his literary labours, at the point of so dramatic a crisis in his affairs, was not due to his skill as a cunning writer, so much as to the skill of a Riffian tribesman as a cunning sniper.

Major de Beaujolais, being guilty of the rashness of writing in a tent, by the light of a lamp, paid the penalty, and the said tribesman's bullet found its billet in his wrist-watch and arm, distributing the works of the former throughout the latter, and rendering him incapable of wielding either pen or sword for a considerable period....

It happens, however, that the compiler of this book is in a position to augment the memoirs of his friend, whom he has called Henri de Beaujolais, and to shed some light upon the puzzling situation. Paradoxically, the light came from dark places--the hearts and mouths of two Bad Men. Their wicked lips completed the story, and it is hereinafter set forth.

* * * * *

The narrative which follows opens at a date a few years previous to the visit of Major de Beaujolais to the Great Oasis.

PART II

SUCCESS

Out of the Mouths of TWO BAD MEN

> *"Love rules the camp, the court, the grove,*
> *And men below, and saints above,*
> *For Love is Heaven, and Heaven is Love."*

THE MAKING OF A MONARCH

CHAPTER I. LOST

Golden sand and copper sky; copper sky and golden sand; and nothing else. Nothing to relieve the aching human eye, in all that dreadful boundless waste of blistering earth and burning heaven.

To the bright tireless eye of the vulture, an infinite speck hung motionless in the empyreal heights of cosmic space, was something else--the swaying, tottering, reeling figure of a man.

The vulture watched and waited, knowing, either from marvellous instinct or from more marvellous mental process, that he would not have long to wait. As the man fell, the predatory bird, with motionless wing, slid down the sky in graceful circling swoop, and again hung motionless, a little nearer to his quarry.

As the man rose, tottered on, staggered and again fell, the vulture repeated its manœuvre, and again hung motionless, nearer to its prey... .

Would the still figure move again? Was it yet too feeble to resist the onslaught of the fierce beak that should tear the eyeballs from the living head?

The vulture dropped a few thousand feet lower... .

§ 2

With a groan, the recumbent man drew up his knees, turned on his side, planted his hands on the hot sand, and, after kneeling prone for a minute, struggled once more to his feet, and bravely strove to climb the long billow of soft loose sand that lay before him.

Beneath the hood of his dirty white *kafiyeh* head-dress, bound round with *agal* ropes of camel-hair, his dark face was that of a dead man--the eyes glazed, the protruding tongue black, the cracked skin tight across the jutting bones. Through the rags of his filthy *jellabia,* his arms and shoulders showed lean and black; his bare legs were those of a skeleton... . An Arab scarecrow, a *khaiyul,* endowed with a spark of life.

At the top of the ridge the man swayed, put his hand above his eyes, and peered out into the dancing heat-haze ahead.

Burning sand and burning sky... . Not even a mirage to give a faint hope that it might not be what it was--a last added torture.

He sank to the ground... .

An hour later the vulture did the same, and settled himself, with huddled head and drooping wings, to continue his patient watch with unwinking eye.

Anon he strutted toward the body, with clumsy gait, and foolishly jerking head, his cruel hooked beak open in anticipation.

§ 3

"Allah! What is that? ... Look, brothers, something white on yonder sand-hill--and a vulture... ."

The speaker reined-in his camel and pointed, his long-sighted gaze fixed on the far-distant spot where he had seen something that to European eyes would have been invisible.

Lowering his outstretched hand, he unslung his rifle as the other Touareg came to a halt around him.

"A trap perchance," growled another of the Wolves of the Desert, from behind the heavy blue veil that hid all but his eyes. He was a huge man, more negroid of countenance than the rest.

"Go, thou, and spring it then," said the leader; and the score or so of raiders sat motionless on their camels while the black-faced man rode off.

Cautiously scanning the terrain from the top of each sand-hill, he circled round the motionless bundle of rags, as the vulture flapped heavily away to alight at a safe and convenient distance.

After a long and searching stare around him, the rider approached the body, his ready rifle in both hands. He brought the camel to its knees.

As he dismounted, the rest of the band rode toward the spot. By the time they reached it, the scout had turned the man upon his back and discovered that he was unarmed, unprovided, foodless, waterless, and utterly valueless. There was not so much as a rag of clothing that was worth the trouble of removing.

"A miserable *miskeen* indeed," said the scout to the leader of the band, as he rode up. "Not a *mitkal* on the dog's carcase. Not even an empty purse... ."

"Curse the son of Satan!" replied the leader, and spat.

"There may be something on his camel, if we follow his tracks back to where he left its carcase," observed a lean and hawk-faced rogue, who was trying to force his beautiful white *mehara* to tread upon the body.

"Yea, a sack of pearls, thou fool," agreed the leader, and added: "Come on. Shall we waste the day chattering around this carrion?"

As the band rode off, he of the negroid countenance jumped on to his kneeling beast, and as it lurched to its feet, he emitted a joyous whoop, and either in light-hearted playfulness, or as a mark of his disgust at the poverty of so poor a thing, he discharged his rifle at the body. The body jerked and quivered, and, as the robber rode off, it writhed over on to its face, to the annoyance of the observant vulture.

Not a man of this band of mysterious blue-veiled robbers, the terrible "Forgotten of God," looked round; and all rode on as heartlessly indifferent to the dreadful fate of this fellow desert-dweller, as if it might not well be their own upon the morrow's morrow.

Life is very cheap in the desert.

CHAPTER II. EL HAMEL

Towards evening of the same day, a desert caravan of semi-nomad Arabs--"peaceful" herdsmen, armed to the teeth, and desiring to fight no foe of greater strength than themselves, followed in the track of the Touareg raiders.

At their head rode their aged Sheikh, a venerable white-bearded gentleman, with the noble face of a Biblical patriarch, and much of the philosophy, standards, ideals and habits of such--a modern Abraham, Isaac, or Jacob.

Beside him rode an Esau, a hairy man, a mighty hunter before the Lord. In his dark face was nothing noble, save in so far as a look of forceful and ruthless determination makes for nobility of countenance.

"Yea--of a surety are we safest in the very tracks of these sons of Shaitan, these Forgotten of Allah--may they burn in Gehennum," said the Sheikh to his companions, and, turning on his camel, he looked back at the long and straggling column whereon the bobbing rolling *bassourabs* showed that prized and honoured women rode hidden from the eyes of men.

"Thou art right, Wise One," replied the burly younger man. "No bullet enters the hole made by another bullet, and no knife nor spear strikes a bleeding wound. No other raiding-party will follow this one, nor will these Enemies of God turn about in their own tracks."

And it came to pass that as the sun began to set, and the old Sheikh prepared to halt the caravan for the evening *asha* prayer--when all would dismount, and, kneeling in long lines behind their leader, would follow him in devout supplication to Allah, their heads bowed to the sand in the direction of Mecca--the eyes of his companion, called Suleiman the Strong, fell upon the bundle of rags on the distant sand-hill.

"By the Beard of the Prophet," he exclaimed, pointing. "A man! And he may not be dead, or that vulture would be at work."

"If it is one of the Forgotten of God he will soon be dead," said the aged Sheikh, laying his hand upon the silver hilt of the curved dagger that was stuck through the front of the broad girdle bound about the long white *jellabia* beneath his *burnous*.

"Not too soon, let us hope, my father," growled Suleiman.

"He may live long enough to suffer something of what my brother suffered at Touareg hands, before his brave soul went to the bosom of the Prophet.... May dogs defile the graves of their grandfathers...."

The two rode to the spot where the man lay, followed by several of the caravan guards, fighting-men armed with flintlock guns, rifles, or long lances, and straight heavy swords.

"He is no Touareg, but a victim of the Touareg," said Suleiman, slipping down from his camel without stopping to make it kneel. "See, they have shot him, and he with scarcely any blood to flow...."

"He may not be dead even yet," he added, after placing his ear to the man's heart and holding the bright blade of his sword to the latter's nostrils. "He is only shot through the shoulder.... Shall I cut his throat?"

"No. Give him water," replied the Sheikh, and crying, "*Adar-ya-yan! Adar-ya-yan!*"to his camel, brought it to its knees. "He who is merciful to the poor and needy is acceptable to Allah."

"Go, one of you, for Hadji Abdul Salam," he added, turning to the impassive fighting-men, who looked on with calm indifference, viewing this evidence of desert tragedy, this agony and death of a fellow-man, with as much interest as they would the fall of a sparrow to the ground.

Is not "Here is a stranger--let us cut his throat" the expression of a sound, safe and profitable principle?

Taking his goatskin water-bottle from where it hung at the high peak of his saddle, the Sheikh untied the neck of it, and dropped a little of the desert's most priceless and precious treasure upon the black lips and tongue.

A fellow-feeling makes us wondrous kind, and the fact that this derelict was a Touareg victim gave him a claim that he would otherwise not have had, and brought him kindnesses he might not have received. Skeletons and dried corpses of men are, in the desert, too common a sight to warrant a second glance; wounded men are a burden; and dying men will soon be dead.

Hadji Abdul Salam, a fat and (for an Arab) jolly rogue, rode up from beside the camel that bore his two wives in a gaily striped *bassourab* (or balloon-like tent), and, putting on an air of wisdom, examined the body. He had a great reputation in the Tribe, by reason of having cured the Sheikh of a mortal sickness by the right use of a hair of the Prophet's beard, a cup of water, in which was soaked a paper bearing a very special extract from the Q'ran, and the application of a very hot iron to the old gentleman's stomach. He also had a most valuable prescription for ophthalmia--muttering another Q'ranic extract seven times, and spitting in the patient's eyes seven times after each mutter.

This learned physician pronounced life extinct.

"Starved to death," he said. "Then died of thirst. Whereafter he received a wound which killed him."

This bulletin satisfied all present, save, apparently, the corpse, whose eyelids fluttered as the blackened tongue moved feebly in a kind of lip-licking motion.

"But I have brought him back to life, as you see," the good doctor promptly added, and his great reputation was enhanced.

§ 2

And alive, just alive, the foundling proved to be. Curiously, and inconsequently enough, and yet again naturally enough, the old Sheikh set great store by the recovery of the man whom he had saved.

Had he not thus thwarted the Touareg, undone what they had done, plucked a brand from their burning, and was not this human salvage his, and a record and proof of his virtue? The Sheikh had reached an age at which proofs of virtue may soon be wanted in the sight of Allah.

He had the sick and wounded man rolled up in *feloudji* tent-coverings, splinted with tent-poles, and slung at the side of a good *djemel* baggage-camel.

"See that the dog dies, you," whispered Suleiman the Strong to the camel-man in charge of the *djemel,* as the caravan moved on again, after the evening prayer had been said. "If he be alive at the next halt, squeeze his throat a little. On thy head be it."

Why add a burden and a useless mouth to a caravan crossing a waterless desert?

A little later the Sheikh sent for this camel-man. "See that this stranger lives," said he. "The succour of the afflicted is pleasing to Allah the Compassionate, the All-Merciful. On thy head be it."

Abdullah, the camel-man, felt that there was altogether too much on his head; but the old Sheikh was still the Sheikh, and he had better "hear his words" and put prudence before pleasure. Abdullah was a good killer, and, like the rest of us, enjoyed doing that which he could do well.

At the next halt, the foundling was still alive, and was distinctly seen to swallow the water that was poured into his mouth.

Suleiman the Strong looked at Abdullah el Jemmal, the camel-man, and, with a decidedly unpleasant smile, touched the hilt of his knife. The old Sheikh praised Abdullah, and said it was well. Of this, Abdullah felt doubtful.

After some hours spent lying flat and still upon the ground, the Unknown was certainly better. He drank camel-milk and opened his eyes.

Doctor Abdul Salam also had time to give proper care and attention to the man's wound.

He wrote a really potent quotation from the Q'ran upon a piece of paper, and fixed it, with blood and saliva, just where it would do most good--over the entry-hole of the bullet.

As the bullet had passed right through the man's shoulder, the good doctor confessed that he was really only wasting time in probing for it with a pair of pliers generally used for gun repairs--though this was, in a manner of speaking, really a kind of gun-repair, as it were.

Doctor Abdul Salam explained further to the old Sheikh, as they fingered the rather large exit-hole, that he would leave it open for a few days--in order that anything in the nature of a devil might escape without let or hindrance--and that then he would close it nicely with some clay, should they be fortunate enough to find any at the next oasis.

This, he explained, would effectually prevent the entrance of anything in the nature of a devil, and so the man really ought to be all right. And, in any case, whatever Allah willed was obviously the will of Allah. Quite so. *Inshallah.*

The doctor thought the Sheikh was getting a bit senile, to pursue a whim to this extreme--but if the Sheikh wished to oblige Allah, the doctor wished to oblige the Sheikh.

After another long rest at the next halt, the Unknown was again better--if his wound was worse. He drank *halib* and water greedily, and looked about him. But if he could use his eyes, he could not use his tongue, or else did not understand what was said to him.

After each halt he grew a little stronger, and by the time the tribe reached an oasis, he could totter about on his feet, and wash his wound for himself.

The good *hakim,* Hadji Abdul Salam, however, washed his hands--of the patient. He would take no further responsibility for the fool, since he thought he knew more about the treatment of gun-shot wounds than the doctor did; and either could not, or would not, swallow the doctor's words--written on wads of paper--precious *hejabs,* warranted to exorcise all devils of sickness and destruction.

Hearing the physician complain, Suleiman the Strong bade him waste neither words nor skill, for as soon as the Sheikh tired of his fancy, he himself intended to cure the Unknown of all troubles, with complete finality. He had a feeling against him, inexplicable but powerful.

And daily the Unknown grew in strength, and by the time the caravan reached its destination, some weeks later, the *qsar* of the Tribe, he could ride a camel, and could almost fend for himself.

But his wound grew worse, and for months he seemed like to die, for he could not get at the hole in his back, whereas the flies could.

The Tribe called him "El Gherib," the Poor Stranger, and "El Hamel," the Foundling, the Lost One, and waited for the old Sheikh to tire of him.

§ 3

But as the months went by, the old Sheikh's fancy seemed to turn to infatuation, and, far from tiring of the man and ceasing to interest himself in his existence, he cherished and cared for him. When, eventually, he recovered, the Sheikh raised him to prominence and importance.

El Hamel was he whom the Sheikh delighted to honour, and Suleiman the Strong sharpened his knife and bided his time--for the Sheikh was getting old, and his sole surviving son was but a boy.

When the Sheikh was gathered to his fathers, the stranger would die, for Suleiman would be Regent of the Tribe.

Undeniably, however, El Hamel was a remarkable person. In the first place, he was Afflicted of Allah and quite dumb; in the second place, he was unbelievably skilful with a rifle and with the throwing-knife; in the third place, he was incredibly strong; in the fourth, he was a most notable horseman and horse-master, even among Arab horsemen; in the fifth, he was indubitably a far better doctor than the *hakim* himself; and lastly, and most remarkable of all, he was a magician--and a magician of power.

This wonderful great gift had come to light in this wise. The Sheikh had lost his *djedouel,* his famous amulet, a silver box wherein reposed a Hair of the Beard of the Prophet, bought in Mecca for an enormous sum; as well as an extremely holy and potent *hejab* or charm--a knuckle-bone of one of the holiest *marabouts* who had ever adorned this terrestrial sphere.

Surely no one could have sunk so low as to have stolen so holy a thing from the Sheikh's own person, and so he must have lost it. Gone it was, anyhow, and great was the commotion throughout the big *douar* (encampment), and great the rewards offered for its recovery... .

On the seventh evening from the day of the loss, El Hamel, that sad and silent man, sat, as usual, before the little, low black tent that was his, and looked remote and wise. Cross-legged, on his small striped carpet, silent and inscrutable, he made a goatskin thong for his sandal, and, anon, regarded Infinity and the doings of his fellow-men.

A goat-herd slave-boy sat and watched him, one, Moussa el R'Orab, Moussa the Crow.

Anon the old Sheikh, terribly upset by his loss, and still more upset by the evil augury of such a loss, strolled past the seated man who salaamed with deep respect.

The Sheikh paused, turned, seated himself beside his protégé, and settled down for a good *faddhl,* the meandering idle gossip so dear to his old heart--as to that of most Arabs. And a gossip with this fine-looking dignified man was particularly agreeable, as the poor fellow's infirmity prevented his taking an active part in it, and rendered him an accomplished listener.

The Sheikh talked on--about his loss; Suleiman the Strong strolled up, accompanied by his good friend, Hadji Abdul Salam, and from time to time various other prominent citizens of this tent-city joined the growing circle of listeners and respectful talkers.

It was the first time since the Sheikh's loss that the evening *faddhl* had taken place outside the tent of El Hamel, a thing that occurred fairly frequently... .

The talk dragged on interminably, and the great full moon rose and illuminated the oasis, and the groves of date palms, the hundreds of low black goatskin and felt camel-hair tents of various sizes, the flocks and herds of goats and camels, the gossiping groups, the women at the cooking-fires, the water-drawers at the *shaduf*, and wide ring of watchful sentries.

Suddenly the dumb man raised both of his clenched fists above his head, pointed to the moon, again to where the sun had set, and then threw his open hands dramatically towards the sky in an attitude of beseeching prayer.

Soon a mass of snow-white foam issued from his dumb lips and flecked his black beard, and his eyes rolled back until only the whites showed.

He looked terrible, and the Hadji Abdul Salam prepared to become professional. The grave Arabs stared in awed wonder at this manifestation of the work of *djinns*, spirits, or devils, and a deep silence fell.

The man seemed to recover, put his hand behind him into his tent, brought out a vessel of water, and drank.

He then stared with starting eyeballs at the ground before his feet. All eyes followed his gaze... . Nothing ... nothing but flat trodden sand, no scorpion, snake, nor hornéd toad was there.

The dumb man made passes with his hands above the spot at which he stared. He poured water on the ground, as though pouring libations to the memory of departed friends.

More passes, more pouring forth of water, more impassioned gesticulations toward the unanswering sky--and then--did their eyes deceive them? Or even as the man sat, with eyes and hands strained beseechingly aloft, did a gleam of silver show through the sand, and *did the lost box of the Sheikh rise up through the earth at their very feet,* before their very eyes, as they stared and stared incredulous?

It did.

The large audience sat for seconds as though turned to stone, and then a shudder ran through it, a gasping sigh escaped it, and, as the old Sheikh's quivering hand tentatively went out towards this magic thing, a great cry went up, so that men came running.

§ 4

The Sheikh summoned up his undoubted courage and seized the box firmly, fondled it, opened it, restored it to its place in his bosom--and then turned and embraced the dumb man as warmly and fervently as he had ever embraced his favourite wife.

"Let him be addressed as *Sidi*, and let him be known as '*the Magician*' henceforth," he said. "*The Dumb Magician--the Gift of Allah,*" and again embracing the Magician, he arose, cast a leathern bag of money into the man's lap, heavy Turkish *medjidies*--and retired to pray apart.

Tongues were loosened.

"No--there was no humbug about it. It was no conjuror's trick."

"His hands were above his head, and his eyes fixed on the sky when it happened."

"No, he had not flung the box there, nor had it been flung from the dark tent by an accomplice. It had suddenly appeared from below the sand and had quietly and steadily risen up to the surface and lain there, while all men watched."

"No, he had not buried it and then shoved it up with his toe. His feet had never been off the carpet on which he sat, and he had never once touched the sand from beneath which the box had risen... ."

It was a plain sheer miracle, worked in brilliant moonlight before the eyes of all! ...

The dumb man sat silent and still, with abstracted gaze, while the rest broke into chattering, gesticulating knots of bewildered men, arguing and shouting in wild excitement.

He then prostrated himself in prayer, upon the site of the miracle, his head upon the ground, and thus the awed crowd left him.

§ 5

"Yea, brother," agreed Hadji Abdul Salam, as he and Suleiman the Strong, followed at a respectful distance by one, Moussa el R'Orab, Moussa the Crow, goat-herd and admiring slave of El Hamel, walked away in the direction of the tent of the former.

"It is, as thou sayest, time that he died."

"I will let that accursed dog Abdullah el Jemmal, the camel-driver, know that unless this dumb devil and father of devils dies before the next moon, it will be the last moon that Abdullah sees," growled Suleiman, grinding his teeth. Not for nothing was he known as El Ma'ian--he who has the Evil Eye.

"He has marvellous powers, and the strength of ten," observed the *hakim*. "But there are draughts which are more powerful than he... . A little something of which I know, in his *cous-cous* or curds ..."

"The cunning dog has a portion of all his cooked food eaten by Moussa, the goat-boy, long before he tastes it," was the moody reply. "The hungry Moussa eats right willingly, knowing that none try to poison him who hath a food-taster... . No, it is a task for Abdullah... . A stab in the dark... ."

"And what would the Sheikh do?" smiled the good *hakim*.

"Impale Abdullah, living, on a stake, after hearing my evidence," replied Suleiman; "and thus shall we be rid of two nuisances at one blow... ."

The two gentlemen discussed the matter further, sitting at the door of Abdul Salam's tent, and--while Moussa the Crow, enthusiastic spy of El Hamel's, lay behind the tent and listened, feigning sleep--Suleiman sounded his host as to his willingness to consider a scheme, whereby their food should disagree with both the Sheikh and the Dumb Magician simultaneously, on the occasion of the next invitation to eat, extended by the Sheikh to his now glorified protégé. There would be no previous "tasting" then.

But Suleiman the Strong quickly saw that he was going too fast, and that he was proposing to Abdul Salam a risky thing, the doing of a dangerous deed for which the *hakim* saw no present reason, and in which he saw no personal profit either. And as he distrusted the Hadji as much as the Hadji distrusted him, Suleiman affected to be jesting, and turned the conversation to the miracle, to which he alluded as a rascally trick.

But it appeared that neither he nor the worthy doctor could offer the slightest suggestion as to how the "trick" was done, nor propound the vaguest outline of a theory in elucidation of the mystery.

Nor could any man of the few scoffers who were among the intimates, toadies, and followers of Suleiman the Strong; and the remainder of the tribe believed in the Dumb Magician to a man.

Nevertheless, there are those who, having beheld a similar miracle in other parts of the world, say that the miracle-worker excavates a hole at the required spot and then fills it with some material that expands rapidly and quickly when made wet--some such substance, for example, as *bhoosa,* yeast, sawdust, grain, or bran.

They aver that the miracle-monger presses the substance tightly together between four stones, covers it with a layer of sand, places the object (which is to spring miraculously out of the earth) upon the pressed expansive material, and lightly covers all with dust, earth and sand. The hour strikes, and soon after the material is wetted--up comes the hidden object.

It is said that Mother Earth has been safely delivered of many brazen gods in this wise, to the credit and enrichment of their even more brazen priests.

But those who talk thus of expansive "material" are obviously materialists, and certainly not of those to whom miracles appeal.... .

That night Moussa el R'Orab had something to tell El Hamel, the latter smiling gently as the boy spoke and gesticulated.

§ 6

As the infatuation of the old Sheikh waxed, so did the jealousy and wrath of El Ma'ian, known as Suleiman the Strong; and it grew apparent to all men that the same *qsar* could not much longer contain both him and El Hamel, the Foundling, the Dumb Magician, the Given of Allah.

Even to the Sheikh it grew clear that one of them must go; so truculent, surly, outrageous, did Suleiman increasingly become; and the old man's heart was heavy within him, for he loved his strong, wise Foundling, this big man of dignity and strength and magic power, whom he himself had found and saved; and he feared the forceful and influential Suleiman.

But one of them must go, or there would be quarrels and strife, parties and factions in that united tribe.... .

It was Suleiman the Strong who went.... .

And he nearly went by *sirath,* the bridge that spans Hell.... .

One evening, the sullen brooding temper that seemed to smoulder behind his cruel eyes, blazed up, and he was as one possessed by *djinns.*

The old Sheikh was standing by the lance (which, planted before his tent, bore his *bairaq* or flag and ensign of rule) talking to El Hamel and others of his favourites.

To him came Suleiman, a *mish'ab* camel-stick in his hand, and a black sullen scowl on his face. He was followed by fat and smiling Hadji Abdul Salam, Abdullah el Jemmal, and certain others.

Thrusting into the circle of gravely conversing elders, Suleiman confronted the Sheikh and poured forth a torrent of indignant and minatory words, pointing as he did so at the impassive, silent El Hamel--his outstretched shaking hand almost touching the latter's face.

The Sheikh rebuked him sharply, and raised his hand to point. "*Emshi!*" he snapped. "Go--thou growling dog--or by the Beard of the Prophet ..."

And then the impossible happened. For, even as the venerable Sheikh uttered the word "Beard," the jealousy-maddened Suleiman seized the long grey beard of the Sheikh in his left hand, shook him to and fro, and raised aloft his right hand, clutching the *mish'ab,* as though about to strike!

But it was Sidi el Hamel who struck.

With incredible swiftness and terrible force, he smote the impious madman with his clenched fist, and men gasped in wonder as Suleiman the Strong reeled staggering back, and fell, apparently dead.

"Bind him," stammered the Sheikh, almost speechless with rage at the unbelievable, unforgivable insult. "I will have him impaled, dead or alive ..." and the old man trembled with wrath and indignation.

Sidi el Hamel ventured to intervene. Touching his breast and forehead, he salaamed to the Sheikh, joined his hands in entreaty and then, stooping, seized Suleiman by the arm, and partly dragging, partly carrying him, bore him to where the women crowded round the *jalib* draw-well, and the *darraja* roller creaked and groaned above the '*idda* superstructure, as a harnessed camel hauled upon the well-rope.

At the foot of a kind of palisade of split palm-trunks that banked up the earth around the stone-built mouth of the well, he flung the man down, and made signs to those who had brought camel-ropes wherewith to bind him, that they should secure him to the wooden wall.

Tearing off Suleiman's *burnous*, El Hamel raised him to his feet, and held him upright while his outspread arms were lashed to the tops of two posts, and his feet secured to a stump by a stout cord that passed round it and them... .

What was the Magician about to do? Would he leave the sacrilegious villain, the almost parricidal criminal to die of starvation and thirst, or was he going to shoot the dog? Men crowded round, with growls of indignant wrath, and the women fled to the tents of their lords.

El Hamel dashed water, from a dug-out trough, in the face of Suleiman, and waited. In a few minutes he recovered his senses, opened his eyes, and stared about him. The Magician stepped back several yards and motioned the onlookers to stand aside. He drew his knife.

Ah! He was going to give an exhibition of knife-throwing, to plant the dagger in the black heart of the dog who had most foully insulted and outraged his Chief and Master, Allah's representative to the Tribe, the Prophet's Vicar upon earth, the Giver of Salt. It was well.

The Sheikh approached and stood beside El Hamel. That great man removed his *burnous*, balanced the dagger upon his hand, and with a swift movement--threw.

The silence was broken by the sound of a swift intaking of breath as the knife stuck and quivered, not in the broad breast of Suleiman the Strong, but in the wood beside his right ear.

El Hamel had missed for once! No matter--the more torture for the foul Suleiman.

With a merry laugh, Hadji Abdul Salam tendered his own knife that El Hamel might throw again.

"This one balances well, Sidi," said he.

El Hamel took the knife, balanced it upon the palm of his great hand, and, with a lightning swoop of his huge arm--threw.

The knife quivered--in wood; beside the left ear of Suleiman the Strong.

Again there was the sound of swift intaking of breath, and the good *hakim* giggled like a girl.

"Try again, my son, and may Allah guide thine arm," said the Sheikh, and placed his great silver-hilted dagger in the hand of El Hamel.

"Make an end, thou squinting, cross-eyed dumb dog," cried Suleiman the Strong, and stared hardily at his slayer, though his face had taken on a sickly greenish hue.

Once again the Magician poised the knife and his great powerful body and--threw.

With a thud the heavy knife stuck in the post above Suleiman's head, and all but touched it. The three knives seemed to hold and frame his face in glistening metal. And then it dawned upon the watchers that El Hamel was *not* missing his mark, and all men marvelled. Suleiman the Strong stood like a statue. Abdullah el Jemmal respectfully tendered a long lean blade. A moment later it stood out from beside the shoulder of Suleiman, its point buried in wood, its blade an inch from his flesh... .

Another stuck exactly opposite that... . A dozen knives were offered to the thrower, and in as many minutes stood in pairs on either side of the motionless man.

Suddenly he cried, "Enough! Make an end, in the Name of Allah the Merciful, the Compassionate," and, as the thrower raised another knife, he collapsed and hung forward, fainting, in his bonds.

But El Hamel had heard from Moussa the Crow of plotted poisonings and the encompassing of the death of the kindly Sheikh by the vilest treachery and ingratitude.

Striding to the man, he again dashed water in his face, and soon Suleiman the Strong was strong once more, and held himself erect.

"Make an end, Sidi," he said. "In the Name of the Prophet make an end."

"*As thou wouldest have made an end,*" screamed Moussa el R'Orab, pointing--and Hadji Abdul Salam eyed the boy sharply.

El Hamel pulled out the Sheikh's knife from where it stuck above Suleiman's head, and Suleiman closed his eyes and awaited the cutting of his throat.

El Hamel took the knife to where the old Sheikh stood, and returned it to him, touching his forehead and breast as he did so.

He then made the sign of a man putting a rifle to his shoulder to fire it, and pointed to his tent, and Moussa the Crow sped thither and brought him the fine Italian magazine-rifle that the Sheikh had bestowed upon his favourite.

Men smiled and nodded. So this was how Suleiman the Strong was to die!

Throwing the rifle to his shoulder, El Hamel pointed it at the face of Suleiman the Strong.

"Look upon thy death, thou dog," cried the Sheikh, and Suleiman opened his eyes.

"*Now* make an end, Sidi," he begged, "in the Sacred Names of God," and El Hamel fired rapidly five times.

Suleiman the Strong sank to the ground--untouched--the cords that fastened his wrists severed against the posts, and hanging idly.

El Hamel pointed out into the desert.

"Yea, go, thou dog," cried the old Sheikh. "Thou bitter tentless dog, go forth and scavenge. With nothing that is thine, begone within the hour... ." And El Hamel nodded in approval, drew his hand across his throat significantly, and pointed again.

The feet of Suleiman the Strong were untied, and with blows and curses he was driven to his tents.

When he departed, well within the allotted hour, he was followed by a flight of stones, some of the best-aimed of which came from the hand of the good physician, Abdul Salam...
.

But Hadji Abdul Salam thereafter fancied that El Hamel eyed him unduly, and perhaps more critically, than a *mou'abbir,* a pious and learned man, should be eyed by a desert Foundling... .

And so the fame and honour of Sidi el Hamel, the Magician, the Given of Allah, grew apace, and his standing and importance in the tribe waxed with them.

More and more the Sheikh depended upon him, and more and more the Sidi strove for the common weal.

He trained riflemen until a few were almost as skilful as himself, many were as good as Marbruk ben Hassan, the Lame, hitherto undisputed best shot of the Tribe, and all (who possessed rifles) were far above the desert average.

Dumb though he was, he also taught them, patiently and slowly, how to attack unscathed, instead of charging wildly into a hail of bullets.

After getting squads of fighting-men to lie in line, flat upon the ground, he would make a few wriggle forward, while the rest aimed their rifles at the imaginary foe; and these halt and aim their rifles while yet others wriggled forward; and so on.

He taught the enthusiastic and devoted fighting-men the arts of volley-firing and fire-control. He made a whistle of wood, like a short *quaita,* and gave signals with it, standing afar off.

He taught selected leaders an elementary drill by signals, and these taught their followers. He showed the horsemen and camel-men many things that they did not know, such as the treatment of ailments, and he scowled angrily and dangerously upon any whom he found saddling a galled beast and neglecting back-sores.

Hadji Abdul Salam, who knew nothing more than the administering of *zarnikh,* an acid concoction, to sick camels, and the muttering of charms over sick horses, looked on with merry laughing face and unsmiling eyes. El Hamel also cultivated the Sheikh's Soudanese soldier-slaves, between whom and the Bedouin fighting-men there is always jealousy, and made a small camel-corps of them, a nucleus of the *élite.*

He also made smiling overtures to an aged wonder called "Yakoub-who-goes-without-water" and his family. He and his three ancient brothers were famous for their gift of living, when others died, if lost in the waterless desert, or on finding the waterhole dried up, at the end of a long and terrible journey.

An ordinary man will make a *girba* of water last five or six days in winter and three in summer, but Yakub and his brothers would double the time--and, as a camel can only carry four *girbas,* this is a valuable gift... . Later El Hamel made these men into a wonderful Desert Intelligence Department, and, as poor old worthless beggars, they hung about oases, *douars, qsars* and desert camps, learning much and bringing invaluable information... .

§ 7

And when the day dawned, of which the old Sheikh feared he would not see the night, he gathered his *ekhwan* and elders and chief men of the Tribe about his couch, and bade them regard the Sidi el Hamel as Regent of the tribe during the many remaining years of the childhood and youth of his son, and commanded that his *aba* should descend upon the shoulders of the Sidi during the boy's minority.

Upon the Sidi's hand he placed his ring, graven with the sacred seal, in token of his power, and lifting up his voice he blessed him in the Name of Allah and of Mahomet his Prophet, ending with the words, "*Rahmat ullahi Allahim*--the peace of God be upon him."

And the first "Amen" was that of Hadji Abdul Salam.

A little later, the old man was gathered to his fathers, and was buried with great honour and much mourning in the *kouba* by the little mosque, which stood near the oasis and *qsar*, the headquarters and depôt of this semi-nomadic tribe.

Shortly afterwards came the great fast of Ramzan, and at the end of that weary month, and on the occasion of the great feast that marked its termination, the Sidi (accepted by all men as Sheikh Regent) worked a new and wondrous miracle.

He worked it upon himself. For, as all stood awaiting the appearance of the new moon of the next month, he strode forth before them, and with upraised arms stretched out his hands towards the horizon.

He then turned toward the watching, waiting assembly and pointed to his mouth. What was about to happen? All stared and wondered in silence.

The moon rose and in that instant the miracle was worked. The dumb Sheikh, Sidi el Hamel, the Magician, opened his mouth, and in deep sonorous voice intoned the *shehada*.

Across the vast silence of the desert and the awe-stricken throng, rolled the solemn words, "*As hadu illa Illaha ill Allah wa as hadu inna Mahommed an rasul Allah*," and, as he turned in the direction of the *kubla* at Mecca and recited the *fatha*, the opening *sura* of the Q'ran, the people fell upon their faces.

The Dumb had spoken.

Thereafter the Sheikh, Sidi el Hamel, spoke seldom and briefly. He uttered only short orders, curt replies, concise comments. It almost seemed as though speech hurt him, and that his long silence--perhaps the silence of a lifetime--caused his Arabic to be halting, like the speech of a man who has sojourned in foreign parts for many years, speaking not the language of his people once in all that time.

But now that the miracle had come to pass and he could speak, his rule and influence became yet more powerful; and more easily he trained his fighting-men; rebuked and punished evil-doers; gave orders and instruction in agricultural industry, animal management, tribal policies, and pursued his strange fads of health-preservation, sanitation, care of domestic beasts, and justice to all prisoners and captives, mercy to slaves, women, and other animals.

Nor would he ever act as *Imam* and lead the prayers, leaving that pious duty to Hadji Abdul Salam, who on such occasions contrived to look as holy as Sidi Mohammed ben Ali, the Reformer of Islam, in spite of his round, fat, laughing face, sleepy narrow eyes and loose lips--for was he not a *hadji*, a man who had made the *hadj*, the journey to Mecca, the House of Allah?

Was he not a *zawia*-trained *khouan*, a holy man indeed?

Who could doubt it, that heard his sonorous call to prayer, "*Haya alla Salat! Haya alla falah!*"--and his leading of the *fedjr, dhuhr, asr, mogreb* and *asha* prayers at morning, midday, afternoon, sunset and night?

Who so fanatical a good Moslem as he, and so fierce against the *Ahl Kitab*--the People of the Book (Jews and Christians) and all other unmentionable *kafirs*.

So good Hadji Abdul Salam, the *hakim,* was the chief *imam,* and, making himself the Sheikh's shadow and echo, aspired to be the Sheikh's *Wakil* and *Wazir.*

§ 8

It was not very long before the value of the Sheikh el Hamel's innovations was proven. One of his wonderful old desert-men, Yakoub-who-can-live-without-water, arrived one night on foot, his camel lying dead a day's journey to the north-west, with news of the great Touareg band that made this the southernmost point of its annual journey in search of plunder.

If unresisted by the Tribe it would rest and feast fatly at the expense of its unhappy hosts, set them to pack camel-fodder, have the date-harvest loaded on to the *hamla* baggage-camels of the Tribe, make a selection of children, young men, and maidens, and depart with such of the camels, horses, asses, goats, rugs, clothing, and money as could not be previously removed or hidden.

Slaughter there might or might not be--probably not very much, and that only in a quite playful spirit... .

Wholesale flight was out of the question. What tribe burdened with women and children, tents, property, goats, asses, and slow *hamla* camels, can flee before an unencumbered *harka* of fierce hawk-like robbers, mounted on swift *mehari* that travel like the wind?

The Forgotten of God, the Blue-Veiled Silent Ones, would leave all their previously gathered booty at a depôt, guarded by their precious and faithful black slaves (whom they breed on slave-farms, like cattle); and their lightning raid upon the fleeing tribe would be like that of eagles upon chickens. Moreover the extra trouble given to these Lords of the Desert would not be easily atoned... .

The *ekhwan* gathered at the tent of the Sheikh el Hamel, and each spoke his mind in turn, the oldest first.

Some were for following ancient custom and leaving the *douar* to unhindered plundering by the Touareg. The sooner they got what they wanted, the sooner they would be gone. The less they were thwarted, the less bloodthirsty would they be. The very pick of the youths, girls, and children might be sent off into the desert, with the very best of the camels, horses, asses and goats--but not too many must go, lest the Touareg wax suspicious and torture the elders until someone break down and confess... .

Some were for drawing up as imposing an array of armed camel-men, horsemen and infantry as was possible, and letting them hover near, in full view of the Touareg, in the hope that, as sometimes happened, the robbers would decide not to over-provoke so dangerous a force, but to rob reasonably and justly, leaving the victims a fair residue of their property, the bare means of subsistence, and many of their young relatives.

One or two, including Marbruk ben Hassan the Lame, showing that the Sheikh el Hamel's lessons in Minor Tactics of War had borne fruit, actually wanted to put up a genuine fight--receive the visitors with volleys of rifle-fire, and if they did not succeed in driving them off, see the thing through and die in defence of tent and child.

"And what of tent and child when you are dead?" inquired the Sheikh el Hamel.

Marbruk ben Hassan the Lame shrugged his enormous shoulders.

"What of them in any case, Sidi?" he asked. "Shall our eyes behold their defilement or, closed in brave death, see nothing of their shame and misery?"

"What says the good Hadji Abdul Salam, the Learned and Holy One?" asked the Sheikh.

The Learned and Holy One thought it would be a sound move for all the wealthy and important men of the Tribe--themselves there present, in fact--to clear out for a space, with all that was theirs. After a sojourn in the desert, away to the south-east, they could return, console the survivors, and help to clear up the mess... .

It seemed sound sense to several aged patriarchs, who had seen too much of the Touareg and his ways to have any desire to see more.

"They cut off the hands of my little son and the feet of my favourite wife," wailed one white-bearded ancient. "Had I fled instead of fighting, they would have been alive now... ."

"Yea, Father," murmured Marbruk ben Hassan, "and the little son would have been a grandfather and the fair woman a toothless hag... . We die but once... ."

And all having spoken and given the counsel that their experience, their courage, their hope and their caution prompted, the Sheikh el Hamel lifted up his voice and gave decision.

"We will not flee," he said. "We will not send the best of what is ours out into the desert. We will not leave the Tribe and go afar off with what is ours. We will not make a show of strength and watch the enemy while he robs us. We will not defend the oasis... ."

All stared in silence upon this enigmatical strong man, the Sheikh Regent of the Tribe, the Sheikh Magician. "We will go and find our enemy," he concluded, "and fall upon him and destroy him utterly."

And in the silence that followed, Marbruk ben Hassan fired his rifle into the air.

"*Wallahi!*" he cried. "Our Sheikh is a *man,* by Allah!"

"We will leave not one of them alive to return and tell the tale," said the Sheikh again.

"*Inshallah,*" murmured the *ekhwan* doubtfully, and the Sheikh strode away, calling for the chosen leaders of the fighting-men and the aged scout Yakoub, who should be their guide.

To these he made a brief speech in short curt sentences, and illustrated his meaning by the ancient method of the writing-on-the-sand. Around a stone which represented the Touareg camp he drew a circle with his knife and then a smaller circle within it, and then another. And to each leader-of-a-score he spoke in turn, each hearing his words, smiling, and replying,

"*Hamdulillah!* It shall be so. *Inshallah!*"

An hour later these men, each followed by a score of men for whom he also had drawn a writing-on-the-sand, assembled at the north-west corner of the oasis and, led by the Sheikh el Hamel and the ancient guide, rode forth in orderly array by the light of the moon.

CHAPTER III. EL HABIBKA

Once again was it proven that attack is the best defence and that an invaluable principle of strategy is expressed in the apophthegm, "Put yourself in your enemy's place, and think as he would think."

The Sheikh Magician was well aware that the Touareg attacks at dawn, and therefore expects to be attacked at dawn.

For this reason he attacked at evening, when cooking-fires were alight, food being prepared, "tents" being made with camel-rug and sage-bush, camels being fed and watered at the *ghadir,* and all men busy.

Well aware, moreover, that the correct and orthodox attack is a wild rush and a hack-and-stab mêlée, wherein mounted men expect to ride down and overcome dismounted men, unprepared and at a disadvantage, he made a most incorrect and unorthodox attack, wherein a complete circle of hidden riflemen opened fire and shot down an enemy who rushed about in great excitement and in full view, as he prepared to receive the said wild rush of mounted men--that never came.

Instead of this, an ever-closing circle of accurate rifle-fire ringed them about, and offered no concentrated body of foemen upon which they might charge.

Always many were firing while some were crawling nearer.

Always many were crawling nearer while yet more were firing.

And from every point of the compass came the thudding bullets and the stealthily approaching men.

At which point of this unbroken circle should they rush? Where was the great ring thickest--or thinnest? ... Nowhere.

From time to time a Targui brave, with a shout of "*Follow me! Ul-Ul-Ul-Allah Akbar!*" would dash forward at the head of a few swordsmen, toward some part of the ring of fire, only to fall with his followers ere steel could be blooded.

And, from point to point of the attack, rushed the Sheikh Magician, and wherever he paused and emptied the magazine of his rifle, men fell fast. He seemed to be everywhere at once, and to see everything at a glance. He both fought and led.

He alone kept to his feet, and scarcely a man of his well-trained force raised more than his head from the ground, even when wriggling forward a few yards that he might fire again from behind bush or stone yet nearer to the foe--silhouetted against his camp-fires or striving to capture and mount his beast.

Thus no attacker shot his brother on the opposite side of the circle, and no attacker suffered from the ill-aimed fire of the Touareg who endeavoured to imitate the tactics of their assailants.

When, here and there, an excited follower of the Sheikh Magician, spurred by his presence to a desire to distinguish himself, would kneel up to rise beside his leader--he found himself flung back to earth and to remembrance of the fact that his sole business was to creep and shoot, to creep ever nearer and to shoot ever straighter, until disciplined co-operative tactics defeated uncoordinated effort, and the well-used rifle asserted its superiority over the sword, the spear and the casual gun.

And so the net drew tighter, the end came in sight, and the cool brain of the Sheikh Magician triumphed over the hot courage and tradition-bolstered invincibility of the terrible Touareg.

Not till the battle was fairly won and the victory inevitable, did human nature triumph over discipline, and his followers, with a wild yell, rise as one man and rush upon the doomed remnant of their foe.

And not till this moment did they sustain a casualty.... .

§ 2

As the moon looked down upon the scene of the battle, and beheld the Sheikh's followers, drunk with joy, intoxicated with the heady fumes of Victory, feasting and rejoicing about the camp-fires that had been lighted by their dead or captured foes, it saw a sight more horrible than that presented by the corpse of any man slain in the fight, more horrible than that of all the corpses piled together, and they were many.

A man had been tortured. His torturers must have been at their foul and ghastly work, even as the first shot was fired by the encircling foe, for he was still incredibly alive, although he had no face and was otherwise mutilated beyond belief or description.

With his own rifle the Sheikh Magician put an end to this defiled creature's sufferings, and then turned to where the shouts of some of his followers indicated that another victim of the bestial savagery of the Touareg had been found.

This man, trussed like a fowl, had evidently been awaiting his turn. He was untouched by knife, but almost dead from starvation, thirst and cruel treatment.

Him, the Sheikh Magician made his own special care. Perhaps he thought of the time when he himself had been saved from death at the eleventh hour, and would mete out to this apparently dying man the measure that had then been his.

With his own hand he poured water from his own *zemzi-mayah* upon the face and mouth of the Touareg's prisoner, cut the cords that bound him, and chafed his limbs. As he did so, his face was suffused with a fine glow of humane and tender sympathy, adorned with a look of brotherly love, and animated with a new and generous fire.

Raising the body into a sitting posture, he put his arms about it, and embraced it,--a Biblical picture of an Eastern father holding the body of his dead son.

Beneath the mask of Arab dignity and gravity, a repressed soul shone forth and sought brief expression in a moment of wild emotionalism.

The moon has seen the fierce tigress paw her helpless cub, the savage lion lick its wounded mate, the terrible and appalling gorilla weep above its slaughtered brother, and it beheld this fierce and blood-stained avenger sit among the dead and croon nurse-like above this inanimate salvage of the slaughter he had made.

Encamped near the scene of his victory--the bodies of his foes given to the vulture and the jackal, the wounds of his followers tended by his own hand--the Sheikh set himself to win back to life the man whom he had saved from the knife of the torturer.

Scores and scores slain, dozens yet dying, and this one to be nursed back to life even as he himself had been; this one to be dragged back from the portals of the House of the Dead, to be snatched from the jaws of Death.

As he himself had done, the almost-dead man made a brave struggle for life, and, one day, opened his eyes in staring wonder upon his saviour.

The Sheikh laid his finger on the bloodless lips, sent all men away, and remained long alone with his piece of human salvage from the ocean of the desert, and its storm of war.... .

They named him *El Nazil,* the Newcomer, and later *El Habibka,* the Friend, as he became the chosen Friend of the Sheikh.

And in honour of his incredible victory over the dread Touareg, they gave the Sheikh el Hamel the name of *El Kebir*--the Lion.

And even as the old Sheikh had delighted to honour his foundling, El Hamel, the Gift of Allah, so did the Sheikh Magician delight to honour him whom he had thus saved and brought back to life.

When he and his fighting-men returned to the oasis-encampment, to be welcomed by the heart-stirring "*Ulla-la-een! Ulla-la-een!*"--the wild shrill trilling of the women, who screamed aloud as they rattled forefingers up and down against the teeth of their opened mouths--he sat the man upon his right hand, decked him in clean robes of respect, and with his own hand fed him, from time to time, with tit-bits from his own savoury stew of goat.

The tribe saw that their great Sheikh, the Great Magician, the Gift of Allah--yea, the Beloved of Allah the Merciful, the Compassionate--delighted to honour the Unknown, even as he himself had been honoured when unknown; and the tribe realized that a great bond of sympathy existed between the Sheikh and the Tentless One, in that the latter was dumb, even as the Sheikh himself had been!

Perhaps the Sheikh Magician would cure him of his affliction, as he had miraculously cured himself? ...

And gradually it was borne in upon all men that the second Unknown had much else in common with their Great Sheikh, for he too was a very remarkable magician, a marvellous shot, a mighty horseman and horse-master, a great physician, and a man of curious and wondrous skill with his hands.

Like the Great Sheikh himself, the man knew that special form of *rabah* in which the empty hand is clenched, the thumb upon the first and second closed fingers, and a blow is delivered by shooting forward the hand in a straight line from the shoulder.

This was a very fine and terrible form of *rabah;* for a man may thus be smitten senseless, and apparently dead, by an unarmed smiter; or in a few minutes be beaten into a blood-stained feeble wreck, with closed eyes, scattered teeth, and horrid cuts and bruises.

Perhaps the Great Sheikh and this Foundling came of the same tribe--some distant southern tribe of great skill in war, great magic, great strength, and great wisdom?

§ 3

Public attention was first drawn to the remarkable powers of the Foundling, the Tentless One, by his calmly and quietly producing cartridges from the ears of Marbruk ben Hassan the Lame.

Marbruk was one of the best shots in the tribe--nearly as good as the Great Sheikh himself--for he had wonderful eyesight, and great strong hands, arms and shoulders.

Perhaps his terrible lameness led him to practise more than most men with the rifle, the one weapon he could use, since he could only hobble about like a half-crushed spider.

One day, as the Sheikh and certain elders and leaders of the fighting-men sat and *faddhled* before the Sheikh's tent, this Marbruk sidled up, patted his loved rifle, showed an empty pouch, and sighed that he had no ammunition.

Promptly the Sheikh's favourite, the Foundling, rose, and, thrusting forth his hand from beneath his *burnous,* produced a cartridge from Marbruk's ear!

Men stared open-mouthed.

He produced another; and then one from the other ear! Men gasped. Marbruk ben Hassan turned almost pale.

The Unknown took two more from beneath the camel-hair ropes that bound Marbruk's *haik.* Marbruk sat down and perspired, and an awed whisper of *Magic! Magic!* rose from the gaping onlookers.

The Foundling concluded this astounding performance by extending an empty hand and a bare arm--and extracting a cartridge from the circumambient air!

He then resumed his seat beside the quite unperturbed Sheikh, who smiled tolerantly as upon the creditable effort of a promising beginner in the science and art of the Magician.

§ 4

For long, El Habibka remained dumb, and when various of the *ekhwan* asked the Sheikh Magician if he would not cure him of his dumbness, the Sheikh replied that such was his hope and his intention.

He explained further that El Habibka was of his own Tribe, from the South; a tribe of men mighty in magic and in fighting, in knowledge and in wisdom,--but much afflicted by the Djinns of the Desert, jealous of the gifts so richly bestowed by Allah, the commonest of all their afflictions being this almost incurable dumbness which came upon them permanently when sick almost unto death.

However the Sheikh had little doubt that he would be able to work a cure in time.

When this was effected it would be found that El Habibka's speech would be halting and strange, even as his own had been since his recovery and return from the very Gates of the House of Death.

He assured the *ekhwan* and the leaders-of-twenty, when *faddhling* with them, that El Habibka would prove a very tower of strength to the Tribe, wondrous wise in Council, a lion in battle, the equivalent of ten wise elders and a hundred warriors.

He also delighted in making El Habibka display his astounding powers with the rifle, with the little-gun, with the knife, and with a long thin cord at the end of which was a slip-knot and loop; his superlative skill on the back of the wildest stallion; his wonderful adroitness and strength at *rabah;* and, above all, his magic.

And indeed the magic of El Habibka swiftly reduced the open-mouthed, staring onlookers to awed wonder, leaving them speechless, save for murmurs of "*Allahu Akbar!*" and "*Bismillah!*"

The things he could do were unbelievable until actually seen. Nor was he any less a physician than the Sheikh Magician himself, for his first great cure, known to all men, was followed by many.

This first instance was the saving of none other than the daughter of the late Sheikh, the Sitt Leila Nakhla, the "Beautiful Young Palm Tree," herself. She had been suddenly possessed of a devil which had entered her head, causing terrible pain and making the head feel as though it would swell to bursting.

To avert this catastrophe, she had bound a stout copper wire so tightly around her head, that it was buried in the flesh. But this gave no relief. The Sitt Leila Nakhla had then sent a message, praying that the Sheikh Magician would come and exercise his wondrous art upon her, or she would die.

If she did not die she would kill herself, for the pain was unbearable and she had no sleep.

The old woman who brought the message prostrated herself at the feet of the Sheikh el Hamel el Kebir,--as he sat on his carpet before his tent and talked to the dumb El Habibka in a low voice,--and implored him to cure the Sitt, her mistress.

And the Sheikh had bidden El Habibka exercise his magic. Nothing loth, that doctor of medicine and science had followed old Bint Fatma to the tent of the Sitt Leila Nakhla, where she lay dressed and adorned in her best, on dyed rugs of camel-hair and soft cushions, awaiting the coming of the Sheikh el Hamel el Kebir.

Seizing her hot hands, El Habibka had stared long into her affrighted eyes.

He had then uttered strange sounds, as the dumb sometimes do; and, with quick passes and snatches, had removed from the girl's very brain--by way of her ears, nostril, mouth and eyes respectively, a rusty buckle, a pebble, a large splinter of wood, and, what was probably the worst offender, a big and lusty beetle, kicking and buzzing like the Devil, whose emissary it doubtless was.

The horror-stricken girl shrieked and almost fainted away.

El Habibka then removed the tightly twisted wire, as no longer necessary, and, presumably to ensure that the breath of life should remain in her, placed his lips firmly upon the girl's, moved them with a slight sound, and then retired swiftly from the tent... .

The Sitt Leila Nakhla never had another headache from that hour, and the reputation of El Habibka grew daily.

Men wondered that the Sheikh el Hamel el Kebir was not jealous, and that he did not slit the throat of one who bade fair to eclipse him as a healer.

Yet far otherwise was it, for the Sheikh moved not without El Habibka, and kept him ever at his side when, after prayers, he sat and *faddhled* before his tent at the hour of sunset, peace and food.

Few sang the praises of El Habibka louder than the pious Hadji Abdul Salam, and none of those who wondered at this fact knew of the Hadji's long and quiet talks with one Abdullah el Jemmal, the camel-man, and the really tempting suggestions that the Hadji made for the poor camel-man's enrichment.

§ 5

The hope and expectation of the Sheikh el Hamel el Kebir that his protégé, El Habibka, would be restored to completest health and fullest enjoyment of all his faculties, was fulfilled--with a strange dramatic suddenness--for Allah suddenly gave him the gift of speech that he might save the life of his preserver!

It happened thus.

One evening, the Sheikh el Hamel el Kebir, El Habibka, the Hadji Abdul Salam, old Dawad Fetata, Marbruk ben Hassan and others of the *ekhwan* and chief leaders of the fighting-men had strolled beneath the palms of the oasis, after the *mogh'reb* prayer by the little white mosque.

Casting their eyes over the irrigation-plots, green with their crops of onions, radishes, bisset, pumpkins, and barley; over the rows and piles of sand-bricks drying in the sun; over the groups of women at the well, in their long indigo-blue, scarlet or orange *tobhs*; over the jostling, noisy, dust-raising flocks of goats at the water-runnels and troughs, the chieftains strode *faddhling*.

Anon darkness fell, the group dissolved (savoury smells of cooking being the solvent), and the Sheikh el Hamel el Kebir returned to his tent, passing as he did so, one before which the Sitt Leila Nakhla sat, with her young brother and two black slave-girls--that she might see and smile as usual at the Sheikh, when he went by.

The boy sprang up and ran to El Hamel, reaching up to play with his big silver-hilted dagger in its curly-ended silver sheath; and, with her soul in her eyes, the Sitt smiled upon the great and splendid man as he knelt and embraced the boy, the future Sheikh, of whom he was fond and proud as a father.

From the door of his tent El Habibka watched the scene, an enigmatic smile playing beneath his beard, and softening his hard eyes as he studied the lovely Leila.

Suddenly he shouted three words in a strange tongue and snatched at the belt of his *gandoura,* as an almost naked man bounded from the black shadow of the palms, straight at the back of the kneeling Sheikh--a long knife gleaming in his right hand.

At the sound of El Habibka's cry--the words of which he evidently understood--the Sheikh swung round, keeping his body between the assailant and the child, but not rising to his feet.

The girl sprang forward like a tigress; up flashed the keen knife of the assassin, and the Sheikh's great fist shot out and smote him terribly, below the breast-bone. As he staggered back, El Habibka's pistol banged twice, and only then the Sheikh rose to his feet.

But El Habibka had spoken, a dozen people had heard, and the Sheikh had understood.

For the moment, this portent was forgotten, as the overwrought girl threw herself upon the Sheikh's breast and entwined her arms about his neck, the boy clung to him in alarm, and men rushed up to seize the murderer.

Gently pushing the girl and child from him, the Sheikh shouted that the assassin was not to be further injured, just as El Habibka seized the wrist of Hadji Abdul Salam, even as the point of that pious man's knife was entering the murderer's neck at the very spot for the neat severing of the jugular vein.

It was surprising with what force the Hadji struggled to execute justice, and with what a remarkable twist El Habibka caused him to drop his knife and yelp with pain.

It was almost as though the Hadji did not want the man to be taken alive.

It was soon seen that El Habibka's two shots had crippled and not killed; and that when the captive had recovered from the Sheikh's terrible blow, he would be able to give an account of himself. Or rather would be in a condition to respond to treatment designed and applied with a view to persuading him to do so.

And when water had been thrown over the man, and, tied to a palm-tree behind the Sheikh's tent, he had been left in the excellent care of El R'Orab the Crow--men's minds were free to turn to the more wonderful, if less exciting, event of the evening--the fact that El Habibka the Silent, the Dumb, the Afflicted of Allah, had been the object of the Mercy of Allah, and had been given speech that he might save his master.

None slept that night, and great was the *faddhling* round every fire--especially when the news spread that the assassin had at length yielded to treatment and confessed that he had been sent on his errand of death by the great Emir, Mohammed Bishari bin Mustapha Korayim abd Rabu, at the instance and plotting of one, Suleiman the Strong, now his *Wazir, Wakil,* and Commander-in-Chief combined!

Curiously enough, the Sheikh el Hamel el Kebir did not torture the assassin--either for the purpose of extracting information from him or in punishment for his murderous attempt.

The sight of certain magics, worked before his astonished eyes by the Sheikh and by El Habibka, appeared to convince him that confession would be good for his soul, even more than the contemplation of preparations for his painful and protracted physical dissolution.

And his story was interesting, particularly those chapters of it that bore upon the professed intention of the Emir Mohammed Bishari bin Mustapha Korayim abd Rabu to assemble his army and make Suleiman the Strong the tributary Sheikh of the Tribe from which he had been cast forth, and to add the Tribe to the small confederation of tribes which the Emir ruled... .

As he began to gain strength and hope of life, the hireling murderer grew more communicative, and under the influence of magnanimous kindness, brain-shaking exhibitions of magic, and the ever-present fear of ghastly torture, became as ardently and earnestly the willing tool of the Sheikh Magician, as he had been of Suleiman the Strong, and the Emir to whom Suleiman had escaped.

Many and long were the councils held by the Sheikh, El Habibka, wise old Dawad Fetata, Marbruk ben Hassan, and the elect of the *ekhwan* and fighting-men; and after a decision had been reached, a great *mejliss* was held, a great public meeting, which was harangued in turn by the wise men and the fighting-men of the Inner Council, while the Sheikh gravely nodded approval of the eloquence of each.

At the end of the meeting, the hitherto dumb El Habibka arose, and in a voice creaking and rusty from disuse, and with words halting, and sometimes almost incomprehensible, cried aloud,

"Hamdulillah! Hamdulillah! Ana mabsut! Ana mabsut!" and, having recited the *fatha* with wide-stretched arms, he fell upon his face before the Sheikh, his body quivering with sobs, or the wild hysterical laughter of a joy too great to bear... .

And the decision of the council approved by the *mejliss* was that at the coming season of sowing, when all the tribes scatter far and wide for the planting of barley for the next year's food-crop, the Tribe should migrate and travel steadily north-west toward that wonderful land where there was known to be a hundred square miles of palm-trees and of all green things, a land flowing with milk and honey, Allah's own Paradise on earth... .

It had always been toward the north-west that the Sheikh had looked, and of the north-west that he had talked, night after night, to the *faddhling* circle and to the eagerly listening El Habibka.

Meanwhile, Yakoub-who-can-go-without-water and his shrivelled colleagues disappeared, and none of them was seen for many days. By the time the first of them returned, much of the organizing work preparatory to the migration had been completed, and the Tribe was almost ready for another of its many moves.

This exodus, however, was to differ from former ones, in that the Tribe was going to move as an army that is accompanied by a big baggage-and-sutler train, instead of a straggling mob of men, women and children, and their flocks and herds.

Four drilled and disciplined Camel Corps, proceeding as an advance-guard, two flank guards and a powerful rearguard, were to form the sides of a mighty oblong; and inside this oblong, the Tribe and its animals would march, each family being responsible for its own beasts and commissariat... .

Great was the sound of the querns throughout the *qsar* as the women of every tent laboured in pairs at the grinding of barley-meal for the filling of the sacks for the journey; and high rose the prices of pitch and *zeit* oil, as leaky *girbas* were made water-tight.

Day-long and night-long was the making and sewing of *khoorgs* for loads of dates and of camel-fodder, since the Tribe would "live on the country" where it could, and be self-supporting where it must, and every fighting-man's date-fed trotting-camel eats a sack of dates a day.

It was a hard and busy time, but a spirit of cheerfulness prevailed, for change is the salt of life, and great was the trust reposed by the Tribe in their wonderful Sheikh, so full of ideas, of organizing power, and of energy; and in his trusted lieutenant El Habibka, now Commander-in-Chief of the fighting-men.

It was felt that the Sheikh Regent would safely and surely lead the Tribe to the conquest or occupation of the Great Oasis, and that he who had defeated a great Touareg *harka,* would defeat anybody who opposed their passage... .

CHAPTER IV. THE CONFEDERATION

A few miles from the Pass of Bab-el-Haggar, Yoluba, the black Wadai slave and fighting-man, nearly seven feet high, and famed for long sight among desert men famous for their long sight, sat sideways on his camel that he might watch the horizon to which all other backs were turned.

He was alone, far in the rear of the rear-guard, behind which rode the Sheikh el Hamel el Kebir.

From time to time, Yoluba of the Strong Eyes would halt and turn his camel about, the while he stared with unwavering gaze along the broad track made by the migrating Tribe... . Suddenly he whirled about, waved his long *mish'ab* stick towards his camel's head, and sent it along at its top pace, until he drew alongside the Sheikh.

"One comes," he said gutturally, from deep down in his thick throat. "A small man on a big camel. In great haste. It will be Yakoub-who-goes-without-water."

At an order from the Sheikh, the rear-guard halted, turned about and deployed. Camels were *barraked* in line, and behind each knelt a man, his loaded rifle levelled... . A piece of drill introduced by the Sheikh, and much enjoyed, when once grasped, by his fighting-men... .

Yakoub it proved to be, and with a tale of weight to tell.

"Well done, thou good and faithful servant," quoth the Sheikh, on hearing it. "Ten silver *medjidies* and the best camel thou canst pick, if all go well... . And so the great Emir will do even as I did unto the Touaregs, and attack at the hour of camp-making, will he?"

"Ya, Sidi! But we will ring the camp about with rifles and await him, *Inshallah!*" grinned Yakoub.

"We will do better than that, Father Yakoub," replied the Sheikh, and sent three of his specially mounted messengers to El Habibka commanding the advance-guard, and to Marbruk ben Hassan and to Yussuf Latif Fetata, commanding the flank-guards, respectively.

The orders were simple. The vast caravan was to push on at its best pace through the deep dunes and vile loose sand that was the only way--churned to fine dust by fifty centuries of caravan-traffic in a rainless land--through the pass between the Bab-el-Haggar rocks, a few miles of precipitous out-crop over which camels could not go.

At the far side of the pass, the advance-guard and flank-guards were to halt and await the coming of the rear-guard, while the caravan pushed on.

§ 2

A few hours before sunset, the Pass of Bab-el-Haggar was silent and apparently deserted, but a quarter of a mile to the north-west of it the camels of an obviously well-drilled Camel Corps were *barraked* in orderly lines, in charge of camel-guards and sentries. On the distant horizon, a mighty cloud of dust indicated the passing of a vast concourse of men and beasts... .

An hour before sunset, a typical Arab *harka* swept like a torrent into the wide pass; hundreds and hundreds of well-armed fighting-men on magnificent buff, grey, and white camels.

At their head rode a splendid group, one of whom bore a green silk flag on which was a crescent and the device of the Lord of Many Tents, the Emir Mohammed Bishari bin Mustapha Korayim abd Rabu, spiritual and temporal head of a small, but growing, confederation of Bedouin tribes.

The pace of the beautiful camels of the Emir and his Sheikhs dropped from a swift mile-eating trot to a slow walk, as they reached the area of flour-like yielding dust-dunes into which even the broad feet of camels sank deeply. The setting sun shone blood-red upon rich silken *caftan,* gay *kafiyeh*bound about with golden *agals,* flowing *burnous* and coloured camel-rugs with dangling tassels... .

After their leaders, ploughed the mass of fighting-men, brave as the lions of the desert and as undisciplined as the apes of the rocks.

"The curse of Allah on this corner of Hell! It will upset my plan," growled the Emir, an impatient man, as his camel dragged one foot painfully after another through the bottomless dust.

"There is no need for haste, Lord," replied Suleiman the Strong, who rode beside him. "*Inshallah,* our ways will humbly resemble those of Allah Himself this day, for is it not written, '*Allah fleeth with wings of lead but striketh with hands of iron*'?"

"This cursed pass will spoil my plans, I say," growled the Emir again.

It did.

A curious long whistling sound was heard, like a sustained note on a *quaita,* the Arab flute, and, as all eyes were raised to the rocks that bounded and formed the defile, a sudden crash of musketry followed, and the pass became a shambles.

Many flogged their camels as though that would give them wings or firm ground on which to tread. Many wheeled about, to escape by the way they had come, making confusion worse confounded.

Many attempted to *barrak* their camels and fire from behind them at the well-concealed enemy, only to find that their unprotected backs were turned to another foe.

"Kismet," groaned the Emir, putting his hand to his bleeding chest. "*El Mektub, Mektub ...*" and fell from his camel.

The man to whom he spoke, this Suleiman the Strong, brought his camel to its knees and then lay flat, close beside it, feigning death.

Wild, almost unaimed, discharging of rifles by fully exposed men, replied but for a brief space to steady, careful short-range shooting by men lying, with resting rifles, behind rocks.

The inevitable end came quickly, and the Sheikh el Hamel el Kebir was prompt to save life.

To the surprise of the vanquished, not a throat was cut; and to each wounded man the same help was given that would have been rendered by his son.

But the defeat was utter, bitter and irretrievable, for not a rifle, a round of ammunition nor a camel remained to the leaderless army of the confederation of tribes, lately strong and arrogant in the mighty hand of the Emir Mohammed Bishari bin Mustapha.

Well acquainted with the truth of *væ victis,* it did not take the Sheikhs of the prisoners long to accept the small change of plan whereby the confederated tribes became attached to the Tribe, instead of the decimated Tribe being attached to the confederated tribes.

Nor did they see any loss in exchanging the leadership and rule of the Emir Mohammed Bishari bin Mustapha Korayim abd Rabu for that of the Emir el Hamel el Kebir who had conquered him in war; who had behaved with the noblest magnanimity to the vanquished, in the very finest Arab tradition, now more often honoured in the breach than in the observance; and who was undoubtedly a great and remarkable man, who might be relied upon to lead the confederation from strength to strength, until it could dwell in unmolested safety, making sure to each his own, that he might reap where he had sown... .

So the tribal Sheikhs gave hostages of their sons and daughters and of their flocks and herds and treasure; and the Sheikh el Hamel el Kebir became the Emir el Hamel el Kebir, the Victorious and Blessed of Allah the Merciful, the Compassionate.

His days now being filled with labours of military and civil organization, the new Emir appointed El Habibka to be Sheikh Regent of the Tribe, and brought joy upon the *ekhwan* and fighting-men by promising that he would himself dwell with the Tribe, and none other.

At a great *diffa* given in the new Emir's honour by aged Dawad Fetata, the Sitt Leila Nakhla delighted to honour him by waiting on him herself.

The Emir was conscious of the honour, but not of the fact that the girl pressed to her own lips and breast, the bowl from which he drank, and let none but herself touch it in future... .

Other nomadic and semi-nomadic tribes, some in wisdom and some in fear lest they be eaten up, sent envoys to the Emir, proposing that they should join his confederation and enjoy his countenance and protection, in return for tribute and the services of fighting-men.

These he visited, accompanied by his famous Camel Corps of men who drilled and manœuvred like the *Franzawi* and other *Roumi* soldiers, and who were reported to be invincible.

And slowly the great and growing confederation moved north-westward to the fabled Great Oasis of a Hundred Square Miles of Palm Trees and green grass, where the Emir el Hamel el Kebir talked of a permanent *douar,* that the Tribe might occupy the land and possess it, waxing mighty, self-supporting agriculturists and herdsmen, strong and safe, as being the centre and focus of a powerful tribal alliance.

He even talked of the building of a walled city with a protected caravan-market, a great *sūq* that should become famous beneath his shadow, and attract caravans from the north laden with sugar, tea, cotton stuffs, soap, needles, scent and sandal; from the south with ivory and feathers and Soudanese "orphans"; from the east with coffee from Arabia; and from the west with the products of Nigeria, Lake Tchad and Timbuctu... . A walled city with schools, mosques, *zaouias, serais, hammams, madressahs,* and cool houses with beautiful gardens... . And the *ekhwan* stroked their beards and smiled at the Emir's pleasing fantasies... .

Inshallah! ...

And, as unto him that hath shall be given, more and more power was given to the Emir el Hamel el Kebir, as more and more Sheikhs sought his protection and countenance; and his Confederation waxed like Jonah's gourd, until its fame spread abroad in all the land, north, south, east, and west.

In the north and west it attracted the attention of certain deeply-interested Great Ones... .

The first intimation that Fame had come to the Emir took the shape of an overture from the great Lord of the Senussi, who sent one of his most important Sheikhs, escorted by an imposing retinue bearing gifts and greetings and proposals for an offensive and defensive alliance, and the exchange of hostages for its better observance.

In full *mejliss* assembled, the Emir listened to the words of the Senussi emissary, and made suitable replies.

After some weeks of intermittent conversations, much *faddhling,* feasting and ceremonial drinking of mint tea, the ambassadorial caravan departed, taking with it a deep impression of the strength of the Confederation, the wisdom and greatness of the Emir, gifts for the Lord of the Senussi, and little else... .

"The Emir would deeply consider of the matter, confer with his tribal Sheikhs, and send his messengers, anon, to Holy Kufra with his reply... ."

CHAPTER V. A VOICE FROM THE PAST

It was the prudent custom of the Emir el Hamel el Kebir and his Vizier, the Sheikh el Habibka, to sit apart from all men, that they might converse of high matters of state in the completest privacy.

This they did upon a rug-strewn carpet, above which a roof-canopy of felt was supported by four poles. At the corners of an imaginary square, four Soudanese sentries, a hundred yards each from the other and from their Lords, watched that no man approached without invitation... .

To them, seated thus one evening, there came the Emir's faithful body-servant, R'Orab the Crow, escorting the aged but tough and enduring chief of the scouts who formed the Intelligence Department of the Emir.

The two men prostrated themselves, salaaming reverently.

"Speak," said the Emir.

"Lord Shereef, thy servant, Yakoub-who-goes-without-water, hath news for thine ear," announced El R'Orab.

"Speak," said the Emir to the ancient.

"Lord Kalipha, a small caravan comes. Its leaders are strange men. One is an Egyptian or an Arab from Egypt. He is of the great Al Azhar *Zaouia* of Cairo. The other speaks and dresses as the Bedouin, but his ways are strange... . The two speak together in a foreign tongue. They seized me and made me their guide"--the old man grinned toothlessly--"and I slept against the wall of their tent for warmth and shelter from the wind--but their talk was in a strange tongue. They have much money and their servants are faithful. Their hired camel-men could not tell me much. They were engaged at Siwah and have come by way of Holy Kufra. They think it possible that the chief leader is a *Roumi*, but he carries papers that great Sheikhs, Emirs, Kaliphas, Shereefs and Rulers kiss and place against their foreheads and their hearts... . It is said that much honour was shown them at Siwa and also at Holy Kufra by the Lord of the Senussi... . I left them at the last water-hole, escaping by night upon my fast camel... ."

Three days later two heavily-bearded strangers sat and talked long and eloquently with the Emir el Hamel el Kebir and his Vizier.

Most of the talking was done by a curious hybrid product of modern civilization who had been a student of the great Al Azhar University at Cairo, and of the Paris *Sorbonne* as well. He had been an employee of the *Bureau Arabe* and had sojourned in Algiers. He had resigned his post and visited Constantinople, departing thence for Baghdad. The wanderlust or some other lust had then taken him to Europe once more.

All that he said was confirmed in terse speech by his master, a man whom the Emir and his Vizier studied more carefully than they did the voluble cosmopolitan Arab-Egyptian.

And what he said was of deep interest--a thrilling and intriguing story... .

He told these simple desert chieftains of a Great *Roumi* King of Kings, one clad in shining armour, who had long since been moved by Allah, in a dream, to see the error of his ways and to embrace the True Faith... . So great was he that the very Father of the Faithful himself had called him Brother and had invited him to Stamboul that he might embrace him... . So great was he that, once upon a time, the very walls of the Holy City of Jerusalem were thrown down that he might enter, when he went there on pilgrimage, using no common gate trodden by the feet of common men.

The simple devout chieftains, much impressed, were too deeply enthralled to talk--until the Emir, stroking his beard, sought enlightenment as to what all this had to do with him.

He received it.

Stirred by the knowledge that there is no God but God and that Mahomet is his Prophet, and shocked by the sight of Islam groaning in bondage--yea, beneath the heel of the *Franzawi Roumi* here in Africa, this mighty King of Kings was about to urge his

Brother, the Father of the Faithful, in Stamboul, to preach a *jehad*, a Holy War, for the overthrow of all oppressors of Islam throughout the world--and especially in Morocco, Algiers, Tunisia and the countries adjacent... .

And to all great Chieftains, Emirs, Sheikhs, Kaliphas, Shereefs, Rulers, and leaders of Tribal Confederations, he was sending word to be prepared for the Great Day of Islam, the Day of the creation of the Pan-Islamic State in Africa, and the utter overthrow and extermination of the *Roumi*... . Already the greatest Islamic power in Africa, the Senussi, were pledged to obey orders from Stamboul, and it was hoped and believed that the Emir el Hamel el Kebir would attack the French when the Senussi attacked the English in Egypt... . Meanwhile--gifts, arms, money, promises ...

This first audience being concluded, and orders having been given for the pitching of a camp for the strangers' caravan, the Emir el Hamel el Kebir and the Sheikh el Habibka el Wazir stared long and thoughtfully into each other's faces.

"D'you place him, Bud?" asked the Emir.

"Search me, Hank Sheikh," replied the Vizier, "but I cert'nly seen him before... . He's got me guessin' and he's got me rattled... . There's a catch in it somewhere... . I'm real uneasy... ."

The Emir smiled; a slow and thoughtful smile indeed.

"He's going to be a whole heap uneasier than you are, Buddy boy... . Remember a sure-enough real thug, way back at Tokotu when we was in the Legion? ... Came to us at Douargala with a draft from the Saida depot. The boys allowed it was him, and him alone, started that big Saida mutiny, though it was never brought home to him... . Same game at Tokotu... . Always had plenty of money and spent it on gettin' popular... . Reg'lar professional mutineer and trouble-brewer ... a spell-binder--and a real brave man... . Get him?"

"Nope."

"He had been in the French Cavalry, he said, and got jailed for mutinying there too, and later, he joined the Legion to carry on the good work... . He was on that march with us from Tokotu to Zinderneuf--the place those two bright boys burnt out and killed old Lejaune--and Old Man Bojolly shot this guy with his empty revolver, and then put him under arrest--for refusing to obey orders... . He tried to work up a mutiny again that time, and he very nearly ..."

"*Rastignac!*" cried the Vizier, and smote his thigh. "*Rastignac the Mutineer!* Good for you, Hank Sheikh... . That's the guy! I knew I knowed him, the moment I set eyes on him... . Had too many drinks out of the old crook not to know him... . Used to wear a pointed beard and big moustache waxed up like you would stick corks on the ends for safety."

"You said it, Bud. It's Old Man Rastignac. And what in hell is the stiff doing in *this* outfit, I want to know. Last we saw of him, he was for General Court Martial and the Penal Battalion."

"Doin'? Earnin' some dirty money again, I s'pose. From the same purse too, I guess... . What'll we do with him, Hank?"

"Teach him poker, Son, and get all he's got... . Think he reckernized us any?"

"Not on your life. I watched him mighty careful. We was clean shaven, those days, and he wore a hairy face... . That's why we seemed to know him and he didn't know us...

. *You* look more like an ole goat in a bush than a soldier, behind that flowin' door-mat of whiskers... . '*Hank!*' Huh! Sure--*a Hank of Hair*... . Gee!"

"And you, Buddy Bashaw, you look just *eggs*actly like a monkey in a haystack... . You ain't a little Man with a beard on him, Son--you're a Beard with a little man in it... ."

The two simple desert chieftains eyed each other critically, their strong faces impassive, sardonic, hard; their eyes enigmatic, inscrutable, faintly humorous perhaps... .

Sending for one Yussuf Latif Fetata, grandson of the High Sheikh, Sidi Dawad Fetata, the Emir bade him bivouac a company of the Camel Corps beside the camp of the strangers, for their honour and protection, and to protect them so effectually that not a man of the caravan left their camp by day or by night. Their camels were to be "minded" for them in the *fondouk,* their rifles were to be taken from them to be cleaned and also "minded"; and daily they were to receive ample rations and water--for that day alone. (No man could leave the Great Oasis without swift camels and a good supply of food and water.)

"On my head and my life be it, Sidi," salaamed young Latif Fetata, and departed to see that the honoured guests were also honoured (and strictly guarded) prisoners... .

But though they could not leave their spacious and comfortable camp, others could enter it--others, that is to say, who had authorized business there--and no one dreamed of hindering that influential and pious priest, Hadji Abdul Salam, chief *imam,* and spiritual head of his Tribe, from paying a ceremonial visit of honour to the Emir's honoured guests.

He paid many visits, in fact, which were not ceremonial and in the course of which this prophet, who was not without honour in his own country, showed that honour might not be without profit also... .

When a certain soldier, one Gharibeel Zarrug, a young man who feared and reverenced the Hadji, and whom the tongue of malice declared to be the Hadji's son, was on sentry over the tents of the leaders of the expedition, the pious Hadji visited them by night, and much curious and interesting conversation ensued.

After one such heart-to-heart talk, and the departure of Hadji Abdul Salam, the Egyptian-Arab, who affected patent-leather dancing pumps, silk socks, scent, hair-pomade and other European vices--and who yearned exceedingly for a high stiff collar, frock-coat, *tarbush* and the pavements of Paris--observed to his colleague and employer:

"Might do worse... . He'd be ours, body and soul, both for the money and because we should know too much... . If he killed this Emir and his jackal, or had them killed, he would be the power behind the throne--until he was the throne itself... ."

"Yes... . Might do much worse," agreed the other man. "He would be Regent for this boy that the Emir is nursing--until the time came for the boy to die... . I don't like this Emir... . He says too little and stares too much... . He's a strong ruler, and no tool for anybody... . And it's a *tool* we want here... ."

"No. I don't like him either," agreed the other, "and he doesn't like us or our proposals, I fancy. I have an idea that the French were here before us. Do you think we are in any danger?"

"*Great* danger, I should say," rejoined the leader, and smiled mockingly at his companion, whose invaluable gifts he knew to be rather those of the fox than of the lion.

"Then we must get down to real business with the Hadji, the next time he comes," was the reply of the Egyptian-Arab. "We shall have deserved well of our masters if we do nothing more here than remove the Emir, a potential enemy of great importance... ."

"We shall do more than that," prophesied the other.

CHAPTER VI. MORE VOICES PROM THE PAST

In pride, peace, prosperity and patience sat the Emir el Hamel el Kebir upon the rugs and cushions of the carpet of his pavilion, a few days later, splendidly arrayed, exhaling dignity, benevolence, and lordship.

Beside him sat his almost equally resplendent Vizier, known to all men as the Sheikh el Habibka el Wazir.

Between their bearded lips were the mouth-pieces of their long-stemmed *narghilehs,* from which they inhaled deep draughts of soothing smoke.

A man came running, halted, and prostrated himself.

"Speak, O El R'Orab the Crow," murmured the Emir.

"Lord," said the man, "the leader Marbruk ben Hassan has returned, with none missing. He brings three prisoners, two of them women. The man prisoner says he comes to the Emir with messages from the Rulers of his Tribe."

"Go to the Hadji Abdul Salam and say that the Emir bids him receive these people and offer them hospitality for three days in the Guest-tents. '*Are not we all the guests of Allah?*' saith The Book... . When they are rested and refreshed, let him bring the man before me... . I have spoken."

The Emir and the Vizier sat in silence, their eyes resting on the pleasant view before them, a scene beautified by feathery palms, green grass and running water, on which rested the benediction of the setting sun... .

Anon men approached, in the midst of whom walked a French officer in full uniform.

The Vizier's elbow pressed that of the Emir.

"Sunday pants of Holy Moses!" murmured the Vizier. "*It's Old Man Bojolly!* ... Run us down at last!"

"Game's up, Bud," murmured the Emir. "This is where we get what's comin' to us... ."

And with severe dignity, and calm faces of perhaps more than Oriental inscrutability, they received the officer, in open *mejliss* or durbar.

§ 2

After the return of the French officer to the Guest-tent, the Emir and the Vizier sat cross-legged upon their cushions, and gazed each upon the face of the other.

"Well, Hank Sheikh, and what do you know about *that?*" asked the Vizier of his Lord.

"Our name's mud," replied the Emir. "Our monicker's up... . Old Man Boje and his '*great and peaceful message!*' ... Be more great than peaceful when his troops arrive... ."

"They say they always get you, in the end," reflected the Vizier. "I wonder what force he's brought and where he's left it?"

"That's what's puzzlin' me, Bud. I allow no desert-column, nor camel-corpse, nor squadron of Spahis, nor company of the Legion, could have got within three days of here without us knowing it."

"Sure thing, Son Hank--if a gang of Touareg Bohunks couldn't, French troops couldn't... . I s'pose it *is* us he's after?"

"Who else? ... It cert'nly isn't this Rastignac guy... . Anyhow, we'll play Sheikhs till Hell pops, and 'see him and raise him' every time, Bud."

"You've said it, Hank. We got better poker-faces than Old Man Bojolly, I allow... . But what'll we do if he gets up in *mejliss* and says:

"'*I rise to remark I've come to fetch you two hoboes outa this for deserters from the Foreign Legion on reconnaissance duty in the face o' the enemy an' the Lord ha' mercy on your sinful souls amen, and you better come quiet or I'll stretch you and call up my Desert Column*,' eh, Hank Sheikh?"

"Bluff him out and say he's got a touch o' the sun and oughter turn teetotal... . If we can't talk anything but Arabic we *can't* be deserters from the Foreign Legion... ."

"Or else tie him up in a neat parcel an' run him into Egypt," he continued. "That's British Territory... . Sit on the walls o' Jerusalem an' sing *Yankee Doodle* to him... . Jerusalem *is* in the Land of Egypt, ain't it, Bud?"

"Yep... . House of Bondage and Children of Israel, an' all that... . But we needn't vamoose any. We can turn the Injuns loose on him, if he starts handing out the rough stuff and is all for marchin' us to the calaboose in Zaguig or somewhere... . Or let his old friend Rastignac get him... ."

"*Can* it, Buddy Bashaw. Cut it out. We don't turn Injuns on to a lone white man, Son... . No, and we don't set 'em up against Christian machine-guns nor Civilized artillery either... . Not after they elected us to Congress like this, and made me President and all... . Put their last dollar on us for Clean Politics and the People's Party, Monroe Doctrine and No Foreign Entanglements... . No, I guess we gotta hit the high places again, and hike. But shan't I laugh some *if he gets Rastignac too*!"

"Gee! Ain't it the hard and frost-bitten pertater, Hank Sheikh--after we been livin' so respectable? Like a Hard-Shell Baptist Minister in a hard-boiled shirt... ."

"It surely would jar you, Buddy... . We had our ups and downs, Son, and now we're booked for a down."

"Some tracking Ole Man Bojolly's done! He's a cute cuss and the fierce go-getter... . He's got a nerve too, to ride straight in here like a Texas Ranger into a Mex village--an' I hand it to him, an' no ill-will... . But I'd certainly like to go and paste him one... . And me just thinking of marrying and settling down and all... ."

"'Nother thing gets me guessing, Bud... . What's he brought the two girls here for? They ain't labelled *A Present from Biskra ... For a Bad Sheikh ...* are they?"

"No. He's French, Hank. Shockin' morals they've got--but I don't see that it's any affair of ours if Bojolly travels comfortable... . But if he does gather us in for the Oran General Court-Martial an' we're sentenced to death, I shall get my own back, sure."

"As how?"

"When he's finished his evidence, I shall say, quiet like, but with all the nacheral dignity and weight of Truth, '*Oh, you Rambunctious Ole Goat*,' I shall say--an' leave it at that... ."

"Well--look at here, Son... . He hasn't showed his hand yet. We've staked him to a hash-party to-night, an' told him to bring the girls. We'll play light till Marbruk ben Hassan comes in--I whispered to Marbruk to scout clever and find out if there was an escort hiding anywhere--and we know for sure whether there's French troops around. And until there is--what we say *goes*... . Gee! Ain't it some world we live in? Major Bojolly and Rastignac the Mutineer, both leavin' visitin'-cards on *us*. It's our At Home day, Son Bud... ."

"We'll be wishin' it was our Go Home day, before long, Hank Sheikh," replied the Vizier. "Anyhow, we'll see that Boje and Rastignac don't meet yet awhile."

§ 3

That evening, after the feast and the departure of their guests, the Emir and the Vizier observed a long silence, each apparently respecting the feelings of the other. At length the Vizier groaned.

"Can you beat it, Son?" quoth he. "Do I sleep? Do I dream and is Visions about? ... Bite me in the stomach if I'm wrong, Hank Sheikh--but I believe I've been talking to an honest-to-God, genuine, sure-enough American girl, and held her hand in mine... ."

"I'm dazed and weak, Bud," murmured the Emir, "but I testify you certainly held her hand in yours. I thought it *was* yours... ."

"*It's goin' to be*," pronounced the Vizier, with a fervour of resolution. "It's goin' to be!" he repeated. "Say, Son Hank--don't go and fall in love with that li'll Peach, or I shall hand in my checks and wilt to the bone-orchard... . *I'm in love,* Hank Sheikh, for the first time in my life! ..."

The Emir emitted a rumble of sarcastic laughter.

"Huh! And yesterday you were going to marry four Arab Janes and settle down respectable!"

"That ain't *Love;* you old fool! Not by a jugful... . That's matterimony and respectability, instead of living like a skylarking lone wolf... . Say, Hank, old Son, you *ain't* goin' to fall in love with that li'll lovely Peach yourself?"

"No, Bud, I am not... . But I'll rise to remark that Old Man Bojolly *is*... . Yep, sure thing! He's fallen for that little looker, all-right."

The Vizier closed a useful-looking fist and shook it above his head.

"*What!*" he ejaculated in a whispering shout. "He'd come here to arrest us an' get us shot--*and* he'd steal our girls from under our very noses too! ... He would? ... I allow that's torn it! ... Old Man Bojolly better git up an' git... . Let's ride him outa town and tell him to go while the goin's good! ... B'Gees! *I'*ll paste him one to-morrow... . Sheikh Hank, Son--I'm goin' to propose to that sweet and lovely American girl, and lay my heart and life and fortune at her feet... . She wouldn't look at that dam' Wop then, sure*ly*?"

"He ain't a Wop. And you ain't got a fortune," replied the Emir patiently.

"Well, he's French, an' that's the same as a Wop or worse... . And I allow I'll dern soon rustle a fortune if she'll have me."

"*That's* the spirit, Son! Good luck to you, Buddy-boy--and I'll back you up. You court her gentle and lovin' an' respectful an' I'll give you a character... . Time you had one too... . But we sure got to tell her all about ourselves, Bud... . All the truth about us, so there's no deception like... ."

"Sure thing, Hank Sheikh, I wouldn't deceive her--not for anything."

"No, Son... . I'll mention about those four Arab Janes--just to show you got the serious marryin' mind, and prob'ly been collectin' the sticks o' furniture for the Home... ."

"Cut out the funny-stuff, Hank Sheikh... . It's fierce, ain't it? I got to talk this Arabic gargle while Ole Boje gets away with it in English--and French--and American too! How I'm goin' to lay my feelin's before her in Arabic? She won't reckernize 'em fer the respeckful love-stuff... . Hell!"

"You got away with it in Agades, Son... . You remember that black Jane... . You was *dumb* then, too... ."

"*Can* it, I tell you, you Hank, or you'll get my goat... . This is different... . This is a girl that's Real Folks... . You don't know what love is, you ugly low-life old moron... . The laughter of fools is as the cackling of prawns in a pot... . You never bin in love, I tell you!"

"Me? Love? No. Sure... . What you know about Miss Maudie Atkinson, Bud?"

"Some looker--if Miss Mary Vanbrugh wasn't there... . An' not bad fer British... . Yep, I'd surely have fallen for her, if the American girl hadn't been there... ."

"You certainly would, Bud... . Thou Fragrance of the Pit!"

"Say--I got an idea, Buddy," continued the Emir. "S'pose we could tell Miss Vanbrugh all about us, and say we trust her not to tell Ole Boje until he springs it on us himself? ... I got a hunch he *ain't* after us, and don't reckernize us either... .

"If I'm wrong, he's got the best bluff and the best poker-face on any man I met yet--an' we're innercent children beside him... . Him an' his *great and peaceful message!* ... We'll wait until Marbruk comes back, an' then we'll force Boje to a show-down... . *I* don't believe the old fox is on to *us* at all... ."

"Then what is he here for, Son?" asked the Vizier.

"You got me guessing, pard," was the reply, and the Emir drained a glass of lemon-water without enthusiasm.

Silence fell. The Emir and the Vizier sank deep into thought. From time to time the solemn face of each was lighted by a reminiscent smile.

"Say, Hank--didn't she just jolly us! I nearly bust with laffin' when she sang that *Bulbul Emir* stuff. Gee! Isn't she a sweet Peach! ... *Allahu Akbar*--she's a *houri*! ..."

"Sure--and that li'll British girl... . '*Oh, Sir, ain't the big one a lovely man!*' ... That's me, Buddy Bashaw--and don't you forget it. *I* got that bokay! It gave me the fantods that I couldn't back-chat with her... ."

"*Lovely man!* ... Sufferin' Moses!" groaned the Vizier. "You ever see a g'rilla, Hank?"

"And I'll tell you something else, Bud," observed the Emir. "I got a hunch that Miss Mary Vanbrugh isn't such a fool as you look... . What about if she was joshing us *double?* ..."

"Eh?"

"Women are funny things, Bud. They see further through a brick wall than you can spit... . They got a sort of second sight and sixth sense, worth all your cleverness, Son. It's what they call ..."

"Instink?" suggested the Vizier.

"Yup, an' something else... . Institootion? ... No. *Intooition*. That's it. An' I got a hunch Miss Vanbrugh saw clean through us--and out the other side!"

"*Gee!* ... Think she's put Bojolly wise--if he wasn't already?"

"No... . No--I think not... . I allow she'd watch and wait... . If we weren't planning any harm to Boje, she'd plan no harm to us... . But I may be wrong. I usually am... ."

"Sure, Son," agreed the Vizier.

"I got to get Miss Vanbrugh alone to-morrow ..." mused the Emir... .

"Me too. *Some*," murmured the Vizier.

Two minds with but a single thought.

§ 4

The next morning the Emir, in the presence of the Vizier, granted an interview to his latest visitor.

Thereafter the two rulers sat in council.

"I said it, Son! *I said it!* He don't know us from Adam," said the Emir, as the French officer returned to his tent.

"Nor hardly from Eve, in these dam' petticoats," agreed the Vizier. "You *said* it, Professor--and I hand it to you, Son... . Sunday pants of Holy Moses, *he ain't after us at all! Inshallah!*"

"No, Judge, he ain't," replied the Emir. "We thought he had come gunning for us with half the French army--and he's come to bring us a million francs... . Can you beat it, Colonel?"

"How much *is* that, Sheriff?"

"Two hundred thousand bucks, Senator... . *Some* jack!"

"*Hamdulillah!* What'll we do with it, President?"

"Earn it, Governor. And do good with it."

"Good to *us*, too, Judge?"

"You said it, Colonel! We'll have our rake-off. The labourer is worthy of his wad... . Says those very words in the Bible... ."

"Sure thing, Pastor. *Allahu Akbar!* ... Yea, verily the face of Allah the Merciful, the Compassionate, is turned unto these, his servants; and Muhammed, his Prophet, hath spoke up for us like a li'll man. Small prophets and quick returns maketh the heart glad."

"Glad goes, Son," agreed the Emir, and the two sat sunk in deep thought.

"We'll go riding this evening," said the Emir at length, "You can ride with Miss Vanbrugh, and I'll take Miss Atkinson... . But let me have a turn with Miss Vanbrugh too-- on the way back, say--and if she starts joshing, I'll own up and confess--if it's plain she's called our bluff... . An American girl won't queer the pitch for two poor American men in a tight place and pulling off a big deal, 'specially if they own up and put it to her honest... ."

"What about the li'll Britisher?" asked the Vizier. "By the Beard of the Prophet she's all-wool-an'-a-yard-wide. *She* wouldn't butt in an' spoil things. 'Specially when Miss Vanbrugh had a talk with her... . Then I can say my spiel to *her* in good old U.S.A. language--bye'n' bye... ."

"Yep--an' by the Beard of the Prophet *and* the Whiskers of Moses I can talk some good he-talk to Miss Mary," agreed the Vizier.

"Sure--but we gotta go careful, Bud... . We don't wanta get lead instead of gold out of Ole Man Bojolly... . And b'lieve me, Son, it's Miss Vanbrugh for his--if she'll fall for him... ."

"I'll cut his throat first," growled the Vizier.

"Cut nothing, Son," replied the Emir. "You're always falling in and out of love... . We aren't goin' to lose two hundred thousand bucks and the chance of settin' these Injuns up for life, just because you haven't got self-control of your passions... . Old Man Boje has come

here in his innocence, wanting to give us a fortune--and we aren't going to hinder him any...
. If Miss Vanbrugh'll have you, Bud, I'll be the happiest Sheikh of the Sahara--and I'll do all I know to bring it off. And if she won't have you, Son, you gotta take your gruel (*and* your sack of gold dust!), an' that's all there is to it.... Get me, Steve?"

"I get you, Father.... But by the Ninety and Nine Names of Allah, I'll sure plaster Old Boje till ..."

"Cut it *out,* I say, you thug.... If she's in love with Bojolly we gotta remember that all the rest of the Universe don't matter a hill of beans to *her*--and the kinder we treat *him,* the fairer she treats *us*.... So go in and win if you can--and keep a poker-face if you can't...."

"Huh! *You* aren't in love, you perishin' politician!"

"Nope? Well then, p'raps I'll have the clearer head to steer us past the doors of the Oran Gaol and through those of the Bank of France, oh, Sheikh el Habibka.... Thou love-sick lallapaloozer."

§ 5

"And you really are perfectly certain that you can bluff it through to the end, and that Major de Beaujolais won't place you?" said Miss Mary Vanbrugh, as she and the Emir el Kebir rode side by side in the desert.

"Certain sure," replied the Emir. "We've been bluffing Arabs with our lives depending on it, and got away with it.... It'll take more than a Frenchman to ..."

"He's one of the cleverest men that ever lived," interrupted the girl.

"Sure thing," agreed the Emir. "But he isn't an Arab. Why should he suspect anything wrong when he sees the Bedouin taking us as Bedouin? It wouldn't enter his head. It isn't as though he was looking for European or American crooks, or ever dreamt there was any about. I may tell you there's another Frenchman here too, who has lived in the same barrack-room with us! *He* hasn't an idea we're not Arabs!"

"How you did it, I don't know."

"Easy enough. Buddy and I were wandering in the Sahara for years--with a couple of bright boys, and with our eyes and ears open. We stayed dumb but we learnt a lot.

"Then I got lost, and this Tribe picked me up--with one foot in Heaven and the other twitching feeble but full of hope.... I stayed dumb until I surely knew Arabic better than American.... Got it from a three-year-old kid mostly. As he learnt to talk so did I.... Then I did a miracle on myself and came undumb. Even then I never said a sentence nor a word that I hadn't heard and learnt by heart. It was easy as fallin' off a log.

"The poor Injuns thought I was from a strange tribe, if they thought anything at all, when my pronunciation was funny, or I hadn't got quite the right religious dope. But I wasn't far out anyway, for I'd been studying that like Hell--for years."

"Your life must have hung by a thread at times."

"Well, it never hung by a palm-fibre rope, Miss Mary Vanbrugh, which is what it deserved," and the Emir smiled.

"And does still," replied the girl.... "And where did you pick your friend up?"

"What, Buddy? Why, he and I have been friends since I was a road-kid. We've been soldiers, sailors, hoboes, cow-boys, hoss-wranglers, miners, lumber-jacks, Wild West Showmen, conjurors, Foreign Legendaries and Sheikhs.... When I got lost in the desert, he got away to safety--and what you think he did? Rustled some camels and a nigger, and *come back to look for me,* right where he'd nearly died himself.... And when I got sort of top-sergeant there, I uster send scouts all round that same country to see if they could get news of another poor Bedouin picked up there like I was.... .

"I never did--but I got news of a gang of Touareg who'd come up that way.... . They'd got him--and I got them, good and plenty and just in time."

"What sort of a man is he? He has certainly got good taste, for he gives me the eye of warm approval.... Virtuous?"

"No. He isn't what I'd call that. I allow he's broken all the Commandments and looks to do it again... . No, he hasn't got any virtues that I know of, 'cept courage, and loyalty, and gratitude, and reliability.... .

"There isn't much to Buddy beyond that he's braver than any lion--for a lion hasn't got imagination--and that he never did a mean thing in his life nor went back on his word or his pal. No. He's only got a fine head and a great heart, and doesn't know the meaning of the words fear, despair, failure, selfishness, nor any kind of meanness.... . Just an 'ornery cuss.' ..."

"You want me to like him, I see ..." smiled the girl, "so you damn him with faint praise. He sounds very like a man to me."

"No, I'm praising him with faint damns like 'ornery cuss.' ... You see, I'm one myself, and so Bud and me suits... . As to your liking him--you couldn't help that--but it would be a dark day for me if you married him an' took-him-home-to-Mother... ."

"Don't worry, Mr. Emir! ... What would happen if you two fell in love with the same girl?" asked Mary Vanbrugh.

"Poor girl would be left a widow like, before she was married. I wouldn't butt in on Bud and Bud wouldn't butt in on me... ."

"And how long do you plan to stay in on this Sheikh game?"

"Till the lill' kid's ready to come into the business and sit on his father's stool. I promised his old Dad I'd see the boy through teething and high-school.... . There's one or two sharks want his job."

"And will your friend stay here with you?"

"Sure.... Unless you take him away, Miss Mary Vanbrugh."

"Keep a stout and hopeful heart, Mr. Emir."

"Or unless Major D. Bojo*lay* takes us both away in the middle of a camel-corps of *goums* and things.... ."

"Why should he want to do that?" asked the girl.

"He wouldn't *want* to, but it would be his painful 'Duty'--when it came out that we were swindlers and Americans, a big man and a little man, the same being wanted for departing from the Legion.... . They'd prove it on us too, as soon as they got our whiskers off. So if you get mad with us any time, and tell him--it's us for big trouble... ."

"It's the very last thing in the world I'd tell him--if you were my worst enemies.... . I'd give *anything in the world* for him to bring off this Treaty successfully.... .

"If you only knew what it *means* to him! ... He has spent his life--and as hard a life as yours has been--in fitting himself for just such a stroke as this. It's not for himself either--it's for France.... . He thinks of *nothing* but France--and Duty... .

"It's his one longing, to feel that he has *done* something for France, and that his labour hasn't been wasted.... . His uncle is Commander-in-Chief and Governor-General and he's almost God to Major de Beaujolais. I think he'd value a pat on the back from the old man more than the Grand Cross of the Legion of Honour... .

"How did you come to know the Major?" asked the girl suddenly.

"He was mule-walloping with a detachment of the Foreign Legion."

"And you actually served under him?"

"We did."

"How jolly--as they say in England."

"Yup. *Beau*-jolais--as they say in France."

"I wonder he doesn't recognize you."

"Well--we were clean-shaven in those days. A doormat of whiskers and a *kafiyeh* make a lot of difference... . He might, yet--but people generally only see what they're looking for... ."

"It must be splendid to serve under him," said the girl.

"We hid our joy," replied the Emir. "We even tore ourselves away... ."

"And of course you'll make this Treaty?"

"Sure. Why not? Provided there's no 'peaceful penetration' nor the Blessings of Civilization, I'll make it... . France protects us, and *we* keep this end o' the Sahara quiet and healthy. We get a rake-off from France, an' we wax rich and prosperous because the caravan-roads and trade-routes'll be kept open and peaceful... ."

"You mean you and your friend will get rich?" asked Miss Vanbrugh.

"I surely hope we make our modest pile... . We aren't in the Sheikh business solely for our health. But what I meant was that these Injuns should prosper and get a bit in the bank. I'd like to hand over the whole outfit as a going concern when the young Sheikh's old enough... . And I'd like to be one of the few white men who have left the native better than he found him. It's a plumb silly idea of mine... ."

"You want to 'make two blades of grass grow where one grew before'?"

"Well--not so much grass, as *loobiyeh*. It's better grazing."

They approached the outlying palms of their corner of the Oasis.

"It's a bargain, then, Mr. Parlour-Sheikh," said the girl. "You'll do your utmost to keep Major de Beaujolais thinking you two are real Arabs, and you'll make the Treaty with him and see that it is kept--and I'll do my best for you... ."

"Sure. I'd sooner face a sack of gold twenty-franc pieces than a firing squad, any day, Miss Mary Vanbrugh... . There's everything to gain for everybody on the one hand, and everything to lose for everybody on the other... ."

"There certainly is, including your beloved Arabs, remember ... I shall be just a tiny bit anxious until we're away again, but, oh, I do enjoy seeing you two solemn boys playing Sheikhs!"

"*Bismillah arahman arahmin. En nahs teyibin hena,*" boomed the Emir el Hamel el Kebir, as they neared the tents.

"Why certainly," replied Miss Vanbrugh. "You've said it, Mr. Emir--whatever it is... ."

§ 6

At eventide, the Sheikh el Habibka el Wazir was dining with his lord, the Emir el Hamel el Kebir, as usual.

In sonorous Arabic these grave men discussed matters of importance to the *haute politique* of the Tribal Confederacy--until the servants had removed the tray of bowls, and brought the earthern cups of black coffee and the long *narghilehs*.

As soon as they were alone, they ceased to express their thoughts in the ancient tongue of the followers of the Prophet.

The Emir, smiling broadly, nodded his head.

"I was right, Son," he said. "Soon as we were alone, I turned a hose of Arabic on to Miss Mary Vanbrugh--best Arabic I ever shot; real Hot Dog.... What did she reply? Tell me that, O Father of Lies and Son of a Gun.... '*Cut it out, Bo*,' says she. '*Talk your mother-tongue and let's get next. What's the game with Major de Beaujolais?*' or words to that effect. And I fell for it, Son. I could not look that young woman in the face and get away with it...."

"You talked *American* to her?" interrupted the Vizier.

"I'm telling you, Bud.... She had me back-chatting like two old Irish women--almost before I knew it...."

"Jiminy!" breathed the Sheikh. "The lill' devil!"

"Why?" inquired the Emir.

"Because she wouldn't talk a word of American when *I* rode alone with her! She only knew French! ... Gee! She surely did get my goat! When I tried a bit of broken English on her, as a sort of thin end of the wedge to letting her know we also were hundred-per-cent Anglo-Saxon Americans from God's own Country, she says:

"'*Commong-vous porty-vous*' an' '*Doo-de-la-day*.' ... I mostly forgot my French since I left the Legion, but I twigged she was pulling my leg.... I said:

"'*You spik Engleesh.... Las' night you spik 'im*,' 'an' she replies, '*Nong Mossoo. Vous étiez ivre*.' (That means *drunk!*) '*Vous parlez Arabique*,' and every time I tried to say something kind and loving in English, she says, '*Parly Arabique, Mossoo le Sheikh. Je ne comprong pas Anglais.*' ... An' she don't know a word of Arabic, I swear."

"How d'you know she don't?"

"Well--she'd have fell off her hoss if she had understood what I said.... And there was me tryin' to talk plain American, and her axin' me in French to talk Arabic.... An' I didn't get any forrader...."

"Gee! Can you beat it?" smiled the Emir. "Well, Buddy, my experience was more joyful than yours. Yea, verily, O Rose of Delight and Charmer of Many ... Thou Son of None--and Father of Hundreds."

"Did you make love to her, Hank Sheikh ... Thou Son of Hundreds--and Father of None?" asked the Vizier threateningly.

"Search me, Son! I hadn't the time nor the temptation. We talked good, sound, solid business, in good, sound, plain American. And let me put you wise, Son, and you quit dreaming love-stuff, and listen.... .

"I've told Miss Mary Vanbrugh that we're two genuine low-brow American stiffs, honest-to-God four-flushers and fakers.... She says she could see that for herself...."

"You speak for *yourself,* Hank Sheikh," interrupted the Vizier.

"I did, Son ... Miss Mary spoke for *you,*" replied the Emir.

The Vizier looked elated.

"She says, '*Where did you pick up that lill' ornery dead-beat that side-kicks with you, Mr. Emir? Did the cat bring it in, or did the wind blow it along, or was it left on the beach by the tide?*' ... or words to that effect, like."

The Vizier's face fell.

"Then *I* spoke for you, Son. I said, '*The pore guy ain't sich a God-awful hoodlum as he looks,* Miss Mary,' I said, and she replies kindly--'*No, Mr. Emir, I'm sure he couldn't be!*' and then I spoke up for you hearty, Bud, and I said there isn't your equal in Africa... ."

The Vizier beamed.

"... to cut the throat of a goat, skin it and gut it, while another man'd be sharpening his knife... . But you interrupted me and I'm wandering around trifles... . Well ... I had to admit that we're Americans, Boy, and wanted by the police ... wanted badly--for doing a glide outa the Foreign Legion... . And I owned up that Old Man Bojolly had got me scared stiff, and that you and I allowed that we'd either got to find Boje a lone desert grave, or get up and hike once more--or else give in and go quietly... .

"Then Mary ..."

"Who you calling 'Mary' so familiar, Hank Sheikh?" asked the Vizier, scowling indignantly.

"Then Miss Vanbrugh put her cards on the table too. A clean show-down, Son... . Boje *ain't* deserter-huntin'. He's got something better to do! ... And he hasn't a notion about Rastignac... . That bunk he pulled on us about '*bearing a great and peaceful message,*' wasn't bunk at all! What he said to us in the Great and Solemn interview was *the Goods*... .

"We must have had uneasy consciences, Son... . He surely thinks he's on a Mission for his Fatherland. He ain't told Miss Vanbrugh too much about it--he being a diplomatist and all, but she knows that much for sure ... And what do you know about *this*, Son? He's a Big Noise in their Secret Service--not just a Major in the Mule-Wallopers... ."

"By the Beard of the Prophet and the Name of Allah *I'll* wallop him," growled the Vizier.

"Well, as I was going to say when you injected that vulgar remark, Miss Vanbrugh and I have done a deal. She won't tell Bojolly that we're genuine swindlers and deserters from the Legion, provided we treat ole Boje kind and loving, and fall in with all his schemes... ."

"We'll fall in with those two hundred thousand dollars without a kick or a moan," observed the Vizier, "and I rise to remark that Viziers are Treasurers in this undeveloped rural State... ."

"So we're on velvet again, Bud... . All Old Man Bojolly wants to do, is to press the dough on us. All we gotta do is sign this Treaty not to let the Senussi in on the ground floor, and to have no truck with low foreigners. That means all people that on earth do dwell who aren't French... . Shall we boot Rastignac out an' tell him to go while the going's good--or keep him around and make a bit on the side? ... But it's old Boje's Treaty we'll sign!"

"You can't sign '*Hank*' in Arabic, Father, can you?" inquired the Vizier.

"I certainly can, and you can sign '*Bud*' too. You only do a lot of pot-hooks upside down, with their tails turning to the left, and then scribble on it... .

"And mind, you gotta do it from right to left, too. I saw that boose-hoisting old rum-hound, Abdul Salam, doing it... . No Arabs can't get their signatures forged, because they never do 'em twice alike, and nobody can read 'em--least of all those who wrote 'em... . 'Sides, I've got the ole Sheikh's family ring... ." and he indicated a great ancient seal ring that he wore on a slightly withered finger, of which the top joint was missing, the only finger that it would fit.

"Well, as I was trying to say, Buddy Bashaw, Miss Mary is as set on Bojolly getting away with it as we are... ."

"Why? What's the graft?" inquired the Vizier.

"Well--as I figger it--he's the golden-haired, blue-eyed boy. Saved her life in Zaguig. Shot up some stiffs who were handing out the rough stuff. Then brought her safe out of Zaguig--where her own brother must have got *his* by now, she says. Whole garrison shot up, and him with 'em... ."

"Old Man Boje must have been mighty set on paying a call here if he lit out from Zaguig while they were fighting... ."

"Sure thing, Son--you spoke the truth for once... . Mary--I mean Miss Vanbrugh--says it's *the* Big Thing of his Life, and if he pulls it off he's a made man... . He wouldn't stop in Zaguig for anything--though his comrades and his life-long pard and chum were in the soup... ."

"Then we raise our price, Hank Sheikh! What's a measly million francs if it's as important as all that? ... Let's keep him guessing, and get some more in the jack-pot... . Tell him we got other offers too... ."

"Well--Son of Temptation and Father of Joyful Ideas--we won't hurry any. I certainly like having the girls around--I could have wept bitter salt tears of joy all down my whiskers when those two girls stepped into our li'll home... ."

"Me too, Hank! I went all wambly in my innards and got a lump in my throat... . I nearly hugged 'em to my bosom... . I may yet... ."

"Not both, Son," remonstrated the Emir. "In the Name of the Prophet let the Reins of Moderation restrain the Stallion of Frowardness. Yup!"

"Only in the way of showing respect, I meant. I ain't a Mormon, am I? If Miss Mary'll marry me... ."

"Well--don't go indulging your mind too much, Bud. It'll only make it worse for you later... . The way Miss Mary talked--I reckon she's a spinster for life or Mrs. Boje for ditto--if he has the sense to ax her... . She wouldn't do us any *harm*--not till Hell pops--but it's Old Man Bojolly's good *she's* thinking of... ."

The Vizier rose to his feet and strode up and down the tent like a caged lion.

"Look at here, Hank Sheikh," he said at last. "Can't we fix it for Mister Blasted Bojolly to take his punk Treaty and *go*--leaving the girls behind?"

The Emir pondered the suggestion.

"We could put it to him, Son," he said at length, "but I don't think you get old Boje right... . I could live the rest of my young life without Boje, I allow--but I believe he's a blowed-in-the-glass White Man, if he is a Wop or a Dago or a Frenchman... . We haven't had a sporting bet for some time, Bud--I'll lay you seven to three in *medjidies* that Boje won't stand for it... . He isn't going to leave two white girls in the wigwams of a camp of Injuns, while he gets away with the goods... . Nope ... I'll make it ten to one on Boje and ..."

"Done! *Shake!*" snapped the Vizier, extending his hand, and the two "shook." "I should certainly enjoy marrying his girl on his million francs... . Teach him not to come here frightening people ... *and--don't forget--he left Dufour and Achmet and the others to die while he made his getaway ...!*"

"But we won't hurry things, Hank," he added. "Let Boje get a bit anxious first. We'll coop him up some--an' pull the fierce and treacherous Sheikh stuff on him. We might pretend we was double-crossing him with the Rastignac outfit."

"You can have it your own way and run it how you like, Son," agreed the Emir, "but I promised Miss Vanbrugh we'd not hurt a hair of his lovely hide, bless him... ."

"He's a brave man, and he's straight. But I say he'd leave the girls in the lurch to get that Treaty," said the Vizier.

A silence fell.

The Vizier, his head on his hand-clasped knees, made the cooing sounds that showed his friend he was indeed again in love.

"Hank Sheikh, old Hoss," he said anon, "she is the plumb loveliest girl from Egypt to 'Frisco an' from Hell to breakfast... . *Yes,* Sir!"

"Mary or Maudie?" murmured the Emir, from the depths of his own long thoughts... .

CHAPTER VII. L'HOMME PROPOSE

Once again the Emir el Hamel el Kebir and his guest Miss Mary Vanbrugh, rode alone.

"... And why do you consult *me,* Mr. Emir?" said the girl. "Unlike yourself, I'm no matchmaker."

"If you're alluding to poor Buddy, I only spoke up for him because you were breaking his heart, Miss Mary Vanbrugh... .

"And why I wanted to consult you about Miss Maudie Atkinson is because she's your hired help, and I don't want to take her away from you while you're in the Desert--if you can't blow your own nose... .

"Also you're a woman--and you'd know better than a rough and common man like me, how a girl'd feel, and if it's a fair proposition... .

"Also you're clever, and can see if it's likely to pan out well for a girl like Maudie--who's been uster living in gay and populous cities... .

"Also if you think you could persuade Major D. Bojol*lay* that it is all right to leave her behind with us low Injuns. In fact what do you think about it? ..."

"Well, I think that Love is the *only thing that matters,*" replied the girl, flushing warmly. "I think that Love is Heaven and Heaven is Love.

"No, I'm *certain* it is... . And if Maudie really loved you and you really loved Maudie, I'd say, 'Go to it, and God bless you, for you couldn't do a wiser thing! ...'"

"It's Maudie I'm thinking about, more," said the Emir.

"So'm I... . And I believe she'd be as happy as the day is long, for she's the most romantic soul that ever lived--and one of the staunchest... .

"I know you'd be kind and good to her, and I know you'd have a splendid wife... . She's real pure gold all through... . And she'd worship the ground you trod on, for she's madly in love with Love... ." The girl gazed wistfully at the horizon... .

"But remember," she continued, "she's very simple, and she's no 'Janey that's Brainy.' She won't brighten your wigwam with high-brow thoughts and bee-you-ti-ful aspirations to make you lead a higher and a better life of culture and uplift."

"Sure--God bless her," agreed the Emir.

"And how long did you plan to deceive her and play this Sheikh-game with *her?*" asked the girl.

"Just up to the day when she realizes that she's fair fed full with Arabs and Desert Sheikhs, and begins to wish I was an ornery White Man.... As soon as I see it in her eye that she misses the shops an' movies an' street-cars an' candy an' the-pianner-an'-canary-home-sweet-home stuff, she becomes Mrs. Hank of the U.S.A...."

"That's sense. She'll want another woman to talk frocks and scandal with, some day, however much she might love you...."

"Sure. But me being willing to pull stakes and light out as soon as she gets real weary of the Injun life--d'you think it's fair to her if I ... ?"

"Yes. If she loves you.... She's seen how you live; and it's been the one great yearn of her young life to behold the Desert Sheikh Sheikhing in the Desert.... Shall I say anything to her? ..."

"Not on your life, Miss Mary Vanbrugh! I'm going to do the thing as I believe she dreams it....

"All women are cave-women at heart, and would like to be swept off their feet once in their lives.... It's when they've got to wash the cave-man's shirt and pants, an' he will leave his nasty stinking tobacco-pipe on the cave drawing-room plush table-cloth; and bawls her out when he can't find his slippers, that cave-life wears thin.... Yep, they do cert'nly like to be swept off their feet and swept right away by a Strong Silent He-Cave-Man, once in their lives...."

Miss Mary Vanbrugh sighed.

"Well, I hope you'll both be very happy--and if Maudie can stand desert life, you *will* be--for you're made for each other."

"And what about Major D. Bojol*lay?*"

"What do you mean?"

"Will he agree to leave her behind?"

"Yes--if I can persuade him that she'll be happy here.... To these European aristocrats she's just a 'servant' and her tastes unaccountable.... Besides, if Maudie *won't* go back, he can't take her by force...."

"Would he leave her if he thought she'd get a bad time? ... *Would he leave the pair of you--in return for my signing the Treaty,* say?"

"I don't think you quite understand a gentleman--if you talk like that...." answered the girl.

"No. Sure. I haven't had much truck with gentlemen, Miss Mary Vanbrugh. Only low common men like me and Buddy.... Sure.... 'Sides--to tell you the truth *I was thinking of Dufour and the others that he left to die,* for the sake of his Treaty! ... I knew old Dufour. He was a man. He was Sergeant-Major with Major D. Bojol*lay* when he was mule-walloping at Tokotu.... I knew Achmet too.... He was a real fine he-man and *some*scrapper...."

"Yes, yes," broke in the girl, "but it was *duty.* Duty is his God...."

"Sure. It's what I'm saying. Isn't this Treaty *still* his Duty? It'll be real interestin'.... All a matter of what's your own private *Bo Ideal* as they call it.... 'Sides, Major D. Bojol*lay's* French, and as you said, he'd give his soul to get that Treaty for his beloved France...."

"His *soul,* perhaps--not his honour," was the proud reply, but the Emir, closely watching, had seen her wince.

398

"I always mistrusted people that go about with a wad of 'honour' bulgin' outa their breast-pockets ... I've found ..."

But Miss Mary Vanbrugh spurred her horse forward and the Emir's further words of wisdom were lost.

§ 2

Miss Maudie Atkinson, bred and born in Cockaigne and the sound of Bow Bells, stood at eventide on a sandhill of the Oasis and gazed yearningly towards the setting sun.

She was a happy, happy girl, but the cup of her happiness was not full. She had, she felt, been, in a manner of speaking, captured by Sheikhs, but not by *a* Sheikh.

True, the great and beautiful man, the *lovely* man, in whose presence she had thrice feasted, had looked upon her with the eye that is glad--and Miss Atkinson, as an extremely attractive girl who had grown up in London, was experienced in the Glad Eye... .

She had had it, she was prepared to swear, from the Great Sheikh, and, moreover, he had held, and squeezed and stroked her hand... .

But, as one who knew joyous days on the Mondays that are holy, Bank Holy Days, at Easter, at Whitsun, and eke in August, Miss Atkinson knew a sense of something lacking.

Young pages and footmen of on-coming disposition had to be slapped and told to Give over, to Stop it, to Come off it, Not to be so Fast, and had to be asked What they thought they were Doing--pulling people about until their back hair came down and all... .

But there seemed to be no hope that the Great Sheikh was going to earn a slap and an admonition to Stop it... .

Not his to chase, with flying feet, a shrieking damsel who fled across the daisy-pied sward to a quiet spot. Not his to hug, wrestle, and mildly punch, a coy nymph, who scolded laughingly.

Not his to behave thus, nor issue invitation to the quiet walk that leads to "walking-out."

No; a calm and dignified man, alas, but oh, so big and beautiful, and so authentic... . And his eyes fair burnt into you... . Just as the lady had written in the book, the lovely Book of Sheikhs... .

Maudie dreamed... . And remembered passages from the Book... .

"*With a thunderous rush of heavy hoofs, the Desert Sheikh was upon her, and ere she could so much as scream, she found herself swung like a feather to his saddle-bow and whirled afar across the desert... . On, on, into the setting sun--while his hot lips found hers and drank deep of her beauty the while they burnt her very flesh like fire... .*"

Ah-h-h-h-h. That was the stuff... .

And even as the Cupid's bow of Maudie's mouth trembled with the words, there *was* a thunderous rush of heavy hoofs, two huge and powerful hands took her beneath the arms, and she was mightily hauled from the ground and dumped heavily on to a hard saddle--("*Oo*-er!")-- ... and whirled afar across the Desert--on, on, into the setting sun... .

Maudie all but swooned. Half fainting with joy, and with the hope fulfilled that maketh the heart too full for speech, she summoned the strength to raise her arms and her eyes.

The latter gazed straight into those of the Great Sheikh Himself, and the former settled firmly about his neck.

His lips found hers in deed and very truth, and with a shuddering sigh of the deepest content and the highest gratitude for the fruition of a life's ambition, Maudie gave the Great Sheikh Himself the First Kiss of Love--a long, long clinging kiss--and was grateful to God for His wondrous goodness.

When Maudie came to earth again, wondering to find the earth still there and Maudie still in the strong arms of this Wonder of the World, she wiped her eyes (and nose) with the sleeve of her *barracan,* sniffed, and gave a little sob.

The Emir reined in his horse, dismounted, and lifted her to the ground. Her knees betrayed her, and she sat down with some suddenness, on the soft warm sand.

The Emir seated himself beside her and took her hand.

"Lill' girl," he said, "will you marry me?" and Maudie cast herself wildly upon his broad bosom.

"Oh, *Sheikh, darling*!" she said, and again flung her arms about his neck.

"We'll get married by the mullah-bird here," said the Emir later. "Then bye'n-bye we'll hike to where there's a Christian marriage-dope man, an' get married some more. Have *another* wedding, Maudie!"

Maudie snuggled.

"And have *another* honeymoon, darling," she whispered.

They kissed until they could kiss no longer... .

Anon she dragged herself from him and stared wide-eyed.

"Why--you spoke *English*!" she stammered in amaze... .

"Sure. I learnt it since you came--so's to talk to you, Maudie... ." said the Emir modestly, and again gathered the girl in a huge embrace.

"But mind you, Maudie," he said impressively, when they rose to go, "that Major de Bojolly mustn't know I've learnt English or else he'd want to talk English all the time--and get me muddled in business perhaps, while I'm a beginner--or p'raps he'd think I wasn't a Sheikh at all!"

"Oh, him!" murmured Maudie languidly. "He's only a Frenchie... ."

§ 3

In the *hareem* portion of the chief Guest-tent were four women, two white and two black.

The black women were slaves, brought as "orphans" from Lake Tchad by a Senussi caravan, and sold to the old Sheikh twenty years before.

The bad old days of the fire-and-slaughter Arab slave-raider are gone for ever, but there is still some slave-dealing carried on--chiefly in children.

These are sold by their parents, or adoptive parents in the case of genuine orphans, to caravan-leaders, who sell them again at a profit in the distant oases, where negroes, other than slaves, are not.

The shocked European Authority confiscates the entire caravan if a slave is found with it--but the caravan does not seek the spots honoured by Authority.

And if Authority goes out of its way and seeks the caravan, it finds none but happy adopted children, staring big-eyed from the backs of camels, or toddling along beside kindly men, or seated patting scarcely "fair" round bellies, beside the cooking-pot.

The unshocked Arab Authority buys the healthy little animal, and treats it well, because it is valuable property; and, when it grows up, puts it in regiment or *hareem* according to its sex--where it may rise to high rank and power as a military commander, or to the position of Sheikh's favourite, and mother of future Sheikhs.

Slave-raiding is the foulest and vilest pursuit ever engaged in by man, but a great deal of misunderstanding exists about slavery as an Arab institution... .

And certainly the two black slave-women, who squatted in the *hareem* side of the guest-tent, were happy enough, as they produced beautiful Arab stuffs and clothing, *henna* for the nails and hands, *hadida* for the hair, *djeldjala* "golden drops," *khalouk* rouge, *koh'eul* for the eyes, and other matters of feminine interest, from the big *bahut* trunk they had carried over from the tents of Sidi Dawad Fetata.

The four women chattered; the chirping sounds of a Senegalese dialect mingled with the Cockney accent of London and the refined tones of a Boston high-school and college; and though in language they were divided, in interest they were one, as the slave girls showed the uses of the stuffs, clothing, unguents, paints and powders that they had brought... .

Anon came the aged Sidi Dawad Fetata, smiling sweetly, and saying that his long white beard was a perfect chaperone and his age-dimmed eyes were blinded by the beauty of the Sitts.

"*Salamoune aleikoume Esseleme, Sitt Roumya,*" he said. "*Marhaba, marhaba,*" and proceeded to hope that life might be as sweet as *Mekhtoume,* the Wine of Paradise; as beautiful as *jahwiyan* daisies in the desert; as satisfying as the dates of Nabt al Saif; and as long and flowing as the Tail of the Horse of the Prophet... .

"The old dear is making a beautiful speech, Maudie, if we could only understand a word of it," said Mary Vanbrugh, and smiled graciously upon the visitor, who promptly produced gifts--a silver *khams* Hand-of-Fatma charm, and silver *maroued* box to hold *koh'eul* for Mary; with a *sokhab* tiara of small coins and *a feisha* charm (to keep a husband's affections) for Maudie.

The old gentleman then announced a *diffa,* clapped his hands, and the slave girls brought in a huge *sahfa* dish, on which was an appalling heterogeny of bowls and platters, of *berkouks,* pellets of sweetened rice; cous-cous; *cherchem* beans; *leben* curds; *burghal* mince-meat and porridge; *asida* dough and onions; *fatta* carrots and eggs; strange sweetmeats, fruits, and drinks.

"As good a death as any, Grandpa," replied Miss Vanbrugh, to the old Sidi's "*Bilhana!* With Joy! *Bilshifa!* With health!" and they fell to... .

"Coming round, Maudie?" asked Miss Vanbrugh later, when they were alone, comatose, replete, bursting with food.

"I'm *getting* round, Miss," replied Maudie.

"We shall be as round as one of those lovely fat Arab babies dressed in a string of beads, if we go on like this, Miss," she added. "I shall fair lose my figger."

"We'll offer a reward for it, Maudie ... Lost--*a lovely figure*... . Anyone returning the same to Miss Maudie Atkinson at No. 1, High Street, Emir's Camp, Great Oasis... ."

"Oh, *Miss,*" murmured Maudie, "may I tell you something? ... I'm not going to be Miss Atkinson much longer."

"You've told me already, Maudie."

"Oh, *no*, Miss!"

"But you have! You've been mad, Maudie, ever since it happened. Perfectly insane--going about like a dying duck in a thunderstorm; trying to do my hair with a tooth-brush; trying to manicure my nails with sand-paper. You don't know who you are nor where you are; nor whether you're on your head or your heels... . Now tell me all about it... ."

Maudie told... .

"If you see Major de Beaujolais, to speak to, don't tell him that some of the Arab Sheikhs know English, Maudie," said Miss Vanbrugh, when Maudie's rapture-recital was finished.

"*No*, Miss," replied Maudie. "The Great Sheikh told me not to. He said the Major might take advantage of his innocence and make him talk English when he was bargaining--and do him down... . It would be a shame to impose on him, wouldn't it, Miss?"

"I don't think the Major will impose on the Emir, Maudie," said Miss Vanbrugh, a little coldly perhaps. "Anyhow--say nothing about it."

"I'd sooner rather *die*, first, Miss," asseverated Maudie warmly.

"Well--if you do let it slip--you'll die *after*," observed Miss Vanbrugh, "for I'll certainly kill you, Maudie."

§ 4

During the days that followed, the Emir noticed a change in the temper of his trusty Vizier.

Perhaps no one else would have seen it, but to the Emir, who loved his friend with a love passing the love of women, including Maudie, it was clear that the Vizier was really suffering and unhappy.

Never, nowadays, in the privacy of the open desert, did he sing,

"O ki yi yip; O ki yi yi,

O ki yi yip; and ki yi yi,

Get along you stinkin' camels, don't you cry,

We'll all be in Wyoming in the sweet bye-an'-bye,"

or any other amended version of any of the eighty verses of "*The Old Chisholm Trail.*" ... Nor did he utter vain longings for his old mouth-organ... .

His hard grey eyes, that saw so much and told so little, enigmatic, ironic, unreadable, humorous, were humorous no longer... .

The Emir was troubled, torn between two emotions, and quite unreasonably ashamed...

The object of his thoughts rode past on a lathered horse, staring grimly before him, looking neither unto the right hand nor unto the left... . He looked dangerous.

"Oh! Sidi Wazir!" called the Emir. "Come and *faddhl*," and El R'Orab the Crow ran and took the Vizier's horse and led it away to its stable of plaited palm-leaves in the *fondouk* horse-lines... .

"Good job this is a Dry State, Hank Sheikh," growled the Vizier, seating himself beside the Emir, "or I should cert'nly lap the *laghbi* this night.... *Hamdulillah!* I'd sure be off the gosh-dinged water-wagon, *some!*"

"What's the trouble, Son?" asked the Emir, although he knew too well.

"Trouble is, I'm going to bust that Sheikh-wrangler, Bojolly.... *Rahmat Allah!* Treaty or no Treaty.... And tell him some talk in the only sensible language there is...."

"What's he done now, Son?" inquired the Emir.

"Put me in Dutch with Miss Vanbrugh.... The Infiddle Dorg...."

"I allow he'd play a square game, Bud."

"I mean it was through him I spoke rude to a lady an' showed myself the low-life ornery bindle-stiff I am."

"You was never rude to any lady, Bud."

"Yes, I was, Hank Sheikh. I axed her if she was engaged to be married to a scent-smellin', nose-wipin', high-falutin dude French officer...."

"What you do that for, Son?"

"She turned down my respeckful proposal of matterimony."

"And then you fired up about Bojolly?"

"Sure."

"And what did Miss Vanbrugh say when you did that? ... She talked American at you all right this time, then?"

"Yep. You bet. When I began to call Bojolly down ..."

"What did she say when you asked if she was fixed up with the Major?"

"She says, '*It's a beautiful sunset to-night, Mr. Man,*' an' she thought she was ridin' with a decent an' courteous American, and that Major D. Bojol*lay* was the finest and noblest and bravest man she'd ever met, an' thank you, she'd prefer to ride back to the Oasis alone...."

"What you do then, Son?"

"I says, 'I thought *you* was American, Miss Vanbrugh,' an' then I over-rode my hoss like the mean coyote I am."

"So you're sore and ashamed, Son. You hurt a hoss an' a woman, the two best things there are...."

"I'm tellin' you.... And I'm goin' to eat sand ... and I'm goin' to bust that Sheikh-wrangler, Bojolly...."

"As how?"

"He can shout his own fancy--knives, guns ... rifles if he likes. P'raps he'd prefer to use that sword he's brought all this way to impress us and the girls.... I'll back my Arab sword against it, if he likes."

"What *d'you* like, Son?"

"Knives. I ain't had a knife-fight since when. And it's a satisfying way of expressin' your feelings to a man you don't much like...."

"And Miss Vanbrugh, Son? Miss Vanbrugh, who you love so much, and who thinks Major D. Bojol*lay* the finest an' noblest an' bravest man she ever saw? ... Didn't I *tell* you, right back at the very first? ... Didn't I say to you, '*Don't you go kidding yourself, you Bud--for she's going to be a spinster or Mrs. Boje'*?"

The Vizier scowled glumly.

"Now I'll tell you something for your good, Buddy Bashaw.... You aren't in love with anybody.... You're just plumb jealous of a better man than yourself, because he's got away with it.... Who was first in the field? ... You talk about busting Boje! And why for? Because you can't get his girl away from him! ... *Gee!*"

"Spill some more, you oozin' molasses-bar'l," growled the Vizier.

"Certainly.... If you haven't got the innercence o' the dove nor the wisdom of the serpent, you *can* have the sense of a louse.... Ole Man Bojol*lay* brought Miss Vanbrugh here, and he's goin' to take her away again.... You made your firm offer of marriage and it was declined with thanks.... Now behave your silly self ... and be ashamed of you."

"Sure. But look at here, Hank Sheikh. I'm *plumb jealous of a better man than me,* am I? Well--no objection to makin' *certain* who's the better man, is there?"

"Yep. You aren't goin' to fight Major D. Bojol*lay*, so don't think it. I dunno what's bitin' *you,* Buddy Bashaw.... *Wallahi!*"

"Why not fight him?"

"Because he's our guest.... Because he's going to give us a wad of jack.... Because we don't want any French army here looking for him. Because Miss Vanbrugh thinks he's the noblest, bravest, and ..."

"Gee! I got a think come!" interrupted the Vizier.... "We'll sure try the brave man out.... We'll see if he *is* worthy o' Miss Vanbrugh--which nobody is."

"'Cept Buddy Bashaw the Wild and Woolly Wazir," murmured the Emir.

The Vizier pursued his great idea.

"You say he's the Almighty Goods, an' *you* seem to want him to marry Miss Mary--well, *we'll try him out. Inshallah!*"

"Now look at here, Son," interrupted the Emir again. "Get this straight.... See that hand o' mine, Boy?"

"*Some! Allahbyjiminy!* I could see it seven mile away, without a telescope neither--an' then mistake it for a leg o' mutton...."

"See that hand o' mine, Bud," repeated the Emir solemnly. "God's my witness, I'd cut it off, if that'd make you an' Miss Mary happy for life. I cert'nly would.... But I got sense, tho' I ain't a clever li'll man like you--an' I say no girl ever did a plumb sillier thing than marry a man she didn't love.... Nor any man ever did such a *damn* silly thing as wanta marry a gal that didn' love him.... I'd sooner see Mary marry you and live on goat's flesh and barley-bread in a tent, than marry the Major and live in High Sassiety, provided she loved you.... But she don't. And won't...."

"Very well, Pastor, an' that's *that*.... Now then! We're goin' to find out how much this French parlour-snake and lounge-lizard *does* love Miss Vanbrugh.... First of all I'm goin' to take ten *medjidies* off'n you, an' if I don't, then you're goin' to take a hundred off *me.*"

"How's that, Son?"

"You forgot that li'll bet we made? We're goin' to knock him up in the dead o' night an' offer him the Treaty, signed, sealed and witnessed--*provided* he saddles up an' lights out to-morrow *without* the girls...."

"Which he cert'nly won't."

"... An' if you're right you get your ten. *And* soon after that, we'll give him a *real* test.... Now I'd lay down my life for Miss Vanbrugh, or any other nice girl ..."

"Sure thing, Son. *Any* girl."

404

"... and if Boje *really* loves Miss Vanbrugh, let him lay down his'n.... We'll give him the opportunity.... He oughta be proud of the chance to do it! ... He won't though, you betcha, and I put a hundred to one on it."

"*Done*. Shake. Put it there, Son," and the two erring men shook hands.

"It's robbing you, Son--and I didn't oughta do it," pondered the Emir thereafter, "but you gotta live and learn."

"You live till to-night and you'll learn you've lost ten bucks, Hank Sheikh," was the cold reply.

"I'll live, Son, if Rastignac don't get me," answered the Emir. "He'd poison our coffee when we visited him, or shoot us unarmed as soon as look at us, if he thought he could get away with it--and nominate his own Emir here.... How *I* didn't shoot *him* when he started in about murderin' Boje and doin' worse for his two female spies, I do *not* know."

"Me, neither," agreed the Vizier. "I promise myself a quiet heart-to-heart wrangle with Rastignac when the time comes.... Reckon we should be layin' up trouble for the tribes if Rastignac was never seen again?"

"Sooner or later.... It's bound to come though, when we hitch up with the French, as we must.... The foul filthy coyote--I'd like to hang him on a tree."

"I allow he's got the face of a shark and the heart of a shark," observed the Vizier.

"No, no! That's an exaggeration, Son," reproved the Emir. "There never wasn't any shark with a face as much like a shark's as Rastignac's is. Nor any shark with a heart as much like a shark's neither.... Still, he's a brave man--and he shall die a man's death if we don't let him go."

"Right, Hank Sheikh," agreed the Vizier. "Let me fight him.... *Knives!*"

"We'll see how things pan out with Boje before we settle Rastignac's hash," replied the Emir. "I should smile to stick 'em in a ring, with any weapons they liked, and say, 'Now fight it out for yourselves'--*after* tellin' Boje what Rastignac offered us big money to do to him *and the girls*...."

"*Rastignac!*" growled the Vizier, and spat in a vulgar and coarse manner.

"You low common man," observed his lord. "You don't seem to improve in your ways although you live with me."

"*No*," replied the Vizier significantly.

CHAPTER VIII. LA FEMME DISPOSE

Yoluba, the seven-foot Soudanese slave, on sentry-go outside the Guest-tent, heard the murmur of voices rising and falling within.

That did not interest him in the least.

Nothing interested him greatly, save to get the maximum of food, love, fighting and sleep. And the approbation of his Lord the Sidi el Hamel el Kebir, Commander of the Faithful and Shadow of Heaven.

To do this, orders must be obeyed promptly and exactly.

Present orders were to prevent the *Franzawi* Sidi from leaving the Guest-tent--firmly but respectfully to tell him he must stay within, because the sun (or moon) was very hot without.

Suddenly the voices ceased and then the *Franzawi's* rose to an angry and abusive shout! Should he rush in?

No--for the Emir and the Vizier were coming out.

"I hand it to you, Hank Sheikh," admitted the Vizier, as the two entered the pavilion of the Emir. "Boje cert'nly spoke up like a man.... He's made good *so far*."

"You can hand me ten chips too, Son," observed the Emir. "And if you go on with it, you'll hand me a hundred. I'll let you back out if you wanta quit.... In fact I'd like you to. I hate playing a low-down trick on a brave man...."

"Cut out the sob-stuff, Hank Sheikh," was the prompt reply. "If he's the blue-eyed hero, let him live up to it--or *die* up to it. He won't know it's a trick either, the way I figger it. 'Sides, you're so all-fired anxious about Miss Vanbrugh--let's see if he's solid, before you give him your blessin' and a weddin'-present."

"What's the frame-up, Son?" asked the Emir.

"Why--we're goin' to be the fierce and changeable, treacherous Sheikhs on him for a bit, and get him buffaloed. Then we'll pay another midnight call on him, an' tell him he's sure hurt our tenderest feelin's--callin' us dorgs an' pigs an' such.... Got to be wiped out in blood.... But we don't want to wipe a guest ourselves--so if he likes to do it himself, we'll let the girls go free and uninjured immediately."

"And if he won't?"

"Then we say, 'Very well, Mr. Roumi. Then the gals come into our *hareems,* the Treaty gets signed, an' you can get to Hell outa this with it....'"

"And if he says, '*How can I trust you to do me a square deal when I'm dead?*'"

"Then we say, '*You* GOTTA *trust us. No option. But when we noble savages give our word on the Q'ran--it goes.*'"

"And how do we work it? ... Tell R'Orab to pull the cartridges outa his gun beforehand, and then let him shoot himself with an empty gun.... When it clicks, our stony bosoms relent and we embrace him in tears.... That it?" asked the Emir.

"Nope. Too easy a death. Nothing in shootin' yourself. 'Sides, he might *find* his gun had been emptied, an' double-cross us. Shoot himself with the empty gun, grinnin' up his sleeve meantime."

"What then?"

"Nasty sticky death. Poison."

"He might drink it, feeling sure it was a bluff and grinning to himself while hopin' for the best."

"He's goin' to *know* it's poison. Good forty-mile, mule-slayin', weed-killer.... What we took off old Abdul Salam.... He's going to see it kill a dorg."

"Well, it'll kill *him* then, won't it?"

"Nope. The poison'll be in the poor dorg's drinkin'-water *already.* Then I'll pour half a gill of *pure milk* into it, an' the li'll dorg drinks an' hands in his checks *pronto*.... Then I give the rest o' the milk to Boje in his cawfee.... Then it's up to him.... *If* he drinks, you get a hundred bucks, an' Boje gets Miss Vanbrugh...."

"An' if he don't?"

"We'll ride him outa town an' tell Miss Vanbrugh that the li'll hero--what was goin' to live for her--didn' see his way to *die* for her."

"*You* can tell her, Bud.... I'll be somewhere else at the moment...."

"Well--we ain't goin' to put him in any danger, nor do a thing *to* him, are we?"

"Not a thing.... And you're going to a girl to bear the glad news that her hero's slunk off and left her because his hide was in danger and to get his Treaty signed. Shake, Son, I admire a brave man."

"But it'll be *true,* won't it?" expostulated the Vizier.

"Yes, Son--and that's what she'll never forgive you," replied the Emir.

"But it won't be," he added. "Boje'll lap that fake poison of yours like you'd drink whisky.... And he'll come outa this job better'n we shall.... I don't like it, Son. Sure thing, I don't--but it'll come back on your own silly head.... Mary'll love the Major all the more, and our name'll be Stinkin' Mud.... The Major'll love Mary all the more, because he tried to die for her...."

"Die nothing!" jeered the Vizier. "He's only a furriner an' a scent-smellin' ornament.... Drinkin' poison at three o'clock in the morning's a tougher proposition than shootin' off guns in a scrap.... 'Sides--s'pose he did play the li'll hero an' drink the fatal draught to save his loved one's life--he won't tell her about it afterwards, will he? 'Specially when he finds it was all a fake?"

"No. He won't say anything, Son. But *I* shall. If Boje swills dorg-slaying poison on an empty stomach in the nasty small hours o' the morning, he's goin' to get the credit for it--an' I'll see he does...."

"Well--he won't, Hank Sheikh, so don't spend those hundred bucks before you collect.... Well, I'm goin' to hit it for the downy...."

The Emir sat stroking his beard reflectively, and murmured, "*Wallahi!* Verily '*he worketh well who worketh with Allah,*' saith The Book.... Bust me if *I* know--Anyway, it'd settle that li'll girl's doubts once for all--an' poor Ole Man Dufour's ghost won't worry her.... If I guess her right, she hates one little corner of Boje and worships the rest of him with all her soul.... It's an awful low-down trick in a way--but it'll settle things once for all for Miss Mary Vanbrugh.... If Boje is a dyed-in-the-wool and blowed-in-the-glass bachelor, with his work as his wife and his job as his mistress, she better know it--the sooner the quicker.... It is a low-down game, Bud--awful mean and ornery--but those Secret Service guys cert'nly spend their lives in bluffing and playing tricks.... It's their job.... And they ought to take it in good part if they're bluffed themselves.... *Bluff!* Gee! What a bluff to pull on the bluff-merchant.... Well, let it rip...."

"Sure thing," replied the departing Vizier. "G'night, pard. *Emshi besselema.*"

§ 2

As the Emir and his Vizier rode back from visiting the camp of the emissary of the Sultan of Stamboul and his great Brother; and from watching the drill of the camel-corps recruits; inspecting the *fondouk* and lines; and generally doing the things that most Oriental Rulers leave to others to leave undone, the Emir asked his Vizier if he had slept well, and if he had risen in a better frame of mind.

"I'm goin' to try Bojolly out, I tell you," replied the Vizier.

"And you got it clear that whether he stands or falls, it won't do you any good with Miss Vanbrugh?"

"Yup. I done with women. My heart's broke--but I shall get over it. I don't ask any girl twice. She refused me flat. Quite nice but quite certain. *And,*when I called Bojolly down-- quite nasty an' still more certain... . No, Hank, my heart's broke, but I'm facin' up to life like a man... ."

"Sure thing, Bud... . Now drop this foolishness about the Major. It won't do any good... ."

"Do some good if it saves Miss Vanbrugh from a fortune-huntin' French furriner, won't it? American girls should marry American men... ."

"And American men should marry American girls, I s'pose?" observed the Emir.

"You said it, Son... . Say--ain't that li'll Maudie-girl some peach? ..."

"She surely is... . Pity your heart's broke, Bud. Still--American men gotta marry American girls, anyway."

"Well--Anglo-Saxon men oughta marry Anglo-Saxon girls, I mean. *Course* they ought... . No frills an' doo-dahs about Maudie, if she *is* British... . Make a fine plain wife fer a plain man... ."

"You cert'nly *are* a plain man, Bud," admitted the Emir reluctantly.

"Maudie may be engaged already," he added.

"She don't wear any ring... . I looked to see ..." replied the Vizier.

"Well--I *have* known engaged girls not wear a ring, Son," admitted the Emir.

"Then they was engaged to mean skunks," decided the Vizier, and burst into song.

His broken heart evidently *was* mending, and cool dawn in the desert is a very stimulating, lovely hour.

The Emir smiled tolerantly as he listened to one more variation of "*The Old Chisholm Trail.*" ... All was well with Buddy when Buddy sang... .

"Wish I got my ole mouth-organ," observed the Vizier.

"Your mouth is an organ in itself, Son," replied the Emir, as the Vizier again lifted up his voice and informed the wide Sahara that,

"Ole Hank Sheikh was a fine ole Boss,
Rode off with a gal on a fat-backed hoss,
Ole Hank Sheikh was fond of his liquor,
Allus had a bottle in the pocket of his slicker." ...'

"How you know I rode off with a girl on a fat-backed hoss, Son?" asked the Emir, as the Vizier paused for breath.

"I didn't," admitted the Vizier... . "Did you? Sorta thing you *would* do... . Many a true word spoken in jest... ."

"Sure, Son. And many a true jest spoken in words," agreed the Emir.

They rode on.

"Sing some more, Son," requested the Emir. "Thy voice delights me, O Father of a Thousand Nightingales... . It's good training for these high-strung Arab hosses... . Make the animals calm in a mere battle... ."

And the Vizier continued the Saga, in the vein of the history-recording troubadours of old:

"Foot in the stirrup and hand on the horn,
Worst old Sheikh that ever was born.
Foot in the stirrup, then his seat to the sky,
Worst old Sheikh that ever rode by." ...

§ 3

Beside a little irrigation-runlet Miss Maudie Atkinson sat--and waited, her mental attitude somewhat that with which she had been familiar all her life at the hour of one on the Sabbath Day, *"For what we are about to receive... ."*

Emerging from the Guest-tent, at what, after much peeping, she considered to be a propitious moment, she had strolled past the tents of her *fiancé (her fiancé!)*, the Great Sheikh, and walked slowly towards a strategic spot. Here she threw off her *barracan* and stood revealed, Maudie Atkinson, in a nice cotton frock, white stockings and white shoes. Much more attractive to Arab eyes, she was sure, than shapeless swaddlings of a lot of blooming nightdresses and baggy trousers.

Silly clo'es for a girl with a figger... .

Would he come?

Sure to, if he wasn't too busy, or hadn't got to take Miss Mary for a ride... . When would that nice Major come up to the scratch, and take what was waiting for him? ... Oh, what happy, lucky girls she and Miss Mary were! ...

Would he come?

A shadow moved beside her and she turned.

Golly! It was the little one. Didn't he look a nib in those gay robes!

"Good-evening, sir," said Maudie.

"'Evening, Miss," replied the Vizier. "Shall we go for a li'll stroll under the trees?"

"*I* don't mind if we do, sir," said Maudie, rising promptly. *(Sheikhs!)*

"I been admiring you ever since you come, Miss," observed the Vizier as they strolled off.

"No! Straight? Have you *reely?*" ejaculated Maudie.

"Sure. All the time," replied her companion with conviction. "In fact, I follered you to-night to say so--an' to ask you if you thought you an' me might hitch up an' be pards... ."

"*I* don't mind, sir," said Maudie. "Fancy *you* speaking English, too... ."

"Yes, Miss... . Er--yes. You see, I sent for a handbook as soon as I saw you that night."

"No! Not *reely?*"

"Sure! Fact! Would I tell you a *lie?* But you must never let Major Bojolly know."

"Oh no, sir. Miss Vanbrugh said she'd kill me if I did... . As if I *would!* Besides, I never see him now. Why are you keeping him a prisoner?"

"Oh, we're just making sure he doesn't run off an' take you two ladies away from us... ."

"He don't take *me! I'll* watch it," asserted Miss Maud Atkinson.

"My heart would cert'nly break if he did... . Miss Maudie, will you marry me?"

"Oh, *sir*! If you'd only spoke sooner!" Maudie looked down and blushed.

"I'm engaged to the other Sheikh... . We're going to be married twice and have two honeymoons... . It's reely very kind of you, sir, but things being as they are, I ..."

Maudie looked up. But the Sheikh had gone... .

A few minutes later he thrust his head into the sleeping-tent of the Emir, where that gentleman, dressing for dinner, was washing his feet.

With a horrible scowl and a display of gleaming teeth, the Vizier gazed upon his Lord.

"O you Ram*bunc*tious Ole Goat," he hissed, and withdrew his Gorgon head from the aperture.

§ 4

But, being a man of noble forbearance and generosity, this was the only allusion made by the Vizier to the human frailties of his Lord.

The soul of determination, and slow to accept defeat, he remarked during the course of the evening *faddhl*:

"Say, Hank--how you like to be a *real* brother-in-law to a Sheikh?"

"Fine, Bud... . You got a sister for me to marry?"

"No, Son. And if I had I'd be pertickler who she married to... . No, I meant a real Sheikh, and I was referring to me bein' his brother-in-law."

"You got me buffaloed, Pard. Spell it."

"S'pose I was to marry Miss Leila Nakhla, then? I'd be brother-in-law to the young Sheikh, wouldn't I?"

"Yup. And own brother to a dam' fool."

"Jealous of me again, Hank Sheikh?"

"You got marryin' on the brain, or where your brain oughter be, Buddy Bashaw... . You had a rise in salary--or feelin' the Spring?"

"It's partly your bad example, an' partly seein' these lovely white girls, Hank... . I'm all of a doodah. I wanta marry an' I wanta go Home... . I sets on end by the hour and sings *The Old Chisholm Trail* ... and then I keeps on sayin' '*Idaho, Montana, Utah, Oregon, Nevada, Colorado, Kansas, Oklahoma, Texas, California*'--till you'd think I was going potty... ."

"No, I'd never think you was *going* potty, Son," observed the Emir, regarding the face of his Vizier benignly. "How long you had this consumin' passion for Leila?" he asked.

"I got up with it this very morning, Hank Sheikh. I s'pose it *is* your bad example? ... *I* dunno... . I think I'll go an' have a talk with ole Daddy Pertater and see what he knows about me an' Leila gettin' engaged... . As you made him guardian, I s'pose he gets the rake-off?"

"Sure, Son... . I allow I'd better go down the bazaar and buy the weddin' present. Have a toast-rack or fish-knives, Brigham-Young-and-Bring'em-Often?"

"Gee, Hank! If your brains was a furnace there wouldn't be enough fire to scorch your hat... . I'm goin' to call on Daddy Pertater right now... ."

But when, after speaking with old Sidi Dawad Fetata of all other subjects on the earth, in the heavens above, and in the waters under the earth, the Vizier inquired--with meaning--as to the health and happiness of the Sitt Leila Nakhla, he learned a strange thing.

"My heart is sore for her, Sidi," announced the old man. "She is possessed of *djinns*... . She cannot sleep... . Every night she rises from her cushions and goes forth to walk beneath the stars. Old Bint Fatma follows her, and she says the girl talks with spirits and *afrits*...

. Always, too, she stands near the tent of the Emir and calls the protection of the Prophet and the blessings of Allah upon him... . No, she sleeps not, and neither does she eat... ."

"Marriage worketh wonders with women," suggested the Vizier.

"Ya, Sidi," agreed the old man. "But the poor Leila's pale bridegroom will be Death... . She will not live to marry my grandson--and he will pine for her and die also... . I am an old man, Sidi, but the grave will close upon her and upon him, while I yet cumber the earth... ."

"And what do you know about *that* for a merry old crape-hanger, my son?" the Vizier asked himself as he strolled to his tent.

§ 5

Hadji Abdul Salam, doctor and saint, entertained visitors that evening.

"Often they sleep in the big pavilion where they have sat and *faddhled* till nearly dawn," he said to the more important of his two guests. "More often they sleep each in his own tent... . There is usually a Soudanese sentry on the beat between the Guest-tent and those of the Emir and the Vizier."

"We can wait till your man is on duty," said Suleiman the Strong, called El Ma'ian, "or if it be a Soudanese, we can kill him."

"There might be a noise, and if you are caught--I do not think you will leave his presence alive, a second time... . He knows it was you who sent the Emir Mahommed Bishari bin Mustapha abd Rabu's assassin, too... ."

"There will be no noise," said Suleiman the Strong, grimly.

"Nor must either the Emir or the Vizier make a sound in dying," warned the good Hadji. "They are lions possessed by devils, and each would spring to the help of the other... ."

"Yea. See to it, thou Abdullah el Jemmal, that thy man dies swiftly and in silence," growled Suleiman.

"Right through the heart, Sidi--or across the throat a slash that all but takes the head off," smiled Abdullah, "according to how he lies in sleep."

"Bungle not--or the Hadji here will put a curse upon thee that shall cause the flesh to rot from thy bones."

"Oh, *yes!*" chirped the doctor. "Surely! ... Be not taken alive in thy bungling, sweet Abdullah. A quick death will be a lovely thing in comparison with what I will arrange for thee, shouldst thou spoil our plans."

"And if I do my part well, I have *medjidies,* camels, women, tents--to my heart's desire, and be made a man of consequence in the Tribe?" said Abdullah the Camel-man.

"Yea! Verily! After the dawn that sees the death of the Emir and the Vizier, thou wilt never work again, Abdullah--never sweat, nor hunger, nor thirst again, good Abdullah."

"Dost thou swear it, Sidi Hadji--on the Q'ran?" asked the camel-driver.

"I swear on the Q'ran, and on my head and my life and by the Beard of the Prophet and the Sacred Names of Allah that thou shalt never hunger nor thirst again, Abdullah, after thou hast slain the Vizier."

"Yes," added Suleiman the Strong, with a sinisterly humorous glance into the merry face of the Hadji, "I myself will see to it that thou shalt *never hunger nor thirst again,* gentle Abdullah," and he displayed gleaming teeth in a smile that quite won the camel-man's heart.

How delightful to bask in the smiles of the future rulers of the Tribe, and to know that one was shortly to become a Person of Quality and a Man of Consequence! ...

"And now--return to this tent no more," said the Hadji in speeding his parting guests, "for it is dangerous to do so.

"At times they visit me--though not often at night--and I have a fancy that the accursed El R'Orab the Crow spies upon me, and also the aged Yakoub... . Let them beware--and watch their food, I say... .

"Go in peace and with the blessing of Allah, and remain hidden with the caravan-men in the *fondouk* of the lower *sūq*... . Gharibeel Zarruk will bring thee word... . *Emshi besselema*... ."

CHAPTER IX. AUTOCRATS AT THE BREAKFAST-TABLE

"Well, son Bud, what you know about *that* for a fight?" asked the Emir of his Vizier as they broke fast after the duel between the French officer and the *agent provocateur* from the East. "What price Boje at the killing game?"

"I allow it was the best sword-fight I ever seen," replied the Vizier. "I never denied that Rastignac nor Boje was real *men*... ."

"And I'll tell the world that if Boje gets Miss Mary, she gets a husband to be proud of," interrupted the Emir.

"Yep--as a he-man that can hold up his end of a dog-fight, all right, Hank. But I tell you a woman wants a man that's something more than a bad man to fight... . S'pose he loves fightin' better than he loves her--what then, Hank Sheikh? And s'pose his real views of women is that they're just a dead-weight on the sword-arm or gun-hand, and a dead-weight on your hoss's back?" ...

The Vizier paused and pondered mournfully.

"Don't stop, Son," requested the Emir. "You remind me of Abraham Lincoln. It's almost po'try too... . I can lend you a bit... . Hark:

"'*White hands cling where your wool is thickest:*
He rideth the fastest who rideth the quickest... .'"

"Where you get that from, Hank Sheikh?" asked the Vizier suspiciously. "'Tain't *Q'ran,* is it? Sounds more like Shakespeare to me."

"No, Son, you're wrong for once. Bret Harte or Chaucer... . I had to say it at school. There's a lot more:

"'Fallin' down to Gehennum or off of a throne,
He falleth the hardest who falleth alone.'"

"Well! I allow he *would*," commented the Vizier. "Because if he weren't alone and fell on the other guy, he'd fall softer... ." he added.

"You're right, Bud, as usual," admitted the Emir. "My mistake. I oughta said:

"'Climbin' down to Gehennum or up on a throne,
He goes by himself who goeth alone!'

"Yes--that's the poem--and, as I said, it's by Josh Billings or a Wop named Dante... . I forget... . They *did* tell me at school, when I had to learn it... ."

"Don't believe there's any such pome, nor that you ever was at school, Hank Sheikh. Put your tail down! And let a yell for some more of this porridge-hash... . Yes--I allow Boje is a good boy--he's straight; there ain't a yeller streak in him; he's got sand; and it's pretty to watch him fight... . But that don't make him the man for Miss Mary Vanbrugh."

"What *would*, Bud?" asked the Emir.

"Lovin' her more than anything and everything else in the world... . Bein' ready to lay down his life for her... ."

"He'd do that, Son."

"*That's* nothing! ... Bein' ready, I was going to say, when you butted in, to give up his army prospects an' his chances, an' his promotion--*you* know--what they call his career and his--future and all... . *To let everything go for the woman he loves--even his country... .*"

"Say some more, Walt Whitman," the Emir stimulated his flagging friend. "I'll lend you a bit for that too. Listen at this:

"'He made a solitude and called it Peace,
(Largely because there weren't no P'lice)
The world forgetting, by the world forgot
He took her to that lovely spot.
Saying I have now but you, my dove, and that's what the papers call
The World well lost for Love.'

"That's Byron, Son. But you shouldn't read him till you're older."

The Vizier stared long and critically at his lord.

"What's biting you now, you old fool?" he asked.

"Miss Mary Vanbrugh," replied the Emir. "Ever since she came here I sit and think of all the things I learnt at school--and how I uster talk pretty an' learn lessons ... and recite po'try ... and play the pianner... ."

"And I s'pose you wore a plug hat and a Prince Albert and a tuxedo and lavender pants and white kid gloves and pink silk socks on your pasterns in those days? Here--get a lump o' this tough goat and chew hard instead o' talking, Hank," advised the Vizier. "You got a touch of the sun or else swallered a date-stone and it's displaced your brain. Chew hard an' listen to me and improve your mind.... What I say is, that Boje's got to do something more than killing Rastignac to prove he's the right husband for a way-up American girl--and I don't agree to it until he shows *and* proves that she's the Number One Proposition of all his life, and nothing else isn't worth thirty cents in the same continent.... Get me? ... And the quicker the sooner, for he's the wounded hero and she's nursing of him--and women always falls in love with what they nurse.... Amateur-like, I mean.... It isn't the same with professional nurses o' course...."

"Right again, Son. I was in a Infirmary once and at Death's Door, and if that old nurse had started lovin' me, I'd certainly have crep' through that Door to escape...."

The Emir was apparently in sardonic mood and of flippant humour that morning--not an infrequent symptom, in his case, of a troubled and anxious soul.

His friend was well aware of this peculiarity, and classed it, in his puzzled mind, with other of Hank's idiosyncrasies--such as his way of being dumbly taciturn for days, and then having a mordantly loquacious hour; or his habit of occasionally speaking like an Eastern dude instead of talking properly like a genuine rough-neck hobo and a he-man. However, whatever Hank chose to say or to do was right in the sight of the man whose narrow, deep stream of affection flowed undeviatingly and eternally towards him, his hero, friend and ideal....

"Well--we better try Boje out as soon as possible or sooner," continued the Vizier. "He only got a bit chipped in the fierce shemozzle this mornin', and he'll be able to sit up and do business to-morrow.... Reckon Rastignac will pull round?"

"No. Rastignac has got his, this time, and a damned good job too, the swine! ... He's for the land where the tomb-stone bloometh beneath the weeping willow-tree, and the wild whang-doodle mourneth for its mate," opined the Emir.

"Well--we and the world can spare him, though I rise to remark he died like he lived, makin' trouble, and seekin' sorrow with a high and joyful heart," and the Vizier turned down an empty cup--of clay--and poured a libation of coffee-dregs. "What'll we do with that mouth-flappin', jabbering, shave-tail breed he brought with him, if Rastignac goeth below to organize mutinies against the Devil?" he asked.

"Send him back with the soft answer that turneth away wrath--and a soft and empty money-belt," replied the Emir.

"You allow Boje's proposition is the best?" inquired the Vizier.

"Sure thing, Son. It is. Yea, verily. And I got a special reason for lending ear unto the words of Boje too. We'll go in solid with him."

"You're right, Hank Sheikh. We don't wanta hitch up with a gang of niggers, Turks, Touareg, Senussi and anti-white-man trash.... We ain't French and we ain't got no great cause to love 'em either--but we got our feelings as White Men.... Yep--and we got some sacks that'd just take a million francs too.... And if ever we got caught out by the Legion hogs, and it was a firing-party at dawn for ours, the French Big Noise would say, 'Forget it--they're good useful boys, and we want 'em whole and hearty in the Great Oasis?' Wouldn't they?"

"You said it all, Son," agreed the Emir, and clapped his hands, that *narghilehs* might be brought by the slave waiting at a respectful distance.

§ 2

"Who *was* this poor creature whom Major de Beaujolais found it expedient to kill?" asked Mary Vanbrugh during the evening ride with the Emir el Hamel el Kebir. "He was a Frenchman too, so why was he treated as an enemy?"

"He wasn't treated as an enemy by *us*, though he soon would have been," replied the Emir. "We received him politely and we listened to all he had to say... . Listened too long for our comfort... ."

"And it was interesting?" asked the girl.

"Some of it certainly was," replied the Emir. "He got to know that there was a French officer here, openly wearing his uniform, and accompanied by two white women... . He told us exactly what I ought to do with the three of them, and offered me quite a lot of money to do it."

"What was it?" asked the girl.

"I won't put it in plain words," was the reply. "But you just think of the plumb horriblest thing that could happen to you, and then you double it--and you'll hardly be at the beginning of it, Miss Mary Vanbrugh."

"Oh!" said the girl... . "And was that why Major de Beaujolais fought him?"

"Partly, I guess--along with other reasons. It certainly didn't help the man's chances any, that the Major knew what was proposed for *you*... ."

"How did he get to know?" asked the girl

"That's what I've got to find out," was the reply, "if I have to pretend he won't get his Treaty unless he tells me... . He'd do *anything* to get that safely signed, sealed and delivered."

"Not *anything*," said the girl, staring ahead unseeingly.

"Well--*that* we may discover, perhaps, all in good time," was the doubting reply... . "Life is very dear--and a life's ambition is sometimes even dearer... ."

The Emir was speaking English, with the words, accent, and intonation of a person of culture and refinement; and his companion eyed him thoughtfully, her face wistful and sad.

CHAPTER X. THE SITT LEILA NAKHLA, SULEIMAN THE STRONG, AND CERTAIN OTHERS

At dead of night, the Sheikh el Habibka el Wazir awoke with the feeling that there was something wrong. For as long as he could remember, this invaluable gift had been his, perhaps because, for as long as he could remember, he had lived, off and on, in danger, and under such conditions that light sleeping and quick waking had been essential to continued existence.

Also the fact that, in the months before his birth, his mother had slept alone in a log cabin, with a gun leaning against her bed, and an ear sub-consciously attuned to the sound of the approach of stealthy terrors--Indians, wolves, mountain "lions," Bad Men, and, worst of all bad men, her husband--may have had something to do with his possession of this animal instinct or sixth sense.

Someone had passed the tent with stealthy steps.... The sentry had done that a hundred times, but this was different.

The Vizier passed straight from deep dreams to the door of his tent, his "gun" at the level of the stomach of anyone who might be seeking sorrow.

"*Min da?*" he growled, as he peered out.

Nobody.... He crept toward the Emir's pavilion.... Nothing.... Yes--a shadow beside the Guest-tent sentry, a young recruit, one Gharibeel Zarrug.

There should be no shadow on a moonless night....

The shadow stooped and went into the tent by the entrance to the men's part of it.

Had it been the other entrance, the Vizier would have fired; for persons wearing black clothing, for the sake of invisibility, do not enter *anderuns* at midnight for any good purpose.

The Vizier circled the Guest-tent in the darker darkness of the palm-clumps, approached, and lay down behind it. Ah! ... The good and pious Hadji Abdul Salam! ... *What* was that? ... *Murder,* eh? ... The low-down, treacherous swine! ...

And Suleiman the Strong was back again, was he? ... And who might *he* be? ... Good old Boje! ... Spoken like a man.... Wouldn't leave the girls, wouldn't he? ... He would--to save his life, and get the Treaty, though.... Wouldn't stand for assassination of the Emir nor the Wazir, eh? ... Yep. Boje was certainly a White Man! ...

The Vizier crept round to the front of the tent and the knees of Gharibeel Zarrug smote together, as a figure rose beside him, and the voice of the Sheikh el Habibka el Wazir gave him sarcastic greeting....

A few minutes later, the Vizier also gave the Hadji Abdul Salam sarcastic greeting, and said he would see him safely home to his tent: he would take no refusal of the offer of his company, in fact....

§ 2

As the Emir el Kebir emerged from his pavilion before dawn the next morning, and strode to where El R'Orab the Crow led his master's great stallion up and down, he was joined by the Vizier.

When the two were clear of the headquarter tents of the "capital" of the Oasis, the Vizier told the Emir of the events of the night.

"The worst of these holy *marabouts* and *hadjis* and *imams* and things is that they *stay* holy in the sight of these ignorant hick Injuns, no matter what they do; and you can't get away from it," observed the Emir. "There'd be a riot and a rebellion if I took good old Abdul and hanged him on a tree.... I'd be real sorry to do it, too.... I like the cute old cuss ... always merry an' bright."

"He's gettin' a whole heap too bright, Hank," opined the Vizier. "But as you say--there's no lynchin' Holy Sin-Busters in this State.... They can cut their mothers' throats or even steal hosses, and they're still Holy Men an' acceptable in the sight of Allah...."

"We better have a talk with old Dawad Fetata," said the Emir. "He knows the etiquette of handling Holy Joes when they get too rorty.... *Bismillah!* We mustn't make any false moves on the religion dope, Son.... There'd be an 'Ell-of-an-Allahbaloo...."

"Sure," agreed the Vizier. "But Old Daddy Pertater won't stand for havin' Abdul plottin' the death of the Emir.... He'll know how to hand it to him.... We'll have a li'll *mejliss*, with Abdul absent, by request.... What are we going to do about this Suleiman guy that's got it in for you? Who *is* he?"

"Don't you remember the gink I told you about--that left our outfit before you came-- and joined the Emir Mohammed Bishari bin Mustapha Korayim, that we shot up--at Bab-el-Haggar? *He* was this Suleiman the Strong, and he sent that thug to get me--the one you shot.... Let him come when he feels like it. I allow he'll get his, good an' plenty, this time," replied the Emir.

"Why not get a posse an' have a man-hunt?" suggested the Vizier. "Man-hunts is good sport, and prowlin' thugs lookin' for your liver with a long knife is bad sport.... Catch him alive, and skin him at poker, Son."

"I allow it was all lies of Abdul's," replied the Emir.... "Suleiman's dead long ago, an' if he was alive he wouldn't come snoopin' round here.... He's on'y too willin' to keep away-- with both feet.... Forget it.... What you do with poor old Abdul?"

"Frightened him white.... *'Lhamdoulah!* ... I certainly did put the fear of God in Abdul... . Did a magic on him.... Produced things from him that he hadn't got.... Told him to watch his eyes and teeth as they'd soon fall outa him; watch his arms an' legs as they'd soon wither; watch his food becos it'd soon turn to sand in him; watch his secret *laghbi* becos it'd boil in his belly; watch his women becos each one had a dancin' partner--secret, like his fermented palm-juice;--an' watch all through the night becos Death an' the Devil was coming for him... . He's *watchin'* all right! ... He surely is a sick man this mornin'.... I reckon he'll die...."

"Poor old Abdul--I must go and hold his hand and cheer him up some," said the Emir. "Promise him a real rousin' funeral and start buildin' him a nice tomb.... Place of pilgrimage for thousands...."

"Say, Son," he added, "I'm glad the Major played a clean game. I told you he was a hundred per cent white."

"He was straight enough," admitted the Vizier. "But I don't like him any.... Too all-fired pompshus.... Thinks he could play his Ace on the Last Trump.... Too golly-a-mighty own-the-earth.... Thinks he's God's Own Bandmaster, Lord Luvvus, Count Again, an' the Baron Fig-tree.... And he's one o' the hard-faced an' soft-handed sort--that women fall for...."

"You're hard-faced, hard-handed, hard-hearted, an' hard-headed, Son Bud.... Yep.... Head solid bone...."

"We'll settle his hash one night, Hank Sheikh," replied the Vizier, ignoring his Lord's rudeness. "Then we'll *see*.... *Abka ala Kheir*."

§ 3

They saw.

Never had the Emir and his Vizier cowered and fled before armed men as they cowered and fled from the wrath of the angry woman who burst into their presence, that night, at the loud choking cry of the man whom they had foully murdered.

She was a raging Death-angel, her tongue a flaming sword.

"My God--*you killed him*! ... You murdered him! ... Poisoned him like a sewer-rat.... What the Hell *happened,* you ham-handed buffalo?" panted the Emir as the two fled from the Guest-tent and went to earth in the pavilion of the latter chieftain....

"Search me!" replied the Vizier, obviously badly shaken. The Emir seized his friend's arm and glared into his face.

"You didn't double-cross me and *poison* that fine man a-purpose? ... Not *poison* him? You wouldn't be such a damned yellow dog?" he asked sternly.

"Don't be a fool," replied the Vizier. "I gave him camel's milk. Part of what we had at supper... . *He's* double-crossed *us*... . Yelped so as Miss Vanbrugh sh'd hear him, an' then threw a fake fit... ."

"Don't be a mean hound... . He saw that dog die--an' he drank what he thought killed the dog... . *And* he choked like the dog did, and then collapsed--he went white an' cold an' limp... . He's *dead,* I tell you... . *God! How'll I face Mary?* ... Bud--if I thought you ..."

"You make me tired, Hank. If he's dead--the milk killed him. 'Nuff to kill anybody too... . I near died myself, first time I drunk milk! ... Hank, Son, you hurt my feelin's... . You seen me kill a few men... . Ever know me *poison* 'em behind their backs? ... You gotta beastial mind, Hank Sheikh... ."

They sat silent for a moment.

"Say, Hank," said the Vizier suddenly. "Think she'd turn crool an' tell Bojolly on his death-bed that we're a pair of four-flushers? ... Or tell him to-morrow if he lives?"

"No, Son, she'd die sooner. She allows the Major would blow his brains out, in rage an' disgust an' fear o' ridicule, if it came out that the Mahdee whom he'd circumvented with his superior Secret Service Diplomacy had circumvented *him,* the Pride o' the whole French Intelligence Bureau, an' signed a treaty for a million jimmy-o'-goblins... . Folks saying he didn't know a Mahdee from an American high-jacker! Gee! ..."

The Emir rose.

"I'm going back," he said. "If he's dead that girl will go mad... . She ain't screamin' any... . She's got a gun too... . Hope she shoots me first... . I take the blame, Boy--for allowin' such monkeying... . I hadn't oughter stood for it... . Shake, Son--you didn't mean any harm... ."

"I sure didn't, Hank pard... . I only meant it for her good... . No I didn't! May I burn in Hell for a liar! I was jealous of a better man. He *is* a better man... . *Was* I mean... ."

"I'll put my gun in his dead hand and shoot myself... . That oughta satisfy him," he added, as the Emir crept out of the tent... .

§ 4

The Emir returned beaming.

"*They're cuddling!*" he cried. "*Cuddling*--fit to bust! ... I didn't mean to intrude, and they didn't see me... . *He was kissin' her face flat*... . You cert'nly brought it off, Buddy Bashaw ... and serve you damned well right! ... They got *you* to thank... . Boje oughta ask you to be Best Man, B'Jimminy Gees! ... Allahluyer! ..."

"But what *happened,* if he didn't throw that fit on purpose?" asked the bewildered Vizier.

"Why--I'll tell you, Son. He was so blamed sure that he *was* drinking poison that *he felt all the effects of it.* He felt just like he saw that dog feel... . I knew an Injun once, an Arapaho or a Shoshone, I think he was, back on the Wind River Reservation at Fort Washakie--no, it wasn't, you goat--it was in the Canyon, and the man was a Navajo breed--and the boys played a trick on him one dark night--stuck a fork in his heel and yelled '*Rattler*'--an' he up an' died o' snake-bite, *pronto.*"

"*Can* it!" said the Vizier. "Cut out the funny-staff."

"Fact, Son! ... Yep--like old Doc' Winter, back in Colorado in the old days. He sent out two letters, when he couldn't go himself--one tellin' a sick man he'd better make his will, and the other telling a Dude from the East he was healthier than a mule... . Put 'em in the wrong en*vell*ups! ... The Dude made his will and died, and the sick man got up and ate a steak... . Never felt another pang or sorrow! ..."

"Sure," agreed the Vizier. "Same sorta thing happened in Idaho... . Only it was a young bride was sick, and a lone ol' bachelor cattle-rustler that*thought* he was... . Same mistake like yours, Hank... ."

"What happened?" inquired the Emir.

"Old bachelor had the babby o' course," was the reply. "Only case on record I believe... ."

"Prob'ly," agreed the Emir... . "And that's what happened to the Major."

"What! Had a ...?" began the Vizier.

"No," interrupted the Emir. "You got a *very* coarse mind, Bud... . He thought the milk was poison, and he thought it so hard that for a while it *was*poison, and it acted according! ..."

"It's a fierce world, Hank... . Let's pound our ears, right here. It'll be daylight in an hour... . God help us in the mawnin', when Miss Vanbrugh gets us! ... I'm glad you're the Emir and not me, Hank Sheikh... ."

The troubled statesmen slept.

§5

Meanwhile, two men of simple passions and simple methods of expressing them, prepared for strenuous action.

Wearing the minimum of clothing and the maximum of razor-edged knife, Suleiman the Strong and Abdullah el Jemmal crept from darkness to darkness until they could see the pavilion of the Emir, wherein burned a single candle in the wind-proof *shamadan* holder, that hung from a tent-pole.

Not far from the big tent, a sentry, one Gharibeel Zarrug, leaned heavily upon his rifle, his crossed arms upon its muzzle and his head upon his arms... .

Rightly considering that the place of the strategist is a place of safety where he may strategize in peace, Suleiman the Strong bade Abdullah the Camel-man reconnoitre the tent and report.

Like a dark snake in the darkness, Abdullah crept to a blacker spot beside the Guest-tent, whence he could see a portion of the interior of the lighted pavilion.

No one moved therein, and, after a period of patient observation, he crawled, writhed and wriggled until he reached the aperture where a hanging curtain of heavy felt did not quite close the entrance to the tent.

Perfect stillness reigned within, and a silence broken only by the sound of breathing.

How many breathed?

It was unfortunate, but intentional on the part of the occupants, that the light hung just where anyone entering would see nothing but the light--the back of the tent being in darkness, and the front well-lit.

Abdullah accepted the situation and moved slowly, silently, almost imperceptibly, across the lighted carpet. Once the light was behind him, he saw that the Emir el Kebir and the Wazir el Habibka lay on their rugs, sleeping the deep sleep of the innocent and just; the Vizier the nearer to him.

What about two quick stabs?

No. These were not ordinary mortals. The Vizier would, perhaps, make some sound as he died, and the Emir's great arm would shoot out and seize the slayer... . Abdullah had seen both these men in swift action... .

No, he must stick to the programme and obey the orders of his leader, to the letter.

He writhed backward as silently as he had come, and wriggled crawling from the tent...

"He did that very neat and slick," observed the Emir, as Abdullah departed.

"Not bad," agreed the Vizier. "He's a bit slow though... . You ain't too near the side o' the tent, Hank, are you?"

"Plenty o' room, Son; but he won't bother to come under while he can come through the front door... . See his silly face?"

"Nope. I allow it's that Suleiman guy what the Hadji was talkin' to Boje about."

"Guess again, Son... . Suleiman the Strong's a real big stiff. Twice the size o' that galoot," and the Emir yawned hugely.

"What you reckon he's gone for, Hank?"

"Why, his bag o' tools or his plumber's-mate, I s'pose."

"Wish he'd hurry up then, I'm real sleepy... . S'pose we'd better hang Mister Gharibeel Zarrug bright an' early to-morrow."

"We'll hand him over to Marbruk ben Hassan and the body-guard. They can use him for a li'll court-martial *mejliss*. Keep 'em happy all day."

"Pore Mister Gharibeel will be Mister Skinned-eel, time they done with him. They'll treat him rough."

"Learn him not to double-cross--but it's poor old Hadji Abdul Salam that oughta hang."

"Sure, Son. He's a bad ole possum... . G'night, boy."

"They are both there, Sidi," whispered Abdullah the Camel-man to Suleiman the Strong. "Sleeping on their rugs like drunken *kif*-smokers, but the Emir lies beyond the Vizier and cannot be reached. El Habibka must die first... ." And he proceeded to explain exactly the position of affairs and of the victims.

"Now listen--and live," growled Suleiman, when all was clear. "Go you back into that tent and crouch where you can strike home--when the moment comes."

"When will that be?" asked Abdullah, whose knife was brighter and keener than his brain.

"*Listen,* you dog," was the reply. "Crouch ready to strike El Habibka at the moment I strike El Hamel. Watch the tent-wall beyond him. I shall enter there... . And our knives will fall at the same moment... . As your knife goes through El Habibka's heart, clap your left hand upon his mouth... . They must die together and die silently... . Then we flee back to the *fondouk*--and to-morrow I will appear to *my* friends and proclaim myself Sheikh Regent of the Tribe... ."

"And I shall be a camel-man no more," said Abdullah.

"No--you will not be a camel-man after to-morrow," agreed Suleiman, and carefully repeated his instructions.

"Now," he concluded, "Dawn's left hand will be in the sky in half an hour.... Remember what will happen if you bungle...."

Kneeling beside the sleeping Vizier, Abdullah el Jemmal poised his long lean knife above his head, and stared hard at the tent wall beyond the recumbent form of the Emir....

In his sleep, the Emir rolled his heavy head round and lay snoring, his face toward the very spot at which Abdullah stared.

A bright blade silently penetrated the wall of the tent. Slowly it travelled downward and the head of Suleiman the Strong was thrust through the aperture, as the knife completed the long cut and reached the ground.

Gently Suleiman edged his body forward until his arms and shoulders had followed his head. As he raised himself on his elbows, Abdullah lifted his knife a little higher, drew a deep breath, and, ere it was completed, the silence was horribly rent by the dreadful piercing scream of a woman in mortal anguish.... A rifle banged....

Abdullah, unnerved, struck with all his strength, and his wrist came with a sharp smack into the hand of the waiting Vizier, whose other hand seized the throat of Abdullah with a grip of steel.

Suleiman, with oaths and struggles, backed from the tent, and the Emir, bounding across the struggling bodies of the Vizier and Abdullah, rushed from the tent, with a low exhortation of, "Attaboy, Bud! Bust him up," and dashed round the tent--in time to see Suleiman the Strong drive his knife into the breast of a woman (who grappled with him fiercely), just as El R'Orab sprang upon the slayer from behind.

Another woman stood and shrieked insanely, sentries came running, and the French officer burst from his tent, sword in hand....

The murderer was secured after a terrific struggle and bound with camel-cords.

As soon as the Emir had shaken the shrieking woman into coherence, it was learnt that it had become the custom of the Sitt Leila, who slept badly, to rise and walk in the hour before dawn--"when she had the world to herself," as the old woman pathetically sobbed, "and unseen could pass the tent of the Emir and pray for blessings on his sleeping head...."

On this occasion, as they went by the road that ran behind the Emir's pavilion, they had seen a man lying prone, with his head beneath the tent-wall and inside the tent.

Realizing that this could mean but one thing, the girl had uttered a terrible scream and thrown herself upon the man.... She had seized his foot and held on, with the strength and courage of love.

The man, moaned the old Bint Fatma, had kicked and struggled, knocking the girl down, had wriggled out backwards, risen, and turned to flee, as the girl again sprang at him and clung like Death....

As gently as any mother nursing her sick child, the big Emir held the dying girl to his breast, her arms about his neck, her eyes turned to his as turn those of a devoted spaniel to its master--and if ever a woman died happily, it was the little Arab girl....

Yussuf Latif Fetata arrived, at the double, with the guard, and, even in such a moment, the man who had made them what they were, noted with approval that it was a disciplined guard under an officer, and not a mob of Soudanese following an excited Arab... .

"Keep that man here and hurt not a hair of his head," ordered the Emir, "I return," and he strode away, with the dead girl in his arms, to the tents of Dawad Fetata.

As he came back, the Vizier emerged from the pavilion.

"Sorry, Son," he whispered, "I croaked him... ."

"Good," growled the Emir. "You'll see me croak the other ..." and it was plain to the Vizier that his friend was in that terrible cold rage when he was truly dangerous.

He himself had enjoyed that for which he had recently expressed a wish--an intimate and heart-to-heart discussion in a righteous cause and with a worthy foe.

Abdullah had really put up quite a good show, the Vizier considered, and it had taken several minutes and several good twists and turns and useful tricks, before he had had his visitor where he wanted him--clasped immovably to his bosom with his hawser-like right arm, while his equally powerful left forced the assassin's knife-hand back and over--until the hand was far behind the sharply crooked elbow, in a position that Nature had never intended it to occupy... .

Abdullah had screamed like a wounded horse as the arm and joint snapped, the knife fell from his hand, and the Vizier seized his neck in a double grip... . Minutes had passed.

"That'll learn you, Mr. Thug," the Vizier had grunted, and released the murderer's throat.

But alas, it was the final lesson of his unlearning misspent life.

"Let the guard charge magazines and form single rank," said the Emir to Yussuf Latif Fetata--who, beyond a greenish pallor of countenance, showed nothing of what he felt. None would have supposed that this stoic had just beheld, borne in the arms of another man, the dripping corpse of the girl for whom his soul and body hungered. "If the prisoner tries to escape, give him fifty yards and a volley... ."

The Emir then bade El R'Orab and the sentries who had seized Suleiman the Strong to unbind him and to chafe his limbs.

"Do you thirst, dog?" he asked.

"For your blood, swine," was the answer.

The Emir made no reply, but waited awhile, that the prisoner's strength and the daylight might increase.

"Give him his knife," he said anon, and gripped his own.

The Vizier drew his revolver and stood near Suleiman the Strong.

"Now, dog," said the Emir, "see if you can use your knife upon a man... . Not upon a girl nor a sleeper, this time, Suleiman the Jackal, the Pariah Cur, the Detested of God... ."

The two men stood face to face, the giant Emir and the man whose strength was a proverb of his tribe; and the staring breathless onlookers saw a fight of which they told each move and stroke and feint and feature to their dying day.

"Yea," said El R'Orab the Crow, later, to Marbruk ben Hassan, who, to his abiding grief, had been absent on patrol, "it was the fight of two blood-mad desert lions--and they whirled and sprang and struck as lions do... .

"Time after time the point was at the eye and throat and heart of each, and caught even as it reached the skin. Time after time the left hand of each held the right hand of other and they were still--still as graven images of men, iron muscle holding back iron muscle, and all their mighty strength enabled neither to move his knife an inch... .

"Then Suleiman weakened a little and our Lord's right hand pressed Suleiman's left hand down, little by little, as his left hand held Suleiman's right hand far out from his body. Slowly, slowly, our Lord's knife came downward toward that dog's throat, inch by inch--and Suleiman sweated like a horse and his eyes started forth.

"Slowly, slowly his left hand grew feeble, and the Emir's hand, which Suleiman held, came nearer, nearer to Suleiman's throat... .

"There was not a sound in all the desert as that blade crept nearer and nearer, closer and closer--till Suleiman uttered a shriek, a scream--even as the poor Sitt Leila Nakhla had done--for the Emir's point had pricked him, pricked him, right in the centre of his foul throat... .

"And then we heard the voice of our Lord saying: '*Leila! Leila! Leila!*' and with each word he *thrust,* and *thrust,* and *thrust,* till Suleiman gave way, and we saw the knife-point appear at the base of that murderer's skull... . Right through! ... *Wallahi!* Our Emir is a *man*! ..."

And from this Sixteenth-Century atmosphere of primitive expression of primitive passion, which from time to time still dominated the Oasis, the Emir slowly returned to the Twentieth Century and received the concise approving comments of his Vizier... .

§ 6

And it was an entirely Twentieth-Century young woman whom they found awaiting them in the Emir's pavilion, when they re-entered it an hour later, after visiting the tents of Dawad Fetata, and then seeing the bodies of Suleiman the Strong and Abdullah the Camelman dragged away by a washerman's donkey, followed by an angry crowd that cursed the evil carrion and spat upon it... .

Miss Mary Vanbrugh requested the privilege, if not the pleasure, of a private interview with the Emir el Hamel el Kebir; and the Vizier departed very precipitately to his own tents... .

The Emir's subsequent account of the interview confirmed the Vizier's preconceived opinion that it was well worth missing.

"I told you I took the blame for that foolishness, Son," the Emir said, "and I cert'nly got it... . I thought I knew the worst about my evil nature, and I thought I'd said it too... . I was wrong, Son... . I hadn't begun to know myself till Mary put me wise to the facts... ."

"Yup! I always said you was a bad ole Sheikh!" agreed the Vizier, stroking his beard.

"And as for *you,* Son ... *Gee!* I wouldn't repeat it, boy! ... That lady surely has got an eye for character! ... When she had done saying what she thought of me--an' it left Bluebeard, Jezebel, Seizer Borjer, Clearpartrer, and Judas Iscariot blameless and smilin' by comparison--when she'd done, she said, '*An' I no doubt you was a fairly decent man till you fell under the influence o' that horrible li'll microbe that's led you astray an' ruined you, body an' soul,*' she said... ."

"Gee! And all becos ole Bojolly got too much imagination, and the Lord have blessed us with the gift of good poker faces!" observed the Vizier... . "Did you tell her it was only our fun, an' we was tryin' him out for her?" he asked.

"Sure, Son. And she said she wished *he*'d tried *us* out--with a gun... . And who were we to presume to dare to think her Major D. Bojo*llay* wasn't the world's noblest and bravest hero? ... If Boje don't have a devoted adoring wife to his dying day, he'll deserve hanging... .

"I said he surely was a real noble hero and a great gentleman. And I praised him fit to bust, and said he also left Napoleon Buonaparte, Abraham Lincoln, Horatio Nelson, Alfred the Great an' John L. Sullivan all nowhere. Got 'em beat to a frazzle... . She said I was quite right, and when I'd said some more she began to get friendly... .

"Time I'd done belaudin' Boje she said I was not *really* a bad man--only misguided--but *you* was the father of all pole-cats and son of a bald he-goat... ."

"Them very words, Hank?" inquired the Vizier, much interested.

"No, Son. I wish to be strictly truthful... . Not those very words, but words to that defect, as they say in the p'lice-court... . She and the Major are going to get married soon as they get away from us savages, and back to civilization--and they're going to start right off, Son, this very day... ."

"Maudie too?"

"No. Maudie told Miss Mary wild camels won't drag her away and Miss Mary agrees... . She's coming to our second wedding. In Zaguig it's to be... . There'll be a White Fathers' Mission there before long... ."

"Ain't they Roman Cathlicks, Son?"

"Yup. Maudie and me's going to be, too--then."

"Wot are you now?"

"Mussulman and Mussulwoman, o' course."

"Then when we retire from business and go Back Home you'll jest be a chapel-goin' Bible Christian agin, I s'pose?"

"Sure... . We're going to get married a third time then... ."

"Well, Hank Sheikh, I rise to remark that you sure oughta find your way into Heaven, *one* trail or the other."

"That's so, Bud."

"Also you an' Maudie'll take a lot o' divorcin' by the time you finished gettin' married."

"That's so, Son. And that's a pleasin' thought. She's the first an' only girl I ever kissed, and she'll be the last... ."

"*Wot* a dull life you had, Hank Sheikh!"

"Won't be dull any more, Son... . Maudie's a live wire and a ray o' sunshine... ."

"She is ... and I don't see why you couldn't ha' kept your heavy hoof outa *my* affair with her, Hank Sheikh... ."

"But your poor heart was broke right then, Son... . I just thought I'd stake out a claim 'fore it mended... ."

"Ah, well! S'pose I'll die an ole bachelor... ."

"Sure, Bud... . Girls are discernin' critturs... . But you might not, o' course. You might get hanged young like... ."

CHAPTER XI. ET VALE

The imposing caravan and escort of Major Henri de Beaujolais and Miss Mary Vanbrugh had departed and a gentle sadness was settling upon the soul of the Sheikh el Habibka el Wazir who was about to be left alone, alone in a populous place, while the Emir departed on his honeymoon.

That forethoughtful man had caused a beautiful camp to be pitched in a beautiful place, far off in the desert, and thither he and his bride would ride alone after a ceremony and a great wedding-feast... . Ride "into the sunset"... into Paradise ... Maudie and her Sheikh! ... Dreams come true! ...

The Emir and the Vizier sat alone for the last hour of the former's bachelor life, and a not too poignant melancholy informed the Vizier's voice as he said:

"Women always come between men an' their friends, Hank, Pard. I reckon I better hike before Maudie does it... ."

"Son, Buddy," replied the Emir, "you're an ol' fool. You always was. If I didn't know Maudie'd love you pretty nigh as much as she does me--I'd never have asked her to marry me... . Son, I wouldn't do it *now* if I thought it would make any difference to *us*... . We're like Saul an' David ... very beautiful in our lives and in our marriages not divided... . Why, Maudie herself said it was almost like marryin' *two* Sheikhs--what she's been set on all her life... ."

"Wot--marryin' two Sheikhs?"

"I'll give you a fat ear in 'two shakes' if you talk blasphemous, Buddy Bashaw... .

"Son," continued the Emir, "I got something to tell you. Something about Miss Vanbrugh that I promised her most solemn I wouldn't tell *anybody*... ."

"Wot you wanta tell me for then, Hank?"

"Becos you *ain't* anybody, see? An' I ain't got any secrets from you, Bud--so cheer up, you droolin' crape-hanger... . You know I said I'd give my hand, for you an' her to marry, *if* you loved each other?"

"Yup. And why was that, Hank?"

"*Becos she's my li'll sister, Mary!*"

The Vizier sat bolt upright on his rug and stared open-mouthed at his friend.

"What you handin' me?" he asked feebly.

"Facts. *She's my li'll sister, Mary.*"

"What a norrible liar you are, Hank Sheikh! ... When did you reckernize her?" whispered the Vizier, and collapsed heavily.

"The moment the Major said, '*Meet the Sitt Miriyam Hankinson el Vanbrugh.*'"

"Then that's your name, Hank!"

"Sure. My monicker's Noel Hankinson Vanbrugh!"

"Sunday socks o' Sufferin' Samuel! That's the first inter*estin*' thing I ever come across in a dull an' quiet life. I surely thought you was born-in-the-bone an' bred-in-the- butter plain 'Hank'!"

"*I*'d forgot it till Boje mentioned it, Bud. Tain't my fault!"

"Won't she *tell* him?"

"No, you old fool. Don't I keep on tellin' you she'd do any mortal thing rather than let Major D. Bojol*lay* know that he's been the victim of a really high-class leg-pull and bluff. He'd die of misery an' shame, thinkin' the whole world was laughin' at him... . He takes himself mighty serious... . *He's goin' to have me an' you come to Paris to meet the President of the French Republic* if we keep the Treaty nicely... ."

"Why, cert'nly... . Very proper... . We'll paint li'll ol' Paris red... . Paris girls like coloured gents I'm told... . We'll surely give the public a treat... . How did she reckernize *you,* Son?"

"She says she took one look at my big nose--got a li'll scar on it, as p'raps you may ha' noticed--an' my grey eyes an' thick black eyebrows, an' then looked for my busted finger... . I got the top shot off'n that, when Pop an' me an' the boys were chasin' hoss-rustlers off the range. She was a bright li'll looker then, and she thought she c'd stick the bit on! ... She knew me most as quick as I did her... ."

"Why you didn't tell me, Hank?"

"Because she made me swear not to tell a soul. She never told Maudie either. She was scared stiff someone might make a slip an' old Boje come to know... . She wants Boje to be the Big Noise of the French African Empire some day ... with her helping... . Neither is she plumb anxious for it to come out that we're the two Americans that quitted the Legion unobtrusive-like, down Zinderneuf way... . They'd get us, Son... . And they'd put us against a wall at dawn too, and take over the Great Oasis as a going concern... . All sorts of boot-leggers, thugs, rollers, high-jackers, gunmen, ward-heelers, plug-uglies and four-flusher five-ace fakers would come into this li'll Garden of Eden then... .

"Well, Son--I better go get Eve an' mooch to the *Beit Ullah.* Come on, Serpent... . You've never been a *good* man, Bud, but you're going to be a Best Man, for once--unless you wanta be a bridesmaid in those gay petticoats."

"An' what about *me* marryin', Adam Hank? ... I reckon I *will* marry those four Arab Janes after all and turn respectable... . Come on!"

"*Four Arab Janes!*" said the Emir. "What *you* oughta do, Buddy Bashaw, is to quit Sheikhing and go to the South Seas! ..."

"Whaffor, Hank Sheikh?"

"... An' be King o' the Can*nu*bial Islands... ."

THE END

BOOK THREE

BEAU IDEAL

"Judge not the Play, before the Play is done
Her plot hath many changes: every day
Speaks a new scene; the last act crowns the Play."
 Hank: All a matter of what's your own private 'Bo Ideal', as they call it.
--Beau Sabreur.
* * *

DEDICATED TO WILLIAM FARQUHARSON THE GOD FATHER OF BEAU GESTE

PROLOGUE

1.

The heat in the *silo* was terrific, and the atmosphere terrible.

A whimsical remark from the man they called Jacob the Jew, to the effect that he wondered whether this were heat made black, or blackness made hot, remained unanswered for some minutes, until a quiet voice observed in good French, but with an English accent:

"It is the new heat Jacob. Red hot and white hot, we know. We are now black hot--And when I have to leave this quiet retreat I shall take a chunk of the, atmosphere--a souvenir--keep it in my haversack."

The man spoke as one who talks against time--the time when sanity or strength shall have departed.

"Good idea," mused another voice with a similar accent. "Send a bit to one's National Museum, too--You an Englishman?"

"Yes," replied the other. "Are you?"

"No--American," was the reply.

Silence. The clank of irons and a deep groan.

"Oh, God," moaned the wounded Spaniard, "do not let me die in the grave--Oh, Mother of God, intercede for me. Let me die above ground."

"You are not going to die, Ramon," said the Englishman.

"No indeed," observed Jacob the Jew. "Certainly not, good Ramon. No gentleman would die here and now--You would incommode us enormously, Ramon--I go the length of stating that I absolutely do prefer you alive--and that's the first time you've heard *that*, Ramon--Worth being put in a *silo* for."

"That's enough, Jacob," said the Englishman; "hold your tongue."

The irons clanked again, as though the sick man turned in the direction of the last speaker.

"You'll keep your promise, Señor Caballero?" moaned the dying man. "You _have_ forgiven me?--Truly?--You'll keep your promise?--And the Mother of God will come Herself and tend your death-bed--If you don't, my dying curse shall blast--"

"I'll see to it, Ramon," said the Englishman quietly. "Don't bother about cursing and blasting--"

"You'll see that I die kneeling!--You won't let me die until I kneel up?--You'll hold my hands together in prayer--my head low bowed upon my breast?--And then you'll lay me flat and cross my hands and make the Sign of the Cross upon my forehead--"

"--I promised, Ramon."

"You'll let God see that I fear Him--_He wouldn't mistake me for my brother_?--He wouldn't visit my brother's sins on *me?*"

"God is just," said the Englishman.

"Yes, my poor Ramon," observed Jacob the Jew, "I greatly fear that you'll find God just--But don't say that you have a brother, Ramon?

"*Nombre de Dios*, but I have, hombre!--" gabbled the Spaniard. "And he is in Hell--*Seguramente*--He was an enemy of God--He hated God--He defied God--And God took him and broke him--*Caramba*! It is not fair the way God--Yes--Yes--Yes--It tis fair, and God is good, kind, loving and--er--just."

"Yes. *Just*--Ramon," said Jacob.

"If I could find your nose, my friend," said the American, turning in the direction of the last speaker, "I would certainly pull it."

"I will strike a match for you later," replied Jacob, a man famous among the brave for his courage; brilliantly clever, bitterly cynical, and endowed with a twofold portion of the mental, moral and physical endurance of his enduring race.

"God will not punish me for my brother's sins, will He, Senor Smith?" continued the Spaniard.

"No," replied the Englishman, "nor him for his own."

"Meaning him, or Him?" inquired Jacob softly.

"We punish ourselves, I think," continued the Englishman, "_quite_ sufficiently."

"Mon Dieu!" said a cultured French voice, "but you are only partly right, *mon ami*. Woman punishes Man, or we punish ourselves--through Woman."

"Bless ourselves, you mean, said the Englishman and the American immediately and simultaneously.

"The same thing," replied the Frenchman. And the utter stillness that followed was broken by a little gasping sigh that seemed to shape a name--"Véronique."

"*Basta!*--My brother!--My brother!--" babbled the Spaniard and sobbed, "God will distinguish between us--*Gracias a nuestra Madre en el cielo! Gracias a la Virgen Inmaculada--Un millón de gracias*--"

"And what of this accursed brother? Surely no brother of yours committed an interesting sin?" inquired Jacob.

"_Cá!_ It was the priest's fault," continued the Spaniard, unheeding. "We were good enough boys--'Only mischievous--Fonder perhaps of the girls and the sunshine and the wine-skin and the bull-ring than of religion and work--My brother was a good boy, none better from Pampeluna to Malaga--if a little quick with his knife and over-well acquainted with the smuggler track--until that accursed and hell-doomed priest--No! No! No!--I mean that good and holy man of God--east his eye upon Dolores--"

"Oh, Mother of God! _He killed a priest_--And he defied and challenged God--And I am his twin brother!--God may mistake me for him."

"God makes no mistakes, Ramon," said the Englishman. "Excuse my playing the oracle and Heavy Father, but--er--you can be quite sure of that, my lad."

"Yes, yes, yes--you're right. Of course you are right! How should God make mistakes?--Besides, God knows my brother, _well_. He followed him--He warned him--When he swore he would never enter a church again, God flung him into one--When he swore he would never kneel again, God struck him to his knees and held him there--Because he swore that he would never make the Sign of the Cross, God made a Sign of the Cross, _of_ him."

"Quite noticed the little man, in fact," observed Jacob the Jew. "Tell us."

"My brother caught the priest and Dolores--In the priest's own church--My brother married them before the alar--and their married life was brief!--But of course, God knew he was mad--As he left that desecrated church, he cried, _Never will I enter the House of God again!_--"

"And that very night the big earthquake came and shattered our village with a dozen others. As we dashed through the door--the old mother in my brother's arms, my crippled sister on my back--the roof caved in and the very road fell from before our little _posada_, down the hillside. My brother was in front and fell, my mother still in his arms--And where did he recover consciousness? Tell me that!--Before the altar_, upon the dead body of his victim, the murdered priest--who thus saved my brother's life, for he had fallen thirty feet from the half-destroyed church-roof, through which he had crashed--Yes, he had entered the House of God once more!--

"It was to South America that he fled from the police--to that El Dorado where so many of us go in search of what we never find. And there he went from worse to worse than worst, defying God and slaying man--and woman! For he shot his own woman merely because she knelt--just went on her knees to God--And one terrible night of awful storm, when fleeing alone by mountain paths from the soldiers or _guardias civiles_, a flash of lightning showed him a ruined building, and into it he dashed and hid.

"It may have been the rolling thunder, the streaming rain, or an avalanche of stones dislodged by the horses of the police who passed along the path above--I do not know--but there was a terrible crash, a heavy blow, a blinding, suffocating dust--and he was pinned, trapped, held as in a giant fist, unable to move hand or foot, or head--

"And, when daylight came, he saw that he was in a ruined chapel of the old _conquistadores_, kneeling before the altar--a beam across his bowed shoulders and neck; a beam across his legs behind his knees; a mass of stone and rubble as high as his waist-- And there my brother knelt--before the altar of God--in that attitude of prayer which he had sworn never to assume--and thought his thoughts--For a night and a day and a night, he knelt, his stiff neck bent, but his brave heart unsoftened--And thus the soldiers found him and took him to the _calabozo_--

"The annual revolution occurred on the eve of his garroting, and he was saved. Having to flee the country, he returned to Spain, and sought me out--Owing to a little smuggling trouble, in which a _guardia civil_ lost his life, we crossed into France, and, in order to get to Africa and start afresh, we joined the Legion--

"_Válgame Dios!_ In the Legion we made quite a little name for ourselves--not so easy a thing to do in the Legion, as some of you may know. There they fear nothing. They fear no thing, but God is not a thing, my friends. _Diantre!_ They fear neither man nor devil, neither death nor danger--but they fear God--Most of them--When they come to die, anyhow.

"But my brother did not fear God--And his _escouade_ of devils realized that he was braver than they--braver by that much--And always he blasphemed. Always he defied, insulted, challenged God. He had a terrible fight with Luniowski the Atheist, and Luniowski lost an eye in the defence of his No-God. My brother fought with awful ferocity in defence of his God--the God he must have, that he might hate and revile Him--the God Who had sat calmly in His Heaven and watched Dolores and the priest--

"In Africa there was little fear of his finding himself flung into a church, or pinned on his knees before a chapel altar! We aren't much troubled with chaplains and church-parades in the Legion!

"But one day my brother saw a lad, a boy from Provence, a chubby-faced child, make the Sign of the Cross upon his breast, as we were preparing to die of thirst, lost in desert sand-storm--My brother, with all his remaining strength, struck him upon the mouth.

"'*Sangre de Cristo!* If I see you make that Sign again,' he croaked, I'll do it on you with a bayonet.'--

"'If we come through this, I will make the Sign of the Cross on you with a bayonet,' gasped the boy hoarsely, and my brother laughed.

"'Try,' said he. Try when I'm asleep. Try when I'm dying--Try when I'm dead--Do you not know that I am a _devil!_ Why, your bayonet would melt--_Me!_ The Sign of the Cross!--_God Himself could not do it!_'

"And next day my brother was lost in that sand-storm, and the Touareg band who found him, took him to the Sultan of Zeggat--And the Sultan of Zeggat _crucified_ him in the market-place, 'as the appropriate death for a good Christian'--Wasn't that humorous!"

Silence.

"Yes, God made a Sign of my brother," said Ramon the Spaniard, and added, "Help me to my knees, Señor Smith, and keep each word of your promise, for I think I am dying."

Silence--

And then a cry of "_Dios apareee_" from the dying man. Jacob the Jew, great adept at concealment, produced matches and struck one.

The flare of the match illumined a deep-dug pit, its floor hard-beaten, its walls sloping to a small aperture, through which a star was visible. It had been dug and shaped, for the storing of grain, by Arabs following a custom and a pattern which were old in the days when Carthage was young.

It was now stored, not with grain, but with men sentenced to punishment beyond punishment, men of the Disciplinary Battalions, the *Compagnies de Discipline*, the "*Joyeux*," the "*Zephyrs*," the *Bataillon d'Infanterie Légère d'Afrique*--convicted criminals.

The light from the burning match revealed a picture worthy of the pencil of the illustrator of Dante's _Inferno_--a small group of filthy, unshorn, emaciated men, clad in ragged brown canvas uniforms which, with the grime upon their flesh, gave them the appearance of being already part of the earth to which they were about to return, portions of the living grave in which they were entombed.

Some lay motionless as though already dead. One or two sat huddled, their heads upon their clasped knees, the inward-sloping sides of the *silo* denying them even the poor comfort of a wall against which to lean.

Beside a large jug which held a little water, a man lay upon his face, his tongue thrust into the still-damp earth where a few drops of water had been spilt. He had drunk his allowance on the previous day.

Another looked up from his blind search, with sensitive finger-tips, for grains of corn among the dirt.

As Jacob held the match aloft, the Englishman and the American gently raised the body of Ramon the Spaniard from the ground. It was but a body, for the soul had fled.

"Too late," said Jacob softly. "But perhaps _le bon Dieu_ will let him off with eight days' _salle de police_ in Hell, as it wasn't his fault that he did not assume the correct drill-position for dying respectfully--

"No use heaving him up now," he added, as the head rolled loosely forward.

Without reply, the Englishman and American lifted the dead man to his knees, and reverently did all that had been promised.

And when the body was disposed as Ramon had desired, Jacob spoke again.

"There are but five matches," he said, "but Ramon shall have two, as candles at hie head and feet. It would please the poor Ramon."

"You're a good fellow, Jacob," said the Englishman, "--if you'll excuse the insult."

Jacob struck two matches, and the Englishman and the American each taking one, held it, the one at the head, the other at the feet, of the dead man.

All eyes were turned to behold this strange and brief lying-in-state of the Spanish smuggler, court-martialled from the Legion to the Zephyrs.

"Pray for the soul of Ramon Gonzales, who died in the fear of God--or, at any rate, in the fear of what God might do to him," said Jacob the Jew.

The Frenchman who had observed that Man's punishment was Woman, painfully dragged himself into a sitting posture and crawled toward the body.

"I have conducted military funerals," said he, "and remember something of the drill and book-of-the-words."

But what he remembered was not available, for, after the recital of a few lines of the burial-service, he fainted and collapsed.

"This is a very nice funeral," said Jacob the Jew, "but what about the burial?"

2.

Suddenly a man leapt to his feet and, screaming insanely, beat the wall with his manacled hands.

"Come! Come! Smolensky," soothed the huge grey-haired Russian who had been Prince Berchinsky. "We mustn't lose our heads; comrade--I nearly lost mine once--Sit down--I'll tell you about it--Hush now--Hush! And listen--Yes--I nearly lost my head once. It was offered as a prize! Think of that! There's an honour for you!

"It was like this--I was with Dodds' lot at Dahomey, you know. He was almost a nigger himself, but he was a soldier all-right, believe me. Faraux was our Battalion-Commander and General Dodds thought a lot of him--and of us. It quite upset Dodds when Faraux was killed at the battle of Glede, but he kept the Legion in front all the same--So much in front that he lost me, _le Légionnaire_ Badineff--

"I was with a small advance-guard and we were literally pushing our way through that awful jungle when the Amazons ambushed us--Wonderful women those Amazons--far better fighters than the men--braver, stronger, cleverer, more soldierly--Armed with short American carbines and _coupe-coupes_, they're no joke!

"I don't want to fight any better troops--Not what you'd call good shots, but as they never make the range more than about twenty yards, they don't miss much!--

"Well, it wasn't many minutes before I was the only man of the advance-guard who was on his feet, and I wasn't on those long--For these she-devils were absolutely all round us, and as three or four rushed me with their _machetes_, one of them smashed me on the head, from behind, with the butt of her carbine--Quite a useful bump too, _mes amis_--for it put me to sleep for quite a while--"

"Lost your head, in fact," put in Jacob the Jew.

"No, no," continued the old Russian, "not yet--but I nearly lost my wits when I recovered my senses if you understand me--For the ladies had divided my property among them to the last rag of my shirt, and were now evidently turning to pleasure after business.

"Dahomeyan is not one of the languages which I speak--I only know fourteen really well--so I could not follow the discussion closely--But it was quite clear that some were for fire and some for steel--I think a small minority-party were for cord--And I was under the impression that one merry lass capped the others' laughing suggestions with the proposal for all three!--

"Do you know, it was for all the world like a lot of nice little girls sitting on the lawn under the trees with their kitten, joyously discussing how they should dress him up, and which ribbons they should put round his neck--

"You know how they laugh and chatter and pull the kitten about, and each one shouts a fresh idea about the dressing-up and the ribbons, and the fun generally--Well, those nice little girls discussed dressing me--for the table--though it wasn't a ribbon they proposed putting round my neck--And undeniably they pulled me about!--

"I could not but admire the way they had tied me up--I was more like a chrysalis in a cocoon than a bound man--They _were_ playful--Good actresses too--as I realized afterwards--When they saw that I had come round, one of them, eyeing me archly, drew her finger across her throat, and the others all nodded their approval.

"The young thing got up, took a bright sharp knife from her waist-belt, and came over to where I lay against the bole of a tree.

"Grabbing my throat with her left hand, she pulled up the loose skin and began to ant, just as the Leading Lady called out some fresh stage-directions--whereupon she grabbed my beard, pulled my head over to one side, and put the point of the knife in, just below my ear--I closed my eyes and tried to think of a prayer--

"When it comes to it, having your throat cut is the nastiest death there is--

"And just as I was either going to pray or yell, there was a loud burst of laughter, and the girl went back to her place in the jolly group--The Leading Lady then, as far as I could make out, said:

"'Now we must really get to business or the shops will be shut'--and told another lassie, who possessed a good useful iron-hafted spear, to put the butt-end of it in the fire, explaining why, with appropriate gesture--

"It was evidently quite a good idea, for the girls all laughed and clapped their hands, and said what a nice party it was--

"While the spear was getting hot, they propounded all sorts of other lovely ideas, and, over the specially choice ones, they simply rocked with merriment--It did seem a pity that one couldn't follow all the jokes--When the pointed haft of the spear was glowing nicely, its owner picked it up, and stepping daintily across to me, held the point a few inches from my eyes--

"Not unnaturally, I turned my head away, but, saying that that wasn't fair, the Leading Lady and the Soubrette made one jump for me and grabbed my head--

"Fine strong hands and arms those ladies had--I couldn't move my face a fraction of an inch--

"And slowly--slowly--slowly--that red-hot point came nearer and nearer to my right eye--It seemed to approach for hours, and it seemed to be in the centre of my brain in a second--

"When it comes to it, _mes amis_, having your eyes burnt out with a red-hot spear-haft is the nastiest death there is--

"But when my right eye seemed to sizzle and boil behind its closed lid, and to be about to burst, my young friend changed her mind, and began upon the left--and when the iron was just about to touch it she remarked, in choice Dahomeyan, I believe:

"'Dammit! The blooming iron's cold!' and, with a joyous whoop, bounded back to the fire, and thrust it in again--

"Shrieks of laughter followed, and loud applause from the cheap seats.

"Meanwhile the ladies hanged me--"

"_Hanged_ you?" inquired Jacob the Jew. "Don't you mean they cut your head off?--You said you lost your head, you remember."

"No, my friend," replied Badineff, "I said I _nearly_ lost it--Not completely--as you have lost your manners--What I am telling you is true--And if you don't like it, pray go elsewhere--"

"There's nowhere to go but Heaven, I'm afraid," was the reply, "being in Hell--and Earth being denied to us--But pray finish your story, as it is unlikely we shall meet in Heaven--"

"Yes--They hanged me as neatly and as expeditiously as if they had had the advantage of an education in Christian customs--They simply jerked me to my feet, made a noose in a palm-fibre cord, threw the end over the limb of a vast tree, hauled upon it and danced around me as I hung and twisted--

"They say a coward dies many times--That was undoubtedly one of the occasions upon which I have died--

"When it comes to it, _mes amie_, being hanged by strangulation--and not by mere neck-break--is one of the nastiest deaths there is--

"But evidently they let me down in time and loosened the rope from about my neck, for bye-and-bye I was staring up at the stars and in full enjoyment of all my faculties--Particularly the sense of smell--

"The intimate smell of Negro, in bulk, is like no other smell in the world--There is nothing else like it, and there is nothing to which one can compare it--and here is a curious fact which should interest the psychophysiologist--Whenever I wake, as we of the Zephyrs do, dumbly sweating or wildly shrieking, from a ghastly nightmare, I can always _smell_ Negro, most distinctly--Very disgusting--

"Curiously enough, these fearless savage fiends, who will charge a machine-gun with the utmost bravery and with a spear, are arrant cowards at night--in mortal fear and trembling horror of ten thousand different devils, ghosts, djinns, ghouls, goblins and evil spirits--And when I came to, they were huddled around me for protection. I was almost crushed and buried beneath the mass of them as they lay pressed round and across me--

"As I was still most painfully bound, I can only suppose that I was, in myself, a talisman, a _juju_, a mascot, or shall I say, an _ikon_.

"And they had gathered around me in the spirit in which simple peasants might gather round a Calvary, and were using me as some might use a Cross, a holy relic or a charm--

"Yes, to this day I smell that dreadful odour--dreadful because of its associations, rather than of itself--in my worst nightmares and delirium of fever or of wounds--

"I can smell it at this moment--

"I have passed some bad nights--one, impaled on bamboo stakes at Nha-Nam in Tonkin--but this was the worst night of my life--almost--

"And in the morning the ladies awoke, made no toilette, and gave me no food--

"But they had given me a faint hope, for I could not but realize that, so far, they had only tortured me by not torturing me at all--and it seemed that they might be keeping me, not only alive and whole, but without spot or blemish, for some excellent purpose--

"They were!--

"And when I discovered it, I was inclined to wish that they had killed me with fire or steel or cord--as they did all of our men whom they took prisoner--

"For some reason, possibly on account of my unusual size--I was a fine specimen in those days, six foot six, and with golden hair and beard--they were taking me to good King Behanzin at Kana, as an acceptable gift for a burnt-offering and a bloody sacrifice unto his gods and idols--

"There was a story afterwards, that Behanzin had been told by his sooth-sayers and medicine-men, that he would undoubtedly beat the French if a strong _juju_ were made with the blood of a white cock that had a golden comb--One of our officers, Captain Battreau, said I probably owed my life to my golden comb--I have a very white skin where I am not sunburnt--

"Anyhow, the ladies took me along--by the inducement of _machete_-points and rhinoceros-hide whips chiefly--to Kana--

"I don't know whether we marched for a day or for a week--Yes--I was strong in those days--for I believe I ate nothing but raw carrion, and my arms were bound to my body the whole time, as though with wire--

"Kana stands on a hill and is built of earth, clay, and sun-baked bricks, inside a great high wall, yards in thickness--

"We entered through a gate like a tunnel, and, by way of filthy narrow red-earth streets, came to a second, inner wall, which surrounded the royal palaces, hareems, temples, and the House of Sacrifice--

"The yelling mob that had accompanied us from the outer gate, crowding and jeering and throwing muck at me--though they kept well out of reach of the weapons of the Amazons--evidently feared to enter this inner city, for that is what it amounted to--

"And I was handed over to a guard of long-speared ruffians and filthy priests who slung me into a big building and slammed the huge double gates--I staggered forward in the darkness, I slipped on the slimy, rounded cobble-stones, sprawled full-length and collapsed--

"There was a loud roaring in my ears--not the conventional roaring in the ears of a fainting man, but the buzzing of millions of billions of trillions of huge flies, that soon so completely covered me that you could not have stuck a pin into my body without killing one. Their blue-grey metallic bodies made me look as though I were clad in a complete suit of chain-mail. And I could not move a finger even to clear my eyes--I could only blink them.

"And as my eyes grew accustomed to the gloom, I saw that the whitish gleaming cobble-stones were the skulls of men, sunk in the red earth--And I realized why I was being nauseated by a terrible slaughter-house stench--

"It _was_ a slaughter-house--The House of Sacrifice, of Kana, the Sacred City of King Behanzin of Dahomey--

"That was another unpleasant night, _mes amis_--Oh, quite unpleasant--We are in clover here--pigs in clover--But, mercifully, I was at the end of my tether, and I had now so little capacity for suffering, that I was not clear in my mind as to whether certain things that happened that night were real or imaginary, fact or nightmare--

"They were real enough--And in the morning I found I was, even as I had either dreamed or realized--actually inside a great wicker bottle or basket, from the top of which my head protruded--

"I could not move a single muscle of my body save those of my face--

"The priests and executioners had been busy during the night, and I was now like a mummy in its bandages, neatly encased in the Sacrificial Basket, all ready to play my helpless part in the bloody ritual of their unspeakable religion--

"Half-dead as I already was, my one hope was that the Service would be short and early--the sacrifice soon and quick--It is most uncomfortable to lie in a bottle with nothing to support your head--

"I could see nothing, and hear little, by reason of the huge flies--but I was aware of tom-toming and shouting without, and hoped that it concerned me--It did--The gates of the House of Sacrifice were thrown open and a number of guards, priests, and executioners heaved me up from that terrible floor and carried me outside.

"Oh, the sweetness of that morning air--even in an African town--It almost made me want to live--And oh, the relief to have one's head freed from an inch-thick covering of flies--

"The great Square of the inner town--a Square of which the sides were formed by, shall we say, the Palaces, Cathedrals, Convents, Monasteries and Municipal Buildings of King Behanzin--was thronged by hundreds and hundreds of warriors, both men and women. As my guards carried me across to the biggest of the buildings, all these people fell back to the sides of the Square, leaving the centre empty, save for me and my guards.

"In front of the palace, an ugly clumsy building of red earth and baked clay bricks, sat Behanzin, King of Dahomey, on the Royal Stool. Around him were grouped his courtiers--I think that His Majesty and they formed one of the least pleasing groups of human beings I have ever encountered--and I have known quite a lot of kings and their ministers--

"As I have already observed, I do not speak Dahomeyan, and at that moment I deeply regretted the fact, and equally so, that none of them understood Russian or even French--However, French I spoke, in the vain hope that a word or two, here and there, might be understood.

"A few were, as I will tell you--

"My speech was brief and blunt--I told Behanzin that he was the nastiest thing I knew--the ugliest--the foulest--the filthiest--the most abandoned and degraded--And I should be much obliged if someone would remove me from a world which he contaminated--

"I had not finished even these few and well-chosen words before I was again seized by my porters and carried to the very centre of the Square, and there abandoned.

"Immediately the Public, obviously well accustomed to these out-door sports and pastimes, fell into perfectly straight lines on each of the sides of the Square, and assumed the position of sprinters at the starting-point of a race--but each with a coupe-coupe, knife, axe or spear in his right hand--and looked to His Majesty for the signal.

"The King rose from his royal stool, raised his spear aloft and gazed around--

"I also gazed around, having just grasped the underlying idea of the National Sport, a game in which I had never hitherto taken part, nor even seen--

"Of course--how stupid of me--it was a race-game, a go-as-you-please, run-walk-hop-or-jump--And my head was the prize!

"I wondered whether His Majesty had gathered that my brief address was not couched in diplomatic language--He certainly now prolonged what was, to me, a painful moment--He stood like an ebon statue, his white ostrich feathers nodding in the breeze, his handsome cloak hanging gracefully from his great shoulders, his spear uplifted, motionless--

"When that spear fell, I knew that every competitor of those hundreds surrounding me, would bound forward like a greyhound unleashed. For a few seconds I should see them race toward me, their bloodthirsty faces alight with the lust of slaughter, their gleaming weapons raised aloft--And I should go down, the centre of a maelstrom of clutching hands and hacking blades--

"I wondered what would be the reward of the proud winner of the King's Trophy--the head of the white cock with a golden comb--the essential ingredient for the making of the strong _juju_ that was to defeat the French--

"That black devil, Behanzin, stood steady as a rock, and there was absolute silence in that great Square, as all awaited the fall of the flag, or rather the shining spear-head.

"A woman, standing in a doorway, giggled nervously, and a crouching sprinter, presumably her lord, looked back over his shoulder--only to receive her sharp rebuke for taking his eye off the ball--

"Another woman dashed forward and handed her husband a _machete_, taking his spear back into the hut--I imagined his saying to her, just before he left the house, Tatiana, my dear, run upstairs and find that new machete I ordered last week--I think it's on the top of the wardrobe in my dressing-room, unless that wretched girl has put it somewhere.'--

"And then I glanced again at the King--Even as I did so, the raised spear-head, which probably bad only been uplifted for five seconds after all, began to travel slowly backward--And there was an audible intaking of breath--Evidently the giving of the signal had began, and in the fraction of a second, the broad, bright spear-head would come flashing downward--

"I closed my eyes--

"_Boom_--BANG!

"I nearly jumped out of my bottle--

"_Boom_--BANG!

"Two shells had burst in Kana, one just above the inner wall, the other in the corner of the Square itself--" Our guns I--Our guns!--

"The runners were running indeed--for their _own_ heads--King Behanzin also ran!--if indeed he did not get a win or a place--

"I was forgotten--before ever the third and fourth shells arrived--Oh, God! I was _not_ forgotten!--There was _one_ competitor left!--I supposed he felt attracted by the walk-over--As he dashed toward me, straight as an arrow, yelling madly, a great spear in his hand, I saw that he was one of the group of courtiers--the man indeed who had stood nearest to the King--

"I admit, _mes amis_, that it seemed to me a little hard, more than a little hard, that with the flight of all hose hundreds and hundreds of murderous slayers, this solitary one should prefer my life to his own--should not realize that the match was abandoned--the race scratched--the proceedings postponed--

"A fellow of one idea--A case of the _idée fixe_--No sportsman, anyhow--The sort of man that steals the Gold Cup--

"I had been through so much, _mes amis_, from the time that that Amazon had hit me on the head, that I really rebelled a little at this last cruelty of a mocking Fate.

"Saved by the bursting of the shells at the fifty-ninth second of the fifty-ninth minute of the eleventh hour, and then this one solitary, implacable madman to fail to realize that I had been saved!--

"Nearer--nearer--he came--and by the time that he was a few yards from me, he and I were alone in that great Square--

"Would he drive that huge spear through my body, and then clumsily hack my head off with the edge of its broad blade?

"How I hoped that the next shell would blow his limbs from his body, though it killed me too--Another bound and he would be on me--I closed my eyes--and the Nightmare Slayer flung his arm round me, and, in execrable French, panted:

"You tell Frenchies I be verra good man, massa--I belong Coast--belong French shippy--I good friend loving Frenchies--I interpreter--I show Frenchies where old Behanzin bury gin, rum, brandy, ivory--

"Another shell burst--And the Nightmare Slayer tipped my basket over, and, flat upon the ground, the lion and the lamb lay down together--

"That, _mes amis_, was how I nearly lost my head--

"We must not lose ours here, for, as you perceive, there are far worse places than this one--I rather like it--"

3.

A long heavy silence was broken by Jacob the Jew.

"The lad we want here is the bold bright Rastignao--Rastignao, the Mutineer--"

"Oh, did you know him?" said the Englishman.

"What about him?" asked the Frenchman.

"What _about_ him? Ho, ho!--He gave the Government some trouble, one way and another--They stuck him in the Zephyrs, but they didn't keep him long. What do you think he did?--

"He used to carry a flexible saw-file round his upper gums from one cheek to the other, and they say he carried some little tool that he used to swallow--on the end of a string, with the other end tied round a back tooth--on search days.

"Well, he filed his manacles and got out--And he killed two sentries, absolutely silently, by stabbing them in the back of the neck with a long darning-needle, to which he had fitted a tiny wooden handle--There is a spot, you know, at the base of the brain, just where the skull rests on the backbone--The point of a needle in _there_--just in the right spot--and _pouf!_--

"Rastignao knew the spot, all-right. And when he was clear, and dressed in a dead sentry's uniform, did he run off like any other escaping prisoner?--Not he--He broke into a Public Works Department shed--took a pot of black paint, and a pot of white, and some brushes, and marched off at daybreak,' as bold as brass--"

"Where to?" inquired the American.

"To the nearest milestone," chuckled Jacob the Jew, "--and neatly touched up the black _kilometre_ figures and their white border--And then to the next--And the next--

"When patrols passed, he gave them good-day and exchanged jokes and the latest news, for cigarettes and a drink--They say he visited several camps and made himself useful, with his paint, to one or two officers, and reported some rascal who had smeared one of his nice black figures because he wouldn't give him tobacco!--

"And so he painted his way, milestone by milestone, to Oran, where he reported himself, produced the dead sentry's _livret_ and leave-papers, and was wafted comfortably, by _Messageries Maritimes_, to France--"

"Well, and what would he do if he were here?" asked a querulous voice. "We may suppose that your Rastignao had neither the wings nor feet of a fly--And if he were here and got us out, where could we go?--More likely to have caused the death of us all--Like those two devils Dubitsch and Barre nearly did to their gang--"

"What was that?" asked Badineff.

"Why, these two unutterable swine were with a working-party in the _zone dissidente_, and at night were in a little perimeter-camp made with dry cactus and thick heavy thorn--Their beautiful scheme--and they nearly brought it off--was to creep out on a windy night and to set fire to these great thorn-walls of the zareba! This stuff burns like paper, and they'd got hold of some matches--It mattered nothing to them that the remaining ninety-eight of their fellow-convicts would inevitably be roasted to death in the process--Those two would easily escape in the confusion, while the men of the escort were vainly doing their best to save the rest of the wretched prisoners--_Their_ position, as you may imagine, would be just that of a bundle of mice tied together by their tails and packed round with cotton-wool soaked in kerosene--

"As luck would have it--the luck of the other ninety-eight, anyhow--the first match was blown out, and a sentry had seen the glare of it--He fired and challenged after, wounding

Dubitsch and so flustering Barre, who had the matches, that he dropped the lot and was unable to strike another before the sentry was upon him."

"What happened then?" asked the Englishman.

"The Sergeant-Major in charge of the escort simply returned them to their place in the gang--but took care that the gang should know exactly what had happened--"

"And then?" prompted the Englishman, when the man stopped, as one who had said enough--

"Oh--they died--they died--They died that same night, of something or other--Judging from their faces, they had not died happily--"

"Sounds as though you saw them," observed Jacob the Jew.

"Quite," observed the narrator laconically.

"Not like poor dear little Tou-tou Boil-the-Cat," observed Jacob.

"What happened to him?" asked the Querulous Voice.

"Oh, he died--he died--He died suddenly, one night, of something or other--But no-one was able to judge from his face whether he died happily or not--"

"Tell us about him," suggested the American.

"About Tou-tou Boil-the-Cat? He wasn't a nice man--Made quite a name for himself, Montmartre way, before he went to the Legion--There was some talk about a Lovely Lady, the Queen of his Band--Wonderful golden hair--Known to all kind friends as _Casque d'Or_--They say he cut it off--Her head, I mean--Got into bad trouble in the Legion too--Life sentence in the Zephyrs--

"A brave little man, but he hadn't the other virtue that one rather demands--No--Something of a stool-pigeon--There were thirteen convicts in a tent--a most unlucky number--but it was soon reduced to twelve, through M'sieu Tou-ton Boil-the-Cat giving information that affected the career--indeed, abbreviated, it--of one of his comrades--

"Yes--thirteen went forth from that tent to labour in the interests of France's colonial expansion that sunny morning, and only twelve returned to it, to sleep the sleep of the unjust, that dewy eve--A round dozen--

"But they did not sleep through the still night, though the night remained quite still--And behold, when another bright day broke, those twelve were now eleven--

"The guard, who was but a simple peasant man, could not make the count come to more than eleven--The corporal--possibly a shade more intelligent, could not by any means make the count a dozen--The Sergeant, a man who could count quite well, swore there were but ten and one--Not the Commandant himself could nuke us twelve!--

"With the help of a bottle of absinthe he might make us twenty-two--but even then he realized that he should have seen twenty-four--

"No--Tou-tou Boil-the-Cat was gone--Gone like a beautiful dream--or like the foul brutish nightmare that he was--

"And that, you know, puzzled our kind superiors--

"For, as it happened, it was quite impossible for anyone to have escaped from the camp that night--full moon, double sentries, constant patrols, and all-night wakefulness and uneasiness on account of expected Arab attack--

"But gone he had--

"We were interrogated severally, and collectively, and painfully--until they must have admired our staunchness and the wonderful cleverness of the missing man--

"We eleven slept in the tent for a month--and the country round was scoured until not one grain of sand was left upon another, and there was not a locust, a scorpion, a serpent nor a vulture, whose _dossier_ was not known--"

"And at the end of a month the whole camp moved on--"

"Did they ever find him?" asked Badineff.

"No--_they_ didn't," was the reply. "The jackals found him--"

"Where?" asked the Englishman.

"Under the sand that had formed the floor of the tent of the eleven--" was the answer.

"Sounds as though you were there--" said the Querulous Voice.

"Quite--" replied Jacob the Jew, and yawned.

4.

The sun had risen and set once more, causing a spot of light to travel slowly across a portion of the interior of the _silo_, with the search-light effect of illuminating brilliantly the tiny area upon which it rested, while leaving the rest of the place in darkness darker than that of night.

There was curiously little movement, and less sound, in the _silo_--the uneasy stirring of a nightmare-ridden sleeper, a heavy sigh, a faint groan, the clank of a chain. Talk had ceased, and scarcely a sentence had been uttered for hours.

The last subject of general conversation had been that of the cause of their abandonment to a lingering and terrible death in that dreadful tomb. Speculation had wandered from sudden Arab attack and the annihilation of the Company, to the familiar theory of wanton malice and deliberate devilish punishment. Men, condemned from the Legion for military "crimes," had advanced the former theory; civilian prison criminals, the latter.

The Frenchman who had attempted to recite the Burial Service had accepted neither of these views.

"We are _forgotten_," he had said, "We are the Forgotten of Man, as distinguished from our friends the Touareg, the Forgotten of God. It is perfectly simple, and I can tell you exactly how it happened.

"As you may be aware, _mes amis_, a list of _les hommes punis_ is made out, by the clerk of the *Adjudant* , every morning, before the guard is changed. The form on which he writes the names is divided into columns showing the class of punishment and the number of days each man has still to do--And the clerk of the *Adjudant* , God forgive him, has written the number of our days under the heading _salle de police_, or _cellules_, or _consigne_, and has left the column 'prison,' blank. So, each day, our sentences are being reduced by one day, in those places where we are not, and the Sergeant of the Guard for each day, observes that there are no men in '_prison_,' for the column so headed is blank--We are _not_ in 'prison' because we are not recorded as being in 'prison'--and therefore we Cannot be released from 'prison.'--"

And Jacob the Jew had observed:

"Convincing and very cheering--Monsieur must have been a lawyer before he left the world."

A rid the man had replied:

"No--An officer--Captain of Spahis and in the Secret Service--about to die, and unashamed--No!--I should say *Légionnaire* Rien of the Seventh Company of the Third Battalion of the First Regiment of the Foreign Legion--I was wandering in my mind--"

5.

"Tell me," said Jacob the Jew (or Jacopi Judescu, the Roumanian gypsy). "What was really your reason for that sloppy feeble 'kindness' to Ramon Gonzales--I am a philosopher and a student of that lowest of the animals, called Man--Was it to please your Christian God and to acquire merit?--Or to uphold your insolent British assumption of an inevitable end natural superiority?--You and your God--the Great Forgivers!--'Injure me--and I'll forgive you and make you feel so damned uncomfortable that you'll he more injured than I am.'--Aren't you _capable_ of a good decent hate or--"

"Yes. I hate your filthy voice, dear Jacob," replied the Englishman.

"No. Tell me," persisted Jacob. "I loathe being puzzled--Besides, don't you see I'm going mad--Talk, man--These corpses--Why did you behave like that to Ramon Gonzales?--He betrayed you, didn't he?--I would have strangled him--I would have had his eyes--Didn't he betray and denounce you after you had found him in the desert and saved his life?--To Sergeant Lebaudy?"

"Yes. He recognized me--and did his, ah--duty," was the reply.

"For twenty-five pieces of silver!--Recognized you as one of the Zinderneuf men he knew at Sidi, and promptly sold you?--

"Consigned you to sudden death--or a lingering death--for twenty-five francs and a Sergeant's favour!--And here the Judas was--wondrously delivered into your hand--and you 'forgave' him and comforted him!--Now _why?_--What was the game, the motive, the reason, the object? Why should a sane man act like that?--What _was_ the game?"

"No game, no motive, no reason," answered the Englishman. "He acted according to his lights--I to mine."

"And where do you get your 'lights'? What flame lit them?"

"Oh--I don't know--Home--Family--One's women-folk--School--Upbringing--Traditions--One unconsciously imbibes ideas of doing the decent thing--I've been extraordinarily lucky in life--Poor old Ramon wasn't--One does the decent thing if one is--decent."

"You don't go about, then, consciously and definitely forgiving your enemies and heaping coals of fire on them because you're a Christian."

"No, of course not--Don't talk rot--"

"Nor with a view to securing a firm option on a highly eligible and desirable mansion in the sky--suitable for English gentleman of position--one of the most favourable residential sites on the Golden Street--"

"Not in the least--Don't be an ass--"

"You disappoint me. I was hoping to find, before I died, one of those rare animals, a Christian gentleman--who does all these funny things _because_ he is a Christian--and this was positively my last chance--I shall die in here."

"I expect Christianity _was_ the flame that lit those little 'lights,' Jacob--Our home and school and social customs, institutions and ideas are based on the Christian ideal, anyhow--And we owe what's good in them to that, I believe--We get our *beau idéal* quite unconsciously, I think, and we follow it quite unconsciously--if we follow it at all--"

"Well, and what *is* it, my noble Christian martyr?"

"Oh, just to be--decent, and to do the decent thing, y'know."

"So, indirectly, at any rate, you returned good for evil to Judas Ramon Gonzales because you were a Christian, you think?"

"Yes--Indirectly--I suppose--We aren't good at hating and vengeance and all that--It's not done--It isn't--decent--"

"But you puzzle me. What of Ramon the Judas--Ramon who sold you? He was a _great_ Christian, you k now--A staunch patron of your Christian God--Always praying and invoking your Holy Family."

"There are good and bad in all religions, Jacob--I have the highest admiration for your great people--but I have met rotten specimens--Bad as some of my own--"

Silence.

"Look here, Christian," began Jacob the Jew again. "If I summoned up enough strength, and swung this chain with all my might against your right cheek, would you turn the other also?"

"No. I should punch you on the nose," said the Englishman simply.

Silence.

"Tell me. Do you kneel down night and morning and pray to your kind Christian God, Englishman? The forgiving God of Love, Who has landed you _here?_" asked Jacob the Jew.

"I landed myself here," was the reply. "And--er--no--I don't pray--in words--much--You won't mind asking questions for fear of being thought inquisitive, will you, gentle Jacob?"

"Oh, no--Let's see now--You forgive the very worst of injuries because you are a Christian, but not _because_ you're a Christian--You do as you would be done by, and not as you've been 'done' by--You don't pray in words, and hold daily communion with your kind Christian God--you regard Him as a gentleman--an English gentleman of course--who quite understands, and merely desires that you be--decent, which of course, you naturally would be, whether He wished it or not--And you'll punch me on the nose if I smite you on the cheek--but you don't even do that much to anyone who betrays you to a dreadful death--And really, in your nice little mind, you loathe talking about your religion, and you are terrified lest you give the impression that you think it is better than other people's, for fear of hurting their feelings--"

"Oh, shut up, Jacob. You'd talk the hind leg off a dog."

"What else is there to do but talk?--And so you are perfectly certain that you are a most superior person, but you strive your very utmost to conceal the awful fact--You're a puzzling creature--What is your motivating force? What is your philosophy? What are you _up_ to?"

"Well, at the moment, I'm going to issue the water-ration--Last but one--" said the Englishman.

"I can't understand you English--" grumbled Jacob.

"A common complaint, I believe," said the Englishman. The quiet American laughed.

6.

"Should any gentleman here survive, I wonder if he would be so extremely obliging as to write to my Mother," said the French ex-officer later. "She is an old lady--quite alone--and she foolishly cherishes a fondness for a most unworthy son--Darling Mother!"

The Englishman and the American memorized an address in Paris, and each declared that he would not only write to Madame de Lannec, but would visit her, give her her son's last message, and assure her of his gentle happy death from honourable wounds received in the service of France, and describe his grand military funeral.

Neither of these two men would admit that he also was already in his grave.

"Been in lots of tighter places than this," said the Englishman.

"I've been nearer death too," observed the American. "Been dead really--In this same Zaguig--"

"Ah--an unpleasant place, Zaguig," said the Frenchman, "I know it well," and added, "I, too, have occasion--ally been in danger--But I finish here--"

"Never say die," urged the American. "Personally, I refuse to die--I've got a job to do, and I intend to live until it's done--"

"Same here," agreed the Englishman. "I must be getting home to tea shortly--My wife--" He coughed.

"Ah, _mes amis_, you wish to live--I, on the contrary, wish to die," whispered the Frenchman, and shortly after became delirious and raved--of "Véronique," of a terrible painter and his devilish picture, of a Colonel of Chasseurs d'Afrique, of a Moor of the Zarhoun whom the speaker had apparently killed with his bare hands, and of his mother--But chiefly of "Véronique"--until he Hank into a state of coma.

In the morning, the spot of light fell on his face and he awoke and, from time to time, spoke rationally, though he did not appear to realize where he was.

He desired the services of a priest, that he might "make his soul." On either side of him, the Englishman and the American did what they could to soothe his passing, and Jacob the Jew produced his last scrap of biscuit for the nourishment of the sick man--He offered to chew it for him if he were unable to masticate--

"It's a privilege to die in your society, _mes amis_," said the Frenchman suddenly, in a stronger voice. "To die with men of one's own sort--Officers once, doubtless, and gentlemen still--I am going to add to the burden of debt I owe you--But I am going to give you something in return--My dying assurance that you are going to live--I most clearly see you walking in the sunshine, free and happy--Walking towards a woman--a truly beautiful woman--She loves you both--but one far more than the other--You fight on her account--your weapons are generosity, unselfishness, sacrifice, self-abnegation, the love of a man for his friend--"

Silence.

"Poor chap," murmured the Englishman, staring across at the almost indistinguishable form of the American. "Wandering again--He seemed better--"

No reply came from the darkness where the other crouched beside the dying man.

"And this is the further request I have to make of you--Will one of you go to the little cemetery and stand by her grave and say:

"'_As he died he spoke of you--He spoke only words of kindness and love--He did not breathe one word of reproach--Only kindness, love and gratitude._'

"She will be able to understand--now--

"And will you take violets--a few violets, from me--Always they were her flower--A few of the beautiful big violets that welcome one home from Africa--Once I kissed an old grandmother who was selling them on the _quai_ at Marseilles, and gave her a gold piece--They were not violets she sold to me--They were _France_--they were _Home_--they were

Véronique--Their odour was the distilled soul of the sweetness of all that is in those three wonderful words--France, Home and Beauty--

"Oh, God--I can smell violets--

"Véronique, did ever you see violets again without thinking of me? Did I ever see them again without trembling from head to foot, without wondering how my frozen brain could function--how my burning heart could beat--

"Forgive me, gentlemen--But you never saw her--.She was God's triumph--Yes, often I called her, 'You Evidence of God'--for such beauty and wonder and untellable glory of womanhood was final proof to me of the existence of a great good God of Beauty.

"And Beauty is Truth--and Goodness."

Silence.

Jacob the Jew crawled painfully toward the spot of light.

"You can give him my water-ration," he croaked.

"Stout fella!" said the Englishman, in his mother-tongue.

The American started, as a slight jingle of iron indicated.

"_Say that again, will you?_" he said in English.

"I said, '_Stout fella_,'" replied the Englishman.

"_Merciful God!_" whispered the American; and the dying Frenchman raised himself on his right elbow, and endeavoured to point with his left hand.

"_Véronique!_" he cried. "I did my best--I *did* save you from Dummarcq--the great César Dummarcq--the world-famous painter, the idol of Paris, the huge vile pig, the half-mad cruel devil--No--_he is there!_--Do not move!--Do not stir hand or foot--a hair's-breadth--or he will shoot--He will shoot *you*, not me, the fiend!"

He sank back upon the ground.

"Dearest Mother!--I nearly broke your heart when I told you I would marry her--And you nearly broke mine when you said that I should not--An artists' model--True--César Dummarcq's model--But a model of beauty and grace--Lovely in all her ways and thoughts and movements--_César_ Dummarcq's model--But a model for all women to copy--Every fascination and charm of mind as well--witty and clever and of the sweetest disposition--With her, one laughed--One laughed the whole day through--

"Oh, but she was _dear_--dear and sweet and a living charm--Was it her fault that she had no heart? No fairy, mermaid, elf, sprite, no magic princess from the golden castle on the crystal hill, ever _has_ a heart!--So I gave her mine--to break--

"Oh, that terrible picture!--Véronique, how was I to know that he had painted us, all save the last few touches?--The jealous devil!--He did not even love you--You were merely his model, his chattel, his property--No one must take you from him--not even to marry you--

"Behind that sinister black curtain--A pistol in his hand--My arms about you as I implored you to be my wife--Your terrible shriek as you saw him appear--smiling--smiling--"

Silence.

The Frenchman's voice changed completely. It was as though an entirely different personality possessed his body.

"No--don't move, my young cub!--Move hand or foot, and our fair and frail young friend will have her beauty marred!--Oh, a _great_ picture!--'FEAR!' _by César Dummarcq_--the greatest portrayer of human emotions, of all time--Yes--'FEAR!'--Do you _fear_, little cockerel?--Do you fear you have brought death to your mistress?--I _am_ Death!--Death the great Artist!--Oh, ho! his macabre compositions!--His lovely colours of corruption and decay!--The great César Dummarcq's greatest picture--'FEAR!'--Now keep still--See, I lay the pistol on this table beside the easel--Ah! _would_ you!--You'd rise from that rug, would you?--_Down_, dog!--Would you murder this woman whom you love so much?--That's better--

"No, my dear Véronique, do not faint. Just a minute--Your glazing eyes staring from the white mask of your face--'FEAR!' Aha!--Wonderful models!--One has to go to some trouble to find them, of course--That's right, popinjay--excellent!--Moisten your lips with your tongue again--See, little pimp, I think I will shoot her, after all--as I have finished her face--Yes--you a little later--Another marvellous picture!--She lies on the divan--same attitude--blood on her breast, a thin stream trickling down her white arm, a stain on the white bear-skin--lovely colours!--And you?--One arm and your head and shoulders across her body--The rest of you on the rug--much the same position as now--A bullet-hole beneath your ear--I am not too near, here, I think--No--What shall we call the second picture?--'REVENGE!' No, a little banal--What about 'FINIS!'--No--No name at all, I think--a--_a 'problem' picture_--

"Oh?--You think I'll make a fine picture on the guillotine, do you?--That's where you're wrong, puppy--This is going to be a _crime passionel_--Glorious advertisement for the great César Dummarcq--Anyhow, the present picture is going marvelously--

"'FEAR!'--Never was FEAR so portrayed before--Hi! Down, dog! There--That bullet stirred her hair--Stirred your heart too by the look of you, you little hound--"

Silence.

"_Ce bon Monsieur César Dummarcq_ would seem to have been a gentleman with a sense of humour," murmured Jacob. "I would we had him here."

"To jest with us?" inquired the Englishman.

"No, for us to jest with _him_, I think," replied Jacob.

Silence.

"Water!" gasped the Frenchman.

"Mine," said Jacob.

"We'll all contribute," said the American.

The Englishman took the jug to the ray of light and carefully measured water into an iron mug.

"A good spoonful each, left," he said, stepping gingerly between two corpses.

The Frenchman drank avidly. Upon this little stream of life-giving water his conscious mind seemed to be borne to the surface.

"Thank you!--Thank you, gentlemen!" he said. "I do hope I have not drunk more than my share--I was not noticing--One of you will see to that for me, will you not?--Get them on the _quai_ at Marseilles, and put them on her grave in the little cemetery--"

"Why certainly, of course," said the American. "Where is it?"

"--And tell her that my last thoughts were of her--She will understand now--She understood nothing when she died--She was like that when I saved her from the Beni Zarkesh--God is very good and He had taken away her understanding--"

Silence.

That roof--In the starlight--He was twice as big and strong as I, that Moor--But I killed him with my bare hands, as I had killed the watchman dozing at the foot of the stair--Oh, that lovely silent struggle, with my hands at his throat--

"And she thought I was de Chaumont, her Colonel of Chasseurs d'Afrique--His name was Charles--She called me '_Charles_' as I carried her to the horses--She called me '_Charles_' through the brief remainder of her life--She died calling me '_Charles_.'--A little hard for me to bear--Yes, I suffered a little--I had thought bitterly of Charles de Chaumont and I had written him a rather terrible letter when, on the strength of his rank and seniority, he declined my challenge to a duel--But I am grateful to him for his kindness to her, and for making her so happy all those years--He must have loved her truly--Who could help it?--And how she loved him!--She must have been happy as the day is long, for she had changed but little--A girl when I lost her--A woman when I found her--Even more beautiful, if that were possible--The mad are often very lovely--An unearthly beauty--Very terrible--But I firmly believe her last days were happy--She had forgotten that _hareem_--And I was her adored _Charles de Chaumont!_--Yes--Unconscious fingers can play a fearful threnody upon our heart-strings--Can break them one by one--_Véronique--Véronique_"

Silence.

"Is he dead?" asked Jacob, later.

"Yes," said the Englishman, and coughed slightly.

"'Yell, do you know," said Jacob, "I think I shall join him. I have always been deeply interested in the Hereafter, and I confess to being a little weary of the Here--Yes, I think it's time to go."

"Are you talking about committing suicide?" asked the American.

"Not at all," replied Jacob. "I am talking about being murdered and taking it upon me to shorten the process. I have no strong views on the subject of man murdering his fellow-man on the scaffold, or against the wall at dawn. But this slow murder is quite indefensible, and I feel justified in expediting my end."

"You'll look a most awful ass if they remember us and a release-party comes, after all," said the Englishman.

"I shall look very nasty, anyhow, by the time a release-party comes," was the reply. "So will you, my friends. And you will have suffered a few hours or a few days longer than I--Either the Company has moved on, and there are a few more miles of the Zaguig-Great Oasis Road, marked, or else there was a sudden raid and the Company is obliterated--Anyhow--I've had enough."

"Don't give up, Jacob. Don't be a coward," said the Englishman.

"No, I will not give up--my right to dispose of myself; the only right left to me," was the answer. "No, I will not be a coward who dare not step uninvited into the next world--What do you do, my friend if you sit on a tin-tack? You promptly remove yourself. I am going to remove myself. I have already sat too long upon this particular--ah--tin-tack."

"Rot," said the Englishman.

"You're beat," said the American.

"You can't commit suicide," said the Englishman.

"It isn't--'decent,' I suppose," smiled Jacob.

"That's it," said the Englishman. "It's a rotten thing to do. One doesn't commit suicide! It's not done. It isn't--er--decent."

"A matter of opinion," said the Jew. "Is it better and wiser to suffer indescribable agonies of the mind, and ghastly tortures of the body, for days, hours, or seconds? It seems to me to be more logical to let it be a matter of seconds."

"Well, logic isn't everything," said the Englishman. Most of our best impulses and ideas are illogical--Damn logic--Love is illogical."

"Surely," said the American.

"Yes. Life is illogical and death is illogical, and God is illogical," said Jacob. "And it is also perfectly illogical to lie here and die of thirst, starvation, heat, suffocation and insects for another twenty-four hours when you can do it in twenty-four seconds--Good-bye, my friends! May we meet again and discuss our discoveries concerning God, Jehovah, Allah, Christ, Mahomet, Buddha and the other manifestations of man's incurable anthropomorphism--_Adieu!_ Or _au revoir_--whichever it may prove to be."

"Hi! Here! Hold on!" cried the Englishman.

"You! Jacob!" called the American.

"Well?" chuckled the Jew.

"Look here," said the Englishman, "be decent, Jacob. You objected to Ramon dying at all."

"Ah--he was the first," replied Jacob, "and there was some hope then--There are only we three now, and one more corpse will not further discommode you. I beg you to believe me that I would not have done this were all the others still alive--not even though I knew there would be no release--

"To have done that would not have been--'decent,'" he added with a chuckle.

"Look here, Jacob, will you do me a favour?" asked the Englishman.

"I shall be most delighted," was the reply. "It will be my last opportunity. And it will have to be soon," he added, his weak voice growing perceptibly weaker.

"Well, I want you to promise to wait another day," said the Englishman. "Only another twenty-four hours. Just till the spot of light falls on the Frenchman's body again--"

"Come on, Jacob," urged the American. "Stick it till then. Please yourself after that. But I believe we'll be saved to-morrow."

"Too late," was the whispered reply. "I have opened a vein--When you want it, you'll find the piece of steel in my right hand--razor-edge one side, saw-edge the other--Pluck up your courage and come along with me, both of you--"

Silence. A deep sigh. The Englishman and the American found it was indeed too late.

7.

"_Now_, my friend," said the American, "we can attend to our own little affairs!--Do you know that our meeting in here is one of the most astounding things that have _ever_ happened?--Do you know you are _the one man in all the world I have been looking for!_--And _this_ is where I find you!--I did my damnedest--and then Providence took a hand--Heaven helps those, etc--"

"I am afraid I don't quite understand," began the Englishman.

"You certainly don't--I don't myself--We're dreaming, of course. It's delirium. We aren't in any _silo_--_You aren't John Geste_."

"But I _am_ John Geste!" gasped the Englishman.

"You aren't John Geste and I didn't spot you directly you said '_Stout fella_,' in English. And I didn't hear you call your wife 'Stout fella' at Brandon Abbas when you were kids and--Oh, my God!

"Where's your hand, man--Oh, _John Geste! John Geste!_--We'll be out of Mere to-morrow, boy--We _can't_ die here. God doesn't mean us to die and rot in this hole that was ordained to be our meeting-place--Ordained from the beginning of Time as the place where I should find you, after all--And Isobel's well and only waiting to be happy as soon as she hears you're corning home to--er--tea, John Geste!--And I was to tell you Michael didn't take the 'Blue Water' from under the cover. It wasn't he who stole it--And I'm going mad, John Geste--mad with joy-and starvation, and weakness, and happiness--"

"Hadn't noticed the happiness much," said the Englishman. "What are you gibbering about, my dear chap? Who _are_ you? How do you know my name--and about Isobel?"

He coughed slightly. "I'm delirious, I suppose--Both delirious--Both dreaming--"

"We're both dreaming the same dream then, John Geste--I want to tell you--"

An ominous clink of metal and a sigh were audible above the feeble croaking of his voice.

"Here, what's up?--You listening?--Here, _wake up_."

The Englishman had collapsed and lay inert, unresponsive, either in a faint or the last sleep of all.

8.

The arrival of the spot of sunlight found the American moistening the lips of the dying Englishman with the remaining drops of water.

"Worn out," he murmured later. "God! I feel as strong as a horse now!--He had given up hope before I recognized him--Oh, Isobel--I've found him and he's dying--No, God can't mean that--I'm talking out loud. I must catch hold of myself--Help me, God, for I am going to help myself--to help them."

The American crawled across to where lay the body of the strange man known to his fellows as Jacob the Jew.

Feeling over the corpse he found the right hand and in it a piece of wonderfully-tempered steel, which, together with a few matches, the man had somehow hidden from those whose duty it had been to search him. Securing it, he returned to the side of the Englishman, and once again endeavoured to revive him.

Panic seized him as he realized his efforts were unavailing. Putting his lips to the ear of the unconscious man, he whispered urgently, and his whisper quickly grew to a hoarse shout.

"_John Geste I John Geste I Come back, John Geste!_ Come _back_, man! You _can't_ die! You can't die, _now_, John Geste! I've _found_ you--_Hi! John Geste!_ Think of Isobel--Isobel!--Isobel!! _Isobel!!!_ Do you hear me?--Do you hear me, John? Fight, man! Fight for your life!--Think how Beau would have fought!--Beau Geste--Think how Digby would have fought--Digby Geste--Fight, John!--Fight for Isobel--Come back--Isobel!--Isobel!!--_Isobel!!!_"

As though the name had reached his semi-conscious mind, the dying man stirred. The other crowed inarticulately, and suddenly fell quiet.

"Wish I knew something more about that blood-transfusion stunt," he murmured in his normal voice, as he deeply incised the side of his wrist, forced open his companion's mouth, and pressed the bleeding wrist firmly against it.

"Excuse me, son," he said, and laughed hysterically.

THE STORY OF OTIS VANBURGH

A lean man, silent, behind triple bars Of pride, fastidiousness and secret life. His thought an austere commune with the stars, His speech a probing with a surgeon's knife.

His style a chastity whose acid burns All slack, false, formlessness in man or thing; His face a record of the truth man learns Fighting bare-knuckled Nature in the ring.

--John Masefield.

A man's place in the scale of civilization is shown by his attitude to women. There are men who regard a woman as something to live with. There are others who regard her as someone to live for.

CHAPTER I

1.

I shall never forget my first sight of Isobel Rivers--a somewhat foolish remark, in view of the fact that I have never forgotten any glimpse I have ever had of her. I don't think I have even forgotten any word that she has ever said to me. Nay, more, I do not believe I have forgotten any word that I have ever said to her.

It was, as was most fitting, one of those truly glorious English spring mornings when one is consciously glad to be alive, and unconsciously aware that God's in His Heaven and all's well with the world.

I was on a visit to the home of my maternal grandmother at Brandon Regis and had that morning walked out from the big old house which was half farm and half manor, where my yeoman ancestors had lived since Domesday Book, or before.

I suppose it was the utter glory of that lovely morning, and not a premonition that this was to be an epochal day in my life, that made me feel so joyously exalted.

I had walked a mile or so, in the direction of Brandon Abbas, and was seated on a gate that opened into one of those neat and tidy English fields that always look to me as though they were tended rather by parlour-maids than by agricultural labourers. I was whistling merrily, and probably quite tunelessly, when a dog-cart, its small body perched high on big spidery wheels, came smartly round a bend in the high-hedged narrow lane to which my face was turned.

On the front seat were two boys, extraordinarily alike, as I saw when the horse was brought to an extremely sudden stand-still at my gate. Back to back with these obvious twins, sat a boy and a girl, the boy an unmistakable younger brother of the twins, and the girl younger still.

They were an astoundingly handsome quartette, and the girl's face was the loveliest I had ever seen.

It is still the loveliest I have ever seen.

I will not attempt to describe her, as it is foolish to attempt the impossible. I can only say that the face was typically Anglo-Saxon in its fair loveliness of pale golden hair, large, long-lashed eyes of corn-flower blue, perfect complexion and tender mouth, faultless and sweet.

The boy who was driving the restless and spirited horse, addressed me in a form of words, archaic and unusual.

"Prythee, gentle stranger, seated pensive on thy gate, and making day hideous with shrill cacophony--"

"Doesn't look coffiny to me," interrupted his twin.

"Nor too blooming gentle," said the boy behind him.

"And I am _sure_ he was making day delightful and wasn't a bit s'rill, and he isn't a stranger now we've talked to him," said the girl.

"Good-morning Madam, and gentlemen," said I, stepping down and raising my cap to the lovely little maiden who had spoken in my defence.

"Have it your own way, pups," cried the first speaker, as the three boys gravely and gracefully returned my salute. "He's not a stranger within our gate, nor on it, now; he is making day beautiful with uninstrumental and unearthly music--"

"Do you mean an unearthly row?" asked his twin.

"No, vulgarian; I meant heavenly music. Music such as ne'er was heard on earth before--let's hope!--But what's all this got to do with the dog? The dog may be dying while we trifle thus--dying of a broken heart."

"Oh, don't say such dreadful things, Beau," begged the little girl.

"Nothing dreadful about that," replied the boy called Beau, manfully checking the horse's obvious desire to bolt. "Compliment to the dog. D'you mean to suggest that the callous brute is not by now dying of a broken heart?"

"Spare a father's feelings," requested his twin, and wiped away a tear. "It's *my* dog--And what we want to know, Sir, if you could be quiet for one second, is--er--have you seen a dog?"

"Often," I replied, trying to enter into the light inconsequent spirit of this joyous charming band.

"Where?" they inquired simultaneously.

"Oh, Wyoming, Texas, Oregon, Nevada--"

"Nirvana?" inquired the owner of the dog. "Then dogs do go there. Good."

"California," I continued. "Boston, New York, Paris, London, Brandon Regis--"

"He's getting 'warm,'" said Beau.

"Brandon Abbas?" prompted his twin.

"I'm not certain," I replied. "I rather think I did, though--" And here the little girl broke in.

"Oh, do stop talking nonsense, Beau and Digby and John--"

"Not talking at all," said John, through whose arm the girl's hand was tucked.

"Well *do*, then, and say something sensible," was the feminine reply, and she turned to me.

"We've lost our dog, and he can't have been in _all_ those funny places you said. Have you seen her here? Will you help me find her--for I do love him so?"

"Why, *of course* I will," I said, and added impulsively, "I'd do anything you asked me. _I'll_ find him if he or she is alive."

And the twins on the front seat, promptly assisted by John, thereupon simultaneously chanted what appeared to be a family cliché.

"Oh isn't--he a nice--boy--He--must--come--and--play--with--us. Won't--Auntie--be--pleased--"

"What's the dog like?" I inquired of the one whom they called Digby. "What breed, if any? And what sex?" as there seemed to be a variety of opinions on this point.

"Sex? Oh--er--she's a bitchelor--feminine of bachelor, you know," replied Digby. "As to what she's _like_," he continued, "that's a difficult question to answer. She's rather like--No, she isn't--She isn't a bit like a giraffe, really--No--She's rather like--a dog. Yes--She is--And she is one of these new Andorran Oyster-Hounds--"

"Oh, good! That's helpful," I said appreciatively, while four pairs of bright young eyes summed me up. I was being weighed, and most earnestly I hoped I should not be found wanting.

"An idea," I exclaimed. "What name does she answer to?"

"She never answered *me*," replied Digby, and turning to his twin inquired, "Did she ever back-answer you, Beau?"

"Never a cheep out of her," was the reply. "Not a word. Sulky beggar."

"Not at all," contradicted John, "merely respectful--Reserved, taciturn chap--Strong silent dog."

"Well, she always answers *me*, anyhow," asserted the little girl warmly. "She always _smiles_--He has a most lovely smile," she added, turning to me.

"Now we're getting on," I declared. "I'm to search for a dog that is very like a dog and answers with a smile--Now what is the likeliest way to win her smile? What shall I call her when I see her?"

"Call her home," said Digby.

"I don't know *what* you'll call her when you see her," said Beau. "Have you a kind nature and a gentle tongue?--You must tell us later what you *did* call her when you saw her--Especially if you called her it in American."

"Darned gosh-dinged gol-durned dod-gasted smell-hound?" suggested Digby.

"I've never heard the expressions," I replied, "but I'll try to remember them if you think them appropriate--But to get back to the dog."

"It's what we want to do," replied Digby, "or to get her back to us. You don't know the state I'm in--Am I out in a rash?"

"No. In a dog-cart," said Beau, "and you won't be in that long, when we start playing chariots--Well, goodbye, old chap. Thanks awfully. I hope you haven't bored us--I mean we haven't--"

"Stop, stop, Beau," cried the little girl, turning round and thumping the boy's broad back. "He's going to be a search-party and we haven't told him what he wants to know, yet--I think he's most awfully kind and nice--And we ought to help him to--"

"Oh, *yes*, Beau," said Digby in a tone of deep reproach, "when he's in such trouble about a dog--Of course we must help him. Now let's see," he continued. "It's got four canine teeth."

"I should think all a dog's teeth are canine," observed John judicially.

"And five toes on his fore-feet."

"That makes twenty," remarked Beau.

"And four on each hind one--He wags his tail from left to right; not right to left--You get the idea, don't you? Like a pendulum. Or an Aberdonian his head, when asked to subscribe."

"But hasn't she a _name?_" I interrupted.

"A _name?_" replied Digby. "Now that's an idea. That's really helpful. Oh, yes, I know she's got a name because I was at the christening--but I've clean forgotten most of it--What's her name, Beau?"

"Well--I always call him Jasper Jocelyn Jelkes, but I think of her as Mrs. Denbigh-Hobbes of The Acacias, Lower Puffleworth."

"Oh, do stop rotting," begged John, and turning to me assured me that the dog's name was Simply-Jones, though generally addressed as Mr. Featherstonehaugh--whereat the little girl was moved to climb down on to the step at the back of the cart, and jump to the ground. Coming round to where I stood, she seized my arm and proceeded to lead me down the lane.

"Come away from those sillies, American Boy," she said, "and I'll just tell you all about it, and you will find her for me, won't you? She is Digby's dog, but it's me she loves, and I know she's grieving and sorrowing like anything, for she has such a nice loving nature and a good heart. Her name is Joss and she's middle-sized and middle-aged and sort of middleish altogether--not exactly a spaniel nor a terrier nor a hound, but just a dog, and if you call '_Joss, Joss, Joss, Joss, Jossie!_' in a kind sweet voice, rather high, she'll run to you and smile like anything. You'll know her by her smile. You will find her, won't you? Our home's at Brandon Abbas--Auntie is Lady Brandon."

"If she's alive on this earth, I'll find her," I said.

"Isobel! _Hi!_ _Isobel!!_ Isobel!! Come on, if you want to be Boadicea," came borne on the breezes, and with a "_Thank_ you, nice American Boy," and a smile that went straight to my heart--and also to my head--Isobel turned and scampered back.

Later, while searching the world for Joss, I had another glimpse of this party.

The dog-cart driven at a reckless gallop across a great lawn-like field, contained a boy and a girl, both wearing fencing-masks, the girl, armed with a bow and arrow, returning the fire of two presumed Roman soldiers who, with javelin and arrow, assailed the chariot, skilfully driven and controlled by a charioteer.

I was relieved to observe that the horse was apparently accustomed to these martial exercises, and that the chariot came round in a graceful curve before reaching the ditch-and-hedge at the end of the field.

2.

Being a strictly truthful person, I cannot say that I found Jasper Jocelyn Jelkes, _alias_ Joss, for it was really she who found me. What her business may have been, I do not know, but she was visiting at High Gables, my grandmother's house, when I returned for lunch.

As I emerged from the shadows of the avenue, I beheld a very nondescript dog sunning herself on the lowest of the white steps of the porch, and smiling, most positively smiling, with extreme fatuity and foolishness, at my Grandmother's tiny Pekinese, a microscopic by-product of the dog-industry, which found no favour in my sight. Lifting up my voice to the level of the hope that rose in my heart, I invoked the smiling caller, in the very tones and accent in which I had been instructed, and in the most mellifluous and wooing way at my command The excellent Joss, for such, beyond peradventure of a doubt, her conduct proved her to be, lolloped straightway to my feet and sitting on end, smiled and smiled and was not a villain, I felt sure.

"Joss!" I cried, patting that smiling head. "*Dulce ridentem Lalagem amabo*; grinning idiot; Minnehaha, Laughing Water; I'm very pleased to meet you--You shall lead me, gentle Jossie, like a blind man's dog, straight to Brandon Abbas, to the house of Aunty, to those delightful boys and to--Isobel. Are you a bit of a card, Jossie? For my visiting-card you shall be--"

Oh, to be seventeen again! Seventeen, on a most glorious English spring day, the day on which you have first encountered the very loveliest thing in all the world--that is to remain, for ever, the very loveliest thing in all your world.

CHAPTER II

1.

After lunch, on that day of days, with Hail Smiling Joss as my sponsor, excuse, and loud note of introduction, I "proceeded," as they say in the British Navy, to the great house of Brandon Abbas, after so feasting the excellent dog that it seemed highly probable she would again lose herself in the direction of High Gables.

Up a few miles of avenue of Norman oaks I tramped, from the Lodge at the gates guarded by heraldic beasts well known to students of Unnatural History--the Returning Wanderer straining at the leash and obviously striving to compose her features to a mask of becoming gravity, tempered by gladness while chastened by shame.

Arrived at a large square of mossy gravel surrounded by a dense shrubbery, I beheld a great porch and an open door through which I had, in passing, a glimpse of a panelled hall, gleaming floor, and suits of armour. A passing glimpse, because it was clearly obvious that Joss intended me to pass, and my will was not brought into conflict with hers, as I heard shouts and peals of laughter from the band of whom I was in search.

Guided by the now excited dog, I crossed a rose-garden and, by a path through some great old elms and beeches, reached an open space of turf which was a view-point overlooking half the county.

As we burst from the gloom of the wood into the sunshine, a hubbub arose; the four, now augmented by several others, converged upon me, and, with a shriek of joy, as she sped forward ahead of the rest, the little girl literally flung herself upon me, threw her arms about my neck, and kissed me warmly. Truth compels me to add that she promptly did precisely the same to the errant Joss, who instantly abandoning her expression, pose, and air of a Misunderstood-but-Hopeful-Dog, stood upon her hind legs, her paws against her mistress, wagged her tail and her tongue, and smiled and smiled to the point of laughter.

"Oh, Stout Fella!" cried Beau. "Splendid! Good scout!"

"Put it right there, Mr. Daniel Boone--or are you Bit Carson? Or Buffalo Bill? Or the Pathfinder?--Anyhow, you're the Dogfinder," said Digby, extending his hand, and wringing mine powerfully. "A father's thanks--The Prodigal Dog--Good mind to _kill_ the fat-headed calf!" and seizing the dog in his arms, he rolled upon the ground in apparently terrific combat with the savage beast, who, with horrid growls and furious barks, worried the throat of her fiercely-stabbing antagonist, and bloodlessly bit him with all her canine teeth.

"In the end, I die, having saved all your lives from a mad dog, and so find a hero's grave," announced Digby. "The dog was born mad," he added, and lay motionless, while the Andorran Oyster-Hound surveyed her tooth-work, wagged her tail joyously, and seated herself upon the chest of her victim.

The youngest brother, meanwhile, having slipped his hand inside my arm, while he critically watched the progress of the fight, stood by my side as I waited--holding the grubby little paw which Isobel had thrust into my hand--and feeling unreasoningly and unreasonably happy.

"I say," said the boy, "you ought to join the Band. Will you? Would you like to?"

"Oh *yes*," chimed in Isobel. "*do*, American Boy--Have you ever been tortured by Indians, or been the Victim of a Cruel Fate, like Mazeppa? Do you think we might roast you at the stake?--We've all got mustangs, and Joss is quite a good wolf or coyote. She's being a wolf now, and she's not mad at all--not even half-witted."

"Not nearly half," agreed Digby, arising. "Er--this is--er--the Captain--Michael Geste, Captain of the Band. I am Digby Geste, Lieutenant of the Band. The object on your right hand is John Geste, or Very Small Geste, or Not-Much-of the Band. The female prisoner is Isobel Rivers, the Music of the Band. The beautiful woman enthroned yonder is Claudia, Queen of the Band; and the gentleman at present struck dumb by toffee-on-the-jaw, is Augustus Brandon, and can't be helped. I may add that, as you doubtless suppose, he is not such a fool as he looks. How could he be?--The small fat boy and girl on the pony are twins, Marmaduke and--er--Marmaduchess. Marmaduke's step-mother, who eats vinegar with a fishhook three times a day, says he is Wholly Bad. We call him the Wholly of Whollies. Marmaduchess is of course the Roly of Polies--These camp followers--scamp-followers--er--no, that won't do, as they follow the Captain, are Honorary Members of the Band. In view of your great services, I have the pleasure--"

"You'll have the pleasure of bread-and-water and six of the best, if you don't take a holiday," interrupted the Captain of the Band, and proceeded most warmly to invite me to become an Honorary Member of "Beau Geste's Band," and to take part in all its doings, for so long as the country was enriched by my presence, and whenever my inclinations prompted me so to do.

Gratefully accepting the Band's hospitality, I was initiated and enrolled, and quickly appointed stage-manager of its activities in its Western American manifestations, and became its authority upon the dark ways of Red Indians, Bad Men, Buffalo Bills, Cow-boys, Deadwood Dicks, and other desperadoes.

I won my spurs (but did not wear them) by finding myself able to catch, mount, and ride a horse that was loose in the paddock. A horse that had never been ridden before and apparently intended never to be ridden again--

After a most delightful tea with these extraordinarily charming young people, I walked back to High Gables feeling happier, I think, than I had ever felt in my life. It was a rather wonderful thing to me, a lonely stranger in a strange land--for there was nobody but my Grandmother and her servants at High Gables--suddenly to find myself a member of so attractive a society, a family so friendly, so welcoming, so uncritically hospitable that, almost on sight, they had admitted me to membership of their Band, with all the privileges attaching thereto--

But as I lay awake in bed that night, the picture most vividly before me was the beautiful face of the darling child who had given me that sweet spontaneous kiss of gratitude and innocence.

It surely was the nicest thing that had ever happened to me.

2.

I shall be believed when I state that I missed few opportunities of accepting the warm invitation to "come again soon" which invariably accompanied the farewells at the end of each of my visits to Brandon Abbas. The more I saw of the three Gestes, the better I liked them, and I knew that I could never see too much, nor indeed enough, of Isobel Rivers-- that lovely little fairy; charming and delightful child; ineffably sweet, and absorbingly interesting, little friend--

Of the boys, I liked John best; for, in addition to all the attributes which he possessed in common with his brilliant brothers, he was, to me, slightly pathetic in his dog-like devotion to the twins, who ruled him with a rod of iron, chastened and chastised him for the good of his soul, kept him in subjection, and loved him utterly. In return for their unwavering and undemonstrated love, he gave them worship. They would have died for him, and he would have died under torture for them.

Yet, at the same time, I like Beau enormously; for his splendour--and it was nothing less--of mind, body and soul; his unselfish sweetness and gentleness, and his extraordinary "niceness" to everybody, including myself. Even when he had occasion to punish a member of his Band, it appeared to me that the victim of his arbitrary justice rather enjoyed the honour of being singled out, even for admonition and the laying on of hands--

But then, again, I liked Digby as much; for his unfailing mirth and happiness. He was a walking chuckle, and those who walked through life with him chuckled too. He was merriment personified; his day was a smile; and if he fell on his head from the top of a tree, the first use he made of his recovered breath was to laugh at the extraordinarily amusing funniness of Digby Geste's falling thirty feet and nearly breaking his neck--He was the most genuinely and spontaneously cheerful person I ever met, and somehow one always laughed when Digby began to laugh, without waiting for the joke.

Isobel was their pet, their fairy, their mascot, their dear perfect play-mate; and Claudia was their Queen--"Queen Claudia, of Beau Geste's Band"--held in the highest honour and esteem. They loved and obeyed Claudia; but they petted and adored Isobel.

I suppose Claudia was of an immaculately flawless beauty, charm, and grace of form and face, even as a young girl--but personally I never liked her. There was a slight hardness, a self-consciousness and an element of selfishness in her character, that were evident--to me at any rate, though not, I think, to the others. Certainly not to Michael Geste, for she was obviously his *beau idéal* of girlhood, and he, her self-constituted paladin and knight-errant. When they played "tournaments" she was always the Queen of Beauty, and he her Champion, ready, willing and able, to dispose of all who disputed his (or her) claim that she was the loveliest damsel in all the world--

Nor could I like Lady Brandon, fascinating as she was to most. She was kind, gracious and hospitable to me, and I was grateful--but _like_ her I could not. She was an absolute re-incarnation of "Good" Queen Bess, and I do not think any living woman could have better impersonated Queen Elizabeth than she, whether on the stage or off. Although beautiful in her way, she was astoundingly like the portraits of that great unscrupulous Queen, and, in my belief, she resembled her in character. She was imperious, clever, hard, "managing" and capable. She was very queenly in appearance and style, given to the cherishing of favourites--Michael and Claudia especially--and extremely jealous. She was a woman of strong character and could be both ruthless and unscrupulous. At least, that is the impression I formed of Lady Brandon--and I am very intuitive, as well as being a student of physiognomy, and possessed of a distinct gift for reading character.

No, I disliked Lady Brandon and I distrusted her--and I thought that she and Claudia were not unlike in character--I was very intrigued when my Grandmother dryly remarked, "Henry VIII is, I believe the '*Rex*' of Brandon '*Regis*,'" when, in reply to a question of hers anent Lady Brandon, I had observed, "She reminds me of Queen Elizabeth--"

She resembled the Queen, too, in her power of inspiring great love in men, a noble love, worthy of a nobler object--

On one of my visits to the Band, I was scolded for my absence of several days--I had been to London, on business of my Father's--and told that I had missed the chance of a lifetime, a chance of seeing and hearing a veritable Hero of Romance, a French officer of Spahis, son of a senior school friend of Lady Brandon's, who had been week-ending at Brandon Abbas, and who had for ever endeared himself to the children, by his realistic and true tales of Desert warfare, and of adventures in mysterious and romantic Morocco.

Promptly we ceased to be Red Indians, Knights of the Round Table, Crusaders, Ancient Britons, Big Game Hunters, or anything else but Spahis and Arabs, and the three Gestes and I spent a portion of our lives in charging--mounted on two ponies, a donkey and a carriage-horse--a *douar* of gorse-bushes stoutly defended by a garrison of Arabs clad in towels, sheets and night-shirts and armed with pea-shooters, bows and arrows, lances, swords and spears, toy rifles and pistols which made more sound than sorrow--

The Band certainly "lived dangerously," but accidents were few and slight, and the absolute freedom permitted to the children, as soon as morning lessons with the Chaplain were finished, was really not abused. Being trusted, they were trustworthy, and the Captain led the Band not into temptation irresistible, nor into more than right and reasonable danger.

This chaplain was a puzzle to me. I felt certain he was essentially good, honourable and well-meaning; but he struck me, in my youthful intolerance, as being too weak and feeble in character to be worthy of the name of man. Certainly he was well-placed in the skirted cassock that he wore; and that, together with his sweet and gentle face and manner, seemed to put him in a class apart--neither man nor woman, just sexless priest. He loved the children devotedly--and was more like a mother than a father to them. Lady Brandon, he obviously adored. He too, was one of this queenly and imperious woman's favourites, and her handsome face would soften to a great gentleness when she walked and talked with him upon the terrace.

It was an extraordinarily interesting household, and when the time came for me to return home and prepare to go to Harvard, I was extremely sorry.

It was with a slight lump in my throat that I spent my last afternoon with the Band, and with a miserable turmoil in my heart that I said good-bye to them. They, too, seemed genuinely sorry that I was going, and seriously considered John's proposal that they should accompany me _en masse_, at least as far as Wyoming, where they might remain and adopt the profession of cow-puncher.

I think I walked back to High Gables that afternoon as quickly as I had ever walked in my life, for I was trying to walk away from myself, from my misery, from the sense of utter loss and desolation.

I was astounded at myself--Why was I feeling this way? What had happened to me? I had not felt so wretched, so bereaved, so filled with a sense of loss and loneliness, since my

Mother died I was like a man who, stricken with some sudden mortal pain, strives to account for it, and cannot do so--

Isobel had put her arms round my neck and kissed me good-bye.

"You will come back soon, nice American Boy?" she had said. And I had positively been unable to answer anything at all. I could only laugh and nod my head in assent.

That night, being absolutely unable to sleep, I rose from my bed, dressed, and, creeping quietly from the house, walked to Brandon Abbas to see, as I told myself, how that ancient pile looked by the light of the full moon--

Next day I began my journey, suffering horribly from home-sickness--sickness for the home of my heart--Brandon Abbas. Each mile that I was carried, by train and ship and train again, from that lovely place, increased my misery, and when at length I reached my Father's ranch, I had hard work to hide it from my sister Mary, that dear determined and forceful young woman. My Father--my hard, overbearing, autocratic Father--was not given to noticing whether others were wretched or not, and my kid sister, Janey, was too young. Noel, the eldest of our family, was still "missing," and my Father professed neither to know nor to care where he was--

However, I soon began to enjoy my sweet unhappiness, and I lived on horseback until the day came when I must go East to college, and leave this free and glorious open-air life behind me.

As a matter of fact, I went willingly enough, for I loved books, and desired above all things to become a fine scholar--I considered "My mind to me a kingdom is," to be a grand saying if one could say it (to oneself only, of course) with real truth--I could never understand Noel's flat refusal to study anything but horses, Nature, and the lore of the Indian and the Plainsman; nor his oft-expressed view that education is not of books but of life. Nothing, according to Noel, could educate one for life except life itself; and books and schooling could but educate one for more schooling and books, the examination-hall, and the realms of false values. And yet he read the books that he liked, my wonderful brother Noel--but to school and college he would not go, and thither not even my dynamic and violent Father could drive him.

"Honour thy father and thy mother"--We could not do otherwise than honour Mother, as well as love her almost to the point of adoration.

What shall I say of my terrible Father? We did honour him. We respected him and most certainly we obeyed him--all of us but Noel, that is. Noel ceased to obey him as soon as he was big and old enough to stand up for Mother.

His refusal to go to school and college was, I believe, due to his wish, that he might be near her and take her part. Nor did he leave home until the day when he found that in his wrath he had pulled his gun on Dad, and realized that he had to choose between that sort of thing--and departure.

He departed, and returned after a quarter of a century in such wise as I shall relate.

My Father was not a bad man. He was a very "good" one. He was not cruel, vicious, nor vindictive; but he was a terror and a tyrant. He crushed his wife and broke her spirit, and he turned his children into rebels, or terrified "suggestibles."

Noel and Mary were rebels. Janey and I were cowed and terrified.

Of all the marvellous deeds for which, as a child, I worshipped Noel, his defiance of my Father, was to me by far the most wonderful.

At different times, my Father in his austerity and tenacity reminded me of Abraham Lincoln; in his rugged and ferocious "piety," of the prophet Elijah, John Wesley, Brigham Young, and John Knox. There was something in him, too, of Mr. Gladstone, of Theodore Roosevelt, and a good deal of William Jennings Bryan at his most oratorical, most narrow, and most dogmatic.

And there was undoubtedly something in him of King David of Jerusalem. Yes, most undoubtedly there were many points of strong resemblance between my Father and that brave, strong, wily man, that pious and passionate king.

And a king, in his own wide realm, my father was, brooking scarcely a suggestion, much less a contradiction, from any man--a king terribly and unhappily aware of the state of sin in which lived all his subjects, especially those of his own household.

He believed that the Bible had been dictated--in English of course--by God, and that to take it other than literally was damnation and death. He almost flogged Noel to death when, at the age of sixteen or so, the latter impiously dared to wonder how Noah gathered in both the polar bears and the kangaroos, for his menagerie, and how he built the fifty-thousand-ton liner necessary for the accommodation of all the animals and their food.

This was after Father's return from a trip to Europe to buy a twenty-thousand-dollar pedigree prize Hereford bull, and the finest pure-bred Arab stallion that money could purchase.

During his absence, Noel had caught out the overseer, a pious-seeming hypocritical rascal, in whom Father firmly believed; had thrashed him, and run him off the Ranch.

Undoubtedly Noel had saved Father a great deal of money and unmasked an unmitigated rascal, and for this, I verily believe, Father hated him the more, and never forgave him.

Yes, Father certainly spoilt Noel's life and made him the wanderer that he became.

To this day, when I have a nightmare, and I have a good many, it is generally of a terrible conflict with my Father, and I awake sweating and trembling with indignation, rage and horror.

For, in the dream, he always rushes at me, bawling invective, his face inflamed with rage, and, seizing me by the throat he raises his cutting-whip to thrash the wickedness out of me, as he so often did in reality. And, to my horror, I find myself clenching my fist to smash that mask of mad ferocity, and then I realize that I am about to strike my own Father, in my indignation that I, a grown man, should be treated thus.

It sounds nothing, but it is a *dreadful* dream.

"Honour thy father"--I believe that Mother worshipped him and feared him, and I believe that I, subconsciously, hated him most bitterly, while I consciously respected and feared him.

To the world, our little western world, he was a great man--a man of his word, a strong man, a dangerous man to cross, a good friend and a bad enemy.

One of Mary's _obiter dicta_ on the subject of Father sheds a great light on his strong and complex character.

"Father has never done wrong in his life," said she, "for whatever Father does is right--in the sight of Father."

Mary inherited much of Father's strength and force of will, as well as much of Mother's attractiveness.

She was a girl of character, and what she set her heart on, she got. If Father's strength were that of granite, iron and adamant, hers was the strength of tempered steel, for she was pliant and knew when to bend that she might not break. She managed Father and refused to be crushed. Where Noel openly defied and fought him, she secretly defied and out-manoeuvred him.

Father certainly loved her--as men do their daughters--and I think Mary loved him, up to a point.

3.

Much as I enjoyed everything, from books to base-ball, at glorious Harvard, I found myself obsessed with the desire to visit England again. Nor was it wholly due to a yearning to see the fine face of my kindly-caustic Grandmother Hankinson once more. Greatly I yearned to revisit Brandon Regis at the earliest opportunity--for Brandon Regis is but a pleasant walk from Brandon Abbas.

I wanted to see the Geste boys again--and I wanted to see Isobel--That's the plain fact of the matter--I wanted to see Isobel. Every single separate day of my life I wanted to see her.

I do not say that, during my Harvard years, I mooned about in a hopeless state of calf-love, a ridiculous young sentimentalist, nor that her lovely little face came ever and ever between me and the printed page, and was always in my mind, sleeping and waking, playing and working--but I certainly admit that I thought of her regularly--

It was my practice nightly, on laying my head on the pillow, to project my mind to the Park of Brandon Abbas, and to enter into a lovely secret kingdom of my own, and there to dwell, happy, remote, and in lovely peace, until I fell asleep.

This kingdom was shared by Isobel, and we two--devoted friends--did delightful things together, had wonderful talks; explored a world of utter beauty; and walked hand-in-hand in a fairyland of joy and fun and laughter--

I am not sure but that this was my real life, at that time; this and the dreams that followed almost invariably, when I fell asleep. Certainly, it was so real that I looked forward to it each day, and if not consciously doing so, was always half-aware and semi-conscious of something delightful that was in store for me, something good and sweet and precious, something "nice" that was coming to me. And when I analysed this feeling of joyous promise I found that it was my soul's anticipation of its visit to the Kingdom of Enchantment where Isobel would meet me and we would walk and talk and laugh together in our Paradise Unlost.

When a sleep-dream followed the consciously induced day-dream, I always awoke from it to minutes of ineffable happiness, a happiness experienced at no other time and in no other way--I felt good--And I realized how singularly blessed was Otis H. Vanbrugh, above other men. Nor did the corollary escape me--how incumbent it was upon me to keep myself fit to enter our lovely secret kingdom, and worthy to meet Isobel there.

I do not think that what are supposed to be the inevitable and terrible temptations of wealthy young men at College, existed for me at all. Late hours would have been hours that made me late for the Secret Garden; the odour of wine was not one that would mingle favourably with that of the dewy roses there'; nor could one who was daily privileged to commune with Isobel, find the faintest possible charm or attraction in the halls of the Paphian dames--So I filled my days with work, read hard and played hard, lived dangerously when living in the West, pursued with ardour there the study of International

Law and of the ways of the mountain lion and of the grizzly bear, and earned the warm approval of my brave and hardy sister, Mary--

And imagine if you can, the frame of mind in which, at the end of my College days, I sailed for Europe--on a visit to a life-long friend of my Father's, who was then our Ambassador to France--and incidentally to visit my Grandmother at Brandon Regis--

As I stepped from the Southampton-London boat-train at Waterloo Terminus, another train was in the act of departure from the opposite side of the same platform, and gliding forward with slowly increasing speed. At a window, waving a handkerchief to three young men, was a girl, and, with a queer constriction of the heart, a rush of blood to the head, and a slight trembling of the whole body, I realized that the girl was Isobel Rivers--the child Isobel, grown up to most lovely girlhood--wonderfully the same and yet different--She had put her hair up--

In the baggage-car of my own train were my cabin-trunks and portmanteaux. In the hands of a porter were already my suit-case and grip. Without ceremony, I rushed across that broad platform, threading my way through the crowd like a football-forward in a hurry. As I reached the now quickly-moving train, seized a door-handle and ran swiftly while I turned it, an official of some sort made a grab at me and shouted, "Stand back! You can't get in there, sir," in fiercely indignant remonstrance, not so much at my daring to break my neck as at my daring to break a railway bye-law.

"Hi! You can't get in there," he roared again.

"Watch me," I replied, eluding him, and swung myself on to the foot-board as the door came open. "I won't hurt your train," I shouted back, as he was left gesticulating in sorrow and in anger, at the end of the platform.

In the compartment that I then entered, were three Englishmen and an Englishwoman. Not one of them looked up as I took my seat, nor spoke to me nor to each other during the long hours of non-stop run that ensued--

Wonderful people, the English!--

And there I sat in that antediluvian non-corridor car through those long hours, my baggage abandoned, my hotel reservation unclaimed, my destination unknown; but with the knowledge that Isobel Rivers and I were in the same train and that I should speak to her just as soon as that prehistoric Flying Dutchman, or Roaring Rocket, reached its destination or first stopping-place.

In spite of cold, hunger, disorientation, and a certain slight anxiety as to the ultimate fate of my baggage, those were, I verily believe, among the happiest hours of my life; and when the train slowed down--it must have slowed down, I suppose, though no change of speed was to me perceptible--to decant its phlegmatic inhabitants at Exeter, I, the last man into that train, was certainly the first man out.

4.

Isobel, I am most perfectly sure, was really unfeignedly glad to see me, and Lady Brandon very kindly pretended to be. I knew that Isobel was glad because, as she recognized me, that wonderful sparkle--a kind of dancing light, that indescribable lighting-up, as though with an internal illumination, that always signalized and beautified her joy--came into her eyes. One reads of people dancing with pleasure and jumping for joy. Isobel did not do these things, but her eyes did, and one could always tell when a gift or a jest or any happening had given her real pleasure, by watching her eyes.

I had often heard John Geste say "_That'll_ make Isobel's eyes shine" when there was something amusing to tell her, or some piece of good news; and I thought to myself that surely no-one could conceive a more glorious and wonderful way of spending his life than in bringing this beautiful light to Isobel's eyes.

Imagine, if you can, the joy that it gave me to realize that I had been able to do it now.

"Why," she said as I approached and raised my hat, "the nice American boy!--Oh, how lovely!--The boys will be sorry," and she gave me both her hands in the most delightful and friendly manner.

Lady Brandon gave me both fingers in a less spontaneous and friendly manner that was nevertheless quite pleasant, and--God bless her--invited me to share their compartment in the train to Brandon Abbas and their carriage which would meet them there. She displayed none of the surprise that she must certainly have felt on learning that there was no luggage problem, as I had no luggage. Beneath her half-kindly, half-satirical gaze, I did my best to conceal the fact that, on catching sight of Isobel, I had abandoned everything but hope, and dashed from one train to the other.

I do not know whether selected prophets, such as Elijah, ever found ecstatic joy in their rides in fiery chariots and similar celestial vehicles, but I do know that my short ride by train and carriage with Isobel, was to me the highest summit of ecstatic joy--a pure happiness utterly indescribable and incommunicable--the higher, the greater, and the lovelier for its purity. And it was not until I was deposited at High Gables after leaving Isobel and Lady Brandon at Brandon Abbas, that my soaring spirit came down to earth, and, it having come to earth, I was faced with the problem of explaining my unheralded arrival and the absence of further provision than a walking-stick and one glove. Also, alas, with the realization that I should not see Isobel again, as she and Lady Brandon were going to Wales on the morrow, and, later on, to Scotland on a round of visits. They had been staying in London with the boys, who were now setting off for a walking-tour in Normandy.

However, _I had seen Isobel_ and received confirmation--if confirmation were needed--of the fact that not only was she the most marvellous thing in all the world, but that everything else in the world would be as nothing in the balance against her.

I have mentioned this trivial and foolish little incident--which ended next day with my return to London and the pursuit of my baggage--because it was on this night, as I lay awake, that there came to me the great, the very greatest, idea of my life--the idea that I might conceivably, with the help of God and every nerve and fibre of my being, some day, somehow, contrive to make myself worthy to love Isobel and then--incredibly--to be loved by Isobel, and actually to devote my life to doing that of which I had thought when her eyes sparkled and shone at seeing me.

It is curious and true that the idea had never occurred to me before, and I had never envisaged the possibility of such a thing as not only loving her, but being loved by her in return, and of actually walking hand in hand along the path of life in the spirit of sweet and lovely companionship, as we did nightly in our Dream Garden--And there, I remember, a little chill fell upon my heart and checked my fond imaginings, as it occurred to me for the first time that the Dream Garden was a creation of my dreams alone, and not of Isobel's as well. There we met and talked and walked and were dear friends, with a reality as great as that of anything in my real and waking life--but of course, it was only my dream, and the real Isobel knew nothing of the Dream Garden.

But did she know nothing? Why should I assume that?

Suppose--only suppose--that she dreamed it, too I Suppose Isobel had this curious and wonderful double life, as I had, and met me in her dreams precisely as I met her, night by night! Absurd, of course, but much too lovely an idea to discard with even pretended contempt. I would ask her the very next time I saw her. How unutterably wonderful if she could tell me that it was so!--Moreover, if it _were_ so, it would mean _that she loved me_--and, at this, even I laughed at my own folly. Still I would ask her the very next time we met--

But the next time we met, I asked her something else.

CHAPTER III

1.

I suppose that among the very happiest days of my whole life were those I spent on my next journey from New York to Southampton and Brandon Regis. I must have seemed insufferably joyous and pleased with myself. When not actually whistling or singing with my mouth, I was doing it in my heart. I loved everybody. What is less certain is whether everybody loved me. I loved the glorious sunshine, the perfect sea, the splendid ship, the jolly food, the passengers, every one of them, the young, the old, the merry, the grumpy, the active, the lazy, the selfish, the unselfish--If all the world loves a lover, surely a lover loves all the world--the great grand glorious world that lies at his exalted feet--The world that contains, and exists to contain, the one and only woman in the world--

I loved the stars, the moon, the marvellous night-sky, the floor of Heaven pierced with millions of little holes through which shone rays of the celestial light--and I sat late and alone, gazing, thinking, dreaming, longing.

I loved the dawn, and late as I may have sat upon the boat-deck at night, I was there again to see the East grow grey and pink and golden, there to welcome and to greet the sun that ushered in one more milestone day upon the brief and lovely road that led to Brandon Abbas and to Isobel.

Brandon Abbas and Isobel!--One day, when a poor rich youth whom I comprehended in my universal love--in spite of his pimples, poor jokes, unpleasing ways and unacceptable views--asked me if I were going to Paris, and I replied, "No--to Brandon Abbas," and he, astonished, inquired where that might be, and I answered:

"Next door to Paradise," he rightly concluded that I was out of my mind or else drunk. Doubly right was he, for I was beside myself with joy and drunk with happiness.

Yes; I loved all things; I loved all men; and greatly I loved God.

At Southampton I let the boat-train go upon its foolish way to London, and-at the terminus hotel of the South Western Railway I awaited the far far better one that meanders across the green and pleasant land of England to the little junction where one may get one better still, one that proceeds thence to Exeter where waits the best of all--the final and finest train in the wide world--that carries its blest occupants to Brandon Abbas.

I was not sitting in a train made with mortal hands, but in a chariot of fire that was carrying me, ecstatic and uplifted, to the heaven of my dreams, my night-and-day dreams of many years.

From the station I drove, in what to the dull eye of the ordinary beholder was a musty, mouldy carriage, drawn by a moth-eaten and dilapidated parody of a horse, to High Gables, and was welcomed with the apparently caustic kindness and grim friendliness with which my wonderful old Grandmother Hankinson hid her really tender and loving nature.

And next day I walked over to Brandon Abbas.

I remember trying, on the way, to recollect some lines I fancied I had read. Were they written by the Marquis of Montrose or had Queen Elizabeth scratched them with a diamond on a window-pane for the encouragement of some young adorer? Was it, "_He either fears his fate too much, Or his deserts are small, Who dares not put it to the touch, To win or lose it all."--?_ Something like that anyhow, and probably written by Montrose.

Well, my deserts were small enough, and at times I feared my fate, but I was certainly going to put it to the touch before I went away, if I stayed for a year or a life-time.

I was going to tell Isobel that I loved her--had loved her unceasingly and increasingly, from the moment that I had seen her, a lovely child sitting in a dog-cart, and much concerned about a dog.

True--I was utterly and wholly unworthy of her, but so was everybody else. I had nothing to recommend me but an absolutely perfect and unquenchable love--but I was not ineligible from the point of view of such a person as Lady Brandon, for example. I was a foreigner, an American, but I had roots in this very soil, through my Mother. I was obscure and unknown, but that could very quickly be put right if I became Isobel's husband. That alone would be a great distinction, but I would undertake to add to it, and to promise that Isobel's husband should one day be the American Ambassador to St. James's, to Paris, to St. Petersburg--any old where she liked--President of the United States of America, if she set her heart on his being that--I was very far from being poor, and should not be far from being very rich, someday.

Thirty-cent things of that sort would be quite germane and material in the eyes of Queen Elizabethan Lady Brandon. To my mind, the only really relevant thing was that I loved Isobel to the point of worship and adoration, and that this love of mine had not only stood the test of time, but had gained from Time himself--for the wine of love had mellowed and matured, grown better, richer, sweeter, nobler, year by year-- Poor boy!--

I turned in at the Lodge gates, and walked up the long drive of which I knew every Norman tree.

Good old Burdon, the perfect butler, fine flower of English retainerhood, was in the hall as I appeared in the porch, and greeted me in the perfect manner of the perfect servant, friendly, welcoming, respectful.

But Her Ladyship was Not at Home--

Miss Claudia was Not at Home--

Miss Isobel was Not at Home--

Mr. Michael, Mr. Digby, and Mr. John were Away from Home--

Nothing for it but to leave my cards and depart, more than a little dashed and damped.

I walked down the drive less buoyantly than I had walked up it. It actually had not entered my silly head that one could go to Brandon Abbas and not find Isobel there--The sunshine was not so bright nor the sky so blue, and what had been the sweet singing of the birds, was just a noise--

And as I rounded a turn in the drive, my heart rounded and turned and drove, for a girl was riding toward me, a little girl on a big horse. The loveliest, dearest, kindest girl in all the wide world--

My heart turned right-side-up, pulled itself together, and let me get my breath again--
Isobel--

The sun shone gloriously bright and warm, the sky was a deep Italian blue, the English song-birds were birds from Paradise--and Isobel held out a gloved hand which I took and pressed to my lips as she smiled sweetly and kindly and said:

"Why! It's our nice American Boy come back! I _am_ so glad--Otis--" and then I knew that something was wrong. Her voice was different; older. Her face was different; older. She was unhappy--

"What is the matter, Isobel?" I asked, still holding her little hand as she bent toward me from her big horse.

"Oh--Otis--How did you know?--_John has gone_--The boys have gone away--"

Her lip trembled and there was a suspicion of moisture in her eyes.

"Can I help?--_Let_ me help you, Isobel," I begged.

"There's nothing you can do--thank you so much," she said. "It's nice of you--I am so glad to see you again, Otis--I have been so wretched. There is no-one I can talk to, about it--"

"There is," I said. "There's me," and I think that moment marked the absolute top-most pinnacle of happiness that I have ever known, for Isobel pressed my hand hard.

"I'll tell you a great secret," she said, and smiled so sweetly through the unshed tears that I could scarcely forbear to reach up and lift her from her horse, lift her into my arms, my heart, and my life.

"I'll tell you, Otis--Keep it a secret though," she added. And then Isobel said the words that in that second cut my life into two distinct halves--

"John and I are engaged to be married--"

No--she couldn't have said that. I assured myself that she had not said *that*. These queer hallucinations and strange waking dreams!--She had not said that--I was not standing staring and open-mouthed, and watching, watching, watching for years and life-times and ages and aeons, while two great tears slowly formed and gathered and grew and rolled from her eyes--One did not splash upon my hand as she said:

"And he has had to go away--And I am so miserable, Otis--We were engaged one evening and he was gone the next morning!--And I have no-one to talk to, about him--I am so _glad_ you have come--"

But a tear did splash on my hand. She *did* say it.

"You and John Geste are engaged to be married, Isobel?" I asked, gently and carefully, very very gently and very very carefully, to keep my voice level and steady, to keep myself well under control--

I heard myself say the words, and I watched her face to see whether I had said them normally--Or had I not said them at all f--I had uttered some words certainly--

Her face did not change--

"Yes, Otis," she said. "And I had to tell somebody!--.I am glad it was *you* . You are the only person, now, who knows. You'll be the first to congratulate me--"

Yes. I should be the first person to congratulate her!

"I congratulate John--and you--Isobel," I said, "and from the bottom of my' heart I hope that every hour of your life will be a happy one."

"Thank you, Otis," she said. "That is nice and dear of you--Oh, I shall be almost too happy to breathe--when John comes back--You'll come and see us again, won't you? Aunt Patricia will be delighted to see you--And we'll go for some rides, you and I--I do so want to talk to you--_about John_."

Words of excuse rose to my lips. I must go to London to-morrow. I must hurry over to Paris. Some business for my Father. After that I must go quickly back to America, and so forth--But before I had spoken, I had a swift vision of a face I knew well, though I had only seen it in dreams. A hard clean-cut cruel face, grim, stern and stoical, the face of that Indian Chief who was the father of my father's grandmother--the face of a man from whom no sign of anguish was ever wrung, a man to whom pain was as a friend, proven and proving.

"Thank you very much indeed, Isobel," I said. "I shall love to ride with you--and talk about John."--

(Thank *you* , also, great-great-grandfather.)

Yes, it would give her pleasure. I would ride with her--and _talk about John_!

During the next month I saw Isobel almost daily, Lady Brandon occasionally, the Chaplain once or twice, and the girl, Claudia, from time to time.

Isobel and I talked unceasingly of John. I thought of things that would please her--dug up what had been fragrant joyous memories.

She did not tell me where he was, being, I supposed, pledged to secrecy, and I asked her no questions as I realized that there was some secret which she was hiding. It occurred to me though, that it must be a mighty strong inducement, an irresistible compulsion, that took John Geste from Brandon Abbas on the day after the declaration of his love for Isobel!

And then, thank God, she went away to stay with friends, and I fled to Paris, plunged into the wildest dreariest round of dissipation (Good God! is there _anything_ so devastatingly dreary as pleasure pursued?) and quickly collapsed as reaction set in, reaction from the dreadful strain of those days with Isobel--Isobel and the ever-present absent John.

I was very ill indeed for some weeks, and, when able to do so, crawled home--dropped back again, the burnt charred stick of that joyous rocket that had rushed with such brilliant soaring gaiety into the bright sky of happiness--

Finished and down--like a dead rocket—

2.

Things were, on the whole, rather worse than usual at home. My Father was becoming more and more tyrannical and unreasonable, and my sisters were reacting accordingly. Strong Mary, the rebel, home from College, was fast approaching both the snapping-point of her temper and the frame of mind in which Noel had cast off the dust of the ranch from his feet and the shackles of his Father from his soul, mind, and body.

Weak Janey, the "suggestible," was fast approaching the end of her existence as an individual, a separate identity, and was rapidly becoming a reed, bending in the blast of her Father's every opinion, idea and wish; a straw upon the eighty rushing waters of his life; thistle-down floating upon the windy current of his mental and physical commotions.

While firmly believing that she loved him, she dreaded the very sound of his footsteps, and conducted the domestic side of his affairs in that fear and trembling of a Roman slave for the master whose smile was sole reward and whose frown portended death.

Filial love is a beautiful thing, but the slow destruction of a character, a soul, a personality, an individuality, is not.

Poor Janey did not think. She quoted Father's thoughts. She did not need or desire anything; she lived to forestall and satisfy Father's needs and wishes. She did not live any life of her own, she lived Father's life and existed to that end.

Janey was abject to Father, and propitiatory to Mary. Mary was defiant and rebellious to Father; and sympathetic but slightly contemptuous, to Janey.

Father was protective, overbearing, loving, violently autocratic and unbearably irritating toward both of them. Apparently he simply could not forbear to interfere, even in things in which he had not the faintest right to interfere, and in which a different type of man would have been ashamed to do so.

Of me, he was frankly contemptuous, and what made me boil with anger was not that, nor the way in which he treated me, but the fact that I was afraid of him. Time after time, I screwed up my courage to face him and out-face him, and time after time I failed. I could not do it. His fierce eye, his Jovian front, quelled me, and being quelled, I quailed.

It was reserved for my Father to make me a coward, so poor a creature that I could not even stand up for my sisters against him.

But the enemy was, of course, as always, within. Deep down in my unconscious mind were the seeds sown in babyhood, in childhood, in boyhood--the seeds of Fear--and they had taken such root, and grown so strong a weed-crop that I could not pluck them out. When I conceived the idea of refusing to obey some unreasonable order, of asserting my right to an opinion, of remonstrating on behalf of one of the girls, I was physically as well as mentally affected.

I stammered and stuttered--a thing I never did at any other time. I flushed and paled, I perceptibly shook and trembled, and I burst into a cold perspiration. My mind became a blank; I looked and felt and was, a fool; I was not sufficiently effective even to irritate my Father, and with one frowning piercing stare of his hard eyes, one contemptuous curl of his expressive lips, I was defeated, silenced, quelled, brought to heel.

Do not think that our Father was deliberately and intentionally cruel to any of his children. Cruelty is a Vice, and Vice was the abhorrent thing, the very seal and mark of the Devil--footprint of the cloven hoof. Did he not spend his life in the denunciation of Vice in every form and manifestation--though with particular abhorrence and detestation of, peculiar rage and fulminations against, _Sex_--its, to him, most especially shocking and loathsome form?

He was not cruel, but his effect upon us was, and it drove Mary and me to the decision that home was no place for us--We had decided independently--I, that I could not work for, nor with, my Father on the ranch, nor live with him in the house: she, that any place in the wide world would be preferable to the house in which her Father intended that she should live and move and have her being, wholly and solely and exactly as he in his wisdom directed.

We discovered our decisions to each other and agreed to act together when the time came; and, as soon as possible thereafter, to rescue Janey from the loving thraldom and oppression that would turn her into a weak, will-less and witless old maid, an ageing servant in her father's house, before she had been a girl.

It was the "old maid" aspect of affairs that particularly enraged Mary on behalf of both Janey and herself. For on the subject of "young whelps loafing round the place," our Father grew more and more unreasonable and absurd. A presentable man was a suspect, a potential "scoundrel," a thinker of evil who would become a doer of evil if given the slightest opportunity. To such we always alluded as--"Means"--by reason of Father's constant quotation of the Shakespearian platitude:

"The sight of means to do ill deeds, makes ill deeds done."

Any sort or kind of non-business communication between a man and a woman was, unless they were married according to the (Protestant) Christian Dispensation, undesirable, wrong, improper; and avowed friendship between them was little better than Sin, Vice--nay, was almost certainly but a cloak for Sin.

Strong Mary, the rebel, suffered most perhaps; weak Janey and I suffered much, certainly. But we stuck on somehow, for some reason--"the inertia of matter," apathy, custom, loyalty to Father, and the feeling that our defection would hurt him more even than his interfering, regulating tyranny hurt us. Most of all perhaps, because we knew that Janey would never have the courage nor the "unkindness" to leave him.

It was a very wretched time indeed for me, apart from the fact that I was so spiritually bruised and sore and smashed. My dreams of Isobel came no more, and my day-dreams of her were poignant suffering. I tried to fight the lethargy, the hopelessness, the selfish sorrow of my soul, and to throw myself into the work of the ranch, to live on horseback a life of constant activity, and to find an anodyne in labour.

But I was selfish--I nursed my sorrow--I thought, young fool that I was, that my life was permanently darkened and that none had plumbed such depths of suffering as I.

And I worked on, hopelessly, sunk in a deep and dark Byronic gloom—

3.

It was a dead hand that released Mary and me from the irksome dependence of our captivity. I do not know whether the hand provided "the means to do ill deeds" in providing us with the opportunity to leave our Father and our home, but it certainly gave us the power to choose our paths in life, and we promptly chose the one that led straightest out into the world of men.

The said hand was that of a Bad Old Man, a meretricious ornament of the city of San Francisco, a gay dog, a buck, a lover of Life, who was, alas, my Father's cousin, once his partner, and known to us from our earliest days as Uncle Joe. He had all our Father's strength of will and character; his ability, grit and forcefulness; his uncanny business skill and his marked individuality. But he had none of his fervid piety; none of his Old Testamental patriarchal self-importance; none of his self-righteous domineering violence; and, I fear, but little of his moral integrity, virtue, and highly-conscious rectitude.

In spite of this latter lamentable truth, we children loved him, as our Mother had loved him--and as Father hated him. He corrupted us with treats, gifts, sympathy, and support; he took our part when, as so frequently happened, we were in disgrace; and he endeavoured to sow in our young breasts the seeds of revolt and rebellion against what he considered harshness and oppression.

For some reason I was his favourite. I amused him intensely, and he apparently saw in me merits and virtues which were hidden from other eyes. And the misspelling of a word in a letter that I wrote to him, changed my life and Mary's life, the lives of my Father and of Janey, and indeed of very many other people--for it was the cause of his leaving me a very large sum of money indeed, the money that was my ransom from bondage--and Mary's ransom too.

It had been my innocent and disinterested custom to write a letter to Uncle Joe, upon the occasion of his birthday. On one of these anniversaries, I, being some seven or' eight years of age--and having just discovered the expression "hoary old age"--wrote my annual letter and concluded by wishing him eventual safe arrival at such penultimate years. But having acquired the phrase by ear and not by eye, I misspelt a word.

The hoary sinner was delighted beyond measure, roared with laughter, shouted with joyous amusement, and swore then and there that he would make me his heir and leave me every last red cent of which he died possessed. He then rushed forth brandishing the letter, in search of all to whom he might impart the jest, and for days and weeks the bars of San Francisco's clubs, restaurants, saloons and hostelries echoed with laughter and my Uncle's shame.

Such conduct gives the measure of the wickedness of the man who had been a thorn in the side of my Father--until the day on which the latter felt that he could prosper without him, that Mammon of Unrighteousness, and cast him forth; the man who had been our dear, dear friend; the man to whom Mary and I owed our salvation.

And at this critical moment he died--and he left me all his money.

Of course, what was mine was Mary's, and at the earliest moment we fared forth together, "to seek our fortunes"--though not in the material sense, and to see the World.

A drop of regret in the cup of our joy was the fact that we found it utterly and completely impossible to induce Janey to come with us. She would not "leave Father"--the simple truth being that she lacked the courage to tell him that she was going with us, the courage to let us tell him that she was going with us, the courage even to slip away with us, or to run away and join us after our departure.

There was nothing for it but to leave her at home, though with the most urgent entreaties to join us at any time that she could induce Father to permit her to come, or pluck up sufficient courage to come unpermitted--

Our idea was, of course, to make straight for Paris--the name of which place, Mary declared, was but an abbreviation of the word "Paradise"--and after sating ourselves with its wonders, make the grand tour of Europe. After that we were going to settle down in Paris, and I was going to obtain employment at our Embassy, for I lead no liking for the profession of rich-man's-son and idler. Mary was going to keep house for me--but I doubted that it would be my house that she would keep for very long, and so I think did she-- Anyhow, that was roughly our programme, and, after what seemed an age of delay, we set forth, without the paternal blessing, to see how far we should carry out the scheme.

CHAPTER IV

Life in Paris was, to Mary, wholly delightful, and to me I was at least as good and as bad as life in Wyoming. In point of fact it was wholly lacking in savour wheresoever I might endure it--but in Paris the heavy cloud, that was our Father, was on the far western horizon and no longer obscured the sun--a further exemplification of the ancient truth that they who flee across the sea change nothing but their sky.

Our friends at the Embassy were more than kind to us, and before we departed for London, Rome, Venice, Naples, Athens and finally Algiers, we had a large and delightful circle of acquaintance, French, American and English.

Mary is one of those girls who are "very easy to look at," and the young men of our circle looked. They also danced, dined, drove and flirted with her to her heart's content, if not to theirs.

As I spent my money very freely, she was soon reputed to be the usual fabulously wealthy American heiress, and the report did not lessen her popularity.

Prominent among her admirers was a much-decorated and be-medalled Colonel of Zouaves, a man who might have sat for a portrait of a typical Sergeant of the Old Guard of Napoleon Buonaparte. He was a middle-aged self-made fighting soldier--a man of the kind that one rather admires for excellences of character than likes for graces of mind and person--and I fear he amused Mary almost as much as he loved her. For he was obviously and hopelessly in love, and I do not think that the dollars in any way gilded the refined gold of _La belle Americaine_ in the eyes of the tough and grizzled Colonel Levasseur--Poor fellow--Bravely playing his part in the ballroom, or at the garden-party, he reminded me, when dancing attendance on my sister, of a large bear heavily cavorting around a young deer--though I realized that the Colonel would remind me still more of a large bear if I saw him engaged upon his real business, which was fighting.

Here again was coincidence or the hand of Fate--or as some, including myself, would prefer to say--the hand of God. For when, after our European travels, we reached Algeria to bask in winter sunshine, Colonel Levasseur was preparing to set forth, as the point of a lancet of "peaceful penetration," to the fanatical city of Zaguig, a distant hotbed of sedition and centre of disaffection, a desert Cave of Adullam wherein the leaders of every anti-French faction, from eastern Senussi to western Ruffian, plotted together and tried to stem the flow of the tide of civilization.

They stood for savagery; for blind adherence to the dead letter of a creed outworn; for ferocious hatred of all that was not sealed of Islam; and for the administration of rapine, fire, and slaughter impartially to those who brought, and those who accepted, northern civilization and its roads, railways, telegraphs, peace, order and cultivation of the soil--

While Zaguig remained secret, veiled, inviolate and aloof, there could be no safety, and, as Colonel Levasseur put it, Zaguig was a boil that the French must lance--that there might be health in the body-politic of a great and growing colony, a future granary and garden and farm for the sons of civilization.

Colonel Levasseur showed better in Algiers than in Paris, and he showed best of all in Zaguig at the head of his men, in his element and on his native heath--or his adopted heath.

For, later on, as I shall tell, I yielded to Mary's impulsive yearnings to go and see a "really unspoilt" desert town, and I accepted Colonel Levasseur's invitation to visit him there, an invitation that coincided with her disillusionment at Bouzen, a spoilt and vulgarized place at the end of the railway, a plague-spot where alleged "desert" Arabs spoke broken French and English to the trippers, and richly earned broken necks every day of their ignoble touting lives.

And to Bouzen from Zaguig came Colonel Levasseur ostensibly to confer with the Commandant of the big garrison there--fairly quickly after learning that Mary was shedding the light of her countenance on that already well-lighted spot.

He took Mary riding on horse and camel, turning a withering Colonel-glare upon the gay and gorgeous subalterns who had hitherto danced attendance upon her--He amused her and he had the inevitable appeal of the strong man who has done things, who has a fine and big job and holds it down.

And he played up to her growing love of the desert, for she had succumbed to its lure and its loveliness of sunrise, sunset, space, colour, cleanness and enduring mystery. Also he told her that _this_ was not the desert--that she had not yet seen the real desert, nor set eyes on a genuine inhabitant thereof, Bedouin, Senussi, Touareg, nor any other--Also, that now was her chance, her chance to cross a tract of the genuine desert-Sahara and see a genuine desert-city, a lion's den whereof he had effectually cowed and tamed the lions--

I asked Mary if the acceptance of his very kind and attractive invitation might not be construed as portending her acceptance of the inevitable proposal of marriage which would most surely ensue, if we entered the said lions' den--whereof Colonel Levasseur was now the lion-tamer--but only to receive the enigmatical reply that sufficient unto the day is the proposal thereof, and that if I did not take her to Zaguig, Colonel Levasseur would.

The which there was no gainsaying--and Mary is a witch whom there is no gainsaying.

The delighted Colonel Levasseur, for some reason, inferred that I had had a helpful hand in Mary's decision to accept his invitation. And he expressed his gratitude to me in various ways, in spite of my denial of deserts.

One took the curious form of insisting upon showing me "life" in Bouzen, by night--_recherché_ "life" not seen of the tripper, but solely of the elect--such as highly placed executive officials, for example, only by whose grace and favour, or ignorance and blindness, such "life" could exist.

Most men accept all invitation of this sort, and offer a variety of reasons for so doing. Some allege that "life" is, and must be, interesting to any intelligent person, and murmur "_nihil humanum--a me alienum puto_," adding that none but the fool misses any rare, genuine "local colour" that may be seen; and that, in any case, one would not like to hurt the feelings of the good fellow who had gone to the trouble of providing the opportunity.

As these were precisely my authentic reasons for accepting the invitation, I went with the worthy Colonel--and mine eyes beheld strange things.

We set forth after Mary had said her good-nights, she imagining that we were also about to seek our respective chaste couches.

Nothing was said to her on the subject of our expedition lest she insist upon joining us, and we be put to the shame of telling the truth or of abandoning the tour of the select improprieties. Incidentally I noted, in my mental dossier of the Colonel, that he was unselfish enough to devote to nie time that might have been spent with Mary had he chosen to announce some different form of nocturnal entertainment, and also that he was of the type that could go straight, from looking upon the face of the beloved lady, to where every prospect pleases only a man who is vile--

Let us, however, concede that it takes all sorts to make a universe, and humbly thank Allah for the diversity of his creatures.

As I had anticipated, I found, once more, that the deadliest, dreariest and dullest pursuit upon which the mind and body of man can embark is the deliberate pursuit of pleasure--that butterfly that flies indeed if chased, but will often settle if ignored--settle and delight the soul of the beholder.

I suppressed all yawns, endeavoured to simulate a polite if not keen interest, and failed to give the worthy Colonel the impression that I was enjoying myself.

So when he asked me if I were doing so, I said:

"Yes, indeed, Colonel"--and added, "It is the only thing I am enjoying"--whereat he laughed, commended my bluntness which matched his own, and promised that I should find the next place stimulating, for I should there encounter the Angel of Death.

I assured him that I was unready, unfit, unworthy; that I did not desire to encounter the Death Angel with all my imperfections on my head; unshriven, unassoiled and unannealed--So young--So promising--

"Wait till you have seen her," replied the Colonel, and I withdrew my objections and listened, as we drove through the silent streets, to his account of the lady whose disturbing and deterrent title was "the Angel of Death," a title well-earned, I gathered, and well-given in return for disservices rendered--

Well, it would be something to make the acquaintance of an incarnate Death Angel, especially if one might then plead fear of anti-climax as an excuse for abandoning the pursuit of pleasure, going straight home, and prosaically to bed.

As the car stopped at a gate in the high wall surrounding a native house and garden, on the outskirts of the town, I, in Hunnish vandal mood, murmured certain lines learned in childhood from Uncle Joe:

"The Death Angel smote Alexander McCloo And gave him protracted repose; He had a check shirt and a number nine shoe And a very pink wart on his nose."

Well, the Death Angel smote me also, that night, but did not give me protracted repose (nor any protracted lack of repose--at the time).

The brightly-lit scene of our entertainment was the typical compound of the typical house of the wealthy town-Arab, the soft-living degenerate *hadri*, for whom the son of the desert has so great a contempt.

Our host, one Abu Sheikh Ahmed, a rotund well-nourished person with a bad squint, a bad pock-pitted face, and an oily ingratiating manner, received us with every evidence of joy, pride and respectful affection. He seemed grateful to us for existing; declared that all in his house was ours; that we were, each of us, his father and his mother both; and that Allah had this night been merciful and gracious unto him in that He had caused the light of our countenances to shine upon him and illuminate and glorify his humble gathering of guests.

Colonel Levasseur received these transports with dignity and restraint--particularly restraint--and informed me in English that Abu Sheikh Ahmed was a carpet-dealer and had the distinction of being the wickedest, most untrustworthy and most plausible old scoundrel that he had ever met.

"He'd be the first to fly to the Commandant with completest revelations of any plot that could not succeed; and the first to shoot him in the back, or cut his throat, in the event of one that did succeed," said he. "So we take him at his true value and use him for what he is worth--He'll give us an amusing show anyhow--"

He did; a show of which there were two items that, as far as I am concerned, proved quite unforgettable; the one for its hideousness, the other for its beauty--and its sequel.

The former was a "turn" by a troupe of Aissa dervishes, and consisted of maddeningly monotonous music and dancing--the twirling and spinning dancers quickly and obviously falling into a state of hypnosis; of a disgusting exhibition of self-mutilation by means of knives and skewers, driven into the arms, chest and legs and in some cases through the cheeks and even the tongue; of the eating of burning tow; and of the genuine chewing and actual swallowing of quantities of broken glass.

It is not given to the Sons of the Prophet to know the joys of a "next morning" head, as teetotalism is a primary essential of Muhammedanism, but I was moved to ponder the sensations of a "next morning" stomach, after an indiscreetly copious feast of broken glass.

Colonel Levasseur had seen this sort of thing before, and regarded it with the cold eye of familiarity, if not boredom.

"Enjoying yourself?" he asked me, when the din and devilry were at their climax.

"Not even myself, this time," I replied, and was very glad when these holy men completed their exhibition of piety, and departed. The odour of sanctity was as un-pleasing as the saints from whom it emanated.

I do not know whether Mr. Abu Sheikh Ahmed was an amateur of entertainment sufficiently skilful to appreciate the value of contrast, and deliberately to preface the beauty of the next item by the bestial ugliness of this one. Probably not--but certainly the vision of loveliness, that now enthralled the gathering, lost nothing by the juxtaposition.

In the centre of one side of a square, three sides of which were rows of Arab notables, and the fourth, the high white house, the Colonel and I occupied plush-upholstered European arm-chairs of astounding ugliness, while our host and his young son sat cross-legged upon the sofa of the same afflicted and afflicting family, the six pertaining small chairs being allotted to his chief friends, or enemies, who awkwardly sat upon them in dignity and discomfort.

In the guest-surrounded square, servants spread a large thick carpet, a carpet whereof the sheer beauty made me blush--for the European furniture that affronted it and the perfect night and the austere grace of the snowy draperies of the assembly--

A current of awakened interest now ran through the hitter, a movement that announced the arrival of an awaited moment. There was an atmosphere of pleased anticipation that indicated both the _piece de résistance_ and the certainty of high entertainment therefrom.

Brilliant teeth flashed white, as bearded lips parted in joyous smiles. Almost I fancied that pink tongues licked, beast-like, anticipatory, appreciative.

Our host beamed upon us, a pleased and pleasing smile of promise and of pride.

"Behold the Angel of Death," murmured Colonel Levasseur, and a woman appeared at the entrance to the house, walked disdainfully to the carpet, threw off a gauze veil and gazed calmly around.

There was a murmur of admiration, wonder, praise--and appraisal; and I heard Colonel Levasseur sigh and Rasp with a little catch of the breath. There was something very simple and elemental about poor Levasseur.

And there was something indescribably arresting, fascinating, wonderful about the real and remarkable beauty of the girl--She was at once pretty, lovely, beautiful and handsome--quite indescribable--Yes--She was astounding--

To begin with, she was so fair that you thought her European until you realized her blue-black hair, unbelievable black eyelashes and eyebrows and the Oriental moulding of the cheek-bones and lips--so brunette and Oriental that you thought her the true Arab Princess of a dream of an Arabian Nights' tale, until you realized her white skin, her rose-pink cheeks, her obviously northern complexion and European blood.

Of her figure I can but say it was worthy of her face. It was perfect, and what was to be seen of her neck and limbs was as white as flesh can be--

She was a human flower--An orchid--a white orchid marked with scarlet and with black. And as these flowers always do, she looked wicked--an incarnate, though very lovely, potentiality for evil.

Catching sight, I suppose, of Colonel Levasseur's gay uniform, she came straight to us, or rather floated toward us on her toes, her graceful arms and hands also appearing to float upon the air, quietly waving around her head and body like thistle-down and like gracefulness personified. One forgot the crudeness of the music, for she subordinated it to her purposes, and, becoming part of her and her movement, it was beautiful.

Straight to us she came, and at me she looked, giving no glance of recognition to the chagrined Levasseur. With a deep, deep curtsy of mocking homage and genuine challenge, that broke her slow revolving dance at my very feet, she sank to the ground, and, rising like a swift-growing flower from the earth--like Aphrodite herself from the wine-dark sea--she gazed straight into my eyes, smiled with the allure of all the sirens, Delilahs, Sapphos, Aspasias, Jezebels and Cleopatras that ever lived, and whispered--to me--as if she and I were alone in all Africa--alone in the gracious night, beneath the serene moon and throbbing stars--alone together, she and I, at the door of our silken tent under the graceful palms of our secret oasis--she and I, alone together upon the silken cushions and the silken carpet spread upon the warm honey-coloured sands--

Good God in Heaven--what was this? I struggled like a drowning man--I was a drowning man, sinking down--down--hypnotized--

"*No! No!*" I shouted. "*No!*--" The only flower for me was an English rose--What had I to do with orchids of Africa? Had I really shouted?--What was she whispering?--French?--

"_Beaux yeux bleus!--J'aime yeux bleus bleus!--Baisez-moi!--Aimez-moi! Venez avec moi--après!_--I lov' you so--_Je t'aime!--Je t'adore!_ Kees me, sweetheart--Crrrush me in your arms, darling--_J'ai attendu Et tu es arrivé--J'ai attendu--depuis longtemps--il y a longtemps J'ai attendu--Et tu es arrivé--Maintenant--Baisez-moi! Embrassez-moi, mon amant Anglais_--ah--"

She was talking French--Was she speaking at all?--Was she talking faulty French and broken English, with the accent of the educated French-and English-speaking Arab?--No. Her lips were not moving--but her eyes were holding mine; burning into mine--Her eyes were great irresistible magnets drawing my soul through my eyes into hers and through them, down into her soul where it would be lost for ever, engulfed, held, drowned, destroyed.

"*No!*" I shouted, and burst into a profuse perspiration as I clung with the strength of despair to--to--sanity, to self-respect, to honour--to Isobel--

And then I shook off the shackles of this absurd folly--or this devilish, hellish danger--and was an ordinary tourist from the north smiling at this ordinary dancing-girl of the south--

But--and I shivered slightly--she was not ordinary--Neither in her evil loveliness, nor in her evil, conscious, or unconscious, hypnotic power, was she ordinary.

Had she actually spoken?

Had I actually cried aloud!

With a real effort, I wrenched my eyes from hers, and glanced around. The Arabs were watching her as a circle of dogs a luscious piece of meat--which is what she was to them.

Levasseur was' roiling cynically and without amusement.

"You are favoured, my friend," he growled, as she floated away on her toes--her hands and her arms floating about her as she did so.

"Did she speak to me?" I asked.

"Not that I heard," he answered in surprise. "She certainly intends to do so, though--Beware, St. Anthony--They don't call her the Angel of Death for nothing--"

I decided that neither she nor I had uttered a sound, that she had paused before me for but a moment--and yet I knew that, if ever she spoke to me, she would speak in faulty French and broken English, with the accent of those Arabs who have learnt a little French and English--as many of the town-dwelling Arabs do, for purposes of business.

This was interesting, a little too interesting perhaps. It was also absurd, utterly ridiculous, perfectly impossible. I could have sworn that I had shouted "*No!*" at the top of my voice, and had recoiled violently.

Obviously I had uttered no sound and had not moved in my arm-chair--But why was I trembling from head to foot, and wet with a cold perspiration that had no relation to the pleasant temperature of the night? Why did I recover my normal serenity and self-control in inverse proportion to her proximity?

While she swayed mockingly before an Arab who sat in the most distant corner of the square, her back toward me, I took my eyes from her and turned again to Levasseur, as the Arab, his face transfigured, his burning eyes riveted on her face, his clutching hands extended, rose slowly to his feet.

"Who *is* she?" I said, controlling my voice as best I might.

"Who *is* she, M'sieu' St. Anthony?" mocked the Colonel, evidently still a little piqued. "She is the Angel of Death, as I think I have already told you."

"Well; tell me a little more about her," I said, shortly.

"Well; she is what you see she is--and a good deal more--Among other things she is the daughter of a very famous Ouled-Naïl dancing-girl--Eh, *mon ami*, but a dancing-girl of a beauty--Of a beauty--of a fascination--of an allure--_ravissante!_" and the Colonel kissed his stubby fingers and waved them at the stars, his somewhat heavy, bovine gaze momentarily aflame.

"Ah! the marvellous--the incredible--the untellable 'Zara Blanchfleur,' as we called her--But *that* was a woman--a houri from Paradise--"

"And the father?" I broke in upon the rhapsody. "A Frenchman I suppose?"

"Said to be an Englishman," replied the Colonel.

"Certainly European," I observed.

"Oh, but yes, it leaps to the eye, that; does it not, *mon ami*? That white skin, those unpainted cheeks--Yes, they say he was an Englishman--The Death Angel believes so, anyhow--and her great desire in life is to meet him."

"Filial affection is a wonderful thing," I observed.

"It'll prove so, in this case," said the Colonel. "For if the little angel gets near enough, she'll cut his throat till his head falls backward--_boump!_--so--Yes; she loves all Europeans--especially the English--for her father's sake!"

"What! Ill-treated her, I suppose?" I said, my eyes again turning to where the girl beguiled the Arab, and was now bending over backward towards him, that he might place a coin of gold on her forehead among the gold coins of the _sokhab_ tiara that adorned it.

"No, no," murmured the Colonel lazily, as he gazed at the smoke that was curling from his cigarette. "She never knew him, I believe. It's her mother she wishes to avenge."

"Ill-treated the mother?" I asked.

"Well; I wouldn't say *that*--He merely did--er--what one does--One tires, of course--of the loveliest of them--One gathers that _ce bon Monsieur Anglais_ took her from the Street 'of a Thousand Delights away out into the--er--Desert of One Delight--An individualist, one perceives--Installed his _chère amie_ in the desert-equivalent of a flat or a _maisonnette_--probably a green canvas tent from London--A desert idyll--

"A great lover, one would say, this Englishman--" mused the Colonel. "Of a certainty he captured the heart of our Zaza--and broke it--No--nothing cruel--He just dropped it--and it just broke--like any other fragile thing that one drops--He left her--

"She was never the same again, our little one--She became positively nun-like--And then, a little strange--_distraite_--Other-world and other-where, one would say--even in moments of love--And, in time, a little mad--And then more than a little mad--And then quite mad--Oh, mad as Ophelia--And through these years, the years of hoping--the heart-sick years of hope deferred--the heart-broken years of realization--the years of growing insanity--the years of madness, she talked of him Always she talked of him and his return--

"Yes, of a truth, he broke her heart."

"One does not somehow imagine the heart of a Zaza Blanchfleur to be very fragile," I observed.

"That is why I say this Englishman was a great lover," said Levasseur. "For certainly the little one's heart had been taken up--and dropped--before--By General and by Subaltern--by civilian and by sheikh--by aristocrat and by plutocrat--by the richest and by the handsomest--Had been dropped--and had gracefully rebounded to be caught by the next--

"But when the Englishman dropped it, it was shattered--and Zaza Blanchfleur lived with a broken heart until she died of a broken heart--

"And the Angel of Death desires _earnestly_--oh, but earnestly--to meet her papa--And, meanwhile, any white man serves her purpose--her purpose of revenge--serves to glut her hate, to fill her coffers and to slake her passion to avenge her mother."

"She must have adored her mother," I observed.

"Everybody adored her mother," said the Colonel sententiously, and heaved a deep sigh, a sigh that, one felt, claimed one's sympathy and the tribute of a tear--

The Angel of Death--and certainly she moved with the lightness and grace of a being endowed with wings--came circling, gliding, floating toward me again.

Row upon row of enigmatic dark faces--Hundreds of hard watching eyes--

The fierce-looking hawk-faced young _Arab, with whom she had coquetted, arose from his place, and came round the outside of the square of intently-staring onlookers, until he was behind the chairs occupied by the Colonel and myself.

"Have you a gold coin?" asked Levasseur. "She is going to favour you again. The correct thing is to lay a twenty-franc piece, or a sovereign, on her forehead, when she bends over backward with her face turned up to you."

Should I avoid her gaze this time--refuse to look her in the face? Absurd--a half-caste dancing-girl of the bazaars of Bouzen--

She was before me again, and I was a captive fly about which a lovely and bejewelled spider was weaving the bonds from which there is no escape but death--Her arms were weaving, weaving, weaving, mesmeric, hypnotic, compelling.

She approached yet closer.

With a great mental and moral effort I wrenched my mind or soul violently from hers, and thrust my hand into my pocket for a coin. I would simply follow the "custom of the country"--signify my approval of her skill in the usual manner, tip this perfectly ordinary dancing-girl--and then tell Levasseur I was more than ready to return to the hotel--

The Angel of Death saw my movement in search of money, but instead of turning her back to me and bending over until her face looked up into mine, she threw herself at my feet, knelt with arms out-stretched, and bringing her wonderful face closer and closer to mine, whispered:

"_Chèri!--Beaux yeux bleus!_--Lov' me!--I lov' you!--Kiss me, Beau'ful blue-eyes--Kiss me!--Quick!"

Now, Heaven knows, I am no saint, and I know I am no priggish pompous fool--There could be no earthly harm in my kissing this girl. No more harm than there is in any snatched under-the-mistletoe kiss. But the last kiss that I had ever exchanged, had been with a dear little child at Brandon Abbas--ah, how dear!--a sweet and lovely little angel; an Angel of Life, if this was the Angel of Death--

I did not want to hurt this dancing-girl's feelings, but neither did I want to kiss her. In fact, I wasn't going to kiss her, whatever happened.

"_Kiss_ her, man," snapped Colonel Levasseur, disgusted, I suppose, at the stupid, graceless and cold-blooded Anglo-Saxon.

"Thanks--but I never kiss," I said, both to the girl and to him.

The Colonel snorted; the girl's eyes blazed; and I felt an uncomfortable fool.

Simultaneously the young Arab made some movement behind my chair, Colonel Levasseur shouted something at him in Arabic, and the girl thrust her angry face almost against mine.

"_Kiss me!_" she whispered tensely, and the eyes, that had seemed to blaze, narrowed, and looked as deadly cold as those of a snake.

I shook my head.

"I never kiss people," I said, and before my lips had well closed, her right hand went to her sash, flashed upward and fell with a sharp and heavy blow on my shirt-front, exactly over my heart--

I felt no pain--That would come--Numbed--

Levasseur sprang to his feet, hurled the young Arab back, and seized the girl's wrist as though to snap her arm.

"You she-devil!" he growled and, as she laughed mockingly, glanced from the knife that gleamed in her hand, to my breast.

I laughed also--a somewhat nervous laugh of relief. She had not stabbed me as I had supposed. She had struck with all her strength, but in the moment of impact she had turned the point of the knife inward, and had merely struck me with the clenched fist that held the knife.

It was over in a second, and she was whirling away again upon the tips of her toes. But few had seen what actually happened--and they had merely seen a girl offer a kiss, receive a refusal, and give a blow.

Turning swiftly from the girl to the jealous Arab, Colonel Levasseur showed something of the tiger that undoubtedly lurked beneath the heavy and somewhat dull exterior of the man.

What he said, I did not catch; but the Arab recoiled from the ferocious glare of the French officer's baleful eye, the gleam of his bared teeth. I thought the big clenched fist was about to crash into the Arab's face, but it shot out with pointed finger, as the Colonel concluded with an order, shouted as at a dog.

"_Imshi!_" he roared. "Get out of it, you black hound--" and the Arab slunk off toward the compound gate.

Impassive faces seemed to harden--hundreds of watching eyes to narrow--

Our host, apparently petrified with terror and amazement, now pulled himself together, rolled off his sofa, and prostrated himself before his guest.

When he had finished his protestations of grief, horror, outrage and alarm--perfervid declarations that he was shamed for life, his face blackened for ever, his salt betrayed, his roof dishonoured, his fame besmirched, his self-respect destroyed, his life laid in ruins--by the action of the vile criminal whom the Colonel had so rightly driven forth into outer darkness--Levasseur quietly remarked:

"*Bien!* I hold you responsible then, that every movement of that seditious, insolent dog, Selim ben Yussuf, is reported to the _Bureau_--And look you, Abu Sheikh Ahmed, if he sets foot in Zaguig without my knowing it, on your head be it--"

"On my head and my life, Excellency," replied Abu Sheikh Ahmed, touching his forehead and breast, as he bowed humbly before the angry Colonel.

Levasseur then thanked him for the entertainment, bade him continue the music and the dance until we were well away; and then, with a brief, "Come along, Monsieur Vanbrugh," marched off to the door, our host trotting beside us, voluble to the last.

"What was wrong with the good What's-his-name--Selim?" I asked as we seated ourselves in the waiting car.

"A cursed great knife, my friend," replied the Colonel, "broad and sharp and curly--That's what was wrong--His hand was on it as I happened to glance over my shoulder--I believe that both he and the girl each thought the other was going to stab you, and so neither did--"

"Oh, nonsense, Colonel," I laughed, "she was only giving me a little fright because I refused her kiss, and he was just being dramatic--to please her--"

"Ah, well, my friend," replied Levasseur, "doubtless *you* know the Arab best--and particularly Mademoiselle the Angel of Death and Monsieur Selim ben Yussuf, who is literally mad for her."

"Who is he?" I asked.

"The son of the Sheikh of an extremely powerful and important tribe," was the reply. "An old man whose friendship is worth a very great deal to us--Make all the difference at Zaguig--Worth a whole brigade--He's very loyal, friendly and peaceable, but things will be different when his mantle descends to Master Selim--if our fool politicians let it--I'd shoot the dog on sight, if I had *my* way--Let's stop the car and walk a bit, shall we? I've been sitting down all day."

I was quite agreeable. We got out, and the Colonel bade the soldier-chauffeur return to his quarters.

"Are these streets at all dangerous at night?" I asked my companion, as we strolled along through the silent moonlit dream-city of whitest light and blackest shadow.

"*that* is, very--in more ways than one," he replied, pointing up a somewhat narrower lane, the entrance to which we were just passing. "There are a good few murders, up there, in the course of the year--We can go that way--It's rather interesting."

"Murders?" I observed, as we turned into the street. "Robbery?"

"Yes. Robbery--Jealousy--Hate--Sometimes the spider kills the fly. Sometimes the fly is a wasp and kills the spider."

It was a strange street. Silent as Death; wide awake and watchful as Life: furtive and secret as Night: open and obvious as Day.

There was no movement, no sound, no invitation; but there were eyes, there were open doors that looked like the mouths of tombs, there were mystery and evil and danger in the black shadows, in the very moonlight, the air--

As we passed the first open door, I saw that it framed a curious picture. Back in the darkness, with which a small native lamp struggled feebly, sat a perfectly motionless figure, bedizened, bejewelled, posed, suggesting an idol dressed up for a barbarous religious ceremony, or the priest of such an idol, watching through the night before its shrine. No movement of the body of this priest or idol caused the slightest change in the reflections from bright jewels, shining gold, or gleaming cloth of silver, the slightest sound from heavy armlets, chains, anklets, girdle or bracelets--but, as we passed, the eyes followed us, gleaming--

And so in the next house--and the next--and the next; so in every house in the silent listening street, the waiting, watchful, motionless street, which the bold and hardy man beside me had declared to be very dangerous. in more ways than one.

"Interesting people, those Ouled-Naïl dancing-girls," observed Levasseur. "They've danced, and they've sat in this street, for a couple of thousand years or so. They danced for Julius Caesar and Scipio Africanus--and for Jugurtha too--as they danced for you and me, and for old Abu Sheikh Ahmed--Roman generals took them to Rome and French generals take them to Paris--There isn't much they don't know about the art of charming--A hundred generations of hereditary lore--Most intriguing and attractive--"

"A matter of taste," I observed. "Personally I'd pay handsomely--to be excused. I don't see how a bedizened, painted, probably unwashed, half-savage Jezebel is going to 'interest, intrigue, and attract,' a person of any taste and refinement."

I spoke a little warmly and wondered whether I did protest too much, as I thought of the Angel of Death.

The Colonel was faintly annoyed, methought. Perhaps he, a person of taste and refinement, had been interested, intrigued and attracted.

"One of them attracted the Englishman to some purpose," he growled. "He took her from this very street--I could show you the house--Zaza Blanchfleur--He treated her like a bride--Regular honeymoon--Fitted out a splendid caravan, and went off a long way into the desert--Oh, yes, she interested _him_ all right, and for quite a while too--And what about her daughter, the Angel of Death f She has interested a few people of taste and refinement, I can tell you!--Some names that would surprise you--"

"And did she sit in this street too?" I asked.

"Of course she did, at first--But she has walked in a few other streets since--Bond Street: Rue de la Paix: Unter den Linden: Nevsky Prospect: the Ringstrasse: Corso: Prado: Avenido: visited nearly all the capitals of Europe, she says."

"What's to become of a girl like that?" I asked.

"Oh--marry a big Sheikh and go out into the desert for good--or a rich Moor and go into a _hareem_ in Fez--stay here and amass wealth--go to Paris, Marseilles or Algiers--she may die a princess on a silken bed in a Sultan's palace, or on the floor of a foul den in Port Said--"

The Colonel sighed, and the subject dropped.

CHAPTER V

At Zaguig, Colonel Levasseur was in his element, monarch of all he surveyed, and greatly he loved playing the monarch before the amused eyes of Mary, who enormously enjoyed the opportunity of "getting nearer to life" as she called it, and "seeing the Oriental on his native heath," unoccidentalized and undefiled--or unpurified and unregenerate.

Zaguig contained nothing European, and it intended to contain nothing European if it could help it. Unfortunately, its representatives had not even that moderate degree of straight speech and fair dealing which prevails in European diplomacy, and hid the bitterest hate and most evil intentions behind the most loving protestations, honeyed words and outward signs of friendship.

I am not a politician nor a world-reformer, neither a publicist nor a sociologist, and I have no views to offer on the subject of the ethics of the "peaceful penetration" of an uncivilized country by a civilized one. But nobody could travel southward from Bouzen, contrasting the Desert with the Sown, without perceiving that the penetration was for the greatest good of the greatest number, and ultimately for the whole world's good, inasmuch as cultivation and production succeeded fallow waste; order and peace succeeded lawlessness and war; and the blessings of civilization succeeded the curses of savagery.

Not always are the "blessings" immediately recognized for what they are, by their unconsulted recipients.

Certainly, in this case, there could be no two opinion on the subject of whether the penetrated approved the process. They were not altruists and they were fanatical Mussulmans with an unfathomable contempt for all Christians and all other God-forgotten Infidels--Particularly was this true of the Zaguigan dervishes, marabouts, mullahs, priests, preachers, and teachers, for Zaguig was what is known as a "Holy" City, and it was wont to make a most unholy mess of any unauthorized intruder--

Probably Mecca and Medina themselves were not more hopelessly reactionary and murderously fanatical than Zaguig, and certainly they could not have approximated more closely to the state of Sodom and Gomorrah than did this Holy Spot--

However, the tide of civilization was encroaching upon the hitherto undefiled sands that surrounded it; waves of progress were lapping against its very walls; and the first wavelets of that irresistible ocean were the men of Colonel Levasseur's Military Mission.

It was in this peculiarly unholy Holy City that Mary met the man who instantly awoke her keenest interest, admiration and approval; who later won her devoted love; and ultimately became her husband.

Mary was--wholly unconsciously, I believe--becoming very interested in the subject of love and matrimony, and had, I feel sure, been wondering whether her twin soul might not be right there, when she sojourned in New York, London, Paris, Monte Carlo, Algiers, Biskra, and Bouzen respectively, where charming eligibles abounded.

To think that he should be in Zaguig where nothing abounded but unwashed Zaguigans, heat, dirt, smells and an almost unadulterated orientalism--

I liked the handsome, hard, clean-cut Major Henri de Beaujolais from the first; and he attracted me enormously. To the simplicity and directness of the soldier he added the cleverness and knowledge of the trained specialist; the charm, urbanity and grace of the experienced man of the world; and the inevitable attractiveness of a lovable and modest character.

He combined the best of two nations, with his English public-school upbringing, and his English home-life of gentle breeding, on the one hand, and his aristocratic French birth, breeding and traditions on the other--I heard that he was as brave as a lion, extremely able, and likely to go very far in his profession--quite apart from the fact that he was the nephew of a most distinguished general and related by marriage (through his uncle's wife) to an extremely powerful and prominent politician.

We first met him at dinner at Colonel Levasseur's table, and I was surprised to note that Mary's attitude to him was anything but encouraging and kind. In fact she rather annoyed me by apparently endeavouring to annoy him I taxed her with this after he had gone, and asked if she disliked him.

"_Dear_ old Otis!" she smiled, and added later. "Why--no--why should I?--I altogether like him--and _then_ some--"

"You certainly hid it," I observed.

"Did I?--Did I?" she asked.

Whereupon I also waxed wily, and remarked:

"He reminded me of d'Artagnan--Just that swaggering self-confidence and assurance--a faint touch of the somewhat gasconading swash-buckler--" and got no further.

"What!" interrupted Mary, "_Are_ you as blind as a mole with a monocle _and_ as stupid as a fish with a headache?--Why I never met a more modest unassuming man in my life!--You couldn't prise a word out of him--about what he has done--Not with a crow-bar--"

"Ah!" I observed profoundly, and chuckled, whereupon Mary marched off to bed.

I love Mary, and I love to watch her at work. What she wants, she goes for; and what she goes for, she gets. Our Red Indian streak is, at times, fairly strong in her, and shows particularly when she is in danger--Then she is the coolest thing invented, and apparently at her happiest--It shows also in a certain relentless tenacity, a determination to achieve her purpose--and, I may add, a certain recklessness--not to say unscrupulousness--with which she handles obstacles and opposition.

The idea that entered my mind that memorable evening remained, and it turned to a certainty. As the days went by, and Mary saw more and more of Henri de Beaujolais, she grew more and more interested in him, and he in her--All his spare time was devoted to "making her visit agreeable," and to satisfying her insatiable thirst for knowledge of North Africa and the Africans.

Poor Colonel Levasseur could but acquiesce, and show a delight that he did not feel, when she assured him of how enormously she was enjoying her stay in Zaguig--thanks to Major de Beaujolais' wonderful knowledge of the place and people, and his extraordinarily interesting way of imparting it.

"Yes," thought I to myself in the vernacular, "Mary has fallen for Major Henri de Beaujolais, and Major Henri de Beaujolais has fallen for Mary--though possibly he doesn't yet know it--But he is certainly going to know it--if the first part of my surmise is correct."

I was filled with hope and joy, for he was just the man I would have chosen for my sister to marry, and I longed to see her married and with a home of her own--A woman needs a home more than a man does--almost more than she needs anything--and our own home in Wyoming was no "home" at all--

It did not greatly surprise me, when, entering the spacious tiled breakfast-room, with its great pillared verandah, one morning, to hear de Beaujolais remark, as he turned to go:

"Well, I have warned you, sir, and done all I can--We're sitting on a powder-magazine and there are quite a lot of lads inside it--_striking matches_--And one of them is our friend Selim ben Yussuf too!--There's going to be a big explosion--and a conflagration as well--and pretty soon--:'

"Won't you stop and have some coffee--before it happens!" smiled Colonel Levasseur in a particularly irritating manner; and, with a haughty salute, de Beaujolais strode from the room, his face set and scowling.

"Wonderful noses for a mare's-nest, these Intelligence people," smiled the Colonel. "Have you seen Mademoiselle this morning?--Been out riding?--Wish I could find all the spare time these Intelligence fellers can--_I_ can't go riding with her every morning--Yes, nothing but mare's-nest after mare's-nest, full of addled eggs--like the Intelligence feller's brains--Yes, addled--Another mare's-nest now--revolt, rebellion, mutiny, murder, massacre and I don't know what all!--I suppose the Secret Service must justify its existence and earn its pay somehow--_Intelligence_, eh? Pity some of them haven't _got_ a little--Ah! Here's Mademoiselle--Bring the coffee at once, Alphonse--_Bon jour, ma chère Mademoiselle Vanbrugh_, you look like the morning itself--only cool--cool--always cool--".

One afternoon within a week of the delivery of these _obiter dicta_ by the wise Colonel Levasseur, I received a message, at the Residency, from de Beaujolais, bidding me hurry to his quarters. The messenger, a fine Spahi, named Achmet, de Beaujolais' orderly, calmly informed me that my sister, the Sitt Miriam Vanbrugh, was in great danger and that I was to go instantly, on the horse that he had ridden. It appeared that de Beaujolais himself had come to the Residency to find me, and had taken my sister's maid away with him--

At least this was what I gathered from Achmet's curious mixture of French, _sabir_ and Arabic.

I rushed down to the street, guided by Achmet, who ran swiftly before me; rode to the house near the Babel-Sûq where de Beaujolais lived, fearing I knew not what, and noting the strange emptiness of the bazaars, lanes, squares and streets, due, I supposed, to the fact that there was a big parade and review in the great Square of the Minaret--

Arrived at de Beaujolais' quarters, I dismounted in the courtyard at the back of the house, gave the horse a smack that sent him trotting to the stable, and dashed up the wooden stairs. I either kicked down or opened the first door to which I came, and found two Arabs in the room. One of them announced himself to be Major de Beaujolais--I recognized the voice after I had heard the name--and said that Mary was in his bedroom with her maid, dressing up as an Arab female--The massacre was to be for that evening, and not a foreigner would survive it, save those who successfully hid themselves--He had sent for me to look after the girls and to share their chance of escape by hiding, in disguise, until a punitive expedition arrived--

So it had come!--De Beaujolais had been right and Levasseur wrong, criminally wrong--And Mary was in the heart of one of the most dangerously fanatical towns in the world, at the moment of a _jehad_, a Holy War upon infidels, their slaughter and complete massacre--Mary and her excellent English maid, Maud Atkinson--And I was to disguise myself as an Arab and hide in a bedroom with them--hide cowering, trembling, sickening, starving, until the arrival of a relief-force from Ain-Zuggout or somewhere!--

One thing was fairly certain, Mary wouldn't consent to do anything of this sort--and I said so--

"What about the troops?" I asked.

"Not a chance," replied de Beaujolais. "They are hopelessly inadequate in number, and they couldn't be worse placed than they are--Scattered about the city--If you hide here, you'll be the only white people alive by midnight--It's absolutely your one and only chance--"

"Mary won't stay hidden here for days," I said. "And I don't like the idea much for myself, either--Let's hear what she's got to say about it," and we went into the next room, followed by the other "Arab"--a Captain in the French Secret Service, named Redon.

Mary, calm and cool as ever, appeared more interested in the Arab clothes than in the prospect of death and destruction.

"Look here, Mary," I said. "What about it? Will you lie low here and keep the place all silent and shut up, and wear those clothes in case anybody gets a glimpse of you--and wait until the relief-force comes?"

"Answer's in the negative," she replied, observing the effect of her head-dress in a shaving-mirror. "These what-is-its over the face don't give a girl much chance, do they?--The just and the unjust--the fair and the unfair--all start from scratch, so to speak--Er--no--Otis, I am not paying a long visit--What's Major de Beaujolais going to do in the massacre? Show great Intelligence and offer us sure, but Secret, Service--or which?"

And then de Beaujolais made the devastating announcement that he was going to clear out, cut and run--before the show started, if he could--He had at that moment got his orders from the dirty, ruffianly-looking "Arab" who was Captain de Redon--

And I, at that moment, got something too--the idea of a lifetime! _He should take Mary with him_, wherever he was going!--It would save her from the massacre, and it would, moreover, throw her and de Beaujolais together in the protracted intimacy of a desert journey.

And that would surely lead to the lasting happiness of both of them! In the imminence of battle, murder and sudden death, I thought of orange-blossoms, bridal veils, and the Voice that breathed o'er Eden--I suppose it was because I knew that it was hopeless and useless for me to think of such things in connection with myself, that I so often thought of them for other people--

And it promptly appeared that my bright idea had not occurred to me alone, for Mary observed that since Major de Beaujolais was escaping, she and her maid might as well escape with him. She said it as one might say: "If you're going to Town too, we might as well catch the same train."

But de Beaujolais apparently had other views.

He declared that it was utterly impossible. He was going on a secret mission of the greatest delicacy, danger and importance--He simply could not take women with him. He repeated his suggestion that I and the two girls should lie hidden in that house, and take our chance of surviving till a French column arrived.

I was glad that Mary did not for one moment suppose that I should do anything of the sort--do anything, in fact, but join my host and his men and throw in my lot with theirs.

For herself, she merely brushed de Beaujolais' refusals and explanations aside, and made it clear that no masculine trivialities and puerilities of politics, Secret Service, or Special Missions, were of sufficient importance to be talked about--much less considered as obstacles in the path of Miss Mary Vanbrugh.

When he waxed urgently explanatory and emphatically discouraging, finishing by an absolute and uncompromising refusal, she merely did not listen, but bade the departing Achmet to take along the portmanteau that Maudie had brought--to wherever he was going--

And so extremely vehement and final was de Beaujolais' negative, so absolutely convincing his reasons for refusing to take her, that I was certain he longed to do it, and was but fighting what he believed to be his own weakness. I conceived him to be in the horrible position of having to leave a girl, with whom he had fallen in love, to the mercies of the men of Zaguig--or else take her with him, to the greater danger to herself and the greatest danger to the success of his mission--

To my mind, the second alternative was wholly preferable, and I set about doing what I could to bring it to pass--for it gave Mary not only a chance of life, but a chance of happiness--Also, I am bound to confess, because it transferred to the broader shoulders of de Beaujolais the terrible responsibility of saving her--

"Take her, for God's sake," I said, "it is her only chance--She will never hide here--She'll come back to the Residency with me, and use a rifle--She is as good as a man--You say there is no shadow of hope--Think of the end then--I can't shoot her--There is at least a chance for her with you--"

"Against my instructions and orders," he said, his face a study of conflicting feelings. "I have to travel as light as possible; as swiftly as possible--and with the irreducible minimum of followers--More people means more kit and camels--more delay--less speed--And she'd never stand the journey--Wholly against my instructions and almost certain death for her--"

"And this is absolutely certain death for her," I said.

I wished I could see Mary's face, but it was hidden beneath the out-door garment that covers the purdah Mussulman woman from the crown of her head to the soles of her feet. Not even her eyes were visible through the strip of muslin that covered the aperture left in the thick material, to permit the wearer to see.

Captain de Redon added his voice to mine--evidently sympathizing to the depths of his gallant Gallic soul with his unfortunately-situated friend; with a girl in terrible danger; and with the girl's brother, pleading for her life. Probably he saw, as clearly as I did, that the one thing de Beaujolais longed to do, was to give way--

And give way he did, with every appearance of reluctance and ill grace.

"Very well," he said. "On Miss Vanbrugh's head be it. She and her maid can leave with me--provided she understands that my business is not to save her, but to serve my country--I shan't let her safety or life stand in the way of duty, for a second--"

I wrung his hand and I knew that Mary was safe--He'd do his duty, all-right, but he'd make it square with the safety of the woman he loved--Yes, he certainly loved her, whether he knew it or not--and a terrific load was lifted from my mind.

A few minutes later, they were all in the street--still empty and silent, I was glad to see--and on their way to the house of the wealthy and friendly Arab, Sidi Ibrahim Maghruf--a party of entirely ordinary and convincing natives; de Beaujolais, a Sergeant-Major Dufour, Captain de Redon, Mary, and Maud Atkinson--the last-named, in her invincible ignorance and cheerful cockney courage, thoroughly enjoying the whole business.

De Beaujolais refused to let me come with them to the house of his friend Ibrahim Maghruf, where the caravan was waiting, as I was not in Arab dress, and begged me (since I refused to quit the town with him, and then take my chance in the desert), to hurry back to the Residency. I was to tell Colonel Levasseur of the arrival of Captain de Redon with orders for de Beaujolais' instant departure, and to try to get the fact into the good Colonel's thick skull that the revolt would break out that very night--

I gave Mary a warm and loving embrace, kissed the place where I imagined her mouth to be, and murmured in the neighbourhood of her ear:

"God bless you, darling girl--" and added a _cliché_ of our childhood anent "a buggy-ride with a nice young man."

That Mary heard and understood my allusion was indicated by the fact that I received an entirely perceptible jab in the sub-central region of my waistcoat, as I took my arms from about her neck.

Crushing down my feelings of loneliness, apprehension and anxiety, I told myself that Mary was in splendid hands, and, hurrying out from that boding and oppressive house, I quickly lost myself, completely and hopelessly, in the maze-like tangle of alleys, bazaars, winding lanes, and crooked streets, that lay between it and the Residency.

The atmosphere of the place was inexpressibly sinister--sly, minatory and enigmatic. There was no-one to be seen, but I felt that I was seen by a thousand watching eyes--What lurked behind those iron-barred window-spaces, those lattices, gratings, slightly opened doors; behind those high blind walls, and upon those screened balconies?--Frequently the lane through which I hurried was roofed completely over, and was a mere tunnel beneath the upper rooms of the houses that formed its sides.

As I emerged from one of these and turned a corner into a narrow bazaar of tiny shops, each but a shuttered hole in the wall, I heard a heavy murmur such as one may suddenly hear when approaching the sea-shore and emerging into the open--

It was indescribably menacing and disturbing, this growing noise as of a hive of infuriated bees, and it quickly grew into the most terrible sound there is--the blended roar and howl and shout and scream of a vast infuriated mob of maddened men, yelling and blood-lusting for rapine, fire and slaughter--The man who can hear it unmoved is a man of iron nerve, a superman indeed--for a mob is infinitely worse and wickeder, more destructive and dangerous, than any single member of it. It is the most wild and savage of all wild and savage beasts; and is infinitely powerful, with its innumerable hands to rend and slay and burn, its innumerable brains to think of evil things for those hands to do.

I was certainly frightened.

The appalling noise increased in volume and came nearer.

I was lost--and knew not which way to turn to avoid the mob nor to rejoin my friends, those splendid soldiers--many of them Africans--who would die to a man, without thought of parley or surrender.

To die fighting with them would be nothing--an exhilaration, a fierce joy--but to be torn to pieces in these stinking gutters, handled and struck by these foul bestial brutes, trampled to a jelly of blood and mud and mess--there could be no more dreadful death--The loathsome indignity of it--a white man struggling impotent in the hands of blacks--his clothes torn from his body!

That was what frightened me, not Death--for he was a fellow I was quite willing to meet whenever he came along--

2.

As the noise made by the mob--the noise varying from the roaring of ten thousand lions to that of a mighty sea breaking on an iron-bound coast in a terrific storm--rose and fell, advanced and withdrew, when I turned corners, entered narrow gullies or crossed open squares, I prayed that Mary was out of the city and safely on her way.

I fervently blessed de Beaujolais and his thought for her; his fetching her maid and me; his final decision to take her with him. I could not refrain from contrasting him with Levasseur--who had invited her to Zaguig that he might impress her and that she might see him in the most favourable conditions.

Well--he had invited her to Zaguig for his own ends and had so been instrumental in bringing de Beaujolais into her life. Long might de Beaujolais remain there!

And suddenly I turned another corner and found, with utter dismay, that I had walked round in a circle; for in the open space where several lanes met, lay a dead horse that I had seen an hour or two earlier, and, not very far from it, lay the corpse of an Arab.

The sight--an unpleasant one--of the man's body, gave me an idea. My object was to rejoin Levasseur and to be of 'use; but it was absolutely certain that I should never reach him in European clothes. I should be torn to pieces by the mob, killed by the first gang I ran into. Dressed as I was, my one chance of life was to creep into some hole and hide. Dressed as an Arab, I might make my way to the Residency, and get into it--if I were not shot by its defenders.

Disguised as an Arab, I might be able to approach and shout, in French, that I was one of them. Dressed as a European, I couldn't shout to the mob that I was really an Arab in disguise--and get away with it. There wouldn't be time to shout, for one thing.

The dead man's clothes were filthy, and they were soaked in blood. He had certainly been in bad trouble--Could he be another Secret Service man, like de Redon One who had fallen by the way? I should somehow feel less compunction about putting on his foul _burnous_, if he were--Should I put his things on over my own, or discard European clothing entirely?--I should have to look "right" about the head and feet, anyway. There wouldn't be much point in going about with European boots and trousers sticking out at one end of a _burnous_ and a European sun-helmet at the other.

But what should I look like, if a gang came round the corner, and saw me sitting in the gutter, swapping clothes with a corpse?

These thoughts flashed through my mind in the moment that I reached the body. Apparently the man had been stabbed, or run through, with a sword.

He had bled very copiously, and I glanced at the trail which connected him with the gate of a compound--No, I couldn't squat down in the open street, pull off my boots and trousers--fancy being caught without one's boots and trousers--and change clothes with a corpse!--Or could I?--

And right here the corpse fetched a deep groan and settled the question. I could not pull the clothes off a dying man--If I could do nothing to help him, I could at least leave him to die in peace.

I turned and hurried away, wondering which of the five streets that entered the square was the one by which I had followed Achmet from the Residency to de Beaujolais' quarters. They all looked alike to me, and I had been too anxious about Mary to take any note of the winding route by which we had come--I found that I was following the trail left by the wounded Arab, and saw that it led into the compound of an apparently unoccupied building, and to the foot of an outside staircase that went up to the flat roof.

As I halted, there was a sudden burst of nearer noise, the sound of men running as well as shouting; and, glancing over my shoulder, I saw that, two or three hundred yards from where I stood, a mob was streaming across the end of the alley down which I was looking. Any one of the running men might at any moment glance in my direction--and in a very few minutes it would be, "Good evening, St. Peter," for mine.

I dashed into the compound, up the stairs to the roof, and found myself in the presence of some half-dozen Arabs--all dead--

"Dirty work at the cross-roads!"

The place was like a butcher's yard, a slaughter-house--also a perfectly private dressing-room provided with an assortment of that kind of fancy-dress of which I was in such desperate need. The garments were all filthy, more or less torn, and plentifully bloodstained; but I realized that this was all to the good, since my object was to make my way through streets swarming with the scum of the city, similarly apparelled, and many of them similarly gore-bespattered. In point of fact it was amazing good luck that I had happened upon this sinister and revolting shambles.

Promptly I divested myself of my outer clothing and boots, and got to work.

It was the nastiest job I have ever undertaken, and there were moments when I was tempted to resume my own clothes, take one of the Arab swords that lay about, and run amok. Still more was I tempted to scurry back to de Beaujolais' quarters and hide--I could find the place by returning to where the dead horse lay--

I suppose that if I were a strong silent man with a big chin (and a thick ear or two), I should have proceeded coolly and swiftly with my task, and should have swaggered forth from that house "every inch an Arab," correct to the last detail.

In point of fact I felt ill and shaken; I was very frightened and nervous; and I could scarcely control my trembling sweating fingers.

Possibly most other ordinary people would have felt nearly as bad as I did!

It was growing dark--The sky was lurid with the glare of great conflagrations--There was a ceaseless nerve-shattering mob-roar, a roar punctuated by hideous howls, rifle shots, and the crashes of volley-firing--I was in the midst of a select assembly of corpses, and their hideous faces seemed to grimace in the waning and flickering light--I had to pull them about, to get their clothes from them--their beastly blood-sodden clothes--and they resented this, and clung to their rags with devilish ingenuity--And there was viscous slimy blood upon my hands--There were knotted strings--and the knots would not come undone-

--and this made the owner of the garment grin and grin and grin at me, and shake his horrible head as I tugged and tugged, the perspiration streaming from me--And once stepping back, I slipped and stumbled and, in saving myself from falling, I trod upon the chest of a man lying behind me, and my weight drove the air from his lungs through his throat, and the dead uttered what seemed a loud cry--the ghastliest, the most loathsome, the most terrifying sound that I have ever heard: the dead voice of a dead man raised in loud protest against the indignity, the defilement of my treading foot--

I hear that sound in nightmares to this day--

From that man I took nothing, though I coveted his _burnous_ and great curved dagger--I dared not touch him, lest his dreadful glazed eyes turn to mine, his horrible snarling mouth shout at me again, his dead hands seize me by the throat--

Yes, I was certainly frightened by the time I had wrested a complete Arab outfit from those reluctant corpses, and I was certainly sick by the time I had rubbed a mud of blood and dust and dirt upon my hands and arms, my feet and legs and--it makes me shudder to think of it even now--upon my face--

Having dressed, I wound a filthy cotton thing about my neck, chin, mouth, nose and ears, almost to my eyes, beneath the head-cloth I had transferred complete from its late owner's head and shoulders to my own; picked up a knife and a sword; and fled from the horrible scene of my unspeakable labours.

As I emerged from the compound, a man dashed from a side-turning into the alley in front of me, and came running swiftly in my direction.

I raised my sword and waited, realizing that my ghastly work up above must, at any rate, have made a terrible spectacle of me, and that standing there, bloody, grim, silent, well-armed, I was scarcely likely to be attacked by one man--nor by any number, until I had to speak, or my disguise was penetrated--

The running man drew near, and I saw that he was a filthy ragged creature, gaunt and wild, carrying a great staff in one hand and a rosary in the other. Flecks of foam lay in white spots on his mangy beard--One of those bestial "holy" beggars, so full of divinity that there is no room for humanity--

As he rushed by, a few yards from me, he glanced in my direction, took me for a fellow tough, and yelled something or other, in Arabic--a profession of faith or an incitement to slay and spare not--and I got a clear glimpse of his face.

It was Captain de Redon.

Dashing after him, I laid my hand on his arm, raised my sword and emitted a meaningless howl. He swung about, cursing me vehemently, and up went his long staff. He looked as pleasant and easy to tackle as a hungry grizzly bear--And he did not know me--nor dream that I was anything but the Arab thing I was trying to appear.

"This one's on you, Captain," I remarked.

His staff and his jaw both dropped as he stared.

"*Mon Dieu!* " he said. "Who are you?--I thought I was the only--"

"Otis H. Vanbrugh," I told him. "Major de Beaujolais introduced us an hour ago."

" *Mon Dieu!* " he said again--"But you have made good use of your time, Monsieur! You took me in completely--What happened?--I am going back to de Beaujolais' quarters to see that everything is all-right--No papers undestroyed--He had to leave rather hurriedly--And I want another bite of Christian food, for I'm starving--Also a scrap of soap if I can find some--Very useful for pious foaming at the mouth--"

As we hurried along, I told him how I had lost my way in trying to get from de Beaujolais' quarters to the Residency, and of my finding the dead men on the roof.

"A queer business," he said. "But corpses will be sufficiently common before to-morrow--And your idea is to rejoin Levasseur and take a hand?--You'll have to be careful. It would be bad luck to get through the mob safely and be shot by the Zouaves--

"Your sister is safely away," he continued, and went on to tell me how he had accompanied de Beaujolais' party to one of the gates, and had been able to divert a mob from that quarter, lead them running to imaginary loot, and, by dashing round a corner and over a wall and through a house and garden that he knew, to get into one of the tunnel-like bazaars and shake them off.

"Perhaps you'd better stick to me for a while," he concluded, as we entered de Beaujolais' place. "If anybody speaks to you, howl and hit him--Sure sign that your heart's in the right place and that you're feeling good to-day--nice and fanatical and anti-French--We'll get as near to the Residency as we can without being shot, and I may be able to get you in--If not, you'll have to manage it, somehow, to-night--Call out in French and say that you want to speak to Levasseur--It'll be a risky business for you, though, between the Arabs and the Zouaves--"

"But aren't you going to join your comrades too?" I asked. "The one of us that got in first could warn them to look out for the other--if we failed to get in together."

"No," replied de Redon. "My job is outside. I'm going to play around with the lads-of-the-village, and speak that which is not true--Just when they are going to start something, I yell that a French army is round the corner--Or I accidentally drop this club on top of the head of the most prominent citizen, at the moment of his maximum usefulness to the community he adorns--Dupe and mislead the poor fellows as effectually as if I were a professional labour-agitator, in fact--"

I liked this Captain de Redon, a cool, competent and most courageous person. As he ate the leg of a fowl, and swiftly searched the two rooms that de Beaujolais had occupied--presumably for papers or other traces of its late occupant--he chatted as though we were not both in imminent danger of a beastly death, and about to go out and look for it.

It was a most interesting and amusing thing to heal a cultured and very delightful voice, speaking excellent English, issue from that dirty ragged scarecrow, skinny, mean and repulsive-looking.

Gazing at him in some amazement, I had an idea, and went to a small framed mirror, a cheap bazaar article, that hung on the wall of the back room.

I was positively startled. Sick and sorry as I had been at the time, I had done my work well--and had so smeared the handful of blood, mud, dust and dirt into my face and eyes that there was not a vestige of my white (or red) skin exposed. The said face was a most revolting, bestial, and disgusting spectacle--barely human in its foul filthiness--No wonder that de Redon had not recognized me nor dreamed that I was a Christian--As I stared at myself, I was glad that Isobel could not see me.

"Ready?" said de Redon, in the doorway. "Excuse my rushing you--We'll get as near the Residency as we can--When we're among the simple villagers, you just follow me and do more or less what I do--If anybody seems offensive or gets inquisitive, hit him--or else spin round and round, and howl--And, look here--if we get in front of the troops, throw yourself on the ground and be a wounded man--If you go running towards them dressed like that, you'll be shot or bayoneted--Wait for a chance to crawl near enough to shout, in French, to Levasseur or an officer, as I said--"

I thanked him and forbore to remark that I had played Red Indians before--and with tame Indians who had themselves trodden the war-path in their time.

We went down into the street and hurried in the direction of the big square, not far from which was the Residency.

De Redon evidently knew every inch of the route, each twist and turn, and he went so fast that I could only just keep him in sight as he kept vanishing round corners and into dark tunnels.

Every moment the horrible noise grew louder and louder as we came nearer to the scene of the fighting.

As we turned from a foul gully into a broader street, a gang of looters came running round a corner a few yards from us.

Waving his staff and rosary of black wooden beads, de Redon howled like a wild beast, and spun round and round, shouted something I could not understand, and dashed on--I at his heels, in the middle of the yelling and excited Arabs. They had evidently come into the city from the outside, being differently dressed from the townsmen, darker and hardier-looking toughs.

Some had long guns and some carried perfectly good rifles.

The street down which we ran, debouched into the big market-square, the Square of the Minaret, and this great place was packed almost solid with people, all moving in the direction of the Residency. Certainly "the heathen raged furiously together," and when we got fairly into the middle of them, I began to feel that it was as safe a place as any, so far as risk of discovery went, and I yelled and waved my sword with the best.

De Redon wriggled, thrust, and fought his way through the crowd aggressively, and with the air of an important person who has very urgent business in hand. In an exceedingly violent and truculent assembly of fanatical ruffians, he seemed the most violent, truculent and fanatical of the lot. I followed him as best I could, and endeavoured to behave as he did.

Suddenly the shouting crowd gave back, just as crowds do when shepherded by mounted police, and, in a few moments, de Redon and I found ourselves in the foremost ranks, and then in front, and ahead of the mob. Turning to face the swaying crowd, de Redon twirled his staff above his head and bawled in Arabic at the top of his voice:

"Back! Back!--Run! Run!--The _Roumi_ dogs--the _Franzawi_ are coming--" and pointed to where from a side-street, a detachment of Zouaves came charging at the double--stoned and shot-at from the roofs, and followed by a howling mob, only kept at bay by the rear-guard-action tactics of a Sergeant, who, every now and then, halted the end squad of the Hal: column, turned them about, fired a volley, and rushed back to the main body, who slowed up during the operation.

Occasionally a soldier fell and was instantly the centre of a surging mob that slashed and tore and clubbed him almost out of semblance to the human form.

As the little column, evidently fighting its way to the Residency, debouched into the square, the officer in command, a young Lieutenant, charging at their head, threw up his sword-hand and shouted:

"_Halte!--Cessez le feu!--Formez le carré!_"

And, in an instant, the company was a square, bristling with bayonets, steady as a rock, front ranks kneeling, rear ranks standing close behind them, awaiting the next order as if at drill.

"Run! Run! My brothers!" yelled de Redon, in the comparative quiet that followed this manoeuvre, a slight lull before the storm.

"Run! Run!--The _Franzawi_--We shall be slain!" and he dashed at the wavering crowd that hung uncertain whether to charge in holy triumph or flee in holy terror.

Following his voice came that of the French officer, full, clear and strong.

"_Attention! Pour les feux de salve!--Enjoue!_--"

"Quick! Quick!--Run! Run--" yelled de Redon.

A huge man, wearing the green turban of a haji, and bearing aloft a green banner, thrust through the crowd, sprang forward, sent de Redon sprawling and yelled:

"_Allah! Allah! Allah Akbar!--Fissa! Fissa!_--Follow me and die for the Faith--"

The crowd howled in response and moved forward,

De Redon, apparently representing a different brand of holiness, and full of the _odium theologicum_, returned the violent assault of the _haji_. He returned it with his club. The haji dropped, and the subsequent proceedings interested him no more.

The crowd rushed forward.

"_Feu!_" shouted the Zouave officer, and either instinctively or because de Redon did so, I flung myself to the ground.

Crash!--rang out the volley of the Zouaves.

"_En joue! Feu!_" cried the officer.

Crash! came the second volley from all sides of the now surrounded square of troops.

The crowd about me scattered like leaves before the wind, and de Redon and I were two of dozens of motion-less figures upon the ground.

"_Garde â vous!_" cried the officer--"_Par files ae quatre!--Pas gymnastique!--En avant!_--"

Before he could give the order, "_Marche!_" a great voice boomed forth from above our heads, as though from Heaven.

On a little balcony at the top of a needle-like minaret, appeared the _muezzin_, and, on a clarion note, fairly trumpeted forth the words:

"_Kill! Kill!--In the name of Allah!--Gazi Gazi!--There is no god but God and Mahomet is His Prophet!--Slay! Slay!--Charge together, in the Name of Allah!--Burn!--Destroy!--Kill!--_"

The mob rallied and from every street, alley, courtyard and doorway poured forth again in hundreds.

"_Charge!_" boomed forth again the great voice of the mullah.

Bang! went a rifle and, as I glanced from the figure of the Iman toward the sound, I saw the Sergeant lower his rifle.

"_Marche!_" continued the officer, even as the body of the _muezzin_ struck the parapet of his eyrie, reeled over it and crashed into the courtyard below.

A terrific yell went up from the vast crowd, and many rushed to the spot, while others turned to pursue the Zouaves, now retreating at the double.

In front of the following crowd, a recumbent figure sprang to its feet, and with extended hand and every appearance of tremendous excitement, pointed away to the opposite corner of the square.

"Beware! Beware!" he shouted. "A trap! A trap--Danger!--Big guns! Cannon! _Boom! Boom!_--Run! Run!"

Bewildered and excited eyes turned in the direction to which de Redon pointed.

"Follow me!" he shouted, and ran toward the nearest street.

I sprang up and dashed after him, waving my sword and yelling, "_La illah ill allah ill Allah!_"

It seemed to me as good a noise as any, and quite fashionable at the moment--in fact, literally _le dernier cri_.

As always happens when a mob is given a lead, a large number followed, and, though de Redon's heroic effort did not prevent pursuit of the soldiers, it delayed it, as our section of the crowd streamed across the front of those who were dashing forward to avenge the death of the holy man who, with his last breath, had incited them to rapine and slaughter.

Keeping as near de Redon as I could, I galloped along behind him, waving my sword and emitting appropriate noises.

Into a side alley dashed de Redon still yelling:

"Big guns! Cannon! Machine-guns!--The French army! The French army--Fly! Fly!" and in a minute it was filled from end to end with the surging rushing river of our followers, each man running because everybody else did.

Out into another street we turned, and into yet another and another, and along them kept the uneven tenor of our way, until before us appeared a city gate, leading out into the desert.

Toward this we streamed, some of us yelling, "_Kill!_" others, "_Fly!_"--others, "_Franzawi! Franzawi!_"--some in search of secular salvation, others the salvation of their souls and life-everlasting, through the slaughter of the Infidel.

Through the gate thundered the yelling mob and, as the inevitable moment approached when those who run begin to ask, "What precisely are we running for?" de Redon began to slacken his pace, drop back into the crowd, and to edge toward the side.

Snatching at my wrist as he did so, he turned about, dropped into a walk, and, a moment later, limped lamely and blindly into a yard-wide opening between two high native houses.

Excited and hurried out of my normal poise and dignified deportment of a perfect little gentleman, I was moved, for no particular reason, to smite him with the flat of my sword where the seat of his trousers should have been, and to hound him along with such opprobrious epithets as I had learned.

"Quicker! Quicker! Misbegotten son of a dog!" I howled; and belaboured the poor half-blind tottering creature in the best Oriental manner.

We rounded a corner, and de Redon laughing heartily, straightened up.

"Splendid!" he said. "But I'll borrow the sword and drive _you_, next time--Splendid!" he gasped--

"Now we'll cut in ahead of Bouchard and his Zouaves and try to get you into the Residency with them--Come on--" and he started running again.

We turned a corner and ran into a gang of looters.

Some were yelling, wrangling, squabbling, in front of a house, while others appeared to be literally turning the house inside out.

As a bed, fittings and occupant complete, came flying over a balcony, de Redon executed a number of those dance-steps which had already won my admiration, while defying emulation so far as I was concerned.

Scarcely slackening his pace, he spun round and round like a top, whooping fiendishly. This interested the looters not at all, and we passed on unmolested--my immediate wonder being whether the occupant of the deciduous bed were an invalid, and my immediate decision being that at any rate he soon would be--

Turning again and dashing through a narrow stinking close, we heard a dreadful scream, that pierced the more distant din of the shouting and fighting.

In a dark and deeply-recessed porch, the back of which was an open door, a man stood with one foot on the breast of a child--a little girl, whose skinny arm he appeared to be turning and twisting from her body in his effort to secure the wide thick armlet of silver, which was apparently too small to pass the elbow.

I have to testify that de Redon was into that doorway before I was.

Turning with a fierce snarl the brute snatched a great knife from his sash, as de Redon, unable to swing his staff up, used it like a spear. The end of the staff went home with a pleasant thud, and drove the man sprawling back against the wall.

Raising the knife, he sprang at de Redon, seizing the staff in his left hand as he did so; and I simultaneously swiped the brute with my heavy sword.

It was the first time in my life that I had struck a man in anger, and I did it unskilfully--so unskilfully that, though he had every cause for complaint, he had no opportunity. The sword was so sharp and heavy, and wrath and indignation had so nerved my arm, that I had split his skull and killed him dead as a door-nail.

" *Mon Dieu!* " observed de Redon, as the man went down, taking the sword with him. "Don't you hit me with that sword any more."

Picking up the sobbing child, I lifted her inside the heavy door, and shut her in the house.

"Papa and the men-servants all gone to the fair, I suppose," observed de Redon, as we ran on down the alley--

This same alley became a tunnel which led into a small square. As we came out into this, the noise became terrific, and, looking down a narrow bazaar which joined it to a main street, we saw that this latter was packed with a dense crowd of armed men all streaming along past the end of it.

"Bouchard will never do it," said de Redon, slowing up. "He should have stayed where he was posted--Perhaps they burnt him out, though--

"Look here," he continued, "if you turn to the right at the end of this bazaar, I expect you'll know where you are. It leads straight to the Residency--Suppose you try to get in, and let Levasseur know what's happening--Tell him Bouchard is fighting his way from the market-square to the Residency, and that I say he'll need help. Then Levasseur can use his own discretion as to whether to make a sortie--I'll go along with the crowd and try the 'French-Army-with-cannon-behind-you' game again--Good luck, *mon ami*--If anyone interferes with you, give him one like you gave our late friend in the doorway--Good-bye--"

And those were the last words spoken to me by Captain Raoul d'Auray de Redon of the French Secret Service.

"Good-bye, old chap, and good luck," I said, and, a minute later, we were into the crowd, de Redon attracting all the attention he could by whooping, twirling his staff, spinning round and round, and howling like the demented dervish he was impersonating.

I, on the contrary, hugging the wall, made my way along in the opposite direction as unobtrusively as possible, and attracted no attention. It struck me as I dodged, elbowed, pushed and evaded the impulsive pedestrian traffic, that, in a way, a fugitive is a good deal safer in time of tremendous public uproar and disturbance than during profound peace, inasmuch as everybody is far too excited to be observant.

Anyhow, not a soul molested me as I went along muttering, gesticulating and foaming at the mouth. It is a curious fact that I did not taste the fragment of soap which I had placed beneath my tongue.

3.

In a few minutes, the throng thinned and slackened and I found that this crowd had detached itself from the outskirts of the vaster one that surrounded the Residency.

Here I made quicker progress, and eventually came, at a run, into a dense mob that filled the street and faced in the direction in which I was going.

Backward and forward they moved, as the front ranks advanced and retired, and into these front ranks I could only make my way by clinging tight to posts, throwing myself down against walls, or diving into doorways, whenever the mob was driven back.

At last I was where I wanted to be, and looked upon a stirring scene of battle, murder and sudden death.

A regular siege of the Residency was in progress, a siege enlivened by constant assault.

From every window, balcony, roof-top, wall, minaret, tower, doorway and street corner, a steady fusillade concentrated upon the building, while, every now and then, a great company of wild death-seeking fanatics rushed at the low wall that surrounded its compound, only to break and wither beneath the blast of the steady rifle-fire of the defenders, and to find the death they sought.

Crisp and timely, crash upon crash, came the volleys from the treble tier of fire of the troopers at the wall, the windows and the roof. Wave after wave swept forward and broke upon that steady rock, throwing up a white spray, as survivors of the ordeal-by-Ere sprang on the low wall, and the bayonets of the French soldiers.

And, the whole time, a ceaseless rain of bullets struck the house, so that it was in a nimbus of its own dust--a kind of halo of its own glory and suffering, as each bullet registered Sits impact with a puff of whitewash, dust and powdered brick--

How to get in there?--

From the surrounding wall, from every window and balcony, and from the parapet of the flat roof, the rifles of the defenders cracked unceasingly. It would be plain and simple suicide to advance openly, dressed as I was, and it would be suicide of a more unpleasant kind to strip off my Arab head-dress and burnous, and so proclaim myself a Christian.

Edging along the walls of houses, crawling on all fours, dashing from doorway to doorway and shelter to shelter, I gradually made my way from among those who played a comparatively safe and waiting rôle--onlookers who would turn to looting murderers as soon as the wall was cleared, and the doors beaten in--until I was among the fighting fanatics who made the frequent hand-to-hand attacks upon the low wall, the wall that must be captured before the house could be set on fire or taken by assault.

There was a hellish din from the hundreds of guns and rifles banging in all directions, and the continuous animal howling of the mob.

It would have been impossible in this inferno to hear what anybody said, and the wild rushes that broke upon the wall were the outcome of herd instinct and mob-intuition rather than of any definite organization, orders and leading.

Suddenly everybody would dash forward, the mouth of every street vomit hundreds and hundreds of men, and a great sword-waving mob would surge across the open, hack and hew and slash as it reached the wall, waver and fall back--and then turn and run for dear life to the lanes, alleys, buildings and compounds from which it came.

And, each time, the litter of dead and wounded increased and lay ever thicker along the wall. Soon the besiegers would be able to charge straight over the wall on a ramp of bodies--

From where I crouched in a deep gutter, my head and shoulders behind a stone post or mounting-block, I could see two sides of the Residency, and did not doubt that it was under heavy fire on its two garden sides.

As I watched and cast about in my mind for a plan, the strange psychology of mobs decreed another sudden simultaneous assault, and I found myself running and yelling with the best--or the worst--in a desperate charge upon the desperately defended wall.

Let it not be supposed that I displayed heroism or strove to find a hero's grave. Far from it. I displayed such prudence as was possible, to avoid getting into the front rank of the rush, and rather strove to keep a hero's body between me and the rifles as we ran. And when at last I reluctantly found myself bounding over the prostrate forms of those behind whom I had hitherto been sheltered, I promptly joined them in their biting of the dust, until a living wall of humanity was once more between me and the wall of stone.

Leaping to my feet again, I made another rush at the spot where the fighting-line was thickest and cast myself at the feet of the brave.

Of the feet of the brave I soon had more than sufficient, for they were planted heavily on 'every portion of my person, as the un-led unorganized hordes again retreated.

Left high and dry by this ebbing tide of horny-hoofed humanity, I found myself within a few feet of the wall, and one of hundreds of motionless, or writhing and twitching bodies.

Of the defenders of the wall I could see nothing save their gleaming bayonet-tips, the occasional képi of some-one who ran crouching along, and the heads of watchful sentries placed at intervals.

A moving cap halted, rose slowly upward and a man looked over the wall.

Now was my chance.

Raising myself on my hands, I shouted:

"_Hi! Monsieur! Je suis Americain!--Je suis un ami!--Aidez-moi!--Je viens--_"

And down I flopped with the utmost alacrity as the worthy man, with a swift neatness, theoretically quite admirable, drew and fired an automatic pistol.

Though he had drawn and fired practically in one movement, his aim was extraordinarily good, for the bullet hit the ground within an inch of my head.

I believe I gave an excellent rendering of the rôle of a dead Arab.

And I decided to play this easy part until there were again some braver men than I, between myself and that wall. Nor did I have long to wait.

With a howl that seemed to achieve the impossible by drowning all other sounds, the mob charged again, materializing with astonishing swiftness, and in astounding numbers.

A shout, a whistle, a sharp order--the wall was lined with heads and rifles--and I fairly burrowed into the filthy dust with my nose, as a volley crashed out--again--again--and I felt as though I should be blown away upon the blast--

With my hands protecting my head, I endured the rush and trample for a few seconds; and then, with a bound and the record sprint of my life, I flung myself at the base of the wall, as a rifle seemed to blow my head off, and a bayonet tore my filthy _kafieh_ just beside my neck.

As I fell and snuggled into the friendly base of that lovely wall, I thought I was blind and deaf and probably dumb, or "alternatively," as the lawyers say, quite completely dead.

Quickly, however, I decided that none of these things was so, as I could see filthy feet and brawny brown legs scuffling around me, and hear the sounds of combat, and shout a curse when a charging, bounding _ghazi_ landed fairly on my stomach, and, for a few minutes, that seemed like a few hours, I was kicked, trampled, trodden and struck until I was almost driven to spring up and take my chance at the wall--

And suddenly I was free, and the feet that had trampled me, were either once more in headlong flight, or else stilled in death.

Free also I was to make all the row I wished, in French, and to tear off my Arab head-dress and reveal myself to whomsoever would lend me his ears--

But I remembered the shoot-first-and-ask-afterward gentleman with the automatic, and restrained my inclination to poke my head over the wall.

Something had to go over the wall, however, so I lifted up my voice and started, more or less tunefully, to bawl in French, a version of a song which I had very often heard on the lips of Colonel Levasseur, and the tune of which I had often heard soldiers singing and whistling on the march. In point of fact, Major de Beaujolais had picked it out on the piano and sung it at Mary's request after dinner only last night--the Marching-Song of the Legion--

Tiens voilà du boudin! voilà du boudin! voilà du boudin! Pour les Alsaciens, les Suisses et les Lorraines; Pour les Belges il n'y en a point, Pour les Belges il n'y en a point, Car ce sont des tireurs au flanc. Pour les Belges il n'y en a point, Pour les Belges il n'y en a point, Car ce sont des tireurs au flanc.

I sang, or rather shouted, and I was heard.

A head suddenly appeared over the wall--Hell! It was my friend of the automatic, and most markedly I did not move.

"_Tiens!_" I cried. "_Voyez!_ and also _Regardez!_ and Ecoutez! and all that, _et ne tirez pas_. Don't shoot the singer, he's doing his best, and have you seen the pen of my aunt, _parceque je suis Americain et Anglais, et Français, et bon garçon et votre ami. Oui! Oui! Je vous aime, Monsieur le Sergent. Comment allez-vous ce matin, et Madame votre femme et tous les petits sergents?_--Kiss me Hardy,' said Nelson, and 'War is Hell' replied Sherman."

The man's head and shoulders came up over the wall, and, placing both hands upon it, he leant right over and stared at me, his mouth open and his eyes starting from his head.

"_Que le diable emportez-vous?_" the Zouave growled. "Who the devil are you and what the hell are you doing there?"

And with a watchful eye upon his empty right hand, I raised myself from the ground, swiftly gabbling that I was a friend and guest of Colonel Levasseur, that I brought most urgent and important information, and that he must either call the Colonel instantly, or let me come over the wall.

The wary man's right hand disappeared from sight, and I flopped back into the dust as it returned holding that beastly automatic.

Damn the thick-headed fool I had torn off my head-dress exposing my fair neck, ears and hair, and the mob would charge again at any minute.

"When I shout '_Come_,' jump over the wall and throw yourself on the ground," bawled the quick-witted clever man whom I had so miscalled. "And lie down quick on this side, or I'll blow your head off," he concluded and disappeared.

"_Come!_" he shouted a second later, and I fairly threw myself over the wall and at the feet of the Sergeant, while he and several of his officious braves covered me with their rifles.

"Colonel Levasseur will be round here in a minute. You stay like that till he comes," said the Zouave Sergeant, and, as he turned away, bade two of his men to shoot me if I moved, or if they felt like it.

I proceeded to play at Living Statuary and tried not to twitch a muscle even when flies endeavoured to explore my brain by way of my eyes, ears and nose.

Among the men who crouched lining the wall were many others who lay at full length upon the ground, dead or too badly wounded to make further effort. The garrison had suffered heavily, both from rifle-fire and from the constant hand-to-hand _mêlées_, when the swords of the Arabs had met the bayonets of the soldiers.

As I watched, a military surgeon, followed by four hospital-orderlies, or stretcher-bearers, came round the corner of the house, and, in spite of the continual heavy fire, had the severely wounded carried away, and the dead laid in a row where they would not cause the feet of the fighting-men to stumble. The less-severely wounded were bandaged where they sat with their backs to the wall.

"What's this?" asked the Surgeon-Major, whom I knew well, as he passed me. "An Arab prisoner. What do you want _prisoners_ for?"

"True," I answered, to his great astonishment, "especially when they are not only civilians but neutrals."

"_Mon Dieu!_" ejaculated the Major. "But you look a pretty bloody neutral and a fairly war-like civilian--" and he bent over the still form of a Zouave--

Colonel Levasseur came round the same corner, cool as on parade, followed by his _officier d'ordonnance_.

"'Evening, Colonel," I called, rising to my feet. "Excuse a certain disorder of dress--"

"Good God It *is* you, Vanbrugh!" he said, seizing my hand and leading me into the house. "_Where's your sister?_"

"De Beaujolais has taken her away with him," I replied, "and Captain de Redon says they have got clear of the town--And I am to tell you that a detachment of Zouaves, under Bouchard, is fighting its way here, and is held up in the Street of the Silversmiths--a huge mob between them and you--"

"And you fought your way in here to bring them relief?" cried the good Colonel, and for one dreadful moment I thought he was going to embrace and kiss me. "You shall get the Cross of the Legion of Honour for that, my brave friend--You have offered your life for Frenchmen and for France--"

"Fought nothing, Colonel," I assured him. "Offered nothing--I snooped around in a great funk, pinched these rags from dead men's backs, and crawled in here on my tummy--But if you'll give me a rifle and a quiet corner, I can hit a running Arab at twenty yards, especially if he is running at *me*."

Levasseur smiled.

"Up on the roof then," he said, "and snipe their snipers. There are some swine with Lebel rifles on neighbouring high buildings, who are doing a lot of damage--Take care of yourself--Better put on a _képi_ and tunic before you go up--you look like the President of all the Dervishes and you might get a bayonet in you before you could explain--Excuse me, I must get Bouchard's lot in--Down the Street of the Silversmiths, you said?"

Outside the room which the Surgeon-Major had turned into an operating theatre, there was a pile of blood-stained clothing and accoutrements. From among these I took a _képi_, regimental jacket, pouch-belt and rifle, and made my way up through the well-known interior--so familiar and yet so utterly different--to the roof, the parapet of which was lined with sharp-shooters who kept up a continual independent fire at surrounding minarets, watch-towers, and roofs of higher houses, which overlooked and commanded this one.

"Hi! Who are you?" cried a bearded officer crouching against the wall opposite the little stone porch, built over the top of the steps that led to the roof.

I knew him by sight but couldn't remember his name.

"Colonel Levasseur's guest, Vanbrugh," I shouted. "He told me to come up here."

"Run across and lie down here," he called back, and I noticed that he drew his revolver as I did so.

"Excuse me," he said, "I didn't recognize you--I don't think that _Madame votre mère_ would do so, either--Now, if you can get the sportsman who is ensconced in the corner of that roof _there_, you'll have earned your corn for the day--He's shot four of my men already, in spite of the bad light--"

So, for a brief space, I was an unenlisted man, fighting for France and my own skin. It was extremely exciting and thrilling, and one was too busy to be nervous. Snapshooting by flickering firelight, mingled with bright moonlight, is very interesting.

The sniper and I 'fought our little duel out--I got quite fond of him--R.I.P--Perhaps my rifle was better than his, though I had no fault to find with the latter when it took my _képi_ from my head, nor when it spoilt the perfectly good collar of my unbuttoned jacket--The light was good enough for him, anyhow--

I was aware of the increasing sounds of approaching volley-firing. Evidently Bouchard's detachment were overcoming resistance and fighting their way in.

The officer in command of the roof was sending more and more men over to the side that commanded the square, so I went across to that side too, chiefly with the object of getting a good view of the show when the Zouaves burst into the open, and charged through.

Cautiously I peeped over the parapet.

Another assault was impending, and down the Street of the Silversmiths came the swiftest of those who were fleeing before the Zouaves.

At their head Was a figure that I recognized--an almost naked scarecrow that spun round occasionally as he ran, and twirled a great staff above his head.

I rushed to my officer and indicated de Redon to him, and then with a brief "Excuse me," cast military propriety to the winds, dashed across to the stairs, and down them in search of Levasseur--I could not run round to every officer, non-commissioned officer, and soldier in the building, and point out de Redon to him individually--but I had some sort of idea that Levasseur might sound the "Cease fire!" while de Redon did his work and then rushed off elsewhere--

I made a swift tour of the upper floor, of which each window and balcony was crowded with soldiers, behind whom lay the bodies of those who would fight no more.

I had expected to find the Colonel on the big wide verandah that ran the length of the front of the house, on either side of the vast roof of the colonnaded porch. This verandah had a low wall or parapet and, like the compound-wall below, was lined with soldiers.

Levasseur was not here, and, as I glanced below, I saw great masses of men gathering to surge across the square in a mighty overwhelming wave once more. I saw a mob come rushing down the Street of the Silversmiths, and de Redon--far ahead of them--bounding, leaping, twirling and yelling in front of the main attack opposite the front of the Residency.

"_Back! Back!_" he howled. "_Beware! Beware!--The big guns are coming--Run!--Run!_--"

I also ran, down the stairs that led to the entrance-hall, and out into the compound, where the soldiers--whose fire-control was admirable--crouched along the wall like statues with levelled rifles, awaiting the volley-signal.

As I rushed past the bearers of a pitiful blinded Zouave, and down the steps under the porch, I saw Colonel Levasseur, standing between his second-in-command and his aide-de-camp, pointing with raised arm, and, as I saw him, I received a tremendous blow that knocked me down. I thought someone had hit me, looked round, and got to my feet, feeling very queer--

What was it that I had been about to do?--Something very urgent and important--De Redon!

As I reeled forward, trying to shout, Levasseur's voice rang out with tremendous volume and authority--He was still pointing--He himself was ordering a volley!--I staggered towards him mouthing silently--

With a great crash, every rifle along that side of the compound was fired--The earth rose up and hit me or else I fell to the ground--

Another great shout from Levasseur--Another volley--

I tore myself from what seemed the powerful grip of Mother Earth, steadied myself, and saw de Redon doing exactly what I was doing, standing, swaying, tottering, his hands pressed to his breast--Why was he imitating me?--Why could I not shout to Levasseur?--

De Redon fell heavily, head foremost--So did L--Why was I imitating him?--A great faintness--A grim fierce face before my closing eyes--An Arab about to slay me?--No, a feathered head-dress--a face more powerful than that of any Arab--Thank you, Chief--Dogged does it--Grit--and grit--and iron guts--

I was on my feet again; breathing more easily too; pulling myself together again; coming round; blood running down my chest and arm--

I reached Levasseur's side somehow--and found I could not speak!

"_Vous êtes bien touché, mon pauvre ami_" he said, in his great rough kindly voice.

I could not make a sound in answer, and he turned from me and bawled another order. The aide-de-camp shouted something about going inside and finding the doctor.

I tried to pull my jacket off and he gave me a hand, thinking I was trying to get at my wound.

Dropping my _képi_ on the ground by the jacket, I made for the wall, wearing only an Arab garment like a long shirt, and very baggy Arab trousers--both garments filthy and covered in blood, mine and that of their late owner.

I managed to get over the low wall without being grabbed by one of the defenders, and a stumbling, tottering run brought me to where de Redon lay in his blood.

Stooping to give him a hand, I found that it would only be a hand, for my right arm had ceased to function. It merely swung numb and useless, as I bent down.

De Redon did not move. I seized him and began to drag him in the direction of the wall--His rotten rags tore away, and I fell--The pain, for which I had been subconsciously waiting, began then, and I think it stimulated me.

I got up again and turned de Redon over. I wanted to get a grip on something he was wearing. Lift him I could not, with only one arm and scarcely the strength to keep myself erect. It seemed beastly to pull him by the arm or leg or hair--He was most obviously dead--Horribly riddled--

None the less, I must get him--I would not go back without him, and, with a word of apology I seized his wrist and began to drag--

I was astonished to find myself alive.

Why was I not shot by one side--or both?

I concluded that the very few on either side who had time to notice me, took me for a friend. The French soldiers were not firing independently but were awaiting the order for the next volley, and they had seen me run out from the compound. The Arabs saw a blood-stained Arab, escaping presumably from the French; but they would begin to shoot at me as soon as they saw me dragging a body to the compound--Or would they think me mad?--Anyhow I was going on the return journey, making good time, and in another minute I should be at the wall--

Was it _possible_ that not three minutes ago I had been up on the roof exchanging pot-shots in a friendly and sporting spirit with a very competent sniper?--

A few more yards and--

There was a sudden deafening crescendo of the infernal d in, a hellish roar from ten thousand throats--a crashing volley--another--and I was hurled headlong, trampled flat, smashed and ground and crushed, a living agony--until a smashing blow upon the head was a crowning mercy that brought oblivion.

4.

I must have been unconscious for a very long time--or, what is more probable, I must have been unconscious and semi-conscious, off and on, for hours--as I have a recollection of terrible battle-dreams, of receiving further injuries, and of being partly buried beneath a heavy weight.

When I awoke, or regained full consciousness, the sun was setting and the battle was over--Gradually I realized that I must have been where I was, for nearly a day--Absolute silence reigned where the very spirit of devilish din had so long rioted--I was lying where I had fallen--The body of a big Arab lay across my legs--The head of another was on my stomach, face downwards--More were sprawled and huddled close against me. All very intimate and cosy together.

With great effort and greater pain, I slowly turned my head in the direction of the Residency, and beheld its charred and blackened ruins affronting the rising sun. The compound wall appeared to be hidden by the piles of dead.

I hoped that the garrison had died in the compound and not in the burning building I thought of the wounded laid out in rows in the corridor outside the operating-room.

My next effort was in the direction of self-help, and was fruitless. What I earnestly desired to do was to remove the head of the dead Arab from the pit of my stomach, where it seemed to have the weight and size of a mile-stone.

I soon discovered that it would be all I could do to remove a fly from the end of my nose, and that by the time I did it the fly would be gone. I don't suppose I could have moved if those two bodies had not been lying upon me. I had lost a great deal of blood, from two bullet wounds in the neck and shoulder, and a bad sword-cut on the head--

It is a truth as well as a truism that we don't know our blessings when we receive them. In fact it is impossible to tell a blessing from a curse. But for those wounds, I should have got back into the Residency and died with the rest. When that enthusiast with the sword did his good deed for the day, he saved my life (and a life worth a thousand of mine, as well) and I never even saw his bright countenance.

That night was just endurable, but to this hour I do not greatly care to dwell upon the day that followed. How much was delirium, nightmare-dream, subjective horror, and how much was real, I do not know. But there were unutterable agonies of thirst and terrible pain, and the unbearable burning of the sun upon one's exposed unmoving flesh; there were vultures, kites and pariah dogs; prowling ghouls who robbed the pitiful dead; times when I gained full control of my faculties and lost them again in paroxysms of screaming terror, pain and fear--silent screams that did not issue from cracked black lips.

And always there were flies in thousands of millions.

At times I was mad and delirious; at times I must have been mercifully unconscious; and at times I was quite clear-headed, and perhaps those were the worst.

I distinctly remember concluding that my father was right and that I was wrong. There was a Great Good God of Love and Mercy who let us be born filled with Original Sin and who had created an Eternal Hell for all that sinned. I had sinned--and here I was, nailed down and being slowly roasted, in unspeakable pain, for ever and for ever. Yes, Father was right, and Noel and I had been wrong in agreeing that such would not be the nature of a God of Love, but rather of a Devil of Hate.

I believe that I slept when kind beneficent Night succeeded hellish torturing Day. At any rate, I was unconscious for most of the time, and remember nothing but occasional glimpses of the stars, and then, with shrinking abject terror, seeing the sun rise.

That was the last of conscious suffering, for I remember no more, and I afterwards learned that I had a very narrow escape of being buried alive when the French relief-force arrived and began clearing up the mess.

It was my white skin that saved me. The men of the burial-fatigue party who were removing my body with those of hundreds of others, noticed that I was some kind of a European, and drew the attention of their Sergeant to the fact. This man informed an officer, and the officer discovered that I was alive as well as white--in parts.

In the military hospital I was most kindly and competently nursed, and, when fit to be moved, I was transferred to Algiers that I might have the benefit of sea-breezes, ice, fresh fruit, better food, and the creature comforts unprocurable in the desert city of Zaguig.

And here I told my tale to the authorities, or rather to the very charming representative of the authorities who visited me in hospital.

Having given all the information that I could, concerning the fate of the garrison of Zaguig, I sought for news of de Beaujolais, but I forbore to mention that my sister was with him--He had seemed so very averse from taking her, and had made the military impropriety of such a thing so clear, that I thought it best to say nothing on the subject--particularly when I found that they knew absolutely nothing as to his fate, and did not expect to do so for weeks or months. My informant professed absolute ignorance of de Beaujolais' destination even.

I decided that, whether the doctors released me from hospital or not, I would remain in Algiers until there was definite news of de Beaujolais. I would then fit out a caravan and go in search of him and of my sister--

After a certain point, I did not progress very favourably. My wounds healed well, but I suffered most appalling headaches--whether from the sword-cut or from sunstroke did not seem clear. At times I thought a splinter of bone must be pressing on my brain, but the admirable surgeon assured me that the bone was not splintered at all, and that the headaches would grow less frequent and less painful.

They did neither, and I decided that I would go to London and see Sir Herbert Menken, then considered the greatest consulting-surgeon in the world.

And while I was slowly gathering energy and still putting of the evil day of travel, Mary arrived, well, smiling, radiantly happy, and engaged to marry Major de Beaujolais.

She had accompanied him to his destination and returned with him to Zaguig, fearing the worst so far as I was concerned. Here they had heard of my escape, and a black cloud had been lifted from Mary's mind--for the joy and happiness of her engagement to the man whom she had "loved at first sight" had been darkened and damaged by her fear--fear amounting almost to a certainty--of my death.

However, she had hoped against hope, and had moreover been conscious of an illogical but persistent belief that I was not dead.

She assured me that one corner of her mind had not been in the least surprised when they got the astounding news that I had survived and was, in fact, the sole survivor of the massacre--

Mary and I took up our temporary abode at the Hotel Splendide at Mustapha Supérieur, and she nursed me while de Beaujolais reported himself and his doings to the military authorities, and obtained furlough for his marriage and honeymoon.

I went with them to Paris after the wedding, where de Beaujolais shopped assiduously with Mary and showed himself not only brave but _foulard_-y, and thence, alone and very lonely, ill and miserable, I went on to London in the desperate hope that Sir Herbert Menken could do something to relieve my almost unbearable headache, insomnia, neurasthenia and general feeling of hopeless illness.

I was quickly coming to the point where either something must be done to me, or I must do something to myself--something quite final, with a pistol.

CHAPTER VI

How shall hasty and impatient Man know his blessings from his curses, his good from his evil?

Good came upon me at this time in most terrible form, and in my ignorance I prayed to be delivered from my good, from the blessing that brought me my life's usefulness and joy--

I arose on this particular morning, in London, feeling ill and apprehensive, afraid of I knew not what, but none the less afraid. I was in the grip of Hell's chief devil--Fearthe fear of something wholly unspecified.

Having dressed, with trembling fingers, I avoided the hotel dining-room and, as early as was reasonable, I set forth, bathed in perspiration, to keep my appointment with Sir Herbert Menken.

"Taxi, sir?" inquired the Jovian hall-porter, as I passed the counter behind which he lurked, all-seeing and omniscient--and it was borne in upon me that his query was absurd. *of course* I could not enter a taxi! What a horrible idea!--I would as soon have cut my throat as get into a taxi--or any other vehicle.

"Good Heavens, no!" I replied shuddering, and passed out into the street, much perturbed at the man's horrible suggestion.

Dreading and hating the throng, the noise, the traffic, I made my way along the street, feeling as I had never felt before, and as I pray God I may never feel again.

I would have given anything to have been back in Zaguig with all its murderous dangers, provided I could have felt as I did there.

I was not in pain--I did not feel definitely ill in any definite part of my body--I was not afraid of anything to which I could give a name--And yet I felt terrible. Every nerve in my body shrieked to God for mercy, and I knew that unless I did _something_ (but what, in the name of Pity?) and did it quickly, I should go mad or fling myself under a street-car or truck--

I fought my way on--

Merciful Christ have pity! This was suffering such as the Zaguigans could never have caused me with knives or red-hot irons--Where was I?--*what* was I?--

Suddenly I knew what I was--

Of course! I was a shell-fish deprived of its shell, and wholly at the mercy of its environing universe. Yes, I was a creature of the crustacean kind, a sort of crab o r lobster, without its armour. Every wave of ether could strike me a cruel blow; the least thing touching me would cause me agony unspeakable--even rays of light impinging upon my exposed nerve-surfaces would be,--nay, _were_ --as barbed arrows, spears and javelins--

If a passer-by brushed against me, I should shriek--a flayed man rubbed with sand-paper--Yes--I was a naked crustacean, and I must find a hole into which to creep--A nice hole beneath a great rock; a hole just big enough to contain, without touching, me--There I should be saved from the eyes and hands, the mouths and antennae of the million-headed--

But I could see no hole into which to creep--

I took a grip upon my courage, and passed on, in search of one--a beautiful dark cave, just big enough--

I reached the end of the block and was about to step off the side-walk when I realized my new danger. If I stepped into the road, the flood of traffic that streamed along it would bear me away irresistibly; away, on and on, into some wild and whirling Charybdis, wherein I should for ever go round and round with accelerating velocity for all eternity, never, never to find the beautiful dark cave that was my great necessity--

I had had a narrow escape from a terrible danger, and I drew back from the gutter, and crouched against some railings. These seemed friendly. At any rate, they did not hurry along, nor whirl round. I clung to them, conscious of the stares of the curious as they hurried past, immersed in their own affairs, but with a glance to spare for mine.

Two errand-boys passed, one in a many-buttoned uniform.

"Blimey! _'E's_ 'ad a 'appy evenin' somewheres," observed one of them. "'E sang '_Won't be 'ome till mornin_'--and 'e ain't."

"Yus," agreed the other, eyeing me with a large toleration, "some people 'as all the luck."

I tried to give them money, to get them to go away and cease to look at me, but my hand so shook that I could not get at my pocket.

I turned my face to the railings and, peering through them, saw that they guarded an "area" or small paved yard on to which looked the basement-windows of the house. And into this yard, some twenty feet below me, opened the door of a coal-cellar, or some such place--a dark, quiet, beautiful cave into which one could crawl and be safe from mocking eyes and jeering voices, from touching hands and feeling antennae, from _everything_ that could, by the slightest contact, agonize one's utterly exposed and unprotected surfaces.

If only I could get to that dark beautiful cave!--But if I loosened my grip of the railings I might fall, or be carried along until I was thrust into the dark river of the roadway and whirled to destruction never-ending.

I moved along the railings, not releasing one hand-grip until I had secured the next, and the perspiration streamed down me as I concentrated every faculty upon this difficult progress to the gate that I could see at the head of a flight of stone steps, leading down to my cave of safety--

And then a Voice smote me, and I looked over my shoulder, my heart in my mouth.

"What's the game, Sir?" said the Voice.

It was a vast and splendid London policeman, one of those strong quiet men, wise, calm, unarmed, dressed in a long authority, the very embodiment of law, order and security, the wonder and admiration of Europe.

Terrible as it was to be addressed and scrutinized, I felt I could bear the agony of it, because these men are universal friends and helpers to all but evil-doers.

"I am an unshelled crustacean--I want to get down to that cave," I said, pointing.

"Crushed *What?* --Want to get home, you mean, I think, Sir," was the reply. "Where's that?"

"In America," I said.

"Longish way," observed the policeman. "Where did you sleep last night, if it isn't asking?"

"At my hotel," I replied.

"Ah--that's better, Sir," said the good fellow. "Which one?--We might get back there perhaps, eh?"

"No, no--I couldn't--I simply could _not_," I assured him. "I would sooner die--I _should_ die--a dreadful death--"

"_Pass along, please!_" said the policeman suddenly and sharply, to the small crowd that had collected. "'Ere, you--_'op_ it--quick," he added to a blue-nosed loafer, who stood gazing bovine and unobedient--

I can remember every word and incident of that truly terrible time, for myself stood apart and watched the suffering wretch that was me, and could give no help, could do nothing but look on--and suffer unutterably.

"Now then, Sir," said the policeman, "if you can't go 'ome, an' you won't go to your 'otel, where _can_ you go?--We all got to go somewheres, y' know--

"You don't want to come along o' me, do yer?" he added as I pondered his dark saying that we must all go somewhere, shook my head in despair, and clung to the railings.

"With _you?_ Where to?" I asked, with a new hope.

"Station," he replied. "Sit down in a nice quiet little--er--room--while we find out something about yer."

"I should love it," I told him. "Could you put me in a cell and lock the door?"

"You'd have to *do* somethink first," the kindly man assured me.

This seemed a splendid chance! Fancy being concealed in a beautiful dark cell until my shell grew again and there was something between my exposed nerves, my bare raw flesh, my ultimate innermost self, and the rough-shod rasping world!

"If I gave you a sovereign and thumped you on the chest, would you arrest me for assault and lock me up?" I asked. "Do--for Mercy's sake--I'll give you anything you like--all I have."

"_Come_, come now, sir," expostulated the officer, "you let me put you in a taxi, and you go back to your 'otel an' go to bed an' 'ave a good sleep--If you don't feel better then, you tell 'em to send for a doctor--

"You a teetotaller?" he added, as I stared hopelessly at his impassive face.

"Practically," I said. "Not in theory, you know, but--"

"Any'ow you ain't drunk _now_," he admitted, sniffing, and added briskly, "Come along, now, sir! This ain't no way for a gent to be'ave at ten o'clock of a Monday morning," and, turning to the lingering passers-by, suddenly boomed, " will you pass along, please," in a manner that swiftly relieved me of the painful stare of many gazing eyes.

One man did not pass along, however, nor go by on the other side--No Levite, he--

He was a small neat man, very well dressed in a quiet way.

"You are like a moth," I said. "For God's sake spread your wings over me--My shell has come off--"

Of course he was like a moth. He had great black eyebrows and deep luminous eyes--sphinx-like, he was--the sphinx-moth--

I had seen moths with just such eyebrows, and eyes shining in the lamp-light--

"Ill?" he asked, and took my wrist between finger and thumb. "What's your name and address?"

"I don't know," I replied. "Do help me--I'm in Hell--body and soul--and I shall shriek in a minute--For the love of God help me to find a cave or a hole--"

"Come along with me," he said promptly, "I've got a beauty--"

He stared hard into my eyes, and in his I saw goodness and friendship, and I believed and trusted him implicitly--

I had fallen into the hands of the greatest alienist and nerve-specialist in England--Coincidence?

Tucking his arm through mine, he detached me from the railings, led me to the house, close by, in Harley Street, where he had his consulting-rooms, gave me a draught of the veritable Waters of Lethe, and put me to bed on a sofa in a back room.

Without troubling to discover whether I was a pauper, a criminal, an escaped lunatic, or a prince in disguise, he took me that night to his far-famed nursing-home in Kent.

And here, my salvation, in guise incredible, most wonderfully awaited me.

2.

At Shillingford House, a great old mansion of warm red Tudor brick, Dr. Hanley-Blythe kept me in bed for a week or so, visiting me upon alternate days and submitting me to an extraordinarily searching cross-examination, many of the questions of which, I was at first inclined to resent. I soon realized, however, that there was absolutely nothing in the specialist's mind but the promotion of my welfare, and I answered every question truthfully and to the best of my ability.

One day, after carefully and patiently extracting from me every detail of a ghastly dream that I had had the previous night--a dream in which I dreamt that I murdered my father--he asked:

"Did you love your father when you were a boy?"

"Yes," I replied.

"Certain?" he queried.

"Er--yes--I think so--" I said.

"*I* don't. In fact I know you didn't," he countered.

I thought a while, and realized that the doctor was right. Of course I had never loved my father. I had respected, feared, obeyed and _hated_ him--He had been the Terror that walked by day and the Fear that stalked me by night--

"Face the facts, my dear chap," said the doctor. "What is, is--and your salvation depends on freeing your mind from repressions, and making a new adjustment to life--The truth will make you free--and whole--Get it up, and get it out--"

I pondered deeply and delved into the past.

"I am sorry to say that I have always hated my father," I confessed. "Feared and hated him terribly--"

"Yes--and you made your God in your father's image," said the doctor--

"I have 'feared God' but not hated Him," I replied.

"Nonsense!" exploded Dr. Hanley-Blythe. "Don't we hate _everything_ and everyone that we fear?--Fear is a curse, a disease, a deadly microbe--the seed of death and damnation--Since we are speaking of God--get rid of that foul idea of 'fear God.'--

"*love* God--What decent God would rather be feared than loved?--Let's have a God that is a _little_ more divine than a damned savage Ju-Ju!--That cursed injunction to _fear_ God!--Killed more souls and bodies than anything else--Love God and fear nothing I--Some sense in that--

"Now look here--get your father in perspective. He's a poor human sinner like yourself and me. A man of like passions with us--Probably always meant for the best--and did his best--by you--Nothing to _fear_--a frail sinner like the rest of us--No power over you now, anyhow--

"When you go to sleep to-night, say out loud:

"'Poor old Dad! I feared and hated you--but now I do neither--I never understood you--but I do now.' Then say, also out loud, 'God means Good, and Good means God--God is Love and Love is God.'--See?"

And another time.

"You are a bachelor?--Well, you shouldn't be--No healthy man has a right to be a bachelor at your age--And you have always lived the celibate life in absolute chastity?--Hm! We shall have to find you a wife, my boy!--I prescribe sunshine and fresh air, occupation and plenty of it, a trip to see your father--whom you will smite on the back and address as 'Dear old Dad--you heavy-father old fraud'--_and a wife_--Yes, a wife, _and_, in due course, about three sons and two daughters--

"What do I think caused your breakdown?--I don't 'think'--I _know_--Your father, of whom you had too much, and your wife whom you never had at all--.Caused a neurosis, and when you got physically knocked out at Zaguig, it sprang up and choked you--And now get up and dress and go out in the grounds and sit in the sun and realize what a harmless old chap your father is, and what a kind friendly fatherly jolly old God made the beautiful jolly old world that we muck-up so much--And think over all the girls you know, and decide which one you will ask to marry you--_Marriage will be your sure salvation_--I prescribe it--"

A couple of nurses--kind devoted souls--helped me into an invalid chair and wheeled me out into the grounds. They found me a beautiful hidden spot among great rhododendron bushes where I should be safely concealed, protected from the rear and on either hand, and have a glorious view of the rolling Kentish park-land before me. They assured me that the path by which we had come was very rarely used, and left me in my wheeled chair to wonder whether I should ever be a man again--

"--Think over all the nice girls you know, and decide which one you will ask to marry you--_Marriage will be your sure salvation_."

There was only one woman in all the world, and she was already married-

I hope no-one in this world suffers as I suffered in mind and body during those days.

3.

I believe that there really are people to whom "experiences" of the psychic and super-normal order are vouchsafed.

I have both read and heard of well-attested cases of dreams and appearances, inexplicable voices, and waking visions whereby information was imparted, or help sought.

Nothing of that sort has ever occurred to me.

I have not, on looking into my mirror at night, beheld the agonized and beseeching face of the woman who needed my help beyond all things, the woman whom I was to love and to marry.

I have not dreamed dreams and seen visions in which such a woman has implored my instant aid and told me exactly what to do, and how, and when and where to do it.

I have not heard a mysterious voice, clear and solemn as a bell, speak in my astounded ear and say, "Come. I need you. Hasten quickly to such-and-such a place and you will find-_"

I have seen no ghost nor apparition that has given me a message.

Nothing of the sort.

But the following fact is interesting.

I sat in my retreat, one day, thinking of Isobel, wondering where she was and what she was doing, whether she were happy every minute of the day, and whether it would be my fate ever to see her again--Long, long thoughts between waking and sleeping--And then with shaking hand and fumbling trembling fingers I opened a book that one of the nurses had left with me, "in case I felt like reading for a little while."

And, opening at random in the middle of the book, I read:

"--his vision of her was to be his Faith and Hope and was to be all his future. She was to be his life and his life was to be hers--For he was a Worshipper, a Worshipper of Beauty, as were they who lived 'or ever the knightly years had gone with the old world to the grave,'--they to whom the Face was not the face upon a coin, the pale and common drudge 'twixt man and man, but the face of a beautiful woman, the Supreme Reality, the Focus of Desire--that desire which is not of the body, not of the earth, not of the Self, but pure and noble Love--God's manifestation to the world that something of God is in man and something of man is in God--This knight thus worshipped God through the woman, with a love that was spiritual of the spirit, with no taint of Self--And his motto and desire was Service--Her service without reward; the service that is its own reward--For he felt that there must come for the World's salvation from materialism and soul's death, a Renaissance, a Reformation--of Love--

"Love that was once the road to all perfection; man's cry to God, to Beauty, to the Beauty of God and the God of Beauty--Love that once leapt free from flesh and cried aloud, not, 'Love me that I may be blessed and comforted and rendered happy,' but 'Let me serve thee with my love, that I may help and bless and comfort thee and render thee happy--' Love that was Service, the highest service of God through the service of His noblest expression--Woman--Love, that divine selfless thing, Man's great and true salvation, the World's one need, the World's last hope--

"He would dedicate his life to the service of this woman, asking of her nothing more than that he might dedicate his life to her service in the name of Selfless Love, the Love that is its own reward, its exceeding rich reward--"

And at the sound of a footstep, I here looked up--and beheld Isobel.

4.

Isobel, actual and alive--looking older and looking ill and pale and too ethereal, and lovelier if possible.

Our eyes met--For a second we stared incredulous.

"*Isobel!*" I cried, still dreaming.

"The dear nice American boy!" she whispered.

Tears came into her beautiful eyes, her sweet and lovely face grew yet paler, and she swayed as though about to faint.

With a strength that I certainly had not possessed a minute before, I sprang to my feet, caught her in my arms and lifted her into the chair. Her need and weakness gave me strength, and I was ashamed--ashamed that I had sat trembling and shaking there--envying any healthy hobo that tramped the road--longing for death and thinking upon ways of finding it--

Isobel!--Here!

She must be a patient of Dr. Hanley-Blythe--ill--.in great sorrow, judging by the look upon her lovely face--

I was shamefully conscious of noting that, by her dress, she was not a widow--And then I rose above my lowest, and strove to put myself aside entirely--*Isobel* was here--and ill--Surely I could serve her in some way, if only by wheeling her about in a bath-chair--.reading to her--

"I can't believe it--I must be dreaming--" she said as these thoughts flashed through my mind.

"Oh, dear American boy--will you help me--I am in such trouble--"

Help her I Would I _help_ her!

My illness fell from me, and I stood erect, and strong--I who had recently been assisted to crawl to that invalid's chair, a wretched trembling neurotic--

"John--my husband--They have taken him--Oh!" Her eyes brimmed over and her trembling lips refused their service--She covered her face and gave way to tears--

Her husband!--

I knelt beside the chair--By the time my knee had touched the grass, I had crushed back the thoughts, "Her husband--' They' have taken him--Dead by now, probably--_'Think of all the girls you know. Marriage will be your sure salvation.'_--"--and I was unselfish and pure in heart--purified by the clear flame that burnt within me, before this woman's altar that was my heart.

"Tell me," I said. "And then believe! Believe with all your soul that I can help you somehow--Be sure of it--Know it--Why--surely I was created for that purpose--"

I was a little unbalanced, a little beside myself, and more than a little inspired--

And I inspired Isobel--with hope--And with faith and with belief--belief in me, her servant.

Under the influence of my assurance and re-assurance, she told me her pitiful tale from beginning to end--

I sat on the ground beside her chair, and she forgot herself and me as she poured out her woe and trouble--poured them out until she was empty of them, and their place was filled by the hope which I gave her, the faith that I had--for the time, even the certainty that I felt.

When she had finished, I took her little hand in both mine, and looked into her eyes.

"I *know* he is alive," I said. "I am as certain of it as I am that we are here together. He is alive and I will find him. I will not only find him but I will rescue him and bring him back. *Alive and well, I will bring him back to you--*"

And at that moment I believed what I said. There is no such thing as "chance;" and God had not brought me to that place for nothing--nor to make a mock of us for His sport--

What Isobel told me on that golden English summer afternoon--as I sat beside her chair, in a short-seen Seventh Heaven of bitter happiness and sad joy, listening to her voice with its soft accompaniment of the murmuring of innumerable bees in immemorial elms--is indelibly written on the tablets of my memory, and I can tell it exactly as she told it to me.

CHAPTER VII

"I shall tell you absolutely everything--right from the beginning," whispered Isobel. "That is the least I can do--after what you have just offered--and promised--Everything, right from the beginning--What it was that caused them to disappear--and caused their deaths--Oh, those splendid boys--And John, my own darling, John--" and she wept anew.

"John is alive," I said. "And he's coming back to you--Believe me--Trust in me--"

"I do," she answered. "Oh, I do--You have given me new life--I always felt that you could and would do anything that you promised--I have always liked you so much--Otis--

"I'll tell you _everything_--You would hardly believe it--You remember Claudia, of course?--The loveliest girl--"

"Yes," I said. "'Queen Claudia of the Band.'--Michael loved her very much, I think--"

"Michael worshipped her," agreed Isobel. "He would have died for her--He did die for her--in a way--Poor wonderful noble Beau--It nearly broke John's heart. He came back so different--poor John. Michael and Digby both--Yes, John returned different in every way, except in his love for me--Oh, John!"

"Michael and Digby _dead?_" I exclaimed. "_Beau Geste_ dead?" This was horrible. What had happened?

"Yes, and Claudia is dead too," replied Isobel. "She was Lady Frunkse. I expect you read that she married Sir Otto Frunkse, 'the richest man in England.'--A motor-smash--You must have seen it in the papers?--She lived--or rather died--for three days--Poor Claudia--she was blinded and terribly disfigured by broken glass, and her back was broken--Her husband went out of his mind for some time. He loved her passionately--and he had bought her--and he was driving the car--and was not quite sober--

"She asked for me on the last day. I was in the room at the time--She knew she was dying--Her mind was absolutely clear, and she did not want to die until she had made a confession--She asked me to tell everybody--after her death. You are the only person I have told--I want you to know everything that concerns John--It was very dreadful--Only her mouth was exposed--In that vast golden room and colossal Chinese bed, poor lovely Claudia was merely a mouth. I knelt beside her and held her poor groping hand and she whispered on and on--and on--

"I'll try to tell you.

"'Is that you, Isobel?' she said. 'There is no-one else here, is there?--Listen--Tell this to my Mother--Aunt Patricia is my Mother--and to John and Otto and George Lawrence, everybody--after I am dead--I cannot tell my Mother myself--Digby knows, now--And poor little Augustus--My Father knows too. I think he knew at the time. The mad know things that the sane do not--Poor darling "Chaplain,"--we all loved him, didn't we, Isobel?'

"'Didn't you love Beau too, Isobel? Really love him, I mean--I worshipped the ground he trod on--But I was only a girl--and bad--I was bad--Rotten. I loved money and myself. Yes, myself and money, more than I loved Beau or anything else--anyone else--

"'And Otto had caught me--Trapped me nicely--It served me right--How I loathed him, and feared him too--and I actually believed he would let me be disgraced--let me go to prison--if I did not either pay him or marry him!--It was more than two thousand pounds--It seemed like all the money in the world to me, a girl of eighteen--

"'And if I married him I should be saved--and I should be the richest woman in England--I thought it was a choice between that and prison--Otto made me think it. I couldn't doubt it after he had sent his tame solicitor to see me--The awful publicity and disgrace and shame--

"'But Michael saved me for a time--He saved me from everything and everyone--except from myself--He couldn't save me from myself--And when he was gone, and Otto was tempting me and pestering me again, I gave way and married him--or his money--

"'Isobel, it was I who stole the "Blue Water"--the mad fool and vile thief that I was--I thought I could sell it and pay what I owed Otto--and a dozen others--dressmakers and people; shops in London. I must have been mad--mac--with fear and worry--

"'Michael knew--before the lights came on again--'"

Isobel broke off here and wiped tears from her cheeks.

"I must tell you about that, Otis," she said. "You heard about the great sapphire, 'Blue Water,' when you were at Brandon Regis, I expect? It was kept in a casket in a safe that stood in the Priests' Hole--and the Priests' Hole is really undiscoverable. Its secret is never known to more than three people, though scores of people are taken to see the chamber. It is said that nobody has ever discovered the trick of it, in four hundred years.

"Aunt Patricia used to show the 'Blue Water' to favoured visitors, and sometimes she would have it out and let us handle it and gloat over it. It lived on a white velvet cushion under a thick glass dome in the steel casket.

"One night--it was not long before I last saw you--we were sitting in the drawing-room, after dinner, and Claudia asked Aunt Patricia if we might have it down and look at it again. We hadn't seen it for ages. The Chaplain--who was one of the three who knew the secret of the Priests' Hole--went and got it, and we all handled it and loved it. Then the Chaplain put it back on its cushion and put the glass cover over it--and suddenly the electric light failed, as it often used to do, in those days.

"When the lights came on again--the 'Blue Water' had disappeared--Everyone denied having touched it--and next day, Beau ran away from home--Then Digby disappeared--Then John--and I was the most miserable girl in England. He told me, quite unnecessarily, that he had not stolen the wretched thing, and of course we also knew that neither Beau nor Digby was capable of theft.

"They joined the French Foreign Legion--and--and--Michael was killed--and Digby was killed--but John came back safe and sound--but oh, so changed--and now--they have got him again," and the poor girl broke down and wept unrestrainedly.

"I'll bring him back," I said, keeping a powerful grip upon myself, lest I put my arms about her, in my yearning ache to comfort her. "I know I shall find him and bring him back--"

"Why--so do I," she smiled. "I believe it--I feel it's true--God bless you--I--I can't--I--"

My eyes tingled.

"I'll finish telling you about Claudia," she said--"Poor Claudia went on:

"'Yes, Michael knew--He came to my bedroom that night--I was in bed, wide awake, and in a dreadful state of mind--I felt awful--Filthy from head to foot--I was a thief, and I had robbed my Aunt, my greatest benefactress--I did not then know that she was my Mother--she only told me when the Chaplain died and she was broken-hearted and distraught--

"'Michael crept in like a ghost.

"'"CLAUDIA," he whispered, "GIVE ME THE _BLUE WATER._ I AM GOING TO PUT IT BACK. THE KEY IS IN THE BRASS BOX ABOVE THE FIREPLACE IN THE HALL AS AUNT SAID."

"'I pretended to be indignant--and talked like the hypocrite and liar that I am. I ordered him out of the room, and said I'd ring the bell and scream if he did not go at once.

"'"CLAUDIA," he said, "GIVE IT TO ME, DEAR--IT WAS ONLY A JOKE, OF COURSE--LET ME PUT IT BACK, CLAUDIA--NO-ONE WILL DREAM THAT IT WAS YOU WHO TOOK IT--"

"'"No-one but you, you horrible cad," I said. "How dare you--How could you--"

"'"DON'T, DEAR," he begged--"DON'T--I KNOW!--YOU BRUSHED CLOSE TO ME AS YOU MOVED TO THE TABLE AND AS YOU RETURNED TO WHERE YOU WERE STANDING--YOUR HAIR ALMOST TOUCHED MY FACE--DON'T I KNOW THE FRAGRANCE OF YOUR HAIR, CLAUDIA?--COULD I BE MISTAKEN--SHOULDN'T I KNOW YOU IF I WERE BLIND AND DEAF AND YOU CAME WITHIN A MILE OF ME?--HAVE I WORSHIPPED YOU ALL THESE YEARS, CLAUDIA, WITHOUT BEING ABLE TO READ YOUR THOUGHTS?--I KNEW IT WAS YOU, AND I WENT AND STOOD WITH MY HAND ON THE GLASS SO THAT IT WOULD LOOK AS THOUGH I WAS IN THE JOKE TOO, IF ISOBEL TURNED THE LIGHTS ON WHILE YOU WERE PUTTING IT BACK--GIVE IT TO ME QUICKLY, DEAR--AND THE JOKE IS FINISHED--OH, CLAUDIA DARLING, I DO LOVE YOU SO-AND I HAD NOT MEANT TO TELL YOU UNTIL YOU WERE OLDER--GIVE IT ME, DEAREST CLAUDIA--"

"'His voice came to me out of the darkness, like that--and I was racked, Isobel--I loved him, you see--And I loathed Otto, and I had to have two thousand pounds or marry him--or go to prison--I verily believed.

"'And I stood out against Michael, and lied, and lied, and lied, and pretended to be indignant--hurt--enraged--wounded--and I called him horrible names, and all we said was in dreadful tense whispers.'

"'"CLAUDIA! CLAUDIA!" he said. "YOU CAN'T POSSIBLY DO IT--I KNOW IT'S ONLY A JOKE-BUT DON'T PLAY IT ANY FURTHER--IF IT DOESN'T BRING HORRIBLE DISGRACE AND HURT UPON YOU, IT WILL BRING DISGRACE AND HURT UPON SOMEBODY ELSE-ISOBEL, DIGBY, JOHN, GUSSIE--AND EVEN IF YOU WENT MAD AND DID SUCH A THING, YOU COULDN'T GET AWAY WITH IT--NOBODY WOULD BUY IT FROM YOU--GIVE IT ME, DEAR. IT IS SUCH A DANGEROUS PRACTICAL JOKE TO PLAY ON A PERSON LIKE AUNT PATRICIA--"

"'And he begged and begged of me to give it to him--and the more certain he was that I had got it, the angrier I grew--Isn't it incredible--and isn't it exactly what a guilty person does?

"'At last he said:

"'"LOOK HERE, THEN, CLAUDIA. I AM GOING AWAY TO MY ROOM FOR AN HOUR--DURING THAT TIME THE 'BLUE WATER' IS GOING TO FIND ITS WAY BACK. SOMEONE IS GOING TO PUT IT IN THE DRAWING-ROOM BEFORE SAY ONE O'CLOCK-AND AUNT WILL FIND IT IN THE MORNING--AND NOBODY WILL EVER KNOW WHO PLAYED THE SILLY TRICK--I SHALL GO DOWN MYSELF, LATER ON, AND SEE THAT IT IS THERE--SPLENDID!--GOOD-NIGHT, DARLING CLAUDIA--" and he faded away like a ghost.

"'I lay awake and lived through the worst night of my life--I could not go down and put it back--tacitly confessing to Michael that I was a thief--I loved him so, and I valued his good opinion of me more than anything--except my beastly self--If he had come back then, I should have given the horrible stone to him--I should--And later I grew more and more angry with him for suspecting me--and I got up and looked my door and bolted it. At about four o'clock in the morning I weakened and grew afraid of what I had done--I saw myself arrested by policemen--Taken to prison--in the dock--tried and sentenced to penal servitude.

"'I added cowardice to wickedness, and at last, overcome by fear, I jumped out of bed, took the "Blue Water" from the toe of a riding-boot where I had hidden it, slipped on a dressing-gown and mules, and crept downstairs. Every board seemed to creak, and my heart was in my mouth. I dared not carry a candle nor switch on any lights.

"'Every stair and board, I trod on, creaked and groaned, and I felt that every soul in the house must know what I was doing--And suddenly I knew I was being followed, and I think that perhaps that was the most dreadful moment of my life.

"'"AUNT PATRICIA," I thought, and I nearly shrieked. I felt that if she turned on the lights and caught me there, with the "Blue Water" in my hand, I should scream myself insane--And then a cold hand touched me, and I did scream--or thought I did--before I realized it was the hand of a man in armour--

"'And then my one need was to get rid of that awful jewel. I rushed to the fireplace and fumbled at the high mantel for the brass box in which Aunt Patricia had put the key. I found it, and hurried on, to the drawing-room door. The noise that I made in opening it sounded like thunder, but by that time, all that I cared about was to be rid of the sapphire, and back in my room before I was caught. It didn't matter to me who was suspected of having taken it--

"'And as I reached the table on which the glass cover stood, someone entered the room.

"'Do you know, I believe my heart really stopped beating as I waited for Aunt Patricia to switch the lights on--

"'And then a voice said," OH, THANK GOD, DARLING--I KNEW YOU WOULD--"

"'It was Michael.

"'And in the sudden and utter revulsion of feeling, I could have cursed him--I had been so absolutely certain that it was Aunt Patricia, that I was utterly enraged at the fright he had given me--

"'And can you believe that I turned about and marched out of that room, to bed, without a word, still clutching the "Blue Water" in my hand?--Later he came and tapped softly and turned the handle. He stayed there for over an hour, tapping gently with his finger-nails and turning the handle--And I lay there trying not to scream--trying to yet up and give him the sapphire--trying not to get up and give him the sapphire--And as the time wore on, I got more and more frightened at what I had done--In the morning, I got up and went out into the rose-garden and he came to me there.

"'"LAST CHANCE, CLAUDIA DEAR," he said. "GIVE ME THE 'BLUE WATER' NOW, AND THERE SHAN'T BE A BREATH OF SUSPICION ON YOU--IF YOU DON'T, IT IS ABSOLUTELY CERTAIN THAT YOU'LL GET INTO THE GHASTLIEST TROUBLE. AUNT IS BOUND TO GET TO THE BOTTOM OF IT--HOW COULD SHE IGNORE SUCH A BUSINESS--EIGHT OF US THERE--I AND SUSPICION WILL BE ON POOR LITTLE GUS--AT FIRST--YOU CAN'T POSSIBLY SELL IT--GIVE IT TO ME AND I'LL GIVE YOU MY WORD NOBODY WILL EVER DREAM THAT YOU--"

"'I burst into tears--I had had such an awful night, and I was so filled with anger and fear and hatred--hatred of Michael and Otto and of all the men in the world--that I broke down--I nearly gave it to him--And after breakfast I did give it to him, too late, and I told him I loathed him utterly, and that I hoped that I should never set eyes on him again I--I never did, Isobel, as you know--And I have never had a happy hour since--'"

Isobel paused and wiped tears from her eyes. I would have left her but that I felt it was good for her to talk and get it all out.

"Poor, poor Claudia," she went on. "She died that night. Sir Otto Frunkse went insane for a time. I thought Aunt Patricia would die too. Claudia was all she had, after the Chaplain died and Michael was killed--She blamed herself for the boys' deaths--And now, John!--Oh, John!--John!"

"Why did she blame herself?" I asked. "Surely it was Claudia's--er--act, that led to Michael's and Digby's going away--?"

"I will tell you everything, as I said," replied Isobel. "It's wonderful to have a Father Confessor and friend--and you are going to find John for me--I know _you_ are--I feel as though I were coming out of a tomb--You have lifted the cover a little already--I shall tell you everything--

"Michael knew that Aunt Patricia had sold the real 'Blue Water'--sold it to the descendant of the Rajah from whom it had been--acquired--by her husband's ancestor, in India--She had a right to sell it, I believe, as her husband gave it to her as a wedding-present--This man, Sir Hector Brandon, used to leave her for years at a time. He was a very bad man--a bad husband and a bad landlord--I know that she put almost every penny of the money into the estate--She had had a model of the 'Blue Water' made before she parted with the original--Michael ran away with this model. He thought it would be a splendid way of covering up what Claudia had done, and of what Aunt Patricia had done, too--and Sir Hector was about to return to England--Poor darling Michael it was just what he _would_ do!--It must have seemed such a simple solution, to him, and the end of terrible and dangerous trouble for the two women he loved--It saved Claudia from shame and disgrace and from Aunt Patricia's anger, and it saved Aunt Patricia from her husband's--Sir Hector Brandon would simply think that Michael had stolen the 'Blue Water,' and Aunt Patricia would think that he had stolen the dummy--in ignorance of its worthlessness."

2.

This Beau Geste!--It was an honour and a boast to have known him! And those two women--that mother and her daughter!--My God!--

3.

"Uncle Hector never came home after all," continued Isobel. "Nor Beau either--Nor Digby--And now, _John_--my John!--Oh, Claudia, the trouble and misery and tragedy you caused that night!"

"Tell me about John," I said.

That would do her more good than anything--I had learnt from Dr. Hanley-Blythe, and from my own experience, what repression can do to one!

"When Michael ran away, taking the suspicion and the blame, and Digby followed him to share it, John felt that he must go too. You see the three boys had always done everything together, all their lives. And John felt that they were shielding him because nobody would dream of suspecting Claudia or me--and there was a reason why Gussie should not be suspected. As a matter of fact, I was in a position to prove his innocence--as well as my own--

--for I had hold of his arm the whole time that toe room was in darkness--So it was _John or Claudia_--and' John went--Then it _must_ be one of the Geste boys--

"John felt certain that Michael had gone to the French Foreign Legion because the very name of it had fascinated him, ever since a French officer had stayed at Brandon Abbas and told us about military life in Africa--Why--you may have met him there!--De Beaujolais is his name. He was the son of an old school-friend of Aunt Patricia's and, at Eton, was the fag of George Lawrence, her second husband--"

"No, I didn't see him at Brandon Abbas," I said. "But I saw him in Africa, in a place called Zaguig--He saved my sister--It's a queer little world--"

"It *is* a queer world--" mused Isobel. "Think of that!--You know Major de Beaujolais!"

"Related to him," I smiled. "My sister married him--I mean he married my sister--"

"W*hat* a coincidence!" said Isobel.

"Not it!" I ventured to contradict. "There are no such things!--It was no coincidence that Jasper Jocelyn Jelkes ran away from Brandon Abbas and came to my Grandmother's place--nor that a Colonel Levasseur became enamoured of my sister and invited us to Zaguig, with the result that I got all broken up--nor that Dr. Hanley-Blythe chanced upon me when I was just enjoying the nervous reaction from it!--Go on about John--"

"He went to the French Foreign Legion, and there he found Beau and Digby as he had felt certain he would--.At the siege, by Arabs, of a fort at a place called Zinderneuf, Beau was killed, and John stabbed the Commandant of the fort, in self-defence--The man had heard that Beau and Digby and John were jewel-thieves and had a huge diamond!--Digby wasn't at Zinderneuf. He came with the relief-party and was sent into the empty fort. He saw Beau's body reverently laid out, beside that of the Commandant--who had John's bayonet through his heart. He went half mad and set the place on fire and escaped to look for John, because John wasn't among the dead--He soon found him, because John had done just the same thing--dropped from the wall furthest from the entrance, and had run to the nearest sand-dunes--Then two friends of theirs, scouting or patrolling on camels, found them, and the four of them got away together--

"Then Digby was killed by a raiding party--"

Her voice broke again and there was silence.

"Poor darling Digby--He was such a kind, happy, _dear_ boy--And after awful hardships and dangers, just when escape seemed sure, the other three were stranded in the desert without camels--And they only had about a quart of water--And one of the two friends, one they called 'Hank,' went off in the night--to give John and the other man a chance--the water--

"Then John and the other--' Buddy,' John called him--got to a desert village and they stayed there a long time, hoping to find the third man or to hear something of him--He had given his life for them--And at last they gave up hope, and found a caravan going south to Kano--There they got into touch with George Lawrence, who was a Commissioner or something, in Nigeria--

"And as soon as they were there, John's companion turned round and went back to look for the lost man--Hank--They were a sort of David and Jonathan pair, and the man said he was going to search until either he found his friend or died--

"John was too ill to go back with this man, Buddy--I have no doubt he would have done so, otherwise, as soon as they had got camels and supplies--Men do such foolish things--But John went down with enteric, and nearly died. As soon as it was safe to move him,

George Lawrence brought him home--Oh, I nearly died of joy, although I cried and cried when I heard about Michael and Digby--

"And we were married--And I was the happiest woman in the whole world--for a time. I was too happy, of course--We aren't meant to be as happy as I was, or we shouldn't want to go to Heaven--"

"Oh, yes, we are," I interrupted, "and you are going to be just as happy as that again. And it's _going to last_, this time--"

Isobel sighed and pressed my hand as she smiled gratefully at me.

"Yes--I was too happy," she resumed, "but it did not last very long--John did not recover properly. He simply did not get fit again--He had had a most terrible time--The deaths of Beau and Digby before his eyes, and the awful hardships he had suffered, ending up with this enteric or typhus, when he was so weak--George Lawrence said he looked like a dying skeleton when he first saw him in Nigeria--And even then of course, he couldn't get proper nursing or invalid food--It was a marvel that he lived.

"Well--we hadn't been married long, before I saw there was something very wrong with John--He hardly ate anything at all, and he scarcely slept--I don't think he ever got any sleep at all, at night. I used to hear him walking up and down, up and down, in the corridor. He would go out there so that he should not wake me, and then he would sit in his dressing-room and smoke for a while and read. He used to be able to doze a little in the afternoons, and I would make him sit in a long chair under the trees in the Bower--you know--where we used to play--I couldn't get him to go to bed in the daytime, as he ought to have done.

"And if he fell asleep in the chair, he had horrible dreams and woke with a dreadful start, or else he would talk all the time--That was how I found out what was really at the root of the trouble. He felt he had left his friend in the lurch--had deserted the man who would never have deserted him, abandoned the David who had gone back into the desert to look for his Jonathan instead of escaping when he had the chance--

"I was so worried and frightened that I got Dr. Hanley-Blythe to come to Brandon Abbas. He wanted John to come here and be under observation, but John wouldn't hear of it--

"Then one night, John was walking up and down in his dressing-room, and, as I was going to him, I heard him say, groaning, '_I shall go mad if I don't go back!_'--I made up my mind immediately, and as I pushed the door wider open, I said:

"'_John, darling, I know what is the matter with you_,' just as though I had had a sudden brain-wave. He stared at me. My heart seemed to turn right over--he looked so ill and so unlike himself, too--and I felt absolutely dreadful at the thought of what I was going to do--

"'_You must go back, darling_,' I said--'_and find them--I shall come with you--as far as Kano anyhow_.'--I meant to stay with him and never let him out of my sight, of course--He stared and stared as though he could not believe his ears--and then his poor sad face lit up with joy, and I thought my heart would break.

"'ISOBEL!' he said, and took me in his arms as though he loved me more than ever, for what I had done. 'You see they may be alive--they may be slaves--they may be in some ghastly native prison--they may be in some place where they'll have to stay for the rest of their lives, for want of camels--Isobel--they offered their lives for Digby and me when they helped us away from Zinderneuf--Hank gave his life for Buddy and me when he went off in the night, and left us the drop of water--Buddy saw me safe to Kano before he went back to look for Hank--And I left them there, and am lining in safety and luxury!--They may be alive--There may be time to save them even yet--I can't sleep for thinking of them--in Arab hands--

"'We'll start as soon as you like, John,' I said--and I felt myself going dead, as it were--dead and cold at the very heart of myself--"

There was silence for a while, a silence broken only by a little sob, and I looked away over the beautiful Kentish scene. Should I let her go on? Was it too painful to be beneficial, or was it her salvation?

"You are distressing yourself," I said, moved almost unbearably by her tears. "Tell me the rest tomorrow."

"Oh, no, no! Let me tell you now--If you are not--tired--Oh, if you knew the relief it is--and the hope that you have given me--my friend-in-need--" she answered at once.

"George Lawrence was wonderful," she went on, "and Aunt Patricia did not raise a word of protest when he said he would come with us--Of course, his help would be absolutely invaluable. He was in Nigeria for about twenty years, himself, and could pull all sorts of strings, give us the soundest advice and assist us in numberless ways--I think that Aunt Patricia realized it was a life-and-death matter for John, especially after what Dr. Hanley-Blythe had said to her--What I did not then realize, was that George Lawrence's real object was to take charge of me, if anything happened to John when he went off into the real desert, right away from civilization and help--He never expected that John would, return alive, and he did not expect that John would ever get better if he did not go--

"Do you know, John began to improve from that night--from the very moment that I had suggested his going back--He went to bed and slept, and I heard him singing in his bath, the next morning!--Several times during that day he actually whistled as he went about his preparations for the journey. He was a changed man, and I got some idea of what he had suffered by sitting idle while his friends whom he had 'deserted' might be dying in the desert, or be living in captivity worse than death--

"On the voyage from Liverpool to Lagos, he put on weight daily, and was almost himself again by the time we got there--And then he revealed the plot hatched by George Lawrence!

"We were to go to friends of his, and I was to stay with them while John and he went on to Kano. After he had seen John off, with a proper caravan--to go to the village where he and his friend had lived while they had been searching for the third man--George was to return to me and take me home again!--These two precious lunatics thought I was going to agree to *that*--and sit down quietly with George's friends for weeks and weeks, and then go quietly home without John.

"'Oh, yes,' they said, 'George's friends are most delightful people; have a charming house in quite the best part of Nigeria; really very good climate at this time of year; plenty going on, at the Club; tennis, racing, polo, bridge and dancing; I should have a lovely time--'

"I didn't argue. I merely smiled and shook my head.

"When they realized, at last, that I was going with John, and that nothing on earth would stop my going with John, there was frightful consternation and alarm! They even talked of abandoning the whole scheme and returning by the next boat--I wouldn't hear of that, and they wouldn't hear of my attempting to make the caravan-journey into that part of the Sahara, one of the most waterless, hot and dangerous of deserts--We compromised eventually--I was to come with them to Kano, and John was to go on with the best guides, camels, camel-men, outfit and provisions that money could buy. He was to take special men, as messengers, too. He was to send a man back with a message, as soon as he reached the village, and send messages at regular intervals afterwards--The men were to report to an English official at Kano, a Mr. Mordaunt--an old friend of George Lawrence, and he would cable news to us--John promised that he would not go further north than Zanout, himself--His idea was to promise a big reward to anybody who brought him genuine news, and he hoped to get into touch with one or two big men, Arab or Touareg chiefs, who are famous and influential in that part of the Sahara--And to tell the great Bilma salt-caravan---thousands of people--about it--

"John thought that the 'desert telegraph'--that mysterious spreading of news which turns even the desert into a whispering-gallery--would soon make it known, far and wide, that a great sum was being offered by a rich European for news of two friends of his--All sorts of canards would soon be flying about, and hundreds of false clues would be discovered--And among tons and tons of chaff there might, one day, be found a grain of truth--

"Poor John!--Oh, my darling John!--He was so hopeful--He was so happy again, now that he was, at any rate, _trying_ to do something for his friends--if only they were still alive--There was hope that the second one was, and just a bare chance that the first one had been found and saved."

"You are tiring yourself," I said again, as Isobel fell silent.

"No, no! Let me finish--unless you are tired yourself," she replied. "It does me good to tell you--and the sooner you know everything, the sooner you may be able to do something--"

"John got to the place, where he had lived with his companion, in about three weeks, and sent back the first messenger. Nothing was known there, apparently, but he had hardly expected to get news so soon, and was still full of hope. Two more messages came, the second from Zanout, where he thought he had found a trace of the man he called 'Buddy.'--It seems the Touareg of those parts know the appearance and brand-marks of every camel, and the full history of every raid in which camels are stolen. John thought that Buddy and his caravan had been captured by Touareg or Tebu robbers, and the next thing was to find somebody who could give details as to the band and where they came from, and whether there had been any survivors of the caravan--And then--And then--We got a cable from George Lawrence's Kano friend, _saying that John himself had been captured_!--Not by raiders--He had been recognized by a French patrol and had been arrested--Oh John, John, dear!--I let you go back there--but you would have died if you had stayed here--"

I could do nothing to comfort her--except reiterate my promise to find him and bring him back.

"George Lawrence was splendid again," she continued. "He took me back to Africa--I would have gone alone if necessary--Before going, he moved heaven and earth--He went to the Foreign Office and the Colonial Office and to see several Members of Parliament and visited the offices of the London newspapers. Then he got into touch with his friend, Major de Beaujolais--who was at our wedding and knew all about John--We went to Paris, and he saw various influential people there, and thence to Algiers to see the Commander-in-Chief--Everybody was most kind and sympathetic and helpless--especially helpless in France and Africa--' Nothing could be done--The law must take its course--We civilian officials cannot interfere with the military authorities--We military officials cannot interfere with the civilian authorities--Fair trial, of course--Court martial--Death penalty generally inflicted--very properly--in cases of desertion in the face of the enemy--Some very peculiar features about this case moreover'--and so-on.

"It was unspeakably dreadful to feel so powerless, baffled and ineffectual--I felt I must get as near as I possibly could to the place--in Africa--I must have every scrap of news--I lasted out--as far as Kano.

"Mr. Mordaunt was so kind and helpful. He had kept the man who had brought the last information--a Touareg camel-driver, hired in Kano--This man had told the whole story to George Lawrence, over and over again--They had found a soldier of the French camel-corps, who had strayed or deserted from a patrol--apparently what they call a _peloton méhariste_, out on a _tournée d'apprivoisement_ through the Touareg country--John had befriended the man, of course given him food, water and a camel, and the man had gone straight off and brought the patrol down on his benefactor--

"From what this camel-man said, George Lawrence and Mr. Mordaunt concluded that the soldier had recognized John and had denounced him, for reward and promotion, or else--having had enough of desertion in the desert--to ingratiate himself with the leader of the patrol and palliate his offence--

"Anyhow, what was perfectly clear, was that John had been captured and arrested in French Territory by the 'competent military authority'--as a deserter from the Legion--

"_Oh John, John, my darling!--Shall I ever see you again!--_

"And when I had learned everything there was to learn at Kano, I collapsed altogether, and only just didn't die--I think it was the belief that I might, somehow, be able to help John, that kept me alive--It must have been a dreadful time for poor George Lawrence--I remember very little about it, but I get fleeting glimpses now and again--

"And here I am, Otis--and can do _nothing_. Everything possible has been done--and all we know, through the kindness of Major de Beaujolais, is that he is alive--or was--and is a convict in the Penal Battalions in Africa!--Eight years!--And then to return to the Legion to finish his five years there!--_Eight years!_ He couldn't survive eight months of that life--And here am I--and I can do _nothing--nothing_--'

"*I* can, though," I said, and arose to begin doing it.

4.

A week later, I was in Sidi bel Abbas--an earnest and indefatigable student of Arabic and of all matters pertaining to the French Foreign Legion and to the French Penal Battalions of convicts, as well--the "Zephyrs" or "Joyeux."

A fortnight later, I was an enlisted *Légionnaire* of the French Foreign Legion, and, secretly, a candidate for membership of the Zephyrs.

It was my intention to see the inside of Biribi, the famous or infamous convict depot of the Penal Battalions, and only by way of the Legion could I do so. Thence, and only thence, could I possibly find John Geste, and until I found him, neither I nor anybody else could rescue him.

CHAPTER VIII

I have very rarely found anything as good as I expected it to be, and almost never as bad. If the joys of anticipation are generally greater than those of experience, the terrors are almost always so, and the man who said, "We suffer far more from the calamities that never happen to us, than from those that do," talked sense.

I had expected life in the French Foreign Legion to be so rough, so hard, so wholly distasteful from every point of view, that I had anticipated something much worse than the reality.

It was hard, very hard; it was rough, wearisome, monotonous and wholly unpleasant; but it was bearable.

I don't think I could have faced the prospect of five years of it--unless, of course, it were for Isobel--but as things were, I contrived to carry on from day to day.

What made things worse for me than for some people, was the fact that I had no military leaning whatsoever, and that the soldier's trade is the very last one that I should voluntarily adopt.

Of course, if one's country is at war, and there is need of more men than the standing army provides, one is fully prepared to learn the soldiering trade, to the end that one may be as useful as possible as quickly as possible. But this was different, and to me, at any rate, the whole business seemed puerile, stupid, and an entirely unsuitable occupation for an intelligent man.

There was not one solitary aspect of life that was enjoyable, and I do not think that I was ever faintly interested in anything but the _salle d'honneur_.

This wonderful museum of military trophies and of concrete evidence of superhuman courage, devotion and endurance, did more than interest me. It thrilled me to the marrow of my bones, and I took every opportunity of gazing at the battle pictures, portraits of distinguished heroes, scenes from the Legion's stirring history--all of them, without exception, painted by legionaries who were survivors of the scenes depicted--or comrades of the men whose portraits adorned the walls.

Every captured standard, weapon, and other trophy, illustrated some astounding story, a story as true as Life and Death, and far, far stranger than any fiction that ever was conceived.

The single exhibit that thrilled me most was, I think, the hand of Captain Danjou in its glass case beneath the picture that told the story of the historic fight of sixty-five against two thousand two hundred better-provided troops; a fight that lasted a whole day, and ended in the capture, by assault, of five wounded survivors--wounded to death, but fighting while strength remained to load a gun and pull a trigger.

What I suffered from, most of all, was a lack of companionship. There wasn't a comrade to whom I could talk English, and none to whom I cared to talk French, or what passed for French, in the Legion.

Stout fellows all, no doubt, and good soldiers, but there was not one with whom I had an idea in common, or who appeared to have a thought beyond wine, woman and song, unless it were food, money and the wickedness of noncommissioned officers.

One of my room-mates, a poor creature named Schnell, who appeared to me to be not only the butt and fool of the _escouade_, but also of Fate, attached himself to me and made himself extremely useful.

For some inexplicable reason, he developed a great admiration for me. He put himself under my protection, and in return for that, and some base coin of the realm, he begged to remain my obedient servant, and was permitted to do so.

I was to meet the good Schnell again--in different circumstances.

Things improved somewhat when, after some weeks, I completed my recruit's course, took my place in my Company and came under the more immediate notice of Sergeant Frederic.

2.

I did not look upon it as a piece of great good luck when I found that my Sergeant was an Englishman, and one of the best of good fellows. I regarded it rather as a Sign.

I never knew his real name, but he was a Public School man, had been through Sandhurst, and had served in a Dragoon regiment. How he had fallen from the Officers' Mess of a British Cavalry regiment to the ranks of the Legion, was a mystery, for he was one of those people in whom one cannot detect a weak spot, and with whom one cannot associate any form of vice or crime.

I often wondered.

It may have been debt, a love affair, or sheer boredom with peace-time soldiering, and I often hoped that he would one day be moved to tell me his story. Naturally I never asked him a question on the subject of his past. It can't be done in the Legion--Not twice, anyhow.

Of course, a Sergeant cannot hob-nob with a *Légionnaire* , walk out with him or drink with him, but Sergeant Frederic, as he called himself, gave me many a friendly word and kindly encouragement when we were alone; and later, when we were away down in the desert, he would march beside me and talk, or come and chat in the darkness of bivouacs. On one occasion, when he and I were in the same mule- *peloton* , he and I were out on a patrol, or a _reconnaissance_, by ourselves, for a whole day, and he laid aside his rank and we talked freely, as equals, and man to man. It did us both good to talk English once again, and to converse with a man of our own level of education, social experience and breeding.

It made all the difference in the world, to me, that my Sergeant was a man of this type, and regarded me with the eye of friendship and favour. Moreover it was not unnoticed by the Corporals that I was a compatriot (as they supposed), and something of a protégé of the Sergeant.

Had I, at that time, proved a slack and inefficient soldier however, I am pretty sure there would have been a prompt end to the favour of Sergeant Frederic and his myrmidons.

Thanks to this position of affairs, I did not in the early days, have too bad a time in the Legion. It was hard, terribly hard, and I was only just equal to the life, physically speaking, when real marching began in earnest, and I took part in some of those performances that have earned the Legion the honourable title of "The Foot-Cavalry" in the XIXth (African) Army Corps.

At first I used to be obsessed with the awful fear that I should fail and fall out, and share the terrible fate of so many who have fallen by the wayside in Algeria and Morocco. But it is wonderful how the spirit rules the body, and for how long the latter will not give in, if the former does not--

Time after time, in the early days, I was reduced to a queer condition wherein I was dead, not "from the neck, up," as we say, but from the neck, down. My head was alive, my eyes could see, my ears hear; but I had no body. My head floated along on a Pain. No, I had no body and I was not conscious of individual parts that had been causing me agony for hours--blistered feet, aching calves, burning thighs, cruelly lame back, cut shoulders. These were amalgamated into the one great amorphous and intangible Pain that floated along in the white-hot aloud of dust, and bore my bursting head upon it.

I used to think that I could be shot, when in that condition, without knowing it and without falling, provided that no vital part were hit, and that I should go on marching, marching, marching--

For, once I had reached this condition, I was almost immune and immortal, indestructible and unstoppable--while the spirit held, high and unfaltering. But when the last " *Halte!* " was cried, and the voice of an officer rang out:

"_Campez_," and the Company Commanders bawled:

"_Formez les faisceaux_," and "_Sac à terre_," and the unfaltering spirit went off duty, its task accomplished, then the poor body had its way--It trembled--it sagged--it collapsed--and it lay where it was, until kindly and more seasoned comrades dragged it aside and disposed its unconscious head in safety if not in comfort.

I fully and freely admit that this marching was the worst thing that I encountered in the Legion, thanks to my good luck in being in Sergeant Frederic's *peloton* . The next worst things were the lack of acceptable companionship and society, the deadly wearisome monotony, and the impossibility of natural self-expression for one's ego. I am no militarist, no "born soldier," and I wished at times that I had never been born at all.

It was on the occasion to which I have referred, the day when Sergeant Frederic and I were alone together, from before dawn to after midnight, that I asked him the question which probably surprised him more than any other that he had ever been asked--We were riding at ease--so far as one can ride at ease on a mule--

"How can a man who wishes to do so, make certain of getting sent to the Zephyrs?" I inquired suddenly. "Just that and nothing worse--nor better--the happy medium between a death-sentence from a General Court-martial, and thirty days' solitary confinement from the Colonel."--

Sergeant Frederic laughed.

"The happy medium!" he said. "Well--they're called the '_Joyeux_'! You're a queer chap, Hankinson--D'you mean you want to join the honourable _Compagnies de discipline_? Don't you get enough discipline here?" and he laughed again. "Well--I dunno--I suppose you'd find yourself in the Zephyrs all-right if if you gave me a smack in the eye, on parade, one morning--"

That was a thing I most certainly should not do--and I little thought, at the time, that it would actually be through this most excellent chap that I should come to wear the military-convict uniform of the African Penal Battalions--

"Better not risk it, though," he continued, smiling. "It is much more likely that you'd be shot, out of hand--It is the law, even in peace time, that the death-penalty be awarded for the striking of any _supérieur_, no matter what the provocation--and no matter what the rank of the striker or the stricken--And you know the awkward rule of the French Army, '_No man can appeal against a punishment until he has served the whole of it._'"

"Yes--Plenty of fellows do get sent from the Legion to the Zephyrs, though," I said. "What's the trouble usually?"

"You've got Zephyrs on the brain," was the reply. "Are you afraid you'll get sent there?--Not the slightest fear of that, unless you wilfully get into serious trouble--What do men get sent there for? Oh, insubordination, desertion, damage to Government property, sedition--or just continued slackness and indiscipline--The Colonel can give six months for that, and the General Court-martial can give you penal servitude, to any extent, for a serious 'crime' or continued bad record--Those who get themselves a term in the Zephyrs earn it all-right, and thoroughly deserve it, as a rule--Almost always--As far as I can remember the wording in Army Regulations, it is, '_The Minister of War has full power to send to the Compagnies de Discipline any soldier who has committed one of several faults, the gravity of which makes any other mode of repression inadequate_--I like that word 'repression'! They _repress_ them all-right, in the Penal Battalions!--Of course, 'Minister of War,' in this case, means the General Court-martial that sits at Oran, and the General Court-martial knows that when the Colonel sends a man before it, something has got to be done with the sin-merchant.

"So they either shoot him, or plant him in the Zephyrs for a few years, and the Colonel is rid of him--

"Naturally the Colonel doesn't want to lose any man who is a ha'porth of good--so you may take it a _légionnaire's_ a pretty hard case and a Republic's Hard Bargain before he gets as far as the General Court-martial."

"Yes," I agreed. "But one hears stories of innocent, harmless and well-meaning fellows who fall foul of a Corporal or a Sergeant, and are so constantly run in, by the non-com., that the Company Officer has to take notice of it, and begins doubling the dose that he finds put down in the _livre de punitions_ against the man's name--By the time the Captain has begun to give the maximum that his powers allow, the Colonel has got his eye on the poor devil, and starts doubling the Captain's dose, and, before long, the man has got the Colonel's maximum of solitary confinement and an ultimatum--reform, or six months deportation to the Zephyrs--And he can't 'reform,' for the Sergeant won't let him--and it's the Sergeant's word against his--"

"One does hear such stories--" said Sergeant Frederic, and changed the conversation.

3.

The days passed swiftly--swiftly as only days of continuous hard work can do, and I began to find myself becoming a routine-dulled *Légionnaire* , with so much to do in the present that I could scarcely think of the future.

This would not do, and I must get action. I had not come to the Legion to settle down, serve my time, and take my discharge! It appeared unlikely that there was anything more about John Geste, for me to learn, and it was high time that I decided on the course which I should pursue to achieve my safe transfer from the honourable ranks of the Foreign Legion to the dishonourable ranks of the working-gangs of the Zephyrs.

The great question was--should I embark on a course of slackness, insubordination, petty "crime" and general unsatisfactoriness, so that by the thorny path of more and more punishment, and increasingly long and heavy sentences of imprisonment, I should sound to their depths the Colonel's powers of "repression," until I touched the very bottom and was repressed from the regiment altogether for the space of six months--or should I conceive, and then commit, some crime for which no punishment was adequate, save such as could only be awarded by a General Court-martial--to wit, penal servitude or Death.

On the one hand, it would be a long and painful--a most distasteful and degrading--business, to play the bad soldier so sedulously that I went through the whole gamut of regimental punishment until the Colonel sent me to the Zephyrs for six months--a disgrace to my Corps, my country, and myself.

On the other hand, it would be unspeakably tragic, if, in attempting to qualify for penal servitude in the Zephyrs, I overdid it, and earned the death-penalty--thus failing in my task of finding John Geste; depriving Isobel of her last chance of happiness; ending in a felon's grave all the high hopes that I had held out to her; and breaking the fine promises that I had made.

In favour of the first course was its comparative safety.

Against it, was its protracted misery and moral abasement, and also the fact that the six months which the Colonel could and would give me, might prove all too short for my purpose--indeed would almost certainly prove too short. Twenty years would probably not be long enough.

In favour of the second course, was its comparative decency and brevity. A serious military "crime," a Court-martial, a sentence.

Against it, was the possibility of the sentence being a death-sentence.

Which to choose?--I wondered whether, ever before, in the long and astounding history of the French Foreign Legion, a man had deliberately endeavoured to earn a sentence in the Penal Battalions, and had solemnly weighed the respective merits and conveniences of a Colonel's short-term sentence, and a Court-martial's penal servitude decree.

4.

I hate to look back upon the period of my life that now began. It was, in a way, almost a worse time than that which I spent in the actual Penal Battalion--as much worse as mental suffering is than physical suffering--for the misery of the constant punishment and imprisonment that I deliberately brought upon myself, was nothing in comparison with what I suffered in _earning_ that punishment.

I loathed myself; I loathed the thing that I had to make myself appear to be-- insubordinate, dirty, untrustworthy, lazy, incompetent and wholly detestable to the normal military mind. What hurt me most, was Sergeant Frederic's disappointment in me, a hurt and bewildered disappointment that quickly turned to scorn and the bitterest contempt.

When I first began to lapse from grace--which was as soon as I had decided that I would lapse by slow degrees and a gradual slipping down Avernus, rather than by the commission of a General Court-martial crime--the good fellow did his best, by light punishment, by appeal to my better nature, and then by sharp punishment--to stay my downward course. He would send for me when I had completed eight days _salle de police_ or some other punishment, and talk to me for my good.

"Look here, Hankinson," he would say, "what's the game?--You're in the Legion and you've got to stay in the Legion for five years, so why not make the best of it, and of yourself? Why not go for promotion? You could rise to Sergeant-Major and re-enlist for a commission--And--other things apart--you might play the game, since you have come here!--And I thought you were such a decent chap--

"It's bad enough when some of these ignorant unintelligent clods are bad, dirty, and drunken soldiers. For a man like you, it isn't decent--I can't make you out, Hankinson--One of the weaklings with a screw loose somewhere, I suppose--Come man, pull yourself together--for the credit of the Anglo-Saxon name, if for nothing else--Dismiss!"

And I would salute, and go, without a word, but with a bursting heart.

Yes, what I was doing now _was_, undoubtedly, by far the hardest of the things I was privileged to do for Isobel.

5.

But, one day, a ray of light and warmth shone into the dark cheerlessness of my life at this period.

Sergeant Frederic had an idea.

He wasn't a brilliant man, but he was one of those sound solid, sensible Britishers who are richly endowed with that uncommon thing, common sense.

He sent for me, and said, as soon as we were alone, "I've come to the conclusion, Hankinson, that for some reason, best known to yourself, you are deliberately trying to get into the Zephyrs!--If so, you're a damned fool--a mad fool--But I can understand a mad fool, if there's a woman in it--

"What I want to say is, I shall punish you exactly according to your deserts--without mercy--But if you are trying to get into the Zephyrs, perhaps you'd better give me a smack in the eye, on parade, and get it over--"

"And now get to Hell out of this," he concluded, with an eloquent handshake.

* * * * *

Fate was in a slightly ironical mood when all my painful efforts to deserve and attain a Court-martial, were rendered superfluous.

A sand-storm--aided by a brief failure of the commissariat, over-fatigue, and frayed nerves--provided me, without effort on my part, with that for which I had schemed and suffered for months.

The battalion formed part of a very large force engaged on some extensive manoeuvres, which were, I believe, partly a training-exercise for field-officers, partly a demonstration for the benefit of certain tribes, and partly a reconnaissance in force.

My Company was broken up into a chain of tiny outpost groups, widely scattered in a line parallel to the course of a dry river-bed which was believed by the more ignorant legionaries to form a rough boundary between Algeria and Morocco.

Small patrols kept up communication between the river-bed frontier line and these groups, and one day I found myself a member of such a patrol.

As it happened, the rest of the _escouade_ consisted entirely of Russians, with the exception of my friend Rien, a Frenchman, and a couple of Spaniards and a Jew. All the Russians were in a clique, except Badinefi, who hated the others.

This man, Badineff, a huge, powerful fellow, was a gentleman, and was commonly supposed to have commanded a regiment of Cossacks. After his third bottle of wine, he would talk of his "children," and say there were no cavalry in the world to compare with them. "My regiment would ride round a whole brigade of Spahis, while it galloped, and then ride through it and back."--After his fourth bottle he would lapse into Russian, and further revelations were lost to his interested audience.

Badineff had re-enlisted in the Legion twice, was now serving his fifteenth year in the ranks, and must have been about sixty years of age.

He spoke perfect English, French and German, and had certainly seen a great deal of life--and of death too.

The other Russians were "intellectuals," political plotters and refugees--a loathsome gang, foul as hyenas and cowardly as village pariah-dogs.

Our patrol started from bivouac, after a sleepless night, long before the red dawn of a very terrible day--one of those days when a most terrific thunderstorm is always just about to break, and never does so.

By one of those unfortunate concatenations of untoward circumstance that render the operations of warfare an uncertain and much over-rated pastime, we had to start with almost nothing in our water-bottles, less in our haversacks, and least in our stomachs.

Sergeant Frederic, however, comforted us with the information that our march was to be but a short one--about ten _kilomètres_--and that the outpost to which we were going was actually holding a well, water-hole or oasis, and was properly provisioned.

All we had to do, was to step out smartly, arrive promptly, eat, drink and be merry, and then lie like warriors taking our rest with our martial cloaks around us.

It was Sergeant Frederic who lied.

The post was quite thirty kilometres away, and we had marched about twenty of them, through the most terrible heat I have ever known, when the sand-storm came on, and we were lost.

It began with a wind that seemed to have come straight from the opened mouth of Hell. It was so hot that it hurt, and one laid one's hand over one's face as though to save it from being burnt from the bones behind it. Dust clouds arose in such density as to obscure the mid-day sun. As the wind increased to hurricane force, the dust was mingled with sand and small stones that cut the flesh, and, before long, gloom became darkness.

We staggered on, Sergeant Frederic leading, and in every mind was the thought, "How can he know where he is going?--We shall be lost in the desert and die of thirst."

Darkness by day is very different from the darkness of night, for at night a man can take a bearing from the stars and keep his direction.

It is difficult to give an adequate idea of the conditions that prevailed. We were deafened, blinded and suffocated.

To open one's mouth and gaspingly inhale sufficient air to rid oneself of the terrible feeling of imminent asphyxiation, was to fill one's lungs with sand; to open one's eyes to see where one was going, was to be blinded with sand; to stagger on, buffeted and bedevilled through that black night-by-day, choking and drowning in a raging ocean whose great breakers were waves of sand, was to be overwhelmed and utterly lost; to give up hope and effort and to lie prone, with face to earth, in the hope of escaping the worst of the torture, was to be buried alive.

Perhaps this was what Sergeant Frederic feared, for he kept us moving--in single file, each man holding to the end of the bayonet-scabbard of the man in front of him, and with strict orders to give the alarm if the man behind him lost touch.

Frederic put Badineff, Rien and myself last--

How long we struggled on, bent double against the wind, I do not know, but I was very near the end of my tether, and feeling as though I were drowning in a boiling sea, when I was jerked to a standstill by the halting of the man in front of me.

A Russian _Légionnaire_, one Smolensky, appeared to have gone mad, and with his clenched fists forced into his eyes, and face upraised as though to lift his mouth above the flying sand, screamed that he would go no further; that Frederic was a murderer maliciously leading us to our deaths, an incompetent fool who did not know in the least where he was going nor what he was doing, and a scoundrel who merited instant death--

A man threw himself on the ground--Another--Another--

As Rien, Badineff and I pushed forward, Sergeant Frederic loomed up through the murk of this fantastic Hell.

"What's this?" he yelled, leaning against the wind.

Another man threw himself on the ground, and the mad Russian began loading his rifle, shrieking curses at Frederic as he did so.

"Let's _die_ like gentlemen, at least," cried Rien, as Badineff sprang on the madman, wrenched his rifle from him and knocked him down.

Another man, a friend of the madman, swung up his rifle to club Badineff, and I seized it as it came back over the man's shoulder.

Rien shouted something that was carried away by the wind, and I received a heavy blow on the head.

I saw Sergeant Frederic draw his automatic, as I stumbled and fell.

Like a prairie fire leaping from tuft to tuft, madness was spreading from man to man, and the unauthorized halt was becoming a free fight. The single-file column had become a crowd--a maddened crowd ripe for revolt and murder.

Sergeant Frederic acted with wisdom and his usual coolness. As I staggered to my feet he roared the blessed words:

"_Halte! Campez!_"

He was instantly obeyed, and everyone sank to the ground. Going from man to man he pushed, pulled, shouted, and exhorted, until he had got all but the weariest and most despairing, crouched on knees and elbows, soles of the feet to the wind, heads tucked in, chin upon chest, and the face in the little space protected by the body.

In this posture, such as the Arab assumes in the lee of his kneeling camel, when caught in a sandstorm, one might hope to breathe, and by frequent movement to avoid burial.

In a few minutes the patrol was almost obliterated and, to any eye that could have beheld it when that awful storm was at its height, it must have suggested an orderly arrangement of sand-covered boulders, rather than a company of men.

How long the sand-storm lasted I do not know, but it was only by dint of frequent change of position that we were not buried alive. Nor do I know how long it had been day when the sun's rays again penetrated the dusty gloom. Whether Sergeant Frederic really had the least idea as to where he was, or where he was going, I do not know, but he bravely strove to give the impression that all was well--that we were not lost, and that a brief march would bring us to water and to food. Encouraging, praising, shaming, exhorting, promising, he got the escouade on its feet and together, and after a brief brave speech, gave the order to march, and as some of us turned to step off, a Russian, Smernoff--a typical sample of "the brittle intellectuals who crack beneath the strain," a loathsome creature, mean as a jackal, and bloodthirsty as a wolf, suddenly yelled:

"_March?_ My God, yes, and where to?--You have lost us; you have killed us, you swine!"

And as Sergeant Frederic strode toward him, the beast threw up his rifle and shot him through the chest. Evidently he had slipped a cartridge in, during the storm.

Frederic fell, rolled over, gasping and coughing blood, drew his automatic, and, with what must have been a tremendous concentration of will-power, shot Smernoff just as Badineff swung up his rifle to club him.

"Hankinson," gasped Frederic as I sprang to his assistance. "Take command--Shoot any man who disobeys you--March straight into the wind--due south--"

Hubbub arose behind me. A rifle was fired, and, looking round, I saw that Dalgaroff had fired at Badineff and apparently missed him, for Badineff sprang upon him and bore him to the ground, his hands at his throat.

In a moment the _escouade_ was in two fighting factions, Smernoff's Russian gang against Badineff, Rient myself, the Roumanian and the Spaniards. I rose to my feet, and, as

I threw open the breech of my rifle, shouted words of command which I hoped might be automatically obeyed. The result was a clicking of breech-bolts as rifles were loaded.

"Rally here, the loyal men," I shouted. "Come on, Badineff," and to my side sprang Rien, Jacob the Roumanian, Badineff and the two Spaniards, and stood shoulder to shoulder with me, between Frederic and the Smernoff faction.

"Now, you fools," I bawled. "Aren't we in danger enough? Follow me, and I will get you out of it--I know the way."

There was a groan and a movement behind us.

"Stand aside," said the brave Frederic, who had struggled to a kneeling position, one hand pressed to his chest, the other holding his automatic steadily.

"Mirsky," he croaked, "return to your duty. Fall in here instantly."

Mirsky laughed, and Frederic shot him dead.

"Andrieff, return to your duty," continued Frederic. "Fall in here instantly."

Andrieff flung his rifle forward and they both fired. Frederic fell back. There was a thunder of hoofs, and a troop of Spahis came down upon us at the charge--their officer riding some fifty yards ahead.

"_Surrender!_" he roared, as he pulled his horse on to its haunches. "_Ground arms._"--And as his troop came to a halt at the signal of his up-flung hand, he bade his Troop-Sergeant arrest the lot of us. Leaping from his horse he strode to where Frederic lay, bleeding to death, and knelt beside him.

"Tell me, _mon enfant_," he said, and put his ear to Frederic's feebly-moving lips.

"Mutiny," he whispered. "Not their fault--_Cafard_--No water--Lost--"

And with a last effort raised his hand, and, pointing to me, said:

"This man is--" And died.

"Ho, this man is the ring-leader, I suppose," snapped the officer, rising and glaring at me. "Tie his hands. Tie the hands of the lot of them," and, drawing an officer's field pocket-book from beneath his Spahi cloak, he entered his observations--quite erroneous, as, at the Court-martial, they proved to be. Having noted that the dead sergeant had shot three of the mutineers in self-defence after being twice wounded by them, and that I was apparently the ringleader, he made a list of the names and _matricule_ numbers of the prisoners, snapped the elastic band upon his book, and returned it to his breast-pocket with a certain grim satisfaction. He then had the prisoners released and set them to work to dig two graves, one for the Sergeant and one for his murderers, while his troop off-saddled and took a mid-day rest--

That evening, we found ourselves strictly guarded and segregated prisoners in the camp, and, after a brief field Court-martial next day, at which our Spahi officer testified that he had caught the lot of us murdering our Sergeant, we were despatched to Oran for the General Court-martial to decide our fate. Out of the mass of perjury, false witness, contradictory statements and simple truth--the latter told by Rien, Badineff, Jacob the Gypsy, and myself--emerged the fact that the _escouade_ had murdered its Sergeant, losing three of its number in the process--Further it was decided that if those three, as might be assumed, were the actual murderers, the remainder were certainly accessories, even if they did not include the actual slayers.

It was a near thing, and I believe that only one vote stood between the death-sentence, and that of eight years' penal servitude, _travaux forcés_, in the Disciplinary Battalions of France.

The President of the Oran General Court-martial was a Major de Beaujolais—

CHAPTER IX

It will perhaps be quite comprehensible that I do not care to dwell over-much upon the time I spent in the Penal Battalions of Madame la République.

I certainly am not going to complain of the treatment I received, inasmuch as I was there by my own desire, and had been at some considerable pains to arrive there.

Each country has its own penal system, and each country can criticize that of the other, if it has nothing better to do. Our own system is not without spot or blemish, and one has heard unpleasant things of the treatment of convict-workers in our coal-mines.

Charles Reade had considerable fault to find with the English convict system, and those exiled to penal servitude in Siberia have a poor opinion of Russian methods of punishment.

And I am the less disposed to assail the French convict-system because Biribi is now abolished (and also, perhaps, the Devil's Island, where Captain Dreyfus suffered, and the Guiana penal settlement), and the worst punishments that we endured were inflicted upon us illegally and in defiance of the law. These latter, generally the outcome of the vicious spite of some local petty tyrant, struck me as rather unnecessary, for the prescribed and lawful punishments were wholly adequate--apart from the fact that life itself was one long punishment.

For example, I personally needed nothing more in the way of correctional attentions than twenty-four hours of la planche. This ingenious device was, as its name implies, merely a plank. To the observer's eye, a simple plank, but to the sentenced man it was something more.

In the first place, the plank was some twelve feet above the ground. In the second place, it was neither sufficiently long, nor sufficiently wide, to enable a man to lie down upon it in anything but acute discomfort and danger of falling. He could merely sit upon it--and he could not do that for long, without changing his position in the hope of finding one less racking and tormenting. In the third place the heat and glare of that white-washed, white-hot prison-yard was a cruel and dangerous torture in itself.

The punishment of _la planche_ sounds mild and moderate. So did some of those of the Holy Inquisition of old--particularly the worst of all, that of water dripping on the head.

Let anyone who thinks it mild and moderate, try it for an hour. Let him not try it for twenty-four hours, however, lest he do not regain his sanity.

But could not one throw oneself off this hellish perch of the devil? One could. One did. But not twice. He was ready, willing, nay positively anxious, to return to that now attractive plank, by the time he had discovered what happened to those who voluntarily or involuntarily quitted the post of dishonour.

Nor indeed was there any real necessity to exceed the simple and lawful punishment of deprivation of water; of standing facing the sun in a white-washed corner from sunrise to sunset without food or drink; or of being chained to a wall with the hands above the head.

In fact one would have thought that "hard labour"--harder perhaps than that known to any other convict in the world--by day, and lying chained to an iron bar and to one's neighbour on the stone floor of a shed, by night, might, with the absence of all that makes life supportable, and the presence of everything calculated to make life insupportable, have rendered even "lawful" punishment unnecessary.

But no. Punishment beyond punishment had to be inflicted, and then illegal and indefensible torture added.

Chief of these were the *silo* and the _crapaudine_, both once permitted by law, and both absolutely prohibited and "abolished" by General de Negrier. I saw both these tortures inflicted, and I suffered one of them myself. But I wish to repeat, and to make it clear, that this villainous brutality was wholly contrary to law and in flat defiance of most definite military regulations.

Also, I wish to repeat that, in any case, I am not complaining. What I got, I asked for.

Further, if the system was severe to the point of savage and brutal cruelty, it is to be remembered that the bulk of the convicts were desperate and dangerous criminals, many of them barely human in their horrible depravity, and far more dangerous to those in authority over them, than any cageful of lions, tigers and panthers to the wild-beast-tamer who ventures among them.

While there was a sprinkling of soldiers whose horrible "crimes" were those of dirty buttons, slackness, drunkenness, earning the enmity of an N.C.O., and being generally and congenitally non-military, there was also a certain number of ordinary criminals who had been, perhaps, more unfortunate than wicked. But there was, as I have said, undoubtedly a very large proportion of the worst and beastliest criminals in the world, prominent among whom was the typical Parisian _apache_, who has no faintest shadow of any solitary virtue, save occasionally the savage courage of the cornered rat.

As is natural and very right and proper, the officers and non-commissioned officers--and more particularly the latter--are chosen with an eye to their suitability for the work they have to do.

Stern disciplinarians are required and stern disciplinarians are selected. Not only did the success of the system depend upon the iron discipline of these men, fierce, unbending, remorseless--but their own lives as well. Many have been killed in the execution of their duty, either by the sudden action of a maddened and despairing individual, or as the result of a cunning plot, planned and executed with fiendish ingenuity and ferocity.

They carry loaded revolvers in unfastened holsters, and their hands are never far from them. In time, they come inevitably to regard the convicts not only as enemies of the State and of Society, but also as personal enemies, and behave toward them accordingly. This is more particularly true of the non-commissioned officers, and in the conditions prevalent in far-distant desert places, where the great French military roads are in course of construction by convict labour.

And to one of these road-making gangs it was my fate to be drafted--the fate "written on my forehead," as the Arabs say--to which I had been destined, as I believed, from the beginning of time, that I might fulfil myself.

The latest road--a Road of Destiny indeed for me--was to run from the city of Zaguig, of horrible memory, to a place called the Great Oasis, a spot now of the greatest strategic importance to France. On this road were working a large proportion of the military convicts.

So, once again, to Zaguig I came, and from Zaguig marched out along the uncompleted high-way that was miraculously to lead me to my goal.

2.

Of that spell of road-work I remember but little.

Each day was exactly like its terrible predecessor. Each night a blessed escape from Hell, if not to Heaven, at any rate to a Nirvana of nothingness.

Often I wondered how men of education and refinement, such as Badineff and Rien, delicately nurtured, were able to bear the horror that was life, inasmuch as it was all that I, with my great sustaining inspiration and need to live, could do, to force my body to obey my will and keep my will from willing death.

In point of fact, it was patent to me that Rien was failing and that both the temper and the body of the giant Badineff were wearing thin.

And then a spell of bad weather, with terrific heat and sand-laden winds, that seemed to have been forced through gigantic furnaces, precipitated, as so often happens, one of those catastrophes of madness, mutiny, murder and heavy retaliatory and repressive punishment.

I am sorry to say that I was the innocent cause of this particular example of these tragedies that are all too common, and indeed inevitable, in such circumstances.

Small beginnings!

As is so often the case, the beginnings of this affair which was to cost the lives of so many men, were small enough, God knows.

A Sergeant, one of those "hard cases" that are naturally selected for their aggressive harshness, merciless severity, and all the qualities that go to make the ferocious disciplinarian and martinet, stood watching me as I swung my pick; with blistered hands, aching arms, eyes blinded with sweat, a terrible pain at the back of my neck, and the feeling that if I bent my body once again, my back would surely break--

As I painfully straightened myself, he stepped towards me, and, with his stick, struck my cap from my head. To be quite just, I think he was only making a sudden raid upon that place of concealment, in search of tobacco, food, paper, pencil, a piece of steel, or a sharp-edged stone.

However, the stick struck my head as well as my cap, and I was still sufficiently near, in memory, to civilization, to find his act discourteous. I must have given expression to this wrong mental attitude, and looked upon him with the eye of mild reproach.

Now, in the ranks of _les Joyeux_, looking can be an offence. A cat may look at a king, but a convict may not look at a corporal--save with the glance of the most respectful, humble and obedient reverence. Any other kind of look may be mutinous; a mutinous look may precede a mutinous act; and a mutinous act precedes death. The red blossoms of wrath must be nipped in the bud, and the Sergeant promptly nipped mine.

In a second I was sent sprawling with a blow that partly stunned and wholly confused me--and it was with a sense of confusion worse confounded that I saw Badineff raise his spade and fell the Sergeant from behind, while Rien snatched the automatic that the man was in the act of drawing.

Ludicrously enough, Rien shouted at the stunned Sergeant, "You insolent dog! How dare you strike a gentleman!" and was himself struck to the ground by a convict, a Spaniard named Ramon Gonzales, a poor mean soul who hoped to curry favour for his virtue, and gain remission for his sins.

At the same moment, a Corporal dashed into the mêlée, kicked me in the face, fired his automatic at Badineff, and was promptly felled by a man belonging to another _escouade_--and, even in that moment, I noticed the splendid straight left with which he took the

Corporal on the point of the jaw, and the fact (which should have astounded me) that he ejaculated in excellent English, "Dam' swine!" as he did so.

As to exactly what happened then, I am not perfectly clear, save that there was a rush of guards and convicts, as Badineff picked up the automatic dropped by Rien, shot the Spaniard who had felled the latter, shot the Sergeant who rose to his feet and pluckily tackled him with his stick, and then shot a guard who charged him with fixed bayonet.

There was a terrific hubbub, some more indiscriminate shooting, and within a few minutes of my original impious glance at the Sergeant, a number of bodies was lying prone upon the sand, whistles were blowing, voices barking orders, convicts shouting insanely, and chaos reigning in the very home of the world's most rigid discipline.

But not for long.

As always, discipline prevailed, and within another minute or two, order was restored. All the bodies but two or three, promptly came to life and were found to be those of wise men who had flung themselves down until the shooting was over, with the double view of dissociating themselves from the evil doings of wicked men, and of having a little nap.

Apart, very much under arrest, stood the villains of the piece, myself, Badineff, Rien; the Roumanian gypsy known as Jacob the Jew; the Spaniard, Ramon Gonzales; the man with the useful left who had knocked the Corporal out, and three or four more.

Well! We'd done it now, all-right! And it was a drum-head Court-martial for ours that evening, and our backs to a wall and our faces to a firing-party at dawn next morning. Except that there wouldn't be any wall.

There would be a grave though, and we should dig it. We should also stand by it and topple neatly into it when the volley was fired. I hoped I should be dead before they shovelled the sand in.

I also thought of a wily convict who was said to have toppled before he was shot, and to have crawled out before he was buried, and I pondered the possibility of contriving these duplicities.

It did not come to this, however, and I am still in doubt on the subject.

Chained together, and surrounded by guards with loaded rifles and fixed bayonets, we were marched from the scene of our sins--a long and miserable march, to the temporary depôt of the slow-progressing, ever-moving Company.

This depôt proved to be a deserted Arab village, and for want of better or worse accommodation, we were hastily consigned to its large underground grain-pit, or _silo_.

Confinement in these _silos_ had been expressly forbidden because men had gone mad in them, died in them, been forgotten in them, had murdered each other in them for the last drops of water. But many forbidden things are done in those distant places where subordinates rule, where public opinion is not, where the secrets of the prison-house remain secrets, where the grave is very silent, and where necessity not only knows no law, but is apt to be the mother of diabolical invention.

Into this grain-pit we were dropped, one by one; those who preferred to do so, being allowed to climb down a rope by means of which a large pail of water and a sack of bread were lowered for our sustenance until such time as a field Court-martial could be assembled.

That might be upon the morrow, or, again, it might not.

I do not think that there was any intention of actually imprisoning us in this *silo* as a punishment--our offence was too desperate for that.

I think that the officer commanding the Company--if he knew anything about it at all--merely gave the order to put us there as the simplest and easiest means of keeping us secure for the brief space that remained to us--probably only a day, or, at most, a couple of days--before we were tried and shot for murderous revolt against authority.

What then happened, above ground, we did not know--and only two of us ever did know--but by piecing together information which, as I shall tell, I obtained later, I came to the conclusion that a whirlwind attack by Touareg or Bedouin tribesmen, upon the Company, drew every man from the depôt to the scene of the fight, where they shared the fate of escort and convicts alike, there being not a single survivor.

What happened below ground may be quickly told, for the worst hours of my life, hours which seemed certain to be my last, hours during which I was compelled to abandon hope of helping Isobel, ended in the greatest moment of my life, _the moment in which I found John Geste_, the moment in which I knew that I had, against all probability, succeeded.

During those dreadful days, we died, man by man, according to our kind; some in fear, some in wrath; some in despair, some in faith and hope; and one by his own hand.

The two Anglo-Saxons survived, whether by tenacity, strength, the will to live, or the Will of God; and on the fifth day there remained alive only myself and the bearded man who had struck and damned the Corporal--_and who was John Geste_.

And then I should never have known him, but that he used an expression that I heard nowhere else but at Brandon Abbas.

Stout fella!

I really cannot, even now, give the faintest idea of my feelings in that hour. As nothing I can say would be adequate, I will say nothing.

I had found John Geste!

Think of it—

CHAPTER X

Alive we were, but only just alive. Thirst, starvation, suffocation, corpses, flies and other attendant horrors had almost done their work on men not over-nourished, nor in too good condition, at the start--and when we were discovered it was none too soon.

We actually owed our salvation, I believe, to the predatory, or at any rate, the acquisitive, instincts of an aged party who, knowing of the existence of the _silo_, came to see whether it contained anything worth acquiring.

It did. And he acquired us.

I was lying beside the inanimate body of John Geste, and doing my utmost to persuade him not to die, when the light from the small man-hole in the roof was obscured suddenly, and I knew that we were either remembered or discovered.

I called out in French, and then in Arabic, seeing what I thought to be the silhouette of the head of a native.

And, in the same tongue, a thin piping voice called in wonder upon Allah, and then in question, upon us. I hastily assured the owner of the silhouette and the voice, that he was indeed the favoured of Allah in that he had discovered us, powerful and wealthy _Roumis_ who would, in return for help, reward him with riches beyond the dreams of avarice.

Apparently my feeble croakings reached not only the man but his intelligence, for the head was withdrawn from the top of the short shaft which connected the *silo* with the ground above, and, a few minutes later, a rope came dangling down into our dreadful prison.

I promptly decided that it would be better for me to attempt the ascent first, for if I could get up I could certainly get down again, and I wanted to see who and what was up above, before fastening the rope to John Geste.

I did not like the idea, for example, of his being hauled up to the roof and then dropped. I accordingly passed the rope round my body beneath my arms, tied it on my chest, and shouted to whomsoever was above, to pull. For several minutes nothing happened--minutes that seemed like hours, and then suddenly with a swift but steady lift, I rose the fifteen or twenty feet to the opening.

I thrust, fending, with my hands and knees, and was Ignominiously dragged out into the blessed light and sweet air of day, at the heels of a camel to whose saddle-tree the end of the rope--the identical rope with which we had been lowered--was fastened.

The man leading the camel halted. I untied the rope, and perceived myself to be in the company of three extremely decrepit-looking old men, and three remarkably fine riding-camels.

It was soon quite evident to me that the leader, at any rate, of this aged trio was anything but decrepit mentally, and he quickly grasped the idea that I was to be lowered again into the pit, that I might bring up another man who was alive but too weak to help himself.

Not only did he grasp my idea, but produced a better one of his own--and I had only just understood it and ejaculated, "God bless you, Grandpa," when my knees gave way, my head spun round, and with infinite regret and annoyance, I collapsed completely.

When I again opened my eyes upon the glorious and wonderful world from which I had been absent for five days in Hell, I was lying in the shade of a mud wall, and John Geste was lying beside me.

Grandpa warmly welcomed my return to consciousness, and explained that he and his young brother had been down quick into the pit, while his youngest brother--a lad who looked about eighty to me--had operated the camel. Also that he had only brought up this one, albeit a doubtful case, as the others were all dead, very dead indeed.

I commended Grandpa most warmly, and promised to set him up for life, whether in a store, a saloon, or a houri-stocked Garden of Eden, and to see both his young brothers well launched in life.

Not only had the excellent old man had the sense to bring up our own pail, and fill it with water, but he had concocted a millet-porridge abomination, which, with some filthy and man-handled milk curd, formed the noblest and most welcome feast which had ever been set before me.

More, and what gave me infinite joy on John Geste's account, he had sent one of the boys for the milk.

While I was wondering where the dairy might be, Grandpa mentioned that there was a Bedouin encampment "just over there ", and any amount of fresh camel's-milk was to be had for the asking, and still more for the giving of a cartridge or two.

When I began to question the ancient as to who he was and whence he came, the light of intelligence faded from his eye, all expression from the mask-like mass of wrinkles which was his face, and he announced he was a very poor man--a _miskeen_ of the lowest type, and that I was his father and his mother.

What he did tell us, and what was of the very deepest interest, was that, five days ago, there had been a sudden Touareg raid upon the road-gangs, a brief fight and a relentless slaughter. Apparently this had taken place a few miles from the deserted village where we lay, and the Touareg _harka_ had swept through it, slaying every living soul they encountered.

As Grandpapa pointed out, it was lucky for us that they had not chanced upon the _silo_. Modestly he contrasted our present fortunate position with the fate that might have been ours.

Excellent as were the ministrations, however, of these three wise men of Gotham, or elsewhere, I doubt whether either John Geste or I would have recovered in their hands. We might have done, for we were both pretty tough and imbued with the most intense yearning to live; but John, I learned, had recently been most desperately ill, and needed something more than curds and soaked millet-seed. That he lived at all, was due, in the first place, to the fact that we had a plentiful supply of fresh camel's-milk, and, in the second plate, that we were promptly captured by semi-nomadic Bedouin, and, in a sense, fattened for the killing.

2.

On the second day after our rescue from the _silo_, as John Geste and I lay in a deserted mud-hut, a tall Arab, followed by our deliverer--volubly explaining that he had just found us--stooped into the hut and favoured us with a long, hard, searching stare, slightly amused, slightly sardonic and wholly unfriendly.

And the Arab was Selim ben Yussuf, that handsome human hawk.

There was no mistaking the high-bridged aristocratic nose, the keen flashing eyes beneath the perfectly arched eyebrows, the thin cruel lips between the canonically clipped moustache and the small double tuft of beard.

In the extremely dirty, dishevelled, unshorn and emaciated creature before him, Selim utterly failed to recognize the "wealthy tourist" whom jealousy had nearly prompted him to stab in the garden of Abu Sheikh Ahmed at Bouzen.

What he did see in me and John Geste, was a pair of French convicts, delivered into his hand--an extremely welcome capture, valuable whether for purposes of ransom, hostage, torture, or mere humiliating slavery.

"_Salaam aleikoum, Sheikh_," I croaked. "I claim your hospitality for myself and my comrade--And listen--He is a great man in his own country, and his father would pay a ransom of a thousand camels, for he is a very wealthy man and loves his son--"

But ere I could embroider the theme further, Selim ben Yussuf laughed unpleasantly, and with a contemptuous:

"Filthy convict dogs!" turned to our ancient rescuer and bade him deliver us alive at the _douar_, whence he had been obtaining the milk for us.

With profound obeisances and assurances of the promptest and most willing obedience, the ancient backed from the hut, vanished into thin air and was seen no more.

When, a little later, a band of ruffians came to fetch us, my strength and temper were both sorely tried. For when I tried to carry John Geste to the miserable baggage-camel provided for our transport, I was tripped up, kicked, struck, reviled and spat upon, by these well-armed braves; bitter haters, every one, of the Infidel, the _Roumi_, the invader of the sacred soil of Islam.

Luckily we were not bound, and I was able to hold John more or less comfortably on the camel. What I feared was that his illness was typhoid fever, and that rough movement would cause perforation and death. Luckily again, it was only a short ride to the encampment of the semi-nomadic tribe of which Selim ben Yussufs father was the ruling Sheikh.

From what I saw and heard of the old man, I got the impression that he was a gentleman--a real courteous, chivalrous, Arab gentleman of the old school, a desert knight of the type of which one often reads, and which one rarely meets.

Unfortunately, like so many Oriental fathers, he was so besottedly devoted to his son that he could see no wrong in him, and would deny him nothing. Further, although the aged Sheikh had by no means abdicated, the reins were slipping from his feeble hand, and were daily more firmly grasped in the strong clutch of his son.

Selim, though not yet ruler, was the power behind the throne--but there was another and a stronger power behind him.

It was before these three, as they sat at the door of a big white and brown striped tent, that we were driven, I staggering along with the unconscious John--who otherwise would have been dragged along the ground by one foot--on our arrival at the _douar_. And, in a moment, it was manifest that the old Sheikh spoke the final word, that the young Sheikh's thought was expressed by that word, while the third person's brain inspired the thought.

And the third person was the Angel of Death.

There, between the father and son, evidently beloved of both, sat the indescribably beautiful half-caste of Bouzen, the daughter of the Ouled-Naïl dancing-girl and the Englishman who had loved her and left her.

She knew me instantly, even as our glances met, and I was apprised of the fact by her long cool stare, and mocking smile, though she spoke no word and gave no sign of recognition.

Remembering the effect produced upon Selim by her previous recognition of my personal attractions, I welcomed her present reticence.

And now what?--Here was a bewildering and astonishing turn of affairs!

I had fallen into the hands of a bitter enemy of France, who was also a bitter and jealous enemy of myself. Behind him, and swaying him as a reed is swayed by the wind, was a girl notorious for her destructive evil-doing--a girl who loathed Christians in general, for her hated father's sake, and me in particular for my lack of response to her overtures at the house of Abu Sheikh Ahmed.

If she had been ready to kill me then, when I was a person of some importance, and actually in the company of the all-powerful Colonel Levasseur, what would she do to me now that I was completely in her power--helpless and harmless--a miserable piece of desert flotsam, an escaped convict, whose killing the authorities would be more disposed to approve than to punish.

I addressed myself to the old Sheikh, throwing myself upon his mercy and appealing to his chivalry and honour--in the name of Allah and the Koranic Law and his own desert custom--for at least the three days' hospitality due to the "guest of Allah," the traveller who is in need.

"Traveller!" sneered Selim. "Convict, you mean--A pariah dog that is condemned even by its fellow dogs--"

Evidently the gentle Selim knew our brown canvas uniform for what it was.

But the old gentleman rebuked him.

"Peace, my son," he gently chided, "the prayers of the unfortunate are acceptable to Allah, the Merciful, the Compassionate, for they are His children--And be who is merciful to the children of Allah is pleasing in the sight of Allah, before Whom all True Believers must one day stand--Let these two men be guests of the tribe for three days, and let them want for nothing--Thereafter let them go in peace, praising God--"

"So be it, my father," smiled Selim. And so it would be, I decided--but I doubted that we should go far "in peace."

"And if they be the condemned prisoners of the _Roumis_," he continued, "are they not then the enemies of the _Roumis_? And are not the enemies of the _Roumis_ thy friends?

"No dog of an Infidel is my friend," growled Selim, eyeing us savagely, and I felt truly glad that the old Sheikh was still master in his own house.

For the next three days we were regarded as honoured guests, and had we been the Sheikh's own sons, we could not have been more kindly and generously treated.

Our food was of the best, we were given complete and clean outfits of Arab clothing, and we shared a tent plentifully provided with rugs and cushions. We were favoured with the services of the Sheikh's own _hakim_, a learned doctor who did us no harm--as I did not give him the opportunity--and who did us much good by decreeing that we be immersed in hot water and then be clipped and shorn by the Sheikh's own barber. It was fairly easy to get the good doctor to prescribe this and whatsoever else I wanted him to prescribe, by pretending to assume that he would prescribe it. And I had only to say:

"I am sure that my sick friend will benefit _enormously_ by hot broth of goats' flesh, provided you will add to it your learned and pious incantations--" to procure abundance of both.

That three days of perfect rest, with unlimited fresh milk, broth, cheese, curds, _cous-cous_, bread, sweet-meats, butter, eggs, lemons, and occasional vegetables, did marvels for both of us, and led me to the blessed conclusion that John Geste was not, after all, suffering from malignant disease so much as from general debility and weakness.

I had only been just in time.

But--Merciful, Gracious, Benignant God--I _had_ found him--I _had_ found him--_I had found John Geste and I had saved Isobel_.

And I was curiously content and unafraid--strangely happy and unanxious, in spite of our position, our almost hopeless position between the upper French and the nether Arab mill-stones--for I knew, I _knew_, I had not been allowed to go so far that I might go no farther--I had not found John Geste to lose him again--by the hand of man or the hand of Death.

Curiously enough, John Geste and I talked but little during this time.

For the first couple of days he was so weak that I discouraged conversation; and when, by the third day, he had turned the corner, and, thanks to his splendid constitution and great natural strength of mind and body, he was making a swift recovery, conversation was difficult.

There was so much to say that we could not say it, and our talk consisted quite largely of those foolish but inevitable repetitions of expressions of incredulity and wonder.

I think it was some time before he really grasped what had happened, and realized who I was; and when he did, he could only lie and gaze at me in bewildered amazement.

And when I had slowly and carefully told him my story from the moment when I had met Isobel at Dr. Hanley-Blythe's nursing-home, to the moment when he felled the Corporal who kicked me in the face, he could only take my hand and endeavour to press it.

As became good Anglo-Saxons, we were ashamed to express our feelings, and were, for the most part, gruffly inarticulate where these were concerned.

Obviously John was worried at his inability to thank me, and, every now and then, he would break our understanding silence with a slow:

"Do you really mean that you actually enlisted in the Legion in order to get sent to the Zephyrs on the off-chance of finding *me*?--What can one say?--How can I begin to try to express--? Isobel shouldn't have let you do that--"

"Isobel had no say in the matter,". I replied. "Entirely my own affair--Gave me something to do in life--"

"It's incredible--" said John.

"Yes--A wonderful bit of luck--No, not luck--"

"I mean it's incredible that there should be a man like you, who--"

"Well, you yourself came back to Africa to look for a friend," I reminded him.

"Yes--but he had a claim on me--I owed him my life--"

"Well--" I fumbled, "a claim--If you're going to speak of _claims_--" and I stopped.

"God! How Isobel must have *loved* you--to let you come." I said.

And:

"God! How you must *love* Isobel--to have come," said John Geste, and from the great hollow eyes the very soul of this true brother of Beau Geste probed into mine.

I looked away in pain and confusion.

His hot and shaking hand seized my wrist.

"Vanbrugh," he said, "you have done for Isobel what few men have ever done for any woman in this world--will you now do something for me?"

"I will, John Geste," said I, and looked into his face. "What is it?"

"It is this--Will you answer me a question with the most absolute, perfect and complete truth--the truth, the whole truth, and nothing but the truth--without one faintest shadow of prevarication or limitation."

"I will, John Geste," said I.

"Tell me then," he begged, "does Isobel love you?"

Let those who can, be they psychologists, physiologists, psychotherapists, physicians, lovers, or plain men and women whose souls have plumbed the depths of emotion--let them, I say, explain why, in that moment I was stricken dumb.

I could not speak.

I could see the lovely face of a girl bending down to me from the back of a horse--I could see the boy, who but those few years ago was myself--I saw her smile--I heard her voice--I felt again the marvellous and mighty uprushing of my soul to the zenith of such joy as is known to human kind, when the declaration of my love had trembled on my lips--and now, _I could not speak_. I was stricken dumb--dumb as I was stricken on that morning of my highest hope and happiness, that morning of my deepest despair and pain.

John coughed slightly.

I fought for words--For a word--I wrestled as with Death itself for the power to shout, "*No!* No! No! A thousand times, no!_" And I was dumb--sitting smitten, aghast, horrified, staring into the tortured eyes of poor John Geste.

His pale pinched face turned impossibly paler and yet more pinched, and from the white lips in that frozen mask came hollowly the words that seared me so.

"Then what I ask of you, Vanbrugh, is this. Get you back safely to England. For the love of God, take care of yourself and get back quickly--And with this message--That I died in Africa--for die I shall--and that the very last words I said were--that my one wish was that you and she would be happier together than ever man and woman had been before."

And then I found my voice, a poor and ineffectual thing, hampered by a great lump in my throat, and after a cracked and miserable laugh, I contrived to say:

"Why now--that's certainly the funniest thing you would hear in a lifetime--Isobel love *me*!--Why she loves any pair of your old boots that you left at home, better than she loves the whole of the human race, myself included--" and I contrived another laugh. "Why, my dear chap, Isobel would rather be on the ground floor of Hell with you, than on the roof-garden of the Seventh Heaven with the greatest and finest man that ever lived, much less with *me*--"

His eyes still burned into mine.

"You're speaking the truth, Vanbrugh?--Yes--you are speaking the truth--Isobel could only love once--How could I doubt her--"

"You're a very sick man," said I.

"I must be," he said, and coughed slightly, again. "But oh, Vanbrugh, you--you--you--_stout fella!_--hero--What can I say to you but that I understand, Vanbrugh--I understand--" and being at the highest pitch of emotion, his English hatred of showing what he felt, came to his rescue, and with an embarrassed grin upon his ravaged face, he squeezed my arm. "Stout fella! You're a stouter man than I am, Gunga Din," he said, and fell back upon his mattress.

Yes, the Gestes could accept generously, as well as give generously--which is a thing not all generous people can do.

3.

During the three days' hospitality and grace, we had received no visits save those of the doctor, the barber, and the servants who waited on us with food, clothing and hot water; and though I had no doubt that our tent was pretty strictly guarded, we had been treated as guests rather than prisoners, in accordance with the order given by the old Sheikh.

On the fourth evening there came a change.

Instead of servants bearing a brass tray laden with excellent food, Selim himself, followed by some half-dozen of his familiars--young, haughty, truculent Sons of the Prophet--swaggered into our guest-tent.

The change which came over his face as he did so, would have been ludicrous had it been less ominous.

Expecting to see two foul and filthy ruffians, shaggy, unshorn--garbed in the tattered remnants of brown canvas uniforms, he beheld two clean and shaven gentlemen of leisure, clad much as he was himself.

And then he recognized me.

"_Allah Kerim_!" he ejaculated. "Our blue-eyed tourist of Bouzen! The contemptuous, haughty _Nazarani_ dog, who had not the good breeding to accept the kiss with which the Angel of Death would have honoured him! She shall be the Angel of Death for you indeed, this time--A kiss?--You shall kiss a glowing coal--An embrace?--You shall embrace a burning brazier--Perhaps that will put some warmth into your cold heart, you dog--And who is this other escaped convict, masquerading in that dress like a jackal in a lion's skin?--Have you slept warm, you _Roumi_ curs?--You shall sleep warm to-night--on a bed of red-hot stones."

And he gave an order that I could not hear, to one of his followers. John Geste yawned.

"Chatty lad," he said. "What's biting him?"

"He doesn't like you much and he doesn't like me a little," I replied, "and I am a bit worried. I don't know exactly how far what he says goes, in this outfit--He's the lad I was telling you about--the lover of the lady who was sitting in papa's pocket."

"And the lady?" asked John Geste. "I dimly remember that there was one."

I stole a glance at Selim. His back was turned--he had gone to the door of the tent and was looking out, seemingly in reflection.

"I am not sure that she isn't the _deus ex machina_--or shall we say the little 'dear' _ex machina_," I replied.

"Or _cherchez la femme_, since we're talking learned," smiled John. "You think she may be our fate, eh? Beware of a dark woman, what?--You know her?"

"I have met her twice, and I am not looking forward to the third time," I replied.

"What sort of a person is she?"

"Well, the gentleman at the front door has been calling as dogs quite freely--shall we say something of a lady-dog?"

"What poor old Digby used to call a bitchelor," grinned John. "Poor dear old Dig--God! I wish he and Beau were with us now--"

"Amen," said I, and was moved to add, "I'll bet they're watching, mighty interested," and, at that moment, Selim's order bore fruit in the shape of some husky negroes.

"Get up, you dogs," he snarled.

"Why certainly, most noble and courteous Arab," said John Geste, as he rose painfully to his feet. "I have eaten of your salt, and I thank you."

"You have eaten of my father's salt and you may thank him--that three days have been added to your miserable life," was the uncompromising reply.

"The arm of the French is very long, Selim ben Yussuf," I said.

"Yes, convict," he replied, "it will reach you, I think, or rather your body--The terms of the reward are 'dead or alive' I believe."

"Selim ben Yussuf!" mused John, aloud. "Son of a famed and noble Sheikh, and seller of dead men's flesh!--Does he eat it too?" he added, turning to me.

"Why no," I said. "He's far too good a merchant--he can get money for it--He sells those who eat his salt too--"

It was a dangerous line, but it _was_ a line--on Selim's pride and self-respect. Torture me he might, but I did not think he would sell me alive or dead, much less John Geste, against whom he had no grudge save that of his nationality and religion.

My last remark had certainly got him on the raw, for he strode up to me, his hand upon the big curved knife stuck in the front of his sash.

"Lying Christian dog, you have _not_ eaten of my salt," he shouted. "It was my father's--'Three days,' he said--and he is no longer in the camp."

"A great gentleman," I observed. "The old order changes--" and I shrugged my shoulders.

I had an idea that the old Sheikh had not gone very far, nor for very long--or our shrift would have been shorter.

"Throw the dogs out," he snarled, turning to his slaves, and we were unceremoniously hustled from the tent, and with sundry kicks, blows and prods with spear-butt and _matratk_-sticks, we were personally conducted to some low mean goat-skin tents, situated at a distance from the main camp and much too near an enclosure obviously tenanted by goats.

Into one of the tents we were thrown, and for the moment, left--but around a camp-fire that burned in front of it, certain unmusical loud fellows of the baser sort rendered night hideous and escape impossible.

A glance round the filthy and dilapidated tent showed it to be entirely unfurnished, nor was anything added unto us save a huge and disgusting negro, who entered and made himself one with us, who were evidently his sacred charge.

John Geste, courteous ever, gave him welcome.

"Take a chair, Archibald, and make yourself at home," said he. "Take three, if you can--"

Archibald, or rather Koko, as we later discovered his name to be, made no reply.

He merely sat him down and stared unwinkingly and unwaveringly.

If he had been told to watch us, he certainly did it. And after his eyes had bored into us like gimlets for a few hours, we were constrained, with many apologies, to turn our backs on him.

For more hours we sat and talked of plans of escape, and could only conclude that, in our weak state, our one hope was the good-will of the old Sheikh.

Nor was this hope a strong one, for however kindly the old man might treat us while we were in his power, it was too much to hope that he would do anything but hand us back, safe and sound, to the French authorities.

Any Bedouin tribe grazing its flocks in the neighbourhood of the Zaguig-Great Oasis Road, would act wisely in giving every possible proof of its innocence, virtue and correct attitude towards the French, in view of the recent attack upon the road-gangs.

CHAPTER XI

That night I was taken horribly ill; so ill that, after thinking it must be cholera, thought departed altogether, and I knew nothing more for several days.

When I did return to a realization of my surroundings, I found that I was back in the guest-tent, and that I was alone.

Where was John Geste?

My last memory was of his helping me in that foul goat-skin hole, while that beastly nigger, callous as an animal, sat and stared.

A horrible panic fear gripped my heart, and feebly I called John's name. And even as my heart almost stopped, I was reassured by the thought, the conviction, the certainty, that this wonderful thing, this finding of John Geste, against all probability, was no chance, no piece of luck--much less a colossal mockery. We are not the sport of mocking Fates.

But I called his name again, with what little strength I had.

Quite possibly the old Sheikh had returned, and, finding that we had been evilly entreated, had had us brought back, not only to the guest-tent, but had given us a tent each. The better sort of Arab is capable of much fineness in the matter of hospitality--a hospitality enjoined by his religion and by countless centuries of desert custom, the outcome of desert need.

At my second feeble call, a man stepped into the tent, in the shade of which he had probably been sleeping. He was one of the servants who had previously waited on us in this same tent.

"Where is my brother?" said I.

"Gone, _Sidi_," replied the man, and promptly departed, returning in a few minutes, accompanied by the _hakim_.

From this gentleman's delight in finding me conscious, I gathered that he had been strictly charged to effect my recovery, the credit for which he promptly awarded himself. To this he was very welcome, as was, to me, the broth which he prescribed--together with pills, potions and Koranic extracts. These last he painfully wrote on scraps of rag wherewith he enriched the mutton broth.

The pills I pushed into the sand beneath my rug. With the potions I watered their burial-place. The rags, in my gratitude and generosity, I bestowed upon the deserving waiter, by way of a tip. For the broth I found a good home, and felt the better for it.

But when, after thanking and congratulating the eminent physician I asked:

"And where is my brother, _Sidi Hakim?_" I got the same unsatisfactory reply.

"_Gone!_" and a gesture of the thin hands and delicate fingers, to indicate a complete evanishment as of smoke into thin air.

In spite of my continued reassurement of myself, I was anxious, worried, frightened, and filled with a horrible and apprehensive sense of impotence.

However, there was nothing to be done, save to recover strength as quickly as might be possible.

"Now let me think--clearly and calmly," said I--and promptly fell asleep.

When I awoke, the Angel of Death was sitting beside me, chin on hand, and regarding me with a look which was anything but inimical.

Staring, startled from my sleep, I read her thoughts.

I am quite certain that at that moment, all that was European in her was uppermost. She was her father's daughter, civilized, white, kind.

She smiled, and while the smile was on her face she was utterly and truly beautiful, more beautiful than any woman I have ever seen, save one.

Extending a gentle--and very beautifully manicured--hand, she wiped my brow with a small and scented handkerchief, product of Paris.

"Ze poor boy," she said softly. "But he has been so ver' ver' ill," and kissed me in the manner and the spirit in which a mother kisses a sick child.

"Thank you--er--Mam'zelle," I said. "Where is my friend?"

"_Gone_," she replied.

For the third time I had received that sinister reply to my question.

"Gone--_pouff!_ Like zat," she continued, and this time the gesture was that of one who blows away a feather.

"I play a trick on Selim, wiz him--Zat Selim think himself too clever--_Oui--Sacré Dieu_--"

"What trick? Tell me quickly--Where is he!" I begged

"Zat Selim?" she asked.

"No, no, no! My friend, my brother! Quick! Where is he?"

She laughed mischievously, obviously quite pleased with herself.

"_Oh, la, la!_ He does not matter--He serve his purpose--He serve my purpose too--Oh! zat great fool, Selim!--But now you go sleep again--"

"Yes, yes, but tell me first, where is my friend? What have you done with him?" I begged.

"What is he to you?" she asked, and her pleased smile faded a trifle.

"My friend! My brother!" I replied.

Her expression changed. A look of doubt succeeded the smile.

"Oh, well!" she shrugged, as she rose to her feet, "--he is only a man!--But _I_ am a _woman!_--" And her smile, as she left the tent, was not in the least motherly.

2.

My state of mind may be imagined.

Against all probability, against possibility almost, I had found John Geste, had thanked God for that miracle--and John Geste had vanished--The cup dashed from my lips. The fruit of my sufferings and labour--dust and ashes.

I groaned in spirit, and I was near despair. But, if I can be understood, I lost hope without losing faith--and did the one thing I could do. I strove to regain my physical strength, while I walked delicately in the path of friendship with the Angel.

That evening she visited me again, all smiles and honey, honey that grew a little over-sweet and cloying.

I learned that Selim ben Yussuf was away, with most of the fighting-men of the tribe, and that the old Sheikh was at Zaguig, presumably by pressing request of the Authorities, who would probably be making life a little difficult for every tribal leader within a hundred miles.

On this and other topics of local interest, she chatted freely, and seemed quite willing to tell me truthfully everything but the one fact I wanted to know.

The moment I spoke of John Geste she became evasive, laughed mischievously, and as I pressed for an answer, seemed first embarrassed and then impatient and annoyed.

After she left the tent, I thought I would see what happened if I attempted to leave it too.

Koko happened.

He made it quite clear to me, though without violence or even truculence of manner, that the guest-tent was my home and that from home I should not stray. As I returned and dejectedly dropped upon my mattress, the _hakim_ entered and I had a bright idea.

I asked him whether he had any personal interest in my recovery.'

He replied that my life was dearer to him than that of his oldest son. I said that that was very nice, but ventured to point out that one would scarcely have thought it, when I lay practically dying, down by the goat-farm.

Ah, that was quite a different matter. Selim ben Yussuf had left no doubt, in reasonable minds, that the news of my early demise would be received with equanimity. Hence something in my _cous-cous_, which had nearly done the trick.

But the news of my approaching demise had not been received by the Sid Jebrail, the Angel of Death, with any equanimity at all.

On the contrary.

She had left no possibility of doubt in any reasonable mind that my death would only precede that of the good _hakim_ by a very few minutes--and hence the fact that my life was dearer to him than that of his oldest son, and that I, being possessed of the feelings of a gentleman would undoubtedly consider the feelings of another gentleman, and live for all I was worth.

This was most excellent, and I returned to my original point.

"So you *do* want me to live, _Sidi Hakim?_"

"I desire nothing more fervently, _Sidi Roumi_."

"Well, I can and shall live, on one condition, and on one only--That I am at once told what has become of my brother, and that I am thereafter at once restored to his society--Get that right plumb in the centre of your intelligent and most noble mind, _Sidi Hakim_."

The good doctor's face fell.

"_Allahu Akbar!_" he murmured in astonishment. "I have heard of these things--People pining for each other--Men for women--Women for men--Even the lower animals--But a man for a man!--Is it possible?"

"It is here under your nose, _Sidi Hakim_," I said earnestly. "I'm going to die right here, to your great inconvenience, I fear--Where is my brother?"

"He is gone, _Sidi_--but do not grieve--He is alive and well--in the best of health, and full of happiness--And he is being _well_ looked after--Oh yes--On my head and my life--And on my son's head and on my son's life--I swear he is being most carefully looked after--Yes--By the Ninety and Nine Names of Allah--By the Beard of the Prophet--"

I shut my eyes and fetched a fearful groan.

"Tell me everything quickly, for I am on the point of Death," I whispered as deathfully as I could contrive.

"_Sidi! Sidi!_" he wailed, "I dare not say a word--_She_ would have my feet set in the fire--"

"All-right--Good-bye," I replied, and, like King Hezekiah, I turned my face unto the wall, continuing this death-bedlamite comedy, in the hope of getting some scrap of information from this gibbering pantaloon.

"_Stop! Stop! Sidi_," squeaked my medical attendant. 'Will you swear not to betray me to her, if I tell you what I know--I know nothing really."

"I will not betray you, _Sidi Hakim_," I said. "And I will not die if you tell me the truth."

"Your brother has gone back to--er--his--er--friends," announced the _hakim_, diffidently.

His information certainly brought me back to life, all right. I shot up in bed and seized him, almost by the beard.

"Do you mean to say that the _French_ have got him again?" I shouted.

"Yes--Yes--" admitted the _hakim_. "He is perfectly safe now--"

I fell back upon my pillows feeling like dying in good earnest. "He was perfectly safe now!"

John Geste was back in the hands of the French and all my work was to do again—

CHAPTER XII

I don't think I gave way to despair. Although my heart sank into the very depths, there was, as it were, a life-line to the surface--a line of faith and hope. I had found John Geste once--What man has done once, man can do again. Evidently this girl knew something, and apparently had some hand in whatever had happened; and almost certainly Selim ben Yussuf had played a part. I imagined myself with my hands at Selim's throat, squeezing and squeezing until either the eyes came out of his head, or the truth out of his mouth.

What had the girl said?

"I played a trick on Selim with him"--and I half-wished it was recognized good form, and quite permissible if not praiseworthy, to serve her as, in imagination, I had just served Selim.

What I must find out was whether the _hakim_ had spoken the truth--which was quite problematical--and, if so, whether John had been taken to Bouzen, Zaguig, or one of the construction-camps on the Road. Of course it was quite possible that he was even now within a few yards of me--either above ground or below it.

What in the name of God could be the trick that she had played on Selim ben Yussuf _with John_.

Followed by a fine-looking Arab, whom later I knew to be Abd'allah ibn Moussa, she again entered the tent.

"Tie his feet firmly, but without hurting him, and his hands in such a way that he is not uncomfortable," she ordered. "He will get strong very quickly now, and I don't want him to run away."

"Will you kindly tell me what has become of my brother, Mademoiselle?" I asked politely. "There can be no harm in my knowing, can there, especially now that you have tied me up so securely?"

"_Eh bien_, how he chatter about zis friend of his I I tell you he has _gone_--gone where you nevaire see him any more--But you see *me*, isn't it?--Don't I look nicer than that friend of yours, _hein?_ "

"You'd look a lot nicer than you do, if you told me everything, Mademoiselle," I replied. "You are a European--you are a woman--we are Europeans--we have done you no harm. Why behave like one of these uncivilized Arabs?"

"_Ah, oui_, zat's so," agreed the Death Angel. "You are both Europeans. I wish all Europeans have only one heart, and I can stab it. I wish all Europeans have only one throat, and I can cut it."

She looked like a tiger-cat, and while I watched, her face changed utterly, and, with a sweet and gentle smile, she dropped to her knees and leant over me.

"All Europeans except you, I mean, Blue-Eyes. You are nice and good and _gentil_. You would _nevaire desert_ anybody, isn't it? _Nevaire would you do that_, I know in my heart." And she kissed me on the lips.

"You kiss me," she said. "You kiss me quick, and say you nevaire run away, and I untie your hands and feet, and take your _parole_, isn't it? Kiss me, _kiss me_, I tell you."

I closed my eyes, set my lips firmly--and received a stinging blow on the face.

2.

What shall I say about this astounding woman, known as "The Angel" among the Arabs, and as "The Angel of Death" to those Europeans who had the privilege of her acquaintance.

She was the most extraordinary and remarkable human being whom I have ever met, yet at the same time there was really no reason that she should astonish and astound, for she was the perfectly logical outcome of her heredity and her environment.

What should the daughter of a hundred generations of savage courtesans--unscrupulous, avaricious and unbridled--sometimes be, but an evil unscrupulous savage? What should the daughter of a blue-eyed Nordic sometimes be, but balanced, self-respecting and amenable to ideas of civilization.

We are assured that in every Jekyll there is some Hyde, and in every Hyde there is some Jekyll; and the best and the worst of us are well aware that the materials of which our characters are woven are not of even quality. But with this "Angel," it was not only a case of a mixed nature reflecting mixed descent, but a case of a complete and undisputed occupation of her body at different times, by two utterly distinct and different personalities.

For part of the time--for the greater part of the time--she was just herself, the Anglo-African, the half-caste, with all the expected attributes of the mulatto. But for the rest, she was either "The Death-Angel," the savage, the African, the lawless and evil native courtesan; or else Mlle. Blanchfleur, the European, the normal white woman, calculable, and, within her sphere, conventional--

Be that as it may, she most certainly astonished and astounded me--this most pathetic, most terrible, nightmare woman--Nightmare indeed--for, thinking of her frequently, as I do--I often dream of her, and though these dreams are not nightmares in the sense that dreams about my father are, their warp is horror and their woof is pity; and the dream is sad, melancholy and depressing beyond belief.

If I could but put the Angel from my mind!

I cannot and I never shall--I think of her, to this day, as frequently as I think of Isobel herself, and infinitely more unhappily. (That is a foolish thing to say, for there is nothing whatsoever of unhappiness in my thoughts of Isobel. What did Isobel ever bring to any living soul but happiness?)

Some of the truth of what I have said of the Angel of Death can be grasped by realizing that her actions ranged from the decreeing and superintending of torture, to the performance of acts of trusting and noble generosity; from venal bestiality, to a high idealism; from a bitter savage vengefulness, to a noble and generous forgiveness.

In short from the worst of her Arab mother to the best of her Christian father.

3.

Whenever Koko, the negroid slave, whose precious charge I was, took his yellow-whited eyes from me, yawned, scratched himself, and stared vacantly out into the wonderful desert night, I gnawed at the palm-fibre cords which bound my wrists. Should I succeed in freeing my hands, it was my unamiable intention to free my feet, and then to do my utmost to incapacitate this gentleman.

He had a long sharp knife, and a heavy stick, short and thick. I had a hard and useful fist. With one of these three weapons something might be done. I did not at all like the knife idea. My own fancy ran in the direction of a swift and knock-out presentation of the fist, followed by a more leisured confirmatory application of the heavy stick. This seemed to me a reasonable compromise between the slaughter of a citizen, who after all was but doing his duty, and my continuation in a position of extreme peril.

"_Eh bien! On dîne donc, n'est-ce pas?_" murmured a silky voice, as I sat with down-bent head, my teeth fixed in the unpleasant-tasting hairy cord.

"'Ow you like it, _hein?_--Eat a bit more then, M'sieur Blue-eyes. P'raps that the las' food you get, what?"

"_Bon soir, Mademoiselle_," I replied, with an attempt at a debonair smile and an air of gay bonhomie that I was very far from feeling. "Won't you join me?--Have a bite--" and I raised my bound wrists toward her.

"Ah, so you say, is it, Blue-eye--Yellow-hair--Laughing face--" replied the Angel, and kneeling beside me, seized my wrists and deliberately bit my hand with the ferocity and strength of a wild beast.

"Laike what you call savage dog, _hein?_" she said, thrusting her face against mine.

"Or a dog of a savage," I observed.

"_Sacré Dieu!_ How I _hate_ you--_hate_ you--hate you!" she cursed, and, even as I was thinking, "Better than loving me, anyhow," she seized my head and crushed her lips violently against mine--

"_Baisez-moi!--Baisez-moi!--Baisez-moi!--_" she cried.

"Soh! You will not kees me, noh?--Naow, leetle Blue-eyes, you kees me, or see what come," and she took me by the throat.

I was revived from the faintness of strangulation by the pain of her setting her sharp teeth in my lip--Darkness, and a roaring in my ears--A voice speaking from very far away--Had I been clubbed on the head--What was that?--Oh yes, the gentle Angel.

"Oah, you _won't_ kees me, _hein?_ You won't lov' me, _hein?_ You won't 'ave me any price, noa? S'pose I say you never kees any other girl, _hein?_" she panted. "S'pose I cut your lips off, yes?" and she seized my ears and shook my head violently to and fro.

Most painful, undignified and humiliating.

"Uh! You say nothing on that, is it! You don't grin some more, _hein?_--What s'pose I say you never _look_ any other girl?--What s'pose I have those blue eyes for myself--'Ave them out your silly 'ead, yes?" and as she spoke, she thrust her thumbs violently and most painfully beneath my eyes. I suffered most horribly in the next few minutes, but I can truthfully say that the idea of surrender to this tempestuous petticoat absolutely never entered my head. I don't know why, but the idea simply never occurred to me. Nor do I think that the reason for this lay in any Joseph-like virtue inherent in my character, nor in any definite feeling that when I did fall from grace, it would not be.

I think my resistance was simply and solely due to the fact that I am one of those stubborn creatures whom you can lead on a hair, but cannot drag with a cable. Also I have Red Indian blood, and my "No" means " *No* ."

Every fibre of my being rebelled against this coercion, and the Angel was beating her head not only upon mine but against a stone wall--compounded of the dogged, unyielding rock of Anglo-Saxon stubbornness, and the cement of Red Indian stoicism, tenacious and prideful.

Not unto me, but unto mine ancestors the credit, if I bore well the sufferings and the temptation--the temptation to escape torture--that were put upon me--

But always I had to remember that a dead, maimed, or blinded Otis Vanbrugh would be of but little service to John Geste--to Isobel--

Springing to her feet, the Angel of Death (by means of a violent kick upon his latter end, tactfully turned towards us) attracted the attention of our chaperon, who squatted in the doorway of the tent, pondering perchance, Infinity, Life and the Vast Forever--or indeed, his latter end.

With a nasty oath and a stream of guttural orders, in Arabic, she drove him from the tent.

During his absence, the Angel gave me what she termed my last chance, and made it clear to me, beyond the peradventure of a doubt, the terms upon which I might retain my right to life, liberty and the pursuit of happiness.

By the time I had made it equally clear to the Angel that, since I was not a person to be led along the primrose paths of pleasant dalliance, still less was I one to be scourged adown their alluring ways, the good Koko had returned and entered with seven devils worse than himself.

By the Angel's clear and explicit direction, I was roughly jerked to my feet, dragged from the tent, and thrown down at the root of the nearest tree.

With promptitude and dispatch, a young palm was cut through, some six feet from the ground.

Impalement! Surely not? It could not be possible that this girl, who had European blood in her veins, who had consorted with Europeans, who knew something of Christian teaching, and who was, after all, a woman--was going to have me stripped and stuck upon the sharpened end of this tapering stump, to die miserably--to die a lingering death of unspeakable agony, while a crowd watched, jeered and gloated.

A woman!--But Hell hath no fury like a woman scorned--If Hell had a fury such as this Angel at that moment, the Devil himself must have felt unsafe--

No, they were not sharpening the top of the stump.

I was again jerked to my feet, held in position and tightly bound to it.

It was to be a stake and not a spear.

Surely she was not going to have me burnt alive--Burnt before her eyes--

A woman!--But a woman scorned--

What should I do as the flames mounted, and death was imminent--Plead to the woman?--Agree?--

Dead, I could not serve Isobel--A hard choice--

No. I saw no preparation for a fire.

Their immediate task completed, the black soldiers stood about--incurious, stupid, animal The Angel gave them a curt order and they went, with scarce a further glance at me--and I and that she-devil were alone.

4.

"Now, my friend," she said when we were alone, "we just see 'ow long you defy ze Angel of Death!--_Sans doute_ you t'ink yourself ver' fine man and bear pain like Aissa dervish, _hein?_ But I tell you somesing. Don't you leave it too late, so that when you say '_All right, Mademoiselle; I finish--I give in--I do what you laike_,' you are not already too spoilt, see?--No good saying zat after you gone blind for always, or after your tongue cut out for always, or you are too burnt ever to walk about any more, see?"

I saw.

"Tell me, Blue-Eyes," this well-named young woman continued, "you rather be deaf and dumb both, or blind only--if I be kind and give you choice?--Perhaps you anger me, and you get all three!--Perhaps I get ver' angry and you 'ave no 'ands and no feets--_Oh, la, la_, zis poor lil' Blue-Eyes!--He ver' proud man until one day he got no eyes, no tongue, no ears, no hands, no feet--Oh, ver' proud man--ver' 'andsome man--till someone cut off his lips and his nose and his eye-lids---not so pretty then--What you t'ink?"

I remembered John Geste's cold iron courage, and yawned. The Death Angel was certainly taken aback.

It then occurred to me to use my lips, while I had them, to whistle a little air. And the first that came to my mind was the one I had sung, or howled, to the Zouave Sergeant as I lay under the wall in Zaguig.

"_Mon Dieu_," whispered the girl. "Is it you are ze bravest man ever I have met--_or is it perhaps you e ink I am making ze bluff and will not torture you?_"

A little bit of both, I thought. I am playing at being a brave man--and surely no human girl could cut a man's eyes out, stab his ear-drums, hammer a wedge into his mouth and cut his tongue out--Not even an "Angel of Death."

"Because if it is zat, I soon show you," continued this she-devil. And drawing her knife she ripped my _jubba_ and _kaftan_ downward from the throat, exposing my chest.

"Kees me," she said softly, rising on her toes, and placing her lips on mine.

"_No?_"--

And on the right side of my chest she made a horizontal gash.

I started and quivered with the sudden pain, and was thankful that she had not, as I had expected, driven the knife into my throat or heart.

She stepped back a pace.

"'Ow you like _zat_--for start?" she asked, and, again placing her lips on mine, whispered "Kees me."

"_No?_"

And again she slashed my breast with a horizontal gash an inch below the other.

"_Now_ kees me," she said, and put her lips to mine.

"_No?_"

And with a sloping cut she joined the ends of the two gashes with a third.

"See?" she asked. "Ze letter Z!--I write my name on you--ZAZA--Always you remember Zaza then--For ze little time you live, I mean--Twelve cuts, it is. I do it ver' neatly now."

Evidently a case of practice making perfect, I thought. "You kees me now, _hein?_"

I tried to think coolly. If I let this fiend kill, or utterly incapacitate, me, there was the end of my search for John Geste--the end of my service to Isobel. I must give way, for their sakes. But, I told myself, were John Geste safe in England, this young woman should not defeat me. Pride is a poor thing to be proud of, and so is stubbornness, but I freely confess to being proud of both.

Well, the dozen cuts would not put me out of action, so she could carry on--But if it really came to blinding, she would win--and, as she felt my unresponsive lips, she changed from cold anger to red-hot rage--which was probably ray salvation.

"_Kees me! Kees me! Kees me!_" she screamed, hammering my face and body with her clenched fists.

"You _won't, hein?_--Then I'll waste no more time!--Now you kees me and say you love me--or you die--and you die slow--and blind," and she pressed the point of her knife sharply in under my right eye.

I saw the grim face of the Sioux Chief, my ancestor, but even to be worthy of him, I must not hold out longer. She was going to blind me--and no blind man could help John and Isobel.

I gave in.

"_Zaza_," I began--and the word was drowned in a scream, as the girl flung down the knife, threw her arms about my neck, and kissed me passionately and repeatedly.

"Oh, forgive, forgive!" she cried. "I was mad--A devil comes into me and I must be cruel--cruellest to what I love best. Forgive me, dear Blue-Eyes, and see--promise me you will come back to me, and I will let you go after your friend--I will do anything for you if you will promise to come back to me--I cannot live any more without you--Look--I will do _anysing--everysing_ if you promise to come back," and, with a slight return of her former manner:

"And I swear to God, on this piece of the True Cross"--and she touched her book-shaped locket--"and to Allah, by this Hair of the Beard of the Prophet, and by my mother's soul, that, if you do not promise, I will stab you to the heart, and then stab myself to the heart also, and we will die together here."

"I promise," I said, only too thankfully--"that I will come back to you as soon as I have seen my friend leave Africa in safety--if you will tell me the truth and give me every help you can."

"Yes, and suppose zat is not in many years--in ten years and twenty years, when I am ugly old woman?

"I give you one year," she added. "You come back to me in one year, or directly you save your friend," and picking up her knife she placed its point above my heart, and I knew with perfect certainty that, if I refused, I should die.

"I will return to you in a year," I said, "or before, if I have found my friend within that time, provided you tell me the truth, and help me in every way."

"And you will marry me?" she asked.

"Of course," I replied.

"And you will take me from this vile country where I am a wicked woman, and neither Arab nor European?"

"I will," I said, "but get this clear--the sooner my friend is found and saved, and sent out of Africa, the sooner will you get what you want--Now tell me--What was this trick you played on Selim ben Yussuf?"

As she cut at the cords that bound me, she told me how Selim ben Yussuf, in jealous rage, had decided to torture me to death, as soon as his father went safely away to Zaguig.

At that moment, a French patrol, a _peloton méhariste_, had ridden into the camp, and Zaza had pointed out to Selim ben Yussuf that a far finer vengeance than mere death by torture, would be to hand me back to the ghastly slavery from which I had escaped!-- Moreover, he would be killing two birds with one stone, for, by giving up an escaped convict, he would be doing a good deal to sweeten the somewhat unsavoury reputation that he bore with the French.

Selim ben Yussuf had agreed that the idea was a splendid one, and had given orders for the _Roumi_ prisoner, in the white burnous, to be brought and handed over to the _goumiers_ of the patrol.

Anticipating this, she had instructed Abd'allah ibn Moussa to take away John's blue burnous and give kin my white one--

So the _hakim_ had told the truth!--

After chafing my limbs, and lavishing upon me the loving tender care and kindnesses of a mother or a wife, Zaza helped me back to my tent--did everything for my comfort, and suggested that, since our bargain was made, I should now relax my foolish and insulting behaviour, and show myself as fond and loving toward her as she was more than willing to be toward me.

The position was a delicate one.

The last thing in the world, that I wanted to do, was to offend her, to bring back her spirit of savagery, to make her anything but my most earnest helper. And the last thing but one, that I wanted to do, was to make love to her.

"Zaza," I said. "Listen. We've made a bargain. Are you going to keep your side of it?"

"Most pairfectly," she replied, "but, oh, most truly."

"And so am I," I said. "When I come back I will be your husband. I will be kind, and gentle, and everything you want me to be to you, but now it is business, work, planning and thinking--not love-making. Do you understand?

"I onderstand," said Zaza. "You will come back to me. Yes, yes, I trust you--I _know_ you will come back--my dear--You would never desert a woman--"

CHAPTER XIII

I suppose that it is a perfectly vain imagining when I wonder whether the Angel's last fiendish outbreak--that so nearly cost me my sight, if not my life--_was_ her last. It would give me very great peace of mind to think that the mood that followed, the mood of remorse and utter repentance, could be thenceforth her normal condition, and that her vehemently expressed hatred of savagery, violence and vice, would last.

Vain imaginings and foolish hopes, I fear. For a temperament is a temperament and she was as much the daughter of her Arab mother as she was of her Christian father.

But the girl that sat the night through, beside my couch, was lovable, gentle, a civilized white woman and rather the ministering angel, "when pain and anguish wring the brow," than the sinister Death Angel of so short a time before. She was, moreover, pathetic and pitiful, and it touched my heart to hear her aspirations to that way of life, way of thought, and way of conduct, that befitted the daughter of her father.

"We will never come near this accursed country ever again, my dear one, when you are my 'usban'--We will go to Paris, and Wien, and Londres, an' I will be so good an' r-r-respectable--An' everyone will call me Madame and Missis, an' not silly evil names like Angel of Death--An' we will have a fine 'ouse an' everysing _comme il faut_--An' all my clo'es shall be make in Paris--An' we will go to the Opera--An' we will ride in ze Bois--An' I will not be Moslem at all, but all Christian--An' scorn all zem _demi-mondaine_ like 'ell--

"You will come back to me--You will start to come back to me ze day your frien' go on board his ship?--Or else you give up ze search for 'im, an' start back to me, one year from zis day, _hein?_--You _promise?_--

"Yes--Yes--I know you speak truth--I know men--I know ze true voice an' ze false voice--Ze true eyes from ze false eyes--From us of ze Ouled-Naïl no man can hide behind his face--No, no--I am _not_ of ze Ouled-Nall--_A bas les Ouled-Naïls_--I am English--I am daughter of Omar ze Englishman--Yes--Yes--I know you speak truth--Your blue eyes are true eyes--Your kind voice is true voice--I _know_ you will come back to me--

"Look, dear one,--will you not swear it for me on Bible and Koran both? Swear it before your God and my Allah--Will you not swear it on zis leetle gold book I wear roun' my neck--Nevaire I take it off--it is a great talisman an' great amulet--One side is my Father and a piece of True Cross--That is God side--On other side is my Mother an' one hair of ze Beard of ze Prophet--Zat is Allah side--Ze Sultan himself gave it to her mother--No harm can come to me while I have such a thing as zis, can it?--I would put it roun' your neck, dear one, an' give it to you, but I dare not let it go from me--All would be good for you, an' that I would laike--But it might not be bringing you back to me--If I keep it, all will be good for me, an' then it will be bringing _you_ back to me--But when you come back to me, you shall have it an' wear it always, night an' day, an' then no harm can ever come to you--I will show you ze pictures of my Father an' my Mother to-morrow--

"Always I am afraid to open it at night-time, lest I lose ze piece of ze True Cross which is only a tiny splinter; or ze hair of ze Beard of ze Prophet--Zat would be too ter-r-rible--I should die--

"Oh, it will be bringing _you_ safe back to me--Yes--Even though I wear it you will be safe, because unless it kept you safe and brought you back to me, it would not be bringing good to me, an' making me happy, isn't it?--Yes--it will keep you safe for me--An' your truth, honour and goodness will make you come--

"Oh I an' I know--Such fun--Old Haroun el Rafiq shall do a sand-reading and tell us--Now I have nevaire spoke your name an' you have nevaire seen him, so he cannot know--We shall see--"

Calling to Koko, she bade him fetch Haroun el Rafiq, and, half an hour or so later, a strange hairless creature of indeterminate age and with the deadest features and the livest eyes I have ever beheld, followed Koko into the tent, salaamed humbly to the Angel, fixed his burning eyes on mine, and squatted cross-legged on the ground. From a small sack he tipped out a pile of sand before him, smoothed it flat with the palm of his hand, made a geometrical pattern upon the surface with white pebbles, and studied his handiwork with rapt attention.

After a minute or so of this contemplation, he wiped out the pattern, smiled as to himself and at his own thoughts, shook his head, rose to his feet and made to leave the tent.

"Stop! Stop!" cried the Angel. "You've told us nothing--"

"What does the Sitt desire to know?" inquired the soothsayer.

"First of all, whether this Sidi will return?"

"Return where?" asked the man. "To this place?"

"Will return to me, I mean," said the girl frankly.

"He will," promptly replied the man, and the enigmatic smile again disturbed the frozen calm of his dead features. "I saw him riding at the head of a goodly company--Riding from the north, straight to you--I saw the _kafilah_ arrive amid scenes of joy and welcome--I saw him stride to your tent and I saw you rush forth and embrace him as a lover--I saw you feasting with him, alone, in a bridal tent--"

The Angel sat with parted lips and shining eyes.

"Did you see more?--More--" she urged.

"No," answered the man, and I knew he was lying. "It is enough--"

"Yes, it is enough," murmured the Angel.

"More than enough," I thought.

The sand-diviner's prophecy elated my companion as unreasonably as it depressed me.

"Yes--You will come back--_C'est vrai_--I feel it _here_--" she said, laying her hand upon her heart.

"Yes, I shall come back, as I have promised," I said, "if I live--But the more immediate question is when shall I _start?_"

"Oh, my dear one--my dear one--my love--_Must_ you leave me at all?--Why must you go?--He is only a convict--a _scélerat_--A what-you-call dam' rascal--"

"He is an innocent man, and the finest man that ever lived," I remarked, "and he is my friend. I only came to this country to find him--And through you I lost him--The sooner I go to look for him, the sooner I shall be able to return to you."

"Oh, my dear one, my dear one, if I had only known!--What a _fool_--What a _devil_, I was--Oh, cannot I come wiz you?--Yes, _why_ cannot I come wiz you?--It is not zat I do not trust you, but I cannot bear zat you should leave me--"

"You cannot come with me," I said. "In the first place, Selim ben Yussuf would be on our track with half the tribe, the moment he returned to find you gone--In the second place, you cannot live like a hunted wild beast, as I may have to do. Besides, I may give myself up to the French again, if I can get news of him in no other way."

And I pondered the fact that there would be no record nor witness of the mutiny that had led to our incarceration in the _silo_, if, as our deliverer had told us, the whole unit had been surrounded and wiped out, to a man. John Geste and I, if I returned, would merely be two of the convicts who had somehow escaped the massacre.

"No, I cannot come wiz you," sighed the Angel "I should be 'indrance an' not ze 'elp, an', as you say, Selim ben Yussuf would capture us and keel you--But I can help you--Yes, I can send you oil wiz ze best of everysing--You shall have my own camels an' men--when you mus' go--"

"You cannot go until you are stronger," she added.

"I must go before Selim ben Yussuf returns," I reminded her.

"Yes--" she agreed. "But you need not go far until you are strong. You could go a day's ride and camp--An' I will tell Selim zat you, zat is to say _your frien'_, as he thinks, died--The _hakim_ will swear it--He fears me greatly--"

"He certainly does," I agreed.

"Yes--I have one or two spells--" she smiled. "Spells an' magics zat you buy in ze chemist's shop in Algiers--An' potions--Ah, _oui_--potions--One drop of which makes e hard stone or e steel, bubble an' smoke--An' I will send Abd'allah ibn Moussa wiz you--My own faithful servant--He is faithful as ze horse of ze Arab, an' ze dog of ze Englishman--He is as brave as ze lion, an' as true as Life an' Death--

"He was ze devoted servant an' frien' of my Mother, an' he nurse me when I am a baby--An' now he lof me laike he lof my Mother--If I say to 'im, '_Go you, Abd'allah ibn Moussa, wiz zis man. He is my lover--die for him, or die wiz him,_' he will not come back wizzout you, an' I will feel corafor'ble in my 'eart--Nevaire, nevaire will he leave you--"

I felt that such fidelity might prove embarrassing. "He'll be a useful guide, anyhow," I agreed. "But I'll send him back as soon as I am well on my way, and feeling fairly strong."

"I shall tell him not to leave you," said the girl. "Well, I may have to leave him," I replied. "But anyhow, the sooner you give him instructions to get your camels and people together, the better."

I knew something of Arab dilatoriness and the utter meaninglessness of time, in the desert.

Without further remark, she rose to her feet, drew her veil about her face, and left the tent.

I followed her to the entrance, with some vague idea of escape from the terrible silken meshes of the dreadful web that this jewelled spider was spinning about me.

"Salaam, Sidi," grinned the unutterable Koko.

"Hell!" I replied, and again flung myself down upon my cushions.

2.

A few minutes later, the Angel returned, followed by an Arab, whose fine and noble face was that of a man of middle age, great intelligence, philosophic calm, high courage, and great determination and tenacity.

I speak without exaggeration. The man's face was noble and he proved to be a noble man, if fidelity, endurance, unswerving loyalty and courage, connote nobility.

"Zis is Abd'allah ibn Moussa," said the Angel, and the man salaamed respectfully. "Zis is a _Roumi_ lord," she continued, turning to Abd'allah.

"Also he is my Lord and my Master, and your Lord and your Master--He is my lover and he will raise me up to be his wife--Go with him, Abd'allah--Follow where he leads--Sleep where he sleeps--Live where he lives--And die where he dies--But he will not die, Abd'allah--for you will guard his life with yours, and you will bring him back to me--"

"On my head and on my life be it," replied the man.

"Go and make ready," said his mistress, and he went away.

There was a commotion of hails, shouting, and men running--alarums and excursions without, in fact.

Abd'allah ibn Moussa turned black into the tent.

"A _kafikih_ comes," he said, and went about his business. The Angel's eyes met mine and her face paled.

"Zat Selim!" she said, as with a bitter laugh, I ejaculated:

"Selim ben Yussuf!"

"I will keel heem, zat so-clever Selim," whispered the Angel, and the European side of her character seemed to fade somewhat.

"I must hide you--I must hide you--He =Lit not see your face--See! You must go back to the goat-herds' tents as soon as it is safe--I will keep Selim in his tents--I will send Abd'allah to take you back--I will tell zis Selim zat e frien' of ze blue-eye Nazarani is dead, an' Abd'allah shall disguise you--Yes, like a poor blind _miskeen_--"

Well, things seemed to be going wrong indeed.

What would I not have given for a few hours of normal health and strength.

I must leave it to the wit and the wiles of the Angel to keep me hidden until I could get away.

The estimable Koko stooped into the tent, very full of himself.

"His Highness, the Sidi Emir, the Sidi Sheikh el Hamel el Kebir, Shadow of the Prophet, and Commander of the Faithful, has arrived with his great Wazir, noble sheikhs, captains, and many soldiers," he announced pompously.

"He calls for the high Sheikh Yussuf ben Amir, and for Selim ben Yussuf his son, and for the Sheikh's captains and _ekhwan_ of the tribe."

The Angel's face relaxed and she heaved a sigh of relief.

"Ze good God be praised! It is not zat Selim!"

"But who is it?" I asked.

"_Oh, la, la!_ He is ze gr-r-reat big man! He is ze chief of ze chiefs--He mak' treaty wiz ze French--He is ver' civilied an' important! He marry English girl--laike me--He is frien' to French an' treats well all _Roumis_--Oh, he is ver' big man--An' often, before, I have want to see him--But now I have you, dear one, I care not at all--"

A pity!

And now, what? How was this going to affect me and my fortunes?

If this Emir were a staunch ally of the French and "kind to all _Roumis_," presumably he would be kind to me--until he handed me back to his allies.

How long would he stay here? What exactly was the extent of his power over this tribe?

Would the _hakim_, or one of the servants, attempt to curry favour with him by informing him that there was a captive _Roumi_ in the camp--or would they fear the Angel more than they feared him?

An idea occurred to me.

If this Emir were truly great, as the Angel implied, might he not be touched by a truthful "David and Jonathan" story?

Suppose I told him everything, threw myself upon his mercy, and begged him to help us--Might he not accede, and, moreover, be a very tower of strength, if his heart were touched and his imagination fired? I would speak of John Geste figuratively as my brother, and quote the Arab proverb:

"The love of a man for a woman, waxes and wanes as doth the moon: But the love of brother for brother is constant as the stars, And endureth like the word of the Prophet."

And if I failed, and if he were inimical, or merely disposed to do his duty to his allies, the French, should I be in any worse position?

If he handed me over to the nearest "competent military authority," I should be promptly sent to Zaguig, and thence to the nearest road-gang, where, in all probability, John Geste had already been sent.

That would be something, but now that I knew of his whereabouts, I could probably help him better from without than from within.

It was almost impossible--it was certainly too much to hope--that another such series of events as had set us free together, could ever happen again, even if he and I were in the same _escouade_.

What to do?

As these thoughts passed through my mind, I watched the face of the Angel, who also was pondering deeply, pinching her lower lip the while--

"I sink I will go an' see zis Emir," she said at last. "Perhaps I will make him do somesing, _hein?_"

Doubtless she had excellent reason for putting faith in her powers of persuasion where Arabs were concerned. It was wholly hateful, but I brought myself to say:

"You know best--If this Emir can and will help us--"

"_Enfin_: If he get your brother for you, _he get you for me_, isn't it?--_Oui!_--I mus' quickly see zis Emir--He will camp close by--I will send Abd'allah to say zat I will pay heem a leetle visit--I sink he has heard of me--Oh, yes--Zen he will make feast, an' I will see which way ze cat jump--If he get _ver'_ friendly, I will tell heem he must help you and your brother--Ze good God grant zat zat Selim does not return before I get you away--Ah, but if I mak' _great_ frien's wiz ze Emir, I could mak' him keep Selim in his camp as hostage for ze good be'aviour of zis tribe--I will tell him sings about zat Selim--

"Now do not let anybody see your face until I come back, dear one--And you go to sleep and get strong while I am gone--I will send some more of ze beef-tea of muttons--"

3.

And sleep I did, long and heavily, possibly by reason of some unusual ingredient in the beef-tea of mutton.

When I awoke, it was as a giant refreshed, and I was filled with an unwonted sensation of hope and confidence.

My first visitor was the _hakim_, followed by a servant bearing hot stew in a jar, and most welcome coffee in a brass bowl.

So much better was I feeling, that I wondered whether my excellent medical attendant, having poisoned me at Selim's request, had administered an antidote when ordered by the Angel to save my life if he wished to save his own.

In point of fact, the creature did not strike me as being of sufficient intelligence and medical knowledge to deal with a cut finger or a blistered heel, but undoubtedly some of these rascally quacks are familiar with poisons unknown to the European pharmacopoeia.

Anyhow, I felt unexpectedly stronger and fitter and, having finished the stew and enjoyed the coffee, I demanded more.

Having fed, washed and been shaved, I peeped from the door of the tent to see what was doing in the great world.

The first object that met my interested gaze was the indefatigable Koko, leaning against the stump of a tree, just in front of the entrance to my tent, and gazing at it--gazing and gazing.

I wondered whether the creature ever shut his eyes at all: Certainly the Angel knew the secret of inspiring obedience and fidelity in her servants.

About a quarter of a mile away, a couple of remarkably fine tents, marquees almost--before which flags and pennons fluttered from the hafts 'of spears stuck in the ground--marked the temporary residence of the Emir.

Near to these big tents was the extremely orderly and well-aligned camp of his followers or body-guard, a camp much more like that of European troops than of a band of Arab irregulars--

Once more I wondered what had taken place in those pavilions--whether the Angel had visited the Emir, and if so, with what success her power of intrigue, allurement and diplomacy had been brought to bear upon the incalculable mentality and character of this powerful lord of the desert.

I was soon to know.

A little later, she entered my tent, threw back her _haik_, and seated herself upon the cushions.

Obviously she had succeeded beyond her wildest hopes.

Seizing my hands in hers she laughed gleefully.

"Oh, my dearest dear one--It goes well--I am so happy--Ze Emir is _gentilhomme_--Oh, he is gr-r-reat man--civilized and good and kind--And oh, zat Wazir of his--_Oh, la, la!_ Oh, he is one naughty little man--Oh, _mais c'est un grand amoureux_, zat one--He mak' lof to me--oh, laike 'ell. But listen--What you sink? Zis Emir, he know all about everysing--He know there is a _razzia_ on the French--He know zat some of you are hiding down in a pit, an' all die excep' two--"

"But how on earth does he know that?" I exclaimed.

"Oh, I don' know--He know everysing zat happen in ze desert--Everysing--They say ze vultures tell him--He know two of you are in zis camp--So when I find zat he know everysing, I tell him ze truth--Oh, he was ver' angry wiz zat Selim--I tell him old papa Yussuf ben Amir go to Zaguig before ze French come to _him_--An' I tell him Selim give back one prisoner to ze French patrol--An' now he want to see you--Do not be afraid--It is good zat you go to his camp, then Selim cannot do anysing at all--An' ze Emir promise me he will not give you up to ze French--Now I tell papa Yussuf ben Amir, an' zat Selim, an' everybody, zat you are *died*."

CHAPTER XIV

Accompanied by Abd'allah ibn Moussa, Koko, the _hakim_, and the Angel's servants who had waited upon me, and knew me to be a _Roumi_, I set forth, my _haik_ well across my face, to visit the Emir el Hamel el Kebir, Chief of the Confederation of Bedouin tribes that inhabited the desert country which extended from Zaguig to the Senussi sphere of influence, and had its capital or centre in the Great Oasis.

His name, titles and position I had learned, as far as possible, from the Angel; from Abd'allah ibn Moussa, who appeared to have for him an admiration almost amounting to veneration; and from the _hakim_, the tribal gossip, scandal-monger, and news-agent.

Seated on a rug-strewn carpet in front of the largest tent, were two richly dressed Arabs. They were alone, but within hail was a small group of sheikhs, _ekhwan_, and leaders of the soldiery.

Sentries, fine up-standing Soudanese, stood at their posts, or walked their beat in a smart and soldier-like manner.

I got an impression of discipline and efficiency not usually to be found about an Arab encampment.

From the little group of officers and officials, a broad squat figure detached itself and came to meet us--a deformed but very sturdy dwarf, whom I knew later as Marbruk ben Hassan, the Lame. He saluted me politely while my following salaamed profoundly.

"His High Excellency the Sidi Emir bids you welcome and gives you leave to approach," he said, and bidding the others remain where they were, he led me to the carpet, whereon sat the man who so mysteriously "knew all things" that happened in the desert.

With a wave of his hand, the big man dismissed the dwarf, and beckoned me to draw near.

The huge Emir, and his small companion, presumably the "naughty Wazir," eyed me with a long and searching stare.

I decided to stand upon what dignity I had, to hold my peace, and let the Emir speak first.

He did.

"Mawnin', Oats," he said casually. "How's things?--Meet my friend El Wazir el Habibka, known to the police and other friends, as Buddy--"

What was this?--Sun, fever, lunacy, hallucination?--Most annoying, anyhow--How could one carry on, if one's senses played one such tricks as this?--One expects to be able to believe one's own eyes and ears. And yet here were my eyes apparently beholding the face of my brother Noel--bronzed, lined, wrinkled and bearded--and my ears apparently hearing his voice. His absolutely unaltered voice. With regard to the face I might have been deceived; as to the voice, never--much less the two in conjunction. Besides, the man had called me "Oats," Noel's own special nickname for me since earliest childhood.

"Pleased to meet any friend of Hank's," said the smaller man, his grey eyes smiling from an unsmiling face.

"He's my young brother," said the Emir.

"Oh?" observed the other slowly. "Still--that ain't his fault, is it, Hank Sheikh? Why couldn't you say nothing, an' give the man a fair chance?

"Don't you brood on it, friend," he added, waving his hand, "and anyway I don't believe it."

Fever, sun, hallucination? Only in dreams and in the delirium of fever do typical Arab potentates talk colloquial English. These men were most obvious Arabs; Arab to the last item of dress and accoutrement; Arab of Arabs in every detail of appearance and deportment.

But could my eyes be normal while my ears deluded me?

No. This was real enough. This _was_ my brother. This man with him was talking English.

"_Noel!_" I said, beginning to recover and accept and believe.

Noel winked heavily, and laughed derisively in a manner most familiar This was real enough anyhow.

"*Noel!*" I said again--helpless but beginning to be hopeful.

"_Know-all!_" ejaculated the little man. "It's what he thinks he is, anyhow--But that ain't his name. B'jiminy-gees, yes it is, though."--

And turning to Noel he said:

"You _said_ your name was Know-all Hankinson Vanbrugh--after Miss Mary come to the Oasis--Gee! I believe you had an accident and spoke the truth, Hank Sheikh--Ain't it some world we live in!"

"_Noel!_" I said again for the third time. "_Hell!_ Am I mad, or drunk, or dreaming or what?"

"Say, sport, if you're drunk, tell us where you got it, quick," interrupted the little man urgently.

"_Oats!_" mocked my brother, my obvious, undeniable indubitable brother, Noel.

"Say, did Mary send you?--I've been wearing mourning for you, Son--Mary said you were all shot up, in Zaguig--In a regular bad way about you she was--only she was in a worse way about her Beau--"

"Sure--Beau Jolly," put in the incredible nightmare Wazir. "Ol' friend o' mine, only he don't know it--"

"Mary been _here?_--Excuse me if I sit down--Will it be in order?"

"No, most certainly not," said my brother. "Common people like you don't sit down in the presence of royalty--don't you know *that* much?--We'll go into the parlour--"

And the two rose and led the way into the tent, the Wazir dropping the felt curtain behind us as we entered.

And then my brother fell upon me, and there was no illusion about the thump and hand-grip with which the proceedings opened.

And Buddy was real. Quite as real as anybody I have ever met, by the time he finished welcoming me as the accepted and undeniable brother of "Hank Sheikh."

And at the tenth or perhaps twentieth attempt, sane and coherent conversation took the place of ejaculation, marvellings, and the callings upon various deities to bear witness that this was indeed a staggerer.

"I am still dreaming, or wandering in my mind, Noel," I found myself saying. "But *did* you say that Mary had been here?"

"Not right here, but down this way--In our home town--"

It was his turn to marvel.

"And she never said a word! Gee! And they say women can't keep a secret--"

"It was to *you* then, that de Beaujolais was coming on his secret mission from Zaguig--And of course brought Mary with him--" I said.

"It certainly was, Boy--But he didn't know it then--And he don't know it now--And as far as you was concerned you wasn't going to know it either, it seems--Gee! What do you know about that, Son?--Good for lil' Mary!"

"She always loved you very dearly, Noel," I said.

My brother smiled.

"Yes, sure," he mused. "And now she loves de Beaujolais a whole heap more very dearly--It's for him, and from him, she's keeping the State Secret."

"What?--Doesn't de Beaujolais know who you are?"

"Not a know to him," replied my brother. He thinks I am the Emir el Hamel el Kebir, Shadow of the Prophet, Commander of the Faithful, Protector of the Poor--Mandi, Shereef and Khalifa--Overlord, Ruler, Spiritual Head and War-Lord of the great Bedouin Confederation of the North South Western Sahara--Friend and ally of France--So I am too--Three loud cheers."

"Don't foam at the ears, Son," observed the Wazir gravely. "Mustn't let no loud cheers in the hearing of the Injuns."

And then I sprang from my cushions and certainly there could have been no sign of weakness about that uprising--and probably my hair stood as erect as I did.

"*Hank!*" I shouted, pointing in Noel's face.

"*Buddy!*" I yelped, pointing in the face of the little man. They regarded me tolerantly.

"*Hank and Buddy*!" I cried. "_The men that John Geste came back to look for!_--Hank went off and left them the water--Buddy stayed by sick John Geste and took him to Kano--Buddy went back to look for Hank--John Geste came back to look for Buddy--"

" *What?* " the two shouted as one man.

" *Yes!* " I shouted in reply. "And *I* came out to look for John Geste and I _found him!_--And Selim ben Yussuf has just sold him back to the French, thinking it was I--"

Both were staring.

"_Hell!_" growled my brother. "I'll take that Selim ben Yussuf on the ball of my thumb and smear him on a wall--the damned dog's-dinner!"

And:

"I'll so take him to pieces that no-one won't ever be able to put him together again," promised the little man. "I'll sure disestablish him."

"God!" breathed my brother, "_John Geste?_"

"Say!" whispered Buddy. "John Geste come back to find *me*?"

"What! Didn't his gel marry him then?" he added.

"She did," I replied. "He went home nearly dead, and they were married--and he could hardly eat, sleep or breathe for thinking of you two in the hands of the Arabs--When he did get a sleep he'd start yelling, '_Hank gave his life for me_,' or, '_Buddy went back and I slunk home_,' until his wife said what he'd been praying God for her to say, and told him to come back and look for you--"

"She must be a fine woman," said Noel.

"She's the finest and noblest woman in the world--the truest, the sweetest and the loveliest--" I said.

Noel gave me a long and searching look.

"Gee! I wisht I were an orayter!" said Buddy. "Sure ain't it the biggest tale you ever heard tell!--And ain't he the White Man?--My God, he's like his brothers!--Come back to look for _me!_--"

And we three sat and stared at each other in silence, each thinking his own thoughts, realizing fresh aspects of this astounding business and trying to grasp the stunning fact that, approaching from opposite directions, and in ignorance of each other's movements, we had met at the heart and centre of this wonderful maze of circumstance.

"And how in the name of the Almighty Marvellous, did *you* come to know John Geste?" asked Noel suddenly.

"I knew all three of them," I said, "--when they were kids--Their home is at a place called Brandon Abbas, a regular castle--only a mile or two from Granny's place at Brandon Regis--"

"If anyone rises to remark that it is a small world we live in, I'll hand him one," observed Buddy. "Gee! Ain't it some world!"

We pondered the smallness of the world and the marvels packed into its limited space.

There literally was so much to be said that there was nothing to say.

"And why on earth did those three boys from the Stately Homes of England come to the Legion?" asked Noel. "The three of them combined couldn't put up half a dirty trick, if they gave their whole time to it."

"Beau Geste ran away and enlisted to shield a girl--she's dead now--and the other two followed him to share the blame."

"Something about a dam' great di'mond, weren't it?" said Buddy.

"Something of the sort," I agreed.

"And how did you come to know that?" continued Noel.

"I met his wife in a Nursing-Home after I had been shot up, in Zaguig," I said. "She was a kid at Brandon Abbas too."

"And she told you that John Geste had come back to look for *us*, she not knowing we were _your_ Brother and Co.?" said Noel.

"He come back to look fer *me*, I tell you," put in Buddy. "He didn't give a curse for you, Hank Sheikh."

"And you offered to come and look for him?" continued Noel, contemplating me thoughtfully. "And you joined the Legion to get sent to the Zephyrs on the chance of getting in touch with him--?

"Good Scout--" he murmured, and sat pondering, stroking and fingering his beard in true Arab fashion.

"Well, Son, the good God Almighty meant you to find John Geste," he observed at length. "Fancy your getting sent to the same Battalion, and then being stuck down in the same *silo* together, and then the Touareg swiping every living Frenchman between there and Zaguig."

"Yes," I agreed. "--And this is what I want to know--How in the name of the Almighty Marvellous once again, do *you* come to know all about _that?_ Who told *you* that there were two French convicts in Sheikh Yussuf ben Amir's hands, and that they were saved from a *silo* after a massacre?"

"Who saved you, Son?" smiled Noel.

"Three aged scarecrows--village beggars, loafers--United ages about three centuries--" I said.

"Meet Yacoub-who-goes-without-water and his two young brothers--"

"Alf and Ed," murmured Buddy, "the Chiefs of my Desert Intelligence Department. You were hardly above ground before I knew that there had been a raid on the road-gangs, and you were hardly in the power of Selim ben Yussuf, before I knew that a couple of French prisoners had been found down a *silo*. I learnt that much while I was on the way here--I'm Keeper of the Peace in these parts--"

"And the pieces--" murmured the Wazir.

"--And I rushed my Camel Corps straight for here when Yacoub sent me word that the Touareg had got busy in my country--I surely will learn Mr. Selim ben Yussuf a lesson he'll remember, and let him know who's Emir of this Confederation--when there are any deals to be done with the French--It was his business to treat you properly and to notify me that he'd got you--

"Yes, damn him," he went on. "It would have been you he'd have handed over, but for that Death Angel girl--And as it is, it's _John Geste_--"

"And now we got to go get John Geste--" put in Buddy. "And that's a game what'll want some playing--Blast Selim ben Yussuf--I'll hang him on his own innards--

"One thing," he added, "I kissed his gel for him, an' that surely doth get the Arab goat surprising--"

Silence.

"Bud," said my brother to the Wazir, "we've built up a big business here--We've put the Injuns wise to a lot of things--We've made the old man's seat safe for the boy--We've taught 'em how to handle the Touareg, and we've got 'em in right with the French--It's a fine, sound, going concern, with me President, you Vice-President, and the Board of Directors hand-picked, and a million francs invested under the old apple tree--We're made for life--We pay our own salaries and we fix our own pensions--also age of retirement--"

"Sure, Hank Sheikh," said his Wazir. "We sure are the deserving rich--"

"--On velvet," continued my brother. "Just made good and got all the lovely things that was coming to us--Why, we're Near-Emperors--Sure enough Presidents of a Republic, anyhow--And now here this John Geste comes along, gets into the Zephyrs, Our Own Representative gets him out, and he gets in again--Are we to lose everything to save him again?--_Let's leave him where he is_--"

"Let's don't, Hank Sheikh," replied the Wazir.

"Are we to undo our life's work?"

"Sure," said the Wazir promptly.

"Are we to lose everything we've worked and toiled and suffered and risked our lives for?"

"Every last thing," agreed the Wazir.

"Are we to break our Treaty with the French?--Break our word to the Tribes?--Break the hearts of the men who love and trust us?"

"Break everything," assented the Wazir.

"Are we to start life afresh at our age?--Take the road again?"

"Sure--Take the road and everything else we can get--What's bitin' you, you ol' fool?"

"You mean you'll throw away _everything_--chuck up the grandest golden success two hungry hoboes ever made--Go back from wealthy prince to tramping beggar?"--

"Ain't our friend in trouble, Hank?" replied Buddy. "What you talkin' about?"

"Shake, Son," said my brother. And the two men shook hands.

"Some folk'd say our duty to the French and these Arabs came first," said Noel.

"Let 'em say," answered Buddy.

"Some folk'd say a man ought not to go back on his word," continued Noel.

"_Word!_" spat Buddy. "Ain't our friend in trouble! What's the word you've spoke, against the word you _haven't_ spoke?--That you stand by your pard through thick and thin--You remember what you said to me, Hank Sheikh?--'_It's all accordin' to what they call your "Bo Ideel._"'"

"Goo' Boy," observed my brother, taking the small man by the scruff of the neck and shaking him affectionately. "When your friend's in need, he's your friend indeed."

"Sure thing, Hank Sheikh--For a minute I wondered if you'd gone batty in the belfry or woozy in the works."

"I was only trying you out, Son--I apologize--"

"So you oughter, Hank Sheikh," snorted Buddy.

"Don't think I doubted you, Son, but I thought I'd remind you that it's a hard row to hoe, and ruin at the end of it."

"Harder for you, Old Hoss," grinned Buddy. "You got a wife, an' I ain't--Me!--I got more sense--"

"Married, Noel?--My congratulations--An Arab lady?" I said. "Why, no, of course, I remember--the Death Angel said you'd married an English girl like herself--"

"An English girl--very unlike herself," replied Noel, and eyed me queerly.

"I shall look forward to meeting her and paying my respects as a brother-in-law," I said, wondering what sort of extraordinary person my brother could have picked up in this part of the world.

"You have met her, Oats," replied Noel, and I stared astounded, beginning to wonder again whether this were not, after all, an extraordinary dream.

No, it was not a dream. It was more like a good dream wasted.

"Met her?" I said. "Where?"

"She was a Miss Maud Atkinson," said my brother with excellent nonchalance, and both he and Buddy watched me expectant, and, I thought, a little on the defensive.

I don't think my jaw dropped, nor my face expressed anything other than what I wished them to see.

"Congratulations again, Noel," I cried. "When I congratulated you before, it was the usual form of words--I can now congratulate you on having married one of the bravest and best little women that ever lived. She went _literally_ through fire to help a friend--in a burning house in England--She's pure gold."

"Thank you, Oats," said my brother, extending his hand.

"Nearly married her meself," observed Buddy glumly. "He butted in, the day before--Stuck his great hoof in our love affair before I--"

Spreading a useful hand across his Wazir's face, the Emir thrust his Minister out of the conversation.

"And Mary never told you *that*--" continued Noel.

"No--She just mentioned that Maudie was married," said I. "Doesn't she rather complicate the situation?"

"Like Hell she does," pondered Noel. "She'd be the first to chase me off to get John Geste--She'd never forgive us if she knew we'd left a friend in trouble--"

"Where is she now?" I asked.

"At my headquarters at the Great Oasis," replied my brother. "In the charge of my Council and a great old bird who is Regent of my chief tribe--At least they think she is in their charge--As a matter of fact she is the best man of the lot."

"Did she marry you as an Arab?" I asked.

"She married me as a Lovely Sheikh, out of a book," was the reply. "Going to marry me again as a common man, out of a job, when we go home--I'm still a bit of a mystery to her--Girls like mysteries--She always wanted a Sheikh and now she's got one--And she's a _houri_--"

"Wicked shame," muttered the Wazir. "Married the gel under false pretences--Tole her he'd bought a book an' learned English so as he could talk to her--the rambunctious ole goat--Spoilt the one and only love affair of my life--"

"Never mind, Son," soothed the Emir. "You started another last night."

"I certainly did," agreed Buddy with prideful mien. "I'll tell the world she fell for me, right there--And she cert'nly is the Tough Baby--I'm going over to call on her, bye-and-bye."

"You certainly made an impression on her," I said. "She spoke of you when she returned from the visit."

"And that brings us to the point," said Noel. "She tells me that Selim ben Yussuf handed a convict over to a _peloton méhariste_ some days ago; and that means that he was taken straight to Zaguig, examined on the subject of the Arab raid, and sent back to a road-gang--Now by the mercy of God, old Yacoub-who-goes-without-water knows his face--and I back him to pick him out from ten thousand--I'll have him and his gang off within the hour, and as soon as John Geste is working on the road again, I shall know it--"

"What will Yacoub do?" I asked.

"Everybody," grunted the Wazir.

"Beg mostly," replied my brother. "Loaf about--.cadge--steal rusty cans and run for his life--look silly--do a bit of water-carrying--pick up a job--hold a horse--lead a camel--They're the three finest old actors that never went on the stage--Believe me, Henry Irving never had anything on Yacoub-who-goes-without-water--"

"And when he locates him?" I asked.

"Them _un_corrigible Touaregs again--" suggested the Wazir. "There'll be another raid and John Geste will be took captive by them--Even the Zephyrs will pity the pore feller--"

"That's the scheme," said Noel. "It'll want some planning--I don't want to hurt anybody, and I don't want to get my people shot up, either; but John Geste's coming right out of that road-gang--"

"I get the idea," I mused. "In the meantime what becomes of me?"

"You're dead and buried, Son. Your ghost turns Injun and stays with us, keeping its face hidden--We'll brown it up a bit--"

"But there are half a dozen people who know I'm alive," I said. "The lot out there who brought me over--"

"That's Miss Death Angel's trouble--" replied my brother. "They're her people--It's up to her to see they don't squeal about her little games, to Selim ben Yussuf, or anybody else--"

"I don't think they'll talk much, when I've had a word with them," he added, and the Wazir chuckled grimly.

"I'm dead of course, as far as the French are concerned," I remarked.

"You perished in the massacre, Son--Poor old John will be in a bad way," he continued. "He can't very well tell the French you're alive and ought to be rescued from the wild Bedouin, and he can't very well leave you to be tortured by Selim ben Yussuf, as he thinks--"

"I suppose Selim ben Yussuf couldn't do any good, if you were to put the screw on him?" I asked.

"No," replied my brother. "_He_ can't do anything. Once he's handed an escaped prisoner back, there's an end of it--I myself couldn't do a thing, although I'm Emir of the Confederated tribes of the Great Oasis, and ally of France.

"--No, Selim can only tell me all about the patrol and then take what's coming to him--The fool!--The damned impudent presumptuous _fool!_--Why, I could prevent him succeeding his father as Sheikh of his Tribe--If I were staying on, that is--" and he smiled wryly. "I'll get him, as it is--if he comes back in time--"

"He's bound to come back soon, I should think," said I. "The girl expected him to roll up at any minute. In fact, when we heard the commotion of your arrival, we thought he had come--"

"What's the position there exactly--d'you know?" asked Noel.

"Yes," I replied. "I do--It's the hell of a position--Selim is madly infatuated with the girl, which you can quite understand--And the girl is apparently madly infatuated with me--which you probably cannot understand--

"I met them both in Bouzen a long time ago, and the trouble began as far back as that--Selim was after her then, and wanted to stab me because she singled me out at a dancing-show--

"I gather that, being heartily tired of Town, she came for 'a day in the country'--Giving Selim a trial trip before marrying him, perhaps--Just as likely to become his step-mama I should say--"

"And then you came on the scene and the scene was changed--" suggested my brother. "Friend Selim did himself some good when he brought you home, didn't he?"

"Yes--And me too--" I sighed. "I paid her rather a high price for my freedom to go off again in search of John Geste--Noel, old chap, _couldn't_ you have come a day sooner?"

"No, Son--nor an hour--Why?"

"Because I made a fair and square bargain with the Death Angel that I'd come back to her as soon as I had seen John Geste out of the country, or else at the end of a year.."

"Come back to her?--What for?" asked my brother.

"To marry her," I said.

My brother stared incredulous, and then laughed harshly. "Marry her?--Well, that's an engagement that'll be broken off," smiled he.

"Not by me, Noel," I told him "It's a 'gentleman's agreement.'--I gave her my word and my hand on it--She has done her part and I'll have to do mine. Just as soon as we've got John Geste out of the country--"

"You'll come too, Son--if you have to come in a sack," affirmed my brother.

"Noel," I said, "listen--Before you came, this girl made a bargain with me. On her side she was to help me get John Geste out of the country--In return for that help, I gave her my solemn promise that I would come back. And I shall do so--"

"I get you, Son," he answered thoughtfully.

Silence fell, and we sat, each thinking his own thoughts--if gazing in wonderment upon incredible but undeniable facts, can be called thought.

The Wazir was the first to break the silence, and the trend of his cogitations was apparent.

"Do I understand that you are reg'larly engaged to this young woman then?" he asked purposefully.

"Yes," I said.

"You _would_ be--" he observed glumly, and in reply to the inquiry of my raised eyebrow, added:

"I was going to propose to her meself, to-day--"

"Then I sincerely hope you'll do it, and be entirely successful," I replied.

"Well, you cut in first, Bo--We'll leave it at that--I ain't bad at heart--"

"No. It's your head that's bad," observed my brother. "Brains went bad long ago--Now stop jabbering and put Marbruk ben Hassan wise--I want Yacoub here quicker than Marbruk can get him--"

The Wazir left the tent.

"Who is he, Noel?" I asked.

"The biggest little man that ever lived--And my friend," replied my brother. "I took up with him when I ran away from home, and we've been together ever since--He's the bravest man I ever saw and there never lived a stauncher--He's true, Son--And when you want him, he's _there_--"

"What's that language he talks?" I asked.

"Well, he was born in the Bowery, New York, and that's his mother tongue--And he got his schooling in South State Street and Cottage Grove Avenue, Chicago, and the slums thereabout, and he talks the dialect--He graduated on the water-front at San Francisco, and learnt some good language there--He was a barkeep in Seattle, and went to the gold-diggings--He was a cow-puncher in Texas and Arizona, and he's used the roads of the U.S.A. a lot--and the railways more so, but I don't think he ever bought a ticket--"

"And why do you talk like him when you are talking to him?" I inquired.

"Because I've got good manners," replied Noel. "And what's good enough for Bud is good enough for me--.

"Now you stay where you are for a bit, Son," he continued. "I'm going to hold a _mejliss_ and get busy--"

A few minutes later, the Emir and his Wazir were seated on the carpet and cushions of State outside the big tent in which I was concealed.

The Oriental Potentate was seated in judgment; if not "in the city gate" as of old, then in the door of his tent and shadow of the palm, as in days far older.

The dwarf, Marbruk ben Hassan, brought to the judgment-seat the party who had escorted me.

"And so there were two _Roumi_ prisoners--" said the deep voice of the Emir, "--and one of them was given up to the French, and the other died--Is it not so?"

"It is so; O, Emir," said the voice of the good _hakim_.

"It is so indeed; O, Emir," said Abd'allah ibn Moussa. And the voices of the servants chorused the refrain.

"And his body was buried in the sand," continued the Emir. "You were all present I think?"

"All; O, Emir--" was the unanimous reply.

"There could be no mistake about it?" suggested the Emir. "I should be sorry for one who made a mistake about it--Sorry for him, and his son, his son's son, and his wives and his children, his camels, his goats, and all that he had."

All appeared perfectly certain that there could be no mistake on the subject.

"Was it a deep grave or a shallow grave, in which you buried this unfortunate prisoner?" pursued the Emir.

And it was the voice of Abd'allah that answered promptly:

"Oh, a very shallow grave; O, Emir. It might be found that jackals had removed the body--should any search be now made for it--"

And the voice of the _hakim_ chimed in with:

"And it was a much-trodden spot, O, Emir, near the camel-enclosure--A very difficult spot to find--even had the jackals not rifled the grave--"

"It is well," concluded the Emir. "Go in peace, making no mistake--for my arm is long--long as the Tail of the Horse of the Prophet."

CHAPTER XV

I spent the following days in a curious condition of mind, and much comfort of body. I had complete and much-needed rest, and freedom from all personal anxiety and fear; and my hope concerning John Geste was rising high--I had had him in my hands and I should have him again--

This brother of mine was a strong man--a strong man armed--influential and powerful, unless he came into deliberate conflict with the French, whose friend and ally he was.

With him I was absolutely safe, and, though idly quiescent myself, I felt that everything possible was being done to further my affairs--which were now equally those of my brother and his friend.

I could lie upon my cushions, resting and relaxed, yet happy' in the knowledge that more was being done to further John Geste's rescue than at any time since Isobel had told me of his capture.

I could not talk with these two without becoming imbued with a feeling of completest confidence. They were so sure that their Desert Intelligence--which had never yet failed them--would speedily discover John's whereabouts, and that their brave and faithful fighting-men would effect his rescue.

Naturally I had my moments of fear, gloom, anxiety and doubt, but I had my hours of hope and joy, and certitude that all would be well, and that I should live to see John Geste step upon the deck of a British or American ship.

And at that point I always awakened myself from my day-dream and refused to envisage the future.

Life--with the Angel of Death as my wife!

Well, I must make the best of it, and the best of her. There is good in everyone, and, probably, in her way--and given a fair chance--she was quite as "good" as I was--And in any case I should be a happy man, if only I succeeded in saving John--

I grew very near to my brother again, during this brief period of waiting, this tiny oasis in the desert of strenuous life, and got to know him very well.

The more I learned, the more was I filled with admiration at his astounding feat--his rising by sheer unaided ability, from being a practically dead man, possessed of the remains of one ragged garment and nothing else, to his present position--as a man of wealth, power and importance.

His was indeed a wonderful story, and in my private mind I ranked him with such men as that Burton who became an Arab and made the pilgrimage to Mecca, earning the title of _Haji_, a Mussulman of Mussulmans.

Little wonder that Major de Beaujolais, with all his Secret Service training, had found no grounds for suspicion, since the Arabs themselves believed him to be an Arab.

His years of wandering in the desert with John and Digby Geste must have been a hard apprenticeship, but the only possible one for such success as this.

And the same applied to my brother's _fidus Achates_, Buddy.

Neither of them was a man of book-education, but both were men of brains, ability, determination and character.

Noel was his father's son there, but oh, how different a man--with his wise broad tolerance.

When I endeavoured to discover Noel's mental attitude to our Father, I was somewhat baffled, but came to the conclusion that if he did not still actually hate him, he thought of him with some bitterness, and promised himself the pleasure of, some day, returning home, and "having it out" with him, "mastering him" as he expressed it--

Not in a spirit of bitterness and revenge, or with the least idea of humiliating him, but rather as a sop to his own self-respect and to meet him on an equality, on his own level, and as man to man; and particularly, I think, Noel wished to demonstrate to him that a son of Homer H. Vanbrugh could, unaided, amount to something, without dwelling for ever in Homer H. Vanbrugh's pocket, or in the shadow of his crushing and overwhelming bulk.

Not only did my affection for my brother increase, as we talked together, but my respect also. And I envied him--He was the Happy Warrior. He had deliberately chosen the way of life that suited him, and for which he was suited, rejecting the job of rich man's son, offered him by circumstance, and going out into the high-ways and by-ways of the world, the open roads that called to him.

He had climbed a steep and rugged path, and he had enjoyed the effort and the danger. He had made contact with realities, looked life in the face, and acknowledged the great God of Things As They Are.

And of all the interesting things about him, what interested me most was the fact that, having literally and actually been crowned with success, he was, without an instant's hesitation, prepared to cast that crown away at a word--a word of a friend in danger.

A crown was not his *beau idéal*.

A man who thought like Don Quixote though he chose to talk like Sancho Panza.

And, too, the more I saw of his friend, the more I liked and respected him, for my brother's standards and values were his in equal measure.

To what extent this was due to the uninfluenced nature of the man, and how much to the fact that my brother was his untarnishable hero, and impeccable model, I do not know--and if the latter, the more credit to him that such a man could be his ideal.

Yes--I liked Buddy. And I wrote him down a bold, unconquerable spirit, sterling and faithful and fine.

2.

"Lie low, Son," whispered my brother, entering my comfortable tent wherein I lay restfully at peace--in the peace of the great desert.

"French patrol coming--You're all right behind that face-stain--your own father wouldn't know you--..No need to chuck your weight about though--If you like to put an eye to one crack and an ear to another, you may have some fun--"

It wasn't exactly fun, but it was very interesting, to hear the officers of the Patrol talking with the Emir el Hamel el Kebir and the Sheikh el Habibka el Wazir, over their three rounds of ceremonial and complimentary mint tea.

Marvellous was the impassive Arab dignity with which the Emir, his Wazir, Sheikhs and chief men met and greeted the French _sous-officier_ and his European subordinates, and with which they conducted them to the rug-and-cushion-strewn carpet before the Emir's tent.

When all customary and proper formalities had been observed, the French _sous-officier_ got down to business.

It appeared that the French authorities at Zaguig appreciated the Emir's prompt action in hurrying to the scene of the massacre, and hoped that, by now, he had some information on the subject of the raiders--

Of course the Touareg at once came under suspicion--but it was easy to cry, "_Touareg_"--and there were certain features of the raid that might or might not indicate Touareg--The said features might have been covered by the Touareg face-veil, so to speak--..

But, and here was a point to consider, might not those veils have been borrowed, and might they not have veiled features that were not those of Touareg faces at all?

There were reasons for thinking so, and if the slaughter had been Touareg handiwork, why was the life of at least one of the road-gang spared?--And how had this man come to be in the hands of Selim ben Yussuf?

The convict himself would say nothing--absolutely nothing--though he had undoubtedly received every encouragement to speak. (My fists clenched as I listened and thought of poor John--I cursed the Angel of Death.)--Of course he may have been knocked on the head and really remember nothing, as he said--But _how_ did Selim ben Yussuf get him?

And what exactly was Selim ben Yussuf doing within a few miles of where the massacre took place?

Old Sheikh Yussuf ben Amir, his father, was all-right, no doubt, but Selim ben Yussuf was quite another coconut--

His record was a bad one, or rather it was a record of strong continual suspicions--It was firmly believed that he had been prominent in the Zaguig massacre, though as there was no survivor of that, except an American tourist, no evidence could be got against him. (Here I was indeed interested.)--Still, Major de Beaujolais had reported that he had seen Selim in Zaguig just before the massacre--and pray where was the gentleman at this very minute?

The Emir stroked and fingered his beard, gravely nodding as the Frenchman talked--And the Emir's Wazir stroked and fingered his beard, gravely and wisely nodding as his master did so.

It appeared that the Emir had himself entertained suspicions concerning Selim ben Yussuf, and had his eye upon him--and in fact, the sole reason why he remained encamped at this spot, with his Camel-Corps, was to see whether Selim returned to the Tribe and, meanwhile, to make wide inquiry as to his whereabouts and movements.

And had the Emir heard the rumour which _l'Adjudant_ Lebaudy had picked up somewhere--that Selim ben Yussuf had had two French prisoners?

Here the Emir stroked his beard very thoughtfully.

"If he has another prisoner, he has taken him with him," he said. "There is absolutely no question whatever of there being another French prisoner in their camp over there--"

"That's certain, is it?" asked the officer.

"As absolutely certain as that Mahommed is the Prophet of Allah--Have a tent-to-tent visitation if you like, but 'twill be but a waste of time--" said the Emir.

"It would be like the young fox," he added, thoughtfully frowning, "if he *did* have two, to give one up in token of good faith, and to keep the other as a hostage--or to torture, if he hates the _Roumi_ as some say--"

"H'm--Give up one to show his love, and keep one upon whom to show his hate, eh?" said the Frenchman.

The Emir then inquired as to this curious rumour, and learned that an Arab _méhariste_ with _l'Adjudant_ Lebaudy's patrol had been told by a boy, a goat-herd, of whom he bought some dates, that there had been two _Roumi_ prisoners, but one was said to have died--

Probably nothing in it--except that one of the Secret Service spies had also brought in a story, admittedly somewhat fantastic, about a _Roumi_. prisoner having been tortured to death by a woman--

The Emir did not appear to be impressed.

"It'll be ten by the New Moon--" he smiled. "However, our young friend, Selim, shall enlighten us--Oh, yes--Selim shall talk--"

"Selim shall squeal, eh?" smiled the French officer grimly.

The Emir looked up.

"What does old Sheikh Yussuf ben Amir say?" he asked.

"He says he knows absolutely nothing about either Selim's movements or about Selim's prisoner or prisoners, and I think he is speaking the truth--"

And the Emir bade the officer rest assured that he, El Hamel el Bebir, would know the truth, the whole truth, and nothing but the truth, as to there having been one or two French prisoners in the hands of Selim ben Yussuf, and as to the precise manner in which that suspect had acquired them.

One more thing--and the officer picked up his riding-switch and _képi_--orders were coming, for Sheikh Yussuf ben Amir's tribe, to migrate at once to the Oasis of Sidi Usman, near Bouzen, there to concentrate and remain until further notice.

Would the Emir facilitate their departure and keep a patrol in the neighbourhood, so long as it seemed likely that Selim ben Yussuf, and the fighting-men with him, might return to where he had left the tribe encamped—

3.

And, next day, as we three sat in dignified isolation apart from all men, a servant came running, spoke to the Soudanese sentry--whose business it was to see that none unauthorized approached within hearing--and drew near.

"Yacoub-who-goes-without-water sends a messenger; O, Emir," the man said, making obeisance.

"Bring him instantly, el R'Orab," ordered the Emir, and, a minute or two later, an aged and filthy beggar approached, a man so old and decrepit that the flesh of his bent and trembling legs seemed covered in dry grey scales rather than brown human skin. His face expressed nothing but senile imbecility and, as his shrivelled lips opened, exposing the toothless gums and a tongue like that of a parrot, one expected to hear nothing but the shrill piping voice of a pitiable dotard, well advanced in second childhood.

Supporting his emaciated frame with the help of a staff, he salaamed profoundly, glanced at me inquiringly, and, on receiving the Emir's kind permission to speak freely, changed astonishingly.

Certainly he was still a dirty old man, but one whose face now expressed shrewdness, alertness, and ripe wisdom. A hopeless, helpless, doddering old pantaloon turned, before my eyes, into an extremely knowing, spry and competent old gentleman.

"May the Sidi Emir live for ever!" quoth he, "and dwell in the protection of Allah and the care of His Prophet--Humblest greetings from his meanest slave, Yacoub-who-goes-without-water, and this message--

"'Know, O, Emir, that the _Roumi_ prisoner sold by Sheikh Selim ben Yussuf to the _Franzawi_ was taken to the city of Zaguig and there cast into prison--At the gate of the prison have I sat, a blind and naked beggar, asking "Alms for the love of Allah! Alms for the love of Allah, the Merciful, the Compassionate--" I have not left this place by day nor by night, and all who have entered in unto it, and all who have come out of it, have I seen--Yea, every one--And behold, three times has the _Roumi_ prisoner been taken by soldiers from this old prison to the new barracks--And three times has he been brought back--Each time did I follow afar off, and what happened when he was taken to the barracks of the _Franzawi_ soldiers, I do not know, save that high officers assembled and questioned him--for I climbed on the back of a passing camel and saw through the iron bars of the "hole through which one looks out.[1]"

[1. Window.]

"'--And the fourth time he was taken from the prison, he marched with others like him, and with soldiers about them, down the Road that the _Franzawi_ build from Zaguig to the Great Oasis--And each night they halted for a night in an armed camp--And now he, and those others with him, have come to the place of the deserted village, and they carry on the work of those that are dead--With my own eyes I am watching this man and with my brother's voice am I speaking these words--And may the peace of Allah abide with the Sidi Emir, and encompass him about--'

"And that is the message of my brother, Yacoub-who-goes-without-water, O Lord--"

And:

"It is well," replied the Emir. "Go and eat."

And as the intelligent old gentleman lapsed back into the idiot centenarian and tottered out of earshot:

"Good God above us!" said Noel. "John Geste! John Geste, himself, is not ten miles away from where we're sitting now, Otis!"

And I could answer nothing.

4.

We instantly became a Council of War.

My brother is a man of prompt action, but he is not of those who act first and think afterwards. I imagine his marvellous success among the Arabs was as much due to his wisdom in the Council-tent as to skill and courage on the battle-field.

In the strange rôle that my brother played at this period of his life, tactics and strategy counted for more than swashbuckling. It interested me greatly to see how he considered the views and opinions of Buddy and myself, and then of his most trusted Arab lieutenants, weighed them carefully, discussed them, and then produced his own, and his reasons for holding them.

Inasmuch as I had worked in the road-gang and knew, to the last detail, the method and routine of the daily and nightly procedure, my advice was asked, my suggestions invited, and I was flatteringly bidden to say precisely what I would do if I were the executive in charge of the work of rescue.

To me, it at once appeared that there were two methods open to us--that of force, and that of guile, and I promptly propounded this platitude.

"Take the force-idea first, Son," said Noel, "bearing in mind it's not to be a raid like this last one. I'll have John Geste if I kill every Arab and Frenchman in Africa, but I intend to get him without killing anybody."

"That rather cramps one's style for force, doesn't it?" I said. "Limits one's scope of action, a little--What would happen if we swooped down upon the working-party in overwhelming strength, but unarmed--Simply kidnapped John by main force--We three seize him, while a hundred good men and true scatter everybody, all ends up, and we ride for it?"

"What would happen, Son?--We should leave about thirty dead--probably including John Geste and certainly ourselves--As I say, I don't want anybody killed, especially my own men--"

"What about a hand-picked party, to surround the spot in the dark, and shoot straight and fast--but high--While they're carefully hitting nobody, we three, armed, say, with 'a foot of lead-pipe' each, dash in and get John--"

"Dash in and don't get John," said my brother. "We get about seven bullets each, instead--"

"Well--what about this idea?--Let your man, Yacoub, get a word of warning to John to be _ready_ at sunset to-morrow--expecting something to happen--Then let Selim ben Yussuf's tribe start their trek in the afternoon, and pass along the road just before the gang is due to stop work--All your men might join in the procession, camels and all complete, and the more dust they raise the better--We three, and a few chosen lads who can be trusted, can be in a bunch, and one of us carry a spare _haik_ and _burnous_--As we pass and jostle along the road, Yacoub gets beside John and says 'Now!' to him, and I shout 'Come on, John.' He just steps into the midst of the crowd and we throw the spare burnous round him to hide his uniform, and he pulls it over his face--Let Buddy be leading a spare camel, and we three push forward as quickly as we can, to the head of the column, and then ride for it--"

My brother smiled.

"Bright idea, Oats," he said kindly. "But it would be 'Keep off the grass' as soon as the mob tried to use the Road--'_At the stiffs in front, at five hundred metres, seven rounds rapid fire'_--No, Son--especially after the recent raid, no clouds of dust are coming near any Zephyr party. Neither along the Road nor across it--"

"Well, let's try guile," I said. "What about old Yacoub slipping John a file and hanging around until John makes a quiet get-away--We're waiting near, with fast camels, and old Yacoub brings him to us--"

"Waiting how long, Son? We might grow grey, or strike roots into the earth before John got his chance--There won't be much slackness for a long time to come--Suppose he's caught using the file?--Suppose he is shot, getting away?--You know about how many single-handed escape-attempts succeed--"

"What about this?" I tried again.

"Supposing you, in your own proper person, as the Emir el Hamel el Kebir, in your whitest robes, heavy corded silk head-dress and scarlet and gold camel-hair ropes round your head, visited that particular section of the Road--with your Wazir, and high Sheikhs, chief executioner, cup-bearer, baker, butler, soothsayer, and holy panjandrum and all--and had an afternoon tea-party with the nice friendly White Men--And while all goes merrier than a marriage-bell, there is a sudden raid by a few score of your best, unarmed--and, as they appear, some of us seize the rifles of our friends, and the rest of us seize the friends themselves--While we hang on to them--grapple them to our hearts with hoops of steel, so to speak--the new-comers guided by Yacoub, simply cut out John from the herd and make their getaway--"

"Leaving us in the soup, like--" murmured Buddy.

"Well--we'd have the rifles, and they'd simply have to 'hands up' while we backed away to our camels and cleared off--"

"Gee! Hasn't he got a mind, Hank Sheikh," admired Buddy. "He sure is your brother--Sim'lar kind o' train-hold-up nature--"

"It's a scheme," mused Noel. "It's an idea, Bud--"

"Or there's that _silo_," I suggested. "Suppose Yacoub provisioned it, and we three made a regular Red Indian swift-and-silent sort of raid, dressed in brown paint and coco-nut-oil--We might get him and rush to that *silo* and lie low there--"

"Down among the dead men," murmured Buddy. "--until the first wild hurroosh is over--That wouldn't lead a pursuit back to your own camp, either. Sneak away from the *silo* the following night to where Yacoub has the camels--"

Noel shook his head.

"Too risky, Son," he mused. "That *silo* may have been discovered and be in use again--And if it hasn't, it sure is an unhealthy spot--What's your idea, Bud?" he continued, turning to his friend.

"Well, Hank Sheikh, I'd like a good up-and-down dawgfight--a free-for-all, knock-down-an'-drag-out, go-as-you-please, bite-kick-or-gouge turn-up--an' run that boy, John Geste, outa gaol--Life's gettin' a dam' sight too peaceful--An' you're gettin' fat--

"But since you've got so partic'lar an' no poor fightin'-man's to get hurt, what about dopin' the guard?--Have a party--Have a supper-party an' hand oat the free drinks generous an' hearty an' doped--You don't taste _hashish_ in coffee, an' if we couldn't do anything else, we could work off three rounds of sweet coffee an' three rounds of mint-tea on 'em not to mention something funny in the _cous-cous_--Nothin' serious--In the mawnin' twenty-five headaches _come_, an' one prisoner _gone_--Hardly worth noticin'--"

"Gee! Hasn't he got a mind, Oats?" admired the Emir. "Filled with treacly treachery, putrid poison, and mouldy mellow-drama--But it cert'nly is an idea--"

He turned to Buddy.

"Don't I seem to remember we already had one misfortunate igsperience with poison, Son?"

"Misfortunate Hell!" snorted Buddy. "It clinched the deal anyhow--That's all the thanks _I_ get--That, and a broken heart--" he added.

"It's an idea, Son--It cert'nly is an idea--" admitted Noel. "The fierce and treacherous Sheikh stuff, eh? Invite 'em to a hash party an' poison 'em--"

"Look here, Noel," I broke in, "excuse the question--But where do you draw the line?--You want no bloodshed, and I can quite understand that, and I entirely agree--But about the treachery part of it, since the word's been used--If I know you, old chap, and I think I do, you'll hate that more than a fair and square fight--openly showing your hand as having suddenly become an enemy of the French--"

"I needn't appear in the fair-and-square fight, Son," replied my brother.

"I could very easily turn a picked lot of my braves into Touareg, and let there be another raid--When the Guard was disposed of, Yacoub could identify John Geste, and they could bring him along--bring the whole lot along, if Yacoub got knocked out--I should never be suspected--It isn't that--I simply don't want any killing, and I'll try everything else first--As to the treachery, that's the only alternative to fighting and that's why I'm considering it--"

"Suppose the French ever find you out?" I asked.

"They're going to find me out, Son--Out of the country--" was the reply. "It's like this, Boy--John Geste came back to save us--I'm going to save John Geste--I'm going to do it without hurting a man, if I can, and that means I've got to play false since I won't play rough--Well--I've taken their money and I've given them good value and a fair deal--

"Now here endeth the good value and the fair deal--so I take no more money--I throw in my hand--I'm a Bad Man all-right, Oats, but I've never double-crossed and I won't start now--The day I break my side of the contract, the contract's broken, and I won't benefit by it any more--I've kept the Treaty that I made with my young brother-in-law, good and proper, but it's got to lapse directly I start monkeying-about with French troops and actin' against French interests--I'm sorry I've got to do it at all--_an' I wouldn't do it for any living soul_, except for John Geste an' you two--"

"Thanks, Noel," I said. "I see--Any trick to get John away--and it's your first and last 'treachery.'--"

"That's it, Son--We don't bite the hand that feeds us, or rather we only bite it once--and that much against our will--"

"And you two will give up everything to save John Geste?"

Noel looked at Buddy.

"Why, sure," said the little man, nodding at my brother. And turning to me, he added:

"It's all a matter o' what he calls his Bo Ideel--"

We talked "about it and about," until my brother said: "Now we'll hear Martruk ben Hassan and Yussuf Latif ibn Dawad Fetata on the subject."

The loud clapping of the Emir's big hands brought a slave running, and he was despatched for the two Arabs.

Marbruk ben Hassan, the deformed, but very powerful-looking, dwarf, heard, apparently without the very faintest shadow of surprise, that the Emir intended to seize a convict of one of the French road-making parties. And, in reply to his master's inquiry as to how he would set about it, were he in charge of the business, replied:

"A swift rush, just before dawn, when sentries are sleeping and all men are at their weakest--Crawl close--Three volleys--and a swift charge pushed well home--"

"And suppose no man on either side is to be killed, on peril of your life; O, Marbruk ben Hassan?" inquired the Emir.

"I am only a soldier, Lord," smiled Marbruk ben Hassan, and fingered his beard.

"A soldier who leads soldiers should have a brain and use it; O, Marbruk ben Hassan," replied the Emir.

Marbruk scratched his right calf with his left foot and reminded me of a discomfortable school-boy.

The other Arab eyed him with a look of affectionate tolerance.

"Taking a hundred men, I would make three parties," said the dwarf at length. "Two strong, and one weak--The two strong parties, each making a détour, should, at sunset, as the men cease work and go to camp, suddenly charge each other, meeting at a spot quite near--There should be much firing, shouting, falling from camels, a _lab el baroda_, a powder-play--but looking and sounding like a great fight--There would be an alarm--The guard would come running and form up in that direction, and while all was in confusion and nothing clear, the small third party should swoop down upon the prisoners and ride off with the man whose life the _Sidi_ desires--Word could be got to him of what was toward--"

"Thou art not _wholly_ a fool, O, Marbruk ben Hassan," smiled the Emir. And the Arab acknowledged the compliment with a low salaam.

"Yussuf Latif?" said the Emir, turning to the other, a lean large-eyed tragic-looking man.

"If guile is to be used and not the sword, I would try France's own pacific penetration," he said. "Open a little market--dates, _sharbet_, fruit, ooked meats--Also a band of holy dervishes would arrive and rest--There might be one or two slave women from the tribe yonder--

"One day, at a given signal, a strong man springs on every soldier, while another snatches his rifle--A small party at once liberates the prisoner and takes him to where two or three of the fleetest camels are waiting, and swiftly they ride hither--"

"And--afterwards--what of those who have seized the guard?" asked the Emir.

"It will be their privilege to die, Emir--All will volunteer--nay, quarrel, for that honour--"

"None are to die, Yussuf Latif--neither in fight nor in willing surrender of their lives--" said the Emir. "Speak again; O, Yussuf Latif--"

"What of this then, Lord? When our peaceful and humble disposition has disarmed suspicion, and we have gradually been permitted to mingle with the soldiers of the escort, every one of these shall be allotted to two of our strong men--Of every two men, one shall have two stout thin cords about his waist, or otherwise hidden--

"At the given signal, every soldier shall be seized by the two appointed to him, and the moment that one has snatched his rifle, the other shall seize him round the arms and body--The rifle-snatcher shall then bind the man's feet together and his arms to his sides--The two shall then carry the man to an appointed place, where all the soldiers shall be laid together unhurt--Except one--This one shall be laid a mile away--his feet most strongly bound and one arm bound to his body tightly--It shall be shown to him that there is a knife stuck in the sand, afar off--

"When we have departed--taking with us the man whom you desire--this bound soldier will roll and wriggle toward the knife, and by the time he gets it and contrives to free himself and his comrades, we shall be very far away, and, making a détour, return hither--"

"Leaving a track for all men to see?" asked the Emir.

The Arab smiled at the joke.

"Nay, Lord," he said, "the détour would take us up the stony Wadi el Tarish where a million camels would leave no trace--"

"Do you like this plan; O, Yussuf?" inquired the Emir.

"Each man thinks his own fleas are gazelles," quoted Yussuf Latif ibn Fetata.

"And what do you think the prisoners will do, when the guards are bound and you are gone?" asked the Emir.

The Arab smiled and put his hand to his throat.

"They must be bound too," he said.

The Emir stroked his beard thoughtfully and pondered awhile.

"You have spoken well; O, Marbruk ben Hassan and Yussuf ibn Fetata--I will reveal my mind later--Meantime, each of you select two score of the best--Yes, yes, I know that all are best--but select the coolest and steadiest--Men who do not fire at shadows nor foam at the mouth as they fight--"

The two withdrew, salaaming profoundly.

"A fine combination, those two," said Noel. "Cautious age and daring youth--And both stauncher than steel and braver than lions--"

"I surely am sorry for that Yussuf Latif boy," observed Buddy. "What's wrong with him is a broken heart--I know the symptoms--none better--"

"That's so, Bud," agreed Noel, and added:

"The wonder to me is that you ain't egsperienced the symptoms of a broken neck--or a stretched one anyhow--"

The smile of the Wazir combined pity, superiority and contempt in exactly equal proportions.

"The point is, have you got a plan--chatterbox? he said.

"I have," said the Emir, and he detailed it to us.

"It ain't perfect," he mused, "but it's the best we can do--It's funny without being vulgar--It oughts succeed--An' there won't be any killing--

"The young woman would help us, all-right, Otis!" he asked, turning to me.

"She certainly would," I assured him "Only too glad to bring me a day's march nearer home--Or right home in a day's march--"

"That's the scheme, then," concluded Noel. "--And we'll bring it off to-morrow night--I'll hate doing it--but I'd hate any other plan worse--And the job's got to be done--"

CHAPTER XVI

In all the changing scenes of life, one of the several that are indelibly printed on my mind, and which I shall never forget, is that of the feast and entertainment, given by the Emir el Hamel el Kebir, to the men of the advance-party of those who were the pioneers on the Road that was eventually to link the Great Oasis with Zaguig, the uttermost outpost of the African Empire of France.

Having a deep personal interest in this Road, the Emir el Hamel el Kebir had, with a considerable bodyguard, come from where he was encamped, to see with his own eyes something of the great Road's swift progress and to greet the fore-runners of its makers.

The feast was, of course, an Arab one.

Surrounded by cushion-strewn rugs, on a large palm-leaf mat, slaves placed a shallow metal dish so vast as to suggest a bath. In this, on a deep bed of rice, lay a mass of lumps of meat, the flesh of kids, lambs, and I feared, of a sucking camel-calf. A sea of rich thick gravy lapped upon the shores of surrounding rice, with wavelets of molten butter and oily yellow fat.

In the centre of the bath was a noble mound of heads crowned with livers, intact and entire. Among the mass of chops, cutlets, joints, scrags, legs, shoulders, saddles, and nameless lumps of meat, were portions of the animals not usually seen on Western dishes. These, however, could be avoided by the prejudiced.

I noticed that the genuine Arabs present, were not prejudiced. Around this dish we knelt, each upon one knee, his right arm bared to the elbow, and, with the aid of our good right hands, we filled our busy mouths, and ate--and ate--and ate--

And ate.

There were present, the Emir el Hamel el Kebir; his Minister el Habibka el Wazir; a gloomy taciturn Sheikh, dark of face and blue-black of hair and well-clipped beard, a man supposed to be under a curse and also suffering from the effects of a highly unwholesome love-potion administered to him by a jealous wife--a potion from which he would probably never recover, as the Emir, indicating my morose and surly self, explained to the French *Adjudant* ; also Marbruk ben Hassan; Yussuf Latif ibn Fetata; and some half a dozen leading Sheikhs of the tribe to which the Emir belonged; and four or five Frenchmen.

From time to time, the Emir would fish out a succulent morsel and thrust it into the mouth of the guest of honour on his right, _l'Adjudant_ Lebaudy, a man who interested me much. I had put him down as very true to type, a soldier and nothing more, but a fine soldier, rugged as a rock, hard as iron, and true as steel--a man of simple mind and single purpose, untroubled by thoughts of why and wherefore, of right and wrong, finding duty sufficient and the order of a superior more important than the order of the Universe--

And by no means stupid--in fact watchful, wary, and fore-sighted, as we were to discover.

We ate in stark silence--as far as speech is concerned that is--lest light converse offend our host with indication that we were finding but light fare and entertainment--When we had finished, and not a stomach could hold another grain of rice, we rose, indicated our profound satisfaction by profound hiccoughs, went to the door of the tent, wiped our greasy hands upon its flap, and then held them forth while servants poured streams of water upon them from long-necked vessels.

Meanwhile, other servants removed the depleted hip-bath, and so re-arranged rugs and cushions that, when two of the wall-curtains were rolled up to the tent roof, each man of the company reclined with his back to a tent-wall and his face to the star-lit night without.

The great guest-tent, in which we sat, was illumined by a hanging lamp within, and the flames of a great fire maintained at sufficient distance to cause no discomfort. A few yards from us, between the tent and the fire, servants laid palm-leaf mats, upon which they placed a rug.

Coffee was brought, glasses and clay cups upon a huge brass tray, and, to do them signal honour, the Emir himself, with his own hand, took glasses of coffee to his European guests.

But _l'Adjudant_ Lebaudy excused himself, and I caught Buddy's eye as the _Adjudant's_ deep voice, in very fair Arabic, rumbled words to the effect that so enlightened and understanding a man as the Emir would not wish him to drink coffee--which disagreed with him--merely for politeness' sake--

The Emir was obviously greatly concerned and somewhat hurt--Never in his two score years of desert experience had he met a man who did not enjoy coffee, or with whom coffee disagreed--_Coffee!_--One of the choicest of gifts that the Mercy and Munificence of Allah had placed at the disposal of man--

Perhaps the *Sidi Adjudant* could not approve such poor stuff as the Emir had to offer?

Not at all, not at all, explained the Frenchman. Doubtless there was none better than that of the Emir in all Algeria, nay in all the Sahara from Kufara to Timbuctu--No, it was merely an affair of the digestion and strict injunction of the _Medécin-Majeur_ against the drinking of coffee--

The Emir expressed deep sympathy and great regret--the latter undeniably genuine.

However--the failure of hospitality could be rectified when the tea was brought--That should be made entirely to the taste of the principal guest--Either with or without _zatar_, which gives tea a scent and flavour so beautiful (to those who like it); thick with sugar--the first cup rich with amber; the second with lemon; and the third with mint--

But, to and behold!--an astounding thing--a shocking thing for any host to learn, the guest of the evening could not take _tea_ either--Tea had the same distressing effect upon his internal economy--

This time the Emir was indeed concerned--Scarcely could he believe his ears--_Not take tea?_ Tea of ceremony!--_Tea_, without which no host could honour a guest; no guest refuse without gravest discourtesy, nay, intentional insult!--

The Emir smiled tolerantly. His guest was of course jesting, as would be seen when the tea was brought--

Meanwhile, at least five men in the tent could scarcely repress the sighs of relief they felt at the sight of the other Frenchmen who sipped and sipped, gave up their empty cups and twice accepted fresh ones--Had they also refused, our plot had been frustrated.

The senior officer's refusal had filled those five with the fear that his continence had been pre-determined and enjoined upon the others. I decided that the incident was merely the outcome of his acquired or inborn mistrust of taking from an Arab host, food or drink so highly flavoured that the taste of a deleterious "foreign body" would be concealed. Also that he had no actual suspicions and had suggested none to his colleagues--

Turkish cigarettes followed coffee. Turkish cigarettes, we learned, were also unacceptable to the digestion of _l'Adjudant_ Lebaudy!

In a quiet gentle voice, the Emir inquired whether a cigarette lighted and partly smoked by himself would be likely to disagree with the digestion of _l'Adjudant_ Lebaudy.

"_Touché!_" smiled Lebaudy to himself, and hastened to assure the Emir that if there were a cigarette in this world that he could smoke and enjoy, it would be such a we--but alas, tobacco was not for him--

Tea followed the cigarettes and, at last, the Emir was brought to understand that the guest of the evening actually _was_ refusing ceremonial tea!

He swallowed the insult in a way which showed that he could not be insulted. Mannerless conduct hurt none but the person guilty of it. Gross discourtesy merely labels such a one as grossly discourteous--

It was well acted, and the other Frenchmen hastened to show the excellence of their manners, and drained their cups--special white-ware cups for the European guests only--at each of the three ceremonial drinkings.

As the third was ended and the cups collected, strains of lively music burst from the adjoining tent, and out on to the carpet floated a cloaked, mysterious form. Her cloak being thrown aside, the lovely and enchanting figure of the Angel of Death was revealed, and _l'Adjudant_ Lebaudy had evidently at length discovered a kind of hospitality prohibited neither by his doctor nor by his digestion.

That is the picture I shall never forget--the Death Angel dancing beneath the desert sky by the light of a great fire, to the insistent sensuous music, the soothing-maddening-monotonous strains of the tom-tom, the _raita_, the _derboukha_ and the flute.

At a respectful distance, in staring silence, sat the soldiers of the Emir's Bodyguard, rapt, enthralled, stirred, excited.

Apart from them, French soldiers off duty--all indeed who were not actually on guard or sentry--also sat and stared, entranced, enchanted.

Only those who have not seen a woman of their own sort and kind, for years, can measure the meaning and appeal to these men of, not merely a woman, but a singularly lovely and bewitching woman, trained and experienced in every art of fascination and allure.

And undeniably the Angel moved more like a winged being from another sphere, than like a creature of flesh and blood.

As the music abruptly ceased, and her dance finished, there was a space of utter silence, followed by wild and tumultuous applause, as the Angel retired to her tent, wherein waited her negro women.

Before this tent sat Abd'allah ibn Moussa, guarding his mistress during her visit to the Emir's camp, but in a position from which he could watch me the while.

I fear that the next item on the programme, the singing of frank love-songs by an Arab youth with a beautiful voice and a remarkable repertoire, fell a little flat.

At its conclusion, the Emir gave orders for fresh coffee to be brought to us, and that yet more refreshment be served to the watching soldiers who had already been regaled with _cous-cous_, mutton-stew, sweetmeats and coffee.

Thereafter the Angel danced again, and her reappearance galvanized into fresh life and renewed interest, the now somewhat somnolent Europeans among the audience.

Again her performance was rapturously hailed and wildly applauded.

During the succeeding turn--some exceedingly clever juggling and conjuring--it was evident to a watchful eye that several of the French soldiers had lain back where they sat, as though overcome by sleep--

For the third time the Angel emerged from her tent and danced, but, on this occasion, introduced a variation. From her dancing-carpet she moved across to that around which we sat cross-legged upon our cushions.

In this confined space she floated, whirling upon tip-toe.

Lebaudy's eyes shone and his lips parted. The Frenchman who sat on the Emir's other side, stared with a glazed and drunken gaze, though drunken he was not. His colleague, next but one upon his left, was frankly asleep. I watched the other _sous-officier_, and saw that he was struggling to keep awake--happy, drowsy, but desiring to see some more of this vision of loveliness before he went to sleep.

Next but one to him, the remaining _sous-officier_ was making an effort to keep awake, while his head nodded abruptly at intervals, as his eyes closed and he relaxed for a second or two.

I admired the foresight of the Emir, who had so arranged his guests that they sat in a straight line to right and left of him, with Lebaudy between himself and the Wazir. Only by craning rudely forward, could Lebaudy see what was happening to his subordinates, who, so far, had not given way to snores as well as slumber. Furthermore, by no amount of craning, could he see the spot where his soldiers sat feasting eyes, ears, and stomachs.

Before _l'Adjudant_ Lebaudy, the Angel paused, smiled seductively, and hovered, dancing divinely with her arms and body, while remaining stationary on the tiny spot covered by the tips of her bare toes. Anon she turned her back and bent right over until her face looked up into his--French _sous-officiers_ do not carry gold coins and place them upon the foreheads of appellant dancing-girls but kisses are another matter, and, taking her face between his strong short-fingered square-nailed hands, he kissed her ardently, and again, with right good will.

With a ringing laugh, the Angel of Death swung her lithe body erect, and began to do her utmost to fulfil her name.

Before Lebaudy she danced, and with eyes for no-one else--not even for the great Emir; and we sat and watched a wonderful exhibition of purposeful seduction--seduction, fascination and captivation.

And, as was her wont, the Angel succeeded in her task. None watching the face of _l'Adjudant_ Lebaudy could think of the simile of the fascination of the rabbit by the deadly serpent, but at least one watcher of this sinister drama thought of Samson and Delilah.

Before my eyes, this brave strong man weakened and deteriorated; ceased to be watchful, wary and alert; forgot his duty and his whereabouts--forgot everything but the woman before him, and succumbed.

Only two of the musicians had accompanied her to our tent, one with a two-ended little drum which he played with palm and finger-tips, the other with the _raita_, and between them and the girl was complete understanding.

I have heard the world's greatest musicians interpret the music of the world's greatest Masters, and I have been greatly moved. But never in my life has European music, rendered on European instruments, _affected_ me, as did that Arab music, played upon the _raita_ and the drum.

Well do the Bedouin call the _raita_, the Voice of the Devil, and I was but an onlooker, while Lebaudy was an actor in this drama of two.

I do not know for how long the girl postured, danced, beguiled, knelt beseechingly before him, sprang away ere his hands clasped her, teased, maddened, promised--all in gesture and dumb-show; but suddenly, after a quick look at four sleeping Frenchmen, she glanced at the Emir, flashing a message, 'I have done my best and can do no more,' and floated backward from us, turned, and disappeared into her tent.

As her intention of departing became obvious, Lebaudy, still but semi-conscious of his surroundings, involuntarily it seemed, rose on one knee as if to follow, remembered where he was, and sank back, "sighing like a furnace."

But only for a moment.

Distracted as was his mind from affairs mundane, he seemed suddenly to realize that he had seen something--and heard nothing.

He had seen a colleague most unbelievably asleep, and he had heard no applause.

Something was wrong--

His trained military instinct of the approach of danger was awakened and, shaking off the last vestiges of the spell, he arose briskly to his feet, with a peremptory,

"Come along! Time we turned in!"--and realized that his four colleagues were all most soundly sleeping.

"_What's this?_" he shouted, half alarmed, half incredulous, and, striding across his left-hand neighbour, he nudged the nearest sleeper with his foot.

To speak more exactly, he fetched him a remarkably sound kick.

"Get up, you swine," he growled in French.

Receiving no response, he knelt swiftly, seized the man's collar, shook him so violently that his head rolled to and fro--and realized the state of affairs.

In that instant all alarm and bewilderment left him. He became as cold and hard as ice, and won my warm admiration.

Without haste or agitation, he coolly raised an eye-lid of the sleeping man, and gave a brief hard bark of disgust.

"_Drugged!_--" he growled in French, and glanced at the other sleepers, the only men now not upon their feet.

The raised tent-walls were lowered from without, and the *Adjudant* Lebaudy stood in a closed tent, and a circle of armed Arabs.

His hand went swiftly to a pocket, and ere he withdrew it with another short snort of disgust, I heard a voice whisper beside me. And the whisper was:

"It hath went before, Bo!"

As a guest, the *Adjudant* had worn no weapons, but he had certainly carried one, and the Wazir, his attentive host, had picked his pocket.

He was a brave man, this Lebaudy.

"Well, noble and honourable host," he said, with a bitter smile, and, with a swift change from sarcasm, added, "What's the game, you dog? You treacherous slinking jackal--What now?--Do you hope for the pleasure of hearing me bawl for help--to my poisoned men?-- What's the game, I say?"

"One that I play with the utmost distaste, with the deepest regret, and with the profoundest apologies," replied the Emir. "A game, I may add, in which you have made the wrong move--from my point of view, that is--

"Huh!--I was to be poisoned too, _hein?_--But I am too old a fox to be tricked by a mangy jackal--"

"No, no, *Sidi Adjudant* --Not poisoned!--No-one has been poisoned--You were to have been our honoured guest--for the night--like these other gentlemen who sleep where they dine--"

"And while I slept?" snapped Lebaudy. "All our throats cut? Rifles and property stolen?--More '_Touareg_' work, _hein?_--"

"No, no, again, *Sidi Adjudant* ," the Emir declared "Not a throat--Not a rifle--Not a mitka worth of property--It was something wholly worthless that I propose to take--a convict--"

"Indeed!--You interest me--" sneered Lebaudy. "And might one venture to inquire which convict you kindly propose to liberate, and why? He must have some very wealthy friends--

"And the sentries--and the guard--?" he continued. "To be stabbed in the back--treacherously rushed at dawn?"

"Not a stab--Not a shot--" the Emir assured him. "One or two of my Chiefs who speak French--sufficient for the purpose--were going to borrow, with many apologies, uniforms from a sleeping Sergeant and Corporal--Half a dozen others, again with many apologies, uniforms from your excellent soldiers, now sleeping so soundly, as you rightly assume--Everything would have been returned safe and sound and, in the morning, my dear *Adjudant* , we should all have awakened together, merry and bright, in the very places where we laid us down to sleep--And by-and-bye you would have discovered that a prisoner was missing--and none so surprised as your simple Arab hosts, on learning the fact!--_Voilà tout_--"

As the Emir spoke, the Adjudant nodded his head from time to time, a thin and tight-lipped smile distorting his face.

"And now?" he asked briefly.

"Ah--now--my dear *Adjudant* --" silkily replied the Emir, "--things are different--You have been so wise--so cautious--so careful of your digestion--that you have changed my plans--The 'game,' as you call it, will be a different one, and you will play the leading part in it--"

"Again you interest me," sneered Lebaudy. "I might almost say you surprise me--I shall play a leading part, _hein?_ And pray what might that be?"

"Listen, my dear *Adjudant* , and listen carefully--lest France have cause to mourn your loss--You will lead a small party of *my* people dressed in the uniforms of _yours_--You will--er--' make the rounds,' do you call it?--reassuring each of your sentries with the countersign and the sight of your countenance, to which you will raise a hand-lamp.

"You will then proceed to the tents of the convicts, and will release the one indicated by the man who will go with you in the uniform of a Corporal, and who will hold a knife within an inch of your back the whole time--That convict you will bring here--I and my followers will at once depart with him--and we shall do ourselves the honour of inviting you to accompany us--"

"And if I refuse?"

"You will accompany us all the same, my dear *Adjudant* --"

"I mean if I refuse to have anything whatsoever to do with your infernal rascality?--To Hell with your sacred 'games.'--Are you a mad dog as well as a treacherous one?"

"At least I am not mad, _>mon Adjudant_," replied the Emir.

"But *you* are--if you refuse--On the one hand, merely a convict the less--and *you* know how easily _they_ can die, be shovelled into the sand, and struck off your roll--On the other hand, the loss to France of a brave, resourceful, and, I am sure, valued officer--"

"Murder, _hein?_" remarked Lebaudy.

"And worse I fear," confessed the Emir sadly. "Torture?"

"Alas!" admitted the Emir.

"And what becomes of *you*, my friend?" sneered Lebaudy. "Are you not forgetting such trifles as the French Republic, the French army--How long will you live, you treacherous rat, after this?"

"Mourn not for me, *Sidi Adjudant*," besought the Emir. "One thing at a time, and first things first--Listen again, I beg--it is for the last time--One of your prisoners is going to be liberated _now_, by me--It will be done more quickly and more easily with your help and presence, but done it will be--Give us that help, and I give you my word, a word I have never broken, that you shall be set free--unhurt--And not only unhurt, my friend, but rewarded--As you remarked, the convict has wealthy friends--and I am one of them--What do you say to fifty thousand francs?--A fortune--Would you care to leave the desert, to retire to your home in France? Beautiful France--And sit beneath the shadow of your own vine and your own fig-tree, a wealthy man--And no harm done, mark you--No betrayal--No treachery--No selling of the secrets of France--Just an act of mercy to an innocent man--What do you say, *Sidi Adjudant*?--What do you say to fifty thousand francs? ."

Profoundest silence in the tent.

Not one of the watchful circle of armed men made sound or movement. All seemed even to hold their breath as they awaited the Frenchman's answer.

"I say _nothing_ to them," he shouted. "I spit on them--And on you--Now, you dog--lay a hand on me as I go to leave this tent, and you have assaulted a soldier of France--obstructed him in the execution of his duty--Already you have bribed and threatened him *you*, calling yourself an ally of the Republic-- *you*, who have made a Treaty with France--*you*, who have taken French gold and would use it to bribe a servant of France--and if I live, I will command the firing-party that shall shoot you like the dog you are--"

"And if you die?" asked the Emir.

"Then with a French rope will you be hanged by another servant of France--"

And upon my soul, I almost whooped "Hear, hear!"

The man was fine, as he stood there surrounded by his enemies, stood firm--wealth on the one hand, and torture on the other.

I felt sorry for Noel, for I knew how he must loathe the part he had to play, and I could not but admire the way in which he played it..

"Believe me, *Sidi Adjudant*, nothing but the sternest necessity could drive me to do this--to offer a bribe of gold or a threat of torture and death, to a soldier of France--"

"Not to mention a guest, I suppose," observed the *Adjudant*. "--An invited guest--The world famous Arab hospitality!"

"Indeed if anything could further blacken my face and make more evil and distasteful my deed, it would be that fact--" admitted the Emir with sincerity. "By the Beard of the Prophet, and the Ninety and Nine Sacred Names of Allah, I loathe what I have to do--Come, come!--It is but a little thing I ask--Just the life of one of those wretched prisoners--And let me whisper to you, a Frenchman, a man of sensibility--_There is a lady in the case--a beautiful woman--a sweet and lovely lady whose heart is breaking--_"

I thought for a moment that Lebaudy wavered then--but he yawned, tapped his mouth once or twice with his open hand, and with a formal:

"It grows late--I thank you for your hospitality, Emir--You must excuse me--" he turned to go.

Noel, Buddy and I seized him--and I for one, hated the job--and the others drew their knives.

"Ah!" said Lebaudy.

And:

"Forgive me," said the Emir, and took him in a huge embrace as Marbruk ben Hassan, swiftly stooping, bound the Frenchman's feet together.

298 BEAU IDEAL

"*Sidi Adjudant*," said the Emir, "I detest doing this--more than I can say--Is there any hope for a parole?--Give me your word to make no effort to escape, and I will not have you bound--Nor shall you be gagged--Nor blindfolded when we shoot you--

"Help us to treat you well--To torture you, to make you aid me, would sadden me for a year--To kill you, to shut your mouth, would sadden me for a lifetime--"

Noel released his grip.

The Frenchman drew back his clenched fist to strike, and his arms were instantly seized by Buddy, and pinioned behind him. "Carry him to the small tent," said the Emir, and the order was quickly obeyed.

Lebaudy made no resistance, but, the moment he was outside the large pavilion, he gave vent to the most tremendous shout I have ever heard from human lungs:

"_A moi!--A moi!_--" he bawled.

And the sound of his voice was enough to awaken the dead.

Marbruk ben Hassan and Yussuf Latif simultaneously drew their knives, and put the points of them to the Frenchman's throat and heart respectively.

"Another sound and you die," growled the Wazir.

"_Garde_--" roared Lebaudy instantly. And the hand of the Emir was clapped over his mouth.

"Into the tent with him, quick," he said. "The sentries may have heard him--"

And in a moment, the brave Lebaudy was hustled into the tent.

"The uniforms!--Marbruk, Yussuf, and the rest of you--Quick--" And all left the tent save my brother, Buddy and myself.

"Now then," he continued, addressing the *Adjudant*, and his voice and manner changed. "You saw that fire out there--Suppose you were bound to a pole and fed into it, feet first?"

"Then I should hardly be able to make the rounds with you, if I wanted to--Even your intelligence might follow that--" was the reply.

"Of course--How foolish of me--Thank you--" replied the Emir. "We shall need your feet, as you say--But we could lead a _blind_ man, of course--Or another idea--We have ten minutes to spare while my men are dressing in the uniforms of yours--Suppose we take of a finger a minute until you change your mind?"

"A bright idea!--Guards and sentries are quite accustomed to seeing their commanding officer approach with both hands streaming blood!" sneered Lebaudy.

"Well then, suppose we agree that you are incorruptible and immovable! Also that as you insist on spoiling our plans and thwarting our modest desire to take but one convict, we are going to give ourselves the satisfaction and compensation of torturing you to death as painfully as we know how--

"That is as you please," replied Lebaudy, "but I shall only get for a few minutes what you will get for all Eternity, you foul dog."

"No, no, Sidi Adjudant ! The removal of an Infidel is an act of merit on the part of a True Believer--"

It occurred to me to feel glad that Lebaudy, whom my brother, of course, had no intention of injuring, much less of killing, had no suspicion that the Emir was other than he seemed. It would be a terrible blow to Mary should her husband's great drama be discovered to be farce.

"We shall know more about that later," growled the Frenchman. "What is not in doubt, is the question of your fate when my countrymen catch you--"

"We shall know more about that later," smiled the Emir. "Meantime your fate takes precedence, Sidi Adjudant --and I will be generous--For, in spite of your recalcitrance, and the trouble and annoyance you have given me, I will let you choose--Shall it be the fire, feet first--Impalement on the sharpened trunk of a young palm--Or pegged out for the vultures?"

The Adjudant shrugged his shoulders.

"It's a matter of complete indifference to me," he yawned.

And before my brother could reply, Yussuf pulled aside the curtain at the entrance to the tent.

"One came running," he said quickly, "a soldier--He heard the cry of this officer--We have bound him--He is unhurt."

"He may have saved your life," remarked the Emir, turning to the Adjudant . "Perhaps he will help us in the little play-acting and give us the countersign, in return for his life."

"If he is one of my _légionnaires_, you will get nothing out of him," was the reply.

"Well, hope for the best, Sidi Adjudant --If the man is amenable, I will not torture you--Perhaps even I will not kill you--"

The Emir then bade Yussuf bring four men and order them, on peril of their lives, to guard the French officer and see that none held communication with him.

He then led the way to my tent, where Marbruk ben Hassan awaited us with a bundle of French _képis_, coats, trousers, leggings, boots, side-arms and equipment.

In a surprisingly few minutes I was a French Sergeant, dark and bearded, it is true--but then the night was dark, and many of the soldiers were bearded--inspecting a guard consisting of a Corporal and eight men.

"Now then," said Noel, "--the captive. No need for him to see me, but he's got to see this guard--You'll talk French to him, of course, Otis--Also let him see, from not too near, the dead bodies of his slumbering comrades and of the _sous-officiers_ in the pavilion--Tell him his top-sergeant is elsewhere, tortured to death--That was his dying yell he heard--If he's only too glad to get his own back on the *Adjudant* , by helping, all's well--If he's staunch, try fright, bribery and corruption."

"Suppose he double-crosses--gives us the wrong countersign, and lets a yell when we get into the convict camp--" said Buddy.

"Well, we've got to take a chance," replied Noel. "It's up to you to be right in judging your man--He may jump at the chance of gaining a few hundred francs and his liberty, especially if Lebaudy is as popular as he used to be.."

"_Used to be?_" I said.

"Yes--Used to be--when Buddy and I were in his *peloton* --"

"He surely was some nigger-driver," confirmed Buddy.

" *What?* --When?" I said. "What _are_ you talking about?"

"When we were in the Legion, Son--You've heard the great tale of the Relief of Zinderneuf, where Beau Geste was killed, and we started out with John Geste and his other brother, and tramped the desert for two years--Well, old Lebaudy was Sergeant of our *peloton* , under our smart-Alec brother-in-law--Lord, yes--Lebaudy is a great old friend of ours!"

"Only he's another that don't know it--" said Buddy, and added:

"It surely hath been a pleasure to twist his tail this night--He's give us many a unhappy night, an' I allow we've give _him_ one, now--"

I said nothing but thought much.

In the best Legion manner, I stepped back, rasped a "_Garde à vous! Par files de quatre. En avant!--Marche!_ " and the drilled men of the body-guard, to whom none of this was new except their unaccustomed uniforms, moved smartly beneath the ferocious eye of the Corporal-Wazir.

We had not marched more than a few yards before I cried:

" *Halte!* "

I had had an idea, and turned back to the Emir's tent. Noel was reclining on his rugs, looking thoughtful and somewhat dejected.

"Son," he said, "I don't like it--I can't sit here in safety and let you go into that camp--If they pinch you, you'll never be seen again--Nor Bud either--The Legion wants him--just like the Zephyrs want you--"

"I'm going anyhow, Noel," I said, "whether you go or not--It's my privilege and my right--I found him, old chap, and I'm going to save him--It's you who are saving him really, but I mean--I must be there--and take the lead too--"

"True, Son--but I don't like it--For two pins I'd come along, as one of your men--But I mustn't be caught and be found to be an American from the Legion--for Mary's sake--And for the sake of my Arabs too--I hate letting Bud go without me--But I can't let you go alone with the men, and Bud insists because John came back to look for _him!_--"

"What did you return for?" he added.

"Why--I had an idea--"

"*No!*" said my brother, in feigned surprise.

"Yes, I've been thinking."

"You aren't here to think, Son--You're here to obey orders, you know--You go and collect the ideas of that man they've caught--"

"What occurred to me," I continued unmoved, "--was this--I'm every inch a French Sergeant--Suppose we put this disguised squad on their camels, and we make a little détour--Then I ride in here again, at their head, and with some more of your body-guard behind us as _goumiers_. We ride in where this prisoner is, and he would at once see, with his own eyes, that we are a perfectly good French _peloton méhariste_. He'll shout for help, and you'll look guilty and confused--I'll be haughty and truculent, and moreover I'll refuse to camp with you--I'll have the man set flee, and tell him to lead us into the convict camp. I'll take command, in the inexplicable absence of Lebaudy and the _sous-officiers_, voice my suspicions that something is wrong, visit the sentries and tell them to be watchful--Count the convicts--and bring one away with me to this camp--With a good nerve and a little luck, that ought to work perfectly--"

Noel smote his thigh.

"Oats," he declared, "you've said something--Go and fetch Buddy--"

I bade my squad--or _troupe_--"Stand easy!" and, in Arabic, told the Wazir that the Emir would fain have speech with him.

In the tent I repeated and elaborated my plan. It appealed to Buddy at once, and he preferred it to the other scheme on account of the human factor.

That was uncertain in both, but less so, perhaps, in my scheme. A bribed and intimidated man might well double-cross us--fearing the French authority more than us, and doubting whether he would ever get his thirty pieces of silver. He would probably agree to all that we suggested and then betray us--instead of his own people--as soon as we were well into their camp, and he in safety.

In a very few minutes my proposal was carried unanimously, the more readily in that none of us was at all enamoured of the debauching of a simple soldier from his duty, if it could be avoided.

"It looks water-tight to me," decided Noel. "So far, the prisoner has neither heard nor seen anything suspicious in this camp. All he knows is that they thought they heard Lebaudy shout--The Corporal of the Guard, or someone, sent him down to see if anything was wanted, and he was seized and held as he came running into this camp--"

"Quite right too," observed Corporal Buddy, with some indignation."--Rushing into a respectable camp like this in the middle of the night--Barging about like a steer at a rodeo--_Course_ he were arrested--"

"Send a man for Marbruk ben Hassan," said Noel.

Buddy stepped out of the tent and, a few minutes later, Marbruk entered with him.

On being questioned by the Emir, it turned out that, as we hoped and supposed, the prisoner had been seized by the guard at the very entrance to the camp, had been put in the guard-tent, and could know absolutely nothing of what had occurred.

All seemed propitious for the success of my plan, and Marbruk was sent back with certain instructions to the guard--one of which was, to place the prisoner where he could see anyone who went by.

Marbruk was then to get my uniformed squad of hard-bitten dependable ruffians mounted, and to have them, with a dozen others in Arab dress, awaiting me at the opposite side of the camp.

Men and camels were of course drilled and experienced members of the Emir's body-guard, picked from his famous Camel-Corps.

"Good-bye, Son, and may God help you," said Noel, as I left the tent. "Keep cool, and act up to me and Bud, and we'll have John Geste here in an hour--Now, don't forget--You're an indignant and suspicious French Sergeant--And you don't hold with Arabs as such--You don't use language _too_ frequent and free, to me, because I'm a Big Noise, and the French Government's very fond of me--Still, you don't like having French soldiers arrested by Arabs, and you want to know all about it--Play up, Son--We'll get away with it--"

His farewell to Buddy was less impressive, for, as that Corporal-Wazir turned on his heel without a word, the Emir's sandalled foot shot up and encountered ill-fitting French trousers.

Yussuf Latif ibn Fetata, in French uniform, stood at the head of my kneeling camel, his foot upon its doubled fore-leg to prevent its rising to its feet. He saluted as I approached and handed me the rein-cord.

I mounted, the camel rose, and I rode away from the camp, followed by my mixed _peloton méhariste_.

The night was dark and very still, and, at that hour--about three o'clock in the morning--_I_ would willingly have been dark and very still, upon the comfortable rug and cushions of my tent--

A quarter of an hour later, I approached the tents of the quarter-guard, and, as we drew near, the Soudanese sentry challenged and brought his rifle from the slope to the ready. I replied with a loud hail and the announcement that we were friends, come in peace.

The sentry turned and shouted, and from the guard-tent a powerful, mis-shapen dwarf came hurrying with a well-tended slush-lamp in his hand.

The guard turned out in fine style.

"_Franzawi!_" cried the dwarf, in great surprise. "Come in peace--By Allah, is it well?"

"*A peloton méhariste Français!*" I cried. "What camp is this?

"The camp of His Highness the Emir, Sidi el Hamel el Kebir, Leader of the Confederation of the Tribes of the Great Oasis--"

"Sir!" cried an indignant voice in French from the guard-tent. "I have been arrested by these Arabs--Been taken prisoner, I have!"

And a man in uniform struggled from the tent, closely followed by two Soudanese.

"Here I What's this?" I shouted, my voice hard with wrathful surprise. "A French soldier in uniform? By whose order was he arrested? Where's he from?--Send my compliments to the Emir--

"Come here, you," I called to the man. "Tell me about it--I'll look into this--"

And with gentle taps of my camel-stick upon its neck, I brought my camel to its knees.

The light from the slush-lamp fell upon my face and upon that of the French prisoner.

"_Hankinson!_" he cried, using the name which had been mine in the Legion.

"*Sergeant* Hankinson, please!" I replied instantly, with stern reproof in my voice. "Have you gone blind, *Légionnaire* Schnell?" And I brought into prominence the gold stripe on my cuff.

Yes--I had been quick!--For once I had risen to the occasion with absolute promptitude and _aplomb_. And, by so doing, I had turned a ghastly contretemps into what might prove a piece of amazing good luck.

It was the miserable Schnell, the butt and buffoon of my barrack-room in the Legion, and, in another second, I should learn whether he had heard that I had been court-martialled and sent to the Zephyrs. It was extremely improbable, as he had gone from Sidi-bel-Abbès to Senegal when I had gone to the Moroccan border.

"I--I--I beg your pardon, _Monsieur le Sergent_," gasped Schnell, saluting repeatedly. "I knew your voice and I recognized your face, and I called your name without stopping to look--I am very sorry, mon Sergent ."

All was well. The miserable Schnell had heard nothing.

"That's enough! Don't chatter like a demented parrot--Tell me how you come to be here--And where the end of the Road is--That is what I was looking for--"

"Oh, close here, mon Sergent ," replied Schnell, standing stiffly to attention. "It's like this, sir--The convict camp is just back there and this Arab--he's a big Chief, a 'friendly'--he gave a _fête_, a feast, and dancing-girls and all that, and invited the Commandant and _messieurs lea sous-officiers_, and all men who were off duty--I was on guard, and me and Schantz and Slinsky and Poggi were sitting outside the guard-tent, when suddenly Corporal Blanchard said, 'Silence, you!--Hark!'

"And we listened, but we heard nothing, and the Corporal said he thought he had heard the voice of _Monsieur l'Adjudant_ Lebaudy. They say he has the biggest voice in the French Army--"

"Oh, for God's sake," I growled, "cut it short--And tell me what you are doing here--You mean you assaulted some harmless Arab I suppose--Or was it one of their women?"

"Oh, sir! No, no, no!" protested poor Schnell. "Corporal Blanchard said he thought he must be mistaken, but said I'd better come across and see whether everything was all-right--And they arrested me--"

"I suppose you came rushing into the camp like a Touareg--like a whole Touareg raid, a host in yourself--" I sneered.

"The Corporal said 'Run across,' sir, and I came _au pas gymnastique_ and--"

"Silence!" I roared. "Don't you back-answer me, you jibbering jackass--How long have you been here?"

"About half an hour, sir," admitted Schnell.

"Well, I'll have you put somewhere else, for about half a month," I bullied. "You blundering half-witted, half-baked, half-bred, half-addled, half-man you."

I was, I fear, beginning thoroughly to enjoy myself. Probably I was uplifted by excitement, hope, fear and tautened nerves. I then turned upon the dwarf.

"And you?" I stormed in Arabic. "How dare you arrest a French soldier on his way to speak with his commanding officer?"

The dwarf spread deprecating hands and shrugged tremendous shoulders.

"By Allah! A mistake--an accident--Such fools as these Soudanese are--But the _Roumi_ soldier came running, and was violent--His Highness the Emir will be distressed beyond words--But the man was very violent. Some say he slew two with his bayonet--others say three--"

"What!" I cried, "absurd!--Was the man drunk then?"

"Well, _Sidi_, this one was not very drunk," replied the dwarf.

"What do you mean?" I cried. "Let your speech be plain--'This one was not very drunk.'--Who _was_ very drunk then?"

A quiet and orderly body of men, several carrying lamps, approached.

The dwarf was flustered.

"Our Lord, the Emir himself," he whispered.

And at the head of a body of Sheikhs, officers, officials, soldiers, and slaves, appeared the Emir el Hamel el Kebir.

"Please Allah! Well?--Come in peace!--The Peace of Allah be upon you!"

I saluted the Emir, military fashion.

"Health and the Peace of Allah upon you, O Emir!--_Le Sergent Hankinson, peloton méhariste, numero douze_, for Number One Construction Camp--I saw your fire and came to ask--In your camp I find a French soldier arrested and detained--I have to request that you hand him over to me at once, with explanation--"

"What is this, Marbruk ben Hassan?" inquired the Emir of the dwarf. His voice was harsh.

Marbruk, with low salaam, hastily repeated what he had said to me.

It appeared that the man had been very violent--some said five had been killed--or gravely injured--The dwarf feared that the man had been under the influence of the strong sharab of the _Roumis_--Fighting drunk, in fact--

Indignantly Schnell denied that he had so much as seen liquor, for years.

"But how _could_ he be drunk?" I interposed angrily. "Where would he get it? Do the wells then contain sharab in this part of the desert?"

The Emir smiled and stroked his beard.

"Nay, I never thought so," replied the Emir. "Until this day I had not thought it--Strange indeed are the ways of the _Roumis_--but let us thank Allah for the diversity of His creatures--Verily wine is a mocker--and well is it prohibited unto us--"

"What is behind your speech, O Emir?" I asked. "Give me not twisted words from a crooked tongue, I beseech you. Let our speech be short and plain."

"Will the Commandant come with me a moment?" asked the Emir with quiet dignity. "And if perhaps he would bring this soldier who has seen no _sharab_--"

"Corporal!" I shouted over my shoulder. "Let the men dismount and take an 'easy.' Each man to stand to his camel with rifle unslung."

And Corporal Buddy's salute and reply were the authentic thing. It would have taken a quicker brain than Schnell's to have found anything wrong with me and my *peloton* .

As I moved off with the Emir, followed by Schnell, the former remarked confidentially, but with care that Schnell should hear him:

"I did not wish to say too much in front of your men, Commandant--And also I thought you would believe your own eyes more quickly than my voice--"

Bidding his followers to halt and to await him where they stood, the Emir led me and Schnell to a tent.

"I regret this most deeply," he said, "--and I would fain have concealed it--I gave a poor feast in my humble camp and invited all who cared to come--It is not for me to make comment--But my men are accused of arresting one who knows nothing of any drunkenness, any imbibing of _sharab_--" and he pulled aside the curtain of the tent.

By the light of the lamp in the tent, we beheld the distressing spectacle of three uniformed non-commissioned officers, deep sunk in drunken slumber.

I shrugged my shoulders and clucked my tongue in disgust.

"Tch! Tch! Tch!--And what of their men?" I asked, shame-faced and angry.

It was the turn of the Emir to shrug his shoulders.

I stirred one of the sleepers sharply with my foot, and shook the other by the shoulder (but not too violently).

"And the *Adjudant* Lebaudy?" I asked.

"Do not ask me, _Monsieur le Sergent_," said the Emir pityingly.

"Where is he?--I will see him--I must satisfy myself--" I said sharply.

"*Légionnaire* Schnell," I added. "Remain in here until I return--Leave this tent at your peril."

The Emir led me away.

CHAPTER XVII

I returned and entered the tent, grave-faced, sad, indignant, but with the look, in my eye, of a good Sergeant who sees promotion in the near distance.

"Schnell," I said, "listen, and be careful--A still tongue runs in a wise head--Get you back at once to camp, and report to Corporal Blanchard that all's well here--_all's well_, d'you understand?--_Monsieur l'Adjudant_ Lebaudy did not call for you--He and the Sergeants are remaining longer--_Remaining longer_, d'you understand?--Be very careful what you say--I should be sorry for you if it were found that false reports--detrimental to _l'Adjudant_ Lebaudy and your superior officers--were traced to you--"

The good Schnell apparently understood very clearly.

"Very good--Get along back then and--oh--report that a _peloton méhariste_--Sergeant, Corporal, eight soldiers and ten _goumiers_--is arriving at once. Tell Corporal Blanchard to warn the sentries--I may as well have the countersign too--What is it, 'Maroc' still?"

"No, sir, '_Boulanger_,'" replied simple Simon Schnell.

"Well, be off then--and don't run like a mad bull into your own camp--Get a bullet in your belly one of these days--"

Schnell saluted and departed with speed, filled with the best intentions.

"Now for it!" I said, as we hurried forth to rejoin my circus of camels and performing Arabs.

"Great stuff! Son, you're The Goods!" whispered Noel, as he gripped my arm--

I gave the order to mount, and, a minute later, I led the *peloton*, in column of files, at a swinging trot toward the convict camp.

Anxiously as I was awaiting it, the sentry's loud:

"_Halte!--Qui va là?_" brought my heart into my mouth.

I switched my mind from thoughts of John and Isobel--and became a French Sergeant again.

I answered, and gave the countersign in correct style--the style with which I was only too familiar--halted my *peloton*, and went forward.

"That you, Schantz?" I snapped.

"No, Sergeant," replied the man. "I am Broselli--"

"Has Schnell just come into camp?" I asked.

"A few minutes ago, Sergeant," was the reply.

"Ah!" I said mysteriously, called my *peloton* to attention, and led them to the camp.

"_Halte!_" I cried at the top of my voice. "Dismount!--Stand easy!"

The guard turned out, the Corporal came hurrying, followed by a man bearing a lamp. He saluted me smartly.

"Urgent and in haste," I said. "Take me to _l'Adjudant_ Lebaudy, at once."

"He's over at the big Emir's camp, Sergeant," replied the Corporal. "A _fête_--a big show--Everybody's there--"

"So I gathered," I said grimly. "A little awkward if there was another raid, _hein_? However, that's the _Adjudant's_ affair--You in command here?"

"Yes, Sergeant--I am senior Corporal," replied the man.

"Well, you'll do," I said. "They want that man back, in Zaguig--The convict who says he was the only item not on the last Touareg butcher's-bill--They seem to think, now, it wasn't a Touareg show at all."

"What! The convicts themselves?"

"No, fat-head--They wouldn't all have killed themselves, would they?"--and I leant over and lowered my voice confidentially. "_Selim ben Yussuf!_--And his tribe one of the Allied Confederation and all!--Yes, that's the latest idea--It was he handed the man back, y'know--And there's about a dozen not accounted for--Smart bit of bluff, what!"

"He hasn't a cold in the eyes, that one," opined the Corporal.

"No," I said. "Come on--I can't stop chattering here all night--You know the man, I suppose?"

"Well--not to say _know_ him, Sergeant--I daresay I can--"

"All-right," I answered. "I know his ugly mug well enough--I had charge of him at the Zaguig Court-martial--We shall be old friends by the time they _do_ make him squeal--"

I turned to Buddy.

"Corporal," I snapped. "We shall be off again in a few minutes--Where's that spare camel? You'll be in charge of it--Tie the man's hands behind him, and the end of the cord to your wrist--The men will mount again in five minutes--

"Come on, Corporal Blanchard," I added. "That damned Court-martial sits to-morrow."

And, preceded by the man with the hand-lamp, we marched off, my heart beating like a trip-hammer.

Apparently this worthy soul was more observant than his Corporal, for if he did not know the desperado by sight or by number, he knew which tent he was in.

With a murmured, "_Tente numero B7_," he led us straight to one of the tents.

"The bird's in here, Corporal," he said, as the sentry came to attention.

"Fetch him out then," said Corporal Blanchard.

"And be quick about it," I snapped.

There were rustlings and growlings within, the kind of sound of movement one might hear on stirring up a cageful of straw-couched feral beasts, at night.

Two minutes later, the man with the lamp reappeared with the sentry--and _John Geste--John Geste!_--ill, and broken and worn, but still firm of lip and grim of jaw.

It was an anxious second--

Just kicked from slumber and flung out into the night, face to face with me, would he cry my name aloud in his incredulous surprise?--If he did, I would take the same line that I had taken with Schnell, but with greater sternness.

I might have known!--I need not have feared--"_Bon chat chasse de race._"--Blood tells--John gave me a quick look, and then stood with the surly hang-dog convict slouch, his eyes on the ground.

"Here, you, put that lamp to his ugly mug--I don't want to take the wrong man," I snarled, giving him what cue I could, and putting my hand beneath his chin, I rudely jerked his head up.

"That's the swine," I said. "Take him along and sling him on the spare camel."

And we marched off.

Buddy's reception of the prisoner was not calculated to raise suspicion in the slow mind of Corporal Blanchard.

With a business-like contemptuous roughness, he pinioned the prisoner. And with a brief:

"_Voilà!_ Undo that if you can!" he pointed with a jerk of his thumb to the spare camel, now attached to his own.

"Get on, and enjoy your last ride in this world," he growled, "and if you so much as _look_ crooked, I'll drag you behind it--"

"Well, good-night, Corporal," I said to the excellent Blanchard, and mounted my camel, every second expecting that the man's detestable voice, with a tinge of respectful surprise, would utter the words for which I had been waiting from the first.

"_What about the warrant, Sergeant? You haven't handed it over._" Had he demanded it, as, of course, he should have done, it had been my intention to say:

"Ah, yes! Of course!"--to feel for it in my inner pocket, and--slowly, reluctantly, with growing horror, consternation, and alarm--to come to the conclusion that I had actually left it at Zaguig! I imagined Blanchard hastening to reassure his superior officer, and disclaim the slightest desire to embarrass him--The warrant could be sent out with the next ration-party--

In that case I would nod my agreement and offer to scribble him a receipt for the goods, as his authority meanwhile.

As I gave the order to march, another idea occurred to me, should he yet remember and yell for the warrant. I would say stuffily:

"Warrant! *you* --How long have *you* been _l'Adjudant_ Lebaudy I think I'll hand it to him, thank you--" (very sarcastically).

But the fool never thought of it at all, God bless him! "_Walk--march--_" I intoned.

The camels shuffled forward, the sentry saluted, and--*John Geste* was free.

2.

During the short ride between the two camps, I kept silence and stared straight ahead into the night.

I could not have spoken without disgracing myself. A choking held my throat, a smarting blinded my eyes, an acute pain stabbed my heart, and I trembled from head to foot.

Nor did I hear a word pass between Buddy and John Geste, close behind me.

I think that both, like me, had hearts too full for speech, and that John was being wary--riding, as it seemed to him, among French soldiers.

By our own guard-tent, I halted and dismissed the *peloton*, the admirable small-part characters of my caste, who hastened away to return their "properties" to their rightful owners. It would not be seemly that any good French soldier should awake to find his trousers missing.

One on each side of John, we marched to the Emir's tent, entered it, closed the opening and stood together--an Emir, a French Sergeant, a French Corporal and a convict!

Three Americans and an Englishman!

Shall I attempt to describe that meeting?--Tell of how John cleared his throat with a slight cough and remarked:

"Thanks awfully, you fellows--These cords are very tight--Anybody got a drink on him?"--and collapsed in a dead faint.

--Of how we worked over him and brought him round, Buddy weeping freely and swearing fiercely--my brother, in grim silence, save when he blew his nose violently--I swallowing, and swallowing, and swallowing, while words of fire capered about my aching brain.

"_John Geste is free--John Geste is saved--Isobel--Isobel--Isobel--_"

Of how, in silence, John Geste put his left hand on my shoulder and with his right gripped mine with what strength he had left to him--

Of how he did the same with Hank, saying nothing..

Of how he did the same with Buddy, saying nothing--

Of how we four men, stirred to our deepest depths, as perhaps never before in our lives, tried to behave as reticent white men should, with decent repression of emotion--though Buddy was once or twice shaken from head to foot by a spasm--followed by a torrent of shocking profanity--though Hank was constrained to blow his nose with a violence that shook the camp and caused Buddy to request him not to wake the Seven Blasted Sleepers though John Geste, from time to time, uttered the slight cough with which he covered what would, in a woman, have been a sob--and I, I could not see properly--

3.

There was a cry without.

The Emir sprang to the tent-door, and we heard the voice of Marbruk ben Hassan.

"Lord, _a raid on the French camp at dawn_! Yacoub-who-goes-without-water hath sent in a rider--Yacoub had news of a big _harka_ encamped, and went thither--He heard the talk around the camp-fires--They are not Touareg. It is Selim ben Yussuf and his band--disguised as Touareg--He knows his tribe moved north as ordered--With an overwhelming rush they will stamp flat the convict camp, shouting Touareg war-cries lest any escape the slaughter and tell the tale--Having slaughtered the guard and convicts, he will loot what he can of rifles, ammunition and stores. And having made another big détour will join the tribe near Bouzen--"

"Man proposeth but Allah disposeth," said the Emir. "Bring me the messenger--" and turned back into the tent where Buddy and I were swiftly resuming our Arab dress.

Noel quickly selected _jubba, kaftan, kaffieh, burnous_ and head-cloth from his own stock of clothing, and John, tearing off his ragged convict dress, assumed them with speed and ease.

I remembered that he had worn Arab dress for a couple of years.

Had it ever been hidden from me, the secret of my brother's rise would now have been revealed. He thought of everything--He ordered everything--He foresaw everything--He was cool, unhurried, supremely efficient, and the policy with which he handled the *Adjudant* Lebaudy was masterly--

Yussuf Latif ibn Fetata came to the tent.

"The French soldiers are again arrayed in their uniforms, save two," and he glanced at the uniforms discarded by Buddy and myself.

"Go like the wind, good Yussuf," said the Emir, "and array those two also--Take note that this bundle belongs to the man lying with three others in the big tent--"

The messenger arrived in custody of Marbruk ben Hassan, and added but little to the latter's précis of his message.

We gathered, however, that Selim was counting on the Emir's being encamped ten miles off, or else on his way back to the Great Oasis, and not only unable to assist the French, but also unable to enhance their admiration and approval of his good-will and good ability in the matter of guaranteeing peace in the desert, and the policing of the new route.

To the Touareg the blame; to the Emir the discredit of inefficiency; to Selim ben Yussuf the loot, and revenge on the hated _Franzawi_--

And as, with beneficent and approving smile, the Emir gave the messenger permission to retire, that ragged wisp of humanity smiled crookedly, displaying his tooth, and with profound obeisance added:

"Also Yacoub bade thy slave tell the Sidi Emir, that the attack will be made from the Zaguig side, as danger would be least expected thence. It will doubly fail because not only will the Franzawi be now expecting it, but Yacoub will himself ride behind the rear of Selim ben Yussuf's _harka_, and as they are about to charge, he will fire his rifle in the air."

"And be himself destroyed by the French volleys?" asked the Emir.

"Nay, Lord, he will be lying flat upon his back behind a sand-dune and his kneeling camel."

The Emir smiled and the messenger departed.

The Emir issued further orders.

"Marbruk ben Hassan," said he. "I need not give thee detailed instructions. A line of men behind a ridge across the Zaguig Road--Camels twenty yards to the rear--Orders to section leaders for ten rounds of rapid fire when Yacoub's rifle goes off, or your whistle blows--Pickets far out, all round the camp--Send out Yussuf Latif with a swift patrol, with Yacoub's messenger as guide--Not a shot to be fired on peril of their lives--We want to be 'surprised'--at fifty yards--"

Marbruk ben Hassan, the happy light of battle on his soldierly face, departed, and the Emir turned back into the tent.

"Here's a pretty kettle of fish!" said he. "Bud, set R'Orab and all the servants to chucking water on that fire, and then on the drunks--See there isn't a light in the camp--You try and fetch the Sergeants round--You come with me, Oats--John, you lie low--Go to bed, in fact, on those cushions--"

John shook his head.

"Can't you find me a rifle?" he asked.

"Onto that bed with you, Boy--I do most solemnly swear that I'll bind you hand and foot, if there's another word out of you--" and he strode from the tent.

As we hurried to the small one in which Lebaudy must have been having one of the worst hours of his life, Noel remarked:

"If I see Selim ben Yussuf over the sights of my rifle, doing the early bird, this morning, it'll be more worms than early bird for his--"

The four men in charge of Lebaudy were ordered to report to Marbruk ben Hassan immediately.

"_Sidi Commandant_," said the Emir, "no man can withstand his fate--To some, good fortune; to some, bad--What is written is written--Your camp will be attacked at dawn--"

"By _your_ orders, you treacherous devil, of course--I quite expected it," was the reply. "Huh! The faith of the Arab!--The noble untamed unsullied Son of the Desert, whose word is better than his bond!--you pariah cur!--Now we know who made the _last_ raid!"

"I think we do, _Sidi Commandant_--one Selim ben Yussuf--It is he who will attack now--"

"By _your_ orders," sneered the _Adjudant_. "Do you take me for a fool--an Afflicted-of-Allah?--By your orders, of course--I, in your power, bound hand and foot--Three-quarters of my men decoyed here and poisoned--and my camp 'will be attacked at dawn.'--I've no doubt it will, you devil, you treacherous hound--you lousy, begging, lying oasis-thief--Attacked at dawn, _hein_?--In other words, when you've cut the throats of everyone of us here, you and your foul gang of murderous ruffians will visit my camp with knives and pistols in your sleeves, and make a massacre--to avoid a fight--That'll be your 'attack.'--My soldiers shot in the back--stabbed in the back--butchered--More '_Touareg_' work, _hein?_--Dead men tell no tales, _hein?_--And all that you may earn some gold for rescuing some rich criminal--

"But you hear my last words, and remember them--The arm of France is long--You'll hang--You'll hang--at the end of a rope, in Zaguig gaol--"

"Are those the _Sidi Commandant's_ last words?--Because, if so, I would fain lift up my own poor voice and utter one or two--" replied the Emir.

"Listen--I have received information from my spies, that Selim ben Yussuf will attack your camp at dawn--A sudden swift raid from the Zaguig side--His object revenge--he does not greatly love the French, as you know--loot, rifles and sport--

"As you have shown me, that would wipe out this night's work, for me, nicely--I have but to saddle-up and go, with all my men--and the convict whom I wanted--and all record of my (shall I say?) impropriety of conduct, will vanish, even as will the aforesaid convict--"

"_Lies!--Lies!_--" roared Lebaudy. "_Lies_--You father of treachery and son of filth--_Words_--"

"Words _and_ deeds, _Sidi Commandant_--" interrupted the Emir. "Time flies--" and he drew a great knife which, with its gold-inlaid hilt, worn upright in the middle of his sash, marked his rank.

"_Deeds!_" sneered the undaunted Lebaudy. "Worthy deeds!--Cut my throat, you Arab hero--" and throwing back his head, he closed his eyes.

My brother cut the cord that bound Lebaudy's feet, and set him free. Lebaudy stared incredulous.

"_Now_ what's the game?" he growled.

"The game, *Sidi Commandant*, is this--You jump on to a swift camel and ride with us--you to your camp to make those dispositions which will mark you as a second Napoleon--I to my men who are by now ambushed across the line of the Road from Zaguig to your camp, awaiting the attack which will come within the hour--

"Meantime the very utmost will be done to revive your sleeping men, and to send them over, on camels, to your camp--"

"Are you speaking the truth?" incredulously asked the astonished Lebaudy.

"Ride with me straight to where my men are protecting your camp," said the Emir.

"I will," replied the Frenchman grimly. "I shall be able to make my dispositions better when I have seen yours," he continued. "Not that I believe a word of it--But I am in your power for the moment, and must play your game, I suppose--"

"It would be wiser, *Sidi Commandant*," said my brother, helping the *Adjudant* to his feet.

"I will put my few men in, to stiffen your line--if there is a line," growled the latter.

"It will need no stiffening, *Sidi Adjudant*," smiled the Emir. "Might I respectfully suggest they be used as a mobile reserve under your command--reconnaissance--pickets--scouts--or even to cut off such retreat as will be left to friend Selim ben Yussuf--"

"Seeing's believing--" growled the *Adjudant*. "I'll make my own arrangements, thank you--And defend my own camp--"

"Not with three men and a boy," smiled the Emir. "I'm going to fight Selim ben Yussuf when he attacks your camp, and you can help me as you like."

"Come on then," snapped the *Adjudant*, half-convinced. "If you are speaking the truth, they may come at any minute now--"

"Arrangements have been made for their reception," said the Emir, and led the way to where the camels awaited us.

As we passed, I thrust my head into the Emir's tent, where John lay at rest upon the rugs.

He was awake.

"Look here, John--orders are that you don't leave this tent till we come back--That'll be all-right, won't it?--Then I can push off with Noel and help save the French camp--He's hopping mad that that young swine, Selim, should have gone on the war-path like this--And on the one and only night when the French can't look after themselves--thanks to Noel himself!"

"Why, no, Vanbrugh, I'm not going to sit here, if Hank and Buddy are going out scrapping--I'm coming too--

"Didn't I come out to Africa to save _those two_?" he laughed, "and now I've _saved_ them, do you expect me to let them out of my sight--scrapping around in the dark and all?"

I grinned at this John Geste.

"Well, and didn't *I* come out to Africa to save *you*?" I asked. "And now I've saved you, do you expect me to let you out of my sight--scrapping around in the dark and all?"

"Better go together then," was the reply.

"Not a bit of it--I must go and back my brother up, and you must have the decency to remember that it's cost us all no end of time and trouble to put you where you are--and you've got to stay put."

"Oh, well, of course," replied John Geste, "if you put it like that--All I can say is--what I said before--" and here he laughed out-right, "we'll go together--"

And we went together--a pair of perfectly good Arabs following their Emir.

4.

A short ride brought us to where we were challenged by one of Marbruk ben Hassan's vedettes, and, a few minutes later, we were being led by Marbruk himself, along the line of his ambush-defence.

If Yacoub's information were correct, and Selim and his raiders were going to attack in this direction, it would probably be Selim's last exploit, and the end of his career of treachery to the French.

The wily and experienced Marbruk had proceeded sufficiently far from the camp to be at a spot where the raiders would still be riding in a crowd. A little nearer to the camp, and they would have spread out into a line--a line that would have outflanked Marbruk's, and soon become a circle completely enveloping the camp.

Already a scout, mounted on a fine Arab horse, had ridden in with information which entirely corroborated that of Yacoub--a _harka_ some two to three hundred strong, had ridden toward the line of the Zaguig-Great Oasis Road, and, turning half-right, had swung on to it.

Having seen this, the scout had galloped back at once.

Adjudant Lebaudy grunted, and, with a guide, rode hard for his camp.

A quarter of an hour later, as I sat beside John, behind the ridge--possibly the most triumphantly happy person in the world--and wished the wretched Selim would hurry up, for I was very cold,--a rifle cracked.

I scrambled to the top of the ridge and looked over.

"Hullo!" said John. "What do you put that at--five hundred yards?"

"Or nearer," I said. "Now Noel will let them know that they don't surprise the camp, whatever else they do--Nasty four-o'clock-in-the-morning shock for Selim--"

A whistle blew near-by. A few minutes later a couple of short blasts were blown, and a crashing volley was fired from a distant section of the ridge.

Almost simultaneously, other volleys followed from other sections, and then the ceaseless banging of rapid independent fire from a hundred rifles.

A pandemonium of noise broke out from what had been the silent mysterious space in front of us--a noise to which wounded men and camels contributed, as well as every subordinate leader who had anything to shout--their cries varying in portent from charge to flight. Some I believe did one, and some the other, for I certainly saw vague blotches of white receding, while vague forms loomed up quite near.

A whistle blew loudly, a long strong blast, and all firing ceased. It blew again twice, and volley upon volley banged clean and crisp. The fire-control was astonishingly good.

The whistle blew again. From our front a few rifles cracked irregularly, and what other sounds could be heard indicated the retreat of our assailants.

"Got a bellyful, as well as a nasty shock!" observed John, as he jerked the empty shell out of his rifle.

"Hullo! There's a side-show," he added, as brisk firing broke out on our left-rear.

Evidently Noel had issued orders, for a section of men, running down the slope, mounted their camels and rode off, followed by myself and John.

Flashes were coming from distant sand-dunes on our left-front. The camel-section was halted in line, the men dismounted, and, a couple of minutes later, were enfilading the crest of the occupied sand-dune.

Undrilled, undisciplined and without any but mob-tactics, this body of raiders, who may have been an independent private effort, or a feint by Selim ben Yussuf, retired in a body to another sand-dune, offering an admirable target in the growing light, as they did so.

Commanded by Lebaudy in person, a small French party pursued in skirmishing order--there was always a number dashing forward and there was always a number firing--and drove them across our front.

As they retreated toward the main body, and in fact, finally fled in that direction, our line swung half-right, prolonging Lebaudy's line until both prolonged that of the Emir, and the whole advanced in skirmishing order from both flanks.

The Emir's aim and object was not, of course, slaughter, nor even the most severe and crushing defeat that could be inflicted upon Selim ben Yussuf. What he wanted to do was to defeat this attack, and in such a way that there would be no fear of its repetition until the French were in a position to deal with it themselves. Selim ben Yussuf's plan had most signally failed, thanks to the presence of the Emir's forces; the raiders were on the run, and the Emir's Camel Corps would keep them on the run. By the time the latter called a halt and returned to their camp, Lebaudy's force would be in a position--and a condition--to deal with any subsequent trouble.

As our line skirmished forward, a long low hill that lay at right-angles to the battle line, cut off Lebaudy's flank from our view. This long low hill, or high ridge, was about a mile in length and a half-section of our men advanced along it's narrow top. Suddenly one of these went running back to where his camel knelt, while another signalled "Enemy in sight," in spite of the fact that there was a retreating enemy in sight of all of us, in one direction or another. The signaller's meaning was made clear, however, when the messenger arrived at a lumbering gallop, and told his tale. Riding to where the Emir sat on his gigantic white camel, on top of a sand-dune, 'he told how there had been a sudden lightning raid, a veritable hawk-swoop, on the left flank of the line. A band of picked fighting-men mounted on the finest camels, and led by Selim ben Yussuf himself, had made a détour, and had approached unseen, by riding up a deep wadi and between high sand-dunes. They had approached sufficiently near the French flank to launch a charge and drive it home with terrific impact, before the flank-section could be swung back into line to meet them. The enemy, using shock-tactics, had broken and scattered Lebaudy's men, and, by the time Marbruk ben Hassan had got the flank-section of the Camel Corps in position to protect his flank and prevent the line from being rolled up, the raiders had wheeled about and fled.

"Fled?" said the Emir. "Then why all this chatter?"

"Yes, fled," said the messenger, and added deprecatingly and as though he were to blame--for every Oriental loathes to be the bearer of bad tidings--"They have taken the French officer with them."

Selim ben Yussuf had captured Lebaudy The Emir raised himself in the saddle and looked behind him.

"Horse," he shouted in a voice that would have done credit to Lebaudy himself, and waved a beckoning arm. Within a minute, his standard-bearer was beside him, and sprang from the back of the magnificent stallion that was the Emir's favourite.

"Oats," he said to me, as he sprang into the saddle, "find Buddy quick, and tell him I am chasing Selim, who's got Lebaudy. Tell him to follow with Yussuf Latif's section. He'll get his direction from the men on that ridge," and he bade the messenger ride back to the hill-top and watch. As he finished speaking, the Emir dashed off like a racing Centaur.

While I watched him go, I was struck by the disquieting thought that, riding at that pace in pursuit of camels, he would very soon overtake them. A camel will always beat a horse in the long-run, but not in the short. The speed is' with the horse and endurance with the camel. To me it appeared inevitable that my brother would overtake Selim ben Yussuf and his cut-throats, long before he had the support of the section that was to follow him--

I quickly found Buddy, in command of the right flank of our line, and following on his camel, with critical eye, the orderly and regular advance of his dismounted skirmishers. I shouted the news to him and, as he shook his camel into movement and wheeled off, he shouted:

"S'pose the old fool thinks he is going to hunt 'em about with a stick!--Chase after him, Son--I'll be along in two minutes--Wish we'd got some more horses--"

CHAPTER XVIII

As I turned to go, I discovered that John had disappeared, and guessed that he was already trailing Noel. Urging my camel to its top speed--an undeniable canter--I took the straightest line for what I supposed to be the scene of the coming conflict. This took me across the ridge from which the messenger had come. From this eminence I could see, in the clear morning light, the fleeing band of camel-riders, a galloping horseman quickly overtaking them, and a solitary rider urging his camel in pursuit--Selim ben Yussuf and his raiders, my brother, and John Geste.

Careering in break-neck fashion down the slope of the ridge, I saw much of what then happened, and learned the remainder later from John and my brother.

2.

At the head of the fleeing raiders, rode Selim ben Yussuf on his famous horse. Its speed was restrained to that of the camels. By him, on a giant camel, also famous in that part of the desert, rode his cousin, one Haroun el Ghulam Mahommed behind whom the unfortunate *Adjudant* Lebaudy hung across the camel like a sack of potatoes, his arms bound to his sides and his feet tied together--a most undignified, painful, and dangerous situation, In a close group round this camel, rode the remaining dozen or so of Selim's selected ruffians, some of whom found time in the lightness of their hearts and the heaviness of their hatred, to award the unfortunate *Adjudant* a resounding blow with a _mish'ab_ camel-stick, or a violent prod with the butt end of a spear. Suddenly, one of the raiders, hearing the drumming of a horse's hoofs behind him, looked over his shoulder and then shouted to his leader.

Selim ben Yussuf looked round, saw, and understood.

Wheeling out from his position in front of the camels, he shouted "_Ride on_," and, lowering his spear-point, charged head-long at the Emir.

Had the latter also carried a lance, the beholders would have seen a tournament like that of the knights of old--a combat belonging rather to the days of Saladin and Richard Coeur de Lion, the days of chivalry, when foemen met in single combat, man to man, horse to horse, and spear-point to spear-point. The Emir, however, carried only the Arab sword which he always wore, and an automatic pistol in a holster attached to the sword-belt which he wore round the sash beneath his _burnous_--

Almost in the moment of impact, the Emir, a most perfect and powerful horseman, checked his horse, pulled it back on to its haunches and wheeled it from the line of attack--so deftly, so exactly, and so absolutely at the right second, that not only did the lance-point merely tear his wind-blown _burnous_, but the furious charge of his assailant missed him completely.

He drew his sword, but not his automatic, and spurred his horse at Selim as the latter was wheeling about, to return to the attack. It was too late for the Arab to attempt to charge, for the horse and man were upon him, and he could only lower his spear-point, that his charging opponent might impale himself upon it. The Emir's sword flashed down with tremendous force, and the deflected lance--either cut through or broken--was dashed from Selim's hand. Again checking and swerving his horse, the Emir wheeled away and gave Selim ben Yussuf time to draw his sword. Had he unslung the rifle from his back, the Emir would have shot him Selim spurred his horse and, rising in his stirrups, delivered a downward out at the Emir's head. The Emir parried, feinted like lightning, and, in his turn, aimed a downward stroke at the head of Selim. Selim parried, but a downward blow from the mighty arm of the huge Emir, delivered with all his strength as he stood in his stirrups, was a different thing from a stroke delivered by the slight but wiry Arab.

It was parried correctly enough, but Selim's sword was struck from his hand as though by a thunderbolt, and the Emir's weapon smote him a heavy glancing blow that caused him to reel in the saddle. Instantly the Emir, dropping his sword, grappled the Arab in his great hands, dragged him from his saddle, dropped him to the ground and fell heavily upon him. For the moment, Selim ben Yussuf was out of action and had ceased to interest himself in the phenomena of this world.

Rising, the Emir took the stunned man's rifle, slung it over his own back, and then took the reins of both horses. Mounting his own, and seeing John Geste and myself approaching, he again galloped off in pursuit of the retreating raiders. It was not long before his race-horse of a charger again brought him near to the band of camel riders. There was now no horseman to meet him on equal terms and charge him, lance in hand. As he drew near, two or three of those whose slower camels kept them in the rear, turned in their saddles and opened fire. But it takes a somewhat better marksman than the average Arab raider, to hit a man on a galloping horse, when shooting from the back of a trotting or cantering camel; nor did the plan of halting and dismounting appeal to any of these stragglers, in view of the fact that he would almost inevitably be cut down or shot, in the act of doing so.

With a wild whoop, and raised automatic, into and through the fleeing band, the Emir dashed. Men shouted, swung long lances round, un-slung long guns, drew swords, fired rifles, wheeled outward from the pursuing Vengeance--did anything but halt.

"_Ride on_" was their last order, and their very present inclination. At anyone who shot, cut or thrust at him, the Emir fired, and, in a tenth part of the time that it takes to tell, he was beside the leading camel--that of Haroun el Ghulam Mahommed. With a curse, the raider thrust his rifle sideways and downward and, without troubling to bring it to his shoulder, fired. Although the muzzle was not a yard from the Emir's body, the bullet missed him, thanks to the movements of both horse and camel. But an automatic pistol is different, and the robber Haroun el Ghumal Mahommed died, as he would have wished to die, weapon in hand and facing his man. With him died his camel which the Emir instantly, though reluctantly, shot through the head--and the band swept on, leaving behind it, its fallen leader, its best camel, and its prisoner, _l'Adjudant_ Lebaudy.

The half-hearted attempt at a rally and a stand was quickly abandoned as the orderly line of the section of the Emir's famous Camel Corps, riding at top speed, came into sight.

3.
L'Adjudant Lebaudy interested me greatly that night, when he returned the Emir's hospitality.

He was not a man of breeding, culture and refinement, but he was a man of courage and tenacity; he was not what is called a gentleman, but he was a strong man. He may have been a petty tyrant, but he was not always and wholly petty. He somewhat pointedly assured the Emir that the latter could drink his coffee without fear, and that he could please himself as to whether he slept where he dined. He was grimly jocular, and his jokes were not always in the best taste, but when we rose to depart, he shook hands with the Emir, stood to attention, honoured him with a military salute, and said:

"You are a brave man, Sidi Emir. You should have the Medaille Militaire for what you did this morning. Instead, you have my complete forgetting of all that happened before dawn to-day--And if there should be a prisoner missing, I shall notify the authorities that it is extraordinary that only one has been killed. Goodbye, Emir el Hamel el Kebir."

Yes, an interesting man, our friend _l'Adjudant_ Lebaudy, and true to type, save that he was perhaps a little bigger than most of his kind, and capable of a certain generosity and magnanimity.

My story grows long--and it might be very, very long indeed.

We set out, next day, for the Great Oasis. Here I did what I had hardly expected ever to do--embraced and warmly kissed my sister's maid, Maud Atkinson--now my sister-in-law and something of a desert princess.

I should love to have time and space to detail our conversations and to describe our Maudie in her new rôle. She obviously worshipped Noel, and confided to me that, much as she loved Sheikhs, she was, on the whole, glad that her Sheikh-like lord had proved (by slow degrees) to be a white man. Repeatedly she assured me that he was a "one," and when, at length, the dear girl realized that I was Noel's own brother, and her own brother-in-law, she could only ejaculate a hundred times:

"Fancy that now!--Whoever would have thought it!--I can't hardly believe it!"

I will not describe the solemn _mejliss_ in which Noel took leave of the assembled Sheikhs of his own and other tribes, after telling them that he was going on a long journey to visit his allies the Franzawi, nor of the really heartrending and pathetic farewells between him and the men with, and for, whom he had striven and worked and schemed and fought.

But, at length, a large well-equipped and well-armed caravan set out from the Great Oasis, and with it went Marbruk ben Hassan and Yussuf Latif ibn Fetata in command of the fighting men of the escort; and, in time, by slow stages and by devious ways, the caravan arrived and encamped not far from a town into whose fine harbour came the ships of many nations--as they had done since the days of the Phoenician tramp and the Roman trireme.

On to a ship flying the French flag, my companions dared not go; and decided to voyage forth beneath either the American or the British flag, according to which entered the harbour first, for the sooner they were away the better.

To the delight of Noel and Buddy, it was an American ship that came--a huge vessel carrying a few hundred tourists and returning to New York from Japan, visiting the ports of the Southern Mediterranean, as she had visited those of the Northern shore, on her outward voyage. A cable to Isobel ensured that she would be awaiting John on the landing-stage at New York.

4.

I feel that I have not told all that I should have done, about John Geste--

This dear wonderful John Geste--This true brother of Beau Geste and of Digby Geste--This man who could not settle down in happiness even with Isobel,--the wonderful and glorious woman who had given my life a purpose, my mind a lifelong dream, my soul a *beau idéal*--could not live even in that Paradise that her presence made for those she loved, while his friends were stranded where he had "deserted" them--The man who loved Isobel so deeply and truly and nobly, as he most surely did--to _leave_ her, after he had incredibly won back to her--to leave her, with little probability that he would see her face again! This is the greater love.

Poor John Geste--

I was almost amused--grimly, sadly amused, when he again tried to thank me and to say good-bye, on that last night.

His repressed emotions, his repressed British soul, almost escaped. His British public-school reserve almost melted--

He, Noel, Buddy and I, had eaten our last supper together, and in silence smoked the last pipe of peace. As the time drew near for us to seek our sleeping-rugs, John Geste rose to his feet, stretched himself and yawned most unconcernedly, and strode from the tent.

As he did so, he glanced at me, and with a jerk of his head, bade me accompany him. I rose and followed him as he strode out towards the cliff. Suddenly he wheeled about.

"Vanbrugh," he said, as he held out his hand. "I want to say--" and his sudden spate of words ended in the little nervous cough that, in him, indicated strong feeling.

"What I want to try to tell you--" he began again, and got no further.

I would not help him. He was suffering an agony of emotional discomfort, and was utterly inarticulate. But I, too, was suffering an agony of pain, misery and grief.

_He_ was going back to Isobel; and I--to the Angel of Death--

I had grown to love him as much, I believe, as one man can love another. I had saved him. By God's grace and mercy and help, I had saved him, and kept my word to Isobel--Yes, I loved him, but I would not help him.

And more than anything I wanted to see whether he would be able to "let himself go."

For myself, I somehow felt that had our positions been reversed, and had he been sending me back to Isobel, I should have embraced him. I should not have been able to refrain from hugging him--

Not so John Geste.

"What I mean, Vanbrugh," he tried again, "is that--

"Well--You understand, don't you--You know what I mean--"

And I heard my knuckles crack, as his grip tightened, and he said it all in four words.

"My God!" he ejaculated--"Er--Oh! _Stout fella_!"

5.

For the sake of his followers, Noel decreed that the three were to remain Arabs until the ship sailed. Those of the passengers, if any, who saw three Arab Sheikhs and a heavily-veiled Arab woman arrive, must have been more than a little astonished to behold them, next day, in the ready-made reach-me-down garments of "civilization," previously purchased in the town.

To this day I hate to think of that parting.

In one way, it was wonderful as being the consummation of a life's work, or rather of the work for which I had been born; in another way it was terrible, tragic, unbearable.

Z admit I was tempted--horribly tempted--and I thought it wad fine of the other three to say nothing whatever to shake my resolution. They knew that I had given my word, and they would not ask me to break it, and when the Devil whispered in my ear, "A dancing girl--a half-caste, half-savage thing from the bazaars of Bouzen--She doesn't expect it of you "--I clung grimly to my poor honesty, and replied, "It's not a question of what she is, but of what I am;--and I do expect it of me." But it was a hard struggle. Nor was my misery lightened by the sights and sounds around me, as the ship steamed out of the harbour.

On a cliff, a mile or two from the town, my brother's followers abandoned themselves to such transports of grief as I have never witnessed before nor since.

With Oriental lack of restraint, they wept--literally rent their clothing, and exhibited every symptom of unappeasable misery and heart-breaking grief. Brief--perhaps as brief as violent--but starkly genuine and very terrible.

It was long enough in the case of a man called el R'Orab, my brother's body-servant, and caused his death. From the moment that he took leave of his master, he neither ate nor drank nor spoke a word. He went about his duties until he collapsed from weakness, and in his weakness he died, refusing even water. Pitiful and absurd as such conduct may seem to the European, it was highly approved by the Arabs, not one of whom dreamed for a moment of urging the man to eat or drink.

Just before he died, he painfully raised himself from his prayer-rug and, seizing the hand of Yussuf Latif ibn Fetata, who, with the help of Marbruk ben Hassan and myself, was nursing him, said:

"We shall never look upon his face again."

Apparently this statement--regarded as inspired because spoken by a dying man--was the last straw upon the load of unhappiness borne by the fated Yussuf Latif.

That night, he left his sleeping-place beside Marbruk and myself, and was seen by a sentry to go forth and stand beneath the stars, his arms out-stretched towards the East. With a loud and anguished cry of "_Leila Nakhla!--Leila Nakhla!_--" he plunged his knife into his heart, and ended the tragic life that had now become insupportable--

My own parting with Marbruk ben Hassan and the rest, near Bouzen, did nothing to cheer my depressed and miserable spirit, and it was in a most unenviable frame of mind that I rode away with Abd'allah ibn Moussa toward the camp of the old Sheikh Yussuf ben Amir at the Oasis of Sidi Usman.

Abd'allah ibn Moussa was to ride in and discover if the Death Angel was still under the old Sheikh's protection, or whether she had returned to The Street, in Bouzen.

We camped, that night, beneath some palms, a far-outlying picket of the great host of trees of the Sidi Usman Oasis, and after a meal of dates, unleavened bread, and curded cheese as hard as stone, Abd'allah ibn Moussa rode off, bearing the message that I had seen my friend set sail, and that I was here to fulfil my promise; also that Selim ben Yussuf was a prisoner in the hands of the French at Zaguig.

At the close of one of the most miserable days that I have ever spent--somehow uncheered even by the realization that I had saved John Geste and sent him back to Isobel--Abd'allah returned. The Death Angel was in the tents of old Yussuf ben Amir. Apparently she went almost mad with joy at the news of my return, and Selim's capture. She was coming out on the morrow, with a small caravan of her own, to where Abd'allah and I now were. Her message to me was:

"Await me there. I send you my heart and my soul, and my life. I have given Sheikh Yussuf ben Amir that which has made him the happiest man in the Sahara, and my slave for ever--that Hair of the Beard of the Prophet that the Sultan brought from Mecca and gave to my Mother. I have done this to show you that I have given up Allah, and now belong to God altogether, and am a perfect Christian because you, my husband, are one."

It may be believed that I did not sleep that night. Perhaps I sub-consciously feared somnambulism, and that I should arise and ride for my life, even while I slept.

6.

She arrived next day.

Certainly her own resources, and those of Sheikh Yussuf ben Amir, had been strained to their uttermost, judging by the pomp and state in which she travelled. Quite a small village of tents sprang up, as I saw when, at the invitation of her messenger, I rode over to the spot where she had pitched her camp. That the Sand Diviner's words might prove true in every detail, it had been her whim that I should come riding into her camp, and that she should run forth from her tent to welcome me.

In her present manifestation she was wonderful--gentle, sweet, submissive, and most obviously longing to be "good"--to play the rôle of civilized and Christian gentlewoman, and be wholly the white daughter of her white father.

It was piteous and pathetic.

Her plan was that we should go to Bouzen, where we should at once be married by a missionary, either Catholic or Protestant, or both if I liked. There she would get her jewels and instruct her Bank--as she was, I learned, quite wealthy. From Bouzen we were to go to Algiers and become European in every detail. From Algiers we were to take ship for Marseilles and become more fashionably European. From Marseilles we were to proceed to Paris and become the last word in European fashion.

We were then to live happy ever after, wheresoever I preferred, but the further we were from Africa, the happier she would be.

Poor little soul

A great feast was provided in the evening, and when we could eat no more, we sat together upon the wonderful cushioned rugs with which her tent was beautifully provided. And when I, unintentionally, evinced my unconquerable weariness, she bade me retire to the tent which she had provided for me, and sleep my last sleep as a lone and unloved man.

As I rose to go, she held forth her tiny hands, and, as I took them, drew me down beside her.

From her neck she took the curious book-like amulet which was her most cherished possession and, putting its thin gold chain over my head, bade me wear it next my heart, for ever. That it would shield me from every danger was her deep certainty and sure conviction.

"My darling husband," she whispered, "I feel in my soul--yes, from the very depths of my soul--that this will save you--"

It did--

With her impassioned kisses warm upon my lips, I retired to my tent and threw myself down upon its sumptuous bed of cushions. The previous night I had not slept at all, and life had been a burden and a misery since I had said "good-bye" to John two weeks ago--two weeks that seemed like years.

I was too tired to sleep. The hours dragged by with leaden feet. Tossing and turning, groaning and cursing, I longed for daylight--and longed that it might never come.

Sitting up, I fingered the locket-amulet, now denuded of its greatest and most sacred of all Arab charms the (doubtless genuine) Hair of the Beard of the Prophet, but still enriched by its (doubtless equally genuine) Christian relic, the splinter of the wood of the True Cross.

Better not to open it now, by candlelight--as she herself had once said, the tiny splinter of wood might fall out and be lost--a loss that I could bear, but one which would probably trouble her beyond measure--

But open it I did. Why, when I had just definitely decided not to do so? The psychologist can, of course, give the reason. I cannot. I know that my fingers opened the locket without any conscious instructions from my brain. I looked at the lovely face, beautifully painted on ivory--of "Zaza Blanchfleur," the Ouled-Naïl dancing girl, whom mighty Rulers had loved, and who had loved an ordinary Englishman, who had deserted her.

Almost in the same second I glanced at the other face, the face of that same man "Omar, the Englishman," the father of the Angel of Death.

I then closed the locket and sat awhile in thought. During that half-hour, my mind was as a leaf upon the sloping surface of a whirlpool; as a straw in an eddy of wind; nay, in a cave of all the winds, blowing in every direction at once.

Twice or thrice I rose to my feet, and then sank back upon my cushions.

Finally I rose, scribbled the Death Angel a message of four words, in French, on a scrap of paper, dressed myself fully, and crept forth like a thief in the night. This was not the camp of the Emir el Hamel el Kabir, or it would have been impossible for me to do what I then did. No wakeful sentries moved, watchful and alert upon their beat; none listened, stared, and challenged. Apparently not a soul was awake in the camp, except myself.

Creeping like a sneaking jackal to where the camels knelt, I thanked God that mine and Abd'allah ibn Moussa's were tethered in charge of our own camel-men, apart from the rest. With ungentle toe, I roused the man who had been in charge of my camel, ever since he became mine, and bade him saddle both it and Abd'allah ibn Moussa's beast. If I took this man with me, he could tell no tales in the morning.

A few minutes later, the camel-man and I were travelling at maximum speed in the direction of Bouzen.

CHAPTER XIX

Arrived at Bouzen, I gave the camel-man money and a letter for the Death Angel, and bade him await me for three days in the market-place, and, at the end of that time, to take the camels back to Abd'allah ibn Moussa and tell him that I had gone on a journey.

I went straight to the railway station and, squatting down, awaited the train for Algiers, as many other Arabs were doing. Arrived at Algiers, I walked warily, gradually accumulating a European outfit, and storing it in the second-rate, or perhaps twenty-second rate, hotel, in which I lived in the native quarter of the city.

It was a different Otis Vanbrugh, who now shuffled about Algiers in _burnous_ and heel-less slippers, from that Otis Vanbrugh who, ages and aeons agone, had descended from his Mustapha Supérieur hotel to escort his sister on her visits to the romantic Oriental bazaars.

In the crowd, hooded and bearded as I was, I was perfectly safe; and in restful peace and safety, I abode until the day when, having paid my bill, I went back to my room, shaved my face completely, dressed myself in my European clothes, seized my suit-case and grip, and marched straight out of the house, picked up a ramshackle carriage and drove to the quay where the good ship _Hoboken_ awaited me and divers other items.

By way of Oran, Marseilles, Gibraltar and Tangier, she ploughed her uneventful way to New York, and, as in a dream, rather stunned and stupid and mechanical, I stepped once more upon my native soil.

My desire was to get home at the earliest moment and to hear, once and for all, that John had, at last, safe and sound, whole and hale and hearty, reached Isobel, and turned her life from a nightmare of suffering into a reality of happiness indescribable.

I endured the long, long train journey; I endured the apparently longer journey by stage; and the third and penultimate lap, by hired buggy, which brought me to where I was right welcome to a night's shelter and the loan of a good horse.

I started at dawn next morning, and a couple of hours' ride brought me on to my Father's land. By afternoon, I sighted the Ranch House, and, soon afterwards, drew rein by the great verandah on which the family spent the major part of what little time it lived indoors.

"Morning, Oats," drawled my brother, without rising from the rocking-chair in which he was seated.

"Hullo, Boy," spake the voice of Buddy, and, as my sun-dazzled eyes penetrated the shadow of the deep verandah, I saw that I had arrived in time to interrupt a family conclave.

There sat my Father, mighty, massive, domineering and terrible as of old, glaring at me with an expression which appeared to rebuke the presumption with which I dared present myself before him unheralded. Obviously he was in a towering rage.

Before him, miserable and shameful culprits, stood Buddy and my sister Janey, tightly clasping each the other's hand--Buddy white under the stress of some emotion, his eyes blazing, his mouth a lipless gash in his set face--Janey, of course, wilting and drooping, and dissolved in tears.

" *Otis* ," cried Mary's voice, and she dashed forward from the side of a tall dark man arrayed in smart riding kit--the wide-cut tight-kneed style of which our Western horsemen are supposed to despise--and, without quite believing my eyes, I saw that it was her husband Major de Beaujolais--(But of course it had been Mary's intention to bring him, sooner or later, to see her home, and something of the life that she had lived almost to the time that she had met him.) Dismounting and dropping my rein over the horse's head, I took Mary in my arms for a brief sound hug, and then followed her up the steps into the verandah.

"What's the row?" I whispered before turning the corner, to enter the grim presence of my irate parent.

"Janey wants to get engaged to Noel's friend Buddy," she whispered. "Says she'll die if she doesn't. Dad says she'll die if she does--and without his blessing--die of poverty, misery, shame, hunger, Father's curse, domestic slavery in a log cabin, disgrace, remorse, housemaid's knee--Puritan Father--Scarlet Letter--"

"In fact, Dad says ' *No* '--and there's an end of it, eh?" I asked.

"Of course," replied Mary. "Naturally he'd say ' *No* ,' and there'd naturally be an end of it!--Who's _Janey_--to dare to breathe, if Dad says she mustn't."

"And Buddy?" I asked.

"He's torn between a longing to pull his gun on the old man before doing a Young-Lochinvar-into-the-West with Janey, and his fear that Janey will never speak to him again if he dares be so impious and blasphemous as to thwart our so-religious Dad."

"So she'll either die of thwarting Buddy by obeying Dad, or else of thwarting Dad by obeying Buddy, eh?" I observed.

"That's the position," agreed. Mary, "and before Dad's much older, he's going to hear something."

"From whom?" I asked.

"*me*," said Mary, with jutting chin, "and Noel--Saintly old man!--While boundlessly hospitable to my husband, he is far from cordial, in fact barely courteous, and alludes to him--not in his hearing of course as 'that Godless Frenchman,' or 'that foreign idolater.' He gets more holy-righteous, every day!--But come on, or he'll think we're conspiring, if you don't come and prostrate yourself before him."

I greeted my Father with a respectful warmth and cordiality that I did not feel, and received a grunt and a contemptuous stare in reply. The old man certainly was in a rage, and in one of his most violently autocratic and overbearing moods.

I kissed Janey, and also gave Maudie a warm fraternal embrace, wrung Noel's hand and that of Buddy, greeted de Beaujolais diffidently--and selfishly obtruded my own affairs immediately. The other matter could wait and I could settle it.

"John safe?" I asked.

"Oh, sure," was the reply.

"And with his wife?" I asked.

"Right there," was the reply from Noel.

"England, I suppose?"

"They wasn't, an hour ago," drawled Noel.

"Where are they?" I said, mastering a desire to hit him.

"Now be reasonable, Son. How should I know where they are?" replied Noel. "They went riding together about an hour ago, and at the present moment they may be here or there, or somewhere else--She met us at New York," he continued, "and as there wasn't a suitable ship for a week, and John was ill, we just naturally brought them along here."

"Then I may see them at any moment?" I gasped.

"You certainly may, Son, at any moment or any other moment."

I sat down heavily on the nearest chair, for all my strength had suddenly gone, and my knees were trembling.

I might see Isobel at any moment!--And John Geste!--Should I mount my horse again, and ride--and ride--and ride--?

I could not ride away from myself, if I rode away from her.

No, I would see Isobel, *once* again--

What was that booming, in my ears? Of course, the voice of my Father.

"And that's that," he was roaring, "and let me hear not another word about it, Janet'--And as for *you* , my friend, you can get out of this just as quick as the quickest horse will take you--and don't you come on to this ranch again until you are quite tired of life. Get me? Good afternoon." Buddy licked his lips, and stood firm.

"Now, Dad," said Noel, laying his hand on my Father's arm. "Remember Janey's a grown-up woman, and Buddy's my best friend, and I say--"

"I'll tell you when I want your say," shouted my Father, "and Janey can sling off with him, and with my curse too, if she likes, and they'd better go while the going's good, and not come back either."

A wail and a fresh shower of tears from Janey, and an oath from Buddy.

"Coming, Janey?" he asked, as he turned to go.

Janey literally threw herself on her knees before her father. Noel rose from his chair, and Mary put her arm round Janey.

" *Go* , my dear," she said. " *Go* , you little fool, and be happy--I'd be ashamed!--Don't you call your _soul_ your own?"

But Janey had no soul to call her own. It was her father's, stamped and sealed. It was not filial love that was working, nor wholly filial fear, but rather the unbreakable habit of a lifetime, the inhibitions of a father-complex.

I conquered my selfishness and, for the moment, thrust self aside.

"Will everybody please go away--for exactly ten minutes," I said, and became indeed the cynosure of neighbouring eyes.

"Come on," I urged Buddy. "Get out, and take Janey with you--and come back in ten minutes. Off you go, Mary? Go on, Noel," and something in my voice and manner prevailed, and I was left alone with my Father, to face him and out-face him for the first time in my life. He gave a bitter ugly laugh.

"Are you graciously pleased to allow me to remain?" he sneered, "or do I also leave my house, to oblige you?"

From sarcasm he leapt to violent rage.

"Why, you insolent half-baked young hound," he roared, springing to his feet, and, meanwhile, I had produced and opened the Death Angel's locket.

As he advanced upon me, with blazing eyes and clenched fist, I held it toward him, and his eyes fell upon the two portraits--It was dreadful.

I thought, for one awful moment, that I had killed my Father.

He staggered back, smote his face with his clenched fist, and dropped into a chair, white, shaking, and stricken. I felt dreadful, guilty, impious--

"_Oh, God!--Where is she_?" he gasped, fearing, I suppose, that she was near.

"Dead," I replied.

He drew a deeper breath.

"_How did you get it?_" he asked, white-faced and frightened.

"From your *daughter*," I answered,--from my *sister*."

"*My God--Where is she?*" he asked again, and I pitied him even more than I hated myself.

"In Bouzen," I said. "Where you bought the Arab stallion--and--other things--"

"*Does she know?*" he groaned.

"No," I replied.

"*To how many have you shown that?*" he asked, and it seemed as though his whole life hung upon my answer.

"To no-one--yet," I replied, and added, as I pocketed the locket:

"By the way, Father, this chap Buddy is one of the very best, a real White Man--He'd make a wonderful overseer for this ranch, and a wonderful husband for Janey--And I might add that Major de Beaujolais is a most distinguished officer, whose visit to us is a great honour; and further, that Noel's wife, Maudie, is one of the best and bravest little women that ever lived--You see, Father?"

A long silence--

"I see, Son," replied my Father, at last, "and you can give me that locket."

"Why, no, I can't do that, my dear Father;" I replied. "When Janey's married, and Mary and de Beaujolais have gone, and Noel and Maudie have settled down here happily, and Buddy has an overseer's job, I must take it back to its owner--"

"_Be careful of it_, meanwhile, Boy," said my Father.

"_Very_ careful, Father," I replied, and shouted to the others to return.

They found Father wonderfully changed, and all went merry as a welling-bell.

2.

John and Isobel returned by moonlight.

John, clasped my hand, held it, stared me in the eyes--his fine level steady gaze--gave his little cough of deepest feeling and embarrassment, and went into the house without a word. Our silence was very eloquent.

I sat down on the verandah steps, and Isobel, who had stopped to give sugar to her horse, came toward me.

She did not know me until I removed my hat, and the moonlight fell full upon my face.

Like John, she said nothing, but, putting up her little hands, drew my head down and kissed me on the lips. She threw her arms tightly about my neck and kissed me again. The embraces and kisses were just those of the child Isobel who had walked and talked and played with me in our Dream Garden--as sweet and dear and beautiful and innocent as those. Her little hands then stroked my hair, and again we kissed, and then, still without a word, Isobel turned and ran into the house.

That is the moment in which I should have died. Instead, I took a horse and rode away.

I rode further and harder than I had ever done in all my life, but I was not cruel to my horse. Who, that had been kissed by Isobel, should be cruel, or ever mean or base or bad?

Am I happy?

Dear God! Who that has been kissed by Isobel is not happy?

EPILOGUE

"He shall know a joy beyond all mortal joy, and stand, silent and rapt, beside the Gate--There is but one Way to that Gate--It is not Love Aflame with all Desire--but Love At Peace--"

THE END